Praise for

FAMILY BAGGAGE

"An endearing and humane story about a family and its sticky web of secrets and misunderstandings . . . one of those rare books you could recommend to anyone and know that they'll love it." —*The Australian Women's Weekly*

"Explores the comic and tragic in family ties, international travel and unexpected romance." —*Irish American Post*

"A book to treasure that is clever, amusing and heart-warmingly touching." —*Woman's Day* (Australia)

Praise for

THE ALPHABET SISTERS

"You'll be laughing out loud one minute and crying the next." —*Cosmopolitan* (Australia)

"Charm, laughter, and tears . . . a delightful story that shows how quarrels can be solved with love and loyalty."
—*Woman's Day*

"The Maeve Binchyish empathy McInerney shows for the changes and chances of family life draws us into this gentle, life-affirming story." —*The Sydney Morning Herald*

ALSO BY MONICA McINERNEY

Family Baggage

The Alphabet Sisters

THE FARADAY GIRLS

THE FARADAY GIRLS

a novel

MONICA MCINERNEY

BALLANTINE BOOKS

New York

A Ballantine Books Trade Paperback Original

Copyright © 2007 by Monica McInerney
Reading group guide copyright © 2007 by Random House, Inc.

Published in the United States by Ballantine Books,
an imprint of The Random House Publishing Group,
a division of Random House, Inc., New York.

BALLANTINE and colophon are registered
trademarks of Random House, Inc.
READER'S CIRCLE and colophon are trademarks
of Random House, Inc.

LIBRARY OF CONGRESS CATALOGING-IN-PUBLICATION DATA

McInerney, Monica.
    The Faraday girls : a novel / Monica McInerney.
        p.   cm.
    "A Ballantine Books trade paperback original"—T.p. verso.
    ISBN 978-0-345-49023-0 (pbk.)
    1. Sisters—Fiction.   2. Grandparents—Fiction.   3. Inheritance and
succession—Fiction.   4. Australians—New York (State)—New York—
Fiction.   5. Domestic fiction.   I. Title.
    PR9619.4.M385F37 2007
    823'.92—dc22

                                                    2007022390

Printed in the United States of America

www.thereaderscircle.com

9 8 7 6 5 4 3 2

Book design by Mary A. Wirth

For Clare Foster

No family can hang out the sign:
"Nothing the matter here."

CHINESE PROVERB

$\mathcal{P}$ART ONE

Hobart, Tasmania, Australia
1979

The day the Faraday family started to fall apart began normally enough.

Juliet, at twenty-three the oldest of the five Faraday sisters, was first into the kitchen, cooking breakfast for everyone as she liked to do. This morning it was scrambled eggs, served with small triangles of buttered toast. She added parsley, diced crispy bacon and a dash of cream to the eggs, with a sprinkle of paprika as a garnish. She also set the table with silver cutlery, white napkins, a small crystal vase with a late-blooming red rose from the bush by the front gate and a damp copy of the *Mercury* that had been thrown over the fence before dawn. The big earthenware teapot that had once belonged to their grandmother had center place on the table, resting on a Huon pine pot holder that sent out a warm timber smell as it heated up.

Juliet stepped back from the table, pleased with the general effect. She'd been asked by her new boss at the downtown café where she worked to come up with ideas for menu items. She made a record of this morning's arrangement in her notebook under the title "English-style Traditional Breakfast???" A smoked kipper or two would have been a nice touch, but they were hard to come by in Hobart. Too smelly, anyway, if her childhood memory served her well.

Twenty-one-year-old Miranda was next up and into the kitchen. She was already fully made-up—black eyeliner, false lashes and very red lipstick—and dressed in her white pharmacy assistant's uniform. She looked around the room.

"Juliet, you really are wasted with us. You'd make some lucky family a lovely maid."

She absentmindedly pulled in her belt as she spoke. Two months earlier, a visiting perfume sales representative had flattered her by mentioning her slender waist. She'd been working vigorously to get it as thin as possible ever since. She worked in the local drugstore, publicly expressing an interest in studying pharmacy, privately thrilled with the access to discount and sample cosmetics.

Juliet was also dressed for work, in a black skirt and white shirt, with a red dressing gown on top for warmth. She ignored Miranda's remark. "English-style traditional breakfast, madam?" she asked.

"I'd rather skin a cat," Miranda answered, reaching for the newspaper.

Eliza, sister number three and nineteen years old, came in next, dressed in running gear. She did a 4k run every morning before she went to university. "That's not how you use that phrase, is it?"

"It is now. I'd rather skin a cat within an inch of my hen's teeth than put my eggs in Juliet's basket."

Juliet looked pointedly at Eliza. "Would you like an English-style traditional breakfast, madam? Toast? Coffee or tea?"

"I'd love everything, thanks. And tea, please. I've got a big day today." Eliza was studying physical education at university. During the week she coached two junior women's basketball teams. On weekends she ran in cross-country competitions. The only time any of her family saw her out of tracksuits was if she went to church on Sundays, and she rarely did that anymore. She took up her usual seat at the wooden table. "Why do you put yourself through this every morning, Juliet?"

"Practice. Research purposes. A strongly developed sense of familial responsibility. It's all good training for when I have my own café."

"Really?" Miranda said. "So if you were training to be an undertaker you'd embalm us each morning?" She was now eating a grapefruit and ignored a yelp from Eliza as her jabbing spoon sent a dart of juice across the table.

"If you get any funnier, Miranda, I'm going to explode laughing." Juliet put Eliza's toast on and stood by the window. She pulled her dressing gown tighter around her body as a sharp breeze came in through a gap in the frame.

It was autumn in Hobart, getting colder each day. Their weatherboard house was heated by open fires in the living room and the kitchen, though they were never lit in the morning. Wood was too expensive. This morning was bright and crisp, at least, the sun strong enough to send gentle light through the red and orange leaves in the front hedge. A scattering of frost lay on the ground. There'd been warnings already that the winter would be a cold one. Possibly even snow, and not just on top of Mount Wellington.

Juliet touched the windowpane as she refilled the kettle. It was icy cold. Their North Hobart house was in the dip of a hilly street, but high enough to give them a view of the mountain, though the trees their father had planted years ago were now threatening to block it. If she stood on tiptoes, Juliet could see the glisten of frost on cars in the street and on the hedges of the houses opposite. She gave a fake little shiver. She liked telling her friends that this weather was nothing like the cold she remembered from her childhood in England. Not that her memories were all that strong anymore. Like their English accents, they had nearly faded away.

The whole Faraday family had emigrated to Tasmania twelve years earlier. The girls' father, Leo, a botanist specializing in eucalyptus plantations, had been headhunted by a Tasmanian forestry company. Juliet could still remember the excitement of packing everything up in preparation for the month-long sea journey from Southampton. None of them had even heard of Tasmania before then.

The toast popped. Juliet prepared Eliza's breakfast and passed it across. She refilled the teapot for the others. Sadie and Clementine's cups were already on the table. Juliet took down her father's cup and saucer from the shelf. It was a delicate blue color, with a border of cheerful red blossoms. Their mother had always had her morning tea in that cup. Juliet could remember her sipping it, closing her eyes and saying, "Ah, that hits the spot." Only Leo used her cup these days.

The kitchen door was pushed open with a bang. "Hell, Juliet. Look at the time." Sadie was still dressing herself as she walked in, her head emerging from an orange and red striped poncho. Her hair, last night the model of current fashion with its teased perm, looked like a flattened haystack this morning. None of her sisters remarked on it. She threw her canvas bag and a pair of cork-heeled boots into the corner of the room with a clatter, then slumped into a chair. Sadie woke up grumpy every morning. "Why didn't you wake me? I told you I have an early lecture."

"You didn't ask me to wake you. Do you want some breakfast?"

"What is it?"

"Cat sick on toast if you keep talking to me like that."

"Sorry, Juliet. I'd love some of your beautiful cuisine. Thank you for getting up early to prepare it for me." Eighteen years old, Sadie was in her first year of study for an arts degree. One month earlier she'd been in her first year of a science degree. She'd also completed one week of a teaching degree, before changing her mind about that as well. "Such a shame there's not a degree in dillydallying," Miranda had remarked. "You'd top the class in that."

"Where's Leo?" Eliza asked, bringing her teacup over for a refill.

"Shed Land. He's been there all morning." Juliet had been up at seven and the light in the garden shed their father used as his inventing room was already shining. He was spending more time in there these days than out looking after his tree plantations. She decided to give him another ten minutes before checking on him.

Miranda pushed the newspaper away and gave a graceful stretch. Her glossy dark-red hair shimmered down her back as she flexed her arms above her head. "If you ask me, we're being replaced in his affections by test tubes and soldering irons. Juliet, call the authorities when you've finished washing the dishes, will you? If it isn't bad enough that we're motherless, we're now heading toward fatherlessness."

"You said you preferred it when he's busy out there."

"Busy out there is one thing. Abandoning his daughters for days on end is another."

Juliet secretly preferred it when Leo was in one of his inventing frenzies. Life was much quieter. He didn't care whether each of them had done their share of the housework, or express dismay about Miranda's too-short skirts, tell Sadie off for playing her music too loudly, remind Eliza to mow the front lawn, tell Juliet to find more uses for mince or tell Clementine to get over her hatred of mince. He hadn't even noticed when Juliet served roast chicken midweek, instead of as a rare Sunday luxury. She'd done it as a test.

If things weren't going well in Shed Land, it was like having a bee in the house. He was always around, offering help that wasn't needed and getting in the way. A real sign of his frustration was when he shut the tin door of the shed loudly enough for them to hear over their pop music, strode into the kitchen, turned off the stove or the grill and declared that he was feeling housebound and was going to take the five of them out for dinner somewhere. They usually ended up at Bellerive beach, eating fish and chips at one of the wooden tables by the water. Money was always too tight for restaurants.

"Morning, everyone." It was Clementine, still in her pajamas, her school blazer over the top, her long, dark hair tied back into a ponytail.

Four voices answered in a singsong way. "Morning, Clementine."

Clementine had barely taken her seat when she stood up again, pushed back her chair and made a dash for the bathroom down the hallway. Eliza and Juliet looked at each other. Miranda kept reading. Sadie began to look ill herself.

Clementine came back, white-faced, clutching a washcloth. "Sorry about that."

Juliet looked closely at her little sister. Clementine was always pale—all five of them were—so that was nothing new, but she did look especially peaky this morning. "Were you sick?"

Clementine nodded.

Juliet guided her gently into a chair and rested a hand on her forehead. She could remember sitting in that chair and having their mother do the same thing to her. It had felt so cool and comforting. It had always made her feel a little better, straightaway. "You don't have a temperature, Clemmie. It must just be a bug."

"Poor Clemmie," Miranda said. As Sadie leaned past her to the sugar bowl, she made an exaggerated face, flapping her hands in front of her nose. "Breathing in Sadie's alcoholic fumes would give anyone a bug. What time did you get in last night, Sadie? I really don't think you are taking your studies seriously, young lady."

"You're just jealous because I have a good social life and you don't," Sadie said, putting three spoons of sugar into her tea.

"I have an extraordinary social life. It's just that I also have an extraordinary working life, unlike you two layabouts. Thank God I decided against going to university. Look what it's doing to the two of you. Turning you into hippies in front of our eyes."

"I'm not a hippie," Sadie said.

"What's wrong with being a hippie anyway?" Eliza asked.

"Nothing's wrong with being a hippie in the same way that nothing's wrong with being a smelly old dog lying around in front of a fire. It's just not what I want to be."

"You think you are so perfect, Miranda," Sadie said. "You're not. You're so superficial. All you care about is makeup and clothes—"

"And perfume," Miranda said. "Don't forget perfume. And I'm reasonably interested in magazines, fake compliments and men buying me drinks."

Juliet stepped in. "Do you want to try some toast now, Clemmie?"

"No, thanks. I'll skip breakfast."

"You're not on a diet again, are you, Clementine?" Miranda said. "The pressures of impending fame getting to you?"

She managed a smile. "Something like that."

"Everything okay with the play?" Juliet asked. Clementine had been out late each night that week doing final rehearsals for her school play, on top of all the weekend run-throughs. She had a walk-on role as a pirate and a credit in the program as assistant set designer. Juliet had been very pleased to hear it. Clementine was usually more scientific than artistic and not usually this enthusiastic about afterschool activities. Juliet had discovered the real reason two weeks earlier, when she spotted Clementine and David Simpson, the boy playing the lead role in the play, holding hands as they walked down Elizabeth Street.

"It's fine. Why?"

Juliet shrugged. "You've seemed distracted the last couple of weeks."

"It's all fine. Just busy. But there—"

"Juliet, are there any eggs left?" Sadie interrupted. She always went for seconds. Miranda called her the Human Scrapbin to her face, Piggly-Wiggly behind her back.

"In the pan. Help yourself."

"Would you serve it up for me? Please?"

"No bones in your arms?" Juliet asked.

Sadie waggled her arms in a floppy way.

"Fall for that and you're a fool, Juliet," Miranda murmured, flicking the page of the paper.

Juliet served Sadie anyway.

"Where's Dad?" Clementine asked.

"Shed Land," Juliet, Miranda, Sadie, and Eliza said together.

"No, he's not, he's here. Morning, my lovelies." Leo Faraday came through the side door, bringing a gust of the cool morning air with him. He was dressed in a wide-lapeled gray suit, a crisp white shirt and a blue patterned tie. His hair had been slicked back, the usual dark-red quiff smoothed over. "And yes, before you feel duty-bound to point it out, I do look extremely smart today and yes, I do have a meeting. Juliet, breakfast smells delicious. Miranda, what is that black stuff around your eyes; you look like a lady of the night. Eliza, have you been for a run already? Sadie, pick up your boots, would you? What's up with you, Clementine? You look like a wet dishrag."

"She's got a stomach bug," Juliet said.

"Poor chicken." His concerned words rang false. He was smiling from ear to ear.

Juliet passed across the blue cup and saucer. "Everything all right, Dad? What's going on out there?"

"Good things, Juliet. Interesting things. Unusual things."

"In your mind, or in reality?" Miranda asked.

"We hardly see you anymore, Dad," Sadie complained.

Leo put down his cup and rubbed his hands together. "Something hot is a-cooking out there, my girls. Something is nearly at boiling point. This time I really think—"

"Good heavens, is that the time?" Miranda said in an overly dramatic tone. They'd all had too many years of his invention talk. The revolutionary motor oil that put their old car off the road for three months. The device designed to repel spiders that had done exactly the opposite. The electronic rain gauge that burst into flames on its first test run. "I'd better finish getting ready or I'll be late."

Clementine stood up and ran to the bathroom again, clutching the washcloth to her lips. They all heard the door slam.

"My word, she's a sensitive soul," Miranda remarked, looking after her. "Clemmie, it's all right, I'll be back after work."

Clementine returned a few minutes later, pale-faced. "Sorry."

"Have you been sick again?" At Clementine's nod, Juliet felt her sister's forehead once more. "Are you sure you're okay?"

Leo felt her forehead too. "You're not hot, but you are a bit clammy."

"Clemmie's clammy," Sadie said.

Miranda gave a bark of laughter. Sadie looked pleased. She liked making Miranda laugh.

"Have you eaten anything unusual?" Leo asked. "It's not food poisoning, is it?"

"No, I'm sure it's not."

"Too many late nights, that's what it is," Sadie said. "The sooner that romance—oh, I'm sorry, Clementine—the sooner that *play* is over, the better."

"What will I wear on opening night?" Miranda asked. "My blue gown or that amusing little lace number my couturier sent over from Paris last week? What about you, Sadie? Will you wear that sweater made of yak hair or perhaps that simply darling little patchouli-steeped handweave I saw you prancing about in last week? How many small rodents died in the making of that, I wonder?"

Leo was still concerned. "Clementine, I'm not sure you should go to school today. You really do look peaky."

"I think she should go to the doctor. That's the third morning this week she's been sick," Sadie said.

"Third time this week?" Miranda raised an eyebrow. "Really? I didn't realize that. Uh-oh. It's morning. She's sick. Put 'em together and what do we see? P-r-e-g-n-a-n-cee."

There should have been a laugh from one of her sisters. There should have been a denial from Clementine. There should have been a rebuke from Leo, and a smart answer back from Miranda.

Instead there was silence.

Juliet knew, right then. Was it Clementine's expression? The fact that her forehead hadn't actually felt that clammy or hot? The knowledge that this David of the play was all that Clementine had talked about for weeks? Whatever it was, Juliet wasn't able to stop the words.

"Clementine? Is Miranda right? Are you pregnant?"

Leo laughed. "Juliet, for heaven's sake. She's sixteen years—"

"Yes, I am."

"—old." He swallowed. "Tell me you're agreeing to the fact you are sixteen, Clementine, not—"

"I'm pregnant, Dad."

"Oh Holy God."

The room fell quiet. No cups being picked up, no cutlery being used, no newspaper being read. Just Clementine at one end of the table and her four sisters and father in the other chairs, staring at her, dumbstruck.

Her expression was calm, even if her hands were clenched. In her pink-and-white-striped pajamas, she looked even younger than sixteen. Her long hair had come out of its ponytail and was now in a tumble around her shoulders. "I'm three months pregnant. I went to the doctor yesterday."

An intake of breath. Juliet didn't know if it had come from her or one of her sisters.

Leo's voice was very low. "Who, Clementine? How?"

She gave her father a withering look. "Dad, please. It's David's."

"David?"

"David Simpson. Her boyfriend," Sadie said.

"Since when did you have a boyfriend?" Leo was staring at Clementine as if she was a stranger at the table.

Juliet answered for her. "She's been going out with David for months. He's in the play with her."

Leo stared around the table. "Why don't I know any of this?"

"You've been busy."

"Oh, I think that might have been worth a little visit to Shed Land. 'Excuse me, Dad, we think you should know that your sixteen-year-old daughter is sleeping around—' "

"Dad!" Juliet and Miranda spoke as one.

Clementine was still calm. "I wasn't sleeping around. I slept with David. Only David."

"Who is this David?"

"He's the pirate king in the play."

Leo stood up abruptly. "That makes it better. That makes it okay. Yo ho ho and a bottle of rum; by the way, I've made your daughter pregnant, Mr. Faraday."

"We did it together, Dad. David didn't *make* me do anything."

"But you're just children." Leo was now behind the chair, his hands on the backrest. His knuckles were white. "I can't believe this. Just when I thought things were getting better for us. Two of you with jobs, two of you at university, you showing such promise at school, Clementine. Good times ahead for us again as a family at last—"

Clementine stood up too. "We're talking about a baby, Dad, not a nuclear war."

"You're sixteen, Clementine. *Sixteen*. Have you any idea what lies ahead of you? Years of nappies and no sleep. It's hell having babies. I should know, I had five of them."

"Thank you very much."

"There were two of us, your mother and I. We loved each other and we wanted all five of you, don't try and twist my words. But it is hard. Very hard when there's two of you, let alone one."

"You've managed alone the past eight years."

Leo's face hardened. "You will not compare my situation to yours. What's got into you, Clementine?"

"David, it seems," Miranda said.

Leo pushed the chair. It clattered against the table. "That's enough, Miranda. Outside."

"No."

"What do you mean 'no'?"

"No, I'm not going to miss this. We need to hear it together. I'll go if Clementine wants me to go, but otherwise I'm staying."

"Clementine?"

"Stay, Miranda. I want everyone to stay. I was going to tell you all soon, I promise. Tonight. Or tomorrow. After I'd told David—"

"You haven't told David yet?" Leo was incredulous.

"I was waiting until after the play."

Miranda snorted. "In case it puts him off his performance?"

"Miranda, I'm warning you. Shut up." Leo reached for his coat. "Right, Clementine. Go and get dressed. We're going to go and tell him now. You and me. See what he's got to say for himself. His parents too."

"I'm not telling him in front of you. It wouldn't be fair."

"Fair has nothing to do with this." The conversation was only between Leo and Clementine now. He ran his fingers through his hair. The dark-red quiff stood straight up. "You'll tell him in front of me, and we'll set a wedding date today if we have to. You're three months, you said. If we move quickly, we can go and see Father Cavalli this afternoon, get everything underway before—"

"Dad, I'm not marrying him."

"No daughter of mine is going to live in sin."

"I'm not going to live with him either. I'd miss you all too much."

"Are you telling me—"

"No, I'm not going to have an abortion."

"Then what the hell are you going to do? Give the baby up for adoption?" He sat down again abruptly. "I didn't even think. Of course that's what you're going to do."

"I'm not doing that either. I'm going to keep it. Keep him or her."

He gave a sharp laugh. "Of course you are. Sixteen-year-olds make wonderful mothers. You'll get a few nannies as well, I suppose? To mind the baby while you go off to discos with your friends?"

"No. I've got other ideas. I was going to talk about it with you tonight. I've had some news."

"More news? I can hardly wait."

"The university course I wanted to do is going ahead."

"The environmental science one?"

"I found out yesterday."

"But that's wonderful. That's really wonderful." It was clear in his face, his pride at her news. Then his expression changed. "But you can't possibly go to university now."

"Why not?"

"Why can't she?" Juliet asked.

He threw out his arms. "Can't you see? She's having a baby. She can't just put it in a bassinet and head off to lectures."

Juliet moved then. She went over and stood behind Clementine, and put her arm around her. "Yes, she can. I'll help her."

Miranda didn't hesitate. "Me too." She moved and stood on Clementine's other side.

Sadie and Eliza followed. All five were at one end of the table, Clementine in the middle, facing their father at the other end. Clementine reached for Juliet's hand and squeezed it.

"You can't *all* help her. You've got work and study too. When are you going to find the time?"

"We'll take it in turns, like we do with the housework."

"I'd rather not change its nappy," Miranda said.

"I'll do all of it," Clementine insisted.

"No, Clemmie, Miranda has to help," Juliet said. "You can't pick or choose, Miranda. What does the poor little creature do if its nappy's full? Wait for one of its less-squeamish aunts to arrive home?"

"It will just need to learn a bit of self-discipline." Miranda's tone was matter-of-fact. "I'll make bargains with it. 'Listen here, sonny, you hold it in until your mother gets home and I'll take you to the park tomorrow.' "

"Girls, you're not being realistic about this. You'll lose interest. You'll be like children getting a puppy for Christmas—bored with it by New Year's Day."

"Of course we won't," Juliet said. "We'll make a pact now. We promise to help you, Clementine, until your baby is at school. You all agree, don't you?" She looked at Miranda, Eliza, and Sadie.

"Of course," Miranda said. "I'm sure the school won't mind admitting her as an early-age student. Six months old, say."

"Until he or she is five," Juliet said firmly. "Miranda? Eliza? Sadie?"

Eliza and Sadie nodded.

"Five, did you say?" Miranda looked alarmed.

"It won't be in nappies for five years."

"All right, but if we're going to help look after it, do we get to choose the name?" Miranda asked.

"You can make suggestions," Clementine said. "If it's a girl, I want her to have Mum's name as her middle name. If it's a boy, Dad's name. The tricky thing is Faraday; it's hard to get a name to go with it."

"I'll pick up a book from the library and we could—"

"Excuse me."

"—take votes on some of—"

"Excuse me." It was their father, knocking on the tabletop. They stopped talking and looked at him. "So that's it, is it? Clementine calmly tells all of us that she is having a baby, that this entire house is going to be turned upside down for the next umpteen years, and you all just accept it? Start bickering already over who gets to call it what and who changes its nappy?"

Five nods.

"As if it's as simple as that? As straightforward as that?"

Juliet spoke on behalf of them all. "It is as simple as that, Dad."

Clementine moved toward him. Not right up to him; halfway. "I'm sorry I disappointed you. But I don't think it's a bad thing. It's a wonderful thing. Don't you think?" She smiled, the great open smile that all five of his daughters had. "A baby in the house. It will be fun, won't it?"

"It will be, Dad." Juliet's voice was soft. "It'll be okay. We'll manage. We know how to."

He shut his eyes. They waited. They had each walked into the kitchen or the living room in the past eight years to the sight of their father having silent conversations with their mother. They knew he wasn't just sending up a prayer to his wife now. He was sending up an emergency flare. Less than a minute later he opened his eyes.

"On one condition."

Clementine waited.

"I never want to change its nappy either. I saw more nappies with the five of you than I ever want to see in my life again."

Clementine stepped forward and held out her hand. "It's a deal."

They shook on it.

CHAPTER 2

Even before Clementine's big announcement, the Faraday house had operated on rosters. It was their father's idea. There were rosters for meals, cleaning, washing and shopping, each task listed in a column with a box beside it to be ticked when the job was done. The rosters changed weekly, the new one pinned on the wall next to the fridge each Sunday night. There were also monthly family meetings to discuss items of interest and review the work schedules.

Miranda had protested once that it was like living in an army camp. She argued forcibly for a new relaxed attitude in the household. Juliet argued back just as forcibly that Miranda's idea of being relaxed was no work being done. Miranda argued back again that a person's home was supposed to be a sanctuary, not a workhouse.

The news of Clementine's baby called for yet another review. No discussion this time. Leo drew up a new roster on a mathematical basis, the tasks divided precisely between them. They would all take turns cooking, cleaning, and washing. Himself included.

"But Juliet loves cooking," Miranda complained when she saw she was rostered to cook dinner every Tuesday. "I don't want to deprive her of an evening's entertainment."

"She has to have one night off. And I don't want any of my daughters going out into the world with only one skill to their name. I want you to be well-rounded, multitalented individuals."

"So how come Clementine only has to do the dusting and dry the dishes?" Sadie asked.

"You know that lump growing out of her stomach?" Eliza said in a bored voice, not looking up from the sports magazine she was reading. "It's a baby. In a few months, she'll hardly be able to move. Dad's just planning ahead."

"I'm actually here listening, in case you've forgotten," Clementine said. "Dad, Sadie's right. I'm pregnant, not sick. I'm happy to do the gardening or the vacuuming."

"The roster stays as it is. I don't want you exerting yourself."

Miranda studied the roster, a look of disgust on her face. "I tell you something, once I get out into the world, I will never peel another potato, lift another broom, or wash another dish."

Leo pushed back his glasses. "How wonderful for you, Miranda. You're getting a slave, are you? And paying them with what? One of your dazzling smiles at the end of each week?"

The other four girls snickered.

"I have plans," she said. "This is no way to live. You treat us like trained monkeys."

"So move out if you don't like it," Sadie said.

"I can't. I've promised Clementine. Besides, you can't have someone who looks like me out loose on the streets. Imagine the uproar. Men crashing their cars after just one look. No, the family nest is probably the safest place for me until I work out a way of disguising my sexual allure."

"That's enough, Miranda. You know your mother didn't like that kind of language."

Miranda abruptly stood up. "Excuse me, everyone, but I feel a sudden overwhelming need for some fresh air. Could we have a short recess in this otherwise riveting family meeting?" As she passed her father she gave what might have appeared to be a playful smile if her voice wasn't so serious. "Face facts, Leonardo, your dictatorship is in its last days. The peasants are revolting. An uprising is rising."

He didn't smile back. "If your mother could hear you. You know how important it was to her for us to stay united."

Only Clementine, in her usual chair at the end of the table, closest to the door, heard Miranda's muttered answer.

"But she can't hear me, can she? And I'm sick of pretending she can."

Clementine found Miranda out on the back veranda a little later. She was smoking and making no attempt to hide it.

"Don't get upset," Clementine said. "Dad's just doing his best."

"She's gone, Clem. She's been gone for eight years but he won't accept it."

"He still misses her."

A flash of anger from Miranda. "And so do I. So would you if you remembered her better." If Miranda noticed Clementine's expression she didn't remark on it. "But when do we move on? Sometimes I think he enjoys it, you know. It's like he's been cast in a lead role as the eccentric brave father of five little motherless girls. You know what people call us, don't you? 'Those poor Faraday girls.' I had enough of it when she died and I've had enough of it now. I heard it again this week, in the pharmacy. 'Is it any wonder that youngest one got pregnant, no mother to mind them, those poor Faraday girls.' "

"Shut up, Miranda."

"I'm not attacking you or your baby, so don't get up on your high horse and start galloping around. I'm just sick of being one of the poor Faraday girls, Clem. Do you know what I think? He's secretly thrilled about you having this baby. He'd love us all to stay here forever, in a cocoon, living life by his rosters, carrying out Mum's rituals at Christmas, at birthdays, at Easter. He treats those scrapbooks of hers like holy relics. He still talks about her as if she was alive. I want to say, 'No, Dad, let's remember that Mum is dead, that she is not coming back and she is not speaking to us through the supernatural medium of bits of colored paper that she stuck into an old book two days before she—' "

"Stop it, Miranda. Don't talk about Mum like that. I like the rituals. I like living together like this. I like remembering Mum as often as we can. And those scrapbooks will be the only way my baby will know her. They're important."

Miranda didn't speak. She stayed looking out over the veranda rail, lifted the cigarette to her lips, then moved it away again. They both watched the red glow of the tip move against the darkness of the garden. There was silence for a few minutes.

Miranda was glad it was Clementine who had followed her out. If Sadie had been there, she would have kept talking, reminding Miranda of how hard it had been for her, that she was the one who had been most in need of her mother at that time, just a few years away from becoming a teenager. Eliza, judgmental as usual, would have called Miranda a cold, selfish, self-serving cow. Juliet would have entreated Miranda to see it from everyone else's point of view. Clementine always said what she felt needed to be said and left it there. She could calm Miranda down by her very presence.

Anyone who said there weren't favorites among sisters didn't have sisters, Miranda decided. Of course there were. The truth of it, though, was that the favorites changed constantly, the alliances shifting back and forth in some unspoken parody of a folk dance, two of them close for a time until a change in tempo forced them to break up and turn to different partners.

At any given time, Miranda was fighting with at least one of her sisters, sharing confidences with another and barely talking to another. There didn't seem to be any real pattern to it either. Sometimes it all happened depending on who was first home from work or school, which sister got the first blast of post-work conversation that sometimes bred confidences or sometimes developed into a row. Five sisters, five different personalities too, regardless of how many times over the years people might have stopped their father and mother, gazed down at the girls in their school uniforms or smart Sunday clothes, and exclaimed how alike they all were, with their dark hair, dark eyes and pale skin. "You Faraday girls, you're like peas in a pod."

No, we're not, Miranda had wanted to snap back for as long as she could remember. She started dying her hair red the moment she could afford to buy hair dye. In fact, she dyed it before she could afford it, begging samples from visiting representatives to the pharmacy.

Beside her on the veranda, Clementine shifted position. It gently interrupted Miranda's reverie. She turned to her little sister. "I'm sorry, Clementine."

"It's okay."

"It's just that I want more than this. Maybe I should move out. Before it's my turn to do the washing again. I hate doing the washing."

"You hate doing everything except flirting and looking at yourself in the mirror."

Miranda laughed. Her temper storms were always brief. She gathered her sister against her and kissed the top of her head. "Dear little Clemmie. And there I was thinking I'd pulled the wool over your eyes."

"Not for a minute, ever. Nor am I little. Or Clemmie. I'm Clementine, I'm about to be a mother of one, so I'm more mature emotionally and physically than you. Now get away from me. You stink of cigarette smoke."

Miranda didn't take offense. She popped a peppermint into her mouth, threw the cigarette butt into the garden and made an exaggerated gesture of straightening her shoulders and taking a deep breath. "Back into the fray we go, Clementine. You go first, so I can follow in your mature about-to-be-motherly wake."

Clementine stopped, her face serious. "You won't move out, Miranda, will you? It will change everything and I want my baby to know you all as much as he or she can."

"I'll visit occasionally, even if I do move out. Fly in from Rio or some glamorous place I'll soon be calling home."

"Don't joke all the time. You keep this family together, you know that."

"No, I don't." Miranda sighed. Her face was serious. "This family is kept together by gossamer threads, lies, and memories, Clem. Nothing to do with me."

. . .

"Anyone home?" Juliet called out as she opened the front door, took off her coat and hung it on top of the others on the rickety row of coathooks.

At least eight coats were always hanging there and no one ever seemed to wear them. It was like the shoe cupboard, full of shoes she never saw anyone wear either. Her fingers itched to have a big cleanup and throw everything out. Not just the clothes and shoes. The faded paintings. The threadbare rugs. Even the now-chipped blue-and-white crockery. It was out of the question, of course. It had all belonged to their mother's mother in Ireland, shipped out with their other belongings when they first moved to Tasmania.

If their mother was alive, there would probably still have been a battle about getting rid of anything. It had been a source of mock-arguments between her parents: Leo wanting to buy new items, Tessa preferring the old, yet the irony was their father hadn't thrown out a single thing since their mother died.

It had come as a shock to Juliet one day, four years earlier, when she hung up one of her father's shirts in his wardrobe and discovered her mother's dresses and cardigans still on the rack. She hadn't mentioned it to the others. It played on her mind for days afterward. Shouldn't he have thrown them out long before? Their mother had been dead for four years at that time. Surely he didn't think she was coming back?

"Anyone home?" she called again.

She went into the kitchen and checked the roster. Her turn to cook dinner again. She spent all day cooking, she came home and kept cooking. She was too tired to do anything special. She decided on spaghetti bolognese, followed by bread and butter pudding.

She wondered where Miranda, Sadie and Eliza were. They hadn't left any notes on the noticeboard. She knew that Clementine was out with David, on their weekly trip to the cinema. Since Clementine had announced her pregnancy four months earlier, she and David had met three times a week, regularly on Mondays, Wednesdays and Saturdays. Like old-fashioned dates, if you ignored the fact Clementine was very obviously pregnant and just as obviously very young. Juliet thought it was quite sweet. Like David himself.

"Sweet?" Miranda had said. "Sappy, more like it. And he's terrified of Clementine, if you ask me. Have you noticed he barely says a word when he's here? Just stares at her."

Juliet suspected it was Miranda that David was terrified of, even if she did secretly agree David was a bit of a sap. A very handsome one, though. If the baby was lucky, it would inherit David's looks and Clementine's composure. She'd always been wiser than her years. When her pregnancy started to show, they'd all had a conversation about how and what to tell people outside the family.

"Just tell them that I'm having a baby," Clementine had said. "You don't have to explain how it happened."

Juliet had felt uncomfortable. She'd wanted to save Clementine from as much shame and gossip as she could. She also had a niggling feeling inside about how it would reflect on her; on all of Clementine's sisters. Struggling to find the words, she'd been relieved when Clementine interrupted.

"Juliet, I honestly don't care what people think. It won't change anything. I'm sorry if you're embarrassed but I promise you don't have to be on my behalf. Just tell anyone who asks that it was a big happy surprise and you couldn't be more delighted."

"Or follow my lead, Juliet," Miranda said. "Tell everyone we woke up one night to find Clementine under a spotlight from a flying saucer being impregnated by aliens. And we can't wait until the baby is born and we've got bets on whether it will have blue skin or scales. Honestly, it shuts people up."

Juliet just marveled at her sisters' confidence, yet again. Some of it was to do with looks, she knew that. Clementine was very pretty, with her long dark hair and big eyes, but it was actually Miranda who was the family beauty. Feature by feature she wasn't: Her nose was too big, her skin a little too freckled, her hair was obviously dyed red and she was more gangly than elegant sometimes, but there was something about the way she presented herself that spelled style. If Juliet was to wear the same clothes as Miranda, she knew she'd feel ridiculous, like a little girl in dress-ups.

As for the other two . . . Juliet secretly thought Eliza would look better if she had a good haircut now and again rather than just pulling it back into that ponytail. It would also be nice if she wore something other than tracksuits occasionally. Sadie had quite a pretty face but she always seemed to look scruffy. She also changed hairstyles as often as she changed university courses. Her current permed look didn't suit her at all.

Juliet knew she wasn't cover-girl material herself, either. She was too round-faced and pink-cheeked.

The ABC news jingle played on the radio. Six o'clock. She'd better get a move on with the dinner. *More haste, less speed.* She'd seen that exact sentiment on a fridge magnet in the café that day. Her English-born bosses Mr. and Mrs. Stottington adored fridge magnets with pictures of kittens and soothing sayings. *It's nice to be important but it's important to be nice* was their current favorite.

Juliet had just started cooking the bolognese sauce when she heard the front door slam. Moments later, the kitchen door opened. Miranda and Sadie walked in. They were in mid-fight.

"Don't even try to deny it, Sadie. I worry for your future, you know that? If you can't even steal makeup from your sister without being so obvious about it, how are you going to get on in the big wide world?"

"How dare you accuse me—"

"I'm not accusing you. I'm stating a fact," Miranda snapped. "Just because you haven't two pennies to rub together because you wouldn't know work if it came up and bit you in the face doesn't mean you can steal my hard-earned goods instead."

"Hard-earned goods? You get them all for free at work."

"I don't get them for free. They are samples, rewards for my hard work."

"Rewards for something, at least."

"Meaning?"

"Small town, Miranda, people talk."

"And what do they say, Sadie?" Miranda had taken a small piece of skin on her sister's arm and was twisting it tightly. The smile stayed in place, her voice was calm but there was a hard glint in her eyes. Juliet remained silent. It was a glint they all knew to avoid.

"Jill's brother works behind the bar in the hotel you always go to." It was the smartest hotel in the city, with a view over the water-front. "He gets to hear and see all sorts of things." Sadie pulled away and rubbed at the spot. The color was high on her cheeks.

"Like what?"

"Like married salesmen leading giggling shop assistants up to their rooms."

"And does he know for sure what goes on in those rooms or is he just a small-minded gossipy big mouth like someone in this kitchen?"

"I'm just telling you what I heard."

"You didn't defend me?"

"How could I? I didn't know the truth." Sadie was almost in tears.

"You'll pay for this." With that, Miranda turned on her heels. They heard the back door slam. Moments later the faint smell of cigarette smoke drifted in through the open kitchen window.

"Don't mind her, Sadie," Juliet said.

Sadie was now sobbing. "You should hear what people say about her. She's getting a real reputation. And it reflects on us as well. How do you think it's been for me around the place? Everyone already talking about Clementine being pregnant and now this as well?"

"It's 1979, not 1879, Sadie, come on."

"I'm sick of it, that's all. It's so unfair in this family. Miranda gets away with murder. Dad's carrying on about Clementine as if she's won the Nobel Prize or something. 'Don't work too hard, sweetheart.' 'Here, Clementine, let me carry your bag for you.' "

Juliet laughed at the mutinous expression on Sadie's face. "What do you want him to do? Shave her head and make her parade down Elizabeth Street in shame?"

"I just think she gets away with it because she's the littlest. She always has. 'Oh, Clementine is so clever. She could read by the time she was four. Top of the class every year, even after her mother died.' I was in the top five percent of my class in high school one term but I didn't get any special praise."

"Sadie, stop that. You know Dad is proud of you."

"No, he's not. Makes me want to go out and get pregnant myself. It'd be the only way I'd get any attention in this house." She stood up. Her chair clattered. Sadie always managed to make more noise than the rest of them put together. "What time's dinner?"

"Seven, as usual."

"It's not spaghetti again, is it? I wish you cooked healthier food. It's no wonder I'm putting on weight." She slammed the kitchen door behind her.

Juliet breathed deeply, fighting a temptation to take the saucepan of bolognese sauce and pour it down Sadie's fat, ungrateful throat.

.   .   .

Out on the veranda, Miranda took a long drag of her cigarette and blew the smoke out into the garden, still angry. She was sick of Sadie. They had never got on. Miranda tried to be kind, tried to be understanding, but there was no way around it. She just found Sadie annoying.

The most annoying aspect of this evening's fight was that everything Sadie had said was true. Miranda had indeed slept with the married salesman. His name was Tom Hanlon. She'd been sleeping with him for the past seven weeks, each time he visited Hobart from his Sydney office. Separated, he told her, though she didn't believe him. He'd been wearing his wedding ring the night they met at an industry dinner in the revolving restaurant at the casino. She'd sat beside him. She'd heard him talk about his wife and children to the person sitting on his other side. He'd reminded her of the big bad wolf from the fairy tale. Dark-haired and heavily built. They had talked and laughed all night. She'd been aware of every one of his admiring glances.

He'd rung her the next day, at the pharmacy. Told her he hadn't been able to get her out of his mind. How her hair, her face, her figure was haunting him. He had sounded quite desperate. "I have to see you again."

"Have to? Or want to?"

"Don't tease me, Miranda."

His words had given her a thrilling feeling. A powerful feeling. She'd been curious—eager even—to find out what exactly she could do with that power. What it could bring her.

A lot, she discovered. A dinner in his hotel. Urgent kissing in the corridor on the way to his room. That must have been when Sadie's stupid barman friend had seen them. As it turned out, it was over in such a short time that she felt short-changed. Tom was so overwhelmed by the sight of her in the carefully chosen lingerie it had lasted less than five minutes. The second time was better. By the sixth time, it was becoming very good indeed.

He had phoned her ten days ago. "Miranda, I'll be in Hobart again next weekend."

"You will? I hope you have a lovely time."

"I'll be at the same hotel, in the same room." He named a time. "I want you there. Ask for the key at reception."

If he had asked, if he had pleaded, she would have said no. It was the statement *"I want you there"* that sold her. She told her father she was out meeting a friend. She arrived at the hotel, collected the key and went to his room. She walked in, expecting to find him sitting at the desk like last time. The room was dark. She tried the light switch, once, twice. Nothing. She felt her way across to the bed, looking for the bedside lamp. She screamed when a voice said her name and a hand reached out and grabbed her.

"Tom, you frightened the life out of me."

"What if it wasn't me?" he said, his voice low in the darkness. "What if you had come to this room and a man started doing this," he slowly unzipped her dress, "and then this," his fingers followed the path of the zip, hot against her bare skin. He kept talking, doing as he said, all with the lights off.

It was unbearably exciting. By the time they were both naked she was desperate for the feel of him. She, or was it him, mentioned something about condoms. They'd been careful until that night. "Are you safe?" he said, his lips hot against her breast. She did a rapid calculation. The last thing she wanted was another baby announcement.

"It's fine."

"Are you sure?"

She was sure. It made it even more illicit, the feel of him without protection. They made love three times that night, all in the dark. She initiated it the second and third times, speaking in a low voice, telling him exactly what she was going to do, describing a scenario: her waking up in her hotel room to discover she wasn't alone, reaching out and feeling him on the side of the bed, her fright turning to desire as she felt his body, felt his lips on her skin, all touch and no talking . . .

"You've got quite an imagination, haven't you?" he said afterward as they lay on the bed, smoking cigarettes.

"I'm surprising myself," she said honestly. It was becoming very good between them. She was only barely letting herself admit it, but she very possibly was just the slightest bit in love with him. It was all hypothetical, of course. He had a wife. Children. He was fifteen years older than her. He lived in a different state. Her father would be appalled, not to mention her sisters. But being with him made her feel bold and free and—

"Miranda, your turn to set the table." It was Juliet, calling from the kitchen.

It made her feel everything she wasn't while she lived in this house.

"Coming," she called. She had five more years of this? It felt like a prison sentence. The sooner that child of Clementine's was born and off to school, the better.

•   •   •

Across town, Eliza was lying on a hard mattress on the floor of a badly lit room on the second floor of an ordinary office block.

"Harder, Eliza, harder," the man said.

Eliza was panting, sweat all over her body. "I can't," she breathed.

"You can. One more time. Come on."

She lifted the weights above her head, held them for three arm-shaking seconds and then brought them to the floor, barely keeping control.

"Good girl. Told you you could do it." Her coach, Mark, took the weights from her and returned them to the stand. Seven years older than her, muscled, tanned, and fair-haired, he had been training Eliza for nearly eighteen months.

"And nearly killed myself in the meantime." She moved across the mattress away from the weights and sat up, reaching for her towel to wipe the sweat from her face.

"Now the run," he said. "Then I have a proposition for you."

"Tell me now."

"Run three kilometers first."

"You're a slave driver, not a coach."

He smiled the slow smile, the one that had got her into his thrall when she first joined his running group. They often traveled around the state together, competing in amateur meets.

"Shame he's got a wife," Miranda had said once, after spotting him at one of the events. "I mean, he's not my type—all that brawn, and his shorts are too tight—but you're the perfect couple. Ever thought about an affair?"

Eliza hadn't met her sister's gaze. The last thing she wanted was for Miranda to guess her secret. She'd been in love with Mark since she'd met him. "He's a married man with two children, Miranda."

"That why it's called an affair, Eliza. If he was single, it would be called a relationship."

"Come on, Faraday," Mark said to Eliza now. "The sooner you get going, the sooner you'll be back."

Eliza was smiling as she ran down the stairs and out into the street. She breathed in deeply as the cold air hit her and then headed down the road. She did the 3K run through the streets in thirteen minutes, a little faster than her average.

He was waiting with the stopwatch as she came up the stairs. At this time of night, they had the gym to themselves. He handed her a drink and talked her through her stretches.

"Okay, what's the proposition?" Eliza asked when they finished.

"You do have a one-track mind."

"You're the one who taught me to be focused. I focused on the run, now I'm focused on your proposition."

"I have to ask you some questions first."

She lowered herself onto the mat. "Go on."

"Do you love living in Hobart?"

"Yes."

"Could you leave?"

"Not yet. Not while I'm studying. And I've made a commitment to Clementine to stay until her baby is at school." After the original shock of the news, Eliza had realized the promise they'd all made to Clementine worked in her favor. She'd already been working on a three-year plan. She'd simply changed it to five years. She'd enrolled in a second course at university, specializing in sports nutrition. She'd signed up for a long-term women's basketball coaching stint. She'd also made a personal goal of competing in—and winning—the statewide cross-country championships for at least three consecutive years. If she was going to be living at home and staying in Hobart, she was going to make use of every moment.

"After that, then. Looking into the future. Could you leave?"

"Of course, if the situation was right."

"Would you miss your family?"

"Very funny."

"I'm serious." He sat down beside her. "Eliza, I'm moving to Melbourne and setting up my own fitness company. I know it's a few years off for you, but I want you to think about coming to join me when you've finished your degree."

Eliza ignored the second part of his question for the moment. "You're moving to Melbourne? Just like that?"

He nodded.

"And what does your wife think?"

"I don't know. It won't really affect her. She's fallen in love with another man and we're splitting up."

Eliza blinked. "Are you joking? What about your boys?"

"I get weekends. Once a month."

"You can't leave Hobart then."

"I have to. I don't want to be here. It's a bit awkward."

"Why?"

"The man she's fallen in love with is my cousin."

"Your cousin?" She stared at him. "And I thought I had trouble with my family."

"You? The Waltons? The happiest family in Hobart? You know what people say: 'Those Faraday girls are so wonderful, so loyal—' "

She ignored that. "I'm sorry, Mark." She was lying. She wasn't sorry.

"Thank you."

"But are you serious about this? Moving to the mainland, offering me a job? This far off?"

He explained in more detail. Everyone knew that the future was in tailored individual programs. "My plan is to get work in a gym to begin with, suss out the market before I take the plunge with my own business. I want to target both sexes and research shows female clients prefer female trainers. So I'm booking you in early. I've given it a lot of thought. We already train well together. I like your attitude, your determination. I think we would work well together too."

"It's a long way off. I'd have to think about it."

"Good, I'd expect you to." He stood up. "You didn't answer my question about your family, though. If you could bear to leave them."

Eliza stood up too. She wasn't smiling anymore. "I can't wait to get away from them."

.   .   .

By the time Miranda finally came back inside, Juliet had finished setting the table.

"Thanks so much for your help," Juliet said.

"I'm sorry, I fell into a trance looking at the stars. At least leave the centerpiece for me, would you?" She reached up past Juliet to the cupboard above the stove and pulled out a bundle of fake holly left over from the most recent July Christmas celebration. The Faradays celebrated Christmas twice a year, a summertime one in

December and a winter one in July. It had been another of their mother's ideas. "Midweek dinner, no need to go to too much fuss," Miranda said, pushing the holly into a jar.

Juliet looked up from the stove. "Did you have to be so mean to Sadie before?"

"Yes, I did," Miranda replied, taking down the water glasses and putting those by the place mats. "Because Sadie can be a mean little sneaking cow sometimes. Please don't talk about her, I'm trying to work up an appetite, not make myself nauseous. How are things at work? Still cooking up a storm in that café of yours?"

Juliet quelled her temper. She hated the patronizing way Miranda spoke about the café, as if working in a pharmacy was any more worthwhile. At least Juliet made something, fed people. All Miranda did was wear a white dress and spray perfume around. "Everything's fine, thanks."

"What's up with you?"

"Nothing."

"You suddenly turn into the Ice Queen and then you won't tell me what's wrong? For God's sake, what is it with you and Sadie tonight?"

"What is it with *us*? Ever wonder whether you and your behavior might be the recurring theme here?"

"Forget it, Juliet. You want to set yourself up as the great martyr, the wise woman of the house, you go right ahead. But spare me the lectures, would you?"

"What are you two talking about?" It was Sadie back again, wearing a sulky expression.

Miranda spun around, her eyes flashing. "Do you know, Sadie, if I was asked to list your ten most annoying habits, and believe me, I'd have no trouble finding ten, your infuriating bloody nosiness would be number one. You want to know what we were talking about? It is None of Your Business. And before you have another go at me as well, Juliet, save your energy. You need it for your mother act. Please don't worry about my dinner tonight. All of a sudden I've decided I'm going out."

"Where?"

"Out. I'm a bit short of spending money, Sadie, so a quick hour's work in the hotel should fix me up, wouldn't you say?" She stalked out of the room.

Three minutes later they heard the front door slam.

"It's all true," Sadie said. "I'm not making it up."

Juliet didn't answer. She didn't want to know if it was true or not.

* * *

Three streets away, Clementine and David were sitting in a small café near the cinema. They'd met for a coffee after school, been to see a film and were now about to have supper and a hot chocolate together. She'd known since they met that evening that there was something on his mind. She wasn't surprised when he finally stumbled his way toward his news.

He almost babbled in his attempt to tell her everything. She half-listened. She felt ten years rather than ten days older than him sometimes. She knew girls were more mature than boys but she was surprised sometimes how obvious boys were. And at that moment, she realized, how boring.

"I got the letter from Melbourne University yesterday and I've been trying to think of the best way to tell you, ask you, I mean—"

She had thought herself in love with him. She'd made a considered decision to sleep with him. She'd wanted to discover sex in a good situation, not in the back of a car, like one of her friends. It had been lovely between her and David. Romantic. He'd lit candles in his bedroom and "borrowed" a bottle of champagne from his parents' wine cellar. He presented it to her, with a red rose in a glass vase. They had laughed a lot, especially when neither of them could get the cork out of the champagne bottle. He'd kissed her first, or had she kissed him? They'd taken their clothes off, item by item, until they were both naked under the sheets. More laughing, lying tangled up in each other, looking up at the football posters on his wall. It was awkward at first but she'd loved the feeling of being so close to him. She was cross at herself for miscalculating the safe dates. She had intended to go on the pill but it hadn't seemed necessary the first time. What were the chances of that, after all? Very high, the doctor had told her later.

". . . I applied for this mathematics course months ago. It's the best in the country and I could defer. You know I want to be around as much as I can. If you want me to turn it down—"

It wasn't her decision. If he'd considered leaving, then his mind was already made up. "It's up to you."

"How can you be so calm?"

That's just the way she was. Her father often commented on it at home. "Clementine, being with you is like being on my own, and I mean that in the nicest possible way. You are the most soothing member of the human race I have ever met. Forget these half-hearted attempts at inventions and world domination. If I could bottle you, I'd make a fortune." Her school reports said the same thing: "Clementine's steady approach to her studies is to be applauded. A mature, good-tempered member of the school community." She often wondered whether it was because she was fifth in the family. Calm was the only character trait left for her. Juliet was hardworking. Miranda dramatic. Eliza determined. Sadie anxious. Clementine calm. There they were, in a nutshell. Mature beyond her years. Losing her mother would make any little girl grow up, she knew that was what people said about her. Old beyond her years, her father described her.

Beside her, David was still tripping over himself to explain, to apologize, to promise that he would always be there for her.

"It's all right, David. Really." She stopped him with a touch to the arm. "I don't mind."

"I'll always love you."

"You might not. You might meet someone else."

"Will you be all right?"

"I don't know yet." Clementine had never been able to lie to make other people feel better.

"I'll get back to Hobart as often as I can."

"You don't have to."

"It's my baby too."

"Yes, I know."

"I want to be as involved as I can."

"I know you do."

She could practically see the relief coming off him now that he'd broken his news. There were lots of things she could say. Point out the facts, to begin with. How could he be involved when he was living in another state? Nappy changing, middle-of-the-night feeding, clothes washing—all of that was out of the question. She had a mental picture of visits in years to come, him awkwardly holding his child. Birthday cards and hastily bought presents arriving days or weeks late. None of it bothered her.

She'd thought about it for a long time, since the day she realized her period was late. She'd kept the news to herself quite deliberately, wanting time to think things through. By the time everyone knew she had felt sure in her head. More than sure. Content. Even excited. As if this was all meant to be. And once she had decided that, and pictured herself with a baby, in the house, with her father and her sisters around her, she had discovered David was not appearing in her mental pictures. She never imagined the two of them strolling along the waterfront, pushing a pram. Setting up house together. Shopping. Sitting under a Christmas tree watching their child unwrap presents. It dawned on her slowly. She would never say it to him, or even to her own family, but she could think of no place in her life for him.

He took her in his arms, awkwardly, uncomfortable with her rounded body and the eyes of the couple on the opposite side of the café who were clearly eavesdropping.

"I'll always love you," he said again. "And if you ever need anything . . ."

She hugged him back. "Thank you, David. For everything." If he noticed she hadn't said she would always love him too, he didn't mention it.

.   .   .

Clementine arrived home just before nine. Juliet looked up from her book as she heard the front door open. She was alone in the living room. Sadie was in the kitchen, noisily washing the dishes.

"You look comfortable," Clementine said, noticing the fire, the book and the thick socks on Juliet's feet.

"Middle-aged before my time, you mean? How was your date?"

"The film was far-fetched but good. The chocolate ice cream was lovely. And David and I split up."

Juliet pushed the book aside. "You *what?*"

Clementine reported the conversation. "I knew he was interested in that course. And he had to do what's right for him, the way I—" Her expression suddenly changed, from serious to a big smile. She put her hand on her belly. "She's moving."

"He is?" They liked switching between the sexes. "Can I feel?"

Juliet put her hand on Clementine's belly, and Clementine put her hand on top of Juliet's. They both felt a little movement, a tiny push against her skin, a pause, and then a stronger movement. Two smiles.

"It's body language from the baby," Clementine said. "Telling me not to worry." She settled into the chair opposite Juliet and put her feet up on the low table.

Where were the tears? Juliet wondered. "Aren't you a little bit upset? The father of your child telling you he is disappearing? Your first great love affair ending?"

Clementine was thoughtful for a moment. "I can't explain it, but it all feels as though it is happening the way it should. It would have been harder somehow if he was staying around. This is cleaner in a way." A pause. "Do you mind about this, Juliet?"

"Mind?"

"It's out of order, isn't it? You're the oldest. You should be the one getting married first, having the baby first."

"Fortunately you've ruined everything by having the baby without getting married. Anyway, I don't think there is some predetermined plan, is there?"

"In nature I think there is," Clementine said.

"Nothing natural about this family."

"It will change everything, won't it?"

"In good ways," Juliet replied.

"In other ways, too."

"What was it like, Clemmie?"

"What?"

"Sex."

"Juliet! You're older than me. I should have been asking you."

"What are you talking about?" They spun around. It was Sadie.

"Nothing," Juliet said.

"Sex," Clementine told her.

"Can I join in?"

Clementine shut her eyes. "No. I'm never doing it again. It got me into enough trouble the first time."

CHAPTER 3

Maggie Tessa Faraday arrived at nine minutes past four on the afternoon of the eleventh of February, 1980. Seven and a half pounds. Black hair. A touch of jaundice but otherwise in perfect health.

"Why do I feel like it was me who was in there having the baby?" Miranda sighed as she leaned against the hospital wall.

"Because you did more shouting than Clementine," her father said.

"Someone had to. They shouldn't have been so slow with the anesthesia."

Juliet returned from the cafeteria with a tray of tea and a plate of cookies. "There's nothing left but these. Will they do?"

Eliza picked one up. "They're a bit bendy."

"I know, sorry. If I'd known it was going to happen today, I'd have organized a picnic basket or something." She wasn't joking.

"How inconsiderate of Clementine to deliver two weeks early," Miranda said.

She had taken everyone by surprise, the hospital especially, when she arrived on her own, white-faced and sweating, complaining of pains. An examination in the emergency room showed she was well into labor. Her contractions were only five minutes apart. She was lucky she'd got there when she did.

Clementine had rung Juliet (in the café), who rang Miranda (in the pharmacy), who rang Eliza (who'd just arrived home), who left a message in block letters pinned on the front door for Sadie, who was out shopping. Miranda, Juliet, and Eliza each then rang their father at work. He moved so quickly he was at the hospital before any of them.

The early admission proved a minor false alarm. Clementine's labor stopped, then started, then came in earnest. Unbeknownst to each, Clementine had asked all of her sisters to be in the delivery room with her. Sadie still hadn't arrived, but the other three were more than willing to help. There was a tense moment when the midwife and then finally the doctor insisted there was room for only one and they'd better hurry up and decide who it was going to be before all three of them were asked to leave. They drew straws. Miranda won.

Outside the delivery suite, Juliet, Eliza, and Leo heard more roars from Miranda than Clementine. It was Miranda who emerged from the delivery room to announce it was a girl and to tell them Clementine was fine. Then they'd all been allowed in, to see Clementine holding the tiny white-wrapped bundle and looking no more exhausted than if she had strolled in from a walk in the Botanic Gardens.

"She is amazing." Leo joined his daughters in the waiting area. He had been in with Clementine and baby Maggie for the past fifteen minutes. His hair was standing on end, his clothes were rumpled, his smile stretched across his face. "What a clever, clever girl."

"To turn an ordinary old father of five into a grandfather in one big push," Miranda said.

"Your mother should have been here."

"If our mother had been here, Clementine wouldn't have been in there," Miranda replied. "She'd never have let this happen, if you know what I mean."

"And you know what I meant. She'd have loved a grandchild."

The girls didn't answer. It was how their father had expressed his emotions since their mother had died. If a meal was particularly wonderful, he would say, "Your mother would have enjoyed this." Beautiful countryside: "Your mother loved this kind of scenery." He used it for negative comments as well: "Your mother would have hated to see you wearing clothes like that."

"Clementine's chosen the name," Leo announced.

That stopped their cups of tea in mid-sip. "Just like that? Without consultation?" Miranda was outraged.

"She wants you to guess it."

The possible name had been a source of constant discussion in the Faraday house since Clementine had announced she was pregnant.

"Is it a song?" Juliet asked. "A book character? Like Mum did with us?"

It mattered very much to them all that it was. Their names were a daily reminder of their mother. She had chosen them from a long list of her favorite songs and fictional heroines. Each of them had a card she had written for them on their baptism day, with just a few lines explaining why she had picked their name and what it meant to her. Juliet had been named after Shakespeare's *Romeo and Juliet*. Miranda's name was also from Shakespeare, Prospero's daughter in *The Tempest*. Clementine's was from the song "Oh My Darling, Clementine." Eliza owed her name to Miss Doolittle, the heroine of *Pygmalion*. Sadie's name came from a short story called "Rain" by W. Somerset Maugham, Tessa's favorite writer. Sadie had imagined her fictional namesake to be a wonderful, romantic heroine and had been very upset to learn the truth. The fictional Sadie was a prostitute. She'd come to Leo in tears. Miranda had snatched the book from her and read it too, in gales of laughter. "Mum obviously had big plans for you."

Their middle names were far more ordinary. Leo had been in charge of them. All saints' names, a nod to his Catholic upbringing: Teresa, Anne, Catherine, Mary, and Agnes. He had written a note on each card too, with a line or two about that saint's life.

He gazed at his daughters, all trying to guess the name of Clementine's baby. "I'll give you a clue. It's a song. Two songs, in fact."

They thought of singers currently in the charts. Blondie, Amii

Stewart, Gloria Gaynor. A shake of the head from their father to each one.

"Give up?"

Three nods.

"Her name is Maggie Tessa Faraday. From two songs, 'Maggie's Farm,' and that Irish ballad your mother loved."

"I think it's beautiful," Juliet said.

"I hate both songs. I'll give it a trial run. If I'm not happy after a month, I'll give her a name myself," Miranda said.

"What would you call her, then?" Eliza asked.

"Boo, because she gave us such a surprise."

Juliet turned to Leo. "Should we let David know?"

"Clementine wants to," Leo said. "In her own time."

David had moved to the mainland five weeks earlier. The formalities had been worked out months before. His name on the birth certificate. Agreed access. Clementine had insisted she didn't want financial assistance from him yet.

"It's not about the money. We'll manage." It was Clementine's answer to everything at the moment. "I think it's better this way. No resentment on David's part. When he's earning money we're going to talk about it again."

Leo had shaken his head in admiration. "You're some stuff, Clementine Faraday."

"Clementine's uterus is contracting even now," Miranda said in a conversational tone, as she browsed through a booklet the midwife had left with them.

"Miranda, please." Leo looked skyward. "One son. Couldn't I have been given just one son? Or even a grandson?" They ignored him. They'd heard it all before.

The maternity unit door flew open. It was Sadie. "Did I miss it? Has she had it?"

"A girl. A healthy, beautiful girl."

Sadie had a stormy expression on her face. "Couldn't she have waited until I was here too? How come I had to miss out?"

"Only Miranda was allowed in," Eliza said. "There were too many of us as it was. We drew straws."

"You can go in and see her now, though," Juliet said.

"It's not the same."

"For God's sake, Sadie," Miranda said with a laugh. "She could hardly hold on until you turned up."

"She said she wanted me to be there when the baby was born."

"She said that to all of us. The baby had other ideas."

"Everything's spoiled now."

"Stop that, Sadie," Juliet said.

"It is. The whole idea was we were all going to be here to welcome the baby into the world. And I wasn't. So it's going to be cursed now."

"The only person who is going to be cursed is you if you keep this up," Miranda snapped. "Stop it right now. Get that ridiculous sulky expression off your face and go in and say hello to your sister and your niece."

Juliet stood up. "It doesn't matter that you weren't here for the exact moment, Sadie, really. I told you, only Miranda was with her, and Clementine was pretty busy. I'm not sure she would have noticed if her entire class from school was here."

Sadie hesitated.

"In you go," Leo said.

Sadie did as she was told. Fifteen minutes later she came back out. Her face had changed, her expression soft where there had been scowls. "She's beautiful."

"She is," Leo agreed.

"And she's all ours."

"Clementine's," Juliet said.

"Ours," Sadie said firmly.

CHAPTER 4

The pram moved forward three inches, back three inches and then suddenly shot six feet across the kitchen floor and slammed into the fridge.

"Not quite there yet, Dad, I think," Clementine said.

"It was working before. Maybe it needs the weight of a baby in it. Would you—"

"No!"

"I'll try the pumpkin again." He tied a small pumpkin to a bigger pumpkin and wrapped the lot in one of Maggie's blankets. He had just settled it into the pram when the door opened.

It was Miranda. She went immediately over to the pram. "Hello, little Maggie," she cooed. She didn't react at the sight of two pumpkins instead of her six-month-old niece. "And who is the sweetest baby in all of Tasmania? Yes, you are. And who is your favorite aunt? Good girl." She straightened up. "Clem, I really think you better pull back a little on the pureed carrots. She's looking a bit orange these days."

"Watch this." Leo pressed the lever again. The pram shuddered forward, rocked from side to side, then stopped.

"That's terrific, Dad. You're going for that earth-tremor effect, I see."

"Dad, really. I'm happy to push her."

"It'll free you up to study or to do other things, though, if the pram moves on its own."

"And the poor child will grow up thinking she lives in a haunted house," Miranda said.

Eliza came in, looked at the pumpkins and frowned.

"My friend Lynetta was in the pharmacy today," Miranda announced.

"Lynetta who used to be called Lyn until she moved to Melbourne and became glamorous?" Eliza asked.

"She was glamorous beforehand, she just hadn't reached her potential. She's started training to be a flight attendant."

"I thought she was going to be a film star."

"She was. But now she's going to be a flight attendant," Miranda said. "She thought I should give it a try too. They're calling for new applicants in a few months."

Clementine looked up from putting Maggie back in the pram. Beside her, Leo was holding the two pumpkins as though they were the real baby. "You wouldn't leave us yet, Miranda, would you?" Clementine said.

Sadie walked into the kitchen. "Is Miranda leaving? Where are you going?"

"I'm not going anywhere. Not yet. Break this fragile family bond? Shatter our perfect harmony? How could I do it?"

From the pram, Maggie started to cry, her waving hands visible over the edge.

"It's all right, Maggie," Miranda shouted over the noise. "I won't go anywhere until I have seen you off on your first day of school, I promise."

Maggie's cry turned into a high-pitched wail.

Eliza put her hands over her ears. "You must be doing something wrong, Clementine. Feeding her too much or not feeding her enough."

"She's a baby, Eliza," Clementine snapped. "Babies cry."

"And I'm an adult, and adults need to sleep. It's not just you who wakes up in the middle of the night, every night, you know."

Maggie wailed again, ignoring Clementine's attempts to soothe her.

Miranda winced. "Eliza's right, Clemmie. Much as I love that adorable child of ours, if she doesn't start putting a cork in it, I'm going to ring David and tell him you and Maggie are coming to Melbourne to live with him."

"I try to keep her quiet. She's just got a temper on her."

"A temper? She's only six months old. She can't even see yet."

"You're thinking of kittens," Leo said. He was back tinkering with the pram's wheels.

"What?"

"It's kittens who can't see when they're first born. Babies can see straight away. Fuzzy shapes for a start, but they recognize everyone: voices, images, features."

"Dad, can you keep out of this? Unless you're planning on building Clementine a soundproofed room."

"That's not a bad idea," Leo said, reaching for his notebook.

Juliet took the opportunity to take a load of washing out to the clothesline at the end of the garden. It was the quietest spot to be found these days. And the cleanest. The amount of noise Maggie made had been the first big surprise after Clementine brought her home from the hospital. The mess had been the second. As for the extra washing . . . how could so small a baby go through so many clothes? Not to mention take up so much room. Sterilizers, nappy-soaking buckets, clothes racks, prams, bassinets, bouncers . . .

Leo was to blame as well. Barely a day went by without him arriving home with a new piece of labor-saving equipment or brain-stimulating toy. The previous night Juliet had come in to the living room to find pieces of brightly colored plastic strewn all over the carpet. It looked like there'd been an explosion. Leo was sitting cross-legged in the center of the chaos, attempting to put whatever it had originally been back together. He'd been trying to make a few modifications, he told them.

"It was a plastic dragon," Miranda had said, exasperated. "A mythical beast. How can you make modifications to something that doesn't exist?"

Juliet finished pegging up the clothes. She really should go back in and put on another load. She heard a wail from Maggie. On second thought, perhaps she would stay outside a little longer.

· · ·

If Leo had wanted a full house for the unveiling of his latest project, three weeks after his attempt at the self-rocking pram, he'd chosen his time badly. Clementine and Maggie were at a friend's house, Sadie and Eliza both had late lectures, Juliet was working overtime and Miranda was meeting a friend. They had all written their whereabouts up on the notice board. Not that Leo had looked at it. As Miranda had said, he clearly preferred to think of it as the "Not-notice Board."

Eliza was first home.

"At last," Leo said, springing out of the armchair in the sitting room.

"Dad, you frightened me! What on earth are you doing hiding there like that?"

"I'm not hiding. I'm waiting for all of you," he said, following her into the kitchen in his eagerness. "It's a landmark day. Where are the others?"

Eliza glanced at the notice board and gave him a quick rundown of where her sisters were.

"Never mind. I'll just have to show them all later. You get to be the first, Eliza. Come and take a look."

Eliza calmly followed him down the hallway, used to these sorts of occasions.

Leo spoke over his shoulder. "I got the idea from one of those music magazines Sadie reads. Or is it you who reads them? Fascinating stuff, I have to say. The names of some of the bands these days—Split Enz, Australian Crawl, Adam and the Ants! How do they think of them?"

They stopped outside the closed door of Clementine and Maggie's room.

"As I mentioned, it's not entirely my own idea," Leo said, beaming at her. "But I bet those rock stars never imagined it being used for something like this!" He threw open the door. "Ta-dah!"

All four walls were covered with empty egg cartons. Hundreds of them. Gray knobbly material all over the previously pale yellow walls. It looked like a set from a science-fiction film.

"Great, Dad," Eliza said. "You've set up an egg factory in Clementine's room."

He ignored her. "It took me all day. I've been collecting the cartons for weeks from everywhere I could think of."

"And no one worried about your mental health?"

"I told them all what I was going to do with them."

"If you don't mind me asking, what *have* you done with them?"

"You haven't guessed? It's soundproofing. So we can all start sleeping through the night. I know it looks a bit dull at the moment, but we can give it all a lick of paint, and we'll hardly notice them."

"Did you ask Clementine if she minded you sticking egg cartons all over her walls?"

"I wanted it to be a surprise."

It certainly will be, Eliza thought. She took pity on him, noting his excited face. "Well done, Dad."

He was oblivious. He'd noticed a carton working loose on the wall near the window and was already putting up the ladder.

Eliza went into the room she shared with Sadie, shutting the door. She changed out of her tracksuit, unpacked her rucksack and tidied away her study notes.

As she had to do every day, she took out a broom and pushed all of Sadie's belongings back on to her side of the room. The line painted down the center of the room was faded but as far as Eliza was concerned it was still in operation. Their father had painted it nearly six years earlier, when Eliza had protested that she couldn't share with Sadie another day. "We're like Jack Sprat and his wife. She can't stay tidy and I hate being messy."

Leo came up with the idea of the line down the middle of the room instead. It worked immediately. Eliza loved it, making a ritual each evening of pushing any of Sadie's belongings over the line. Sadie hated it then and still hated it, but she made no attempt to be any tidier.

As she finished neatening the cover on her bed, Eliza realized that was one more thing to look forward to. Her own space. Mark had made vague mentions of them sharing a house when she moved to Melbourne but Eliza had told him she would rather not. It would be expensive, but she was determined to begin their business lives as separate people. She was also longing for her own place, no matter how small. The idea of her own kitchen and bathroom filled her with a strange excitement. No tripping over other people's clothes and boots, or finishing dishes only to discover cups hidden behind sofas, underneath beds. Clean floors staying clean. All that, and working with Mark, every day. It would be a kind of heaven.

. . .

Sadie was at the cinema on her own. She had decided to skip her lecture. She hadn't finished reading the book they'd be discussing so it was really a waste of time.

. . .

In a bar on the waterfront, on a high seat next to the fire, Miranda took a long drag of her cigarette, crossed her legs, and blew smoke at her own reflection in the mirror behind the bar.

"Another drink, Miranda?" The elderly barman knew her well. Miranda and her friend Liz came here as often as they could afford.

"Yes, thanks, Richie. Two gin and tonics."

One for her and one for Liz, if she ever came back from her flirting session in the corner. She'd been talking to that man for the past ten minutes and it was supposed to be her round. With a sigh, Miranda reached for her purse. Farewell to her latest savings plan, then. Thank God Leo had told them all he would waive their board for the time being, on account of them all being such a help to Clementine and Maggie. Not that Miranda had been able to offer much help in any practical sense yet. She saw herself more as an emotional support to Clementine. Juliet, Eliza and Sadie were much better at that hands-on work. Clementine seemed to be managing very well, too, juggling her studies with looking after her daughter, either taking Maggie to her lectures or organizing babysitting rosters between Eliza and Sadie for the few hours she was away.

It was just a pity Leo hadn't decided to pay them all for helping Clementine. Even without the expense of paying board, Miranda still found it hard to keep herself in the manner to which she dearly wanted to become accustomed. Perhaps she should be grateful for Leo and his obsession with keeping the family together.

The barman delivered the two drinks and took her money. "Everything going well for you, Miranda?" he said as he delivered the change.

"Great, thanks."

It was and it wasn't. She'd had a phone call that day from Tom. A lying phone call. He was ringing to let her know that it broke his heart to tell her, but he was being moved to another sales area. He'd be looking after Victoria and South Australia from now on.

"Your wife asked for that, did she?"

He went silent.

Miranda laughed. "It's all right, Tom." And it was. He was too old for her anyway. She thought about telling him that, but decided she'd save that line for another time. He'd been becoming a little possessive anyway. Ringing her nearly every day at the pharmacy, even at home once or twice. Tom's wife had obviously been checking the phone records. Miranda had thought herself in love with him, but she realized then she'd been mistaken. She'd miss him, but not too much. And after all, there were plenty of visiting salesmen fish in the—

"Miranda, I'd like you to meet Kevin. He's down from Sydney on business and said he'd love to buy us both a drink." It was Liz, back at last.

Miranda spun around on her stool, put out her hand and gave a big, welcoming smile. "Kevin, it's a pleasure to meet you. Welcome to Hobart."

* * *

Clementine was in trouble. She thought she'd known what to expect. From the moment she knew she was pregnant she'd decided to be organized about it. She'd read all the books. She'd spent the final weeks of her pregnancy talking to maternity nurses. She'd arrived at her doctor's appointments before Maggie's birth with lists of questions and taken down the answers in her neat handwriting. She borrowed an idea from her mother and started a scrapbook, filled with handy tips on minding a newborn, coping with a three-month-old, what to expect at nine months. She knew what to do if the baby had colic, wasn't sleeping or developed a rash. She knew the symptoms for more than a dozen rare childhood diseases.

She'd coped with all the talk at school and the gossip among the neighbors. As the pregnancy progressed, she'd become used to her changing shape, to being rounded where she had always been thin, heavy when she had been light. All her sisters had started stroking her bump as though it was a cat she had sitting in her lap. She'd wanted to ask them to stop until she realized she actually quite liked it. From them at least. It was the stroking from near strangers that she didn't like so much. She was almost an exhibit at school. She thought about charging her classmates five cents per touch.

She turned seventeen the week before she sat her final exams, at a table that had to be brought into the exam room specially because she was finding it difficult to fit behind the usual desks.

The birth had been painful but, as the books said, once it was over she truly had forgotten about it. The midwife told her she had the right idea to have a baby when she was so young. The body was supple then. It would practically ping back into shape afterward, you wait and see.

It hadn't "pinged," but she had got her old figure back more quickly than she expected. She'd breast-fed as advised. All things considered, everything was going as expected.

Except one thing.

Maggie.

Clementine may have read all the books, but her seven-month-old daughter definitely hadn't. Maggie did as she pleased. She cried for no reason. She slept one night and not the next. She fed happily one day and then wasn't interested the following one, gazing about with her dark, bright eyes instead. She roared if she was left alone. She roared if she was put into her room to sleep. Sometimes she just roared for no reason at all. If she wasn't vomiting, she was weeing or pooing. Sometimes all three at once. Clementine felt her own body was out of control too. Her breasts leaked at the first cry from Maggie, sometimes at just a passing thought about her daughter. Some days her clothes were no sooner washed and on than they were covered in little calling cards of white milky vomit, first one shoulder, then the other. Although nothing could beat the incredibly sweet, brand-new, fresh smell of Maggie when she was clean and dry and dozing in Clementine's arms, sometimes it felt like she was surrounded from the moment she woke by the combined odor of washing powder, baby vomit and nappy contents.

The first few months it was as if Maggie had five mothers. Juliet, Miranda, Eliza and Sadie couldn't do enough for her, competing over who got to hold her, dress her, bathe her. One afternoon Juliet and Eliza almost came to blows about whose turn it was to change a nappy. Clementine caught Sadie waking Maggie up, after Clementine had spent nearly an hour getting her to settle.

"I missed her," Sadie said in explanation.

Miranda offered to mind her for a couple of hours another day, while Clementine caught up on some sleep. "We'll have a little cuddle and then I'll lay her down, I promise," Miranda said.

When Clementine emerged from her bedroom two hours later it was to find Maggie still wide awake on Miranda's lap, with her hair—what there was of it—tied into dozens of little ponytails.

"She's a baby, not a doll," Clementine said.

"You mean she's real? I thought she had very lifelike eyes."

Week by week, though, her sisters had drifted away. Clementine couldn't blame them. They'd put up with enough disruption in the early months, especially the long sleepless nights when Maggie's crying kept everyone awake, before Leo had the brain wave about the egg cartons. They had their own lives, after all.

Leo was still the doting grandfather—he was besotted with Maggie, Clementine knew that—but his attention wavered depending on what was happening in Shed Land. He'd started a new project and went out there straight after dinner most evenings. Clementine had once been able to rely on him to help with the nightly bath. She now found she was doing it on her own.

She hadn't said anything to any of them. She was conscious of not upsetting anyone, and making Maggie blend as seamlessly into the family as possible.

The only consolation was Maggie seemed happy enough. Her eyes were bright, she was putting on weight, she was lively and when she did deign to sleep, it was deeply and calmly. It was Clementine who hadn't slept properly in weeks. Her hair was in its long plait down her back day after day. She didn't have the time or energy to wash it regularly.

That's what she hadn't expected: the constancy and intensity of looking after a baby, the loss of time to herself. Before Maggie, she could go for a walk whenever she wanted. Arrange to meet friends. Go to the library. Study. Sleep. Now nothing could be done without planning and preparation. And even if she did organize everything, have Maggie dressed and ready, a sudden nappy change or a vomit or a crying fit and everything was delayed, postponed or canceled.

David had flown back from Melbourne twice to visit them, once in the hospital just after Maggie was born. He had looked at the baby in his arms as if it was a large slug. Clementine saw him try to hide it, but his youth overwhelmed her again. He wasn't ready for this. Swept up in the aftermath, the attention, the presents, the fun of a homecoming to the newly decorated bedroom, she told herself it didn't matter that she was on her own as a parent.

It was only in the middle of the night, when she finally got Maggie to sleep, that she let herself be upset, shedding silent tears into the pillow. All the things her father had said kept coming back to her. Her life was on hold now, buried under an avalanche of nappies, wipes and bibs. She had insisted that of course it wouldn't be like that; of course she could manage everything.

She told herself that again now, as she sat in her bedroom trying to get Maggie to sleep. She put her in the cot, but Maggie started wailing as though she was being dropped into hot water. She paced around the soundproofed room—the cell, as she had started to think of it—to no avail. If Maggie had been sleepy after the last feed, she was nothing of the sort now. Her eyes were alert. Clementine spoke to her in a low voice, urging her to sleep, for both their sakes. The unblinking gaze back. Clementine stroked her little face, her nose, her eyebrows. The eyelids flickered and for a moment she was optimistic. A second later, Miss Bright Eyes was back again.

Clementine took her into the living room, where the fire was lit. Even though it was late spring, the nights were still cold. She turned off the main light, lit the lamps, made it as peaceful as possible. She changed position, holding Maggie up on her shoulder. She liked the way her head felt, tucked into her neck, the tiny tickle of Maggie's breath on her skin, the sound of her breathing. She had lain there night after night listening to it, fearful at first, almost counting the breaths, urging each one on. She had read about cot death, about sleep apnoea, measles, chicken pox. All the childhood diseases. She was so well informed she was filled with as much anxiety as love.

Because she did love her daughter, didn't she? Is that what she called this feeling she had for her? She didn't know for sure. She'd thought she had loved David, after all. She rarely thought of him now.

She felt something so strong for Maggie, something that made her want to be with her, yearn for the feel of her warm little body against her own. Hours passed when all she wanted to do was stare into Maggie's eyes, marvel at the almost-blue of the whiteness around her dark irises. Long minutes passed stroking her soft cheeks, counting the tiny spiky eyelashes, tracing her almost invisible eyebrows, touching the tiny—so tiny—fingernails and toenails. She could smell her constantly, a soft, powdery smell of . . . what? Washing powder? Baby powder? Not just that. It was as if Maggie had her own special scent that only Clementine could smell. The same way that her head seemed to be shaped to fit exactly into the curve between Clementine's chin and shoulder. All those moments were beautiful. But the physical side of it, the sheer work of it, was taking up room in her head that she'd expected to fill to overflowing with love and maternal feelings.

But she couldn't complain. She wouldn't complain. She didn't want any of them saying, "We told you so," or "Didn't we say this would happen?" If she had to keep up this being-capable act, she would do it, until it killed her.

As she sat up in the small hours, night after night, trying to get Maggie to settle, she realized what she wanted was her own mother. She wanted to go to her mum and ask, How do I do this? What does it mean when Maggie cries? What is that rash? Am I burping her right? Can she sleep on her side like that? Should I be getting these pains in my breasts?

She tried to imagine her mother across the living room now. It was difficult. What would she be doing? Knitting? Sewing? Clementine couldn't remember if her mother had ever done either of those things. Would she be watching TV, the sound turned low so as not to disturb Maggie's light sleeping? Would she be reading? Doing a crossword?

Clementine attempted to summon up an image of her mother's face. If she turned around she wouldn't even have to try. The entire back wall was covered in framed photos: first day of school, family holidays, birthday celebrations. More than half of them featured their mother. Clementine didn't want to look at photos of her mother. She wanted her here, now. Alive.

She heard a thump in the hallway and silently cursed, checking to see if the noise had woken Maggie. It hadn't. Sadie always jumped the last few rungs of the attic ladder onto the bare floorboards below, no matter how many times Leo asked her not to. She'd been up there looking for the Christmas decorations, even though it was three weeks off. Moments later she came into the living room, carrying a dusty box. "I do love having two Christmases a year, don't you? I'd eat roast turkey every week if I could."

Clementine put her finger to her lips, gesturing toward Maggie. Sadie pulled a face, mouthed the word "Sorry" and sat on the floor in front of the fire, emptying the box of decorations with a clatter. "Sadie!" Clementine hissed.

"Sorry," Sadie whispered.

Clementine watched as Sadie carefully sorted the decorations into types, stars in one pile, tinsel in another. Her sister looked more peaceful than usual as she went about her work. Clementine decided the time was right.

"Sadie, what was Mum like?"

"What?"

"What was Mum like?"

"Look behind you."

"I know what she looked like. I can't remember what she was like, though. Her personality."

"She was . . . she was Mum, you know." Sadie looked uncomfortable. "What's brought this on?"

"Nothing especially. I just feel like talking about her. Tell me something about her, Sadie. Something you liked doing with her."

Sadie put down the length of tinsel she'd been untangling and thought for a moment. "I used to like sitting in the bedroom while she got ready to go out. Miranda would always be there too. Mum would go through her wardrobe and say, 'Well, Miranda, will I wear this one or this one?' And I'd watch her put her makeup on. She wore lots of it. Lipstick especially. That's obviously where Miranda got it from."

"Why can't I remember that?"

"You were just a little kid, I suppose."

"You were only two years older than me."

Sadie shrugged. "I don't know, Clementine. Maybe those are the two years when you get a memory." She stood up, picked up the box and left the room.

A few minutes later, Juliet came in. She made a pretense of looking for a magazine, straightening a cushion, looking at a row of books on the bookshelf, before coming over and sitting beside Clementine on the sofa.

She spoke in a whisper. "Are you okay?"

Clementine nodded.

"Sadie said you were asking her about Mum."

"I'm allowed to, aren't I?"

It was unusual for Clementine to snap like that. "Of course. But why out of the blue like this?"

"I just need to know about her."

"Because of Maggie?"

"Because of me and because of Maggie. I can't seem to remember anything about Mum, Juliet. And it feels wrong that I'm a mother and I can't ask my own mother what to do. It's not fair."

"No, it's not."

"And I hate that I'm the only one who can't remember her well. You've all got proper memories. All I have are the photographs."

"You don't remember her at all?"

"I remember her being in the house. Having someone to go to, to ask things, walking to school with her. But then it gets mixed up in my memory. I think it's Mum I'm remembering and then I realize I have the timing wrong, and it's you taking me to school or you packing my lunch."

"I'm sorry, Clemmie."

They were quiet for a moment, both looking into the fire. The burning wood made a spitting, crackling sound. Clementine adjusted Maggie on her shoulder and tucked the blanket a little closer around her.

"She was a busy person," Juliet said after a moment. "She was always doing something or planning something. Dress-ups. Elaborate parties for our birthdays. She liked organizing things, visits to markets or trips out of town. She had lots of energy." She smiled. "That's how I remember her. She almost hummed with energy."

"And what was wrong with her? Those are all good things. There must have been things wrong with her as well."

Juliet hesitated. "She was a bit distracted sometimes. So many of us, I suppose. It was hard to get time on your own with her. She could be a bit moody sometimes too. Get cross out of the blue, with Sadie especially. With Miranda too, now and then."

Clementine smiled, gently stroking Maggie's head, the movement ruffling the soft black hair. "Did she ever get mad at you?"

"No, never with me. That's one good thing, I suppose. She died before we had a chance to have too many fights."

Clementine hesitated. "Juliet, did you know Dad still keeps all her clothes in his wardrobe? After all this time?"

Juliet smiled. "I thought it was a secret. That only I knew."

"Is there something a bit funny about that, do you think, after all these years? Shouldn't he have, I don't know, given them away or given them to us?"

"Maybe. I don't know. I don't know what's normal. Maybe it helps him."

"I'd love to have something of Mum's. Something to give Maggie as well."

"Me too. But don't you remember what happened that time Miranda asked if she could borrow her—" She stopped. "Sorry, you probably don't. You were still a little kid."

"Tell me now."

"It was about eighteen months after Mum died. Miranda had her end-of-year school dance and she needed a gold scarf or a wrap, that kind of thing. She told Dad she remembered Mum wearing something like that and about five minutes later he came back into the room and handed the scarf over. Miranda was all kisses and hugs, as if Dad had presented her with a Tiffany necklace."

"But that's so unfair. How come she got to have something of Mum's and none of us did?"

"She never wore it. When she came out the next night all dressed up in it, Dad freaked out. Said he was sorry but she couldn't have it. It was Tessa's, and he shouldn't have given it to Miranda. And that was that. She handed it back and he never offered anything again."

"But he let us have the scrapbooks. And her recipe books. You use them all the time."

"I suppose because we helped her do them. They were different."

"But all the other things she started. The July Christmas. That was her idea, wasn't it?"

A pause. "She only had the idea for it the day before she died."

"I can't believe I didn't know any of this." Clementine turned to face Juliet. "What about all the other things we do in her memory? The birthday chair? The treasure hunts at Easter time? Did she ever do those with us?"

"Those ones, yes," Juliet said. "You've seen the photos stuck in her scrapbook."

Juliet had a sudden memory of sitting in a living room with her mother—but was it here in Hobart or in London before they emigrated?—when Tessa announced she wanted a purple page in the latest scrapbook. She'd given Juliet, Miranda and Eliza scissors and magazines each, set a kitchen timer to ten minutes and shouted "Go!" When the time was up, there were snippets of shiny paper all over the room.

Miranda had won, helped by a cookery magazine. She'd cut out aubergines, grapes and plums. It made Juliet sad to think Clementine had none of those memories of their mother. The rushes of excitement, the spontaneous games, the fun. They were the bright moments. The dark side was the mood swings that often followed. Every high day had a low day, when Tessa wouldn't want to play with them, when Leo would cook, when the bedroom door would be shut for most of the day. "Your mother's just tired," Leo would say. "She needs a sleep-in." Protecting her, as he always did. Treating her like some precious object. In awe of her, almost. He still was now.

"I should be able to remember more than I do," Clementine said. "I read a book that said you learn to mother the way you were mothered yourself. And I wasn't mothered properly if I can't remember it happening, was I? So does that mean I'll be bad to Maggie? That I won't know how to look after her properly?"

"You do look after her properly. You're a great mother. Everyone says you are."

"Everyone is wrong." She was not lowering her voice now. "I'm a terrible mother. She needs someone better than me."

"Oh, Clemmie. Of course you're not a terrible mother. You're a lovely mother. Go easy on yourself. It's the early days. She's not even a year old yet. You're tired. You're still learning. You have to be patient. You can't know everything all at once."

"This isn't learning. Learning is facts. This is—" She searched for the words. "This is like chaos theory and algebra and trigonometry and Latin and cross-country athletics and mental torture all rolled into one."

"All that? Well, you're the family brainbox. You should be able to pick it up in a second."

"I don't know if I can."

"Of course you can."

"I don't like being like this, Juliet. Out of control. It's not me."

"This is out of control?" Juliet laughed and leaned across, kissing Clementine and then Maggie on the tops of their heads. "You're doing wonders. It's us who need to lift our game. Do you want a hot chocolate or something? It might help you sleep."

"Don't go yet, Juliet, please. Tell me, when Mum would take us on those trips, where would we go?"

Juliet sat down again. "Funny places. She drove us to the top of Mount Wellington one day. She told us we had to pretend it was the top of Mount Everest and that we were Edmund Hillary and his sherpa. We got right into the spirit of it. I remember coming back to the car after about an hour—Mum had got cold so she'd left us to it. She was sitting in the car listening to the radio, and Sadie was so excited, telling Mum about the other climbers who had perished on the way up, and how emotional it had been when she planted the flag on the summit and—I'll never forget Sadie's face—Mum said, 'Sorry, darling, I'm not sure I know what you're talking about.' It had been her idea to do the make-believe and she'd forgotten. Poor Sadie was so upset."

"Tell me another story."

Juliet started to smile. "I remember Dad's first boss was over for dinner once and he had a great turn of phrase, really Australian. It was all, 'I was flat out like a lizard on a rock,' or 'Fair suck of the sauce bottle.'" Mum kept trying not to laugh, I know, and then she started getting up and down from the table every ten minutes or so, excusing herself, hinting that she had to go to the bathroom. But of course I knew she was going into her bedroom to write it all down. She liked collecting funny comments like that. In the end Dad said to her, 'Tessa, would you just bring that diary of yours into the dining room once and for all, or the poor man will think you've got cystitis.' "

"Dad said that?"

"Mum was horrified."

"I didn't even know Mum kept diaries. Has Dad still got them? Have you read them?"

"No, of course not. You don't read other people's diaries."

Clementine was sitting upright. "You do in a situation like this. Juliet, can't you see? If Mum always kept diaries, she probably wrote about what it was like to have us. About being a mother. I need to read them. When was the last time you saw them?"

"In the hospital." She hesitated. "After she died, I had to collect her things. Her diary was there with her other books."

"Didn't Dad do that?"

"No, he couldn't." She didn't tell Clementine it was because he had locked himself in his bedroom for two days after Tessa died. It was fifteen-year-old Juliet who spoke to the hospital about her mother's body, to the priest about the funeral.

"So what did you do with the diary?"

"Dad told me to leave it in their bedroom. In the wardrobe. When I put it away I saw there were loads of other ones. All the same, small blue notebooks. She must have been keeping them for years."

"I need to read them."

"You can't."

"Why not?"

"Because Dad won't let you. And I know because I asked him myself, a few years ago." It was the year she turned twenty-one. Her father's expression had changed instantly.

"No, Juliet," he had said. No discussion, no argument. He had walked out of the room. There'd been no further mention of the diaries.

"But she's our mother," Clementine said.

"And she was his wife."

"I need to read them, Juliet."

"No problem. I'd say they're in Dad's bedroom somewhere. You go and help yourself while I distract him." Her eyes widened as Clementine stood up, a dozing Maggie still on her shoulder. "I'm joking. Of course you can't read them. I realized afterward that I couldn't have, even if he had given them to me."

"Why not?"

"They're diaries. They're secret."

"But what if they are the only way you'll ever find out what someone was like?"

"Clementine, I know what you mean, but if Mum had meant for us to read them, she'd have said something to Dad, or left a note—"

"Mum didn't know she was about to die, though, did she?" Maggie made a snuffling sound, wriggled under the cream blanket and then was quiet again. Clementine gently rubbed her back for a few moments before she spoke. "I'm going to ask Dad. Not just about her diaries. About all her things."

"You're a braver woman than me."

"Will you hold Maggie for me?"

"You're going to ask him now?"

"It's important."

"Maybe you're right. Maybe it is time. But if we're going to ask Dad about Mum's things, then I think all five of us should be there."

"He has to let us, Juliet. She was our mother as much as she was his wife. He'll understand, won't he?"

Juliet hoped so.

CHAPTER 5

Their mother had gone into the hospital for a simple operation. "Women's problems," was the phrase used.

Juliet, fifteen at the time, happily took over the running of the household. It would only be for a week or so. As all their neighbors said, the rest would do Tessa a world of good. Running that house full of girls, the poor woman must be exhausted.

Tessa was in a small ward, just three other women. Her daughters took turns visiting her, not wanting to crowd the room. Thirteen-year-old Miranda especially grew tired of the remarks that would greet any group visit.

"Ah, the Von Trapp family are back again," one cheery hospital porter would always say when the five of them filed into the corridor.

Their mother was due to come home on the fifteenth of April. None of them could wait, Juliet especially. The adventure of keeping the house running without Tessa had paled after a week. Even the routine of coming home from school, having a quick dinner and going into the hospital to visit her each night had started to lose its luster. The hospital had asked if they could restrict the visits to two children at a time. It was Miranda's fault, they all knew, though they hadn't told their father. The nurse in charge of their mother's ward had caught her in the storeroom, opening up boxes of bandages and turning eight-year-old Clementine into a little mummy. "We wanted to cheer our mother up," she said, unabashed, when the matron caught her. Clementine—or at least what was visible of Clementine—stood motionless beside her, her dark eyes peering through the white bandage. "Laughter is the best medicine, isn't it?" Miranda said.

It was the thirteenth of April. Two days until she'd be home. Leo had hung a calendar on the wall by the rosters and had been marking off the days. He took a final sip of tea after his dinner, stood up and reached for his coat. "Visiting time. Come on, Juliet and Clementine, your turn."

"Freedom awaits, alleluia," Tessa said as they walked in. Despite being in the hospital, she was fully made-up, her dark hair curled, her eyes lined, her lipstick red. "You must be as sick of coming to see me as I'm sick of being in here." She had the ward to herself again. The other beds had been through several different occupants in the time she had been there. She was working on one of her scrapbooks.

"You're more of a magpie than a mother," Juliet said, as she took in the clippings, photographs, glue and scissors spread over the bed.

"I like to have bright things around me. That's why I had the five of you. Now, what about this for an idea," she said as they settled in the uncomfortable chairs around her bed. "Let's start celebrating Christmas in July. As well as in December."

"Two Christmases?" Clementine said. "Two lots of presents and trees and everything?"

"Exactly. We could have our usual summer Christmas and then our own special Christmas in wintertime, like it would have been if we still lived in England." Tessa showed them an article about expatriate July Christmases in the English *Woman's Own* to which she subscribed. It took three months to arrive in Australia and was always out of date season-wise as well as calendar-wise.

"Let's start this year. What do you think, Leo? Can you get us a tree? Of course you can get us a tree. You can get us thousands of trees. Clementine, will you be in charge of the decorations? Will you help me with the puddings, Juliet?"

Leo said it sounded great. He said that to all of her suggestions.

There was nothing unusual in the way they said good-bye to their mother an hour later, or in the way they had a light supper of hot chocolate and cookies when they got home. There was nothing unusual in the way Juliet made sure Clementine's school clothes were ready for the morning, or in the way Leo went out to his shed, already distracted with a new idea.

It was 3:15 in the morning when Juliet heard the phone ring. She sat upright, heard her father get up to answer. "No," he said, too loudly. Over and over again. She got up and went into the hall. He was listening to whoever was on the other end of the phone, shaking his head, still repeating "No" again and again. Juliet's first thought was that something had happened to his brother Bill in England.

He hung up. She saw in the dim light that his hand was shaking. Not just his hand, his whole body. The expression on his face frightened her as he turned around.

"Dad?"

"It's Tessa."

Not "Your mother," the way he usually referred to her. "What did she want? What's happened?"

"She's dead."

"No."

"A nurse found her. They—"

"No, Dad."

This was a nightmare. She had seen her mother that night. Been laughing with her. Talking about July Christmases. How could she be dead?

Movement behind her. She turned. Miranda, yawning. "What's going on?"

"Wake the others, Juliet."

*   *   *

They all went into the hospital. There was no thought of leaving anyone behind. Clementine was still in her pajamas. Juliet carried her. There was a doctor waiting for them. Yes, Tessa had recovered well from the hysterectomy. What none of them had expected was sudden heart failure caused by an undiagnosed blood clot. The doctor sympathized briskly, then talked at them, a constant stream of words from his too-full lips. There was no way anyone could have foreseen it, he said. We did everything we could. There was no comfort in his words. Juliet noticed he kept checking his watch as he spoke to them. He was waiting for his shift to be over.

Word spread before dawn. Neighbors crowded in. There were whispered comments. It's a scandal. Sue the doctor. Sue the hospital. In there for more than a week and they didn't detect a blood clot? What kind of hospital is that? Their father shook his head to every suggestion. The local priest was there nearly every day. He was the one who kept saying, "Yes, it's a tragic mistake, but going to the courts about it won't bring her back."

More days, more visitors. The funeral. After days of sharp autumn sunshine, the weather turned cold and gray. There was a tracing of snow on the mountain. The wind was like ice. Juliet stood beside her father, holding a weeping Clementine close against her, Sadie, Eliza and Miranda sobbing next to them, all watching as their mother's coffin was lowered into the wet, dark soil of the Cornelian Bay Cemetery.

When Juliet thought back to the first days and weeks after her mother's death, it felt like life seen through a frosted window. Everything was blurred, shapeless, unclear. She remembered crying for what felt like hours, every day. All of them did. Tears would turn to anger, bringing more tears. They came together, closed in around each other, trying to soothe one another, then one of them would snap under the strain and go out with friends, until it was too much being away. They would almost hurtle back into the house. It didn't feel safe outside.

Their father became a different person overnight. Juliet was more conscious of it than the others. As the eldest, she heard more from the whispered conversations of visiting friends. They stopped talking when the other girls came in. It was an honor of sorts that they considered her old enough to listen. The same phrase over and over again. "Poor Leo and those poor little girls . . ."

Leo didn't even try to hide his heartbreak. Juliet saw him griev-ing, heard the sobs that seemed to tear from inside him. There was no comforting him. There were rare moments when he returned to being their father, thinking of their loss more than his own. It didn't last long. The other person, the man who had loved Tessa, was stronger, more desperate. She didn't like to admit it, but the depth of his sorrow shocked her. The helplessness of it. The desper-ation of it. Didn't he know they needed him to be strong for them?

Juliet gradually found herself in complete charge of the house, and the family. There was no system, no rosters, no order at that time. She did everything. In the early weeks there was no need to cook. Casseroles, stews, pies, buns, cakes and cookies were regu-larly left at their front door. Leo couldn't walk down the street with-out someone coming up and murmuring their sympathies. For the first month, every Saturday morning saw a small group of women at the door, carrying mops and dustcloths. They ignored the shocked looks on the girls' faces and Leo's protests. Before they quite real-ized what had happened, the six of them found themselves out tak-ing a walk. On their return an hour later, the floors had been swept and washed, the cupboards tidied, the refrigerator organized and restocked, their beds made with fresh sheets, the clothesline at the end of the back garden a mass of linen billowing and snapping in the wind.

It was Juliet who called a halt to it after the fourth week, explain-ing that it was time the family started looking after themselves again. Miranda complained bitterly. "Couldn't you have told them not to do it any more after they'd done it once more, instead of be-fore they started?"

Juliet ignored her. She was ignoring Miranda as much as possi-ble. She couldn't understand how Miranda could still be spiky and full of attitude. Juliet herself felt as though her clothes had become too tight, pressing hard against every organ, especially her heart. It was hard to breathe, to talk, to smile, to get out of bed, to keep going when all she wanted to do was cry, howl, blame someone. She wanted to go to her mother and tell her how bad she was feeling, and that was the one thing that was impossible.

Eliza shut herself away. Juliet noticed she was losing weight, but the truth was she didn't really care if Eliza was eating properly or not.

Sadie seemed to be watching each of the others to gauge the best way to behave. Some days she was in tears from the moment she woke up. Other days she was as angry as Miranda, snapping at each of them, pinching Clementine so hard she cried, roughly wiping the dishes. Juliet saw her deliberately drop two glasses and barely react as they shattered on the floor.

Clementine was bewildered. She hadn't been able to completely understand why their mother was in the hospital, let alone what it meant when Leo took her on his knee and told her Mummy had gone away, that her heart had got worn out and that she now lived in heaven. Clementine kept checking around the house as if she expected to find her, sitting in the living room or standing by the kitchen sink. When time came for her to go back to school, Juliet found her standing in the kitchen with her lunchbox. Not crying. Waiting. It was Tessa who had always made Clementine's lunch. Juliet managed not to cry in front of her that moment but once the sandwich was made—with extra butter and jam—and packed into the plastic box, she had to go outside and cry until her chest hurt.

Their father was no help. If he saw Juliet that morning from the kitchen window, her eyes red-rimmed, he didn't comment. He just locked himself away from them, physically and mentally. He barely spoke in the mornings as they got ready for school and he got ready for work. He had decided to go back just a week after their mother's funeral. Before she had gone into the hospital, he had often worked back late, either in the laboratory or visiting the eucalyptus plantations in the hills beyond Hobart. He used to take one or more of his daughters with him, showing them the rows of tiny seedlings and talking about the different species, why it made more sense to grow trees especially for harvesting rather than cut down the old-growth forests that had been there for hundreds of years.

Juliet wondered who was looking after those seedlings and plantations now. Certainly it wasn't their father. He was working only the minimum hours and spending all his spare time in his shed. The light was always on.

The day three bills arrived in red-bordered envelopes was the day Juliet realized something had to be done. She was trying to study for her exams. She couldn't do everything for everyone. She didn't have room, or time, to cope in her own way. It was all crowding in on her. She wanted to mourn and grieve and cry for her mother too.

She decided to wait until after dinner to talk to her father. The three overdue bills lay on his placemat. She was too tired and too angry to be subtle about it. As she picked up the old pottery casserole dish to carry it to the table, one of the clay handles snapped off. In slow motion it tipped out of her hands, spilling hot gravy, meat and vegetables onto the floor and their mother's handwritten recipe book. She didn't try to stop it. She stood and watched as it formed a pool at her feet and soaked into every page of the recipe book. Miranda appeared at the door.

"Are you all right? I heard a noise—"

Juliet brushed past her, saying nothing. She opened the back door, walked across the veranda, onto the lawn, already damp with dew. She didn't knock at the shed door. He was sitting at the bench. Not working at anything. Just sitting.

"I can't do it anymore, Dad."

"Do what?" He didn't turn around.

"Be Mum. You have to help."

"I can't."

She saw it in his shoulders, slumped. His hair scarcely combed.

"We're sad too, Dad. We miss her too."

He turned. His eyes were red. He was angry. The most feeling she had seen from him in weeks. "Not as much as me. You can't be as sad as me."

She kept her temper. Just. "Different sad."

Silence.

"We need your help."

He was about to speak, about to say something important, she could tell from the breath he took. There was a noise beside them.

Clementine, in her pajamas and dressing gown, without slippers. Her feet were wet and she was already shivering.

"Clemmie, what are you doing out here?"

"I cleaned up the mess."

"What mess?" Their father speaking.

"Juliet threw our dinner on the floor."

"I dropped it. Not threw it."

"I could make toast for our dinner if you like," Clementine said. "If someone else will get the toaster out of the cupboard for me."

Juliet wasn't hungry. All she wanted was to go somewhere, curl into a tight ball, cry and then sleep. But her little sister was waiting. "Good idea, Clemmie." Juliet summoned as much brightness into her voice as she could. "Let's have toast and cheese."

She and Clementine were on their way back to the house when their father appeared in the doorway of his shed. "No," he called after them. "Not toast and cheese."

Juliet stopped. "Pardon?"

"Not toast and cheese. We'll go out for dinner."

Their father was talking, even smiling. Juliet recognized that same fake optimism she heard in herself. "Come on, get the others."

Miranda didn't want to come. Eliza said she wasn't hungry. Sadie was napping and was upset about being woken. Clementine was the only one who seemed excited.

Juliet cornered Miranda, Sadie and Eliza in her bedroom. "You have to come out. This is important."

Miranda rolled her eyes. "Oh, yes, very important. A life-changing moment for our family. I can see the magazine articles now. 'We were all so unhappy after our mother died until the night we had a meal in one of Hobart's finest pubs. We haven't looked back since. Who needs a mother? It's so much better without her, cheaper too, one less mouth to fee—' Oww!"

Juliet was as shocked as Miranda at the feel of her hand slapping her sister's face. "Shut up, Miranda, do you hear me? Just shut up for once, can you?"

"Don't you ever hit me again." Her voice was icy.

"Don't you ever talk about Mum like that again."

Miranda's eyes were like slits. She held her hand to her cheek.

Sadie and Eliza were shocked, staring back and forth at the two of them.

The despair swept over Juliet again. "One hour. That's all I'm asking. One hour of pretending to be a family out in public."

"I'm not going." It was Eliza talking now. "Everyone whispering about us. 'Those poor Faraday girls.'"

"They won't even notice us. Come on. It's the first time Dad—" She stopped. "It's important for Dad."

"Dad?" Miranda, recovered again. "Who's that? Oh, that man who lives in the shed?"

"I'm ready."

It was Clementine, dressed in the same clothes she had worn at their mother's funeral. Her Sunday best. A blue wool coat. Dark-blue boots. She looked like a child from an English Christmas card. All that was missing was the robin sitting on her shoulder.

"Are we still going?"

Juliet dared her sisters to defy her. "Yes, Clementine, we are."

The dinner was a disaster. The dining room fell silent when they walked in. Three women came over during the meal to give their sympathies. Leo kept speaking in a fake bright voice, asking Clementine for too much detail about her schoolwork.

The food was terrible. Overcooked fish and chips. Burned steak. Lumpy sauce. Canned vegetables.

"Dessert, anyone? This is a special night out," Leo said, so up-beat he sounded like a preacher from the American South.

"You don't have to lay it on so thick, Dad." It was Miranda.

"I'm not sure what you mean."

"You don't have to pretend to be our caring father. We're used to life without you. I mean, it's nice of you to give us an hour of your time, but please don't feel you have to bother again. Not for a year or so. Mum's anniversary perhaps. Or at Christmas, if we are still together as a family. Or shall we give that July Christmas a go? You all saw it in her scrapbook, didn't you?" Her eyes were too bright, her smile too forced. She looked like an actress on the brink of a breakdown.

"That's enough, Miranda." Leo's voice was quiet.

"Oh, what fun we'll have. I can hardly wait. You don't look too pleased, Dad. Have I spoiled a surprise? Come now. We can do it. What have we got, six weeks to organize it?"

Sadie, Eliza, Juliet and Clementine were still and quiet. This was between Miranda and their father.

She continued, in the same conversational tone. "Sorry you got left behind when Mum died, Dad. And that you got stuck with us. I'd like to spend all my time in the shed too, and not talk to anyone. Let's get five more sheds, will we? One for each of us? That way we don't have to talk to anybody; we can all just lock ourselves away. Clementine, you can visit me whenever you like—" she had noticed her youngest sister's shocked expression "—but I really think this is the best way forward."

"I don't know how else to be."

"Oh no, of course not, you're only our—" Miranda's tone had turned sharp. Then a glance from Sadie and a sudden touch on her arm from Eliza halted her.

They could barely hear their father's voice. "This wasn't supposed to happen to us. She was supposed to come home. You saw her, Juliet. You too, Clementine. That last . . . that night we visited her. She was happy, wasn't she? Talking about the future? About that Christmas idea?"

A nod from Juliet. Clementine stayed quiet, but she slipped her hand into Juliet's.

"We didn't get time to talk about what I was supposed to do next, if . . . if something like this ever happened. Whether we should go back to England. It just happened." He looked directly at Miranda. "You're right. I don't know what to do. I think about all the years stretching ahead without her, and all the advice she would have given you, and the shopping you would have done together, and your weddings and your babies, our grandchildren. The whole picture that we had in our heads of what our lives would be, and she is in every single picture. I didn't see this gap, this space that I am supposed to fill. I can't be her. I don't know how to be without her."

He cried again then, in the dining room, tears streaming down his cheeks, oblivious to open stares from the other people around them, from his daughters.

None of the girls spoke. He cried, soundlessly, for what felt like many minutes.

Clementine got down from her seat and went over to her father. "Do you want a tissue, Dad?" He took them from her outstretched hand. He wiped his eyes. Juliet, Miranda, Sadie and Eliza watched in silence. After a minute or two, Clementine held out her hand again. Leo handed back the tissues and she returned to her seat.

Miranda picked up the menu. "I would like dessert after all, thanks, Dad." Her voice sounded normal. Only the high flush in her cheeks gave anything away. She beckoned the waiter. "Five large chocolate sundaes, please. Dad, one for you?"

He nodded.

"Make that six," she said.

That night their father didn't go back out to the shed. He called a family meeting.

"Miranda hit the nail on the head tonight. We need to get this show back on the road. We owe it to your mother." It would be a phrase they would hear many times over the next years. "Now, let's get those rosters out and let me take a look at how your mother used to do these things. And no shirking on my part. I'm adding my name to it this time."

There was a muffled exclamation from Miranda. Juliet sent her a warning glance. Miranda rolled her eyes in answer but didn't say what she was obviously thinking.

"Each of you has been given a special gift," he was saying. Then he stopped. Gift was a word their mother had often used.

"Are they like Christmas presents, Dad?" Clementine said. "Those sort of gifts? Are we going to do Mum's July Christmas?"

He seemed relieved to change the subject. The hearty voice emerged again. "What do you think, girls? Juliet? Are you up for it especially? I mean, I'm happy to give the turkey a go myself, but your mother always said you were a born cook."

Juliet felt like an actress too, stepping in and picking up her lines just in time. "I'd like to do it. It could be fun." She didn't know if she had the energy for anything to ever be fun again.

"Mum said she wanted me to do the tree." Clementine ran out of the room and came back with the final scrapbook. "I'm going to make a fairy like that one, see."

Their mother had clipped pictures of eight different fairies from the English magazine and stuck them all neatly on a page. The sight of the neat work, the thought of her mother carefully sticking down the pieces of paper, was too much. It hit Juliet like a punch, a great roaring rush of feeling that seemed to come from her feet upward. She barely made it outside before she was violently ill.

Sadie, or perhaps it was Eliza, came up behind her. She didn't turn around, just felt a soothing hand on her back. She shook her head, shook their hand away. "I'm all right. Just leave me alone."

A pause, another brief touch, and whoever it was went away.

When she came into the kitchen ten minutes later, it was all organized. Clementine was jumping up and down on the spot in excitement. The first Faraday July Christmas was going to take place in six weeks' time. A turkey and all the trimmings. A tree. A pudding. All of it. They'd promised Clementine.

That night, Miranda came into Juliet's room. She sat on the edge of the bed.

"I hate all this, Juliet. I hate it so much it hurts. I want her back. I want our old life back."

"Me too."

The door opened. Clementine was there, with her favorite rug.

"Juliet, can I come in?"

"Of course, Clemmie."

She gave a deep sob. "I miss my Mum."

"Oh, darling. Come here." She held back the blankets and Clementine clambered in beside her. Juliet opened her arms and held her little sister tight as Clementine wept even harder. "Don't worry, Clemmie. I'm here. I'll look after you."

"Promise?"

"Promise."

"Can I sleep here with you tonight?"

"Of course you can." Juliet stroked her hair back from her face, as Clementine's sobs lessened. Her breathing changed until she slowly fell asleep. Juliet continued to stroke her hair.

"Juliet?" Miranda's voice was soft in the darkness.

"Mmm?"

"Will you look after me too?"

"Of course."

"Promise?"

"Promise," Juliet said.

CHAPTER 6

It took Juliet three days to get the five of them together. In the end, she'd had to slip notes under Miranda, Sadie and Eliza's pillows: *Need to talk about something important, out of Dad's hearing. Meet you at the park at 2 p.m. Saturday?*

"I feel like I'm one of the Famous Five," Miranda said when she arrived. She was the last to get there, straight from work, still dressed in her pharmacy uniform. "What next? Chasing robbers and searching for counterfeit money? You be Julian, Juliet, seeing as you almost have the same name. I'll be Dick. He was the best one. Sadie, you be George because you look like a boy with that new haircut. Eliza, you're Anne, just because. Clementine, you have to be Timmy the dog."

Juliet ignored her and waited a few more minutes for Clementine to give Maggie a feed and put her back in her pram. When she finally had everyone's attention, she explained what the meeting was about. She didn't go into detail about her conversation with Clementine the previous week.

"I can see Clementine's point, but isn't it Dad's business if he has kept Mum's belongings all this time?" Eliza said.

"It's not just his business. She's our mother. Was our mother." Miranda looked like she was ready to confront their father there and then.

Sadie wasn't happy. "But what if he only lets Clementine have a look at her diaries and choose some of her clothes, because she's got Maggie?"

"For God's sake, Sadie," Miranda snapped. "You sound like a six-year-old sometimes."

"Leave her alone, Miranda," Juliet said. "We have to decide whether we all want to do this. Because it has to be all or none of us. I'll take a vote. Miranda, do you want to ask Dad about this?"

"Of course."

"Sadie? Eliza?"

Two nods.

Juliet already knew Clementine's feelings.

They were walking back to the house, taking turns pushing Maggie's pram, when Miranda stopped. "If he does say yes, do any of you actually want to read Mum's diaries?"

"Yes," Clementine said immediately.

"Of course," Sadie said. "Why wouldn't we?"

"What if we don't like what we read?" Miranda asked.

"Isn't it better we know her as she was?" Eliza said. "I'd rather know more than less, wouldn't you?"

"Could we get someone to read them for us first, and edit out the unsavory parts?" Juliet suggested.

"How do you know there'd be any unsavory parts?" Eliza said.

Juliet shrugged. "That's what diaries are for, aren't they? To put down all the secret fantasies and evil thoughts that you can't share with anybody else?"

"Do you keep a diary, Miranda?" Sadie asked.

"You think I'd tell you if I did?"

Eliza spoke. "I can tell you all one thing about the diaries."

"What?"

"Wherever they are, they're not in Dad's wardrobe."

Juliet, Miranda, Sadie and Clementine stopped and stared at Eliza.

She glared back at them. "I'm not the only one who goes in there, so don't look at me like that."

"She's right," Miranda said. "I used to go in there all the time. I liked looking at her dresses. That blue evening gown especially. I loved her in it. I tried it on once."

"Miranda!"

"What was wrong with that? What girl wouldn't want to try on her mother's best clothes?"

"What did it look like on you?"

"Terrible. Two inches too short and two sizes too small."

They walked on a little farther before Juliet spoke. "I wore one of her rings the day I was sitting my final exams."

"Juliet, you didn't!" Clementine was shocked.

"It made me feel better. I put it straight in the jewelry box when I got back, I promise."

"Did you pass the exam?"

"With flying colors," Juliet said.

Miranda turned. "Eliza? Do you have anything to confess, my child?"

Eliza shook her head. "I never tried on anything. I just liked going in there, sitting in the wardrobe."

"You'd *sit* in there?"

"I used to think I could still smell her perfume on some of her clothes."

"Clementine?" Miranda asked.

"Never. I always felt too guilty even looking in the wardrobe, let alone sitting in it."

They were nearly home.

"You haven't asked me if I ever went in there." It was Sadie, looking unhappy.

"Sorry, Sadie." Juliet ignored Miranda's rolling of eyes. "Did you?"

Sadie nodded, then lifted her shirt to show the top of her jeans. A brightly colored scarf was wound through the belt loops. "This scarf was Mum's."

"Sadie!" Juliet was shocked.

"When did you take it?" Miranda asked.

"Last year."

Juliet wasn't happy. "Sadie, that's not right."

"What's the difference? You borrowed her ring. Miranda tried on her dress."

"For less than an hour," Miranda said, "and it was only for that long because I couldn't get the damn thing off."

"And I only had the ring for the day."

Sadie pulled her shirt down. "You're all just jealous because you didn't think of it first."

. . . .

Leo was in the shed. Clementine left a sleeping Maggie in her pram on the back veranda, within hearing distance. The shed light wasn't on but they could hear him humming. Juliet knocked.

He opened the door with a smile. "Girls! Five girls in fact! What a delegation. To what do I owe this pleasure?"

The others looked to Juliet. "Dad, we need to talk to you about something. About Mum," she said.

"I see." His expression instantly became wary. "Will we go inside?"

They settled in the living room, Leo in his usual armchair, the five sisters taking up all available space on the two sofas. Maggie's pram was now outside the living room door. They were all so quiet her baby snores were audible.

Miranda looked at Juliet, urging her to start. She took a breath. "Dad, we've been talking—"

"Better that than fighting, I suppose," he said, too cheerily. "You know, when you all appeared at the shed door like that my first thought was, oh no, another one's pregnant . . ."

Juliet ignored that. She decided to launch straight into it. "Dad, we think it's time you let us go through Mum's clothes. Through all her things. And we'd like to have the choice to read her diaries. We think it's important."

"No."

"Just like that? Can't you at least think about it?"

There was no sign of his joking face now. "What's brought this on? We're just getting on top of things; Clementine's doing so well with Maggie—another hurdle crossed as a family. Why—"

Juliet interrupted him. "Because we need to. We know everything of Mum's is still in your wardrobe."

A faint flush appeared on his cheeks.

"We need you to share it," Eliza said.

"But why now?"

"Because of me, Dad." Clementine looked directly at him. "I need help. I want to ask Mum questions about being a mother, about looking after a baby, about how it feels. And I can't. I think having her things around us, talking about her more, even seeing her diaries, will be the next best thing."

"Ask me about having babies. I fathered all five of you, remember."

"It's a woman thing, Dad. Please don't take offense. But—" She faltered as his expression became stony.

Sadie stepped in. "It's been nine years, Dad."

"You think I don't know that? You think I haven't missed her every single day of those nine years?"

His raised voice silenced them. Maggie began to whimper. All of them watched as Clementine moved across to the pram and settled Maggie again. No one spoke until she was back in her seat.

Juliet tried again. "This will help all of us, Dad."

"We're doing just fine as it is."

"I'm not."

They all turned to Miranda. Confident, dramatic Miranda.

"Well, I'm not. Dad, you're not the only one who misses her. I wish every day that she were here, that I could talk to her. Feel that she was around."

Leo ran his hand through his hair. "I know that. But seeing her clothes, reading her diaries . . . that won't bring her back."

"So why have you kept them, then?"

"I haven't kept them."

"Your wardrobe is full of her things. We've all seen them," Juliet said.

"The clothes are still there. But the diaries are gone." He hesitated. "I burned them. She always said to me that if anyone ever read them she'd be in big trouble. She made me promise to get rid of them if she . . . if anything ever happened. I took her by at her word. I had to. They were her private thoughts. Perhaps I shouldn't have, but I did. I burned them all."

Juliet glanced at Clementine. She was biting her lip.

"When, Dad?" Eliza asked.

"A month after she died."

"Didn't you think of us?" Clementine's voice cracked. "Think that we might like to read them one day?" Beside her, Juliet reached for her hand.

"I wasn't thinking straight about anyone at that time. I'm sorry." He looked wretched. "I should have thought that you might want to read them one day. I didn't. Everything else is there still, I promise." He was silent a moment. "I thought it would make it easier. I hated the thought of opening the wardrobe to take out a shirt and her side of it being empty. It would have—" He stopped. "I liked them being there. They reminded me of her every single day."

"We'd like that reminder of her too," Eliza said.

"Please, Dad." Clementine's voice was soft.

Leo stood up. "I need to think about it for a little while."

. . .

The next day was Sunday. At the breakfast table, Leo waited until they had finished their once-a-week treat of bacon and eggs. The newspaper had been passed between all of them. Clementine had just given Maggie a feed. The mood was warm, relaxed. No one had mentioned anything about the previous day's conversation.

"We could start on it today if you like."

Five heads shot up.

"I thought about it last night," he said. "I imagined asking your mother about it. I'm sure she'd have told me I was being silly, keeping everything for this long."

"She's right," Miranda said.

He stood up. "Ready when you are, then."

They made it fun. They turned it into a fashion show. There were some tears from each of them, but there was no teasing, not even from Miranda.

There were dresses, coats and skirts hanging in the left-hand side of the wardrobe. Shirts, jeans and scarves in the drawers. Her shoes were in bags, each one polished, many pairs with shoe horns. There were two jewelry boxes, one with rings, the other with necklaces and earrings. "All costume jewelry," Miranda announced authoritatively.

Leo left them to it. It made it easier on everyone. Juliet took charge, taking the items out one by one, holding it up as they passed remarks or asked to try it on. It helped that none of them was the same size as their mother. She had been at least two sizes smaller than Sadie, two inches shorter than Juliet and Miranda. It also helped that each of them had different taste in clothes. They decided anything they couldn't wear would go to a charity shop.

The scarves, rings and necklaces were divided between them. The shoes—too small for them all—went into the charity bags, except for one pair each as a keepsake. Clementine chose a pair for Maggie too.

The final drawer yielded a surprise. A box wrapped in silver and rose colored paper, with a bow on the top.

Juliet called her father back in. Leo took it, holding it in one hand, moving it to the other, awkward again. "This was for her. For your mother. I bought it the week before she died. It was supposed to be a welcome-home present. I've never known what to do with it."

"What was it?"

"Perfume. A new perfume that had just been released. She loved perfume."

"See, I take after her," Miranda said.

"Open it, Dad," Eliza urged.

He did, carefully taking off the sticky tape, now yellowed with age. He opened the box. Inside was an elaborately shaped purple glass bottle, with the name of the perfume in gold curving writing across the front. "Moonstruck," Leo read. "That's right. It was called Moonstruck. I loved the smell of it too."

"Can I try it?" Miranda put out her hand. Leo handed over the bottle, his attention taken by the card attached to the box. Juliet watched as he opened the envelope and read the message inside, then silently slipped the card into his pocket.

Miranda sprayed the perfume onto her wrist and waited a moment before smelling it. "Oh my God!" she said, pulling a face and waving her wrist dramatically. "It's disg—"

"Distinctive?" Juliet said hurriedly, nodding toward their father. "Here, let me try."

Miraculously, Miranda picked up the cue. "Incredibly distinctive. I've never smelled anything like it," she said, too effusively.

Juliet tried it. So did the others. Miranda was right. It was disgusting. Too flowery, too musky, too spicy. Whether time was to blame, or whether it had always been disgusting, they didn't know.

"Beautiful," Eliza said.

Sadie nodded. "So memorable."

"It takes my breath away," Clementine added.

Miranda snorted.

Leo looked delighted. Almost reverentially, he packed the bottle back into the box. "I know you will all want to share this, but I think it should stay with one person to begin with." With great solemnity, he held it out. "Juliet, as the oldest—"

"Honestly, Dad, I hardly ever wear perfume. Miranda?"

Miranda took a step back. "No, no, you're the oldest."

"Dad, are you sure?" Juliet didn't look happy.

"It would mean a lot to me to know you were wearing it. I should have done this years ago."

The last of their mother's clothes had just been carefully folded into a bag when Miranda spoke. "Dad, while we're all here, doing this, I think there's something else we should say."

Leo waited.

"If you ever meet someone else, a woman, someone you like, then it's fine with me."

"What's fine with you?"

"If you want to have another relationship. You're still young."

"Young? I'm fifty-two years old."

"I know you loved Mum and I know that wouldn't change if you did meet someone else."

The telephone rang. Leo looked relieved. "Thank you, Miranda," he said as he hurried out to the hallway.

"It is okay with everyone, isn't it?" Miranda asked, looking around the room.

"No, it's not," Sadie replied. "Well, maybe it is, but you shouldn't have sprung it on us like that."

"It wasn't fair, Miranda," Eliza said. "You didn't check with the rest of us first."

"Don't you agree? Don't you think it would be all right for Dad to meet someone else? To get married again if he wanted?"

"Have someone else live here?" Clementine looked alarmed. "With all of us?"

"We're not all going to live here together for the rest of our lives, are we? I know I'm not. And before you say anything else, Clementine, I'm not about to move out and abandon you and Maggie. But we need to look to the future."

"I don't know if I would like Dad to get married again," Clementine said. "I can't imagine someone else sleeping in here with him."

"That's because you're not supposed to imagine your parents having sex. But if he wanted to, he should be allowed to. He's a young man, he's got a good job, he's got all his hair, even if it is red. He's a catch."

"A catch?" Eliza scoffed. "A man who comes complete with five daughters and a granddaughter? Any sane woman would run for her life."

"I think it's still too soon, for Dad and for us," Sadie said.

Juliet turned back to the bed and fastened the bag of clothes. What would it mean? A guilt-free handing over of responsibilities to another woman?

"I think it would be wonderful," she said.

●　●　●

The next morning, before it was quite light, Miranda came out of her bedroom, wrapped in her silk dressing gown, groaning inwardly at the faint throbbing in her head. Her own fault, she'd downed too many gin and tonics during late drinks with her friend Liz. Without turning on the light, Miranda made her way to the cabinet in the corner of the bathroom, in urgent need of the headache tablets she kept on hand for mornings like this. She reached inside her cosmetics bag and rummaged around. The tablets were there, thank God. But so was something else. Something hard and smooth. It felt like a glass bottle. She switched on the light. It was a glass bottle. A purple glass bottle. She grinned, despite the headache. "Oh no, you don't," she said out loud.

•   •   •

Two days later Clementine was trying to find a matching pair of socks for Maggie. She'd done a big load of washing but hadn't had time to sort everything yet. Hers and Maggie's clean clothes were still in a tangled bundle. She had an essay on the nesting habits of eastern black-billed gulls to write and a lot of reading to do. The juggling act between her studies and looking after Maggie was getting more difficult every week, but she was determined not to let on.

She emptied the basket onto the bed, a multicolored tumble of T-shirts and little socks spilling across the bedspread. As she moved a small pink onesie, something purple rolled off the cover onto the floor below. Something hard. A glass bottle.

She was laughing as she picked it up.

•   •   •

Four days later, Eliza and her coach were on their way to an athletics festival in Launceston. Although he was now based in Melbourne, Mark returned regularly to see his sons and check on her training. Conversation flowed easily between them. They talked tactics, discussed the possible results for the day. As they passed through the midlands town of Bothwell, they started talking about the plans for their fitness company. In the warmth of the car, Eliza felt her excitement build again. Not about the race, not just about their work, but about their future together. It was several years off yet, but they spoke about it as if she was due to start work the next day.

She was still in love with him. She wondered whether he had guessed yet. It was like a lovely secret, something warm buried inside her. There was no rush. She felt the same way about Mark as she did about her training. It was a matter of long-term planning. Being sure of where you were headed. And being patient. She didn't care how long she had to wait for him. It was as simple as that.

They arrived and parked alongside the other cars. She took her bag out of the trunk, heading for the changing room. "Good luck," Mark said, briefly touching her back as he passed her. Even a fleeting caress like that made her feel like a cat, wanting to stretch with pleasure, press up against him. The day would come when she would do exactly that, tell him how she felt, she knew it. It made it all the more exciting.

In the changing room she nodded at the other women, put her bag in the corner and reached inside for her running gear. As she pulled the shoes out she noticed a glint of color inside the left one. She frowned. Whatever it was had been pushed right inside the toe. She pulled it out. It was a purple glass bottle.

Three of her competitors turned around at her sudden burst of laughter.

*   *   *

Sadie spent more time in the library than any of her sisters. She liked the peace and quiet. She liked the fact she could read the latest newspapers and magazines for free. She liked their extensive reference section. She didn't look up information on Jane Austen or the Romantic poets, though. She spent her time there looking up parenting manuals, childhood development reference books and mother and baby magazines. It was fun to read about the stages a baby went through in theory and then to see Maggie do it in reality. She wasn't imagining it, either. Maggie was definitely more advanced than average. At her age, coming up to eleven months, she should be just crawling, have several teeth and general dexterity. Maggie had not only been crawling for months, she was even starting to walk, had lots of teeth and was already able to build little towers of blocks.

It continually surprised Sadie how fascinating Maggie was. When she had first come back from the hospital with Clementine, Maggie had done little but sleep, eat and fill her nappies. In the past few months, though, she had become something. Become someone. Sadie was entranced. It wasn't something she had admitted to any of her sisters, but it had never really occurred to her that Maggie would be her own person. Have a distinct personality, even as a baby. Yet she did. Those dark eyes of hers would fill with laughter sometimes, especially when Sadie did a silly dance in front of her. She could also look bored. Annoyed. Curious. All the things human beings could look. Sadie could hear Miranda's mocking tones: "Of course she does things a human being does, Sadie. That's because she is a human being."

Sadie simply hadn't expected to find her niece quite as bewitching as this. A five-year-old, yes. A teenager, definitely. But a baby? It had been a wonderful surprise. She never minded any more when Clementine asked her to look after Maggie for a few hours while she tried to catch up on sleep, or meet a friend, or try to have something close to a normal teenager's life even for just a few hours. Sadie had begun to offer to babysit, and to her delight Clementine accepted every time. Sadie would play with her niece or hold her in her arms as she watched TV, loving the warm heavy weight of her, the gentle rhythm of her breathing. She even read to her, despite the fact that Miranda, again, told her she was being silly, but Maggie did respond to stories and colors, Sadie was sure of it.

Sadie liked to gently bite on her niece's chubby little fingers. She liked the smell of her, fresh from the bath. She liked how sweet she looked in her different outfits. She liked the dark lashes against her skin, the silky smoothness of that skin. There was something so perfect about every part of her.

Sadie settled herself into her favorite corner. This was her first

visit to the library in two weeks and a great selection of new magazines had come in, filled with fascinating articles. Once she'd had a
good read of those, she'd have a browse around the children's section upstairs too. She thought it was time Maggie moved beyond
the board books she had been borrowing for her so far.

As she reached into her carry bag to take out her library card,
her fingers brushed against something. It was a small bottle. A purple bottle.

Her snort of laughter earned her a stern look from the librarian.

*   *   *

Juliet had discovered many years earlier that routine was essential
if she was to keep her family fed. Let them complain about her
planned menus, she'd decided. If they found it too boring, they
could take over. Especially now she was so busy at the café. The
Stottingtons kept introducing new ideas and new menus. For a
near-retired couple, they had great business brains—Juliet was
learning a lot from them. She also had the feeling they were
grooming her for something. Her family better watch out, she
thought, or the day would come when she wouldn't have time to
cook for them at all.

Thursday night was always pasta night. If she had time she exper-
imented with different sauces—creamy mushroom or spicy bacon
and tomato—but usually the most variation she could offer was the
type of pasta. Long strands of spaghetti, little pasta shells or sometimes thick tagliatelli. The previous year she'd found the perfect
pottery storage jar in a housewares shop in the mall. It held enough
pasta for three meals, with a nifty measuring ring for spaghetti built
into the lid. She took it down. She'd already checked the notice
board. Everyone would be home tonight. There should be enough
spaghetti, she guessed from the weight in the jar. She took off the
lid, set up the measuring ring and poured the strands into her
hand. As she did so, something slipped out and landed on the table
with a clatter. Something purple. Something made from glass.

She started to laugh. "Oh no, you don't," she said out loud.

CHAPTER 7

"What I don't understand is how in less than two years that child has managed to infiltrate all our lives, take over our house, have us all running after her and now has ten times as much luggage as any of us. Where am I supposed to put my bag?" Miranda was disgusted and making no bones about it.

"There's room, love. You just need to push a bit harder." Leo put a shoulder against the suitcase on top of the luggage compartment of the station wagon and heaved. The suitcase moved, flying over the divider into the backseat.

"Perfect. Plenty of room. And I don't need a seat. I'll just run along behind the car."

"That might be the best thing, actually."

Clementine came out of the house with another bag. "Is there room for this?"

"Clem, tell your daughter she needs to learn to pack lighter. Catwalk models have fewer clothes than her."

"I tried, I promise. But I've brought all her birthday presents with me."

"What's the point? She won't know if she's opening boxes of cereal."

They were on their way to a house in Bicheno on the east coast for a week's holiday, timed to celebrate Maggie's second birthday.

Their mother had found the house years before while traveling with Leo as he visited tree plantations. They'd heard the story many times. How she had grabbed his arm, pointed out over the rocks and the coastline. "It was just like that at Grandma's," she had said. Her grandmother was Irish, from the northwest of the country. As a child, Tessa would go every summer to her two-story house just outside the small village of Glencolmcille in County Donegal. She'd pick blackberries, go swimming, make cakes and help her grandmother do the summer chores, like whitewashing the walls around the house.

. That first day in Bicheno, Leo and Tessa had parked the car by the shore and gone walking. From the beach Tessa had caught sight of a two-story house, back in the bush. It was brick, not stone, and modern—not over a hundred years old like her grandmother's house—but it had delighted her. They'd called into three nearby shops and houses until they got the name of the owner. Yes, they did rent it out.

A month later the whole family had come up for a week's holiday. It had been the middle of winter, unfortunately. They spent the week inside, looking out at the driving rain. They played card games, Monolopy, Cluedo, Twister, charades and consequences. They fought constantly.

Clementine didn't remember that visit, although everyone always told her that was where she had first fallen in love with penguins and other birds, after Leo took her to see the colony that lived in the rocks nearby. They had gone to Bicheno twice after their mother died. The first time had been too sad. They'd come home early. The second holiday was better. The owners had redecorated. It didn't feel too much like the place they had visited with their mother.

The mood this time was bright. The seven of them finally crammed into the station wagon, three in the front, four in the back, Maggie and her baby seat taking up more than one space. As they took the highway out of Hobart, heading through hills, looking forward to the first dramatic glimpse of coastline, they waited for their father to tell the same story of the day he had first seen the house. How sad it was that Tessa hadn't got to see that beloved Donegal house again.

They all knew that Leo and Tessa had been planning a trip back to the U.K. for the whole family. Only Tessa had returned after they emigrated, making the trip home every two years to see her parents, arriving back after the fortnight away laden with English biscuits, magazines, jams and her favorite chocolates. They would pore over photos of places she'd been and people she'd seen: her parents, old friends from school days, as well as snapshots of their old house, even the corner shop she used to love visiting. Tessa had promised to take them to all her favorite places as soon as they could afford it. There'd been a tin in the pantry with a notice on it: "Holiday Fund," and a little picture of a plane, drawn by their mother.

"Seven of us to the U.K.? You don't need a tin of change, you need a swimming-pool full," Miranda had said.

After Tessa died, the tin was pushed to the back shelf of the pantry. What money there was in it had been used to buy groceries. There'd been no more talk of a trip to the U.K.

It wasn't just the expense or their study commitments. Their links with family over there were fading. Leo's parents had died when he was in his midforties. Their mother's parents were in a retirement village in north London. They'd been too unwell to come to her funeral. Her mother was apparently prone to high blood pressure and her father wouldn't travel without her. There were occasional letters, phone calls at Christmas, but they had never been close. Leo hinted once that Tessa, an only child, hadn't got on well with her parents, her mother especially. The Faradays' closest relative in the U.K. was Leo's brother Bill, a doctor. He'd been out to Australia twice to visit them, the first time soon after they emigrated, the second time just a few months before Tessa died. Juliet could remember him well: all jolly, great company, as outgoing as her father was gentle. He'd reminded her of a character in a war film, with his short hair, Errol Flynn looks and flamboyance. He and Tessa had been great friends, singing and even dancing around the kitchen one night, to the delight of the girls. "Come on, Daddy," a nine-year-old Miranda had allegedly shouted. "You dance with me too. I be the lady and you be Fred the Stair."

Bill had phoned every day for the first two weeks after he heard the news Tessa had died. Juliet spoke to him most days, her father unable to take the call. Her uncle often sounded drunk, Juliet thought, though she hadn't said anything to her father. "She was a beautiful girl," he would repeat. "This is a tragedy."

There'd been few calls since. No more visits either. Perhaps Bill hadn't wanted to come all that way to see his brother without his lively, dancing, singing wife beside him.

"Your mother loved Bicheno so much because it reminded her of her grandmother's house in Donegal," Leo announced, the road ahead of them rising into the hills.

In the backseat, squished between Clementine and the door, Miranda made a loud snoring noise. Juliet glared at her.

"Dad, you tell us this every time we drive this road," Clementine said mildly.

"Do I?"

Miranda shook her head and turned and looked out the window. "This is an appalling state of affairs. Me, twenty-four, trapped in a car with too many members of my immediate family, including a very stinky child." She blocked her nose with her fingers and spoke in a nasally voice. "I know, Dad, why don't you invent a really huge nappy with compartments, and the baby could wear it all day, with little tubes that funnel the waste into the separate areas, therefore saving the mother many hours of nappy-changing time and—"

"Not a bad idea. By the way, have I told you about my latest project?"

Miranda put her hands over her ears. "No, but please do."

Eliza returned to the book she was reading. She'd always been able to read in a moving car without getting carsick. Sadie went back to playing peekaboo over the front seat with Maggie. Beside her, Juliet was making a shopping list. They'd have to buy everything in Bicheno, she'd realized. There had been no room in the car for groceries.

Leo talked on, oblivious to his lack of an audience. "I actually got the idea for it watching Pete next door doing his mowing. He must have refilled the petrol tank three times in the space of an hour. There had to be a more efficient way, I thought. So what I've been working on is a—"

Miranda shut her eyes. She was asleep within five minutes. She didn't wake up until they pulled into the laneway of the holiday house.

•   •   •

"I'm worried about Clementine," Juliet said a few days later. The weather had been mixed, rain in the morning, sunshine in the afternoon. There had been a lot of lying around reading. Maggie was everyone's plaything. Juliet had noticed Clementine leaving her with them more and more. She had said she was using the time to study but Juliet noticed her books were still in their bag. "I think she's depressed."

"I don't know about depressed, but she's certainly clean," Miranda said.

"What do you mean by that?"

"Have you noticed she's started taking two showers every day? Not just here, but when we're at home too? And she's in the bathroom for nearly an hour each time. She asked me to mind Maggie for her last week while she nipped in for a shower, or so she told me. She took forever. I was late for work because of her."

Eliza joined in. "She did that to me too."

"She's finding it hard," Juliet said.

"We're all finding it hard," Eliza said. "But do you hear me complaining?"

"No, but I don't hear you offering to help. She hasn't said anything, but I get the feeling her study is suffering," Juliet said.

"She shouldn't have taken that university program, then. Or she should have thought about this happening before she got pregnant."

Miranda snorted. "And from high judgement, Eliza Faraday

speaks. How nice of you to drop in from Mount Olympus to pass on your words of wisdom."

"I'm not condemning her. I'm just being realistic. If I pull a muscle in my leg and have to withdraw from a race, I can't blame anyone else. It's my fault."

"Thanks for that touching insight into the mind of an athlete, Eliza, but what does that have to do with Clementine and Maggie?"

"She needs to work it out for herself. We won't be around to help her all the time, will we?"

Juliet looked shocked. "She's our little sister, Eliza."

"I know who she is. And I know Maggie is our niece." Her expression was defiant. "But I'm sorry, someone has to be realistic here. All five of us can't become full-time mothers just because Clementine decided to have a baby."

"She didn't decide to have a baby." Juliet was angry now. "God, Eliza, what's got into—"

Sadie interrupted. "I'm happy to do more. I'll do Eliza's share. I don't mind. I think Maggie is beautiful."

"I think she's beautiful too." Eliza was exasperated now. "I'm not suggesting we hand her over to an orphanage. I just think Clementine has to find her own way out of this mess."

"I've had an idea."

They all turned to look at Sadie.

"Why don't I become Maggie's part-time nanny? I can juggle my lectures. Defer one or two subjects if I need to. My course is different from Clementine's. She has to keep up the research if she wants to pass." Clementine's main project was an investigation into the impact of airborne pollutants on seabirds in Tasmania. "The world can wait to find out what I think of Jane Austen's use of metaphors. That would give me lots more free time. I'm happy to do more looking after Maggie."

"Really?" Eliza said. "For payment, you mean, or for free?"

"I'll do it for free. We're doing all right financially, aren't we? We could try it for a year, anyway. And it will get easier the older Maggie gets, once she starts kindergarten or school."

"Why would you do this, though? Why would anyone volunteer to spend more time crawling on the floor picking up bricks and changing smelly squares of cotton flannel nappies?"

"Out of kindness, Miranda," Juliet said. "Ever heard of that?"

Miranda just flicked the page of her magazine.

. . .

Clementine protested about Sadie's offer at first. It wasn't fair, she said. She'd feel guilty leaving Maggie. She wasn't leaving her permanently, just for a few hours every day, Sadie reminded her. It was too much to ask, Clementine said. I'm happy to do it, Sadie insisted. Thank you, Sadie, Clementine said. You're welcome, Clementine, Sadie answered.

. . .

The new arrangement coincided with Sadie's latest attempt to lose weight. She'd been talking about losing a stone—fourteen pounds—for as long as any of them could remember. It wasn't that she was overweight, though Miranda enjoyed telling her she was. She just hadn't inherited the slender figure and fast metabolism her sisters had. It was so unfair, she told them all as often as possible. Every week she made an event of weighing herself and every week she was disappointed. "There must be something wrong with me. I'm exercising more and I'm just staying the same."

"That's because you work your way through at least five packages of cookies each week," Eliza said.

"I'm hungry when I get back from my walk," she said defensively. "I've earned a few cookies, haven't I?"

"To lose weight you have to move more and eat less. You're moving more and eating more. They cancel each other out. Ipso facto, status quo."

"What have they got to do with it?"

"I don't mean the band. I mean nothing will change."

She sighed. "I'll have to forget about it for now, anyway. I won't be able to go on a diet when I'm home looking after Maggie. I'll find myself picking all day."

"So get out of the house more," Eliza said.

"And do what?"

"Look at things. Walk. Show Maggie the world."

"We like it here. All her toys are here."

Miranda roused herself from her position on the sofa. "Your problem, Sadie Faraday, is you just don't want to lose weight. In fact, I bet you can't lose weight."

Sadie narrowed her eyes. "You bet me? How much?"

Juliet looked at the two of them and laughed. "You should see your faces."

"Fifty dollars if you lose fourteen pounds by Christmas. That's December Christmas, not our July Christmas."

Juliet was appalled. "Miranda! You can't afford that."

"I won't have to pay up. Sadie will never do it."

"Let me get this clear," Sadie said. "You'll pay me fifty dollars if I lose fourteen pounds in the next eight months?"

"That's it in a nutshell. Except nuts are fattening. That's it on a crispbread."

Sadie held out her hand. "It's a deal."

*   *   *

Sadie started both projects on the same day. Over breakfast—she had grapefruit, dry toast and coffee—Clementine ran through all the arrangements: what time Maggie liked to have her daytime nap, what to give her for lunch, which were her favorite toys. Sadie eventually called a halt to it.

"Clem, I've watched you with her every day for the past two years. I love her as much as you do. I know how to look after her."

"You'll ring me at the university if you need to? If anything happens at all?"

"Straight away, I promise. It's only for a few hours. You'll be back in the afternoon. Forget about us. Go and worry about your feathered friends."

Things went beautifully for the first two months. Clementine slowly relaxed into the new arrangement. They all noticed the change in her. The tense look disappeared. Her study books appeared in her room again. She spoke about her course research over dinner, about her lecturer, about the latest findings.

Miranda leaned back in her chair. "What is this I see before me? A normal student? A young woman able to speak of something more than toilet training? Boring us rigid with tales of Tasmanian bird life instead? Oh, happy day. Welcome back, Clementine."

Meanwhile, Sadie spent an hour every day walking with Maggie in her pram. She took a stopwatch with her and sent away for a pedometer.

"I'd start getting worried for that fifty dollars of yours, Miranda," Juliet said one evening as Sadie ate a small serving of Juliet's roast beef, said no to potatoes and had a fresh peach rather than the apple pie everyone else was having.

Maggie's clothes were washed each day, her toys tidied away. Sadie did more than her share of the housekeeping. They all agreed it was working very well.

Ten weeks after the new arrangement had started, Clementine came home from university to an empty house. That was unusual. Sadie and Maggie were always waiting for her.

She checked the notice board. A note from Sadie said they'd gone walking and would be back by four p.m.

It was after five by the time they arrived at the front gate. Clementine was distraught. She'd been up and down the road and had already called the police, who hadn't been helpful. "Where in God's name have you been? I've been worried sick."

"We went for a walk. And she was so happy we kept walking, through town, down to the waterfront and then up to Battery Point. I stopped at the shop there."

"That's miles away. What if something had happened?"

"But it didn't. We had a lovely stroll around and then we met a group of other mothers and got chatting to them."

"*Other* mothers?"

"They meet every Thursday in that little park there. They were so friendly. I told them all about Maggie. One of them has trouble putting her daughter down in the afternoon as well. I said I'd found that singing to her helped."

"*You'd* found?"

Leo arrived home. "There you are, Sadie. I told Clementine you'd be fine, that she wasn't to worry."

"You rang Dad? Don't you trust me with Maggie?"

"Yes, I trust you, but this wasn't on."

"I'm trying not to stay at home. It's good for both of us to be out and about. I just lost track of the time."

"Yes, sitting in a mothers' group, talking as if Maggie were your daughter."

Sadie's cheeks reddened. "I meant to tell them she was my niece but then they all assumed she was my daughter so it was easier to go along with it."

"They thought she was your daughter because you didn't tell them otherwise. Sadie, she's my daughter."

"I know that. Settle down, Clementine. I'm sorry we worried you. If we're ever late back again, I'll ring and leave a message, I promise."

"There won't be another time. I knew this wouldn't work."

Leo stepped in. "Clementine, please calm down. It's all been going so well. I've been so proud to see you back studying again."

"I'm going to put my studies on hold. I should be looking after Maggie full time."

"What about your research? Your professor's plans? You told me you thought there could be an international paper published about this if you keep it up."

Clementine wavered.

"Clem, I'm sorry," Sadie said. "I really didn't mean to worry you." She watched as Clementine took Maggie out of the pram. She was fast asleep. "I thought it would be the best thing for her, lots of fresh air, and I really think she liked it."

"Then please don't do that again. Stay away longer than you said. Or say you're her mother."

"Of course she won't," Leo answered for her. "It was just a little misunderstanding."

Clementine moved Maggie to her other shoulder. The little girl shifted in her sleep, a hand coming up and clutching her mother's chin. Clementine kissed it.

"See, she knows who her mother is," Sadie said. "Of course she does."

Clementine relaxed. "Sorry for overreacting. I was worried."

"Sorry for coming back late. I was only trying to help."

Clementine collected Maggie's blanket and bag of toys. "We'll be in the living room if anyone's looking for us."

Leo waited until the door shut behind Clementine and Maggie. "Well done, Sadie. You handled that really well."

"Did I?" Sadie glowed with the praise. "Thanks, Dad."

CHAPTER 8

As her third birthday approached, Maggie turned into a whirling dervish. She started spinning in a circle when she was excited. She talked nonstop. Not a lot of it made sense, but she talked nevertheless. She got cross if she didn't get her own way but any temper tantrum would pass in seconds. She also liked to be in charge, being the first to open the front door when they all came home from somewhere; the one to change the TV channels; the one to ring the bell Juliet had bought to call everyone to dinner.

Clementine threw a small birthday party, inviting the family and three of their neighbors' children as guests. One child for each year of her age. Sadie had read the tip in one of the magazines she often quoted. There were jelly cakes, swiss rolls, chocolate crackles and ice cream cake. The adults ate most of the food, except for Sadie. She was still on her diet. She had lost the weight she said she would and received her fifty dollars from Miranda. She and Miranda had made a further bet. Sadie had to keep the weight off for a year or she would have to pay it back to Miranda.

Sadie had secretly drafted in help from Eliza. "Think of me as one of your guinea pigs," she'd said. Eliza had drawn up a simple weekly exercise and nutrition plan for Sadie to follow. Combined with all the walking she did with Maggie, she was finding it easy. Especially with Eliza in the same house keeping an eye on her. All Eliza spoke about these days was exercise and fitness. Her own trainer Mark was doing brilliantly in Melbourne, she kept telling them.

"Anyone would think you're in love with Mark the way you talk about him all the time," Miranda said one day. Everyone was in the kitchen. Leo was in his seat at the end of the table, reading a newspaper.

"I told you, he's married," Eliza snapped. She hadn't told them anything about Mark's separation.

"So, does that make him instantly repulsive?" Miranda said.

"You're just jealous that Eliza has a man in her life and you don't," Sadie said from the sink.

"I don't have a man in my life?" Miranda's tone was frosty. "And how are you so sure of that? Your remarkable network of spies might just be letting you down for once."

Sadie turned, her gloved hands covered in bubbles. "Where is he, then?"

"You seriously think I would bring a boyfriend home to meet all of you? Let me return the favor, dear Sadie. Where are all the boys beating a path to your door, may I ask?"

Sadie's cheeks colored. "It's none of your business."

Miranda snorted. "Oh, so you have got a boyfriend?"

Sadie lifted her chin. "Yes, I do as it happens."

"What's his name?"

Sadie hesitated just for a moment. "Anthony."

"Anthony? And what does Anthony do?"

Another pause. "He's a plumber."

"How fantastic. Handy with his hands and those hard to negotiate bends, so important in a man. And where did you meet this Anthony-the-Plumber?"

"Here. He came to fix the shower."

"And fell in love with you on the spot?" Miranda leaned back in her chair, folding her arms. "Then how come we haven't seen him call for you?"

"I meet him in town."

"Oh, how sweet. And what does he look like? Is he tall? Short? Thin? Fat?"

Leo was now listening.

"He's just regular," Sadie said, all her attention on the dishes.

Miranda laughed. "You're a terrible liar, Sadie. You always have been."

Sadie didn't look at her. "Shut up, Miranda."

"Dad, did you hear that? That nanny Clementine hired to look after Maggie just told me to shut up."

Leo shook his head, fighting a smile. "I second her motion. Shut up, Miranda. Leave your sister alone."

"Oh, you spoilsport," Miranda said, standing up and sweeping past him, ruffling his hair as she did so. As she passed Sadie, she pointed at a plate on the draining board. "You missed a spot, by the way."

．　　．　　．

The week after Maggie's birthday Miranda held a party for the pharmacy's wholesalers and best customers. Six months earlier, she'd been promoted to head buyer. The new position suited her, for many different reasons. She got to travel interstate on buying trips twice a year. She'd also had a pay raise. She needed the extra money to pay for her increased social life. Since Tom, she'd decided not to mix work with pleasure. It helped that his company had sent a pimpled twenty-two-year-old down to replace him. Not Miranda's cup of tea at all.

She and Liz spent most of their nights out at the casino. It was the most glamorous place in the city. The bars were always filled with visiting businessmen. Miranda had enjoyed several dalliances, one with a visiting academic. He was a mathematician. Also married. She and Liz had sighed about it to themselves the next day when they met for a drink and report-sharing.

"He's lovely but there's no future."

"No? Good."

They'd both laughed.

"Any presents?"

"Dinner, very fine wine."

"And?"

"And none of your business." Miranda needed to keep some things to herself. What had happened after dinner was nice sex in his hotel room. Something about hotel rooms excited her. Of course, what was the alternative? Bringing her lovers back to the family home? The mental picture of it made her laugh.

As the party got underway, Miranda glanced around the newly decorated shop, now filled with their best customers, crammed in against the displays of cosmetics and shampoos. She circulated. There was a combination of elderly customers who visited three times a week for their prescriptions and the chance of a chat, and the younger group who bought all their makeup and perfume at the pharmacy.

"Miranda Faraday, as I live and breathe, are you still working here?"

"Lynetta." Her friend, the flight attendant. "What are you doing here?"

"I gate-crashed. My great-aunt's one of your best customers so I hitched a ride with her. Get me some champagne, would you? I hope it's real French stuff, not some appalling Australian version."

As Miranda passed Lynetta a glass, she gave her the once-over. The other woman's hair was glossy and expertly cut. She was trim, her clothes and makeup perfect, her shoes high. "You look amazing."

"Thanks," Lynetta said. She didn't return the compliment.

Miranda straightened her spine that little bit more. "So, how's life in the sky?"

"Best thing I ever did. I'm in charge of the cabin now."

Miranda didn't ask what that meant. "You don't get sick of being a glorified waitress?"

"That's such a cliché, Miranda. I thought you had more wit than that. The work is the least part of it. I've never done so much socializing in my life. Limousine rides to and from the airport, luxury hotels . . ."

"Are you a flight attendant or a call girl?"

"Those are our normal working conditions. We're the public

face of the airline. Of course they have to look after us. We're also in charge of safety. Dismiss it if you must, but it's an extremely important job."

"I'd have thought the pilot's job was a little more important."

"Don't start me on the pilots." She assessed Miranda. "Seriously, you should think about it yourself. You have the looks, the height, the attitude."

"I've just been promoted here."

Lynetta didn't ask for details or say congratulations. She looked at her watch. "I better go. Mum and Dad are taking me out to dinner at the casino. Thanks for this. Bye for now." She put her glass on the counter and left.

"Enjoy the flight home," Miranda said sourly. She took a sip of champagne. The bubbles had gone out of it.

*   *   *

"Two more clients, Eliza. I'm on my way. We're on our way, I should say."

Eliza smiled into the phone. She was in the gym after hours, on her own, updating the membership records. Mark had rung her from the gym he worked in part time. "Will I ring Fortune 500, or will you?"

"I know, I'm getting carried away. But it's a great start. How are you?"

Missing you, she wanted to say.

"You'll love it here in Melbourne, Eliza. There's a different attitude. Everyone lives and breathes sports. If we could just get involved with one of the football clubs, we'd be set up."

"Don't move too fast. I have to graduate first, remember."

She waited for him to say he missed her. He didn't. He was too busy talking about the latest program he'd developed. This type of personalized, multilayered approach was the future, he was sure of it.

"So when will you be down in Hobart next?"

"Look, it could be a month or two. Especially now I've got these new clients. One of them wants weekend sessions, and I can't just leave them in the lurch."

"But how will your kids get on without seeing you?"

He hesitated for a moment. "They're not without me at the moment."

"Pardon?"

"They're here in Melbourne with me."

"But I thought you said your wife wouldn't let them travel without her."

"She won't." A pause. "Belinda's here too."

"Your wife and your cousin and your children? It's a bit crowded there, isn't it?"

"My cousin's not here."

Eliza needed to sit down. She moved the membership records off the desk and found a place. "Mark, what's going on?"

"We're just spending a bit of time together, for the sake of the kids."

"And where is your wife sleeping, for the sake of the kids?"

"Eliza, don't be like this."

"Like what? Truthful? I'm working all hours every night to get a double degree so that you and I can set up a business and you're over there having a reunion with your wife?"

"It's for the sake of the kids."

"You weren't thinking about the kids six weeks ago."

It was the last time he'd been in Hobart. She'd believed everything he'd said to her. That it was all over with his wife. That being in Melbourne was the fresh start to his life. His enthusiasm had been so infectious she had let her guard down.

After they had finished their business catch-up that day, she had calmly got up, walked across to the gym door and locked it.

"You're locking me in?"

She nodded. "I don't want anyone to catch us."

"Catch us doing what?"

"This." She kissed him.

He smiled slowly. The smile that got her every time. "What's this all about?"

She had told him. That she was in love with him. That she'd been in love with him for years.

"Wow," he'd said.

She laughed. "Wow what?"

"Wow, that is fantastic news."

Just that. That and his smile. It was all she needed. She put aside all her thoughts about waiting until he was divorced, waiting until she was in Melbourne. She was sick of waiting. She kissed him again, and this time he kissed her back.

They were soon doing more than kissing. Eliza had imagined this for years. What she hadn't realized was how much better the real thing would be. He kissed her lips, her face, her neck, lower. He lifted off her top. She took off his T-shirt. There was no talking, just whispers and moans of pleasure. He hesitated once and she urged him on. She was ready for this. She had been ready for four years.

It was fast, hot love-making. It was so good they did it again, soon afterward.

"Would you say we've just christened our new business partnership?" he asked her, smoothing back her hair, kissing her neck, touching her body again.

"Something like that," she said, moving against him once more.

He went back to his parents' house that night, ready for his youngest son's birthday the next morning. When he called that afternoon from the airport he made no mention of what had happened between them. She guessed—and he confirmed it in a phone call the next day—that his parents, his children and his ex-wife Belinda were at the airport saying good-bye to him. He told her again that everyone was trying to keep the breakup as amicable as possible. It seemed he hadn't been joking.

"How long has this been going on, Mark?"

"My cousin moved out of her place three months ago. Belinda's been coming over to Melbourne every second weekend."

"And when you've been down here, you've been staying with her, not your parents, haven't you?" His silence gave her the answer. "So when were you going to tell me? When I'd packed up my whole life to come over to Melbourne to go into business with you?"

"Look, Eliza, I didn't know—I still don't know—if it will last with Belinda and I. We've got lots of problems we need to work through."

"But what about me? About us?"

"Eliza, you know what I think of you."

She hung up on him. She cried, out of anger at first, and then the heartbreak took over. Nothing had prepared her for this. What did she do now? All her plans, all her thinking had been directed toward Mark, toward Melbourne, toward them being together. He had been her escape route, the thought that kept her going through all the suffocating times with her family. Now . . . nothing. It hurt, deep inside her. She prided herself on always being strong, staying determined, putting her best foot forward, but there was no one here to see her now. She let the tears flow, hugging herself into a ball.

It felt like hours had passed before they finally eased. She went into the changing room, washed her face, soaked tissues with cold water to try and fix her swollen eyes. She made herself go back to the desk, pushing down the hurt voice inside that wanted to start crying again. She wouldn't cry for him. Not again tonight, not ever. A sticker on the side of her gym bag by the door caught her eye: *Set your goals. Aim high. No one can do it but you.*

She reached for a piece of paper. Gym letterhead. She did some scribbled calculations. She was midway through her university studies and had nearly completed a nighttime accountancy course. She had some savings in the bank.

She would happily have given up everything for him. He had chosen his wife over her. But it didn't mean her future plans had to be thrown away as well.

She'd do it anyway. Move to Melbourne and start her own business. As soon as she could. The minute Maggie started school.

Sadie stepped on the scales, gave a whoop and stepped off again. Beside her, Maggie stood in her stockinged feet watching, her large dark eyes the image of Clementine's. She was wearing a red corduroy dress and a red knitted cardigan with a blue flower on the pocket. Sadie thought she looked like a particularly sweet pixie. The new haircut added to it, the dark strands a spiky halo around her head. Her sticky-out ears also added to the effect. Sadie loved Maggie's ears. Miranda had remarked earlier that week—out of Clementine's hearing, of course—that if Maggie's ears got any bigger she'd be able to fly across Bass Strait on her own. "It's evolution at work, isn't it?" she'd said, looking down at Maggie sitting on her lap, taking her ears between her fingers and making them stick out even more. They all laughed as the light from behind shone through them, making it look as though Maggie did indeed have magical glowing ears. Maggie had laughed too.

"Clap your hands, Maggie," Sadie said. "I've lost another two pounds."

Maggie clapped her hands, lost her balance and fell onto the scales. "Ow," she said.

Sadie picked her up and looked down at the scales again. "Look, that's what you and I weigh."

"We weigh."

"Good girl! We weigh! Are you the cleverest girl in the world? Yes, you are." She hopped off and put Maggie on the scales on her own. "See, that's how much you weigh. The perfect weight, because you are the perfect girl, aren't you?"

There was a noise at the front door. "The postie's been. Come on, Maggie. The postie."

Maggie ran to the door and picked up the mail. "Five letters," she said.

"So there are. Good girl. Thank you." She leafed through and handed a circular back to Maggie. "This one's for you, Maggie. It's from the Queen. She says she wants you to be the Princess of Tasmania and she's going to build you a castle to live in."

Maggie took it and appeared to be studying the letter—a catalog for seedlings—very carefully. "Oh," she said.

Sadie left mail for Leo, Miranda and Clementine in the basket on the hall table. In the living room, she took out some blocks for Maggie to play with—she ignored them and kept reading her seedling catalog—and opened her own letter. A formal white envelope with the University of Tasmania letterhead. An equally formal letter inside. Sadie scanned it first, then read it again more slowly.

It was a personal letter from her tutor, expressing concern at her nonattendance at lectures that semester. "Please telephone me at your convenience to discuss this further," the tutor finished.

A form letter, Sadie decided. There had been none of that formal language when she had called the tutor several months earlier and explained she was going to take time off to mind Maggie each day.

The tutor hadn't been happy.

No one seemed to understand. It wasn't a hardship. She loved it, in fact. The secret truth was Sadie felt far more at ease being at home with Maggie than she ever had sitting in a lecture hall, trying to find hidden meaning in novels that had already been pored over by hundreds of thousands of students through the years.

Perhaps it would be different if she'd had a thirst for specific knowledge. But she didn't. She'd signed up to an arts course because it looked like a good excuse to do a lot of reading for three years. Her fellow students were fired up with ideas for careers afterward. When Sadie looked beyond her graduation day, all she saw was fog.

Offering to look after Maggie had been a spur of the moment decision. Part of her had offered simply because she was dreading writing a 6,000-word essay the following month on the First World War poets. The surprise had been discovering how much she loved staying at home looking after Maggie.

"So much for women's lib," Miranda had retorted when Sadie made the mistake of trying to explain it. "Women all over the world burning their bras, and you, Sadie Faraday, at the forefront of modern womanhood, with a lifetime of learning stretching out in front of you, throw up your arms, throw in the towel and say, 'No thanks, I don't want a brain, I want to graduate in Pram Pushing modules one, two and three.' "

"You're letting other women down by saying those things," Sadie replied. "Women's liberation is about giving us the choice to work or be educated, opening up new paths."

"Exactly. New paths. Not old ways." Miranda leaned down to where Maggie was playing on the colored mat in the middle of the floor. "Nothing against you, Maggie. You know that I truly believe you are the most enchanting child ever to have been born, but you really should start lifting your game in regard to life skills. Can you change a tire yet, for instance? Mix a martini?"

Sadie leaned down and picked Maggie up. "Don't listen to her, Maggie. She's a bad influence."

"I'm a bad influence? You're the one who waits on her hand and foot. Clementine doesn't even do that and she's her real mother, not some pretend stand-in like you."

"How dare you."

"How dare I what?"

"Talk to me like that, especially in front of Maggie."

Miranda rolled her eyes. "Two facts, Sadie. Number one, Maggie wouldn't understand if I called you a whore of Babylon. Number two, you're not Maggie's mother. It's Clementine who is the important person in her life."

"She spends just as much time with me as she does with Clementine."

"You're not getting this, are you? Clementine is her mother, Sadie. You are her babysitter. Keep it in perspective." Miranda glanced down at the elegant gold watch on her wrist. "I'm late. I'd better get going."

"Where are you going this time?"

"Out to talk to people taller than two feet about subjects more fascinating than kittens, building blocks, colors and numbers. Like you should occasionally."

Sadie scanned the letter again, then put it back into the envelope, folded it in two and pushed it deep into the pocket of her jeans. The tutor didn't care if Sadie came back to lectures or finished her degree. It was all about making his attendance records look good. And besides, she could go back and study any time. For now, it was better for everyone if she continued as she was.

Sadie knew she was doing a good job. Clementine had said as much the previous night. She'd come in late, after a field trip to the east coast, rushing through the door, calling to Sadie as she threw down her coat and bag. "I'm so sorry, Sadie, we got held up. I'll get her dinner ready now."

She'd walked into the kitchen and found a freshly bathed Maggie on Sadie's lap. Maggie held out her arms. "Mummy. Mummy."

Clementine had scooped her up, given her a kiss and held her tight. "Poor Maggie. I'm so sorry. What kind of a mother am I?" She stopped, taking in the sight of the dinner dishes already washed and draining on the sink. "Have you done it already?"

"Dinner done, bath done, nappy changed, story read."

To her amazement, Clementine's eyes filled with tears. "What would I do without you?"

"Take Maggie everywhere with you?"

"I'm serious, Sadie. You don't know how much this means to me. It's like the best of both worlds, and I couldn't do it without you. Thank you."

"Thank you," Maggie echoed.

Clementine sat down opposite Sadie, holding Maggie on her

lap. "Is it still working out for you as well? Are you managing to get to all the lectures you need to? And your essays? I haven't seen you writing anything for weeks."

"I'm writing them when I'm in at the university," Sadie lied, "while I'm still in study mode."

"So you're happy to continue looking after her? Really?"

"Of course," Sadie said. "We have fun together, Maggie, don't we?"

She put out her arms toward her niece. Maggie turned around and nuzzled into Clementine's neck. Clementine kissed her.

"Want me to hold her while you get your dinner?" Sadie had asked. She'd been surprised by the sudden spike of hurt. Of course Maggie would want to stay with Clementine. She hadn't seen her all day.

Clementine had shaken her head, standing up and lifting Maggie up into the air, then down, up and down, to Maggie's giggling delight. "No, I'm not hungry yet. We'll go and have a play in the garden together. Come on, Maggie. Come and tell me everything you did today."

Sadie decided to put that moment from yesterday out of her head. She had her niece to herself today, after all. She sat down next to Maggie and her blocks, and handed her a red one. "We're perfectly happy as we are, aren't we, Maggie? We get on great together. And who needs silly old university when I've got you to play with?"

Maggie reached up and pulled at Sadie's nose. "Sadie." The word was crystal clear.

Sadie beamed at her. "That's right, I'm Sadie. Good girl, Maggie. You're my gorgeous, clever little girl."

B y the time Maggie was four, Sadie was looking after her five days a week. The hours had increased three months after Maggie's third birthday. Clementine had been offered a position in a research team cataloguing the bird life on Maria Island, off the east coast of Tasmania. It wasn't a small project, either, but a long-term ecological study.

Clementine was very excited about it. Sadie had tuned out after a while, getting lost in the details of wind-stream effects and nesting habits. It was Clementine's final remark that seized her attention.

"I'm going to have to put Maggie into kindergarten full time. I can't ask you to increase your hours, Sadie. I don't know how you're managing to get any study done as it is."

"Put Maggie into kindergarten? Don't be mad. I'll talk to my lecturer again. I'd love to look after Maggie some more."

"Oh, Sadie, are you sure? I feel like I'm asking too much of you as it is, but this project—" her face lit up, "it's like a dream come true."

"I'm one hundred percent sure," Sadie said. "You can't turn down an opportunity like this."

"You're positive, Sadie?" Leo asked her when they were alone in the kitchen washing up after dinner.

"It just makes sense, Dad. And I enjoy it."

"Good girl. Your mother would be very proud of you too."

What Clementine didn't know—what none of them knew—was Sadie hadn't been anywhere near the university in months. She'd telephoned her tutor and invented a long story about Maggie not being well, an unusual strain of childhood measles, she thought. A quarantine situation, just for a few months. If the tutor had sounded skeptical, Sadie did her best to ignore it.

She'd also changed the hours of her part-time housecleaning job. She'd answered an ad in the paper two months earlier, after tiring of always being short of cash. Leo now gave her an allowance in exchange for looking after Maggie, as well as waiving her board, but what with buying little treats for Maggie as often as she could, she needed to earn some more. The house owners didn't mind when she did the work, as long as it got done. When Clementine was home looking after Maggie, Sadie did the cleaning. And if Clementine assumed Sadie was at her lectures those times, there wasn't much Sadie could do about it.

Lately, Sadie had been reading up on the importance of social interaction between preschool children. Contact with other children a few mornings a week was ideal, according to one article. Flicking through the piles of newspapers in the library one afternoon, she found a copy of the weekly newspaper for Sorell, a small town sixteen miles east of Hobart. An ad in the back pages caught her eye: Calling at-home mothers—is your child five and under? Are you looking for a break in your routine? Like to chat with other mothers?

Sadie had rung the number from a phone booth later that day. A friendly woman answered and bombarded her with information. It was a casual setup, for company and advice, and especially to give their children the opportunity to play with others the same age.

"Our first meeting is on Friday. Why not come along? Here's the address." The woman on the phone kept chatting. "So we'll see you and your daughter soon! Sally, is it? And Maddie, age four. I'll write that down now. Great, looking forward to meeting you!"

She'd hung up before Sadie had the opportunity to explain that it was Sadie, not Sally, and that Maggie, not Maddie, was her niece, not her daughter. There wasn't the chance to explain when she arrived at the woman's house in Sorell two days later, either. She pulled up in Leo's car right at ten o'clock, just as three other cars arrived. The mothers of Sorell were punctual. Maggie was shy at first, clinging to Sadie, until another little girl around the same age held out a small battered doll and Maggie just as silently took it. Five minutes later the two of them were engrossed in a game of make-believe while Sadie fell into easy conversation with the other mothers. It was such a relief to hear that their children were also fussy eaters, that they didn't always go to sleep at the right time. No one asked Sadie where she lived, what she did for a living or even if she was married. All the focus was on the children, with a side order of talk about TV shows and fashion.

She told Clementine most of what had happened. That she'd started taking Maggie to a weekly playgroup. That she seemed to enjoy it.

"Are the other children good fun, Maggie?" Clementine asked, smoothing Maggie's hair over her ears. Sadie's fingers itched to unsmooth it. She loved the way Maggie's ears stuck out through her hair.

Maggie took a deep breath and told Clementine everything that had happened that day. "We went in the car and then another lady got there too and she had a little girl with her and there was a blue doll so I had that and then the boy hit it so we put it in the tree then we had apples and came home."

Clementine and Sadie shared a laugh. Sadie intended to tell her that the group was in Sorell, and that the other mothers had made the embarrassing mistake that Maggie was her daughter, not her niece, and not only that, but they insisted on calling them Sally and Maddie, not Sadie and Maggie, but the opportunity passed. In the same way that the moment passed to correct everyone in the group as well. She'd decided it was easier to leave things as they were.

She'd only just managed to get away with Maggie calling her Sadie. She told them it was Maggie's best attempt at saying Sally. She also told them Maddie sometimes called herself Maggie. It was so funny the way children mixed up letters, wasn't it? she said, before telling them that Maddie also called her grandfather Tadpole. It was the closest she'd been able to get to saying Grandpa.

"Tadpole? How gorgeous," one of the women said. "But you don't mind Maddie calling you by your name, instead of Mummy?"

"No, I think it's sweet," Sadie said.

"Oh, I'd hate it," another woman joined in. "I love hearing my daughter say Mummy. Tell you what, here's my number. Why don't you and Maddie drop down to us one weekend? Or what about you give me your address. We're up and down to Hobart quite often, we could drop in on you."

The woman wouldn't take no for an answer. Sadie had no choice. She wrote down a false address and phone number. She changed the subject. She also decided not to go back to that group again.

She took Maggie out on other day trips during the week instead, to the outer reaches of the city, sometimes even to towns an hour or two's drive from Hobart. She checked with Clementine first, of course. Sadie loved those trips. She and Maggie would make up songs as they drove. All of Maggie's songs were about cats. She'd just learned to rhyme and specialized in a song about the cat and the rat and the mat, sung to a tune a little too much like "Jingle Bells." Sadie often found herself humming it throughout the day.

They drove to many of the beaches around Hobart, collecting shells some days, writing numbers on the sand on other days, or lying sunbathing, having picnics and reading books if the weather was warm. On cooler days, Sadie took Maggie to the library or to shopping centers. She saw other mothers dragging squawking children down supermarket aisles and marveled once more at Maggie's wonderful temperament. She started bringing the family camera with her. Clementine was grateful when Sadie gave her a packet of photos, souvenirs of all the places she and Maggie had been to that month.

That gave Sadie the idea. She decided to put together a special gift for Clementine. A Maggie scrapbook, just like the scrapbooks their mother used to keep.

It was a fun project. She started working on it while Maggie was watching TV or having a daytime nap. It would be a whole collection of different things, she decided. Snapshots of Maggie's life.

She started with a photograph of Maggie's favorite toy, Red Monkey, perched up on the back veranda, with the garden behind. It looked like he had climbed there. Maggie had firm ideas about her toys' names. As well as Red Monkey, she had Brown Bear, Orange Lion and Green Turtle. Her choice of names had an effect on the whole family for a while. "Has anyone seen the red tablecloth?" "Who moved my blue leather bag?"

"We've all got adjectivitis," Leo had said.

She devoted two pages to Maggie's love of dressing up. It had reached an obsession in the past year. She'd gone through a Goldilocks stage (six weeks), a Little Miss Muffet stage (eight weeks) and a superhero stage (five weeks), each one characterized by constant reading of stories about each character, night after night, combined with the wearing of clothes as close to those in the books. Fortunately she lost interest in each one not too long after Sadie or Clementine tired of the same story each night.

Sadie sprinkled notable dates and events from Maggie's life throughout the pages of the scrapbook. She already knew her birth date, of course. She casually asked Clementine and her sisters questions until she was certain of the dates of Maggie's first tooth, first step and first words. She wrote down the dates Maggie had the chicken pox. She wrote about the day Maggie broke her left wrist, when she fell off the ladder Leo had left leaning against the plum tree. She wore a plaster cast for six weeks and didn't cry when it was cut off. It was still in the cupboard in her and Clementine's bedroom. Sadie slipped in one afternoon, cut off a tiny sliver and stuck that in the scrapbook too.

She decided to devote three pages to Maggie's remarkable talent for numbers. She had been the first to notice it. Looking after her one rainy afternoon, when Maggie was only three years old, she'd watched in amazement as her niece lined up her toys in a row in the living room—dolls, cars, bears and all—then walked alongside them in what Sadie could only describe as an inspection parade, tapping each one on the head and counting aloud. She reached twenty-nine.

"Twenty-nine!" Sadie told Leo and her sisters later. "It means she's a child genius, doesn't it?"

Miranda was impressed. "Either that or she's got too many toys. Clementine, have you been sneaking her into some accelerated schooling?"

"I've been teaching her how to count, of course." Clementine watched as Maggie repeated her counting trick for them all. "She'll be going to school the year after next; I can't have her turning up not knowing anything."

"I've been teaching her too," Sadie said. She'd been showing Maggie how to count for months now. She'd known the day would come when all that accumulated knowledge would kick in.

"It's not surprising she's advanced for her age," Clementine added. "I read to her every night before she goes to sleep too."

"Read her what, though? Your essays on the endangered birdlife of Tasmanian islands?" Miranda said. "No wonder the poor child is asleep by seven."

"All her favorite books are about numbers, now I think of it," Sadie said eagerly. "You know, *Goldilocks and the Three Bears, Five Little Ducks.* I've been reading her books about colors and letters too. She'll be reading herself before too long, you wait and see."

Over the next few months Leo produced a set of magnetic numbers that he stuck to the fridge. Miranda gave her numbered blocks. Sadie gave her a blackboard with numbers painted across the top. Eliza gave her a bag of rubber numbers that floated in the bath. Juliet got her number-shaped cookie cutters and made her a batch every week.

Each night after dinner, Clementine would lie on the couch with Maggie nestled beside her, holding up fingers and doing addition. "What's your fingers plus all of my fingers, Maggie?"

"Twenty," Maggie said.

"What if I add these fingers to these fingers? Three plus four plus two. How many fingers?"

"Nine fingers."

"And if I take away three fingers from ten fingers?"

"Seven fingers."

Sadie made up lots of number games when the two of them were together as well. Before long, Maggie was doing simple sums in her head without anyone having to hold up fingers. It became a family party trick. Maggie the Marvelous Performing Mathematician, Miranda called her. The adults would toss her additions and subtractions as though she was a family dog catching biscuits.

"Nine plus one, Maggie," Juliet would say as she prepared dinner or swept the kitchen floor, with Maggie acting as kitchenhand beside her.

"Ten. Ask me another."

"Eight divided by two."

"Four. Another."

"I didn't even know what the word 'divided' meant when I was her age," Miranda said.

Leo was delighted. It sprang from his side of the family, he insisted, until Clementine gently reminded him that David, Maggie's father, had graduated in applied math and physics from Melbourne University. "He had something to do with it, all right, I'll grant you that, but it's nurture versus nature, if you ask me. Maggie arrived with the seed of maths genius and between us we have coaxed it into full, glorious blooming life."

David called in each year, whenever he was back home in Hobart. The visits were as awkward for him as they were for everyone else watching him. He didn't seem to know how to behave around Maggie. Maggie hadn't shown all that much interest in him, either. She wasn't frightened of him—Clementine had made sure to show her photographs and talk about him occasionally—she just wasn't that interested. The previous year she had kept on playing with her doll's house when he came in.

"Maggie," Clementine had said, "say hello to David, your dad."

Maggie hadn't spoken, just looked at him for a long moment, then solemnly reached up and handed him a wooden block.

Clementine told the others later she was quite touched to see him put it in his pocket.

There were birthday presents each year from him, even if it was obvious to all of them that they were spur-of-the-moment buys. But they had all agreed the contact was better than none.

Sadie decided to keep the David section of the scrapbook quite small. She filled other pages with drawings of Maggie counting her toys and solving sums. She loved drawing Maggie in cartoon-style, dressed in her little red coat, with her big dark eyes, short dark hair and, of course, her sticky-out ears.

She filled a page with funny things Maggie had said. She drew little cartoon strips setting the scene, drawing everyone in the family with speech bubbles coming out of their mouths. She had plenty of examples to choose from. Her favorite was the time she'd told Maggie she had a tummy ache. Maggie had pulled a sympathetic face and said, "I've got a tummy ache too, a tummy ache in my head."

Once Sadie started filling the pages with mementos and snippets of Maggie's life, she found it hard to stop. The difficulty was what to leave out, not what to put in. She decided to go back even further than the past year. She crept into Clementine's room one day and went through the basket of bits and pieces about Maggie that Clementine had been keeping. Her birth notice from the newspaper. Her birth certificate. Prints of her feet and hands from her first days in the hospital. Sadie made photocopies of everything, stuck the copies in the scrapbook and put the originals back, all without Clementine knowing. It would make a wonderful surprise, Sadie knew. Not just because it was carrying on their mother's tradition of scrapbooks, but to have everything collected in one place like this.

She'd present it to Clementine and Maggie on the little girl's fifth birthday. It would be the perfect occasion. She pictured Maggie's delight to see a whole scrapbook all about her, Clementine's gratitude and amazement that Sadie had gone to so much trouble. The others would be just as impressed, Sadie knew it. She could hardly wait.

"That's your mummy up there, Maggie. Look, wave at her!"

Maggie waved up at Clementine, on the stage with other students from her course, all recipients of excellence awards. The Faradays were in the left-hand side of the hall, in their best clothes. They had already been to Eliza's graduation ceremony in the same hall earlier that day. She now held two degrees, one in physical education, the other in accountancy.

"Very convenient of the two of them to get this over and done with in one day," Miranda had said. "Thank God you're only a part-time student and we're years off your ceremony, Sadie. I don't know if I could handle another one of these this century."

Sadie didn't say anything. She was too busy trying to avoid her tutor, and hoping he didn't see her father. In her last letter she had painted a sad story about her father having been hit by a car and being wheelchair-bound. It meant she was needed at home much more, limiting her study and lecture time. She had been granted a further leave of absence. She hoped she had only imagined the skeptical tone to the reply letter, in which her father was wished a speedy recovery.

This was a triple celebration day, though they didn't know it yet. Leo had received good news two days earlier. He was saving it for the celebration lunch.

He had booked a private room in one of Hobart's best restaurants. It looked beautiful. Red walls and velvet curtains at the window, opened to give them a clear view of the water. The table was set with white linen, gleaming glasses and shining cutlery. Miranda said it was like being in a castle banqueting hall.

Eliza and Clementine arrived, still in their graduation gowns. Sadie followed behind them, carrying Maggie. The little girl was wearing Eliza's mortarboard and getting cross that it kept slipping off.

Leo was last to arrive, carrying a large box. It was only after everyone was seated and a toast had been drunk to Eliza and Clementine that he revealed what was inside. He called on Maggie to help open it. Inside were six smaller boxes, each with a name tag. Maggie delivered them, one by one.

On his signal they all opened the boxes. Each one had a plastic bag containing a handful of grass inside.

"Dope?" Miranda said. "Interesting approach to fatherhood, Dad."

"What's dope?" Maggie asked.

"Never mind," Sadie whispered.

"I'll tell you later," Clementine said.

"Tell me now." Maggie stood on her chair. "What is dope?" she shouted. She was going through a shouting stage.

"Maggie, sit down," all four of her aunts and her mother said as one.

Maggie sat down.

"It's not *that* grass," Leo said. "It's grass grass. Lawn grass."

Eliza poked at the bag, lifted it out and turned it one way, then the other. "Thanks, Dad. That's a really thoughtful present."

"And to think you're a university graduate. All of you, take the grass out and look underneath," Leo instructed.

They all did as he asked. Folded at the bottom of each box was an envelope. Inside the envelope was a check. Each check had their name on it. Beside it, a sum. One hundred dollars.

"A hundred dollars! Each! Dad, what's happened?"

"You have the grass of the world to thank." He paused. "Girls, one of my inventions has been accepted."

There was a rush of congratulations and a scramble of hugs, Leo beaming amid it all.

"Which one is it, Dad?" Clementine asked. "What does this one do?"

"Turns poor families into not-so-poor families," Miranda said. "No wonder people want it."

Leo didn't even notice Miranda's remark. He'd been working on this invention for months, he told them. His idea had been to improve the performance of lawn mowers, not through faster blade speeds, but by improving the flow of petrol into the engine. After several false starts, he'd had success. With his fifth prototype he'd noted a fifteen percent increase in fuel efficiency.

"That's when it started to get serious, with lawyers and meetings and—"

"You've had meetings about this? And you didn't tell us?"

Leo explained. He'd spoken to his lawyer who had liaised with interested parties. A representative of one of the lawn mower companies had flown to Tasmania to meet Leo. A preliminary deal was signed. While the process was still going through, Leo had developed a new, improved version. One that he realized could be used in other areas and with other liquids. He ran more trials and built other prototypes. He'd sent details to his legal team in Sydney. His lawyer spoke to another patent lawyer, who spoke to a petrochemist who spoke to an industrialist. Leo's hunch was correct. His updated invention had even more possible applications in the gas and oil industries worldwide.

"A miniature oil rig?" Miranda asked. "That's what you've been building out there?"

Not an oil rig, he said. A new way of measuring flow and viscosity and velocity of a liquid while simultaneously measuring input and output. All in something the size and shape of the human ear. In fact, not dissimilar to the human ear, with its valves and tubes and unbelievably delicate mechanisms . . .

"Put simply, my girls, not just lawn mowing people want what I've invented. Big multinational organizations are interested too."

"To pollute the world even more?"

Leo ignored Clementine. Three very large companies had expressed further interest, he reported. The lawyer had visited Leo in Hobart twice, as recently as last week. It was the biggest deal he had ever been involved in, he'd told Leo.

What really had everyone excited, Leo added, were all the possible applications. Medical research. Food science. But that was in the future. For now, the focus was on the petrochemical industry, the pièce de résistance being the gadget's likely use in one of the most common petrol-using devices in the world. "Can you guess what it is?" he asked.

Eliza tried first. "A car?"

"No, not a car."

"Tractors?" Clementine suggested.

"Chain saws?" Juliet said.

"Petrol pumps!" Leo nearly shouted. "Petrol pumps measure gas. And my invention will help them measure it more accurately. And do you know how many petrol pumps there are in the world?" This time he didn't wait for their guesses. "No one does. Because there are so many of them. Millions and millions of them. And the lawyer thinks every single one of the companies who own those petrol pumps will want to have my invention."

"That's a lot of petrol pumps," Clementine said.

"A lot of money," Eliza added.

"A lot of everything," Leo said cheerfully.

"I can't believe it." Juliet looked shocked. "I just can't believe it."

"I believe it." Miranda clapped her hands and gave a whoop, beaming at everyone. "Just wait till I tell the girls at work about this!"

"No, Miranda."

"No what?"

"No, you can't tell anyone. None of you can breathe a word about this to anyone. Not now, not ever."

"What?"

"I've signed a secrecy clause."

"Oh, phooey," Miranda said with a laugh. "You may have. We haven't. Dad, don't be mad. We can't keep quiet about something like this."

"You have to keep quiet. All of you have to."

"Dad, come on."

"I'm not asking you. I'm telling you. I need you to swear that you won't tell anyone. Swear on your mother's grave." He had never, ever said that before.

"So how do we explain our new house, our new car, our new glamorous clothes?" Miranda asked.

"There's not going to be a new house or car or glamorous wardrobes. Not for years yet."

"Years!"

"I'm afraid so. It could be five years. Ten, even. These things take an enormous amount of time, protecting copyright, registering patents. It's important that I move slowly, protect all our interests. That's what I've been doing the past few months, ensuring my idea remains my property. Our property." While the negotiations were underway with the lawyers he'd had time to think about the possible impact if it was a success, he told them. He had decided they weren't going to radically change their lives, buy a bigger house, get expensive cars or take extravagant holidays.

He launched into another speech. It sounded as though he had been preparing it for some time. He talked about their mother, how excited she'd been when he'd got the job with the forestry company in Tasmania and the whole family had moved across the world, what an adventure it was for all of them, how they'd made Hobart their home. He said he knew her wish would have been that they stay together as a family, no matter how hard it might be. To help each other. To stay friends. He talked about how well they had coped with everything life had thrown at them. How wonderful it was to have Maggie in their lives. How proud he was of each of them. "We've done it together as a team. I want to make sure the money doesn't change things. I could just divide it all up, hand it over—"

"What an excellent idea," Miranda said.

"I'm serious, Miranda. We could have gone to pieces when your mother died, but we didn't. We stayed a family. I want us to stay a family forever." He looked solemnly around the table. "What would make me very happy is this. If we were all to promise, together, today, that we will always have an annual family celebration together, paid for out of this windfall. Maybe not always here in Tasmania, maybe back in London, maybe even somewhere else. It's something I would love to be able to look forward to, to think about during the year, to help plan. And it would make me very happy if that's what this money was used for. Something solid and long-lasting for us as a family."

"A new mansion for each of us to live in would be solid and long-lasting."

"Miranda, give up, will you?" Juliet said.

"I can't. It's the Faraday blood in me. The same blood that kept Dad locked in Shed Land before and after work for the past ten years working on his inventions until he finally hit pay dirt."

Leo acknowledged her words with a faint smile. "So, then. Christmas together, every year?"

"A July Christmas or a December Christmas?"

"Either one or both. We'll play that by ear. And we don't need to worry yet about where or how long or who cooks. It's the idea of it I hope you'll agree to. What do you think?" he prompted again.

"Of course," said Juliet.

Nods from Sadie, Eliza and Clementine.

"Of course," Miranda added after a moment.

Leo held up his glass in a toast. "Thank you, my chickens."

"Turkeys," Miranda said.

"Turkeys?"

Miranda nodded. "If we're agreeing that we don't get to touch any of this wonderful fortune and we're promising to have Christmas together once or twice a year for the rest of our lives, then we're definitely turkeys."

．　．　．

Juliet's first sight of Myles Stottington, the man who would become her husband, wasn't a good one.

She'd gone into the café early on a Monday to catch up on the menu writing and to redo the blackboard. She usually did it after work on Saturday, but she'd been busy getting final instructions from Mr. and Mrs. Stottington. They were heading back to the U.K. for an eight-week holiday and were keen to go over every detail with her before they left.

They'd been talking about this long trip home for months. Usually they just went back for a fortnight each year. They'd been concerned about going away for so long, despite Juliet's insistence she was happy to manage without them. One morning Mrs. Stottington had come in to work in high excitement. Their son in England, Myles, had come up with a wonderful idea. He'd come out to Tasmania and keep an eye on everything while they relaxed and enjoyed their holiday. After all, he'd grown up in cafés. He could do it with his eyes shut.

Juliet noticed the light on as she got closer to the café. Surely she hadn't forgotten to switch it off on Saturday afternoon?

She pushed the door. It was already unlocked. Had she forgotten to lock it as well? She heard a noise from behind the counter, where the hatch led into the kitchen. There was someone in there. The someone stood up. A man in a dark hooded sweater. He was tall. Broad. Juliet's heart began to beat faster. A burglar? The only weapon she had was her umbrella.

Another noise. The chest freezer being opened. She crept up to the counter and looked through the hatch. The man was taking out packages, piling them up on the bench beside him. He was stealing their food. All the buns, cakes and bread she had made herself.

She pointed the umbrella at him. "What do you think you are doing?"

The man leaped. The freezer lid dropped, hitting him on the head.

"*Ouch!* Who are you, sneaking up on me like that?"

"Who are you, more to the point?" She inched backward, toward the phone to call the police.

"Are you planning on attacking me with that terrifying weapon?"

"If I have to. Come out with your hands up." What cowboy movie had she heard that in?

He came out, both hands held up. He now had a big smile on his face. "Mum and Dad told me they had a burglar alarm. They didn't tell me they had a highly trained security guard as well."

His accent registered. It was a Manchester one. She noticed his coloring. Dark-brown hair, like Mrs. Stottington. A large nose, prominent but finely shaped chin, like Mr. Stottington. It was a good-looking face.

"You're Myles?"

"I'm Myles," he said.

She was cross. "Why didn't you say that to begin with? You terrified the wits out of me."

"You're one to talk, with that umbrella. Does it fire bullets as well?"

She started to smile. "I haven't tried. You can put your hands down now if you like."

He did. "Let me guess—you're Juliet."

"I'm Juliet."

He grinned. "The Wonder Girl." He stepped closer and held out his hand. "Pleased to meet you, Juliet."

"Pleased to meet you, Myles." They shook. His hand was warm, with a sure grip. She relaxed. "If you don't mind me asking, why were you excavating our freezer at eight o'clock in the morning?"

"I was fixing it. Well, trying to fix it. Mum said you've had trouble with the thermostat. I couldn't sleep so I thought I'd make a start before you all came in this morning."

"You know how to fix freezers?"

"And refrigerators. And cars. And motorbikes."

Juliet was surprised. She'd heard the Stottingtons talk about Myles and his business sense, how clever he was. She'd always assumed it was an office job, like accountancy or even law.

"And could you fix it?"

"No problem."

"Can I make you a coffee as an apology?"

"Make it two and have one with me."

Twenty minutes later Juliet hadn't written up the daily specials or set the tables. She had laughed a lot instead, as Myles told her of his journey to Australia—he'd flown via Hong Kong, encountering every traveling nightmare possible, from long delays to flu-ridden fellow passengers. He somehow made it sound fun. He'd asked her lots of questions too.

"Five sisters, a father and a little girl? It must be bedlam. How does your father cope?"

Juliet told him about Shed Land and about Leo's inventions. She didn't mention the lawn mower one, but there were plenty of others to choose from. The hairdryer. The spider catcher. The self-rocking pram.

At first he laughed. Then he started asking questions about the pram. Had her father used a hydraulic mechanism on it, or was it spring-based? What about the brakes? Had he thought about a push-pull device, using weights?

Juliet told the truth—that she didn't have a clue. It could have been fairies moving the pram for all she knew. The invitation was on the tip of her tongue. Her father would love to hear another person's ideas. God knows he'd had enough of his daughters' eyes glazing over as he tried to explain how this mechanism would work or that device would revolutionize the house. She watched as Myles reached for a paper napkin and started scribbling on it. He was actually serious.

She felt a glow inside her. He was so easy to talk to. And attractive, too, the more she looked at him.

The front door of the café opened. Mr. and Mrs. Stottington were standing there, beaming.

"Didn't I tell you, Reg?" Mrs. Stottington said, nudging her husband. "They're getting on like a house on fire. I knew they would. Isn't he lovely, Juliet? And he's single. Why don't you ask him out? Show him around Hobart? He'd love it, wouldn't you, Myles? Go on, Juliet, ask him."

Juliet couldn't stop herself. She went bright red.

"Go on, Juliet," Myles said. He had a lovely sparkle in his eyes. "Ask me out."

So she did.

*   *   *

A month later, Juliet knew she needed some help. It wasn't in her nature to confide in her sisters. Especially not about men. She had friends from school that she talked boy-talk and work-talk with over cheap pizzas and red wine. But two of them had moved to the mainland, another was expecting her first child and the other three had long-term boyfriends and were often otherwise occupied these days. A part of her didn't want them to know everything about her, either. She didn't like appearing—or feeling—uncertain.

She needed help from someone now, though. Perhaps she was mistaken, perhaps it was some kind of hormonal rush, but whatever she did, no matter how much she tried to talk herself out of it, she couldn't deny it. She was in love with Myles Stottington.

It was ridiculous, she told herself many times each day. She'd only known him for a month. She was just a family employee. He was only in Tasmania for a short time, while his parents were away. Just because they'd gone on a few dates and spent the entire time talking and laughing didn't mean anything, surely? And just because she literally went weak at the knees when he kissed her didn't mean anything out of the ordinary, either, did it?

It wasn't just the dates. They worked so well together in the café too. He encouraged all her ideas. He praised how organized she was, how good she was with their customers, what a great cook she was. He was decisive. He not only knew how to mend freezers and cars, but he also knew all there was to know about menus, stock control and customer relations. She almost ran to work these days she was enjoying it so much.

She truly didn't know how to deal with what she was feeling. She'd not had a proper boyfriend before. A few dalliances at school, including a half-serious relationship with a fellow student for a few months, but they'd never progressed beyond meeting with groups of friends and the occasional kissing session in his car.

She couldn't even remember breaking up with him. They had simply drifted apart.

All she knew for sure was that something inside her changed when Myles was around. She felt better. Sparkier. More alive. Happier. She loved being with him. She knew he enjoyed being with her. He'd said it. He'd told her that he wished he'd known she was here; he would have been out to visit his parents much more often. That had to mean something.

He was only going to be in Hobart for another month. Juliet didn't have time to waste. She needed advice. She mentally ran through her sisters. Could she talk about it with Clementine? No, she was too caught up with Maggie and her birdlife at the moment. Sadie? No, it would quickly turn into a discussion about the fact that Sadie herself had never had a boyfriend. Eliza? She barely seemed to notice men. It had to be Miranda.

Her chance came the next night after dinner. Miranda had gone to her room. Juliet waited a few moments and then knocked on the door and entered.

Her sister was lying on her back on the floor doing sit-up exercises, dressed in only a black satin slip. Her face was covered in a green creamy mask. She kept exercising, managing to point to the bed in between sit-ups. "I'll be with you in a moment. Do take a seat."

Juliet perched on the edge of the bed, preferring to look at the room rather than her sister's trim body effortlessly stretching.

As usual, Miranda's bedroom looked like something out of a magazine. She changed it around on a monthly basis. The dressing table surface was covered in skin creams, lotions, makeup and small bowls filled with costume jewelry. More than a dozen bottles of perfume were arranged on a shelf. The bed was piled with silk cushions of different shades of green and blue. The rug was tufts of colored wool, reds and pinks. It was like being inside the genie bottle on *I Dream of Jeannie*. Stylish and sexy.

Juliet thought of her own room. It had the same curtains that had been hanging there when she first moved in years earlier: blue-and-white check ones that didn't quite meet in the middle. The bedspread was chenille, with many areas of the pattern picked bald while she was reading. There was a bookshelf, a dressing table and a small stool that badly needed re-covering. Nothing matched. It had never bothered her especially. But perhaps that's where she was going wrong in terms of men. She simply wasn't feminine enough.

Not that Miranda ever went into detail, but Juliet knew that her sister was never short of boyfriends or admirers. Juliet could tell when she was seeing someone. A kind of mood—a haze almost—would surround her. Glamor. Excitement. Confidence.

Miranda counted the final sit-ups, reaching one hundred, before coming to her feet in a graceful movement. "So then, Earth Mother, what can I do for you?"

"Stop calling me that for a start."

"Your spikes are out. What's wrong? Soufflé didn't rise today?"

Juliet couldn't snap at her. "I need you to help turn me into a *femme fatale.*"

Miranda burst out laughing. "Oh, that's all? No problem."

"Please don't laugh at me. I feel silly enough coming to you for help as it is."

"I'm not laughing at you. Not much anyway."

Juliet took a breath. "Miranda, I don't know for sure if you're a virgin anymore or not—"

"Good. It's none of your business."

"—but I am. And I don't want to be anymore."

"You want me to help you lose your virginity? Juliet, you're barking up the wrong tree. I'm a woman. I'm your sister. There are laws against that kind of thing."

"I'm in love with someone and I want to sleep with him. And I don't know how to make it happen."

"Now we're talking." Miranda elegantly arranged herself on the bed. "Tell all. Who is the object of your affection?"

"His name is Myles Stottington."

"Oh dear. Unfortunate surname. Too many *t*s."

"He's Mr. and Mrs. Stottington's son from Manchester."

"Myles Stottington, Mr. and Mrs. Stottington's son from Manchester? That's not a man, that's a speech therapy exercise." As Juliet rose and headed for the door, Miranda reached out, laughing. "Come back. I'm sorry. Remember that thing called a sense of humor?"

Juliet sat down again. "I'm too serious about it to be able to laugh."

"This isn't a new thing? You've actually managed to keep a man hidden from us?"

Juliet explained about the past month of working and going out with him. "I'm mad about him, Miranda."

"So what's the problem? It sounds like it's going swimmingly. Stottington-ly, even. Is he mad about you?"

"I think he might be."

"Even better. So all you need to do is create the right environment for it to happen."

"What sort of an environment?"

"Well, a bed is usually a good start. Ask him to come away for a weekend with you. Pack your nicest nighties or, even better, don't pack any at all. And let nature take care of the rest. It's as simple as that."

"I don't just want to sleep with him, though. I want more than that."

Miranda raised an eyebrow. "Marriage and babies?"

Juliet nodded. "But if I sleep with him now, will he think that's all I want out of our relationship? That I'm one of those kind of women?"

"What kind of woman would that be?"

"You know, those cheap ones who sleep around just for fun."

"The women are the cheap ones, you mean? What about the men? It's all right for them, is it?" Miranda's tone of voice changed. "You've been locked in your kitchen for too long, Juliet. Ever heard of a thing called the sexual revolution?"

"Yes. No. Oh, you know what I mean." Juliet was too agitated to take her up on the argument. "Look, forget it. I shouldn't have said anything to you. I should have known better."

Miranda softened. "Oh, don't get mad again, Juliet. I'm excited for you."

Juliet was shocked at the sudden welling of tears in her eyes. "You're not excited. You're making fun of me. It's hard enough for me anyway. Forget it. I shouldn't have breathed a word of it to you. I'll forget about him and go back to spending my whole stupid boring life stuck here cooking stupid boring meals for—"

"Stupid boring us?" Miranda offered, reaching across to soothe her sister. "I know, sweetie. It's like working in a women's prison sometimes, isn't it? We're all inmates and Dad is our prison warden. Why didn't he and Mum have a boy, introduce a few more male hormones into this throbbing, emotional mix?"

Juliet shook her hand away. She wiped her eyes, angry at herself now. "Forget all of this, would you? Forget Myles."

"I will not. That name of his is seared on my memory. Have you got his number?"

"Yes, of course." Juliet knew it by heart.

Miranda reached across and picked up the phone extension beside her bed. "Call him, Juliet. Call him now."

"And say what?"

"Say you're free this weekend and you'd love to go away with him. Tell him you want to show him some of our beautiful scenery. Stay overnight somewhere together."

"Just like that? Tell him the truth?"

"It's worth a try."

Juliet took the phone. She rang the number. Myles answered. He sounded very happy to hear from her. She asked him the question. She didn't even falter. Miranda sat opposite her, smiling. Juliet barely had time to finish the question before he answered.

It was a yes.

.   .   .

Four days later, on Sunday morning, Juliet woke up just before dawn, in unfamiliar surroundings. It took her a moment to get her bearings. She was in a cabin near Cradle Mountain, in a double bed beside a large window looking out over the lake, mountains and forests.

She wasn't alone. Myles was beside her. Naked. They had barely managed to unlock the door and put down their bags before it had happened. She'd felt it building between them the entire journey from Hobart. They'd talked as much as they usually did. Laughed as much. A lot of work-talk, at first. As they drove north, he'd asked her to tell him what changes she'd like to make to the way the café was run.

"I wouldn't be so presumptuous. It's your parents' café."

"It's our café while they're away."

Our café? She liked his use of "our."

"Mum and Dad are great businesspeople but they get stuck in their ways. Let's experiment while we can, for the next month. New menus. New décor. Nothing radical. We need to bring our customers with us."

"You've done this before?"

"I grew up in these places, remember. Every time Mum and Dad bought a new café, they'd move us lock, stock and barrel to the new town."

"They own other cafés?"

He laughed. "Oh, just a couple." His expression changed. "You don't know about them?"

She shook her head.

"They haven't told you about the business they left behind in the U.K.?"

She shook her head again.

"Juliet, Mum and Dad own more than thirty cafés, all around the U.K."

"Thirty?"

"It's our family business."

"But they never mentioned it."

"It was probably Mum's idea. The whole reason for the move was to reduce Dad's stress, take his mind off things." He explained. His grandfather, Mr. Stottington's father, had started the business years ago, in market areas in Manchester. Cheap and cheerful cafés, big servings, low prices, early openings, late closings, catering just for workers. "Then they expanded, especially in the sixties when it became fashionable to eat in places like ours. Dad took over, and then when he met Mum, they changed it some more. Moved into London as well. Went up a notch quality-wise, better menu and décor, opened more in other city centers. But the market cafés are still the main earners for our company."

"You're in the family business too? I thought you said you were a mechanic."

"No, I'm just interested in how things work. I'm self-taught. I work for Mum and Dad. We work together, at least. I do all the acquisitions. That's one of the other reasons I'm here, to see if the Stottington empire could expand into Australia."

"The Hobart café is a launching pad?"

"Perhaps. I'm not sure yet. I think we need to make some changes to the model first. That's why I'm keen to hear your ideas."

"My ideas?"

"I already know you'll have great ideas. Tell me, Juliet, if this was your business and you wanted to expand across the country, what would you do?"

Their conversation changed from a casual one to something akin to a business meeting. All the thoughts Juliet had mulled over in recent months leaped into her head. An extended menu, she suggested. Mrs. Stottington had often asked her for ideas but never acted on them. Myles was decisive. Did she have examples? Could she draw up some possibilities and costs? Yes, that would work, he said to her plan to offer set specials on weekends. Outside catering to businesses and parties. Certainly worth investigating, he thought. He'd get her to do a trial run.

She felt she was talking to a different man. She felt different too. He was listening to her ideas, asking for her suggestions. He'd been watching her at work the entire time, she realized.

"Our core business is fast, cheap, wholesome food in unfussy surroundings. That's what's worked in the U.K. and what we think will work here too."

They were looking beyond Hobart already. He'd already made inquiries about setting up their base in Sydney.

"Your base?"

He nodded.

"You're not going back to Manchester?"

"Just for a few months to finalize things, but then I'll be coming back here. Well, coming back to Sydney, anyway."

Sydney was only a two-hour flight from Hobart, she thought.

"Would you come up and see me there, Juliet?"

"I'd love to," she said.

He smiled at her. "I think Mum was right. We make a great team."

She didn't blush. She didn't contradict him. She just smiled back. "Yes, we do."

"I'm not just talking about work," he said.

"Nor am I," she replied.

They'd talked in a rush after that. She didn't know how to play games and she didn't want to. She told him, outright, that she had fallen in love with him. He told her that he felt the same way about her. He'd stopped the car then and kissed her. For a long time, until a truck driver going past honked his horn at them.

They hadn't been able to get to their cabin quickly enough.

She felt him wake beside her. She turned in his arms and smiled.

"Good morning."

"Good morning." He sat up, looked around and then went under the covers again, pulling her close to him. "I like it here," he said.

She was glad. "I hoped you would. It's one of the most beautiful parts of the state," she said. "There's a fantastic walk that goes right around the lake and if we time it right—"

"That's not what I meant." He kissed her. "I meant I like it here, here. Here in bed with you here."

"You don't want to go out sightseeing?"

"Do I have to? Can't you describe it to me, as I do this," he kissed her again, "and this?"

She closed her eyes. His fingers started to move across her body. His kisses followed. She realized she couldn't even begin to describe it.

•   •   •

It was on their way home on Sunday night that she asked him the big question. The one that had been hanging over them since they met.

"Myles, would you like to meet my family?"

He laughed. "At last. I've been longing to meet your family. They sound fantastic."

"They do?" Uh-oh. "What about lunch next Sunday?"

"I can't wait."

•   •   •

The dining room couldn't have looked better. Everyone had dressed up. Miranda had left off the more dramatic elements of her makeup, wearing only a little blush and a pale pink lipstick. All four of her sisters and Leo looked suspiciously bright-eyed, but Juliet could handle that. She had given everyone a talking-to that morning.

"Please, everyone, just behave. This is important to me. If any of you say anything stupid, or try and ruin it, or embarrass me, or make a smart remark—"

"That's me mute for the afternoon," Miranda said.

"—I'm going on strike. Never cooking another meal, ever again."

Myles arrived at five to one. They were all looking through the living room window at him. He was carrying a bottle of wine and a box of chocolates.

"Punctual. That's worth one point," Miranda said. "A bearer of gifts too. Two points. A little excessive, but noted for its range and generosity."

He greeted Juliet warmly, kissing her, touching her arm. Five pairs of eyes noted that. He shook Leo's hand. (A good, firm handshake, Leo reported later.) He said hello in a friendly way to the others. Even more impressively, he remembered their names throughout the lunch.

He was nice to Maggie, "but not creepily nice," as Clementine put it. He was polite. He asked everyone questions. He complimented Juliet on her cooking, three times. He complimented Miranda on the table decoration. It was a pot plant. He asked Eliza for advice on running spots in Hobart. He did his best to find a book that he and Sadie had both read.

After lunch he and Leo disappeared out into the shed together. Pleased as she was that they were getting on so well, Juliet began to worry. What if it was Leo he wanted to meet and spend time with from now on? If Myles ever did come to visit again, he would spend all his time out in the shed . . .

They all looked out the window, toward the garden.

"I like him," Miranda said firmly. "He's a real man. All man. He's Manly Myles the Manly Man."

"I like him too," Eliza said.

"Me too," Sadie and Clementine agreed.

"Me too," Maggie said. She was standing on a chair, also looking out the window.

"But?" Juliet asked.

"But what?" Miranda asked.

"What's the catch?" Juliet said.

She looked at her four sisters. They all looked back.

"No catch," Miranda said. "I approve. And if I approve, so do the others."

They nodded. Maggie nodded too.

"Really, Juliet, what do you take us for?" Miranda said. "We're your sisters, you have lured your potential mate into the house, we have given you our approval. Prithee, what more dost thou ask of us?"

"They're coming back," Clementine hissed.

The two men were greeted with six innocent smiles.

CHAPTER 12

S adie had never been busier. Looking after Maggie filled five days a week and the occasional weekend. The scrapbook took up any other time she had to herself. That was nearly finished. She'd prepared more than forty pages of drawings, photographs, notes and scraps of memorabilia. There was just the cover to do now. In the meantime, she'd discovered she had another project to look after, this one just as secret. The hiding of the Moonstruck.

The purple bottle had turned up suddenly three weeks ago, hidden inside her pillow case. Since the first time she'd found it in her library bag, more than four years earlier, it had appeared out of the blue in her room or hidden in her belongings more than a dozen times. It had never been spoken about among them, not since that very first day Leo had handed it to Juliet so solemnly. There was no pattern. Sometimes weeks went by without her seeing it. The longest period had been four months, but she'd guessed it was moving back and forth between her sisters during that time. The previous winter she had found it hidden in her things three times in less than a month.

It still thrilled her to come across it. She found it in the bottom of her bed one cold winter's night, hidden inside her hotwater bottle cover. Whoever had done it had been quick. She'd only been in the bathroom brushing her teeth for less than a minute. She received it once in a parcel delivered by their postman, her name and address typewritten, the postcode Hobart and no clues about the sender inside. In turn, she had come up with some inventive hiding places of her own. Tucked deep in the lining of Eliza's all-weather coat. In the bottom of Miranda's "touch at your own peril" box of organic muesli that she kept in her bedroom should anyone steal so much as a bran flake. She engaged a school friend to deliver it to Juliet in the café one afternoon, in the guise of a large coffee can. She'd had fun the past week or two trying to decide who would get it next and when.

The following Saturday afternoon she had the house to herself for once. There had been a clatter of activity that morning, shouts and conversations and doors opening and slamming. Sadie lay in bed, pretending to be asleep, until they had all gone and the house was quiet.

She ate a quick breakfast—plain toast and tea as usual—eager to get started. She began with a little poke around each of her sisters' rooms, ostensibly looking for hiding places. Juliet's was always worth a look, especially now she had a boyfriend. Miranda's was usually the most interesting, with new perfumes and creams cluttering her dressing table and new decorative items appearing every few weeks. Sadie sprayed on a bit of scent, then ran her fingers along the new lamp on the bedside table. The shade was made from strings of beads in blue, red and green. Sadie turned it on, admiring the multicolored light it sent out into the room. She put her hand inside and noticed the shadow it cast on the wall. The perfect shape of her hand, in three color hues . . .

It was trickier than it looked. She tried to rest the Moonstruck bottle inside the lampshade but it kept dropping out. Sticky tape would melt in the heat. String would be too obvious. She needed fishing line or something invisible. Leo would have some in Shed Land, surely. It was out of bounds when he wasn't there, but he'd never know, would he? She'd be in and out in less than a minute.

The shed was locked but they all knew where the key was kept. The door opened smoothly. It was funny to be in there on her own. Scary and exciting, all at once. There was no fishing line in sight. She tried the door of the wooden cupboard that took up one wall. It was locked. She tried the second key on the keyring. It worked. There were five shelves, each as tidy as the other. The first held files. There were pieces of metal, tiny bottles of liquid and soldering material on another shelf. Bundles of Leo's notebooks, boxes of test tubes, an old-fashioned weighing scale on another. On the bottom shelf was a bright-red basket with a lid, made from woven straw. It stood out against all the gray files, plastic boxes of wire, screws and unidentifiable objects on the shelf beside it.

She knew even before she reached for it that the basket had belonged to her mother. She remembered seeing it in her parents' room, on the bedside table on her mother's side of the bed. Why had Leo kept it in his shed, though, instead of in the wardrobe with the rest of their mother's belongings? Did any of her sisters know about it? Should she wait until they came home? Tell them, so they could ask their father about it together? Or be first at something for once? She hesitated for only a moment. She checked the windows of the house. No sign of life. She still had time.

She slowly took the lid off. On top were three magazines. *Woman's Own*s from the U.K., still in their wrapping, dated 1971, the year their mother had died. They must have kept coming for a few months before someone canceled the subscription. Sadie moved them to one side, resisting a temptation to open and read them. She found a scrapbook, just like the ones their mother used to fill. She opened it. The pages were blank. Underneath the scrapbook was a colored plastic box. She picked it up. It rattled. She pried off the lid. Inside was glue, scissors and colored pens. All the items their mother had used to create her scrapbooks and recipe books. Sadie didn't take them out. She just touched them gently, thinking of her mother using those scissors, those pens.

There was another cardboard box at the bottom of the basket. She lifted it out, her heart beating faster. She didn't know how, or why, but when she thought about it afterward, she realized she knew in that moment what was in there. She was right. Inside were two bundles of small blue notebooks. Her mother's diaries.

Sadie looked at them for a long time. Perhaps she was mistaken. Perhaps these were blank ones that her mother hadn't started writing in yet. Wiping her hands on her jeans first, she lifted out a bundle and slid one of the diaries out from the rubber band. *"Tessa Faraday"* was written in curving writing across the front. Sadie opened the cover and turned to the first page. There was her mother's signature again. She flicked to the first page. To a second page. A page at random in the center. Her mother's distinctive writing sprawled across each page, words jumping out at Sadie. She shut that one, opened a second one. Another year, each page filled to the edge with writing. She did a quick count. There were nine diaries. She checked the dates on the inside cover. Each one covered a two-year period, the earliest from 1953, the last one the year she died, 1971. Eighteen years of her mother's life documented in these pages, here in front of her.

The dog that lived two houses down started barking. It meant someone had walked past the front fence. As swiftly as possible Sadie put the diaries back into the cardboard box, replaced the lid, the plastic box, then the magazines, moved it all back into the cupboard, shut and locked it. Her hands were shaking. It took three tries to lock the shed door.

She was down at the end of the garden, pulling dead leaves off the lemon tree in what she hoped was a purposeful-looking way, when Miranda appeared on the back veranda.

"Is Dad there?" she called out.

"Haven't seen him," Sadie called back.

"It's your turn to do the washing, remember."

"I was going to do it later."

"Don't forget." Miranda went back inside, slamming the door behind her.

Sadie stayed where she was for a few more minutes, thinking hard. She had intended to tell Miranda what she'd just found. To tell all her sisters. But in that moment she decided not to. Not yet, anyway. She pulled off a few more leaves, then joined Miranda in the house.

The others came back later, Leo last of all. Sadie was sure they could tell from looking at her. It must have been obvious. She imagined standing in the middle of the room and shouting, "I've found Mum's diaries! They're in Dad's shed!" Just as strong was the feeling that it was her discovery, her secret and that it was best she didn't say anything at all.

She lost interest in the Moonstruck and the fishing line after that. The next time she was in the house on her own she pushed the purple bottle inside one of Eliza's drink containers, zipping up the gym bag. She then hurried down to the shed. Her hand was shaking as she unlocked the doors. She had barely taken the diaries out of their hiding place in the cupboard when the dog began barking. Cursing under her breath, she put everything back as quickly as she could, locked up, ran through the garden, on to the veranda, through the back door and into her room. She had just landed on her bed, pulling down a book at random from the shelf, when Eliza came in.

She took one look at Sadie's face. "What have you been up to? You look guilty as hell."

"Nothing. And it's none of your business anyway."

"You've been snooping at something, Sadie. You always get exactly the same look when you've been up to something you shouldn't have."

Sadie nearly told her. It was on the tip of her tongue. But then what would happen? Eliza would tell Juliet, who'd tell Miranda, who'd tell Clementine and then they'd all go in a delegation to Leo who'd say no, they couldn't read them. Perhaps this time he really would burn them. Sadie would get into trouble—huge trouble—for being in Leo's shed without permission. She knew in that instant she couldn't tell Eliza. She also didn't want to tell her. She wanted to be the one to read their mother's diaries first.

"Tell me," Eliza said, pinching her.

Sadie looked, very obviously, at Eliza's gym bag. Back at Eliza. Then at the gym bag again. "I don't know what you're talking about." She thought about adding, "You're carrying on as if you've been moonstruck or something," before deciding it was too obvious. Eliza got the hint anyway. Sadie slipped off the bed and went into the living room, turning on the TV.

Eliza was quite different when she came and joined her a few minutes later. Sadie knew the look. The secret, amused look they all wore now and again, whenever the Moonstruck had changed hands.

"Cup of tea, Sadie?"

"Thanks, that'd be great," she said.

Over the next days Sadie returned to the shed as often as she could. The opportunities were rare. She was minding Maggie full time during the week and couldn't risk taking her in with her. Her niece was talking so much these days—and noticing just as much. She was sure to say something over dinner about her and Sadie being in Tadpole's shed together looking at the old books. On the weekends Leo was there most of the time.

She didn't dare take the diaries out of the shed. She barely dared to read them. But once she started it was hard to stop. It gave her great comfort to touch the pages her mother had touched. It was even more exciting to read the words her mother had written. Fate must have brought her to the cupboard that day. She had started reading from the first diary. It had been an odd feeling to realize she was older now than her mother had been when she was writing those first entries. Tessa was writing about her work as a secretary, nights out in London, outings with girlfriends, shopping expeditions. There were little quotations Tessa must have loved. A theater ticket stuck on to a page. Some of it was a little uncomfortable to read. Tessa was obviously the prettiest girl in her group of friends, and there were lots of references to her looks and her clothes, alongside occasional dismissive remarks about her friends' outfits. Sadie guiltily enjoyed every word. Her mother had a very good turn of phrase, whether she was describing a dress or being a little mean about someone she knew.

Sadie allowed herself ten pages each visit. It was a little like reading a novel when she already knew the plot—the last pages she had read had been descriptions of Tessa getting ready to go out dancing with friends, about a crush she had on a boy in her town. Sadie had done the calculations and worked out her mother was about twenty years old. It meant she was only eight months away from meeting Leo. Even though Sadie was dying to read about that, she kept herself to the ration. It was her own lovely secret.

CHAPTER 13

I n later years, Leo referred to the family meeting held the day after Maggie's fifth birthday as the Night of the Bombshells. It was as if a giant had come stomping along, he said, picked up their house and shaken the contents until half of the family flew out of the windows and landed hundreds of miles away.

Miranda told him that was a bit fanciful.

The family had been in an uproar as it was. Maggie had been very excited about her birthday party. She'd chosen her own theme (rabbits), her own menu (fish fingers and ice cream), her own music (Christmas carols, for some reason) and had invited five friends from school.

There had been the usual excitement the night before—Maggie asking time and time again if the birthday chair would be there, if everyone would sing "Happy Birthday" to her five times, one for each year; all the Faraday family rituals. Clementine was up studying late the evening before and somehow managed to sleep through her alarm. When she woke up, Maggie's bed was empty. She heard laughing from the kitchen. She found Sadie and Maggie sitting at the table together, Maggie in the birthday chair, wearing a little coronet of flowers, beaming. She was already dressed, in clothes she must have chosen for herself—a yellow T-shirt, red pinafore dress and a pair of blue trousers.

"At last, you're up," Sadie said.

Clementine ignored that, going to Maggie, giving her a big kiss, saying happy birthday five times and adjusting the coronet so her ears didn't stick out so much. It annoyed her to see that Maggie had already opened up one of her presents—from Sadie, by the looks of it. A wooden jigsaw puzzle. She loved jigsaw puzzles.

"Sadie's got another present, Mum, for both of us. Hurry up and open it with me."

"Don't you want to wait until the others are up?"

"No, I want to do it now. Sadie said it's really special."

It was a scrapbook of Maggie's life. Clementine stayed silent as she and Maggie looked through the pages together. Every milestone of Maggie's life was documented. There were photographs and drawings, with commentary and dates alongside. There were other markers—a tiny fragment of one of Maggie's early teeth. A scrap of her cast from the time she broke her wrist. Maggie was flicking through the pages quickly, pointing at herself on every page, counting the photographs.

"See the numbers on the pages, Maggie?" Sadie said. "Take a close look."

Clementine and Maggie looked. Each letter was done in large outline, the inside filled with little drawings of things Maggie loved, all the way up to the fortieth page. On page one, the number one was filled with a Red Monkey. There were two little cakes inside the number two on page two. Maggie was entranced. She ignored the contents of the pages and flicked back and forth looking at the numbers, counting each time.

Everyone thought it was fantastic. Sadie basked in their compliments all morning. No one noticed that Clementine didn't seem as happy about it as them.

Leo had been expecting something big at the meeting the following day. Three of his daughters had come to him to share important news. He'd asked each of them to wait until they were all together. He already had an inkling. Maggie's fifth birthday had been a landmark date for all of them, he knew that.

It started normally enough, with Maggie in charge as usual, taking her mother, aunts and grandfather by the hand and leading them one by one to their chairs. She had started doing it eight months earlier, first each night at dinnertime and then at any family meeting. It was a ritual for her. Once they were all seated she would walk around the table counting them. Only when they were all there and all counted would she let them start talking. If they tried to do it before, she would start wailing and stamping her foot. The foot-stamping was funny, the wailing wasn't. She had a shriek that could break glass.

"I haven't counted you," she would say crossly. "You have to let me count you first."

Once they were gathered around the table to Maggie's satisfaction, Leo opened proceedings. Not with a prayer or a speech, but with a simple, "Anyone got any news to tell?"

Three hands shot up. Maggie looked cross for a moment, then put her hand up as well.

"We'll start with Maggie," Leo said, smiling at his granddaughter. "What's your news, little one?"

Maggie kept her hand up in the air. "It's a secret, Tadpole."

"What kind of secret?"

"A secret secret."

"Do you want to tell us what it is?"

Maggie shook her head.

"Good girl. You'll grow up to be a spy, for sure." Leo turned back to his daughters. "So, anyone else like to start?"

There was silence for a moment and then Miranda stood up, straightened her spine and spoke in a deep, modulated tone. "Welcome aboard your flight from Hobart to Melbourne."

Clementine leaped up. "You got accepted? You're in?"

Miranda grinned. "I'm in!"

"Into what?" Sadie asked.

Miranda made a theatrical bow. "I, Miranda Faraday, have been accepted into the next intake of flight attendants with our esteemed national airline carrier."

"You're going to be an air hostess?" Sadie looked shocked.

"At your service, madam."

"But what does this mean, Miranda?" Leo asked. "Flying everywhere, I realize that, but you can't be based in Hobart, can you?"

She shook her head. "That's news item number two. I'll be moving to Melbourne."

Eliza started to laugh. Miranda turned. "What's so funny about that?"

"We can share costs on a moving company." She waited a beat as the others around the table stared at her. "I'm moving to Melbourne too."

Leo put his hands to his head. "Two of you gone, just like that? Without any discussion?"

"Dad, I've been thinking about it for months, you know that. Years. I've been offered a position with a one-on-one training company." The lie came easily. "It's just starting up, I'll be in it from the bottom. It's exactly what I want."

"I don't even know what personal training is," Leo said mournfully.

"It's a form of prostitution, except you do it in tracksuits," Miranda told him.

"What's prostitution?" Maggie asked.

"I'll tell you later," Clementine said, with a glare at Miranda.

"I bet you don't," Miranda said.

Eliza explained what the company did.

"But aren't there unfit people in Hobart?" Leo asked. "Why do you have to move to Melbourne?"

"There's more there." Eliza told them about her proposed training programs, the trend toward personal fitness consultants and her research into different methodologies.

Leo had the look of a dazed man. "I just thought you liked to run."

"Of course I do. But fitness is more than that. Healthy body, healthy mind. Do you know that studies in the U.S. have shown—"

Leo interrupted. "Eliza, perhaps you and I could have a separate meeting about this later. In the meantime, I need to know something. Is anyone else abandoning the family ship?"

Juliet slowly raised her hand.

Leo shut his eyes. "When and where, Juliet?"

"I don't know when but I'm moving to Sydney," she said. She couldn't help herself. Her face burst into a grin. "Myles has asked me to marry him."

There was an explosion of congratulations, hugs and excitement around the table. Clementine fired questions. "What did he say? Did he get down on one knee? Produce flowers? Violins?"

Miranda was watching her very carefully. "It was romantic, wasn't it? I can tell."

Juliet blushed. "It's none of your business."

"That's exactly right, Juliet," Leo said. "You keep your happy memories to yourself. It makes them more special."

"So when is the wedding?" Eliza asked.

"We're not rushing into it. There's plenty of time."

"Not much," Miranda said. "If you want to start a family, you're going to have to get cracking, aren't you? I certainly want to be an indulgent aunt to more than Miss Maggie here."

"Of course we want children, but there's plenty of time for that too." She and Myles had spoken about that as well. He wanted three. She wanted five. They'd compromised on four. Not straightaway. They wanted time together first, to get themselves settled in Sydney. There *was* plenty of time. She wasn't even thirty yet.

"Where will you get the baby from?" Maggie asked.

"They have wonderful shops in Sydney that sell all sorts of things like babies, Maggie," Miranda said.

"Oh." Maggie seemed content with that.

Clementine glared at Miranda again.

Leo looked pleased. "That's marvelous news. He's a fine man. When we finish the meeting, this definitely calls for champagne." He counted off on his fingers. "That's me, Miranda, Eliza, Juliet—" He stopped and looked expectantly at Sadie and Clementine.

"My turn," Clementine said. She reached into her bag beside her, pulled out a letter and read. " 'Dear Miss Faraday, We are pleased to announce your grant application has been successful in regard to the study program specified in the supporting documents.' "

"Which means what, exactly?" Miranda said.

"It means that our Maria Island study has gone up a level. For the next three years and maybe longer, I'll spend two weeks every year studying the birdlife there, with full field team backup. It's part of an international study. My professor suggested I apply for it. We're world leaders in this kind of environmental, theoretical and practical study—"

"Hold it there, Clementine," Miranda interrupted. "Use words of one syllable."

"It's an international study into a rare species of Tasmanian bird and I'll be leading my own team."

"At twenty-two years old?" Miranda said. "Have they taken leave of their senses?"

Clementine gave them the details. The project would cover the effects of weather changes, risks to habitats, the impact of airborne and waterborne pollution. The results would be shared with universities around the world, the data to form the basis of a major ecological study.

Leo looked like he might cry. "Clementine, I am so proud of you. I'm so proud of all of you."

"No, you're not. Not yet." It was Maggie speaking. She pointed across the table. "Sadie, you haven't had your turn yet. Tadpole, ask Sadie what her news is."

"Sadie, I'm so sorry. What's your big news?"

"I don't have any."

"Well, I know it might be hard to top some of that."

"I don't have any, really. I'm finishing my degree, staying in Hobart, looking after Maggie." She shrugged, appearing casual, though there were two spots of color high on her cheeks. "If you want me to keep doing that, that is, Clementine?"

"Of course I do. You know I couldn't have got this far if it wasn't for you. But there's something I need to talk about with all of you, about exactly that." Clementine leaned down to her daughter.

"Maggie, would you run into the living room for me and pick out six books from the bookshelf that have the word 'the' in the title? I'll count how long it takes you, okay?"

"Six books? Can I get ten?"

"Of course."

"You treat that child like she's a dog. A very well-trained dog, mind you," Miranda said after Maggie had hopped off her chair and run out of the room.

Clementine looked around the table at her family. "I've got something big to ask all of you, something about Maggie." She hesitated. "I can't tell you how much it's meant to me for Maggie to grow up here with all of us; to get to know all of you so well. It could have been so hard for me, but you all made it so much easier. And I'd hate that to change. What I want to know is would you each take it in turns looking after Maggie while I'm away each year? Wherever it is you are living? So she doesn't lose touch with any of you?"

"But you don't need to do that, Clementine," Sadie said. "I'm here. I'm not going anywhere. I can look after her while you're away."

"I know you could, Sadie, but it's too much to ask."

"It's not too much. I love looking after her."

"I know, but I want to make sure she spends time with all her aunts, especially now. I just like the whole adventure of it for her. Coming to stay with each of you, you spending proper time with her. The idea of all of us sharing her still."

"I think that's beautiful, Clementine," Leo said. "Your mother would have loved that."

"I do, too. I think it's a great idea," Miranda said.

"But what about your work?" Sadie asked. "You won't be able to do it, Miranda. Not if you're a flight attendant. Be realistic."

"They have these incredible things in the airline industry called holidays, I believe. I'll use those. We'd get plenty of notice, wouldn't we, Clementine?"

"Of course," she said. "I'll know my schedule for the next three years."

"Oh, you are a clever girl. Then definitely, count me in."

"Me too," Juliet said.

"But won't Myles mind?" It was Sadie who asked, not Clementine.

"He thinks Maggie's great. And it would be too bad if he did mind."

"I'd love to have her to stay with me too," Eliza said. "I don't know yet where I'll be living, though." She laughed. "A minor point, but I'll let you know as soon as I do. You're sure you trust us?"

"Of course I trust you. I'd love it, and I know Maggie would love it. I love the idea of her moving between all of us."

"But this is mad. She doesn't need to," Sadie said, her voice loud. "I'm here. Maggie wouldn't have to be disrupted. What about her schooling?"

"It won't matter too much, not in the early years, I'm sure. It'll be fine. I'll get schoolwork from her teachers if I need to." Clementine smiled at them all, looking like her teenage self for a moment. "It means so much to me. Thank you."

"But, Clementine, seriously," Sadie said. "I think you're rushing into—"

"I did it," Maggie announced from the doorway. They could hardly see her over the pile of books in her arms. "Twenty-two. Who wants me to count them?"

She beamed as Leo, Clementine, Juliet, Miranda and Eliza applauded. Only Sadie wasn't smiling.

CHAPTER 14

Sadie thought about it constantly for two days. She was trying not to be angry. But it was hard. It felt like she and Maggie were being punished for getting on so well together. How could Clementine not see she was making a big mistake? Didn't she realize that Sadie would do anything to keep Maggie happy?

She had a special bond with her niece, she knew that. One the others didn't. Some of it was because she'd spent so much time with Maggie, but there was more to it than that. It was a true connection.

It was no good. She was deeply hurt. She couldn't let it rest. She waited one afternoon until she knew Clementine was in her room alone. Maggie was out helping Leo in his shed.

She knocked on Clementine's door. "Can I talk to you about something?"

Clementine looked up from her desk, books spread in front of her. "Of course."

"It's this whole business with Maggie." Sadie took a breath. "I've tried to understand and I can't. I thought you were grateful for everything I'd done. Putting my studies on hold, looking after Maggie as much as I have, and then—" She faltered. "It feels like you think I haven't done a good enough job."

She wanted Clementine to fall over her, to tell her she had done a wonderful job, that she hadn't realized this would hurt her, that of course she wanted Sadie to take sole care of Maggie each time she was away. Instead, Clementine gave her a long look, sat down on the bed. She seemed to be choosing her words carefully.

"I'm sorry if you feel hurt. You know I think you do a great job with Maggie. But I want the others to spend time with her as well, and this is the best way to do it."

"What are you two talking about so seriously?" It was Miranda, just arrived home from work. Normally Sadie would have snapped at her, told her it was a private conversation. She needed to talk about this more, though. If Clementine kept refusing to understand, maybe Miranda's input would help.

Sadie realized seconds after filling her in that she'd made a mistake. Miranda wasn't on her side.

"Sadie, of course you've done a wonderful job with Maggie," Miranda said. "But she is Clementine's daughter and it's up to her to decide what she thinks is best. Besides, you can't have her all to yourself. We all want to spend time with her."

"But it's a crazy idea. You'll be in Melbourne or flying all over the country. Eliza will be there too, busy. Juliet will be in Sydney. You can't put a child on a plane on her own. She'll get scared."

"Maggie isn't scared of anything. Besides, one of us takes her to the airport, another meets her at the other end and we ask the flight attendants in between to watch her. I still don't understand why we're talking about this. She is Clementine's daughter and this is what Clementine has decided. Since when did you set yourself up as Maggie's gatekeeper?"

"When I became her primary caregiver."

"Her what?" Clementine's voice was icy.

"The person who spends the most time with a child is called the primary caregiver," Sadie said sullenly.

"Forget it." Clementine rarely lost her temper but she did now. "Sadie, go back to university full time. Thank you for all you have done. It's clear I made a big mistake. I'll put my research on hold and I will look after Maggie myself."

"Clementine, you can't," Miranda said. "After all these years of work. And you can't pass up this opportunity."

"I have to put Maggie first."

"You are putting her first. You always have done. But you're allowed to have a career *and* be Maggie's mother. We're just fighting over what scraps of her are leftover. Sadie, you have to learn to share."

"I don't want her routine disrupted," Sadie said. "It's her I'm thinking of, not me."

"That's too bad because I don't want months to pass without seeing my niece."

"Then don't move to Melbourne. Stay here like me."

"Oh, the martyr. No, there's a whole world out there and I want to experience it."

"It's always about you, isn't it? Well, I'm talking about a little child's life."

"No, you're not, Sadie. You're talking about my daughter."

Miranda glanced between the two of them. "Look, I can see both sides, astonishing as that may sound." Miranda realized she was quite enjoying the position of peacemaker between Sadie and Clementine. "But it's really up to Clementine to decide the best approach. We have to do whatever she thinks is right. Okay, Sadie?"

Sadie didn't answer.

．　．　．

In her room later that night, Clementine thought over the conversation with Sadie. She had to stay levelheaded. It was true, she couldn't have got to where she was without Sadie. All mothers had to make sacrifices. "You'll feel pulled between your baby and your own life from the moment they're born," one book had cautioned. "Whatever choice you make, you'll wish sometimes you'd made a different one."

Clementine loved Maggie dearly. Completely. She treasured the time they spent together. She couldn't remember what life was like before Maggie arrived. But—and that was the word that triggered all the feelings of guilt—she also loved her study. She loved the feeling of being the first to discover data about the bird species they were studying. The unpredictability of it, not knowing what they might learn, the beautiful order of their work, the meticulous planning, the timetables they followed, the minute detail of the data they were collecting. When she thought about Maggie, it was with a rush of loving feeling but also, if she was honest with herself, a feeling of confusion, uncertainty and, yes, exhaustion. That had been Sadie's gift to her—taking on so much of the day-to-day minding of Maggie, allowing Clementine to enjoy the bedtime stories and cuddles—leaving her plenty of time and room in her head to do her work.

She was grateful to Sadie. But she was feeling something else as well. A feeling of competitiveness mixed up with guilt that she had been able to go to university full time while Sadie only went part time. All of that, combined with resentment. Too often these days it was as if Sadie viewed Maggie as *her* property. More than her niece. Her surrogate daughter, almost.

She thought back to the morning of Maggie's fifth birthday.

Clementine knew she should have been grateful for the scrapbook. She should have been touched that Sadie had gone to so much trouble, but she wasn't. Her reaction was so powerful and so sudden it shocked her. She was angry. How *dare* Sadie do this, appoint herself the documenter of Maggie's life like this?

She managed to say thanks. She managed to turn the attention from her by saying to Maggie what a lucky girl she was to have an auntie like Sadie. Then she excused herself and went into her bedroom to try and calm down, be rational about it. It was just a scrapbook. But a voice inside kept saying, yes, the scrapbook *you* should have done for Maggie.

Clementine had kept smiling, even as she realized the scrapbook hadn't just made her feel guilty. She actually felt uneasy about it. Sadie should have been doing things for herself, not spending so much time gathering material about Maggie. Clementine also realized Sadie must have gone through her room to find the birth certificate, for example. How *dare* she?

She didn't feel this way when any of her other sisters gave Maggie gifts. She loved seeing their different ways with Maggie, as well. Juliet's spoiling, Miranda's teasing, Eliza's teaching. She also loved seeing Maggie with Leo. Theirs was a special friendship. Full of rituals and games, her adoration of him as obvious as his deep affection for her.

She tried to be rational about it. It would have been worse, surely, if Sadie didn't love Maggie so much. Clementine knew she should be thankful. She was.

But she still didn't like it.

*   *   *

In her room, Miranda was sorting out clothes. It was still weeks before she left, but now the decision was made she wanted to get on the plane and go. Her real life was about to start, she knew it. No more days spent on her feet in the pharmacy, dressed in an unflattering uniform, smiling politely at sniffling customers, cranky old people, demanding salesmen, crying children . . . She stopped short, remembering her conversation with one of the trainers at the airline interview. "You have to be realistic about it. Yes, a lot of it is glamorous—luxury hotels, constant travel and excellent pay—but remember, much of the time you'll be on your feet, dealing with rude people, scared people, drunk people. Once they see that uniform you're their slave, not a human being." Miranda laughed out loud. She was swapping one job for another very similar one, she realized. The difference was she'd be handing out drinks, food and safety tips rather than hemorrhoid treatments, tablets and skincare products. And of course she'd be high in the sky rather than earthbound on a Hobart shopping street.

She sat in front of the mirror and smiled at her reflection. "Good afternoon. Welcome aboard." The smile turned into a grin.

*   *   *

Eliza was walking briskly down to the gym. Since she'd made her announcement about moving to Melbourne she'd been spending more time than usual working out, and not just because it helped keep her nerves at bay. She wanted to keep away from the house in case anyone asked for more details.

The truth was there was no job waiting for her. She hadn't spoken to Mark in a long while. She'd heard from a friend in her running group that he and his wife and kids were still in Melbourne, doing well. Still together. For a short time she'd considered going somewhere else. Sydney. Adelaide. No, she finally decided. She'd been focused on Melbourne for all these years and she wanted to see it through. She had a list of ten gyms there and she was going to go to them all and beg for a job if she had to. She'd get experience that way. Work as a waitress at night if she needed to as well. She'd save her money. Do her own research. Explore her business ideas. Make contacts. Then, when the time was right, she was going to start her own company, hire her own staff and build up her own group of clients. She didn't care how long it took. She couldn't wait to get started.

·   ·   ·

Leo went out to the shed after dinner as usual. He didn't do any work, just sat at the workbench, thinking about the week's events. He did a mental rollcall through his daughters, as he had done every day since they were born, thinking about each of them in turn. Juliet first. He was very happy for her. He liked Myles. A true gentleman. Juliet had her head screwed on, in any case. She deserved happiness.

He imagined Miranda as an air hostess. It was perfect for her in a way, with her glamour, sharp wit and need for constant stimulation. Not to mention those looks and that temper. He worried about her more than she knew. But she had got this far without getting into any serious scrapes. If anyone could look after herself, it was Miranda.

Eliza was different. Secretive. She always had been, even as a little girl. Prone to be judgmental too. But so determined. If anyone could make a success of a business like this fitness thing, it was her.

And Clementine. His clever Clementine. She consistently amazed him. To think that the work she'd be doing would be a world first. Even her solution to the care of Maggie while she was away on the field trips was inspired.

Leo had noticed Sadie's reaction to Clementine's suggestion. She'd been unhappy about it. She'd never been good at hiding her feelings. He would never say it to her face, but deep down he thought of her as the runt of his litter. A terrible word, but sometimes when he watched Sadie trying to keep up with the others, his heart would almost break. In her adolescent years, he had seen her comparing her own qualities with Juliet's hard work ethic, Miranda's fizz, Eliza's determination, Clementine's intelligence and finding herself wanting each time. He and Tessa had often talked about Sadie. "We'll need to watch her," Tessa said once. "She's not like the others."

"Life's harder for her, that's all," Leo said in her defense. "Poor little thing just sees the world as an unfair place."

He knew better than most how unfair it was. At least he could now think of Tessa's death without the same shudder of despair, the desperate overwhelming sadness. Time did heal. Time changed things. Life went on. All the clichés were true. What they didn't say was that you never stopped missing someone. He missed Tessa every day. He didn't need July Christmas or birthday chairs to remember her. He'd been glad to discover he didn't need her clothes in his wardrobe, either. He wished he hadn't taken so long to share everything with the girls. They occasionally wore the different items that they'd divided between them, a scarf here or a necklace there. He liked seeing it.

Not that he'd shared everything with them. He'd kept one thing back himself. A small, silly thing. A brooch. He had given it to Tessa the first day they met, after winning it in that sideshow stall. He could remember it so clearly. He still thought of it as the day his life had changed. His brother Bill calling from college to say he was coming to visit for the day, bringing a good friend of his.

"Another girlfriend?"

"The latest in a continuing series," Bill had laughed, always the smoothie. "You'll like this one."

Leo had more than liked her. He was a scientific man, but he would swear with his hand on his heart that he had fallen in love with Tessa on the spot, the moment she stepped out of his brother's car. She reminded him of Elizabeth Taylor, with her heart-shaped face, pale skin, dark eyes, and dark wavy hair. She was dressed in a light pink suit with three-quarter sleeves and a knee-length skirt. Leo noticed every detail of her appearance, down to her shoes and her bag, all of it so feminine. There was something fragile about her, something that made him want to protect her, but a spark in her eyes at the same time. She was laughing as she got out of the car, and he felt like he was basking in the warmth of her smile as they were introduced. "And I thought Bill was handsome," she said. "Good looks certainly run in your family."

"Didn't I tell you she had fine taste?" Bill said.

Leo couldn't remember what he'd said back to her. All he recalled was a sudden feeling of happiness, as though someone for whom he'd been waiting for a long time had finally arrived. It hadn't bothered him to see Bill link arms with her, pay her the courtesies of the dating gentleman he was. Leo had known in his heart that Tessa was just a passing dalliance for Bill.

They'd gone to a local fair, Tessa smiling between the two of them, linking both their arms. At the hoopla, Tessa had picked out a lovely brooch. She had two tries to win it, before Bill told her she wasn't meant to have it. Leo had never told Tessa this, but that afternoon he'd spent more than ten pounds throwing hoops until the man behind the stall took pity on him and handed over the brooch.

That night the three of them went to dinner. Leo learned Tessa wasn't just lively and beautiful, she was also smart. Funny. A great storyteller. An even better flirt.

When Bill and Tessa left him back at his lodgings, he felt a stab of jealousy—sharp and pure—when he saw Tessa lean her head on Bill's shoulder, when he saw the silhouette of their kiss before Bill started the car and drove away.

The next day he surprised them, and himself, by catching a bus and arriving unannounced at Bill's house before ten o'clock. "I had so much fun yesterday, I want more. Shall I fix breakfast?" he'd said when a sleepy Bill answered the door.

He'd followed his brother into the kitchen, trying not to react at the sight of Tessa's clothes strewn on the sofa in the living room. Of course she and Bill were lovers. Hadn't it been obvious? What he hadn't expected was how much it hurt.

"So you and Tessa are serious?" he asked from the stove, cooking eggs while Bill smoked cigarettes and read the paper. Tessa still hadn't appeared, though Leo had heard movement upstairs.

Bill twirled an imaginary mustache. "So many women, so little time. What do you think?"

"She's special."

"She is," Bill agreed.

"Don't hurt her."

"Of course not."

Tessa finally came down, kissing Bill on the cheek and touching Leo on the arm. "Lucky me," she said. "Two Faraday brothers for the price of one." They spent that day together as well. They fell into a pattern over the next few months, Leo joining them on an outing most weekends or a night out at least once a week. Leo lived for those meetings. Even if it was Bill's arm she took, Bill's shoulder she leaned on, it was enough for him to be close to her.

One Saturday afternoon, twelve weeks after he'd first met Tessa, Leo arrived at Bill's house as expected. He knocked at the door and waited nearly five minutes before his brother answered.

"Tessa won't be coming today. She may never be coming back." A long drag of his cigarette. "We had something of a fight last night. Or was it this morning? It was dark when she stormed off, anyway."

"You didn't do anything to her, did you?"

Bill laughed. "The other way around, more like it. She was hurling cups around the kitchen like nothing else."

Leo noticed then the pile of broken china pushed into a corner of the kitchen, the broom resting beside it.

"She said I'd been flirting with another woman."

"And had you?"

"I tell you, Leo, I'm starting to think she's a bit—" He made a gesture with his finger close to his forehead.

Leo chose to misunderstand. "Excitable. That's one of the lovely things about her."

Bill laughed. "Excitable? Bonkers was the word I had in mind." Another slow drag of his cigarette. "No, I've been giving this some thought. She's too intense for me. When she comes back to get her things, I'm going to call it quits."

Leo hadn't stayed at Bill's for long after that. He caught the bus home and sat in the living room, close to the phone. He'd known she was going to call. Some sixth sense, he had never been able to explain it. When she did, in tears, he was there, saying the right things. He caught a bus straight to her house. When he knocked at the door, she opened it.

"Oh, Leo," she said.

He'd taken her in his arms. Nothing had ever felt so good.

It was that simple. He told her the truth that same day. That he loved her. That he thought she was the most beautiful woman in the world. That his brother must have been mad but thank God he was, otherwise this would never have happened.

Miraculous event followed miraculous event. He kissed her for the first time, kissing the tears away from her eyes, then responding as hungrily as she did when she kissed him back, wrapping herself around him. They made love for the first time that day. He wanted to ask if it was too soon, hadn't she only just broken up with Bill? But he silenced himself. This was what he wanted, more than anything.

They were married within four months. Bill was the best man. "Of course I have to be," he'd said. "And of course I'm not heartbroken. I was Cupid, wasn't I? A roadtesting Cupid, no less."

A rush of anger. "Never say that about her."

"Leo, come on. It happened. I had her first. There's no denying the facts."

Leo had walked out of the room before he said something he'd regret.

Bill's history with Tessa had something to do with Leo's decision to pack up everything and move to Tasmania. He couldn't deny it.

He wanted to put as much distance between them as he could. Not that he could stop Bill from visiting. He just wished he hadn't noticed Tessa change when she knew Bill was on his way. A shimmer, was how Leo described it to himself. He also knew she saw Bill when she went back to the U.K. to visit her parents. It would have been worse if she'd been secretive. More suspicious. Even so, he'd once dared to ask her the question.

"You don't feel you made a mistake, do you? Think you married the wrong brother?"

"Of course I don't," she'd replied, with that laugh he loved, the upward glance. "I was just practicing on Bill, waiting for you to turn up."

He'd wanted to ask her again and again, to hear her words cancel out every bad feeling he'd had when he heard the two of them laughing together during Bill's visits, or when he heard her talking to him on the phone, on the rare occasions Bill called. It was a terrible thing to be jealous of his own brother. But it had all come good in the end, hadn't it? He and Tessa had truly fallen in love. A proper, enduring love, a mature, serious love, not the flash-in-the-pan days she and Bill had shared. He and Tessa had produced five beautiful daughters. A wonderful future ahead of them, cut so short.

He remembered Bill calling when he got the news about Tessa's death. Juliet took the call. It wasn't until weeks later that Leo was able to speak to him. He hadn't wanted to hear what Bill had to say. He was terrified that Bill would mention something that he and Tessa had done together, something Leo would never be able to get out of his head. Something he and Tessa would never be able to replicate. That was the only way he had been able to cancel out Bill's history with her. Anything she and Bill had done together, Leo had made sure he and Tessa had also done. Weekends in Paris. Dinner at the most expensive restaurant in London. Train trips to Brighton. Once they were done, he'd felt confident enough to start making their own life together.

His contact with Bill was now down to an occasional postcard. Bill drank too much, Leo knew that. If he wasn't an alcoholic, he was just one or two glasses away from it. But if he was to arrive in Hobart, or if Leo were to go to England and track him down, he knew the feeling of rivalry would start in a moment. One wisecrack from Bill and Leo would be twenty years old again, in his brother's shadow.

Oh yes, he understood how it felt to be jealous of a sibling. To want something a sibling had. Which was why he had been able to recognize in Sadie something he'd experienced himself. It was the one shadow over what Leo thought of as a beautiful time for his family, after all those years of sadness. Maggie's arrival had been a blessing, and not just to Clementine. She had given them all so much enjoyment. Looking after Maggie had also given Sadie real purpose in her life, Leo thought. He had been pleased to see it. She definitely had a gift with children. With her niece, at least.

But all that aside, he still had an uneasy feeling. It had been slowly building over the past few years. Small things had triggered it at first. Sadie watching with an almost hungry expression as Clementine and Maggie shared a close moment. Sadie taking Maggie to get new shoes, to the dentist or to buy new clothes, without checking with Clementine first.

There was also the unsaid battle over how Maggie wore her hair—her ears covered or uncovered. Such a small thing—Leo personally loved Maggie's sticky-out ears—but he knew Clementine didn't. He could always tell which of them had just been with Maggie when she came to visit him in Shed Land by whether her ears were showing or not.

There had been the incident with the mothers' group, in the early days, when Sadie and Maggie turned up late. Clementine had been beside herself with worry. Leo thought nothing of it when it happened. It was easy to lose track of the time, but more recently Sadie had been telling untruths about something else, he suspected. Telling him she and Maggie were taking short trips across to the eastern shore or up to Mount Wellington. If that was the case, why was the mileage on his car so high? He'd started keeping a record. Sadie was traveling almost forty miles every week. What could he do, though? Follow her? And wherever they were going, it certainly wasn't doing Maggie any harm. He was a doting grandfather and completely biased, of course, but he'd never seen a happier, brighter child.

If Sadie was telling lies, there wasn't much he could do about it. He hoped he'd brought them all up to tell the truth, but he was a realist. People told lies. He was guilty of it himself. He was reminded of it every time he came into this shed. Every time he opened the cupboard and saw the basket containing Tessa's diaries.

He could still remember the day the girls asked him about their mother's diaries. He'd told that lie so easily. Of course he hadn't burned them. But neither had he read them. It was enough to know they were there and that one day, if he wanted, if it felt like the right thing, he would read them. He didn't need to yet. Tessa was still clear in his memory. He could summon up her way of speaking, the expressions she used, with ease and with pleasure. The diaries were his insurance policy against forgetting her. One day he would read them. But not yet.

"So are you feeling like Little Miss Stay-at-Home?"

Sadie turned. The question had come from Liz, Miranda's friend, home from Perth for a week's holiday. She was almost shouting in a bid to make herself heard over the noise. Every room in the Faraday house was filled with people. Leo had decided to throw a combined party to celebrate Juliet and Myles's engagement, to congratulate Clementine on her Maria Island project and to bid farewell to Miranda and Eliza as they left for Melbourne. People had begun arriving at six p.m. and now, at eleven, the chat and the music were boisterous. Leo made a beautiful speech and proposed a toast to everyone. Maggie insisted on making a toast too. It involved her saying "To the Faraday girls," and clinking her glass with everyone at the party. She was still doing it long after the formal part of the evening was finished.

"I'm not sure what you mean," Sadie answered Liz's question, though she knew exactly what the other woman meant. She'd heard different variations on the same theme all evening long: "No big news from you, Sadie?"

Liz had the grace to look a bit uncomfortable. "You know, all your sisters escaping out into the world. Are you tempted to do something yourself?"

Sadie realized she'd never liked Liz. She didn't like any of Miranda's friends much. They were all brittle and sharp-tongued.

"No, Liz. I'm going to stay here and become Leo's housekeeper. Pass the news around for me, would you?"

She walked off in the direction of the kitchen. Too bad if she seemed rude. She was sick of everyone. Between all the packing of Miranda and Eliza's belongings and the constant phone calls with moving companies and friends in Melbourne sorting out accommodation, not to mention Miranda's new and infuriating habit of carrying on the whole time as if she were already on a plane, prancing about in air hostess-mode . . . Sadie had had enough.

The one good outcome was that Leo had been so occupied that he was barely setting foot in Shed Land. Sadie seized every opportunity to slip in and read some more of her mother's diaries.

It truly was fate that she had found them. They were the only thing keeping her sane at the moment. She was having trouble filling her days, now that Maggie had started school and she didn't have an excuse not to be at university. She was spending hours in the library, hiding there in case any of her family got suspicious that she was hanging around the house so much. She'd started taking a risk, smuggling the diaries out of the shed. It was easier to do that than sit huddled on the shed floor, nervously alert for a noise from the house or the sound of the neighbor's dog barking. Once she was in the library with them she could settle down properly. Her ten-pages-a-day ration had been cast aside long ago. She was reading as much each time as she could.

It was so strange to read descriptions of her own father and her uncle as young men. That had been the biggest shock so far—to discover that her mother had gone out with Uncle Bill before she met Leo. If the others were to know that!

Tessa hadn't been that impressed with Leo at their first meeting. "*The puppy dog*" she called him in the first diary entries about him. "*Bill's shadow*" in later ones. Tessa had guessed Leo had a crush on her early on. "*He blushes whenever I talk to him. So sweet.*"

There were pages about her feelings for Bill and their on–off relationship. Sadie was embarrassed to read some of them. She really shouldn't know these intimate things about another person, especially when the other person was her uncle and the narrator was her own mother. What must Leo have thought when he read them? Sadie wondered. Of course, he would have already known about Bill and Tessa, but even so . . .

Tessa certainly hadn't been bowled over by love-at-first-sight for Leo, Sadie was just as uncomfortable to discover. She started going out with him only as a way of getting back at Bill. It worked in the early days. Bill had been jealous and he and Tessa had a short, disastrous reunion. A weekend away to Manchester together. *"So wonderful to feel Bill's arms around me again."* But they had fought all weekend. *"I would be crazy not to stay with Leo. He's so devoted. It's so nice to be loved so much by someone."* There was an engagement followed weeks later by a wedding. A honeymoon in Paris. *"Romantic,"* Tessa wrote. *"I didn't tell Leo, of course, but Bill and I once stayed in the same hotel."* Once again, Sadie winced as she imagined her father reading these same words.

While Clementine continued to make preparations for her Maria Island study and Juliet, Miranda and Eliza finalized their packing, Sadie kept reading. The diaries were turning into an addiction. Her mother had a very sharp wit, Sadie was discovering. A nasty wit, even, now and again. Sadie had been reminded of Miranda more than once. Tessa wasn't just dismissive of Leo occasionally, but about some of their friends too. Sadie was fascinated all the same.

Juliet noticed something was going on. She surprised Sadie one afternoon as she was sitting in the living room, thinking back to the entry she'd read the week before—Tessa's description of being pregnant with Juliet, as it happened: *"I feel so full, in an odd but good way, as if every part of me is made from cream, all rich and smooth."*

"What are you sitting here all daydreamy about?"

Sadie jumped. She'd been so deep in thought, imagining her mother pregnant, imagining that same feeling in her own body, that it was almost a shock to see the grown-up Juliet beside her. "Nothing," she said.

The next time Sadie was in the shed she was tempted to skip past several diaries, to get to her own arrival into the family. How many people got to read what their mother thought about being preg-

nant with them? Or what they were like as children? Especially in
this sort of detail.

As the family began to grow, there were comments about Juliet,
and Miranda, as infants, then toddlers. The funny things they said.
Observations about how different they were to one another, how
Juliet reminded Tessa of Leo, how she saw more of herself in Miranda. In the last entry Sadie read, Tessa had just discovered she
was pregnant again. She wasn't completely happy about it, complaining of tiredness and nausea already. *"I'm like clockwork, one baby
every two years. Leo barely needs to look at me and I'm pregnant. It must be
the Catholic in him."* She mused over whether she wanted a boy or a
girl and what names she might choose. She had decided all the
names would come from books or songs. *"I loved knowing my own
name was from* Tess of the D'Urbervilles *so I'm carrying on the tradition. Leo can choose their middle names. If this one is a boy I think I shall
call him Darcy."* Sadie had to stop herself saying to the page, "It's a
girl! You're going to call her Eliza!" It meant Sadie's own birth was
only one diary—two years—away now.

Occasional feelings of guilt still crept up on her. Not just about
reading the diaries, or going in and out of Leo's shed without asking, but about keeping what she knew from her sisters. She nearly
told Clementine one afternoon, when they were sharing a peaceful
moment together in the kitchen. It didn't happen often these days.

"Do you still wish you could ask Mum what it was like to have
children?" she asked.

"Of course," Clementine said. "It still hurts when I see other
mothers with their own mothers. I wish it for Maggie as much as for
me. I'd love her to have known her grandmother, to have heard all
her stories."

Sadie was surprised by Clementine's honesty. A little shamed
too.

As she kept reading, Sadie came across snippets she knew
Clementine, of all her sisters, would liked to have heard. The fact
that Juliet hadn't slept properly through the night until she was
four years old. That Tessa had been beside herself with tiredness,
caring for a small girl and a new baby—Miranda—at the same time,

not to mention two years later, after Eliza's arrival, when she had three daughters under the age of five. Days had gone by without diary entries. Sadie took special delight in reading that Miranda had been a bad-tempered baby, slow to learn to feed and covered in milk-spots. She also produced the most evil-smelling nappies. In the diary Sadie was presently reading, Eliza was two months old. She was already active, Sadie had been amused to read. *"This baby kicks and wriggles all day long,"* Tessa wrote.

Leo was barely mentioned. He seemed to work a lot, come home for lunch and help Tessa with some housework, return to work, then come back home again before six for his tea. She hardly referred to his job with a tree nursery based outside London. She wrote about the weather, about snowfalls and about new recipes she had tried. *"Juliet a great help in the kitchen."* Sadie smiled at that too. Mentions of Bill turned up occasionally in the pages, a report that he had phoned, or that a letter had arrived. Sadie was trying to read between the lines as much as she could. She was sure she wasn't mistaken. Her mother still carried a torch for Bill.

Clementine, Juliet, Miranda and Eliza would love reading all of this too, Sadie knew. And they *would* get to read it. Not just yet, though. In a month or so. She wanted to read all the diaries first. And as soon as she had, she would tell her sisters she'd found them. She wondered how they would react. Whether they would decide to ask Leo if they could read them, or if it would happen in secret? They'd have to decide that among themselves.

For the time being, Sadie would keep reading. The really good stuff was about to happen, after all, she thought with a smile. *She* was about to arrive.

CHAPTER 16

Maggie was used to hearing voices filtering down the hallway while she tried to get to sleep. Usually it was her mother and her aunts. Sometimes her mother had friends over from the university. Sometimes she could hear Tadpole's voice too, the nights he wasn't out working in his shed.

She loved the sound of their voices. It made her feel happy. Tonight she knew all the voices well and could get a picture of each of them in her head. She also knew she was the one they were talking about. Her mum had told her earlier she was going to discuss it tonight, while the five of them were still together. She had cleared it with Maggie first. That was how she put things. "It's just the two of us, Maggie, so I want to clear it with you first, to make sure you know what I am going to talk about. I know you're only five years old, but it affects you more than anyone."

Maggie really liked it when her mum talked to her like that. She liked lots of things about her mum. The fact they looked really alike: dark-brown straight hair and dark-brown eyes. The way her mum would tuck her into bed, stroke her hair and say, "Tell me about your day, Maggie." The fact her mum was only seventeen years older than her. She liked how clever she was, the way she had found out all these things about birds before anyone else did and the way she was in the magazines sometimes. Not pop magazines or magazines with recipes in them like her friends' mothers had in their houses. Science magazines from the university, with photos of the birds she studied, and the thing she had discovered that was happening to their feathers because of too much dirt in the air, and the research she wanted to do.

"Won't it be boring?" Maggie had asked when her mum said this study could last at least twenty years.

"That's the fantastic thing about it, Maggie. I'll be able to really test my research, make sure what I am saying is true, not just guess-work. And I'll be there on the ground, not getting other people to do my work for me."

"And tell me again what will happen tonight?" Maggie had asked.

"We'll decide who you go to stay with while I'm away on Maria Island in a few months' time. And who it will be the next time and the time after that. It's going to be a battle, Maggie. Your four aunts will fight about who gets you first."

Maggie turned in the flannel sheet, hugged the hotwater bottle in its cuddly penguin-shaped cover against her body and smiled a little secret smile. She didn't mind which of them won the fight. She was happy whichever way it went.

●   ●   ●

"It's all organized, Maggie," Clementine said to her the next morning at breakfast. "You'll stay with Miranda in Melbourne when I first go away, then Juliet and Myles in Sydney, then Eliza in Melbourne, then Sadie here in Hobart. We did a draw and that's how it came out. What do you think?"

"I love it," Maggie said simply.

●   ●   ●

There were lots of things going on in the house after that. Eliza and Miranda packing up their suitcases, putting other things away in boxes in the attic. Maggie went halfway up the ladder once but then got a bit dizzy and came down. She'd go all the way up the ladder when she was seven, she decided.

There were three trips to the airport. The first time to say good-bye to Eliza. The second time to say good-bye to Myles and Juliet. The third time to say good-bye to Miranda. Maggie was put in charge of making the farewell cards. She drew a picture of herself with an unhappy mouth and tears coming out of her eyes. The amazing thing was that everyone else had tears coming out of their eyes too these days. Especially at the airport.

"Is the airport always a sad place?" Maggie asked Sadie on their third visit. "All we do here is cry."

The house went quiet then. Maggie found it strange at first that Juliet, Eliza and Miranda weren't there anymore. They rang all the time though. She talked to each of them every week.

"Is Juliet Myles's wife now?" Maggie asked Leo one morning at breakfast.

"No, not yet," Leo said.

"Is she allowed to live in the house with Myles if she isn't his wife?"

Leo coughed. "It's not an ideal situation, Maggie, but they are adults."

Maggie liked the words "ideal situation." She said them as often as she could over the next few weeks until Sadie, and then Clementine, asked her to stop.

Eliza and Miranda were both in Melbourne, but Eliza was living with a friend near the beach and Miranda was staying near the airport with lots of other people from her work. Clementine explained that Miranda had talked to her bosses and they had told her she could have a break between her training finishing and her real job starting. "And that's when you'll be there," Miranda said. "It's worked out perfectly for everyone."

Maggie liked those words too. For the next week she said, "it's worked out perfectly for everyone" as often as she could.

She started visiting Tadpole in his shed more often. Apart from Clementine, Tadpole was the cleverest person she had ever met. He knew the answers to everything. She had a question she wanted to ask him. She'd asked her mother about it a long time ago but she had forgotten the answer. She did the special knock to let Tadpole know it was her—five little raps on the center panel of the shed door, one rap for each of her years.

He put down the small silver tool he was holding. There was a little roll of wire beside him and next to that, a pincushion with what looked like hundreds of pins stuck in it. "Yes, Maggie?"

Her attention was captured by the pincushion. She got that feeling, like an itch, to count them. She was like that whenever she saw lots of things in a row. Trees in a park. Birds on a wire. Sometimes her mum was patient about it and would wait until she counted them, but sometimes not. Sadie always let her count things.

"Maggie?"

She turned her attention away from the pins. "Tadpole, where did I come from?"

"Let me guess. The kitchen?"

"No, where did I come from to be here, in this family?"

"We all got together and decided it was too quiet so we got you to make things noisy for us."

"Really?"

"Not exactly. What's brought this on, Miss Maggie?"

"A boy at school told me I grew in Mum's stomach like an alien and then she vomited me up."

"What a silly boy. Of course that's not where you came from." He stepped away from the stool and with a groan crouched down until he was at eye level with her. "Do you remember me talking about that dog we had once? When your grandmother was still here with us and your mum was a little girl?"

Maggie nodded. There was a photo of that dog on the pinboard. It was a black-and-white one called Beckie.

"Well," said Leo, "one day Beckie had pups in her kennel and we said, Wouldn't it be nice if we could have one of those pups to live with us? So I went down and looked at them and there was one little one, with dark-brown hair and dark-brown eyes, looking up at me, with a mischievous glint in its eye." He touched the end of her nose with the tip of his finger. "What color eyes have you got, Maggie?"

"Dark brown," she said.

"What color hair?"

"Dark brown," she said.

He leaned down and whispered. "Nothing's changed since the days when you were a puppy."

She opened her eyes wide. "I used to be a puppy?"

He nodded. "You were a beautiful puppy. But you're an even more beautiful little girl. Now, what would you like for dinner? A nice dog biscuit to chew on?"

She screwed up her nose and poked out her tongue and her grandfather did exactly the same back.

Maggie waited to see if they would talk about anything else, but he went back to his work at the bench and stayed quiet. She sat on the little chair he had put there for her, swinging her legs.

Tadpole was writing, lots of numbers in rows. She copied him sometimes, in the notebook he had given her, sitting beside him here in his shed, writing down all the numbers she knew. Not as many as Tadpole, but she had filled four pages of her notebook. She leaned across to the shelf beside her, picked up the little row of test tubes and hit them gently with her fingernail, the way Tadpole had taught her. She counted them as she hit the glass, one, two, three, four, five, six, seven. Clink, clink, clink, in different notes. A scientist's xylophone, Tadpole called it. Maggie knew what a real xylophone was. She'd been given one for Christmas. She couldn't play a proper tune yet, but she liked it when Clementine played "Baa Baa Black Sheep."

Tadpole had said Maggie could move into her own room if she wanted. Miranda's and Juliet's rooms were empty now. Maggie thought about it and then told Clementine that she would rather stay in her room with her, if that was okay.

"You can come and sleep in my room sometimes with me if you like, Maggie," Sadie said, but Maggie didn't want to. That was Eliza's bed.

If her mum was at the university when it was time for Maggie to come home from school, Sadie would pick her up instead. They still had lots of fun together, like they used to do before she went to school. She liked being with Sadie. They played skipping or singing games and sometimes they would hold hands and climb up the hill to their house pretending it was really steep.

One night Clementine had to work late at the university. Sadie read Maggie a story and put her to bed, saying good night and leaving on the night-light like Clementine did. Maggie couldn't get to sleep, though. She lay there holding Red Monkey, rubbing her bare feet against the warmth of the flannel sheet. She reached under the pillow and found the tiny photo frame she kept there. It was a picture of her mother. Maggie had cut it out and put it into the frame herself. It had been her mum's idea, when she'd found out that she'd have to go away to that island to study her birds.

Sometimes she thought she could hear her mother's voice come out of the photo. She tried it the night Clementine was away. She was midway through telling her mother what had happened at school that day when she heard someone at the door.

"Are you okay, Maggie?" It was Sadie. "Are you having a nightmare?"

"I'm talking to my mum," Maggie said.

"Oh, poor Maggie. Are you lonely?"

Maggie shook her head. "I'm just talking to my mum."

"I'm here. You can talk to me if you like, about anything. You know that, don't you?"

"No, I can't."

Sadie sat on the bed and said, "Of course you can. Is something wrong?"

Maggie shook her head.

"When your mum's away, Maggie, I can be your mother, okay? So if there is ever anything you want to tell her and you can't because she's away somewhere else, then tell me, okay?"

Sadie stroked Maggie's head, the way her mum did when she was saying good night. It didn't feel as nice, though. Sadie's hand felt a bit cold and she was doing the stroking in the wrong direction. Maggie was too tired to say anything, but she was secretly glad when

Sadie stopped, leaned down and kissed her forehead, told her she loved her—Maggie whispered back "I love you too"—then switched off the light.

She did love Sadie. She loved all her aunts, and Tadpole.

She loved secrets and surprises too. She and Sadie had a good secret going at the moment. It had happened one day when just the two of them were home alone. She was sure that Sadie had gone into the garden but she couldn't see her. She must be playing hide-and-seek. Maggie went outside and checked in the usual places, behind the water tank and in a corner of the veranda, but Sadie wasn't there. She was about to go back inside when she heard a sniff, and then another. From inside Tadpole's shed.

She went to the door. It was open. She knocked anyway. Sadie did a jump and looked cross. "Maggie, I told you to wait inside."

"I wanted to see what you were doing." Maggie saw a blue notebook in her aunt's hand. Then she saw something else. "Are you crying?"

"No."

"Yes, you are. What's the matter, Sadie? Are you sad?"

Sadie shook her head, stood up, and pushed the notebook into her pocket. "Let's go back into the kitchen, Maggie."

"Okay." She looked around at the shed first. "Tadpole said we can't come in here if he's not here."

"I know. But this is different."

"Why?"

"Because I'm doing a surprise for Tadpole."

"A surprise? What kind of surprise? About that book you have in your pocket?"

Sadie got down on her knees and pulled Maggie close to her. "It's a really big secret, Maggie, so you have to promise not to tell, okay?"

Maggie nodded.

"Do you remember the scrapbook I did for you, for your fifth birthday?"

Maggie nodded. She loved that scrapbook. She looked at it nearly every day.

"Well, I'm doing another scrapbook, just for Tadpole. Full of all the things he loves. But it's a big, big secret so you're not to tell anyone that you saw me in here, okay?"

"Okay."

"Promise, Maggie?"

"I promise." Maggie made a sign on her chest. "Cross my heart and hope to die."

"Good girl," Sadie said.

● ● ●

From then on when Maggie and Sadie were home together, Sadie would often go into Tadpole's shed.

"It's going to be a great surprise," Maggie said when Sadie came back inside one afternoon.

"What is?" Sadie said.

"Tadpole's scrapbook."

"Oh. Yes," Sadie said.

Maggie thought that was strange. It was as if Sadie had forgotten all about it.

● ● ●

The night before Maggie was due to go and stay with Miranda she heard the phone ring. She heard her mother say, "Oh no. That's terrible. No, of course I understand. We'll sort something out, don't worry. I know you had, yes, she was too. Let me talk to Eliza. Maybe she can do it. Honestly, don't worry."

She heard her mother make another phone call. "Eliza, it's me. Miranda's got a crisis at work, some sort of flu epidemic, half the crew down. All non-urgent leave has been canceled. Exactly. No, I can't. I leave for Maria Island tomorrow. Is there any way you can—? Of course you can't. Sorry, I forgot all about that conference. Look, don't worry, I'll think of something. I know, she's been really excited. We'll let you know. See you."

Maggie wondered what that was all about. She turned over in her bed again and started thinking of all the things she and Miranda were going to do in Melbourne together. Miranda had been sending over lists in the post each week. The last list had fifteen things on it, one for every day she'd be in Melbourne and one spare. They were all counting things. Maggie couldn't wait to go to the zoo and see fifteen animals. They were also going to go to a place called St. Kilda and count as many palm trees as they could.

Miranda had also sent a photo of the room she had ready for Maggie. She had moved to a flat of her own on the tenth floor of a big building in St. Kilda Road. From her window she could see all of Melbourne, as far as the sea. Maggie's room was usually the iron-ing room but Miranda was turning it into Maggie's Palace, she told her. It had red curtains, a blue bedspread, and a yellow rug on the floor. "Bring your favorite toys, but I'll have you so busy you won't get a chance to look at them."

In turn, at Miranda's request, Maggie had sent a list of her fa-vorite foods and the things she didn't like eating. Clementine had helped her to write it.

I like:
1. Fish fingers
2. Ice cream
3. Beans
4. Lollies
5. Vegemite sandwiches

I don't like:
1. Cabbage
2. Peas
3. Toast with bits in it
4. Eggs
5. Sultanas

Bits of what? Miranda had written back on a postcard.

Maggie had forgotten what she'd written by then.

As she turned over in bed again, she heard the front door shut. She knew from the thump of the bag on the floor a few seconds later that it was Sadie.

"Sadie?" That was her mum's voice. "Can you come here?"

The kitchen door shut. Maggie thought about getting up and pressing her ear to the door the way she sometimes did, but it was warmer in bed. Clementine would come and tell her in a little while anyway. They talked all the time about everything.

Once Maggie told her about a fight she had, when one of the kids called her a basket.

"A basket?" her mum had said. "Are you sure that's what they said?"

Maggie was fairly sure. "They said I'm a basket because I don't live with my dad."

Clementine got mad and told Maggie that if anyone ever called her that again she'd come and sort it out. Then she asked her about her dad and if Maggie wanted to see him more. Maggie didn't mind. He was nice when she saw him, but she didn't have to have a dad all the time.

"All your friends have dads."

"They don't have you and lots of aunts or Tadpole, though," she said.

Maggie was nearly asleep when she heard the doorknob turn. She opened her eyes wide, as wide as they would go, so she would look really awake. Clementine came over and knelt beside the bed.

"Maggie, are you awake? Sadie and I have got some great news for you."

CHAPTER 17

Maggie woke up the next morning with a feeling of excitement in her stomach. Today was the day she was going to Melbourne. Even better, Sadie was coming with her now, on the plane and then staying in Miranda's apartment for the whole time.

"We'll have lots of fun, Maggie, I promise," Sadie had said.

Maggie had woken up in the middle of the night. She called across to her mum a couple of times but Clementine wouldn't wake up. Maggie wanted to talk to her about Melbourne. She called out again. Clementine just rolled over and kept sleeping.

Maggie hopped out of bed. She'd go and get a glass of water. She went into the kitchen, pulled a chair across to the sink and had a drink. She looked out the window and got a surprise. There was a light on in Tadpole's shed. She'd just decided she would go down and say hello to him when the door to the shed opened and Sadie came out. Maggie quickly put down her glass, hopped off the chair, ran back into her room and jumped into bed. She shut her eyes tight and pretended to be asleep, just in case Sadie happened to look in.

Leo had to go into work early the next morning, so he told Maggie he was going to say his farewells. He picked her up and gave her such a tight squeeze she made a squeaking sound, which made them both laugh. "Have a wonderful time and come back as quick as you can. It won't be the same without you here. I'll miss you every day."

She gave him an extra hug. "I'll miss you too, Tadpole."

Leo grabbed his overcoat and headed for the door. He was halfway out when Sadie spoke. "I'm going too, Dad."

Leo turned. "Sadie, I'm sorry, of course you are." He came back in, leaned and kissed the top of her head. "You have a great time too."

.   .   .

At the airport, Maggie danced back and forth between her mother and her aunt. She had a little backpack on her shoulders, with a bottle of water, the two bread rolls that Clementine had made for their lunch, one with her name on it and one with Sadie's name on it, a book, her teddy and the picture frame with Clementine's face in it.

They were sitting in a café waiting to get on the plane. Maggie kept kicking her legs she was so excited. Clementine asked her three times to stop it, as she was making their coffee spill. She took out the book from her backpack.

"Are you okay, Sadie?" she heard her mother ask.

"Fine, thanks."

"You seem a bit preoccupied. Are you sure you're okay to do this?"

"I'm fine, I said."

"Okay."

Maggie turned over a few pages. Her mother and her aunt didn't say anything for a little while.

"You'll call and let me know you've got there safely, won't you?"

"As soon as we get there."

"And let me know how you're getting on?"

"How can I? You'll be out in the wild, won't you?"

"We'll be out in the camp for the first week, but they'll be able to get a message to me if anything happens."

"We'll be fine."

"Sadie, are you sure you're okay?"

"I'm not," Maggie said. "I can't wait."

She gave her mum a big hug at the farewell gate. She got a bit sad when she saw her mum was crying but she didn't feel like crying herself. She was too excited.

"I love you very, very, very, very, very much, Maggie," Clementine said.

A very for every one of her years. Maggie started to say twenty-two verys for every one of Clementine's years but Sadie stopped her and said they had to get on the plane.

Maggie kept looking back at her mum as they walked across the concrete and up the twelve metal steps onto the plane.

"I'm excited, Sadie," she said as they found their seats, numbers 10A and 10B.

Sadie was staring out the window. Maggie tugged at her sleeve.

"Sadie, are you excited too?"

Sadie nodded.

"You don't look it," Maggie said.

"Sorry, Maggie." Sadie smiled. "Is that better?"

"Much better."

.   .   .

They rang Clementine from a phone box as soon as they landed in Melbourne. Maggie almost couldn't speak. "We were high in the sky and I could see clouds and water and we had an orange juice and an apple on the plane. Sadie bit her roll and there was something in it, a purple bottle of— What? What, Sadie?" Maggie stopped. "Sadie said I'm not allowed to tell you about that. Is it still the same day in Hobart?" She listened for a little while. "I'll put her on."

Sadie took the phone. "Hi. Yes, she was great. No, not scared at all." She listened for a long time. "You think I don't know that? I'd better go. This is costing a fortune."

.   .   .

They went on a long bus trip and then did a walk to Miranda's house. Maggie couldn't believe it. It was really high up and she could see for miles and miles through the windows. Miranda had put a sign saying Maggie's Palace on her bedroom door. She'd left a basket filled with her favorite things in the fridge—fish fingers, beans, ice cream, lollies and Vegemite sandwiches. There was a note next to them. Sadie read it aloud.

" 'WELCOME TO MY HUMBLE ABODE, MISS MAGGIE AND SADIE. PLEASE FEEL FREE TO MAKE YOURSELF AT HOME, MAGGIE. WHAT'S MINE IS YOURS. SADIE, PLEASE MAKE YOURSELF AT HOME TOO, BUT WHAT'S MINE ISN'T YOURS, OKAY? WILL RING AS SOON AS I CAN. HAVE FUN! LOVE MIRANDA XX' "

Dear Mum, Maggie wrote after her first three days in Melbourne. It took her a long time, with Sadie showing her how to do each of the letters first. *We are having great fun. We go on the tram every day.*

"Good girl. Your writing is lovely. Now we take it to the mailbox," Sadie said.

They took the lift all the way down, out into the street and walked down the busy road until they got to a mailbox. They passed ten trees on the way. Maggie counted each of them. Sadie lifted her up so she could reach the slot in the mailbox.

"Pop it in. Good girl. Now what?"

"I'm hungry."

.   .   .

They did something good every day. Maggie showed Sadie the list Miranda had sent to her.

"Is this what you want to do?"

Maggie nodded.

"In that case, we'll do it."

They went to the museum and to the art gallery. They rang home every day. Clementine wasn't there. She'd gone to the island, but sometimes Tadpole answered and they told him what they'd been doing. Sometimes when they rang he wasn't there either, so they left their voices on the answering machine. Maggie liked doing that.

"This is Maggie. We're having great fun. Bye."

*   *   *

One time Maggie went out into the lounge room and Sadie was crying. She went over and gave her a big hug. "Don't be sad, Sadie."

Sadie gave her a big hug. "Thanks, Maggie."

"Are you missing Tadpole?"

"No, it's not that. It's a long story."

"Do you want me to read to you?" Miranda had left lots of books in her room. Maggie ran and got one now. It was about five ducks. She didn't know all the words but she read it as best she could. At the end, when all the ducklings were with their mother again, she looked up. Sadie was crying and smiling at the same time.

"Thanks, Maggie."

Maggie pointed at the ducks on the page. "That one can be Miranda, that one is Juliet, that one is Eliza, that one is Clementine and that one is you."

"And who's that one?" Sadie pointed to the mother duck. "Tadpole?"

"No, that's your mother." Maggie thought for a moment. "Where's your mum, Sadie?"

"She died, Maggie. About fifteen years ago."

"My grandmother died too. Tadpole told me. He's still really sad."

"I know. Your grandmother was my mother, Maggie."

"She *was*? How?"

"Because Tadpole is my father. And his wife was my mother."

Maggie thought about that for a little while. "What was she like?"

"I don't know. I thought I did, but I got it wrong."

"Did you love her? Like I love my mum?"

"I don't know."

"Did she love you?"

Sadie stood up, brushed crumbs off her jeans. "No, Maggie, she didn't."

"But she was your mum. All mums love their kids."

Sadie didn't answer her that time.

•   •   •

The next three days they caught trams, went to the beach and visited the zoo. They ate whatever they wanted, whenever they wanted. They sat up on the couch in Miranda's living room and watched videos. Maggie fell asleep, curled across Sadie's lap. When Sadie went to move her into her room, she sat upright, opened her eyes wide and stared at the TV screen. "I'm awake, I'm awake."

Sadie started to laugh. "No you're not. You've been asleep the past hour."

Maggie held her eyes open with her fingers. "No, look how not asleep I am."

Sadie did it too. "This is what you look like." She shut her eyes tight. "And this is what you looked like about a minute ago. You were snoring so loudly the whole room was shaking."

Maggie started to laugh. "Even the chairs?"

"The chairs were shaking, the table was shaking, I looked out the window and all the buildings on St. Kilda Road were shaking. You must be the noisiest snorer in the whole world."

"Like this?" Maggie made five grunting noises, then burst out laughing again.

"Now you're a pig. You're not my niece, you're a little piglet that caught the plane from Hobart with me."

Maggie made the noise again and then reached up and flung her arms around Sadie's neck. "This is fun."

"You're right, it is." Sadie gave her a big hug back. "You know what, Maggie? I love you very much."

"I love you too." Maggie decided to tell her something. "I have to tell you a secret, Sadie."

"Do you, Maggie? What is it?"

Maggie clambered up on to the sofa, put her hands around Sadie's left ear and whispered. "You're my favorite auntie."

"Am I?" Sadie gave her a big smile. "Really?"

Maggie nodded.

Sadie pulled her into a hug. "Can I tell you a secret? You're my favorite niece."

"I'm your *only* niece."

"You'd be my favorite even if I had one hundred nieces. I know, Maggie. Let's live here for the rest of our lives, watch TV all the time and catch trams every day—"

"And eat chips and lollies and go to the beach—"

Sadie nodded. "And have as many ice creams as we want. You'll never go to school and we'll just have lots of adventures all the time."

"Will we climb the Faraway Tree?"

"Of course we will. The Faradays have to climb the Faraway Tree."

"I'd love to do that."

"Would you really?"

Maggie nodded.

"Me too," Sadie said.

*   *   *

Miranda rang the next morning. She was in Perth. She spoke briefly to Sadie, then asked to talk to Maggie.

Maggie started giggling as soon as she took the phone. Miranda always made her giggle. "Yes, and I saw ten seagulls. We had fish and chips. I had twenty-four chips. No, you didn't. I don't believe you. I'll ask Sadie." She turned. "Sadie, did Miranda once balance fifty chips on her nose and then eat them all?"

"I can't remember."

"She can't remember," Maggie said into the phone. She listened and laughed again. "Sadie, Miranda said you would have eaten all the chips, not her."

"Very funny," Sadie muttered, not looking up from the news-paper.

Maggie kept talking to Miranda for a little bit longer. When she finished she turned to her aunt. "Do you want to talk to Miranda again, Sadie?"

"No, thanks," Sadie said.

. . .

A postcard arrived the next day. Clementine must have posted it the same day Maggie and Sadie left.

> DEAR MAGGIE, I LOVE YOU AND I MISS YOU. I HOPE YOU
> ARE HAVING FUN. LOVE CLEMENTINE XXXXX

"She didn't put your name on it, Sadie. She must have forgotten."

"Yes, she must have," Sadie said.

. . .

Maggie was doing some drawings in her bedroom that night when Sadie came in. She got down on her knees so she and Maggie were at the same height. "Maggie, that was Tadpole on the phone just now. He rang to—"

"Tadpole! I want to talk to him!"

"No, sweetheart, he's gone now. He could only talk for a minute because he needed to pass on some news. Maggie, you know how your mum is up on that island, sleeping outside and watching those birds? And you know how cold it is there?"

Maggie nodded.

"Well, I'm sorry to say that your mum has caught a bad cold, you know, with lots of coughing and sneezing? And the doctors think she might have something else as well, called pneumonia. And Tadpole says she's going to be fine but that the doctors think it wouldn't be a good idea for her to travel home yet, or see other people in case they catch it."

"But if my mum is sick, I have to help look after her."

"We can't, sweetie. We need to let the doctors do that. And they're really good doctors and they'll make sure she gets better really soon. But it means we won't be able to talk to her for a little while."

"Can I write to her?"

"Of course you can. We'll do a get-well card for her tonight and put it in the post first thing. She'll have it in a few days. And she'll write to you too, I'm sure. But what it means is we can stay away from Hobart for a little bit longer. And I've had an idea, Maggie. Tadpole and I were talking about it on the phone and he thinks it's a great idea too. You know how we were talking about having a big adventure?"

Maggie nodded.

"Let's have a real one. Starting tomorrow. Just you and me. What do you think?"

Maggie sat up. "A real adventure? What kind of one?"

"The best kind. The kind with lots of surprises."

"But Miranda was going to come home and see us."

"She was?"

"She said on the phone she would surprise us and be in Melbourne for a day next week."

"Oh, that's right, I meant to tell you. Miranda rang late last night after you'd gone to sleep, Maggie. She said she's really sorry but she has to keep working and she won't be in Melbourne. And the other news was that one of the other girls from her airline needs this apartment. So you and I are going to go and stay somewhere else. And guess what, we have to catch a train to get there."

"A train!"

"A train with big windows and even a carriage with a restaurant in it so we can have sandwiches and a drink as we're going along."

"Will Mum know where to write to me if we're on a train?"

"Of course she will. I'll send her our new address as soon as we get to where we're going. But she might not be able to write for a little while, because she is sick. But I want you to keep writing to her and telling her what you're doing and how happy you are, okay? Will we draw her a picture now?"

CHAPTER *18*

T hey caught a train the next morning. The journey lasted six hours. Then they caught a bus for another two hours. Maggie got sick of it. It was only when Sadie promised she could have as many lollies as she wanted that she stopped crying. They got out at a bus stop near lots of trees, and started walking. Maggie didn't feel like walking. She kept starting and stopping.

Sadie waited for her every time. "We're nearly there, Maggie. I promise."

"Where are we?"

"It's a surprise. We're having an adventure, remember?"

"I want to go home."

"We'll have an adventure first, and then you can go home."

"I want to go home now."

Sadie came back and crouched down to Maggie's height. "Do you know where we're going to sleep tonight?"

Maggie shook her head, her bottom lip trembling.

"We're going to sleep in a caravan. A caravan is like a doll's house for people. And you know what else it will have, if we're really, really lucky? A campfire."

"What's that?"

"It's a fire outside that we can cook our dinner on. Won't that be fun? We can have potatoes and beans and sit around and sing songs."

"What songs?"

"Any songs you like."

Maggie started walking, then stopped again after ten steps, her backpack falling off her shoulder. "I'm tired."

"We're almost there, I promise." Sadie pointed ahead. "See, up there?"

"What does the sign say?"

"It says the Happiness Bay Caravan Park."

"Which word is 'happiness'?"

"The first word."

"But that's a *B*, not an *H*."

"It's just the way they've done the writing."

· · ·

Maggie loved the caravan. She opened all the cupboards, laughed at the little stove, climbed into the bunk bed. "Even the TV is little."

"Imagine if we were really little too?"

"I am little."

Sadie laughed. "So you are. So do you like it? Will we stay here for a while? Have an adventure?"

"My mum is sick."

"I know, sweetheart, but don't worry, she'll be better soon. And she'd be much less worried if she knew you were having fun, wouldn't she?"

A nod.

"So let's have fun and have a picnic dinner tonight, and tomorrow we'll send her more get-well cards, okay?"

"Okay."

Sadie reached into her bag. "And what do I have here but Vegemite sandwiches!"

Maggie clapped her hands.

· · ·

They spent the next day playing on the lawn near the caravan and swimming in the little pool that was there just for them. They were lying in the sun, drying their bathing suits and their hair when Sadie asked her a question.

"Maggie, have you ever wondered what it would be like to have red hair?"

"Like Miranda?"

"Not just like hers. I found a box at the shop here. We could change the color of our hair if you want."

"Mum might not like it. She and I have got the same color hair."

"Just while we're having our adventure."

"Okay."

· · ·

Maggie wrote to her mother the following day. It took her a long time to do all the letters. Sadie had to help her with most of them.

> DEAR MUM WE HAD GOOD FUN TONIGHT. WE HAVE GOT
> RED HAIR. SADIE MADE TOAST WITH CHEESE AND
> TOMATO SOUP. I LOVE YOU. LOVE MAGGIE XXXXX

"Will we take it down to the mailbox now?"

"No, I'll drop it down tomorrow when I go to get the groceries. It's a bit rainy out there tonight. Are you having fun, Maggie?"

Maggie nodded. "I love it."

"Me too."

"I wish we could live like this all the time."

"Me too."

· · ·

They stayed in that caravan for five sleeps. Maggie wrote to her mum three times and told her all they'd been doing. Swimming. Reading. Playing hide-and-seek. Playing I spy. Drawing in the sand.

Maggie only cried three times and that was because she wanted to see her mum and got sad that she was still sick. The rest of the time she was really good. Sadie told her that every day. "You're the best girl in the world, Maggie. Did you know that?"

Maggie nodded.

The next day Sadie said it was time they had another adventure. They caught another bus. They were on it for half a day. Sadie told her half a day was twelve hours. Maggie wrote those numbers in a new notebook Sadie had given her. The bus had a little toilet in the back of it. Maggie thought that was funny. She went three times.

They got to a new place that was by the sea, with even more caravans in it.

"I wish my mum was here," Maggie said. "And Tadpole. And Juliet and Miranda and Eliza."

"I do too, Maggie. It'd be fun, wouldn't it? But just for now it's only you and me, so what shall we do?"

Maggie shrugged. "I don't care."

"In that case, I'll decide. We're going to cook more sausages, and bake apples, and if you're really good, we're going to have ice cream tonight, too. As much as we want."

"As much as we want?"

"Even more than that."

•   •   •

"Good morning," Sadie said the next day.

Maggie did a big yawn.

"Guess who I just spoke to?"

Maggie sat up, still half asleep.

"Your mum," Sadie said.

Maggie woke up properly. "My mum!"

"Your mum! She sends you lots of love and says she misses you and that she hopes you're having lots of fun. I told her you have been the best girl in the world and we're having a real adventure."

Maggie clambered down from her bed. "Can I talk to her?"

"I'm sorry, Maggie. She could only talk for a minute this time before she had to go back to bed. She was coughing a lot, the poor thing. But she said to tell you she loves you very much."

"She wouldn't say that. She says 'very, very, very, very, very.' Five times. Not once."

Sadie smiled. "Sorry, Maggie. I forgot. That's exactly what she said. Now come on, get dressed and come and have breakfast."

• • •

"Maggie, you know how we were playing that game and pretending to be other people? What about we play one where you're my daughter?"

"But I'm your niece."

"It's just easier to say 'daughter' sometimes. If I say you're my niece, people always say, 'Where's her mum?' and we have to answer all their questions, and the whole day passes answering their questions instead of having our adventure."

"I miss Mum."

"I know."

Her tears started. "I want my mum, Sadie."

"Oh, darling. I'm here."

"I want Mum."

"You can't see her, sweetheart. She's in the hospital."

"But if she's sick, I want to look after her."

"She's got good doctors."

"I want to talk to her. I don't care if her voice is funny. I want to talk to Tadpole, too. And Juliet. And Miranda. And Eliza. I miss everyone."

"We'll ring them, then. But I've only got a bit of money. Would you like to talk to them, or to your mum?"

"My mum."

"You wait here, and I'll go and talk to the man in the office, okay?"

Maggie sat in the office. The man wasn't there, but his wife was. She was old too. Sadie told her she had to go and buy some groceries, and then she'd be right back.

The phone rang. The lady answered it and handed it to Maggie. "It's for you."

"Maggie, hello!"

Maggie thought her voice sounded funny. "Mum! Where are you?"

"I'm in the hospital, but I'm fine. I'll be out soon." Her mum started to cough. "How are you? Are you having fun with Sadie?"

"I miss you."

"I miss you so much. But I'll be better soon. What have you been doing?"

"Our hair is red and we're having an adventure. Tomorrow we're going to go to the beach. We can't call Tadpole, because we haven't got enough money, but he could call us, couldn't he?"

"He's very busy at the moment, but he sends you lots of love." Her mum started coughing again. "I have to go. I love you very, very, very, very much."

"That's only four times."

"What?"

"That's only four times. You have to do it five times."

"I love you very, very, very, very, very much."

When Sadie came back, Maggie was sitting in the chair still, swinging her legs and talking to the lady. She had a lollipop in her hand. "Sadie, the lady said there are penguins here sometimes and even a seal."

"Let's go and look for them tomorrow, then. How was your mum?"

"Good. What's for lunch? I'm hungry."

．　．　．

The next day Maggie had just finished lining up ten little stones, eight feathers, and twelve shells when Sadie appeared beside her, with both hands behind her back. "I've got something for you. Guess which hand?"

Maggie pointed. Sadie's left hand was empty. Maggie pointed again. Her right hand had a piece of paper in it.

"It's a letter from your mum and from Tadpole. It came today. Want me to read it to you?"

Maggie forgot about her counting. She nodded.

"It says, 'Dear Maggie, It was lovely to talk to you last night. I hope you are having lots of fun with Sadie. Aren't you lucky to be having such an adventure? It is like something from an Enid Blyton novel. You will be going up the Faraway Tree next. All is well with us. We miss you. Lots of love, Clementine and Tadpole.' And there are five kisses, see?"

Maggie counted them. "Mum forgot to put the heart."

"What heart?"

"She always puts a heart over my name when she writes it."

·   ·   ·

That night Maggie cried herself to sleep. The next day there was another letter from her mum, saying she hoped Maggie wasn't feeling too sad, that she didn't need to be. She should just have lots of fun with Sadie. This time there was a heart over her name.

·   ·   ·

Most days they had the beach to themselves. Today there were just two people up the other end, a man and a woman.

Maggie found a piece of string, got Sadie to tie a piece of driftwood to it, and started dragging it up and down the beach. Grains of sand flew onto Sadie's book.

"Maggie, careful!"

"It's my tiny dog called Tiny, and I'm taking it for a walk."

"Don't take it too far. Only as far as the five trees. And make sure you can see me the whole time, okay?"

"Okay."

Maggie made all sorts of shapes in the sand as she and Tiny walked along. She picked up shells—four red ones and six white ones—and put them in her pocket. She looked back every time to make sure she could see Sadie. She had just counted the five trees and was turning Tiny around to head back when she heard her name.

"Maggie? Maggie Faraday? Is that you?"

It was the lady. She came closer and leaned down, smiling. "It is you. Maggie, I'm Lucy. Do you remember, I worked in the library at your school last term?"

"Hi, Lucy."

"I didn't know you were up here on holiday too."

"I'm here with my auntie Sadie." She pointed to Sadie down the beach. It looked like she was reading. "Mum's sick in the hospital at the moment, so we're having an adventure."

"Your mum's in the hospital? What's wrong with her?"

"Something bad. She coughs a lot."

"That's terrible. I hope she gets better. We're heading back to Hobart tomorrow, so I might call in and visit her."

"You won't be allowed to. She's too sick."

"I'll drop her some flowers, then."

By the time Maggie got back to where Sadie was sitting, she had found ten pink shells, nine black shells, and four pieces of seaweed. She could hardly carry them and pull Tiny at the same time.

Sadie started laughing when she saw her struggling with everything. "Haven't you done well! Will we make a picture?"

They had so much fun making the picture that Maggie forgot to tell her about the lady from Hobart.

*   *   *

Two nights later she and Sadie were sitting by the little fire outside their caravan, pushing foil-wrapped potatoes around in the coals with long sticks.

There'd been another letter from her mother that day. Maggie had asked how the postman found them, and Sadie said that postmen were amazing. They always knew where to find people.

They'd just eaten the potatoes, right out of the blackened foil, adding lots of butter so it ran all over their fingers, when Maggie heard her name being called. She thought it was the lady from yesterday at first. She and Sadie both looked up. Then she realized who was shouting. It was her mum. Her mum!

"Maggie! Maggie!"

It *was* her mum. Running across the lawn, in between all the other caravans. And not only that, Tadpole was behind her, running as well!

Maggie leaped up. "Mum! Sadie, look!" She started to run. Sadie grabbed her arm.

She pulled away. "Sadie, look, it's my mum. Let go."

She started running. Her mum was running toward her too. Clementine was crying. Maggie started to cry too. She met her in the middle of the lawn, near the taps. Before she knew what was happening Clementine had pulled her up off the ground, into her arms, squeezing her so hard it hurt, saying her name over and over again. "Maggie, Maggie, Maggie."

"Mum, you're hurting me."

She didn't let go of her. "Maggie, are you all right? Are you okay? Is everything all right?"

Maggie pulled back a little bit. It was her mum! "Are you better? Has your cough gone?"

"Are you okay, Maggie? Are you okay?"

She nodded. Of course she was. Maggie couldn't work out why she kept asking her that. Her mum had been sick, not her. She clambered down out of her arms and took Clementine by the hand, skipping now she was so excited. "Come and see our caravan."

Maggie looked toward the fire. Tadpole was already there, standing next to Sadie. They weren't laughing or talking. Tadpole had Sadie's arm in his hand, holding her. Then something strange happened. Her mum took her by the shoulders, said to her in a funny voice, "Stay here, Maggie." As Maggie watched, Clementine walked up to Sadie and hit her, on her face, then on her body, then on her face again. Not just once. Again and again, until Tadpole stopped her.

Maggie couldn't believe it. She had never seen her mum hit anyone. She started to cry. "Mum, don't!"

Tadpole appeared next to her. He leaned down and swung her up into his arms. "Come with me, little Maggie."

Maggie was still crying. She tried to look over his shoulder, but Tadpole moved her around and she couldn't see them anymore.

Tadpole kept walking with her, down toward the beach, rubbing her back and saying, "Shh, shh, shh. It's all right, Maggie. It's all right."

"But why did Mum hit Sadie, Tadpole?"

"Don't you worry about that." He hugged her tightly again. It hurt as much as her mum's hug had. "Are you all right, Maggie? Have you been having a good time?"

Maggie nodded. They were on the beach now. He knelt down on the sand, still holding tight to her. She had so much to tell him. She told him about making their hair red and about eating fish fingers. She was halfway through telling him about doing pictures in the sand when she saw a funny look on his face. She thought he would be smiling, but he wasn't.

"Tadpole, what's wrong? Are you sad?"

He shook his head. "Not anymore, Maggie."

She flung her arms around his neck. "I missed you, Tadpole."

To her big surprise, Tadpole started crying, the tears falling down his cheeks. "We missed you, too, Maggie."

PART TWO

CHAPTER 19

Greenwich Village, New York
2006

Maggie Faraday stood in the middle of a small studio apartment, on the sixth floor of a building two blocks north of Bleecker Street. It had been her home for twelve weeks and five days.

"Nearly there," she said aloud, as she gazed around at her morning's work. She often spoke to herself these days. More worryingly, she also answered herself. She took out a notebook from her jeans pocket and checked her list. Ten tasks done, three to go.

She drew the red curtains, sending a warm cozy glow through the apartment. She'd already finished polishing the old wooden table in the center of the room. She'd salvaged it from a sidewalk sale the previous week. A local bar had been selling all its contents. She'd begged for help from the Irish barman to carry it up to her apartment, waiting for him to ask her why she wanted an old thing like that, to remark that it didn't match the rest of the elegant furniture in the living room. All of the things Angus would have said if she'd brought something like it home to their apartment in London. "You silly, funny thing," he'd have said.

She didn't think the table was silly or funny. She loved the old look; the smell and feel of it. It had scratches on top from bored patrons, as well as scuffs on its legs and edges. She imagined hundreds of conversations, arguments, beginnings and endings of love affairs taking place over it. It reminded her of the old wooden table that had stood in the middle of the kitchen in her family home in Hobart.

"You're too sentimental, that's your problem," Angus would have said. "That family of yours has a lot to answer for."

She lit the scented cinnamon candle and placed it in the center of the table. A pot of mulled wine was simmering on the stove in the small kitchen, sending out a hazy, steamy scent of wine, cloves and spices. Bing Crosby was crooning Christmas carols from the sleek stereo system in a corner of the room. She'd looped tinsel over the curtain rail and hung a slowly spinning three-dimensional foil star from the light fixture. There wasn't room for much more. It was a tiny apartment. There wasn't even space for a twenty-four-hour bed—it spent the daylight hours folded up in a large cupboard in the living room.

The apartment had five great things about it. Maggie had counted them:

1. It was safe. Not only was it on the sixth floor of the building, but the doorman downstairs was the human equivalent of a suspicious doberman. It had taken her ten minutes to convince him she had a right to move in when she first arrived three months earlier with her one suitcase. He'd asked to see her ID. "You don't look twenty-six," he said. "Really? Thanks," she replied, as though she hadn't heard that comment a hundred times before.

2. It was quiet. The bars and clubs of Bleecker Street were only meters away, but there was no loud music or shouts from patrons, just the constant humming sound of New York—millions of conversations and car noises softened into an underlying murmur. That had surprised her. She'd expected a soundtrack of car horns, shouts, and fights, not that comforting hum.

3. It had a wall of windows. The living room was light-filled, all year round. It meant people could see in if the curtains

weren't drawn, but she could also see out. It was a good exchange.

4. It looked out over the communal park. That had also been a
surprise. She'd expected an apartment in New York to look
out onto more buildings, concrete, and sidewalks, not this
oasis. There were many different species of tree, so there was
always something in bloom or in leaf. There were also fifteen
benches. She'd sat on each of them.

5. It had a balcony. To be accurate, half a balcony, but the divid-
ing wall made it private enough, and she rarely heard anything from her neighbor on that side.

There were only three bad things about it:

1. The kitchen was so small there was only room for a two-
burner stove and the larger of the burners was faulty. She'd
put in a call to a repair company about it that morning.

2. Her next-door neighbor on the other side was odd. Up at all
hours, given to loud conversations with him or herself, and
addicted to far too many loud game shows on television.

3. The couple down the corridor ate nothing but burgers and
fries, so there was always a mist of deep-fried fat and meaty
smells outside their door. Maggie had started running from
her apartment to the lift any time she went out, blocking her
nose to avoid the smell.

Five positives, three negatives, so the positives won. It was the
way Clementine had taught her to think; her grandfather Leo's
creed as well. "Look on the bright side." "Count your blessings."
"Things could be worse." Could they? Maggie hoped not. She was
having enough trouble staying afloat in New York as it was.

"Think of it as a holiday," her aunt Miranda had said when she
offered her the use of the New York apartment. "A hideaway. Yours,
rent-free, flatmate-free."

Work-free, friend-free, old-life-free. It had seemed like a lifeline
at the time, the only option open to her. She needed to leave her

house, job, Angus, everything behind. Make a dramatic gesture to try and cancel out a terrible event. The problem was, it had come with her. She still thought about it every day. And her head was the same head, her face was the same face, her body was the same body. She was the same person in a different place.

"You can't blame yourself, Maggie." Everyone had said it to her, from her boss at the company, to Leo, to Clementine, to Juliet, Eliza, and Miranda.

But she had to blame herself. Because what the man had done that day was her fault.

If only she had picked up the signs when she was talking to him in the conference-room foyer beforehand. She noticed him as she was making herself a cup of tea. He seemed agitated. She put it down to the bad traffic jams outside. There had been grumbling about long delays and traffic snarls from a lot of the people as they arrived and took their seats in the large hall. She passed him a jug of milk. He mistook her for a waitress. She was used to it. She was always being told she looked like a student. It had become a joke in the firm, to send Maggie into the boardroom first and watch people's faces when they realized she was the head of finance, not the girl hired to wash the cups.

She felt like she had made a connection with him that day. Was it fate that had brought them together even for a few minutes? Could she have stopped him?

Miranda had been impatient about that. "How could you have? You're a mathematical genius, not a psychiatric genius. His own wife said she hadn't realized how distressed he was."

Eliza had plenty to say about it, too. "That was his life path, Maggie. He probably didn't even notice you."

Juliet had also tried to console her. "Sweetheart, you couldn't have done anything. He had made his decision. It had nothing to do with you."

It had everything to do with her. He made it clear when he stood up in front of all the shareholders and said that he was doing this because his livelihood was gone, because some faceless, heartless accountant had decided to close down his business with one stroke of a pen. Before anyone had a chance to stop him, he reached into the bag beside him and—

Even now she couldn't think of the moment without feeling physically sick. She knew it was her fault. It had been her decision—her work, her analysis of the figures—that had led to his branch of the company being shut down.

"You were just doing your job," Leo had said.

Her job? Then how many times had this happened before without her realizing? What she had thought was simply a great skill, something that had enabled her to breeze through school, through university, to be headhunted from job to job—had she been ruining lives all this time? That's what had kept her awake night after night since it happened. How could she have been so naive?

Even more naive to think Angus would support her through it.

"Look on the bright side," Miranda had said. "You got two of the bad things that were going to happen to you in your life over with in one day. A double whammy, if you like."

It had felt like a quadruple whammy. Leaving the company offices in a state of shock after what felt like hours of interviews with the police and her employers, wanting nothing more than her own house, her own bed, Angus's sympathy and support. Getting the black cab to her door, letting herself in, going to his home office, and walking straight in on another scene she wanted to forget. Her boyfriend of three years, naked except for his socks, moving energetically on top of a completely naked woman. Not just any woman. A pretty, blond woman called Lauren, until that moment Maggie's closest girlfriend in London.

"At least you did something dramatic about it," Miranda said when Maggie told her what happened next. "I would have been more upset if you'd just burst into tears in front of them."

Maggie had screamed and roared and shouted at both of them. She had grabbed their clothes and tossed them out of the window. She had thrown the water from a nearby vase over them.

"Good thing you don't keep hydrochloric acid in the house," Miranda said.

Maggie had grabbed two suitcases, filled them with her clothes, and called another black cab. Ten minutes later she'd found herself sitting in the back of it, trembling with delayed shock, barely able to speak. It took the driver several minutes to find out where she wanted to go. She eventually named a hotel in Mayfair that she remembered from Miranda's visits to London.

It was only when she'd entered the hotel room and fell onto the king-size bed that she allowed herself to cry. Not for Angus. She realized later that not one of the tears that night had been for him. They'd all been for that poor man at her office. She'd realized then she hadn't told Angus about him. Two days later, when she had a formal meeting with him to finish everything between them, she still didn't tell him. She didn't need to. If he was interested, he could have read about it all in the newspapers. While she and Angus spent a chilly hour disentangling their lives, Miranda waited outside in the limousine she had hired especially for the day, smoking cigarettes and flirting with the handsome thirty-year-old driver. When Maggie eventually emerged carrying a small bag of belongings, Miranda took her to lunch at the most expensive restaurant she knew in London.

Maggie didn't know what she would have done without Miranda by her side at that time, or without the phone calls every day from her mother in Tasmania, or the cards and flowers from her other aunts. That time had gone by in a strange haze. It was only now, three months later, that she felt she was slowly getting back to normal.

She hadn't told any of them, but during her first week in New York, she'd barely left the apartment. She was too scared. She found herself in tears nearly every day and kept telling herself off for being so feeble. She found a box of opera CDs in one of the cupboards and played those over and over again, the drama and beauty of the music sparking more crying. She stopped fighting it, and let the tears flow in time to the music.

After six days inside she ventured out into the communal garden. It soothed her to count the trees (there were forty-five) and sit on each of the benches. It wasn't until the second week that she braved the busy streets and the mysteries of the subway system. It felt good to be surrounded by people again.

She made a list of all there was to see and forced herself to visit at least two sights every day. Back in the apartment at night, she crossed them off her list: the Empire State Building, Carnegie Hall, the Chrysler Building, Grand Central Station, Wall Street, Ellis Island, the Statue of Liberty. She joined tour groups, walking tours, read every word of every leaflet, looked up at the skyscrapers, down at the sidewalks, immersed herself in the sights and sounds of yellow cabs, rushing pedestrians, immaculately dressed shoppers, horse-drawn carriages in Central Park.

She collected tiny details, memorizing them, like mental snapshots. A glint of gold from the roof of the Chrysler Building vivid against a sharp blue sky. A row of six people at a pedestrian light, each with bags in their left hands, talking into phones held in their right hands, like a real-life chorus line from a Broadway musical. A dog walker in Central Park, two handfuls of hounds dragging her along, like a husky team in the North Pole. A fleet of yellow school buses, crammed with well-dressed children from private schools, being directed by a middle-aged woman with a walkie-talkie. She patted the Wall Street bull. She ate three oysters in Grand Central Station. She stared silently at the site of what was once the World Trade Center. She filled her head with Manhattan in the day to help cancel out thoughts of London in the night. She could have written her own tour guidebook—*New York City for the Bewildered.*

She put on a bright voice whenever any of her family phoned. They'd been speaking to one another about her, she could tell. They kept using the same phrase, as if they'd agreed on their approach.

"It'll do you good to have some time out, Maggie."

"You mustn't blame yourself, but everybody needs some time out now and again."

It wasn't time out Maggie needed. It was time over. How far back would she go, though? Had everything she'd done in her life been leading up to that awful moment in London? If she'd failed one exam at school or university, been late for one job interview, done

one thing differently, would she somehow have stopped it happening that day?

"You can't go over and over it, Maggie," Clementine had said. "You'll drive yourself mad."

But she had to go over and over it. She couldn't stop herself. That's what she'd been trained to do in her professional life: go over and over details; analyze graphs and spreadsheets; find the missing link, the rogue figures, the incorrect numbers. She did it in her own life too much, she knew that. Reviewed each day, wished she'd said things in a different way, worn different clothes, reacted in a more mature fashion. She proofread her life. It wasn't something she could just turn off.

She had never thought doing something she loved would lead her to this. She, Leo and Clementine had often spoken about how lucky they were to work in fields they loved: Leo with his inventions, each one more successful than the last, even though he should have long retired; Clementine with her groundbreaking research into more than a dozen rare bird species and their habitats. She had been all around the world, had set up studies on islands off the coast of Australia and in some of the most remote places in the world. For Maggie it was a love of numbers. She had been that way for as long as she could remember. She'd looked forward to math classes at primary school. She was at the top of the class at high school. She was fast-tracked into university when an alert teacher recognized she had a rare gift. "The world is your oyster," a career advisor said. "You can go into research, economics, teaching, business . . ."

She'd chosen business. Big business, specifically. Miranda had been disgusted, of course. "So dull, darling. I had such high hopes for you. Why don't you set up your own company?"

She didn't want to. She liked the security of working for a big organization. She liked having her own office; being left alone to pore over balance sheets, to review budgets, to analyze sales figures and projections. She liked knowing she was close to the humming heart of a business.

"You are getting enough exercise, aren't you?" Eliza would always ask. "I don't like to think about you holed up in an office for hours and hours every week." That was before Eliza had her accident, when she was running five kilometers every day and making sure her personal training clients ran twice that distance. Even after the accident, when Eliza's focus changed, she took a close interest in Maggie's well-being. Maggie still couldn't walk past a gym without feeling guilty. She was just grateful she'd inherited her mother's slight frame.

"You just do whatever you want to do, Maggie," Juliet would say. "It's your life. As long as you make sure you're eating properly and come and visit Myles and me as often as you can."

Opportunity had followed opportunity for her. After graduating top of the class from the University of Tasmania, she'd done postgraduate studies in Sydney and been headhunted by a large firm that sent her on training courses all over the world. She became used to frequent air travel, business class—but then she'd been traveling on planes since she was a child, flying interstate once a year to stay with her aunts. She went home to Tasmania to visit Leo and Clementine as often as possible, and joined the whole family for at least one, sometimes both, of their annual Christmas celebrations.

Three years earlier, her Sydney company had taken over a London-based company specializing in wholesale supplies for supermarkets. She'd been offered a relocation package. An extraordinary relocation package. They had high hopes for her future with them, the managing director told her. She'd rung her mother, her grandfather, and all her aunts.

"Of course you have to take it," they all said. "What an opportunity for someone your age."

She'd liked London immediately. Her employers found her a house in a good part of the city, gave her a car, rewarded her long hours with an excellent salary. They also introduced her to Angus. He was the stock control manager for a subsidiary company. They met at a staff Christmas party, and he pursued her romantically and persistently from the following day. They had moved in together three months after that. It was Angus who encouraged her to work even harder, apply for promotions, network with the heads of the company; his ambition so much stronger than hers.

Each step leading her, unaware, closer to that moment in London.

"It wasn't your fault, Maggie."

It was her fault. They hadn't heard what the man said.

"You read the police report, Maggie. He was seriously unbalanced."

Perhaps he was. But it was her work that had sent him over the edge.

A spirited ringing of synthesized church bells made her jump. The CD of Christmas carols had come to an end. She pointed the remote control at the stereo system, restarting the CD player for the third time. It had been playing all morning as she wrapped her presents. She sang along with Perry Como, Ella Fitzgerald and Frank Sinatra, taking the occasional sip of mulled wine. She was nearly done. One more ribbon for Eliza's present, a few more layers of protective wrapping around Juliet's gift, and everything would be ready for the post office.

She did her best to ignore the spike of sadness that she wouldn't get to see her presents being unwrapped this year. That was her second favorite part of Christmas. Her favorite part was the looking. She had never been one to race out the night before. She bought presents all year round, tucking them away until the time was right. This Christmas was different. The early presents she'd bought had been left behind in London. Angus had probably thrown them out by now.

Now that the wrapping was done, she took down a large bag from the top of the fridge, and began to load up the parcels, saying good-bye to each of them as she put them into the bag.

Her grandfather's parcel was first. She gave it a pat. "Happy Christmas, Tadpole." His gift was a gold cardboard box filled with a handpicked selection of chocolate. For a thin man, he had an enormous appetite for sweet things. He savored his chocolate, making one block last for days. He'd always kept a store in his in-

venting shed, too. He liked to produce studies that showed the ingredients in chocolate had a direct impact on the working of the
brain, as well as stimulating the hormone that produced a feeling
of happiness.

"That's in mice, Leo," Miranda would say. "Not mad inventors."

Maggie got into the habit of sending her grandfather regular
parcels of souvenir chocolates as a child, when she first started
going away to stay with her aunts. She'd kept it up into adulthood.
He received regular parcels of chocolates from Sydney when she
was studying at university there. She sent him parcels from Canada
when she was there on six months' work experience. From London
he received monthly parcels: boiled lollies, traditional creamy tof-
fee, or the quirkily named sweets from Marks & Spencer that he
loved: Fantastically Fizzy Fish, Squealingly Fizzy Piglets.

She'd been assembling his Christmas present for the past six
weeks, searching the United Nations of sweet shops New York offered. In Little Italy she came across a small delicatessen that im-
ported rich dark Venetian chocolate, shaped like hearts and
wrapped in red cellophane. The twenty-four-hour supermarket
across the road from her apartment sold Hershey's bars, the American chocolate Tadpole loved. He said it had a different texture,
rougher to the tongue and therefore more interesting. But he also
loved smooth Swiss chocolate. She found bars of that beside the
counter of a small restaurant called Edelweiss, on 59th Street, two
blocks back from Broadway. There were chocolate-covered Brazil
nuts from a Spanish deli on 34th Street; sugary almonds from Chi-
natown; and homemade Turkish delight, pink and smelling of
rose water and icing, from a crammed, brightly lit delicatessen off
Orchard Street. The final addition was a small box of square fudge
decorated with Aboriginal artwork in gold paint that she'd unexpectedly found in an equally unexpected Australian-themed ice
cream shop in the East Village. "Seven different countries for you
this time!" she wrote on the card, before signing it as she always
did, "with love from your Maggie xxxxxxxxxxxxxxxxxxxxxxxxxxxx."
Twenty-six kisses for her twenty-six years. Another long-standing tradition between them. Leo kept his to one X with his age beside it in

brackets, seventy-eight at his last birthday. He said it would take him a year to draw all the kisses otherwise.

She touched the second parcel. "Happy Christmas, Juliet." After ten years in Sydney, Juliet and her husband now lived in Manchester, running their chain of cafés from an office in the back of their big three-story terrace house, the walls covered with shelves piled high with cookbooks, organized into alphabetical order. It led into a test kitchen, sleek and stylish, stocked with the best saucepans, cookware, ovens, and baking equipment. Maggie had seen several magazine articles featuring photos of Juliet against a backdrop of the kitchen. She looked just like a cook should, Maggie thought. All curves and smiles and twinkling eyes, like her picture should be on a box of custard powder or a carton of cream. Wholesome and good for you.

Away from the kitchen, Juliet collected delicate glass vases. Maggie had bought her dozens over the years. Since arriving in New York, she'd browsed in curio shops and homeware stores in Manhattan. Two weeks previously she'd caught a train to Boston from Penn Station. On a side street near Boston Common, she stopped in front of an antiques store. In the window was a beautiful pale blue vase. She knew Juliet would love it. Maggie had gone in, deciding on the spot to go beyond the budget she had set herself. The woman behind the counter barely smiled a welcome, assessing Maggie from top to bottom, clearly finding her wanting, with her faded chain-store jeans, her long-sleeved T-shirt, her ordinary bag, her shoes made for walking, not parading. She'd not said hello or "Can I help you?" or responded to Maggie's smile and greeting; merely watched her closely, half shop assistant, half store detective.

If it had been three months earlier, if Maggie had come in wearing something from the wardrobe of clothes she'd had in London—a sleek designer suit or shift dress or even her casual clothes from that time: expensive jeans; a tailored, handmade shirt; a cashmere cardigan; leather boots—she knew there would have been a very different welcome. She left within seconds, not looking back at the shop or the vase. She always needed to like the shop as-

sistants from whom she bought presents. Especially if the present
was for Juliet.

As it turned out, she'd found the ideal vase in a homeware store
back in Greenwich Village, only three streets away from her apartment. The woman who'd sold it to her was the woman who had
made it. She'd explained how she produced the dramatic effect in
such a delicate piece of work, shimmers of red against deep strokes
of green. Maggie had liked her as much as she liked the vase. She
wrapped it very carefully, choosing paper that matched the vase's
colors. Perfect Christmas colors. Juliet would love it.

The third parcel was much smaller. "Happy Christmas to you
too, Eliza." It was easy to buy presents for Eliza. Maggie got her the
same thing every year: a necklace. Eliza had dozens of them, and
she wore one every day: long strings of beads, heavy dramatic pen-
dants, delicate gold chains. Maggie loved buying or finding them
for her. As a child, when she was staying with Eliza, she'd even
made necklaces for her, carefully threading wooden beads onto
cotton thread, stringing papier-mâché shapes onto yarn, or making
her own beads: tiny strips of colored paper wound tightly around
matchsticks, left to dry, and then glazed.

On Maggie's last visit to Melbourne, over two years ago now,
she'd been touched to see those homemade necklaces on a specially made board in Eliza's bedroom. Her aunt had a place for
everything in her Art Deco flat, which was on the ground floor of
an old house in the beachside suburb of Elwood. Her decorating
style was minimalist—bare floorboards, white walls, carefully posi-
tioned paintings. Eliza's own fashion style followed similar lines—
straight silhouettes; mostly in black; always in linen, cotton, or
wool; never man-made fibers. Her makeup was similar—simple,
understated. She wore her hair in a sleek, short crop. It was about
looking in control, she'd said to Maggie. It's what people expected
from a life coach.

Maggie knew Eliza would love this year's present. She'd found it
in a students' gallery on Lafayette Street. The girl behind the
counter had bleached hair and a big smile. She told Maggie stories

about each of the students as Maggie looked at their work. The one who had made Eliza's present (ten shades of blue beads on three strands of thin wire) had grown up by the sea. The necklace was called *Oceanscape*. Maggie had written all of that on Eliza's Christmas card. She knew Eliza would like the fact her necklace had a name.

Her aunt Miranda's gift was in the next parcel. There was never any need to buy her jewelry, perfumes, makeup, scarves, bottles of gin or sweet-smelling soaps either. Miranda had spent her life awash in personal beauty products and luxuries. She'd been flying the world for twenty years. She now lived in Singapore, the home of duty-free shopping. Her luxurious apartment on the thirty-fifth floor of an upmarket block overlooking the bay had felt like a department store to Maggie the one time she visited. Miranda's jewelry box was piled high with pearls and gold chains, her bathroom cabinet lined with bottles of perfume, below it a large basket of guest soaps from all the high-class hotels she'd stayed at over the years. On the shelves were enough skincare products to stock a dermatology clinic.

Five years earlier, at the age of forty-three, Miranda had accepted a lucrative invitation from her employer, one of the more exclusive Asian airlines, to stop flying full time and become a training manager instead. Still based in Singapore, she'd swiftly moved up five floors in the same building to an even more luxurious penthouse apartment. She announced cheerfully to Maggie during one of their regular phone calls that she didn't miss the early starts or the dry skin for a minute, and she was much happier on the ground. More time to socialize, too. Singapore was filled with airline pilots with time on their hands, she declared.

The arrangement was perfect for Miranda. If she wasn't traveling, she was socializing. She was certainly too busy to do something as time-consuming as browse in bookshops. The task of finding good books had been handed over to Maggie many years before. When she was young, she'd chosen the books either by their covers or by explaining to bookshop assistants that she was there on behalf of her aunt and what could they recommend? (Miranda had coached her on the speech.) She still did it, relying more on news-paper reviews than bright covers these days. This Christmas parcel contained three books, with explanatory notes, as ordered by Miranda. Maggie had spent hours in New York's new and secondhand bookshops. She'd found a debut novel from a young Mexican writer, a rising star in the literary world; "earthy and exuberant storytelling," Maggie had written. There was a book of quirky facts about manners; "the author is the sister of one of the English royal's nannies and seems obsessed with the proper use of a fork," and a nonfiction study of the impact of cotton-growing on the world; "stand-out fact: cotton = pollution—a third of the world's pesticides are used in its cultivation." Maggie knew Miranda wouldn't read all of them. She could almost hear her aunt's amused voice. "Read them? Darling, when will I get time to do that? But I have to *know* about them; that's far more important. And pick ones with smart-looking jackets that will look good on my shelves, won't you?" It was an act, of course. Miranda was very well-read. Scarily well-read, sometimes. Or perhaps just scary.

Maggie touched the fourth parcel. "Happy Christmas, Sadie." She was the hardest of her aunts to buy for. You couldn't buy a gift for a person's house if you didn't know whether they had their own house. Or makeup or jewelry if you didn't know whether they wore any. Or luxurious hand creams in case it went against all they believed in. Or even a sweater or a nice scarf if you hadn't seen them in twenty years and didn't know what colors they might like or even what size they were. The only things you could buy someone who you now knew only through her annual cards were notepaper and beautiful pens. The Christmas present contained both, as it had done every year for as long as Maggie could remember. "Hope to see you soon. Lots of love, Maggie," she'd written in the card. She'd written the same thing in every card for the past twenty years. A quick summary of what she'd been up to that year, and then the farewell message.

"Are you sure Sadie gets all my news?" she used to ask when she was much younger. "How do we know when we don't hear any back from her?"

"She passes a longer message through Father Cavalli at the church," Leo said. "He lets us know how she's getting on. He says she loves your news reports, you know that."

She'd been the only girl at her school in Hobart with an aunt who'd run off to join a hippie commune. It had been quite a novelty. Not as good as her classmate whose uncle was a news broadcaster on one of the TV stations on the mainland, but worth something. Maggie had often talked it over with her friends.

"What do hippies actually do?" one of them asked once.

Maggie hadn't been too sure. "They look after dolphins," she'd said, thinking of the necklace Sadie sometimes wore.

"Really? How do you look after dolphins?"

"Feed them, wash them."

"They don't need washing, do they? They're already in the water."

"That's salt water. Sadie washes them in nice, soapy water." She'd changed the subject quickly after that.

As a teenager Maggie had asked Clementine if Sadie's decision had been connected with her in any way. It had been preying on her. After all, Sadie had gone off to become a hippie just after Maggie had stayed with her for those few weeks, the time Clementine was sick. Maybe spending too long with an almost six-year-old had put Sadie off her family.

"Of course it had nothing to do with you, Maggie."

"Does she miss us, do you think? Do you miss her?"

"It's not about missing her. It's her life. She has to do what she wants with it."

Maggie checked her watch. She'd better get to the post office. She put all the parcels into the large bag, placing her mother's gift on top.

It was the oddest-shaped of them all—as always, a jumble of gifts, like a lucky dip. It was a treat, shopping for a mother who was only seventeen years older. Their tastes were very similar. The main gift this year was a vintage brooch, a mixture of delicate gold wire and bright red, green, and orange stones, in the shape of a penguin. Maggie always sent her mother something to do with a bird, obvi-

ous as it was. There was also some American chocolate (Clementine loved it as much as Tadpole did), a secondhand CD of opera
music, and practical items: thick socks, thermal underwear, heavy-
duty moisturizer, and a new watch to replace the one she'd lost last
time she was "down south," as Clementine and her fellow scientists
called Antarctica.

Maggie wondered whether Clementine had gotten word yet
about her next trip. In the old days in London, she e-mailed or was
on the phone to her mother every day, up-to-date with every piece
of news. Since her move to New York, she'd tried to be more independent. She managed it well in a practical way, phoning only once
a week, not using e-mail at all, and only rarely sending text messages. She wasn't managing so well emotionally; all the questions
about her family were still buzzing around her head. It's just they
weren't getting answered.

She toyed for a moment with sending the parcel to Antarctica
rather than Hobart, just because she still got a kick out of seeing
the address:

CLEMENTINE FARADAY
DAVIS STATION
ANTARCTICA

Even though she knew the reality—that the parcels were only
delivered once or twice a year, depending on weather conditions—
she still liked imagining a polar post office, staffed by penguins, the
mail delivered by sleds. Once she heard from Clementine when the
next Antarctic trip was on, she'd send another parcel to that address. In the meantime, she addressed this one to the family home
in North Hobart, adding a quick sketch of a Christmas pudding
and sprig of holly to the label. She was glad Clementine had decided not to join the rest of the family this Christmas. Her mother
had assured her it had nothing to do with Maggie's own decision;
that it was work-related. Maggie wondered about that. Either way,
it made it easier for her that Clementine wouldn't be joining the
family either.

She'd just gathered up her keys when the intercom buzzed. It was Ray, the doorman, to let her know a repairman was on his way up. She waited outside her door for him.

"Thanks for coming so quickly," she said as she led the man to the tiny kitchen. "It's the stove. The large burner just won't seem to work for me."

"Like all of us, breaking down with age. What's that accent of yours? British?"

"Half British, half Australian," she said.

"Nice mix. I'm half Irish, half Polish myself." He stopped in the middle of the room and rubbed his shirt-sleeved arms. "You'd want to talk to your super about that air-conditioning. It's freezing in here."

As the repairman spoke, Bing Crosby burst into a chorus of "Jingle Bells." The man looked around, taking in the decorations, the table piled high with Christmas parcels, and the air rich with the scent of cinnamon and other spices.

"Are you early or am I late?" he said.

"I beg your pardon?"

"All of this." He gestured at the room. "It's the middle of summer out there. Old people all over New York are dropping like flies in the heat, and you're living here in Santa's grotto, wearing that getup."

"It's a family thing," Maggie hurried to explain. "We always celebrate Christmas in July." Embarrassed now, she took off the Santa hat and duffle coat she'd had on all day. She caught sight of her hair in the mirror. It was standing up in dark tufts, her ears far too visible. She quickly smoothed it down. "I was just getting into the spirit of it."

"Some sort of spirit, anyway. Where'd you say that family of yours was from? The North Pole?"

She managed a weak smile. Maybe he was right, though. Maybe she'd gotten a little bit carried away. She pressed the off button on the CD and crossed the room to draw back the curtains. Bright summer light flooded in, bouncing off the tinsel and foil decorations. The sky outside was blue. The garden below was filled with sunbathers. She blew out the scented candle and turned off the flashing Christmas lights too. What had she been thinking? That doing it like this would make her less homesick?

The man watched her, an amused look on his face. "That's Christmas for you. All that work, and then it's over in an instant. So, want to show me that stove of yours?"

Maggie led him to the kitchen and watched as he inspected the burner. He didn't mention the mulled wine in the saucepan on the other burner. Neither did she.

"So do you like it here in New York?" he asked, as he lifted up the wires and removed the fuse.

She nodded. "Yes. Yes, I do. It's great."

"You're here for work?"

"No." She paused. "More of a career break." She had a sudden urge to sit him down, make a cup of tea, tell him everything. She was longing for a conversation with someone apart from herself. But she was worried that if she started, she wouldn't stop. Besides, she'd made a deal with Miranda not to talk about it too much.

"The apartment's yours for as long as you want to stay there," her aunt had said. "But on condition there's no going over and over everything, all right? If you want to keep blaming yourself for something that wasn't your fault, I can't stop you, but I'll tell you now, hair shirts are right out of fashion in New York this year."

She'd been just as outspoken when she heard that Maggie had decided not to join them for their July get-together. "But you have to be there. You know Christmas isn't Christmas without a child around to marvel at the lights and get excited at the presents."

"I'm twenty-six, Miranda. I'm not a child." She'd been in no mood for teasing.

Juliet had been more sympathetic when they spoke on the phone the day before. "Maggie, please, change your mind. It's not too late. Get a flight and come and join us. It'll do you good. It's not right for you to be on your own like this, not after everything that's happened."

Maggie had been tempted. She pictured herself arriving at Belfast airport, getting a rental car, and heading west, driving across the bare landscape, seeing the yellow gorse and the purple heather against the dark brown of the peat fields, the mountains appearing to her left, the glint of the sea now and again, that sweep of view as the road opened above Glencolmcille. She imagined the drive through the village, the winding road, the narrow stone bridge, the steep climb up the laneway, seeing the house for the first time, walking in to find the living room fire lit, even though it was summer, the kitchen filled with cooking smells, the decorated tree in the hallway, having fun arranging all the presents underneath . . .

"Please, Maggie," Juliet had said again. "Come and celebrate with us. The pudding is perfect this year. I've tried a new recipe."

She'd told Juliet that she was sorry, she'd made up her mind.

She'd had a text message from Clementine within the hour.

Maggie, are you sure about this? Isn't it just what you need at the moment?

Juliet had obviously phoned or texted Eliza as well. Maggie's phone rang ten minutes later. It was a bad line, the echo traveling from Melbourne to New York.

"Maggie, is it true?" Eliza didn't bother with a greeting. "I'm about to travel all that way to see the best niece in the world and she won't be there?"

"The others will be there, Eliza."

"It's not the others I'm coming to see. I saw enough of them when I was growing up. Would you like to talk about it? Do you think you might be overreacting? You had a terrible shock. It might still be manifesting itself."

Angus's voice came to Maggie's mind again. "Those aunts of yours think they control you. Think for yourself for once."

She'd told Eliza there was someone at the door and she needed to go. She had a stomachache for half an hour afterward. The phone rang twice more, and she didn't answer. She knew it would be either Miranda or Eliza again. When she checked the machine an hour later, she was right; both of them saying the same thing, that Christmas in Donegal wouldn't be the same if she wasn't there.

Two days later, she'd just walked back into the apartment when the phone rang. It was Clementine, telling her she'd decided not to join in the family Christmas that year either. Her work commitments were just too heavy, she said. No, of course it had nothing to do with Maggie's decision. She'd just hung up with Clementine when the phone rang again. Eliza, telling her she'd made the same decision.

"How do they always know the right time to ring you?" Angus had asked once. "Do they have you on radar screen or something?"

"All done, Mrs. Claus." The repairman had finished. It had taken him less than a minute.

She paid him the fee and added a generous tip. "Thanks again," she said as she opened the front door.

"You're welcome. Merry Christmas."

She managed a smile, then shut the door. She looked at the parcels, the wrapping paper gaudy in the bright light, the decorations in a bundle on the floor. The mulled wine smelled sickly sweet. So did the cinnamon candle.

"Merry Christmas," she said to the empty room.

CHAPTER 20

Glencolmcille, Donegal, Ireland

Juliet finished making the last of the beds, straightening up with a soft moan, holding the small of her back. Some days her fifty-year-old bones felt like they were a hundred years old.

At least the house was almost ready now. It helped that she hadn't had to heat it from scratch or spend her first day in the garden, mowing the lawns and hacking a path up to the front door through the gorse and the long grass. It had been the right decision to get a local caretaker and start renting the house out to other people when they didn't need it. It wasn't good for a house to stay empty for too long. The soul seeped out of it. The landscape around this part of Donegal was testament to that, with abandoned shells of houses and crumbling drystone walls here and there in the small green fields. Abandoned by families through emigration, death, or, more optimistically, for the comfort and pleasure of a new home.

The Faradays' holiday house had been built in the early 1900s. It was halfway up a steep hill, two kilometers from the village, reached by a short but curving laneway lined by trees that scratched and stabbed at the gray sky in the winter months, and formed a light green tunnel of leaves in the summer. The house was called *Radharc na Mara*—"Sea View," in the Irish language. The words were there in black paint on the whitewashed pillar by the front gate. Juliet had touched up the paint yesterday when she arrived. It was the first thing she did each visit, followed by the cutting back of the fuchsia bushes lining the short path to the front door, creating a dark pink carpet of flowers at her feet as she worked. Fuchsia was the national flower of Ireland, in her opinion, the delicate flowers springing out of all the hedges and stone walls in the area, their bell-like petals fluttering in the breezes.

The original house had been a traditional-style two-story building with four windows—two up, two down—with a heavy wooden front door protected by a porch. A family of eight had first lived there, the Faradays had been told, all of them sharing just three bedrooms and one bathroom. The next owner had added another wing, in the same gray stone, with two more bedrooms and a second bathroom, creating a protected courtyard at the same time. The owner after that had rewired, reroofed, and painted the gray stone white. But the new kitchen, the modern laundry room, the ivy growing over the low stone wall at the front, the tubs of fuchsia and honeysuckle at the entrance and the beds of flowers and heathers all around had been added by the Faradays.

The new windows were theirs, too. When Leo had first inspected the house, the windows had been the originals. Small, shuttered, deep in the stone walls, protection against the wind and rain that buffeted the hills and mountains most days of the year, fresh and fierce, straight off the Atlantic. It was the first thing he had asked the young man showing him the property. Would the structure of the house handle new windows? Not only new glass and frames, but larger, wider windows, double glazing, too, of course. The young man, "scenting a sale, there and then," as Leo had put it, hadn't hesitated. Of course the house could handle it. It would also improve the house comfort-wise ten-thousand-fold, not to mention add considerable value. With great aplomb, he had then given Leo a business card for his brother-in-law, a glazier based in the nearby fishing port of Killybegs.

The work was done before the family had their first holiday there. Juliet now couldn't imagine it any other way. The wide windows were what made the house, opening it up to the view and the light. The four back windows looked onto sweeps of mountainside, green tumbles of gorse, and stonewall-edged squares of field beside scoops of shale and smudges of purple heather, the green and brown of the mountainside dotted with black-faced sheep. The side windows faced the nearby village—a sprinkle of whitewashed houses, a pub or three, a garage, two shops. Across from them was a curving beach, reached by a clamber up a small slope, and then another clamber down some rocks. The Faraday house looked right over to that beach. Juliet lost hours each day sitting in one of the low, comfortable armchairs, staring out, watching the weather, hearing the wind, gazing up at the clouds in the sky in ways she never did at home in Manchester, hadn't done in Sydney, not even in Tasmania when they had lived the life of islanders, surrounded by water and sky. It was wild here. She always had a sense that they—visitors and locals alike—were clinging onto the earth by their fingertips, that a gust of wind could easily come and whip them away, carelessly.

"That, my love, is why I got double glazing," Leo had said the first year they stayed there, when she tried to explain to him how close to nature she felt in Donegal. "Not to mention underfloor heating, wool carpets for the bedrooms, and a six-burner stove so you can keep us well fed."

"No poetry in your soul at all, is there?"

"Not when I'm hungry." He had gone to the stove then, lifting up the lids of the pots, breathing in the fragrant steam from a simmering soup, opening the oven door to inspect the baking apples, currants and sugary syrup bubbling in the dish around them. "Those ten years in that Le Cordon Bleu college we sent you to weren't wasted, were they?"

"I loved every minute of it," she answered distractedly. She had never been within ten miles of a Le Cordon Bleu college. Or even a weekend cooking course. She was a self-taught cook, a self-taught businesswoman, a self-taught wife, sister, daughter . . .

"And thank God for that," Leo said.

She didn't thank God for it. It had nothing to do with God. If she traced it back, it had everything to do with the moment when Leo was told by a colleague about a job in a place on the opposite side of the world in Tasmania. Was that when her fate, not to mention the rest of the family's fate, had been sealed? If they hadn't moved to Tasmania, would their mother still have died so young? If they hadn't decided to stay in Tasmania afterward, would Juliet have learned to cook so well, which had led her to work in the city-center café, which was where she had met Myles, which had gotten her to today, where the two of them ran a company and were in charge of more than forty cafés in Australia and the U.K.? Would Leo have kept up his inventing, producing dozens of useless gadgets until the day everything finally came through with his petrol filtration device and he had more money than he knew what to do with?

Life wasn't an accident. It was a series of dominoes, each event making another happen, which led to another and another. Even this house. The last place any of them would have expected to have a family gathering was in Donegal, the wild, northwest county of Ireland.

Leo had been staying with Juliet and Myles in Manchester six years earlier when he switched on a television program. The sound had been turned low. To this day they still didn't know what the program had been about. The three of them had been attracted to the scenery: wild, bare mountains; green fields running down to the sea; long, empty beaches. It's like Tasmania, Juliet had said. They watched the credits and saw that it had been filmed in Donegal.

She later learned that after leaving them, Leo had flown to the small regional Donegal airport, called into property offices in the town itself, and spoken to several young property salesmen. The day after that he drove around the county with the brightest of them. It only took two conversations with local people to learn which house had once belonged to Tessa's family. Unfortunately he was too late for it. It was a wreck of a building. The house for sale two fields away—sharing the same view—wasn't, however.

Miranda had been on one of her flying visits to Juliet's house when Leo broke the news.

"I have a surprise for us all," Leo announced after dinner, placing a brochure in the center of the table. "I decided it was time we had a holiday house. Somewhere special for our Christmas gatherings. Have a guess where."

Miranda and Juliet glanced at it. A large house surrounded by green fields, with a glimpse of blue sea.

"Byron Bay?" Miranda asked. It looked like coastal Australia to her.

"Somewhere in Victoria?" Juliet suggested. "Near the Great Ocean Road?"

"Wrong country," Leo said, a grin appearing on his face. "I'll put you out of your misery. It's in Donegal."

"Donegal, as in *Ireland,* Donegal?"

"As in Mum's grandmother's Donegal?"

The grin was now a hundred-watt beam. "The very place."

"Well, that's convenient," Miranda said. "We can decide on the spur of the moment to have a getaway weekend, and it will only take us thousands of dollars and two days of travel to get there."

He ignored her. "Your mother grew up just a walk from that very house. Don't you remember her talking about it? There was a beach down the road, and a little stream and a stone bridge where blackberries grew, and they'd pick them and make jam and pies and—"

"Leo, it wouldn't have been like that," Miranda said. "You know what she used to say about her holidays. It rained every summer. There were probably flies."

"She said the wind would always howl, and they had to spend most of the time indoors," Juliet added.

"She loved it there," Leo said firmly. "You'll love it too once you see it."

"He's lost his marbles completely," Miranda hissed to Juliet when they went out into the kitchen together. "More money than good sense. I thought the sports car he bought last year was a worry, but this is ridiculous."

"Let him be. He sold the car, remember? It's something he has

to do, you know that. He gets like this every year around her anniversary."

"So let him fly back to Hobart and put hundreds of dollars'
worth of flowers on her grave. Not buy a house on the spur of the
moment in the wilds of northern Ireland."

"It's Donegal. It's part of the republic."

"Juliet, I don't care if it's in the middle of Beirut. What's he
doing spending our inheritance on some house none of us will
ever visit?"

"Because this house means something to him. He thinks it's important."

"It's all right for you. You live just an hour or two's flight away.
What about me and Clementine and Eliza, on the other side of the
world? It's ridiculous."

"It's not ridiculous." Leo had followed them into the kitchen.
"It's my treat to you all. I can afford to buy it. I can afford the air-
fares to get you all there. Even if it's only once a year, for one of our
Christmas get-togethers. Please, girls. It would mean a lot to me."

And so it happened. Through some miracle of schedules, each
year for the past five years, they had somehow managed to gather
in the Donegal house for one of their Christmas celebrations. Miranda still complained about it every year.

"One year, Juliet, just one year I'd like to say no to him. Just to
see what would happen."

"He's an old man. He's our father. Family's everything to Leo."

"And after he's gone? Then what?"

Juliet never liked to think about that. She moved from the bedrooms to the living room now, filling the vases with flowers she'd
bought in Killybegs that morning. She had just finished arranging
them when her mobile rang. She checked the number and
snatched up the phone.

"Leo!" She'd starting calling him by his first name the year she
turned forty. Her sisters had followed her lead. "At last! Where are
you?"

"Hello, chicken. I'm in Paris, about to board the Chunnel train."

"Paris? What are you doing there? I've left a dozen messages for you in your London hotel."

"I only just got them. I heard about a wonderful museum in the north of France and got talking to the man who runs it. He invited me over and showed me the most marvelous things that never go on public view. We were about ten floors underground, I'm sure of it. Could have stayed there for days. I can't wait to tell you all about them. Now, have you got pen and paper, and I'll fill you in on my travel plans."

"I need to tell you something—"

"Hold on a moment, Juliet, would you? We've got a terrible line. I'm going to try another spot."

She moved over to the window, watching the progress of a thick, creamy wave into the bay as Leo came back on the line and kept talking. He was going to spend a night or two in London, he told her, then fly into Belfast airport and hire a car for the two-hour drive to Glencolmcille. He'd be with her by the end of the week, he said.

"This will be one of our best Christmases, I can feel it in my bones. When do the others arrive? Don't tell me, Maggie's already there, is she?"

"Well, no." Juliet cursed her family yet again, leaving it up to her to break their news. "Leo, she's not coming."

"She's not *what?*"

"Maggie's not coming. She rang on the weekend. She's sending everyone's presents by special delivery, but she said she just can't be here with us this year."

"But she loves these gatherings. Perhaps if we ring her again once we're all there? Maybe it wouldn't be too late for her to—"

"I've got news about the others too."

Leo laughed. "Don't tell me they're not coming either."

"Okay, I won't."

His voice became serious. "Who's not coming?"

"Eliza and Clementine. They both rang yesterday. Miranda's decided to come for only two nights. It'll just be you and me here for the rest of the week. Won't that be nice?"

"Juliet, no offense, but of course it won't be nice. When did this happen? What reasons have they given? It's because of Maggie, isn't it? Because she won't be there."

He was right. It was no coincidence that her sisters had found reasons to change their plans after hearing that Maggie had decided she definitely wouldn't be joining them.

"It just wouldn't be the same without her," Clementine had said from Hobart. "And I'd hate to think of her imagining all of us enjoying ourselves without her. It was going to be a rushed trip for me as it was. I'm going to save up my holidays and have a proper break with her in the new year."

"I've got four new clients," Eliza had said from Melbourne. "It doesn't seem worth traveling all that way just for a few days, especially when Maggie won't be there."

"Maggie's the only thing that makes those gatherings bearable," Miranda had said from Singapore. "If she's not going to be there, I'm not coming for a whole week either. I'll spare you a day, maybe two."

Another year Juliet might have argued with each of them. Pleaded on their father's behalf. The fact was, she felt the same way. It wouldn't be the same without Maggie.

"We have to make Maggie change her mind," Leo said. "It's not too late for the others to come. I was counting on you all being there."

Juliet laughed. "Good luck, Leo. We've spent twenty-six years teaching Maggie to know her own mind and think for herself, and you're going to overturn it with one phone call?"

"But I've got plans. Things I need to talk to you all about." Leo was quite agitated now. "And what if Sadie turns up this year and none of you are there?"

"I'll be here." She fought to keep her temper. Of course she would be there. Dutiful, reliable Juliet. "And you know Sadie won't turn up."

"She might. I sent an invitation to her care of the priests in Hobart. They promised to send it on to her. My credit card details, the address, everything. You haven't heard anything, have you? I put your phone numbers, as well as mine, on the letter."

Juliet rubbed at the mark on the windowpane with added vigor. "Oh yes, now I remember, she rang last week. Did I forget to tell you? You know how things like that slip the mind, the sister we haven't seen for twenty years deciding to drop by for some midyear mulled wine."

"It's not a joking matter, Juliet."

Juliet sighed, searching inside herself for some patience. Leo had been talking about Sadie a great deal recently. "I'm sorry. No, we haven't heard from Sadie either. As far as I know, she won't be surprising us with a visit."

"Sadie and Maggie are alike, in many ways, aren't they? Carrying guilt like this. Cutting themselves off from everyone."

"The two situations are completely different, Leo, and you know it."

"Poor little Maggie."

"Not so little, Leo."

"When will this New York exile of hers end?"

"I don't think there's a time limit. Although Miranda did mention something to me about another friend wanting the apartment next month, so Maggie may need to move out after that."

"Then what? She goes back to London, to her old job, back to that Angus of hers?"

"I don't think Angus is part of it anymore. And she never mentions work. She's living off her savings, I think."

"I might just make a little trip over to see her, after I've caught up with you. Yes, that's exactly what I'll do. I know she told us she wanted to be left alone, but she'll make an exception for me, surely."

"Could you let me know what time you'll be dropping by here, Leo, if it's not too much trouble?"

"Don't be hard on me, Juliet. I'm an old man, reviewing my life, counting down the days to the grave. Humor me. Who's cooking this year, by the way?"

"Who? Let me think . . ."

"What country is it this year?"

"Thailand, as you very well know. You had the deciding vote, re-member?"

"Thailand, of course. I'll call you as soon as I get to Belfast Air-port, I promise. Let you know when I'm on my way."

"That would be great." He was already distracted. She could hear it in his voice. "See you soon, Leo."

She hung up and returned to the kitchen. Even if she'd wanted to, it was hard to stay cross with Leo for long. How could she not ad-mire a seventy-eight-year-old father who'd taken up gallivanting as his primary hobby? Myles wouldn't have agreed, of course. They'd had this fight many times over the years. "Yes, he's a charmer, but he also manipulates you all. You know that, don't you? Never lets you forget how much he's done for you."

"How can you say that? You know how generous he is with his money, with everything. We couldn't have expanded half as quickly as we have if it wasn't for Leo's money."

"Leo's money, that came with far more conditions than any hard-nosed bank manager would have attached. 'Thou shalt all gather each year for at least one Christmas celebration, whether you like it or not—' "

"We do like it."

" 'Thou shalt keep a spare room in thine house for Leo to drop in whenever it suits him.' "

"Of course I'm not going to turn my own father away if he wants to come and stay. He's an old man, Myles."

"He's an old man who is used to getting his own way. The five of you—the four of you—have been dancing to his tune for as long as I've known you."

Juliet had been furious with him. Because, perhaps, he was just the tiniest bit right. But how dare he? It was all right for him; both his parents living the life of Riley in retirement in Spain. Family was important to Juliet. More important than anything. It always had been.

It was time to get back to work. Block those negative thoughts out. A saying from the old days in the Hobart café all those years

ago came to mind: "Make the best of what you have." It amazed her
sometimes how consoling those clichés actually were. She was sure
there had been one about busy hands making a light heart. Even if
there were just three members of the family here this year, there
was still lots of work to be done.

She'd already unpacked some of their supplies into the large
freezer, but half of the wooden shelves and the big table in the center of the room were still covered with boxes and paper bags. The
small shop in the village had the essentials, but she couldn't expect
them to have the sorts of ingredients she needed this year—
coconut milk, coriander, and lemongrass, for starters. Last July
they'd had a Spanish Christmas. The year before it had been German. Or had it been Austrian? She remembered lots of sauerkraut
and Wiener schnitzels. And Leo singing a passionate version of "O
Tannenbaum."

She only had herself to blame. The multicultural July Christmases had been her idea. She'd decided on it twelve years before,
when the Hobart family home was still their gathering place for the
two Christmas celebrations each year, one in July, one in December. The July menu hadn't changed in years: roast turkey; crispy,
golden-brown potatoes; four different vegetables—freshly shelled
peas, brussels sprouts, parsnips and carrots—roasted to crunchy
tips the way they all liked them. Bread sauce and a homemade
gravy. For dessert, a traditional plum pudding made two months
previously from directions in their mother's handwritten recipe
book. Juliet would keep the bowl on the darkest, coolest shelf of
the pantry, as her mother had done, each week tipping a little more
brandy into the bowl, taking a moment to breathe in the rich, cur-
ranty fumes. She'd make a fruitcake and her own thick, white
icing. She'd have Maggie beside her nearly every step of the way, a
mini chef's apprentice, watching solemnly as she made the pastry,
helping her measure out the sultanas and mixed fruit peel for the
mince pies, letting her take charge of sifting the powdered sugar
on top of each golden pastry lid, arranging them onto serving
dishes, finishing each display with a little sprig of artificial holly.

It was as she and Maggie started to ice the mince pies that year that she'd been overcome with a feeling of absolute boredom. How many had she iced over the years? She made an average of thirty of the little pies each year. That had been their twenty-fourth July Christmas.

She'd turned to her niece. "Maggie, what's thirty multiplied by twenty-four?"

"Seven hundred and twenty," a then fourteen-year-old Maggie said without hesitation.

More than seven hundred mince pies. Two dozen cakes. Two dozen puddings and turkeys, hundreds of brussels sprouts . . . It was time for something new. Before she had time to change her mind, she'd gone out to the shed and spoken to Leo.

"Will you cast us all out if I change the Christmas menu a little?"

"Of course not. As long as we eat together and I get to laugh at you all in silly hats, I'm happy."

"So I don't have to cook a turkey tomorrow?"

"Not if you don't want to. It's about being together, not what we eat."

She'd called in the others. "You won't complain if there is no turkey on the table?"

"I won't. And I bet the turkey won't either," Miranda said.

Eliza had taken some convincing. "I thought the whole point of the July Christmas was to have turkey in wintertime rather than summertime."

"Mum never specified the menu," Juliet explained. "It was the idea of it she loved."

It hadn't felt like she was being dishonorable to her mother's memory, not even for a minute. It had been a feeling of change, of moving on, even if just in a small way. A strange relief. The turkey—already bought, alas, so the change in menu was no last-minute reprieve for it—went into the freezer. The vegetables were chopped into tiny pieces and made into soup, which she would freeze as well. The plum pudding would keep for another month or two; another year or two even, considering the amount of brandy it was steeped in. She'd shut her eyes tight and thought of the most delicious meal she'd had recently. She got an immediate sensual memory of a wonderful three-course meal she and Myles had enjoyed six weeks earlier in Leichhardt, Sydney's Little Italy. Perfect. They'd have an Italian July Christmas. Antipasto to begin, pasta for second course, meat for third course, rich creamy tiramisu for dessert. A long, leisurely Italian meal, just like all the ads for pasta sauce on the television.

She got organized quickly. She was almost too late. The supermarket was closing when she drove up. Almost defeated, she remembered the deli in West Hobart that stayed open late, no matter what day it was. She went in with intentions of buying everything she needed for an Italian-flavored feast, and then got talking to Freddie, the Indian man behind the counter. Half an hour later she left, carrying three crammed bags of fresh vegetables, spices, meat, and two handwritten pages of recipes.

The next day the Faradays sang Christmas carols and pulled their crackers over a feast of samosas, chicken tikka, naan, chutneys, cucumber raita, and saffron rice. The next year they went French (caramelized onion soup, slow-cooked chicken, tarte Tatin), the following year Spanish (spicy prawns with parsley, oven-baked fish with cumin), after that Vietnamese, Moroccan, Irish, German, and, at last, Italian. They were slowly working their way around the world, each of them taking turns to pick a country. Each of them except Sadie, of course.

It still amazed Juliet that they'd been able to continue with the traditions without Sadie being there. It was Maggie who had insisted. Proof again that they'd been right to make light of what had happened to her that summer, to turn the whole thing into an adventure. She had started talking about the July Christmas the day after she came back home, as though things were perfectly normal. She hadn't even seemed bothered that Clementine barely let her out of her sight, that all of them kept touching her, hugging her, saying how much they'd missed her.

It was Miranda who made up the story to explain Sadie's sudden disappearance. It was two weeks after they had gotten Maggie back. Their neighbor Mrs. Freyn had stopped Miranda on her way into town. She'd noticed everyone was home for the weekend again.

"I haven't seen that Sadie for a while," Mrs. Freyn had said. "Clementine's been taking her daughter to school every day lately, I've noticed."

Miranda said she didn't know where the idea came from. It had simply popped into her head. "Actually, Mrs. Freyn, she's made a big life decision. She's decided to drop out. Join the counterculture. Take up an alternative lifestyle."

Mrs. Freyn had just stared at her.

"She's become a hippie," Miranda had said helpfully.

"You should have seen her hurry to get away from me and pass on the news," Miranda told them when she'd gotten home.

Clementine stayed stony faced, as she always did back then when Sadie was mentioned. Eliza thought Miranda had gone too far. Leo hadn't been at all amused.

"Well, what should I have said?" Miranda had said defiantly. "The truth? She kidnapped Maggie, so we've banished her from the family for the foreseeable future?"

"Of course we can't tell people that," Eliza had said. "Imagine the talk around town."

"Miranda's right, Dad. We have to tell people something," Juliet said. "But for God's sake, Miranda, why say she's become a hippie? Of all things. The closest Sadie has ever gotten to being a hippie was that mohair sweater she bought at the market."

"You really have gone too far this time, Miranda." Leo had run his fingers through his hair. Another time they might have laughed at all the tufts standing up.

Miranda crossed her arms. "So, you come up with a better story."

"Clementine, can I have a word?" Leo had asked.

The two of them had been gone for nearly ten minutes. When they'd emerged from the kitchen, it was obvious from their expressions that there was no change in the situation. Clementine's jaw had been set. Leo's hair had been standing on so many ends, it looked like he'd been electrocuted.

"Perhaps you're right," he'd said. "Perhaps this is the best option we have."

It was sealed the next day when Maggie came home from school. One of her classmates had asked where Sadie was. They were used to her collecting Maggie after school.

"Is Sadie coming back soon, Juliet?"

"Not for a little while, Maggie."

"Why not? I miss her."

Juliet shot a glance at Clementine. "Ask your mum, Maggie."

"She's decided she wants to live a different sort of life," Clementine had said. "Away from us for a while."

"But will she be back at Christmas?"

"I don't think so."

"But when will I see her again?"

"One day. Just not yet."

"Then can I write to her?"

"No. I don't think she wants us to."

Maggie had become upset. "But she'd want me to write to her. I know she would."

Leo had come in and overheard. "Of course you can write to her. What a great idea. You go and get your pencils, and we'll write her a letter now."

Clementine had barely waited for her to leave the room. "I don't want Maggie writing to her, Dad."

"If Maggie wants to write to her, Clementine, Maggie can write to her."

"How can she?" Juliet said to Leo after Clementine left the room. "We haven't a clue where she is. She made it clear to you she doesn't ever want us to know where she is."

Leo had come up with a tangled solution to use a friend's address as a halfway house. It would be easy enough to do. One of them would post Maggie's letter to Leo's friend, enclosing a brief reply to it, hoping Maggie wasn't old enough to know it wasn't Sadie's handwriting. A week or so later the letter would arrive back.

Before they'd had a chance to put that plan into action, though, out of the blue they heard from Sadie. A card arrived, delivered by Father Cavalli. He turned up at the house one day, asking to see Leo.

Leo filled them all in later. Sadie had rung Father Cavalli. She'd asked him to be a go-between.

"She wants to stay in touch?"

"Not with us. With Maggie."

"No, Dad."

"Clementine, she wants to be able to write to Maggie. And Maggie wants to write to her. I want this to happen too. I want to know she's all right."

"I don't want her anywhere near Maggie, ever again. She's lucky I didn't press charges."

"Clem, we don't know why she did it, but try and understand—"

"There's nothing to understand. She kidnapped my daughter."

"She didn't see it like that."

Clementine had stood up. "There's no other way to see it. You think I could ever trust her near Maggie again?"

"It's just a letter, Clementine," Juliet said. "And it's important to Dad. He needs to know she's all right."

Clementine hadn't been happy about it, but she finally agreed. Leo rang Father Cavalli. The first letter came a week later, sent via the priest's address, delivered to the Faraday house by the priest himself. It was an ordinary sixth birthday card, with a drawing of six mice in fairy costumes on the front. The note inside was short, just five lines: "Dear Maggie, A very happy birthday to you! I hope you had a great party. I am having fun too. Lots of love, Sadie xxx."

Maggie was delighted with it. She put it with all the others on the mantelpiece. Clementine didn't read it. Leo, Juliet, Miranda, and Eliza all did, trying to glean more information from the envelope, from the card itself. There was none to be had. No postmark, no address.

It was Leo who put the card away safely after Maggie's birthday had passed. It was also Leo who helped Maggie write a reply, and dropped it back up to Father Cavalli, to send on to whatever address Sadie had given him. "Dear Sadie, Thank you for the card," Maggie wrote. "I had a great birthday. I miss you. Hope to see you soon, love Maggie xxxxxx."

The cards arrived from Sadie each year. Even after Father Cavalli retired, his successor kept delivering them, and also sending on Maggie's reply. Leo enclosed a letter each time, passing on messages from Juliet, Miranda, and Eliza. Each year Juliet knew Leo hoped Sadie's card would acknowledge their letters, contain more news about her life, or say she was coming for a visit. They never did.

Juliet found it hard, especially as the years passed and the awfulness of that time when Maggie was missing faded. What remained was a gap in the family, an empty space at every mealtime, at every Christmas celebration. Juliet read once about an amputee describing his missing limb, how sometimes he woke up and imagined it was still there, that if he were to look down he would see his leg. Sadie's absence felt like that. That all of this had been a silly joke and she would walk into the house at any moment, as if nothing had happened.

Juliet had never told her sisters or Leo, but she had tried to find Sadie many times. At first, she'd called hospitals, worried that Sadie had had a nervous breakdown, that something had happened to make her take Maggie in the first place. The stress of university exams sparking it, perhaps, until they discovered to their additional shock she hadn't done a university exam for years. Juliet had rung directory inquiries for every state in Australia. She'd tried the electoral roll in every state as well. Nothing. In recent years she'd regularly done Internet searches. Still nothing. It was as if Sadie had disappeared off the face of the earth. Except for the annual cards and the fact that twice a year, at both of their Christmas celebrations, they would lift their glasses and let Maggie propose a toast to Sadie. "To Sadie," they'd all echo.

One more tradition added to the already overflowing Faraday family vault.

· · ·

The sun was streaming through the front windows by the time everything was unpacked into the fridge, freezer, and cupboards. Juliet went outside into the yard, enjoying the sound of the gravel crunching under her feet, the feel of the sunshine on her face, the light breeze. She'd better enjoy it; the weather in Donegal was contrary at the best of times.

She leaned against the stone wall, idly picking at the moss growing in the cracks, wondering as she often did whether her mother had ever stood by the wall at that old house up the road, doing this same thing. She wondered what Tessa would think about her July Christmas idea still being celebrated, all these years later.

Juliet herself had tried to call a halt to the Donegal gatherings three years ago. That awful year, when she and Myles had been doing nothing but fighting. She'd had no energy for family. She'd phoned Leo to tell him, and also to ask him to let the others know. There had been an uproar, loudest of all from Miranda, of all people.

"What do you mean you're calling it off? You can't. It's our Christmas, not just yours."

"Then you organize it."

"But you're the cook. You do it so well. It would kill Leo. And you know how much Maggie loves it. She'll have bought all the presents already. Juliet, how can you be so selfish?"

That was rich, coming from Miranda, the queen of selfishness. The woman who had never done anything in her life if it didn't suit her plans. Juliet had been very angry about it. If Myles still had the patience to hear her talk about her family, he would have said, "It's water under the bridge, Juliet. Let bygones be bygones." But she couldn't. She could let a skin grow over it, she could try to get on with her life, but these fights and disagreements felt like little tumors, still inside her, festering away.

She'd gone ahead with the July Christmas that year, of course. Flown to Ireland the week before as usual, spent the whole time cooking, and of course Miranda had breezed in, spent most of the weekend on the phone catching up with old friends in Ireland and the U.K., then breezed out again. Juliet had barely had a conversation with her.

When she brought it up with Leo, she got even more frustrated with his response.

"That's just what Miranda is like, Juliet, you know that. A flibbertigibbet."

"Why do we let her get away with it? Year after year after year?"

"Because we just do."

"What if I started behaving like that? Forgot to do the shopping? Decided I felt like sleeping in rather than cooking?"

"But you wouldn't, Juliet, that's the difference. We've always been able to rely on you."

"How do you manage it, Juliet?" Miranda had drawled the previous year. "So effortlessly, too."

Effortlessly? she had nearly shouted back at her. There was nothing bloody effortless about this. It was nothing but effort. But Miranda had moved away to unpack, or phone one of her endless bloody male admirers who filled her perfect bloody life . . .

Her phone beeped to alert her to a text message.

Myles. He was in Glasgow on a business trip.

ALL OK?

"Fine," she texted back. No point telling him the truth. He had long ago tired of her family dramas.

Juliet returned inside, made herself a cup of tea, and carried it into the living room. She didn't sit down, preferring to stand in front of the window, staring out at the water and the sky. The weather had changed dramatically even in the last ten minutes, the blue now covered in a gray haze of mist. She'd seen violent rainstorms in the middle of July here, and had spent unexpectedly warm days on the beach in October. She had a longing to stay on beyond Leo and Miranda's visit this time. Perhaps she would. The business didn't need her anymore. It hardly needed Myles either. It practically ran itself these days. She checked all the weekly reports, of course, attended meetings with their bright-eyed area managers, studied the figures, queried some decisions, but if she and Myles had wanted to—financially, at least—they could have retired several years earlier. They had more money than they knew what to do with. And it wasn't as if they needed to keep any tucked away for their children's education, or to set them up in business, or to give them a lovely nest egg to buy their first home.

The truth was, of course, that money only protected you from things you expected. You could build a big house against cold weather, buy plenty of food to stop yourself from getting hungry, prepare detailed plans for your business. But what good had money been to any of them when the truly sad, unexpected things started happening to the Faradays over the years? The terrible time with Sadie, twenty years ago. Eliza's accident. The awful events Maggie had been through this year. All that had happened between herself and Myles, too. No protection at all. The rooms upstairs that would remain empty this week were testament to that.

Juliet forced herself away from the window and from that train of thought. The worst was over, surely. All right, this July Christmas would be hard without Maggie, but they had to respect her choice. As they'd had to respect Sadie's choice to leave the family all those years ago.

Respect. Understand. Forgive. Were they one and the same thing? She still didn't know the answer. She didn't know if she ever would. Not for the first time, she decided to bury her thoughts under a pile of food and housework. She turned away from the view and walked back to the kitchen.

CHAPTER 21

On runway five, gate thirty-three of Singapore's Changi Airport, Miranda Faraday was buckling herself into her business-class seat and looking with pleasure around the small upstairs cabin. Twelve hours to Heathrow, a quick jaunt across to Athens, a delicious week in an island villa before she flew over to Ireland and God-only-knew what kind of weather. Why hadn't their mother been born in Tuscany to olive-growing, wine-making Italian parents? She loved Donegal, and she loved staying in Sea View—or Cloud View, as she called it to annoy Juliet—but only in small doses.

She would enjoy the journey. She always did. Read a bit, watch one film, doze. She had removed all her makeup and applied the rich moisturizer to her lips, the special light cream to her eyelids, the super-strength cream to her face. She was wearing a soft tracksuit and pure cotton socks. A bottle of distilled water was in easy reach. The pretakeoff champagne was the only alcohol she ever drank on a flight. She also knew to eat only one of the meals on offer. There definitely was such a thing as jet lag, but it was easy enough to repel if you had enough self-discipline. And that, as she proudly liked to tell her students, was practically her middle name. There didn't have to be a use-by date for flight attendants. Keep yourself trim, well-groomed, and fit, and you could fly for years.

That had been her intention, at least. Now she had the best of both worlds—six months of the year spent training new attendants in the airline's training center in Singapore, two months off, the remaining months spent in charge of first- and business-class cabins on the best flights between Singapore and the Gulf States. Varied, interesting, and wonderful for her social life. She had met her past three paramours (she had never liked the term "boyfriend," and "partners" signified something much more long-term than she had ever managed) on those flights. "Lovers" would have done equally well as a term, she supposed, but she liked all that "paramour" suggested: expensive gifts, romantic dinners, sad but swift endings . . .

She took a sip of the champagne, staring out of the window, idly taking in the view of the runways bathed in the hazy, orange tropical light she loved.

"Madam? More champagne?"

"Why, thank you, young man. I don't mind if I do."

"It's all right for some," he whispered as he topped up her glass and placed a crisp copy of that day's *International Herald Tribune* on her tray table.

"Play your cards right with me and one day all this will be yours," she whispered back. The young man serving her had been one of her earliest students and knew her habits well—champagne and newspapers were the start. "Full capacity today?"

"Ninety percent." He lowered his voice some more. "There's a spare seat in first class. I can move you across if—"

"I'm fine here."

"Are you mad? There's a vacancy in economy too, if you're that relaxed about where you are."

She laughed. "Darling, I haven't turned right when I got on the plane in twenty years, and I'm not about to start now."

She shut her eyes then. Glen didn't need his training to tell him that meant the end of the conversation. He turned to greet another passenger with his best white-toothed smile.

She felt someone approach her seat and half opened an eye to take a look. A businessman, unsurprisingly. About her age, late forties, perhaps a bit older. A quick glance. No wedding ring, although that didn't mean anything these days. His suit was well cut. He carefully removed his jacket. The steward was there in an instant, offering to hang it up. A gracious thank you. A good sign. He was a man of manners and intelligence. Miranda herself had been at the receiving end of too many patronizing thank yous, or no thank you at all, not to mention imperious orders, sleazy pickup lines, or blatant groping.

If there was ever a job with an image problem, it was that of a flight attendant. Glorified waitresses, trolley dollies, sex-mad men and women—she'd experienced all the prejudices over the years. If they only knew what went on behind her perfect makeup and wide smile. It was akin to being a psychiatrist sometimes, she thought. She could judge a person's personality in moments. As the flight lengthened she'd watch all the protective layers fall away. The brusque arrogant businessman who'd fall asleep after one too many brandies and let his guard slip, mouth slack, head lolling, showing his true self. The businesswoman who spent the first three hours of the flight engrossed in paperwork and spreadsheets later found sleeping with a small cuddly toy slipped out of a designer handbag. It was also surprising how many men on flights slept with their hands tucked inside their trousers. A comfort thing, she gathered. Off-putting, though, to say the least.

The flight attendants on each plane were as varied. Some had joined the airline straight from university. Some were models, actors, performers. Some just wanted to travel and get paid for it. Others, like Miranda, just wanted to escape.

The social life was what made the job. Miranda had been enjoying herself for years. Planes were like dating clubs in the sky. She had read once that Marilyn Monroe was able to turn her sex appeal on and off at will. Miranda had discovered she could do the same. Some flights she was the consummate flight attendant: professional. But if she was in the mood, if she had a two-day stopover ahead of her or was in need of some attention, it was like flicking a switch on inside of her. As she greeted passengers at the doorway, she would make special eye contact, a flirty remark, linger that little bit longer over a passenger's boarding pass. Only business-class or first-class passengers, of course. Phone numbers exchanged at the end of the flight, or sometimes even at the beginning. Sometimes more than two or three phone numbers were exchanged. She had never joined the Mile High Club, though; a woman had to have some standards.

The wages were good, but she realized early on they weren't good enough for her to be able to afford the jewelry she aspired to wear, the clothes she liked. So it was a charming thing to discover that rich businessmen often liked to give pretty flight attendants expensive gifts in exchange for their good company, and sometimes more than their good company. Rich men also often had houses around the world, and were more than happy to make them available to friends. Rich men away from home also liked to have a beautiful, witty, well-groomed woman join them for dinner, for a night at the theater, a day at the races—the Hong Kong Derby was Miranda's personal favorite. It had been fun when it first began all those years ago, and it was fun now. No strings attached.

Her sisters were appalled, of course. She'd given them enough information to whet their appetites, and then turned the conversational tables. "What they didn't know wouldn't hurt them" had always been her motto. She felt so much older and worldlier than them all. But she always had, hadn't she? Juliet might be older in years, but there had always been something innocent about her. Eliza and she had never really had much in common. Miranda found her far too humorless, when it came down to it. Judgmental, too. Clementine was different, of course—as driven as Eliza, but Miranda had always had a soft spot for her littlest sister. And Sadie? What could she say about Sadie? If all of that business hadn't happened, if Sadie hadn't pulled that ridiculous stunt with Maggie and walked out on them all, if she'd stayed in Hobart as Miranda had expected her to—would she have still found her as annoying?

She thought about Sadie often. She knew all her sisters did. She looked out for her on planes, in airports, in the different cities she traveled to. She tried to imagine what she'd look like these days. The idea of her being a hippie had become so entrenched, Miranda often pictured her sister in baggy rainbow trousers, braless in a T-shirt—images she knew herself were long out-of-date.

She'd never told her father or her sisters, but she went looking for Sadie once, when she found herself at a weekend house party in Byron Bay, not far from where Leo and Clementine had discovered her and Maggie that time. If Sadie truly had become a hippie, she couldn't have chosen a more beautiful place. It was all sky and sea and green hills, the light changing from hour to hour, the atmosphere relaxed, the shops on the main street dedicated to crystals, whole foods, chakras, and chanting. Miranda couldn't get out of the place fast enough. Not before making a few casual inquiries, though. She asked at four of the shops, in two of the pubs, in one of the caravan parks. No one had heard of a Sadie Faraday. Two people did ask her if she wanted a massage, though.

Miranda had been glad when the cards started arriving each year from Sadie. The unspoken thought in the family was that she'd done something drastic. Really gone off the deep end. Taken to drink or drugs, or fallen into some black pit of despair. The annual cards didn't point to that, though. Brief as they were, Sadie's tone to Maggie was always cheerful. "Things are going great with me," she often wrote. She never mentioned Leo or any of her sisters in her cards. It was as if she had wiped them from her life.

"Excuse me, but may I take a look at your newspaper?" It was the gentleman beside her.

She turned. "Of course you can. Help yourself," she said in what she liked to think of as her sexy voice, pitched just that bit lower than usual. She watched his smile widen. Honestly, all men were the same. She'd lost count of the times she'd been asked about her newspaper—the best onboard conversation starter, it seemed. This was a twelve-hour flight. No point in engaging in too much conversation with him yet, though. She'd read instead.

She picked up her book from the seat pocket in front of her. Maggie's latest card was tucked inside as a bookmark. She thought of the last time she'd seen her niece, three months earlier. She'd been in France on holiday when she got the distraught phone call on her mobile, Maggie in such floods of tears it had taken Miranda some time to understand what she was saying. She'd almost made a joke about it: "Let me get this straight, Maggie. A man at work put a gun to his head, and then you came home to find Angus and your best friend at it on his office floor. You're sure you're not channeling *Days of Our Lives*?"

Maggie had been serious. Miranda rapidly realized that. After assuring Maggie she'd be there as soon as she could, she called her sisters. She couldn't get in touch with any of them. Miranda tried to get to London from Paris that night. Unfortunately there was bad fog. It wasn't until late the next morning that she was able to get a flight. She caught a cab directly from Heathrow to the hotel Maggie had run to.

Maggie was waiting inside her room, her hair standing on end, her shirt and skirt crumpled. Her suitcase was beside the bed, unopened. She'd obviously slept in her clothes. Miranda pulled her straight into a long hug. Maggie began to talk, not needing any prompting. The whole story spilled out of her.

She was still in a state of shock, Miranda realized. She suggested they leave the hotel, go back to Maggie's house. It would do her good to be surrounded by familiar things. Maggie said she couldn't. It was all over between her and Angus.

Miranda moved across to hug her niece, but Maggie recovered, sitting up, wiping her eyes. "I've decided to resign. I can't go back there. I can't be in that place every day."

"Maggie, slow down, please. You've had a big shock. You have to give yourself time."

Maggie got off the couch. Only five foot three and slight in figure, pale-skinned, and dark-eyed, she reminded Miranda of Clementine as a teenager. "I don't need any time. My boss at work told me to take a couple of days off, Miranda. See the counselor he hired. As if that was enough. As if everything goes back to normal after that. But it can't go back to normal, can it? I'm not that same person."

"Maggie, you are."

"I'm not. It's as if I let everything sweep me along before now. I didn't stop to think about anything. I can change things, though. I can decide to get off the roundabout, can't I?"

"But what will you do? Stay in London? Look for another job?"

Maggie rubbed the end of her nose. "I don't know yet. I need to think everything through. I can't fix what happened, but I can do whatever I can for that man's family. I have to try and make amends. I've got savings. They'll need it more than I will."

"Maggie, you're moving too fast. Think things through some more."

"I don't need to. It all couldn't be clearer. Do you know what my boss said the man was? Collateral damage. 'Put him out of your mind, Maggie. You've got a great job. We're grooming you for even bigger things.' " She broke down again. Miranda held her close.

"It's all right, Maggie," Miranda said, smoothing the dark hair away from her niece's face. "Don't worry about him or about Angus or about anything. None of that matters at the moment."

"It does matter." Maggie sat upright. It was as if she'd just had a series of revelations. Out it poured. She'd been having doubts about Angus for months. She'd been seduced by the side of life he'd shown her, she confessed. Tickets to Covent Garden, to West End plays. It had been like playing dress-up. It had been fun. Until she realized that all the things that mattered to him didn't matter to her.

"He was the one who wanted to live in that expensive area, who insisted we had to have this brand-name furniture and wear only designer clothes, and I went along with it. How can I have been so weak?"

"You're not weak. The last word I would ever use to describe you is weak."

"But I have been, Miranda. I'm twenty-six. I should have had more sense. What was I doing going out with someone like him?"

Miranda bit her tongue. She'd thought exactly those things the first time she had met Angus, but had decided to say nothing. She had been so pleased that Maggie was finally going out with someone. Her long-term single status had been a source of much discussion between her mother and aunts. She'd hoped Angus would grow on her. In fact, he had become more annoying each time they met. He didn't like her either, Miranda knew. She'd been pleased with that fact.

Miranda tried again to advise caution, to take things slowly. As she reported to Clementine in one of their many phone calls, she might have been trying to stop a landslide with a broom. "When that daughter of yours makes her mind up, there's no stopping her, is there?"

By the time Miranda and Maggie met for lunch the next day, Maggie had handed in her notice. She'd also written a large check and arranged to have it sent anonymously to the man's family.

Miranda herself had come up with a solution to Maggie's living arrangements. Racking her brains, trying to decide on a good bolt-hole for her niece, she remembered her friend Ramona's apartment in New York. She and Ramona had flown together for years, until Ramona finally married the American businessman she'd been having an affair with for nearly a decade. The Greenwich Village apartment was the smallest of nearly a dozen investment properties the pair owned in Manhattan. Ramona rarely rented it, offering it instead to close friends for their personal use. Miranda herself had stayed in it many times. Fully furnished, secure, and private, it would be perfect. It had taken only two phone calls to determine it was available and that Maggie could have the use of it for at least three months, possibly longer. Maggie accepted the offer immediately.

Miranda left London the next day to fly back to Singapore for a new training intake. Maggie flew out to New York three days later. It had all happened with speed and ease.

"As if it was meant to be," Juliet had said in some wonder when Miranda filled her in.

"No, it's not," Miranda had said. "It's about knowing the right people."

In Miranda's opinion, and she knew her sisters agreed, the one good thing to have come out of the whole tragic episode was Maggie's breakup with Angus. None of them had ever liked him, from the moment they first met him in Donegal two years earlier. One look at Maggie's well-dressed, good-looking boyfriend and Miranda had thought of five words: "spoiled," "opinionated," "arrogant," "ambitious," and "stupid." Maggie had appeared blind to all five qualities. Her first serious relationship, it was no wonder.

Angus only stayed in Donegal for two days. By the time he left, Miranda's face hurt from smiling so falsely. It hurt as much to lie to Maggie when Maggie asked her within minutes of him leaving whether she liked him.

"He seems to treat you very well and that's all that matters." Miranda winced inside at her own priggish tone. She waited until Maggie had gone inside before she turned to Juliet. "I'm lying. I don't like him one bit. He's using her."

"I don't like him either, but it's her choice who she goes out with."

Miranda canvassed everyone else's opinion. "Do you like him, Leo?"

"I only talked to him for a moment. He certainly has a keen business mind."

"Eliza, did you like Angus?"

"If he's good to her, I'll like him."

"She can't marry him, though," Miranda said.

"Why not?" Eliza asked.

"I came across this last night." Miranda produced a scrapbook with *Flotsam and Jetsam* written in her own writing on the cover. She hadn't come across it. She'd gone looking for it. She knew Juliet had shipped all the recipe books and scrapbooks from Hobart to the holiday house. It was the only time they all got the chance to look at them. "See, on page fifteen. She can't get married unless she gets permission from all of us. And she's not getting my permission."

"That would really hold up in court."

"What would?" Maggie had come back into the living room after seeing Angus off.

"That little document we made you sign eight years ago. You do know you can't marry him unless you get permission from us all?"

Maggie laughed. She'd forgotten all about that, she said. She leafed through it before finding the page Miranda mentioned. They had drawn it up one winter's evening, when everyone happened to be home in Hobart. There had been a lot of teasing that Maggie was growing up too quickly, getting out of their control.

There'd also been a lot of red wine drunk. Miranda, or perhaps it had been Eliza, said it was time they laid down some ground rules. She asked Maggie to fetch one of the scrapbooks, opened it to a blank page, and scribbled down ten points. In a flash of wine-fueled wordplay, she dubbed them "The Ten Comm-aunt-ments."

This document constitutes a formal agreement that Maggie Tessa Faraday must hereby and henceforth obey her all-seeing, all-knowing aunts (and, okay, mother) and undertake the following commandments to the best of her ability for the rest of her life:

1. Floss her teeth daily.
2. Eat her greens.
3. Exercise.
4. Read a lot.
5. Sleep in occasionally.
6. Smoke only for appearances not out of habit.
7. Help old people across the road whenever possible.

The last three were more serious.

8. Work in a field she enjoys, for love not money, although if the money's good, that's a bonus.
9. Always be prepared to drop anything and rush home if any of her family calls.
10. Only marry for love and with the express preapproval of her mother and aunts.

All four of them had signed their names underneath. Juliet, Miranda, Eliza, and Clementine.

"I'll sign for Sadie. I'm sure she'd agree," Maggie had said.

It had been a fun night, Miranda remembered. Even Leo joined in. They'd all had bad hangovers the next day.

She wished again that Maggie was joining them in Donegal this year. It truly wouldn't be the same without her.

A low snore sounded beside her. Her neighbor, the businessman, was sleeping. He was quite handsome, now that she looked closely at him. Perhaps she would have a little chat with him later on . . .

She decided it was time to stretch her legs. She walked forward into first class and moved elegantly down the center aisle. She was turning when she saw the man seated in 2A. All the details registered in an instant—the stocky figure, the still-dark hair, the tanned face. Twenty-six years had passed, but she knew him straightaway. Her heart began to beat faster.

She moved silently up the aisle past his seat again, glad of the dim lights, sure her reaction would be obvious on her face. She'd been expecting this moment ever since she'd started flying. He was a businessman, after all. He surely flew all the time. Once she thought she'd seen him in Sydney Airport. She'd felt a quickening of her pulse that time too, but then the man turned and she realized it wasn't him.

She took another look, willing him not to glance up from his newspaper, to give her the opportunity to study him closely. Was it him? She was uncertain now. A quick word with the steward in charge of the first-class cabin and the passenger list was handed over. Her pulse slowed again. She was mistaken. The gentleman in 2A was a Mr. Richard Foster, not Mr. Tom Hanlon.

She returned downstairs to her own seat. How ridiculous that her legs were shaking, after all this time. She hated the fact she kept doing this to herself. For all she knew, he was long dead. Or as good as dead, stuck in some dull, suburban life in Sydney, in the same house he had lived in all those years ago, with the same wife, the same job selling cheap cosmetics to bored pharmacy assistants . . .

But if that man upstairs in first class had been Tom Hanlon, what would she have done? What would she have said to him? Shouted at him, even? He probably had no idea of the legacy he'd left her.

Miranda remembered sitting across the desk from her doctor, in the bright surgery office on St. Kilda Road. It was the day after her thirty-fifth birthday. She'd been having problems with her periods. At first she thought it was because of all the flying that she did. Her doctor thought it might be early menopause. He ran tests. Then more tests. He arranged for her to have scans. He'd finally called her in to tell her the news. She had bad scarring and blockages in both fallopian tubes.

"How could that have happened? I hardly even know where my fallopian tubes are."

He explained. He used terms she remembered from booklets in the pharmacy. She'd never cared about them back then. Pelvic inflammatory disease, most likely caused by an undetected and untreated chlamydia infection.

She tried to joke about it. "Chlamydia? What is that, a Greek Island or a disease?"

"A bacterial infection. A serious infection, I'm afraid. You catch it by having unprotected sex."

"But I've never had unprotected sex."

"Are you sure? It's the only way it is transmitted."

She remembered then. Yes, she had had unprotected sex. Once. That night with Tom, in the Hobart waterfront hotel . . .

Miranda felt the color rise in her cheeks. "There was one time—"

The doctor didn't ask for more details. "It only takes the once, unfortunately."

She needed to deal with this quickly, move on, put it behind her, and then forget all about it. "So what do I take? Tablets? Medicine?"

She sat in disbelief as the doctor explained the effects of pelvic inflammatory disease were irreversible. Not only that. She stared as he explained the legacy of the disease. "But how can I be infertile? I haven't even tried to have children."

"It may be possible. We make medical advances all the time. IVF might be an option. But that's the heartbreak of this disease. By the time you find out you have it, it's too late to do anything about it."

One night in a hotel room and her life had changed.

She didn't tell anyone. Three weeks after the doctor's appointment, she broke up with Benedict, her boyfriend at the time. They had always used condoms, so she could at least be certain she hadn't passed it on to him. It was scant consolation. She never told him the truth about why she ended it. He worked in the industry too, and the last thing she wanted was word to go around.

She'd had to break up with him. She decided she could cope with this news, but she wasn't going to drag Benedict down with her. A year after she finished it between them, she heard that Benedict was getting married. A year later she heard that he and his wife were expecting twins. They now had three children, she thought. Possibly even four. He'd left the travel industry now.

That could have been her with Benedict and a family. If it hadn't been for that night, if it hadn't been for Tom Hanlon . . . She'd had plenty of nights to mourn about it, to get angry, to try to rewrite history. She truly had come to terms with it, she thought. Either that, or done a good job convincing herself that it had been her choice not to have children.

And, thank God, she had Maggie. Maggie had made the knowledge that she would never have her own child easier to come to terms with. She'd known Maggie all her life. She'd been at the hospital when she was born. She'd watched her learn to walk, talk, climb, swim, read, count. She'd watched her go off to her first day of school. She'd cheered her on at dozens of math competitions. She'd helped her get ready for her first high-school dance. She'd comforted her when she had her first unrequited crush, attended her university graduation ceremonies, and even wept openly—to the rest of her family's surprise—when Maggie received the student of the year award. Miranda had been part of every milestone of Maggie's life.

All the good parts of motherhood with none of the bad parts. That's what she told herself whenever she found herself feeling sad. Whenever the sight of a mother and daughter together gave her a sudden, painful ache deep inside. Whenever she stopped moving long enough to ask herself, What would my daughter have been like? Or would I have had a son? Two sons? Three of each? What kind of mother would I have been?

It was a strange kind of consolation that Juliet and Eliza had never had children either. Not that the three of them ever sat around declaring, "Isn't it wonderful to be childless!" Miranda knew Juliet and Myles had tried for years, going down the IVF route for at least six cycles, as far as Miranda knew. She had quickly learned not to ask Juliet about it, after Juliet had turned on her one afternoon in Sydney. "It's all right for you, Miss Bloody Glamour Queen who never wanted children anyway. Well, I did, Miranda. I *longed* for them. So mind your own bloody business, because you will never, *ever* know how it feels to want something so badly and know you will never be able to have it."

There had been a moment, a split second, when Miranda had nearly told her that yes, actually, she did know how that felt. But Myles had come in and Juliet had clammed up. Miranda had never spoken about it with Juliet again.

As for Eliza, who knew whether or not she wanted children? As far as Miranda knew, Eliza had never even had a long-term relationship. Nor had she ever expressed interest in children. Perhaps if she hadn't had that accident, things might have been different. Miranda wondered whether Eliza was even able to have children after the trauma her body had gone through. It wasn't the sort of question you asked Eliza. She had a way of setting her jaw and making her face go very still that quickly put a halt to any personal questions. Miranda wasn't surprised she'd made such a success of her life-coaching business. Her clients were probably terrified of her.

And Sadie? Miranda allowed herself a moment to think about her. Was she happily living in the suburbs somewhere, a dozen children gamboling around her, like the old woman who lived in the shoe? The proud mother of triplet boys? The devoted carer of adopted children, perhaps? Or so traumatized by the events of twenty years ago that children were the last thing on her mind?

The man in the seat beside her moved, and she caught a faint scent of a very expensive aftershave. It was one of her favorite male fragrances. She'd had enough introspection for one flight, she decided.

She turned and gave him her most engaging smile. "So, tell me, are you traveling for business or pleasure?"

CHAPTER 22

The lights were low. Soft music was playing in the background. Although they were by the sea, there was no sea view. Eliza had compensated by decorating the room with seascapes and painting the walls a soothing light blue.

She waited as the man across from her searched for the right words. "It's not that I don't love her. Of course I do."

"So what's stopping you, do you think?"

"It's the idea of committing." He gave a grin. Eliza imagined it having quite some effect on women through the years. "The thought that I won't ever sleep with another woman in my life again."

The clock behind her gave a subtle buzz. "Richard, that's our time up this week. If you feel like you need to talk about it some more, please make an appointment outside."

"Thanks, Eliza."

"You're welcome." She stood up, doing her best to hide her wince as her leg protested at the movement.

She took the ten minutes between appointments to check her e-mails. There was one from Leo, sent from his Blackberry.

> Have just spoken to Juliet and heard the news. If it's a matter of money, you only have to ask.

She wrote the reply without thinking, knowing she would never send it.

No, it's not about money. It's about wanting to stay sane.

What if she kept writing?

I always hated the July Christmases. If Maggie was there, I could just about bear it, but why would I want to put myself through it otherwise? A twenty-six-hour flight from Australia; another flight from London to Belfast; a two-hour drive; seven nights in an uncomfortable bed in a room with rattling windows; more food than is healthy because Juliet can't stop cooking; tension in the air because Miranda can't stop fighting with her; Sadie, the elephant in the room that none of us mention; you stringing us along with tales of delays in that big jackpot payment to keep us coming back year after year. It sounds like the tenth circle of hell to me.

For a moment she was tempted to send it. Her secretary's soft voice on the intercom stopped her. She pressed delete and cleared the screen.

Her second appointment for the day was a woman around her own age, late forties. Eliza reviewed her case file, then asked the woman to tell her what had happened since their last appointment. Had she started looking for a new job? Begun the exercise program as part of her goal to lose twelve pounds before her fiftieth birthday? Stopped cleaning up after her teenage son?

The woman admitted she hadn't done any of those things.

"Katherine, it's your choice. It's your life. You can make things happen or not happen."

"It just overwhelms me sometimes."

Life coach or a psychologist? It was a thin line sometimes, Eliza thought. "That's why it's important to break it down into manageable-size pieces."

"You're my role model, you know," the woman said, energized.

"You have it all. Independence. Your own business. And I know it hasn't been easy for you. Your secretary was telling me all about your accident, how you had to start from scratch after that, but look at you now—"

"Let's talk about you, not me."

She finally left the office at six p.m. She'd had a quiet word with her secretary, told her firmly that her job was to be a secret-keeper, not a secret-sharer.

In her car at the traffic lights, Eliza checked her mobile phone again. No message yet. As she watched, it started to ring. She smiled. He was nothing if not punctual.

"Eliza."

"Mark."

"Does now suit?"

"Perfectly," Eliza said. "See you soon."

He was first to her apartment, in the kitchen pouring them both a glass of wine by the time she arrived. "How was your day?"

"Better now. Come here."

She knew exactly what he liked. He knew exactly what she liked. Slow kissing in the living room, clothes being removed in the hallway, naked in the bedroom. She arched up against him, feeling his body weight on her, running her hands down his back, feeling his fingers stroke her thighs, higher. Afterward, she lay with her head on his chest, idly playing with the hair there. He stroked her skin too, her back, her thighs, not hesitating when her skin changed in texture, the marks still visible even all these years later.

She had long ago stopped being self-conscious about the scars. He said he barely noticed them. She had never told him as much, but she was grateful to them. If it hadn't been for the accident that gave her the scars, she and Mark would never have made up. They wouldn't still be together now.

They had managed to live in Melbourne for more than eight years without bumping into each other. She had known where he was, of course, and exactly what he was doing, as he had known about her. The fitness industry in Melbourne was small enough then for it to be easy to keep tabs on one another. He'd had a head start on her, of course, setting up his training company exactly as they'd discussed. In the early months, she'd begun to have doubts. The fire of getting her revenge on him by building a more successful business ebbed sometimes. It had been harder than she expected, arriving in a new city, putting all the theory she'd learned into practice.

They had seen each other just once, at an industry function, five years after she moved to Melbourne. The woman she was with had waved across at him.

"Mark's from Tasmania too. Do you know him?"

"No," Eliza had said, quickly turning away, her heart thumping.

There was room for both of them, it turned out. Mark concentrated on sporting teams, devising fitness regimes. In sports-mad Melbourne, he found plenty of clients.

Eliza targeted female executives. "Healthy body: Successful mind" was her slogan. She offered one-on-one training, in-home sessions and nutrition advice. She lived the life her clients lived— up at six, finishing at nine. She watched other women juggling work commitments, family responsibilities, society's expectations, wanting the impossible—a perfect body, perfect relationship, perfect job, perfect family life. As she jogged alongside her clients, she heard tales of exhaustion and organizational hell. In the gym with other clients, she watched them strain to reach personal goals, heard talk about glass ceilings and male-dominated workplaces. As she helped their bodies get stronger and fitter, she learned more about the business world than she had in any of her courses at university.

Her family life was different than her client life, though. She rarely saw Miranda, even though they lived in the same city. Miranda was always too busy. Eliza went back to Hobart twice a year, for each Christmas celebration. It was enough. It was so different there these days, with only Leo, Clementine, and Maggie at home. Maggie came to stay with her in Melbourne once a year, sometimes for a fortnight, sometimes longer, depending on Clementine's schedule. Eliza always enjoyed those times. Maggie hadn't ever been a needy child or a sullen teenager. You could talk to her. She knew how to be quiet. She was interested in the world. She also had a lovely sense of humor. Miranda had claimed credit for that, of course.

"That's just how it's worked out," she'd said in her annoying, theatrical way. "We've each played a part in molding Maggie, passing on our own gifts to her. Leo and Clementine have made her clever; Juliet's taught her to cook; Eliza has taught her about fitness and self-discipline; and I have taught her to be wonderful."

Eliza was driving back from Tullamarine Airport after dropping the then thirteen-year-old Maggie off for a flight back to Hobart when it happened. A wet road, bad driving conditions; there was no way Eliza could have avoided it. The truck driver came out of a side road without stopping, and plowed directly into Eliza's side of the car. She was knocked unconscious by the impact. Her left arm broke with the impact against the steering wheel. Most damaging of all was the large piece of metal from the truck's bumper bar that buckled on impact and turned into a knife, slicing her thigh, through muscles and skin. Ironically, that same metal saved her life, stopping the blood flow until the ambulance men were able to cut her out of the car.

She was in the hospital for three weeks, and then in a rehabilitation center for two months. An uncertain future stretched in front of her. Leo came to Melbourne for the first month, visiting every day. Clementine and Miranda took turns taking time off work after Leo went back home, visiting just as often. Maggie came over for weekends and sent cards every few days.

Eliza didn't want sympathy. She wanted the truth. A doctor finally gave it to her. "If you do all the exercises, if you stay strong enough through the pain of the rehabilitation process, you'll walk again, but you'll never be able to run."

It was the week before she was discharged that Mark appeared. News of her accident had spread. She'd had cards and flowers from all her clients in the early weeks, and then, when it became clear that her recovery would be slow, tentative phone calls asking if she would understand if they went elsewhere, only until she was better, of course.

Her first thought when Mark walked in was that he had come to take her clients. He must have seen the fire in her eyes and guessed what she was thinking.

"I'm not a vulture."

"Why are you here then?"

"I heard you'll never be able to run again."

"That's what they're saying."

"Bullshit."

"I beg your pardon?"

"I said bullshit, Faraday. Of course you will."

"Who's going to make me?"

"I am."

Just like that, their friendship was rekindled. She didn't ask about his wife or his sons for nearly a month. He eventually mentioned them in passing.

"You're still together?" A nod. That was the last time he spoke of them.

He kept to his word. He did help her walk again. Mark and two physiotherapists. He also made her run. She would never be as fast or as fit as she had been. The injuries were too severe; her body wasn't strong enough to take the weight in motion. But she still proved the doctor wrong. She slowly regained tone. She built up her muscles again. The day came, ten months after her accident, when she finally managed to run one kilometer. It was ungainly, and she was nearly crying with the pain, but she finished it. Mark was at her side.

He drove her home from the sports ground that day, carried her training bag in, said no to her offer of a drink. He was about to leave when she asked him, "Why did you do this?"

"I've always liked a challenge."

"Why, Mark? Was it guilt?"

She waited for a glib answer. He looked at her for a long moment, and then answered. "Because I love you."

Her heart flipped in her chest. "Love? You never loved me."

"I did. I do."

"Are you going to leave Belinda?"

"No. But I don't want to leave you again either."

"So it's my choice?"

He nodded.

She'd stared at him. He was so familiar to her. The long, lanky body; the tanned face; the blue eyes. She had never stopped loving him either. "How would it work?"

"However you wanted it to. I'd take whatever you could give me. And I'd give you whatever I could in return."

She hesitated only a moment, before walking across the room, closing the gap between them. She reached up and kissed him.

He kissed her back. A long, hungry kiss that quickly became something more. It was slow, sensual, extraordinary.

They met again two nights later. Again a week after that. There was no more training together, no more encouraging from him to get fit again or to exercise. What was happening between them now was something new. Eliza tried to find a name for it. A sexual relationship? A love affair? Or both.

They had now been together for nearly fourteen years. They saw each other at least twice a week. It was Mark who had encouraged her move from fitness training into life coaching, when she had finally realized her body would never completely recover from the accident. She'd eventually found her new career just as rewarding. It was the same principles, after all, except she was encouraging her clients to be disciplined, organized, and focused about their whole lives, not just their physical fitness. The hours were better too. She and Mark had managed four holidays away, less than a week each time. She never asked him what he told his wife and sons, how he explained his absences. She didn't want to know. She also never asked him what his plans were with his wife, now that his two sons were getting old enough to leave home. Not because she dreaded the answer. She simply didn't want to know. What they had was enough for her.

Something had changed inside her after her accident. She had come so close to dying, so close to losing everything, that she had hardened. She knew that. She knew there was just one chance at happiness, one chance at a full life, and in all the long, lonely, painful hours in the hospital and during the physiotherapy after-ward, she had made a promise to herself. If she wanted something, she was going to do all she could to have it while she still could. And she had always wanted Mark. Always loved Mark. And she knew he loved her too. He told her often. He thought she was beautiful. He loved her determination. Her courage. Her intelli-gence. Once or twice he had tried to explain why he hadn't been able to leave his wife and sons, but she'd stopped the discussion. She didn't want to know any details. Eliza thought of his life with his wife and sons as a foreign land, one she didn't want to visit.

She knew she and Mark had something other couples didn't. Passion that lasted. It had never been diluted by discussions about putting the trash out, running out of milk or whose turn it was to drive the kids to swimming lessons. They didn't nurse each other's colds and flu. They didn't discuss budgets for renovations or trips abroad. They had the cream at the top of a relationship, without all the tedium. And who knew—perhaps Mark and his wife would have broken up again if it hadn't been for Eliza adding the color he needed in his life.

Only one person in Eliza's life knew about Mark. Her best friend in Melbourne, a former client called Louisa. She had arrived to visit Eliza unexpectedly one summer afternoon, just as Mark was leaving. It had been obvious what they had been doing.

To Eliza's surprise, she told Louisa everything that afternoon. Louisa had been shocked and disapproving. She didn't care how fantastic the sex was, she said. Or whether Eliza believed Mark was her soul mate. "What makes me so angry is you've put your whole life on hold for him."

"I haven't. My life is good."

"You could have met another man."

"I didn't want to meet another man."

"Eliza, he's married. He's got two kids. What about you and kids?"

"I've got Maggie."

"Maggie's your niece. Not your daughter. You don't know what you're missing. It's the most incredible feeling, that bond with your own child. It makes me sad that you'll never experience it. It's what women are born for."

"So my life is worthless otherwise?"

"That's not what I'm saying."

"Yes, it is. That's exactly what you're saying. I'll need to break that news to my sisters too. All of us childless and pitiful, except for Clementine. Thank God Clementine decided to get pregnant at sixteen or we would all be truly sad old women."

"I'm saying it because I care about you. You have to see the situation as it is. You're supposed to be the expert on living the ideal life. What if one of your clients came to you and said she'd been having an affair with a married man for years, but there was no chance of them ever being together in any fulfilling way? What would you advise *her* to do?"

She and Louisa hadn't spoken for nearly a month after that conversation. Eliza had been too angry about it at first. How dare Louisa make those judgments? How dare she assume that just because she wanted a life filled with children, that Eliza wanted the same thing? Because she truly didn't want children of her own. Perhaps Maggie's sudden arrival all those years ago had fulfilled any maternal instinct she might have had. Perhaps it was the knowledge that her injured body might not be strong enough to bear a child. Or that even the mention of children might change everything she had with Mark. Whatever the explanation, she was sure of her decision.

It was Eliza who broke the silence. "I miss you," she said when she rang Louisa. "I miss you telling me off."

"You're not going to listen to me, though, are you?"

"No. So will you take me as I am?"

Louisa had. They were best friends again. But she still didn't approve of Mark.

Eliza lay in bed now and watched as Mark dressed. A farewell kiss, a touch of his hand to her face, a "See you soon, my love," and then he was gone. She dressed slowly, made herself a coffee, and then decided not to drink it. She'd go and get some air instead.

Usually she headed in the direction of the beach. This afternoon she took the opposite route, past the big houses, under the trees. She loved this area, the mixture of ordinary red-brick flats next to gracious old mansions, the snap of the sea in the air. She liked the fact there were cafés in one direction, restaurants in another and everything else she needed in between: a laundrette, a chemist, a bakery and a shoe-mender. There was also a Catholic church, a Jewish synagogue, and a meeting hall for the Church of Seventh Day Adventists. As Mark had said once, if the end of the world was to happen, she had plenty of places to flee to.

She found herself outside the Catholic church today. Intending to walk farther, perhaps even to the shopping village, she surprised herself by walking through the gate, up the gravel path, and in through the side door. It was her first time in there. Inside it was cool and dark, the air still redolent of incense from a ceremony earlier that day. The smell was immediately familiar from childhood. She began to do the sign of the cross before catching herself just in time. It was hypocritical enough for her to be inside a church let alone to start going through the rituals. She stopped at the back pew, lowering herself, with some difficulty, onto the wooden kneeler. There were other people in pews beside her. The priest was hearing confessions, she realized. She turned and saw the old-fashioned confession boxes, watched as a man her father's age emerged, a short pause before a woman Eliza's own age took his place.

It was a very long time since Eliza had been to mass, let alone made her confession, but all the prayers came to mind in an instant. She could join that queue, wait her turn, step into that box and say all the words.

"Bless me, Father, for I have sinned. It has been about twenty-five years since my last confession."

"And your sin?"

"I've been having an affair."

"Who with?"

"A married man. The love of my life."

"Are you sorry about it?"

"Not one bit. I'd do it all again tomorrow."

"Any other sins?"

"I've been lying to someone for the past twenty years."

"Who to?"

"My niece."

"What about?"

"My sister Sadie."

"Can you change that?"

"Tell her the truth? And tear the family apart even more? No, thanks."

She'd been thinking about Sadie a great deal recently. She knew it was partly to do with the time of the year, the run-up to one of their Christmas gatherings. She went through it every year around this time. Something else had sparked it this year, though. Five months ago, while shopping in Bourke Street Mall, Eliza thought she saw Sadie. It was a woman of the same height, the same build, with dark-brown hair. She looked as Eliza had imagined Sadie to look, twenty years on. She called her name. "Sadie?"

The woman didn't turn. Eliza started to follow her, cursing her bad leg. The old Eliza would have been able to catch her in a minute. The woman turned a corner and Eliza briefly lost sight of her. Mercifully, she had stopped to browse in a shoe store.

"Sadie." She put her hand on the woman's arm. She turned. Close up, she looked nothing like Sadie. "I'm sorry. I thought you were someone I knew." *Someone I knew. The sister I haven't seen for twenty years.*

If it had been Sadie, what would she have said? "Hi, how are things? Fancy a coffee? And by the way, sorry for all of us ganging up on you like that all those years ago. You were right to cut all ties. But what about we let bygones be bygones?"

That would make for a lovely Donegal gathering, if Eliza was to turn up with Sadie by her side.

She had never told the others, but she had tried many times over the years to track Sadie down. She had to respect Clementine's point of view—that awful time when Maggie was missing had affected her more than anyone else, after all—but the simple truth was she missed Sadie. Yes, it had been terrible what she had done.

But also understandable. Hadn't they all fallen in love with Maggie?

Eliza had often wished she'd been there when Leo and Clementine found Sadie and Maggie in that caravan park. In the endless postmortems when they were all back together in Hobart, Leo had gone over what had happened and his conversation with Sadie, all of them still trying to make sense of it.

Leo said he had tried to talk to Sadie. Tried to make her understand how worried everyone had been, that leaving brief messages on the answering machine hadn't been enough. Tried to make her understand why Clementine was so upset. It was like talking to a wall, he kept saying. She wouldn't explain; just kept asking to be left alone.

He did as she said, left her there. He, Clementine, and Maggie returned to their rental car and drove to a motel in the nearby town. Maggie was perfectly normal, happy and chatting away as though it was also perfectly normal that Clementine and he should have just turned up like that.

The next morning Leo went back to the caravan park. He was too late. Sadie was gone. He checked with the man in the office. Sadie had left nothing but Maggie's belongings crammed into a plastic bag.

They had all been worried that she'd done something drastic. Killed herself. Leo had spent days on the phone to police stations and hospitals in the area. They'd been mildly sympathetic but not helpful. A domestic dispute, they inferred. Young women had fights with their family members and headed into the unknown every day of the week.

When the card arrived from her for Maggie's birthday, Eliza had been as relieved as everyone else. The following year, another card arrived for Maggie. The year after, another. Even though they never contained any news, they gave them all some solace. Leo always asked Father Cavalli, and in later years the other priests, if they had any more news of her. They obviously knew where she was. Surely the priests understood what her absence was doing to the family. The priests had been understanding but unhelpful. They had to respect Sadie's decision, they always said. Over the years Leo and all of Sadie's sisters had written letters to her, enclosing them with Maggie's letters and Christmas cards. They'd never been acknowledged.

Eliza still often tried to picture Sadie, to imagine where she might be and what she might be doing now. She did it with all of her family. She pictured Leo on his travels, Juliet working hard in England, Miranda clinking champagne glasses in some sophisticated bar, Clementine out in the bush or perched on a rock by some coastline. She thought of Maggie—until three months ago—in a glossy office in London. But Sadie? The picture was always blank. Where could she be? With whom? What state of mind? Happy? Sad? Disappointed? Fulfilled?

Eliza could ask herself the same questions. She knew the answers. She spent enough time thinking about it. She was all of those things at the same time.

"Can I help you?" An elderly man in a dark suit and white collar was standing at the end of the pew.

"No, thanks, Father." She gave him the briefest of smiles, then got up and walked as quickly as she could out into the bright sunlight.

CHAPTER 23

Clementine wasn't prone to whoops of delight, especially when she was home alone, but the letter that had just arrived called for something special. She'd been waiting six months to get her research grant approved, and today she'd had the confirmation. She automatically went to ring Maggie in London to tell her the news, stopping herself just in time. Maggie wasn't in London anymore and, in any case, Clementine was trying not to ring her too often at the moment.

She imagined a conversation instead. "Maggie, I got it!"

Maggie wouldn't need to ask what "it" was. "That's fantastic! When do you leave? How long this time?"

She'd be away for fourteen months, her longest stint yet. The previous three times she'd been to the Antarctic had been for summer trips, heading down in early November and coming back in February.

"You're sure you don't mind, Maggie?" She'd been asking her daughter that same question for as long as she could remember. At first it had been about local trips, when Maggie was just a child. "You're sure you don't mind me going to Maria Island?" "You're sure you don't mind me going to Devonport?" The locations had changed each year as Clementine's field of study widened, as more opportunities opened up and as her reputation grew. "You're sure you don't mind?"

She'd asked the question of Maggie three years before, when she first applied to go down south. It wasn't as if she was just a plane trip away if something happened. It wasn't as if Maggie could nip down and visit her. It wasn't as if e-mail and telephone calls were always the most reliable.

"You have to go," Maggie had enthused. "Mum, it's brilliant."

Clementine knew Maggie meant it then. Most of the time she called her "Clementine." "Mum" was just for special occasions.

Clementine had loved her three trips there so far, from her first sight of the continent, like a massive white dome on the horizon. It had been hard to tell whether it was cloud or land. It had taken two weeks to get there on the ship from Hobart, longer than that on one of the journeys when the ice had been so thick they'd had to slowly break their way through it. She'd been based at Davis station, studying Adélie penguins. Her first encounter hadn't been encouraging: lots of them running around the base, looking bedraggled and grumpy. The second trip, she'd spent weeks off station at the rookery, studying their breeding habits. It had been so comical to watch them building the nests. They would waddle off, pick up a stone, waddle back, place it in a pile, then waddle off for another one. In the meantime, another penguin would waddle over and steal one of those stones. There had been plenty of serious research, too. She'd worked with a team of people from the U.K., Germany, Spain, and Sweden, as well as Australians.

The trip was months off still, but Clementine couldn't resist it. She started to make her checklist. As she wrote down the different items, she absentmindedly reached back for her plait, getting that familiar dart of surprise to find it gone. She'd had it cut off earlier that year, the same week she'd submitted the application for this research trip. She'd decided it was time, now she was in her early forties. It would also make sense from a practical point of view, if she was to go to Antarctica again. Showers on station were limited to three minutes each, barely time to wash her body, let alone a head of long hair. She liked the new short cut, a cap of dark locks, with a slightly longer fringe. Maggie loved the new look too. Leo said she and Maggie could pass as sisters. He'd been saying that since Maggie was a teenager.

Clementine kept at her list for twenty minutes before deciding to take a break. If someone else had been home, she'd have opened a bottle of champagne. Instead, she settled on a cup of green tea and one of Beethoven's piano sonatas. She liked to play it loudly, and these days she could do whatever she wanted in the house. She'd had it to herself almost all year. Leo was rarely in Tasmania these days. He was marvelous. A man in his late seventies, still so active and engaged with the world. In all her years, the only occasion they'd ever fought was the terrible time with Sadie. It had broken both their hearts. In the end they'd made a mutual decision not to talk about her.

As the kettle boiled, she stood in front of the notice board by the fridge. The housework rosters that used to cover it were long gone. It was now covered with Maggie memorabilia. Over the years it had held school reports, notices about sports days and drawings. Articles in the Tasmanian newspapers about the various statewide math competitions she'd won. A clipping from one of the Sydney newspapers when she graduated with perfect marks, the youngest to do so in the university's history.

Not just articles. There were so many photos, there were triple layers in some places. The most recent one showed Maggie and Angus on holiday together in the Yorkshire Dales. Clementine took it down. Then she changed her mind. It was a lovely photo of Maggie. She got the kitchen scissors, cut Angus out of the photo, put him in the bin, then stuck Maggie back on the notice board. The dozens of Maggies pinned all over the board smiled out at her, as if in approval.

The notice board was a pictorial history of Maggie's life. Photos of her on holiday in Bicheno as a two-year-old next to photos from trips to Sydney to stay with Juliet and Myles. As a teenager in Melbourne with Miranda. A baby photo next to one of her with Eliza at the MCG in Melbourne on the day of the AFL grand final. Dozens and dozens of snapshots of her life.

All that was missing were photos of Maggie and Sadie together. Clementine had taken them down twenty years ago. Even after Maggie had been found and brought back home, no one had ever put them back. Perhaps they didn't dare to. Or perhaps they didn't need to.

The truth was, they all probably thought of Sadie more since she'd been gone than they had when she was with them. As much as they could think of her without knowing any true details.

Maggie had only occasionally questioned the whole situation. Why was it that Sadie never told them where she was? Why didn't she ever come and visit? It had been frightening in a way how easy it had been to keep the lie going, year after year. Equally frightening that a person could just step out of their life and start a new one. Leave their family and everything they knew behind.

They didn't talk about it much anymore. Hints over the years, occasional mentions and careful reactions to innocent comments by Maggie about Sadie. Maggie had asked once why her aunt never rang her, and without missing a beat, Miranda explained that Sadie believed all modern technology was immoral.

"So she wouldn't watch television? Go to the cinema? What would she do?"

"Dance, mostly," Miranda said.

Maggie started to laugh. "Sadie can't spend every day dancing. She must have a job. How else would she buy food and clothes?"

"They grow a lot of their own food. And they only wear second-hand clothes, so they're quite cheap."

Clementine told Miranda off about it later. It was like water off a duck's back.

"As I've always said, if you want to come up with a better story, go right ahead. God forbid we should ever tell Maggie the truth, after all."

Many times Clementine had wanted to tell her the truth. She wanted to tell everyone the truth, get it all out in the open. Sadie had done a stupid, dangerous thing, but everything had turned out okay in the end, hadn't it? Wasn't it as simple as that?

She'd talked to Leo about it, but his response surprised her.

"There are two sides to this, Clementine. Sadie isn't away from us just because of what happened with Maggie. She wants to be away."

"But if we told her we wanted to see her again—"

"We have. I have, at least. In every letter I've ever sent with Maggie's. She's never replied to any of them."

"It's my fault. It's all my fault."

"No, it's not, Clementine. It was no one person's fault. You're not to blame yourself."

She would never have believed it possible, but Clementine missed Sadie. She wanted to see her again. She would welcome her back into the family. She had felt that way for years now. That terrible time so long ago had almost faded from her memory. It almost felt unreal, as if it hadn't ever happened. Maggie hadn't been harmed. She had still grown up bright, happy and confident. All that remained from that time were questions. Clementine wanted to know why Sadie had done what she'd done. She would be able to ask her about it in a calm way now, she knew. Out of genuine curiosity, without any of the rage and fury that had surrounded any thought of Sadie in the early years.

She often tried to picture her sister and wondered whether she had ever been back to Hobart. Had they been sitting in the house, unaware that she was outside, observing them? Had she and Maggie walked down to the Salamanca market, or enjoyed a coffee at one of the cafés looking over the water, without realizing that Sadie was sitting nearby, watching them?

Sadie's latest card to Maggie had arrived on time as usual, a week before her birthday. The current parish priest, Father Huang, had delivered it to the house. He wouldn't answer any questions about where Sadie's card had come from or if he had spoken to her recently.

"We have to respect her privacy," he said.

They'd all been frustrated by the priests' secrecy over the years, but as Leo had said, if Sadie didn't want to be in contact with them beyond the annual card to Maggie, there was nothing they could do about it.

They had gone on without her. That had been the surprising

part of all this. Life had continued. Having Maggie in their midst had made it easier. She'd been a distraction, a focal point and a delight. Clementine was the first to admit she was biased, but there was something special about Maggie. There always had been, ever since she was a child.

Clementine thought she knew her daughter intimately, yet Maggie constantly managed to surprise her. That's what astounded Clementine about motherhood. Maggie was completely her own person. She had her own distinct personality. Her own attitudes. Her own brain. Clementine saw elements of herself in Maggie. Not just the physical likeness—they also had a similar approach (an obsession, Miranda called it) to study. There was also quite a lot of her father, David, in her. His coloring. His intelligence as well.

Not that Maggie or Clementine saw much of him these days. He was living in Perth with his wife and family now. He had four other children. Maggie had met them, and it was all very civilized, but there had never been and would never be a close bond between them. He had helped them out financially for several years, until Leo's increasing success with his inventions had made his contribution unnecessary. He still sent Maggie a birthday card each year, as she sent David and his family Christmas cards. Beyond that, it was as if he didn't really exist. Clementine's intuition the day she discovered she was pregnant had proved true.

She had spoken to Maggie about him occasionally. Checked she was all right about David; that she wasn't hurt not to see him more often.

"Should I be?" Maggie had asked. "I know who he is. I know where he is. That's enough, isn't it? If I need to know any male things, I can ask Tadpole, can't I?"

"Well, yes," Clementine said, taken aback.

Juliet had laughed at her later. "You're the queen of being sensible. You can't be surprised when your daughter turns out the same way."

Clementine couldn't claim complete credit for Maggie's upbringing. As hard as it had been to admit at the time, Clementine knew that Sadie had been like a second mother to Maggie in her first five years. Juliet, Miranda, and Eliza had helped guide her out of childhood, through her teenage years, and now into adulthood. After what had happened with Sadie, Clementine had been so wary to let her out of her sight at first, but the arrangement worked beautifully for all of them, Maggie especially. She blossomed under everyone's attention.

"It's no wonder she's as wonderful as she is," Leo had remarked once. "She's a hothouse child, that's why. Like one of those rare orchids that is watched twenty-four hours a day and has a dozen gardeners caring for it."

It hadn't just been her aunts spoiling Maggie. Leo had doted on her. He filled her head with stories of inventors. By the time she was a teenager, Maggie knew about the origins of electricity and could have done lecture tours about Michael Faraday, the inventor of the electric motor and, Leo insisted, a distant relative. It was Leo who heard about the math competitions. It was Leo who drove Maggie all over the state to enter them. No one was prouder than he was when she won them. He built a new shelf in the living room to hold all the trophies she kept bringing home. He also put up the industrial-size notice board in the kitchen to hold the newspaper articles and photos.

"You're lucky she's not beautiful as well as smart or she'd be the world's most annoying child," Miranda had remarked one day.

Clementine took offense at the time, declaring that of course Maggie was beautiful. She later admitted to herself that Miranda had a point. Maggie *wasn't* conventionally pretty. There was something special about her, though. The bright expression, the dark eyes, the strong eyebrows, the big smile, the slight figure, even her fairy-folk ears, which had resisted all of Clementine's attempts to hide them over the years. Maggie herself had a love-hate relationship with them. At the age of seventeen and in her first year at university, Maggie had declared they were her best feature and got a perky haircut that showed them off. She spent the next few years getting even quirkier haircuts, more suited to the lead singer of an alternative band than a top-of-the-class mathematics student. She started dressing to suit the look as well: vintage dresses, heavy Doc Marten boots, antique jewelry.

"You're like *My Fair Lady* played in reverse," Miranda declared in disgust one visit when Maggie arrived dressed in a 1960s-style purple shift dress, dark tights, and knee-high boots. She also had three earrings in her left ear and two in her right ear. "I do all I can to make you into a lady and you turn into this?"

Maggie became more conservative when she began working in the business world. She started wearing expensive Italian boots. She still shopped in small boutiques and vintage clothing stores, though. On the surface her clothes were conservative—shirts, skirts and jackets. It was only on closer inspection the unusual details emerged—ragged hems, appliquéd flowers and handmade fabrics. She kept her hair short—neat and tidy at first glance, up close the quirky fringe or barely noticeable colored highlights giving it character. She still fidgeted with it, though, tugging at strands and covering her ears. Eliza had told her off about it once. "You're too old to do that now, Maggie." Eliza had never been the most lighthearted of them, and the older she got, the more serious she'd become.

"She wouldn't know a good joke if it came up and laughed in her face," Miranda said once.

Clementine wondered what the weeks in New York had done to Maggie's dress sense. She hadn't sent any photos yet. Occasional phone calls and texts, a couple of postcards. She rarely went into detail about what she was doing there. She'd made it clear—nicely but firmly—that she wanted to be left alone. They'd all had to respect her wishes.

Clementine looked up at the clock and did a quick calculation of the time difference between Hobart and New York. There were only a few hours each day when they could call each other, and this wasn't the right time. She shut her eyes, brought a picture of Maggie to mind instead, and sent her what she could only describe as a beam of love. It wasn't something she would ever admit to her sisters, but Clementine often sent what she thought of as ESP messages to Maggie. It made sense to Clementine. Maggie was in her mind so much, it seemed like a logical step, almost a possibility. She could be immersed in the most detailed research, far away in Antarctica or alone on an isolated island, and yet thoughts of her daughter were only ever the smallest of distances away. She would get sudden flashes about Maggie, images and memories of her weaving in and out of her other thoughts. How could she describe it? A spiritual link, a bond, the equivalent of an emotional umbilical cord? It didn't matter if there were thousands of kilometers between them. It didn't matter that Maggie was now an adult, facing her own problems, making her own decisions. The connection between them was still as strong.

She'd never wanted another child. She'd had several relationships since David, but nothing too serious. She was seeing someone at the moment, a fellow scientist called Peter, whom she'd worked with in Antarctica. The isolation down there led to many a fling, Clementine had noticed. But it didn't look like lasting their return to real life. He was already getting too serious.

"You're married to your work, Clementine," a previous boyfriend once said. It was true. She already had everything she wanted in her life: Maggie. Her family. Her work.

Especially her work. She pulled her thoughts back to the matter at hand. In four months' time she'd be onboard the ship to Antarctica. Two weeks after that she'd be back at the station, at the very bottom of the world, surrounded by ice and snow and that sharp wind. She couldn't wait. She loved it there. It was fascinating and nerve-wracking at the same time. Not unlike motherhood, she realized.

She turned the CD of Beethoven up even louder and returned to her list making.

CHAPTER 24

The temperature in the corner office on the fifth floor of a glass building in Dublin's Dame Street was reaching uncomfortable levels. After three weeks of wet, gray summer weather, Ireland had switched to blue skies and sunshine. The insurance company that owned the office building made record profits, but none of it was directed toward efficient air-conditioning.

Sadie Faraday reached across the desk, turned off her noisy fan, switched off her computer, then leaned back and stretched. It had been a long week. She'd put out an offer for a new advertising agency the previous month and had spent the past three days listening to pitches from the companies on the short list. So many promises, so much enthusiasm, so many sets of whitened teeth gleaming at her from the end of the boardroom table.

"You're the market leader in your field. Your company name is known all over the country," the first agency had said. "It's time to tell your story. Add the personal touch."

"We've done the research, and your number-one asset is your reputation," the second agency said. "We want to highlight that."

The third agency had presented something so artistic, so obscure, a million miles away from what the company actually did,

Sadie found it difficult to keep a straight face. What on earth did bluebirds in a tree have to do with a company whose business was cleaning pubs and restaurants?

She'd promised them all she'd have her decision made by Tuesday the following week. It would mean a weekend looking over the submissions again, but she didn't mind. She didn't have anything else planned.

The calendar on the pinboard beside her caught her eye. It featured colorful photographs of beaches all over the world. The July picture showed an exotic scene from Barbados. Sadie did what she should have done before today and tore the page off the calendar. She was a week early, but it made her feel better to do it. August was always a much easier month to look at than July.

"Anyone alive in here or has the heat killed you, too?"

She turned at the sound of the voice. It was Dennis, the head accountant. He'd been with the company since the early days. Sadie had interviewed him for the position herself. He was carrying his briefcase and light jacket.

"The poor weather can't win in this country," Sadie said. "It's either too wet or too hot. Aren't you ever satisfied?"

"Of course not. If we didn't have the weather, what would we talk about? We're all heading to the pub for a few celebratory pints. Want to come?"

"What's the occasion?"

"Lorna's thirtieth birthday."

"I thought her birthday wasn't until December."

"It's not. We're getting in some early practice."

Sadie grinned. "I'll meet you there. I just need to make a call first."

"I'll order you one. Glass of chilled white wine?"

"Perfect, thanks." As Dennis shut the door, she dialed the number. It went straight to an answering machine. She left a message. "Darling, it's me. Just to let you know a few of us are going for a drink after work, so I'll be home a little later. There's a chicken salad in the fridge if you want to get started before me. See you soon. I love you."

She pulled the dust cover over her screen, turned her phone to voice mail, picked up her handbag, and left the office for the day. The door, with her nameplate, SALLY O'TOOLE, MANAGING DIREC-TOR, slammed shut behind her.

CHAPTER 25

The phone started ringing just as Maggie reached the door to her apartment. By the time she realized it was her phone, juggled the shopping she was carrying, found her bag, and extricated the key, it was too late. The ringing had stopped.

She pressed the button on the answering machine as soon as she got inside. A warm, male American voice filled the room.

"Hi. This is a message for Maggie Faraday. Maggie, it's Gabriel West, calling on behalf of Rent-a-Grandchild. Could you call me when you get this message?"

Maggie put down her parcels, found a notebook and pen, and called him back. "Gabriel? It's Maggie Faraday."

"That was quick. You carry your answering machine around with you?"

She laughed. "If you'd left a longer message, I'd have gotten there before you hung up."

"I'll make a note of that on your file: 'Leave long pauses when speaking to Maggie Faraday's machine.' So, how are things?"

"Good. Busy," she lied. "You're filling in again?"

"Mom has a conference in Seattle. Avon ladies of the world unite. She bribed me."

It was the third time Maggie had spoken to Gabriel, although they hadn't met face-to-face yet. She usually dealt with his mother.

She'd met Isadora West after seeing a leaflet in a café down the street.

New York City—City of Loneliness?

More than two hundred thousand elderly New Yorkers spend day after day alone, with no visitors; no human contact. Can you help? Please give up just an hour of your time twice a week and help bring the outside world into their lives.

Lonely in New York? Maggie knew only too well how that felt. She would never have thought it possible, but she'd started to want to do more than sightseeing. After six years in full-time work, she didn't know what to do with herself without a job. She rang the number listed on the leaflet that same afternoon. At eleven o'clock the next morning she found herself in a small office on the second floor of a building in the Flatiron District. It was above an Indian restaurant. Maggie could smell the rich spices through the floorboards.

Across the desk was Isadora—"but please call me Dora"—West, in her late fifties, impeccably dressed in a white linen suit, beautifully made-up, and with the fastest-speaking voice Maggie had ever heard. She gave Maggie a potted history of her company and her own life within a minute of her arrival. As well as the Rent-a-Grandchild project, she ran a thriving Avon agency, a dog-walking business and a window-cleaning enterprise. She had a desk for each, she explained to Maggie. Maggie glanced around. Sure enough, there was a desk in each corner of the room, all four of them impeccably neat, with organized files, different-colored filing trays and vases of flowers neatly arranged on top.

"You saw one of my Rent-a-Grandchild leaflets, you said? Good, good. You don't get paid, you realize that? It's a public service. I make enough money with my other businesses. Do you know the city well? Have you got references? What experience have you got with older people? When can you start?"

Maggie started to answer, but Dora interrupted. "They're just formalities. Don't look so anxious. You'll be great, I can tell. I can point out a lunatic a mile away, and you aren't one. Now, male or female? No, not you, I know you're female. That skirt you're wearing is kind of a giveaway. I like it. Good fabric. I like your hair, too. You've got that kind of asymmetrical quirky look going on. Funky. I meant, would you prefer to visit a male or female?"

Maggie was trying to keep up. "Female, please." She already had a grandfather. It would be good to meet an older lady, hear her advice, her life story, get her insights.

Dora ticked a box on the form in front of her. "Good. I've dozens more females than males on my book. They outlive men three to one. Or is it four to one? There's more of them, anyway."

Dora had called the references and put Maggie to work quickly. She had already visited three clients. The first, a white-haired woman called Lily, with a matching white-haired dog called Lolly, had been so grandmotherly Maggie expected to see apple pies cooling on her windowsill. She lived in a fifth-floor apartment overlooking Gramercy Park, had worked as a teacher in an exclusive private school, and liked to talk about dead English authors. Maggie enjoyed her twice-weekly visits very much, and was disappointed when the woman's grandson in Florida invited her to come and live with him and his family just a month into the arrangement.

Her second lady was an icy-faced German woman called Greta. Unbeknown to Dora, Greta had also signed up to an agency called Lonely Old European Hearts. She resigned from the Rent-a-Grandchild scheme the day after she met Klaus, an Austrian butcher the same age as her. The two of them moved to Klaus's daughter's home in New Jersey three weeks later. Greta sent Maggie a postcard a week after the move, in care of Dora's office.

It was Dora's son, Gabriel, who rang to say the postcard had arrived. He introduced himself, explaining that his mother was away for a few days and that he was managing the office in her absence.

Maggie hadn't talked to anyone yet that day. She was hungry for conversation. Gabriel seemed just as happy to talk. She didn't tell him she'd been feeling as lonely as the old people. She mentioned what a wonderful service she thought it was and that she liked his mother very much.

"She likes you, too," Gabriel said. "I've got your file in front of me. She's put a gold star on the front cover. That's a very good sign."

"I don't know how she manages to run all those businesses at once."

"Nor do I. I get very nervous when she's away. What if I get confused? Sell window cleaner as the ideal makeup remover? Send one of the dogs to visit a poor, lonely, old person?"

He was amused by Greta's postcard. "It's got a picture of a large sauerkraut on the front," he told Maggie. "And she's written across it in block letters, 'Wish you were Herr.' "

Maggie offered to come in and collect it rather than have him forward it on. When she came in the next day, Gabriel had gone. Dora was back behind the desk.

"The gods were shining the day you walked in to see me, Ms. Maggie," Dora said, already flicking through her client lists. "From now on you're getting all my difficult clients."

She was true to her word. For the past three weeks, Maggie had been visiting a terrifying woman called Dolly Leeson.

Dora had briefed her beforehand. "I have to warn you, this is a tough assignment. This one's worked her way through everyone on my books. Stand up to her; she likes that. And let me know how you get on."

Maggie visited Dolly for the first time the next day. "Tough assignment" was an understatement. Maggie walked out of Dolly's Garment-District apartment feeling like she'd spent an hour in a dryer. Dolly was in her midseventies, overweight, and opinionated. Her apartment was in chaos, with books and newspapers spread over every surface. There were paintings on each wall—an odd mixture of delicate landscapes and kitschy ones of crying clowns and dogs playing pool. There was an oxygen tank on a hand truck in one corner. Dora had alerted Maggie to that. "She's supposed to be on it for six hours a day. If you hear her wheezing, remind her, would you? She does need it. She's in terrible health. It's her temper that keeps her alive, I'm sure of it." Dolly hadn't been wheezing that day. She'd been complaining. She started the moment Maggie arrived until the hour was up. Her targets included the state of the world, the state of the Union, global warming and zippers that stuck. She insulted Maggie in between, picking on her clothes, her accent and the fact she was in New York. Maggie expected her hair to be blown back by the sheer force of the invective.

Her next visit was no better. Dolly answered the door, grunted at her, let her in, then continued doing her crossword. Maggie asked several questions and received no answer. The phone rang twice. Dolly ignored it. When Maggie asked if she wanted her to answer it, Dolly ignored her too. Maggie waited patiently until her hour was up, said thank you and left. The last thing Maggie heard as she left the apartment was Dolly shouting, "And don't come back! You're fired!"

Maggie rang Dora as soon as she got home. She was too late. Dolly had already rung the Rent-a-Grandchild office to complain about her.

"Complain about what? I barely said a word while I was there."

"That's what she was complaining about. I told you she's a toughie," Dora said, unperturbed. "It's just her way."

The third visit Dolly didn't let her in at all. Maggie stayed outside the door for half an hour, trying to persuade her, until Dolly eventually opened it, keeping the security chain on, shouting at her in a cloud of whiskey and canned tuna breath that if she had wanted to see her, she would have opened the door. "Can't you take a hint, you silly jug-eared girl? Leave me alone."

"But you signed up to the agency. I'm only here because you asked for someone to visit you. Are you sure you don't want me to come back?"

"Today, no. Next week, come back. We'll see how I feel then."

Maggie was at the end of the corridor when Dolly called her back. "I've changed my mind. See you tomorrow."

"This is about Dolly, isn't it?" Maggie said to Gabriel on the phone now. She'd been expecting the call. She'd been to see Dolly that morning, and it hadn't gone well.

"She's just left a message complaining about you. Quite a long message, in fact."

"Oh dear."

He laughed. "Can you tell me what happened?"

"Of course."

"Dolly said you wouldn't do what you were told. She said you were"—he paused, as if he was checking some notes—" 'insolent, inarticulate, insubordinate and indolent.' "

"That's right," Maggie agreed. "She also called me 'feckless, foolhardy, frivolous, and fey.' "

"Fey?"

Maggie decided this wasn't the time to tell him that Dolly had said Maggie's ears were creepy and made her feel sick. "You're like something from *The Hobbit*," is how she'd put it. Maggie had needed to turn away, so Dolly wouldn't see her laughing.

"She likes alphabetical insults," Maggie explained. "It's from reading the dictionary for all the crosswords she does, I think."

"You might want to keep her away from the *F* pages, then," Gabriel said. "She also said she begged you to help her with something and you refused."

"I had to." Maggie needed to explain. "I love doing this job, Gabriel, I promise. Your mother would tell you that. I'm happy to sweep rooms, clean birdcages, empty trays of kitty litter if I have to. But Dolly is a law unto herself."

"Can you tell me exactly what she wanted you to do? For the purposes of correct reportage, of course."

"She wanted me to get drunk on whiskey with her, and then make an obscene phone call on her behalf to her nephew, because she thinks he is after the contents of her bank account."

"And you wouldn't?" The smile was back in his voice again. "Maggie, where's your sense of fun? What about her cigarettes? Didn't she ask you to get her some of those as well? Tell you there's nothing like a cigarette with a fine, full glass of whiskey?"

"How do you know about the cigarettes?" Dolly had asked her to buy two packs, one for each of them. This was despite the fact Maggie didn't smoke and Dolly had an increasing need for the oxygen machine.

"She used to ask me to do the same thing."

"You were Dolly's Rent-a-Grandchild too?"

"For six months. When I first moved back to New York."

"How did you last it?"

"I took up smoking. I learned a lot of swears. I developed a taste for whiskey. We had a ball together. The only drawback is I've been in rehab ever since."

"Can I please have another one like Lily?"

He laughed. "No, you're stuck. Much as I'd love to let you off the hook, I can't get anyone else to call on Dolly. Except you."

"But she really fired me this time."

"She did, yes. But I told her she has to have you; that we've got no one else on our books who can cover her area."

"What did she say?"

"She swore—from the *B* page in the dictionary. She also told me I must really be scraping the bottom of the barrel."

Maggie laughed. He did a very good impersonation of Dolly. "But you defended me?"

"Of course I did. I told her you were a living angel. I also told her that if she didn't watch herself, you'd show her the sharp side of your hitherto sweet tongue the next time you visited. She said she'd quite like to see that. So the scene is set, really."

"Thanks, Gabriel."

"Thanks? For sending you back into Dolly's jaws? You're not being sarcastic, sardonic, and supercilious when you say that, are you?"

"No. I'm being grateful, gullible, and gormless."

He was laughing as he hung up.

* * *

Maggie decided to visit Dolly the next day. It was a ten-minute ride on the subway and a five-minute walk to her apartment. One of the many good things about joining up with Rent-a-Grandchild was that she'd had to find her way around the city. She found it surprisingly simple, in seventh heaven with all the numbered streets farther uptown. It appealed to the orderly number counter inside her.

Maggie got off at 34th Street, stopping en route to buy a bottle of water. It was another bright, blue-skied day, with the temperature forecast for the high nineties. She was already hot and sticky, despite the fact she was wearing her lightest cotton dress. The sunlight was reflecting off the windows of the skyscrapers, and the air was filled with exhaust fumes from the constant traffic, not to mention the jostling and hustling against the crowds of people on the sidewalks. She promised herself a long, cool shower as soon as she got home.

Dolly's apartment was on the fifth floor. There was a lift, but it was cramped and a little smelly. Maggie preferred to take the five flights of stairs. She walked down the hallway and knocked at Dolly's door. After several minutes she heard a shuffling of feet, a latch being unlocked, and then the door opened, the security chain firmly in place. Dolly peered out. Her hair was in curlers. She was wearing an orange housecoat. She didn't look happy.

"You again."

"I'm afraid so."

"That Gabriel or Gloria or whatever his name is warned me you were coming back. As I said to him, talk about sending me the scrapings from the bottom of the barrel."

Maggie was too hot to be polite. "I know. I said the same thing to Gabriel about having to visit you."

To her surprise, Dolly gave a roar of laughter. "At last. A bit of spark. About time, too. Your choirgirl act was really getting on my goat. So, are you coming in or going out? Don't stand there all day." Dolly turned and shuffled back into the room.

Maggie followed. She looked around the apartment. It was only a day since she'd been there and every surface was already covered in newspapers and magazines. She suspected Dolly had just spread them all out. "Would you like me to tidy this up a bit for you?"

Dolly glared at her for a moment, and then agreed. As Maggie began, Dolly watched her closely.

"If you're going to hang around, you may as well answer a few questions."

"Ask away," Maggie said.

"What's that accent of yours? What do you do? And why are you in New York?"

Maggie blinked.

"Don't have much to say for yourself, do you? That's the problem with young people these days; so self-absorbed they don't know how to conduct a conversation."

"I would if you let me get a word in occasionally."

Dolly clapped her hands. "Alleluia, a bit more spirit. So what are you, then? When you're not being a do-gooder harassing old ladies like me?"

"I'm a mathematician."

"A math teacher?"

"No, a mathematician. I work with numbers, in big companies."

"You're an accountant, you mean? Why didn't you just say that? So where are you working now?"

"I'm not working at the moment. I'm on a career break."

"How can you be on a career break? You don't look old enough to have a career, let alone have a break from it. How old are you? Fifteen?"

"Twenty-six."

Dolly made a scoffing noise. "Liar. So what was your last job? Why did you leave it?"

Maggie busied herself with the last of the newspapers. She noticed a pile of washing in the corner. It looked clean. "Can I fold up these clothes for you?"

"Hit a sore point, did I? Did you get fired, is that it? Where was it? Here? Or in Tanzania or Transylvania or wherever it is Dora said you were from?"

"I'm sorry, Dolly, but I don't like to talk about my personal life."

Dolly was grinning now. "You're trying your best to be mild-mannered, but you've a temper. I can see it. I like that in a person. I'm starting to like you, as it happens. So what happened in the job? Did you cook the books? Sleep with the boss?"

"I'd really rather not talk about it."

Dolly reached over and picked up the Rent-a-Grandchild leaflet and read from the front page. " 'Company and conversation in your own home.' I'm going to sue that Genevieve and his mother for false advertising. I've had better conversations with that cushion over there."

Maggie was starting to enjoy herself. "His name is Gabriel, Dolly, and you know it. He told me he used to visit you."

"He did. He was as disobedient as you. At least he would chat to me, though. About politics, mostly, but that was better than nothing. I can't even get you to do that. I think I'll fire you again."

Maggie gave up any pretense of tidying.

Dolly continued. "Then I'll hire you again. A woman my age has to make her own fun. And I like the way you keep coming back. It shows great strength of character. So what happened at your work? When I asked you, your whole expression changed. You're trying to hide something, but I think you also want to talk about it."

Maggie sat on the edge of an armchair. She had no choice, the seat was piled high with crossword puzzle books. "Did you used to be a psychologist?"

"Of course not. Think I'd be living in this squalor if I was? So what happened in your job? No, don't tell me. Let me try and guess."

"I'll just tell you."

"No, no, I want to guess. Humor me, I'm an old lady."

"I don't want you to guess. I'm happy to tell you. Not happy. I want to tell you."

"Go on, then. All the details please. Make it juicy."

Maggie told it as it had happened. As she spoke, all the details returned in her mind. The look of the London conference room, the rows of seats, the noise from the whispered conversations among the two hundred people present. The tiny squeal from the microphone as she stood up to present her report.

She had Dolly's full attention. "I'd just announced our trading figures for the year, and explained to all the shareholders that the dip in profits meant the closure of one of our area offices. And then . . ." Maggie paused.

"Go on," Dolly said.

Maggie had ignored the man at first. Thought he was going out to the bathroom, or to make or take a phone call. She had kept talking as slide after slide of spreadsheets appeared on the big screen behind her. She had been looking down, reading off her notes when she heard a ripple of something, conversations, confusion from the audience. She'd looked up, and the man had been standing less than three meters away from her. She'd recognized him from the morning tea break. He'd been right in front of her now, his hands shaking.

Dolly was waiting. "Come on, then."

Maggie swallowed. "A man, one of our employees, came up to where I was standing at the microphone, took a gun out of a bag beside him, and shot himself in the head."

"Shot himself dead?"

"That was his intention. The police found a suicide note later. But he survived. The bullet passed through his skull, into the left side of his brain, and lodged there. He's been in a coma ever since. He's got a wife, two young children. The doctors said it's doubtful he'll ever recover. If he does gain consciousness, he'll have severe brain damage."

"How awful."

"Yes, it was."

"I bet he's annoyed. Goes to all that trouble, and it doesn't work."

"Dolly!"

"I can see how it would upset you, but why did it make you resign?"

"Because it was my fault. I was the one who made the decision to shut his office."

"So you were doing your job? And this man reacted in this extreme way. So you decide to react almost as extremely?"

"I had to leave the job. And I had to leave London. How could I stay there after something like that had happened?"

"Are you always this prone to melodrama?"

Maggie fought to keep her temper. She regretted telling her any of it. "I shouldn't have told you."

"Don't get snippy just because I'm not showering you with sympathy. Did you hate your job, anyway? Was this just a handy excuse to leave it?"

"I loved my job. You're twisting my words."

"You didn't want to be in London, anyway, did you?"

Maggie was silent for a long moment. Something about the directness of Dolly's gaze made her tell the truth. "No. Things hadn't been going well for me."

"Outside of work, you mean? Boyfriend trouble?"

Maggie nodded.

"What was his name?"

Maggie told her.

"Scottish, was he? From Glasgow or Edinburgh?"

"Edinburgh. You do a very good Scottish accent."

"I do a very good any accent. That's what I used to be, a voice coach on Broadway. So what happened with Angus?"

Maggie explained about walking in and discovering Angus and Lauren. Dolly laughed.

"It wasn't funny, Dolly."

"Of course it was. It's always funny to see people at it. The beast with two backs, as Shakespeare called it."

Dolly was right, Maggie admitted. It had looked comical. She started to smile.

Dolly looked pleased. "So what did you do then?"

Maggie told her. Dolly especially liked the fact she'd thrown water at the pair of them. "Like people do with mating dogs?" She was laughing so much, she started to wheeze. Maggie fetched the oxygen and stood beside her as Dolly breathed deeply for nearly a minute.

Dolly took another breath, and then gave Maggie a long look. "An attempted suicide in front of you and an unfaithful boyfriend in your own home. I wonder what the next bad thing will be for you. Bad things come in threes, you know."

"I know," Maggie said. She knew every saying there was about numbers. She and Leo had been collecting them for years. One in a million. Two's company, three's a crowd. Seventh heaven. A stitch in time saves nine. At sixes and sevens.

"So is that why you're here? You're on the run?"

"I'm not on the run. I'm taking a break." Assessing her options. Reviewing her life.

"And picking on charity cases, like me."

"That's right."

"You're not doing a very good job. Where's my cup of tea? And make one for yourself while you're at it, would you?"

Maggie prepared a tea tray, using surprisingly clean and delicate teacups and a teapot she found in one of the cupboards. She sat opposite her. Dolly barely took a sip ("Ugh, disgusting") before she started firing more questions. She wanted to know about Maggie's upbringing. About her family. "If you're going to be annoying me twice a week with these ridiculous visits, I want to know who the hell you are."

Maggie answered every one, to her own surprise. She was like a person just out of solitary confinement, desperate to talk. She told Dolly about her mother, her absent father, about all four of her aunts, even about Sadie the hippie who had run away. She told her about Leo and his inventions. She showed Dolly the family snapshot she always carried with her, the one taken at the airport the day she flew out to London, with everyone—everyone except Sadie, at least—there to see her off. She told her about the house in Donegal, about the July Christmases. How she had decided not to go to the July Christmas this year.

"Why not?"

Maggie decided she'd said enough for one day. "Can we talk about you now, instead of me?"

Dolly laughed. "All right. I'll leave you alone. We'll do my life tomorrow."

"You want me to come back so soon?"

"You have anything better to do?"

"No. I'd like to come back. You're sure you don't want to fire me first?"

"Not today. I'll ring and tell Giselle—"

"Gabriel."

"Whatever his name is, I'll tell him you're not as bad as I first thought."

"Can I get you anything else before I go? A cool drink? More oxygen?"

Dolly waved her hand at her. "Get out. Before you overstay your welcome. Stop blaming yourself about that man. And start being truthful to yourself. You wanted to leave London. All you have to do now is decide what you want to do next."

There was nothing to say to that. She was right.

*   *   *

It was now even steamier outside. It would have been cooler to take the subway, but Maggie wanted to walk. She needed to think about everything Dolly had said. She'd gotten so much of it wrong, of course. Hadn't she?

Maggie made her way down Tenth Avenue, sticking close to the buildings, trying to get some shade at least. She found herself near a small park, and went in through the gate. There wasn't much in the way of greenery. It was more a dog run, with two areas marked out—one for small dogs, one for large dogs. There weren't many takers for either. It was too hot for hounds as well as humans today. She spotted an empty bench in a corner by the fence, shaded by a spindly tree. She took a seat, leaned her head back, and looked up through the covering of leaves at the office buildings all around her. She imagined herself inside one of them, in her corporate clothing, at her computer, going through pages of figures, meeting with company directors. Feeling confident. Comfortable.

Claustrophobic.

Dolly was right. She'd had enough of that job, that life, London, and Angus. She had wanted to change it all months before she did. What had stopped her? Thoughts of her family? Fear of their reaction? They would have been worried, Maggie knew. That wasn't how she behaved. They were used to her succeeding, impressing and achieving. Not turning her back on everything.

She had been relieved to have an excuse not to go to Donegal this year. Not because she didn't want to see everyone. She loved her family. She loved those gatherings. But she hadn't been ready for their questions, not en masse. It had been hard enough on the phone with each of them. What was she going to do next? Was she sure she'd made the right decision? All these questions asked out of love and concern, she knew that, but overwhelming all the same.

"They all treat you like you're their little toy," Angus had said once, after a stream of calls from her mother and aunts about something as simple as her latest haircut. "Why don't they mind their own business?"

She'd defended them vigorously. But maybe he'd had a point?

"You don't have one mother, you've got four of them. Just because you lived with them when you were little doesn't mean they have ownership rights. Say no occasionally, Maggie."

She hadn't wanted to. She liked hearing their opinions and advice. Didn't she?

She rubbed at her nose. She knew she didn't regret leaving her job. She regretted the circumstances, but deep down, right deep down, had she been secretly grateful for being handed a simple exit? If she had handed in her resignation without a dramatic reason like that, there would have been an uproar: from her employers, her family, Angus. From her aunts particularly. Without that terrible day happening, she might have let it drift on with Angus even longer, too.

It was uncomfortable to think this way. She much preferred feeling she was the wronged woman, painting Angus as the villain.

"I would have ended it with him soon, anyway, I know I would have," she said out loud. She ignored a puzzled look from an elderly man walking past her.

There was a message from Gabriel waiting for her when she got back to her apartment, asking how she'd gotten on with Dolly. She called him back straightaway.

"We got on great today. I liked her."

"You liked her? She must have decided she liked you, too."

"I don't want to get too carried away. She tolerated me, let's say."

"So you're happy to keep seeing her?"

"She's asked me to go back again tomorrow."

"And you're going? So soon? Good luck. I'll make a note on your file for Mom. You'll get two gold stars after this."

Still sweaty from the long walk home, Maggie showered and changed into fresh clothes. The rest of the day stretched out in front of her. Talking to Gabriel had reminded her that she didn't actually have any friends here. If something were to happen to her, in fact, who would know? Who would come looking for her? Days could go by without anyone phoning, or if they did and got the machine, they might think she was just away on a day trip or lying low. She wondered if there was the equivalent of Rent-a-Grandchild for someone her age. Rent-a-Friend. Perhaps she could suggest it to Dora. Perhaps she could suggest it to Gabriel? Ring and ask him out for a drink?

No, she'd go and buy some fruit and vegetables, make a healthy salad, maybe go for a swim. Practical, day-to-day things. Self-reliant things. That's what this whole New York stay was about, after all. Being independent.

It was when she was at the checkout of the supermarket across the road that she realized her purse was missing. She had an awkward minute with the woman at the cash register, realizing she'd have to put everything back. She retraced her steps. It wasn't at the deli counter. It wasn't in the shopping cart. She returned to her apartment. It wasn't anywhere there, either. It was as she stood in the middle of the room that she remembered. She'd taken it out to show Dolly the family photo. She could picture exactly where she'd left it. Damn.

She rang Dolly's number first. No answer. It just went straight to the answering machine. She could picture Dolly in the middle of a crossword puzzle, ignoring it. Maggie had nothing else to do. She decided she might as well go and collect it now. Surprise Dolly with a second visit in the one day.

Her MetroCard was in her purse. It meant another long, hot walk back to Dolly's street. Up the five flights of stairs again. Down the corridor. She knocked at the door. No answer. She knocked again. "Dolly?"

Still no answer.

"Dolly?"

She tried the door. It should have been locked. The security chain should have been across it. It opened.

She knocked again. "Dolly?"

Dolly was there, sitting in her chair. Her arms were on her lap, her head lolling forward. Maggie didn't need to check her pulse to know she was dead.

CHAPTER 26

I t was after six by the time Maggie was back home in Greenwich Village. She had stayed in Dolly's apartment, sitting beside her body until the emergency workers arrived in response to her phone call. She explained who she was and why she was there. There'd have to be a post-mortem, they told Maggie, but it seemed straightforward. No suspicious signs. Heart failure from what they could tell.

"Good thing you're forgetful," one of the men said, picking up her purse and handing it over to her.

"Did you know her for long?" one of the police officers asked as they walked down the corridor together.

"Just a few weeks." She explained the situation. "She always used to fire me. Tell me not to visit her again. Except today she didn't. She asked me to come back."

"Maybe she knew."

Maggie stared up at him. "Do you think people know?"

A shrug. "I don't think so. Would we all live such messy lives if we knew our time was almost up?"

His words stayed with Maggie as she left Dolly's apartment building, joined the crowds on the pavement, down into the muggy scent of the subway. She stared across at her fellow passengers on the train, averting her gaze if anyone made eye contact, staring instead at their reflections in the dark windows. If there was a way of knowing they were going to die—if they had even the smallest inkling—what would all these people do? she wondered. What would she do? She knew the answer straightaway. Run to her mother, to Tadpole, to her aunts and surround herself with them, as quickly as she could.

She was coming up out of the subway when she realized she hadn't rung the Rent-a-Grandchild office. It seemed urgent to let them know. She took out her mobile phone and dialed the number. It was after hours. She wasn't surprised to get the answering machine.

"Dora, Gabriel, it's Maggie Faraday. I've just left Dolly Leeson's house." She paused. "Dolly died this afternoon." She briefly explained what had happened. "I called the ambulance. And the police. They've taken care of everything." She couldn't think of anything else to say after that, so she hung up.

Back in her apartment, she showered for a long time, scrubbing her skin hard, using a lot of body lotion afterward, trying to add another layer of scent and sensation around her instead of the memories of Dolly's locked-up flat. About to put on jeans, she heard Dolly's voice. "Why don't you dress up when you visit me? You'd look much prettier."

She put on the best of the three dresses she'd brought with her. It was dark red, a simple design, but beautifully cut. She put on pretty silver earrings. Makeup. Lipstick. "That's more like it. If you've got it, flaunt it," she could imagine Dolly saying.

She needed air. She went across to the windows, opening each of them as wide as she could, opening the door wide as well, letting the hot air into the apartment. She sat out on the balcony. She didn't smoke, but she knew there were cigarettes inside. She scrabbled in the drawers, found the crumpled pack. God knows how old they were, or who they had belonged to. She needed to do something, mark Dolly's passing in some way. Whiskey would have been better, a big flamboyant slug of Irish whiskey, or a gulp of rough Spanish wine—something Dolly herself would have liked. Maggie had nothing alcoholic, and she didn't have the energy to go out again to buy a bottle of wine. She managed one long drag on the musty-tasting cigarette, coughed, and put it out before lighting it again and making herself finish it.

She was in the bathroom, brushing her teeth to get rid of the taste, when the phone rang in the room behind her. She let it ring. She hadn't turned the answering machine on again since Gabriel had rung that morning. She'd turn it on soon. Just not yet. Her mobile rang. She let it go to voice mail too, not in the mood to talk. When she checked it a few minutes later, the caller hadn't left a message.

Nearly thirty minutes passed. She was sitting out on the balcony again, listening to the sounds of a city on a hot night when the apartment intercom rang. She leaped at the sound.

"Ray?" Her voice sounded odd, she realized.

"Hi, Maggie," the doorman answered. "You have a visitor."

"Who is it?"

"A man called Gabriel." He lowered his voice and chuckled. "Better than a boy named Sue, I guess."

"Gabriel's downstairs?"

"Want me to send him up?"

She hesitated. "No, I'll come down."

She took the lift, staring at herself in the mirrored walls of the small space. The nice dress and the full makeup looked incongruous.

There were a few people in the foyer, two talking to Ray at his desk. On the bench by the window, a gray-haired man was sitting. He was dressed in a faded green T-shirt. Jeans. Black runners. He was the only person watching the lift.

Maggie stepped hesitantly toward him. "Gabriel?"

"Maggie?" He stood up. He was tall. Serious faced. She realized then the gray hair was premature. He was only in his early thirties. "I got your message about Dolly. I called your cell phone and your home number, but nobody picked up."

"I'm sorry to put you to all this trouble. You didn't have to come."

"I did, actually. Legally. It's part of the arrangement. If something happens, we need to make sure you're okay. It's not fair for you to have to handle it on your own. And I knew Dolly too, re-member. . . ."

The tears came then. She hurriedly wiped them away. "Sorry. It's ridiculous, me carrying on like this. I only met her a few weeks ago."

"But she got under your skin."

"We got under each other's skin."

"Don't take it personally. She hated everyone, remember."

"But to die on her own like that. Gabriel, what if you hadn't called me? What if—"

"Maggie, I did call you. You went back to visit her. So there are no what-ifs."

But there were. Maggie could picture them all in her mind. Sad, lonely pictures.

"Maggie, do you want to go and have a drink? We can talk about Dolly, tear her to shreds. Have our revenge."

She badly wanted a drink. She badly wanted company. She wanted to talk to someone, and this kind man was offering all three things. "Are you sure? If you've got time."

"I'm very sure." He checked his watch. "And yes, I do have time. I have exactly three hours, then I need to go to work."

"You're working tonight?"

He gestured to the bench by the window. A guitar case, covered in stickers. She could read the writing on one of them: *"Buskers do it in all weather."*

"You're a busker?"

"One step up. I play in an Irish bar in midtown every Tuesday night."

"You don't sound Irish."

"Oh, I do when I need work in an Irish bar. 'And here is a song my great-grandfather taught me. Will you join me in "The Fields of Athenry." ' "

Maggie smiled. "That's very good. A bit of Dublin, a bit of Belfast."

"Not bad for a man who's never set foot in the place. I watched *The Commitments* a lot on DVD. Learned more swears than I'll ever be able to use in one lifetime. It was that or *The Field* over and over again." He grinned, switching back to his own accent. "I'm also Spanish when the tapas café in the West Village hires me. I'm a walking linguaphone CD. So should we go? Will three hours of drinking be enough for you?"

"Plenty."

"We'll have to start with whiskey, you realize. In Dolly's honor."

"Irish whiskey?"

"The very thing." A perfect Irish accent again.

She went back up to her apartment and gathered her bag and a jacket. Gabriel was waiting by the front desk when she returned. They walked out into the warm evening together.

Upstairs, in her apartment, her mobile phone started ringing.

* * *

At JFK airport, Leo hung up without leaving a message. He tried her home number, but it just rang out. These young things, too busy with their social lives to even answer a phone call. He'd wanted to check Maggie was there first, not just turn up and surprise her. Now it looked like he had no choice. He just hoped there was a comfortable chair in her lobby. He picked up his suitcase and the briefcase he hadn't let out of his sight for weeks now, and walked out toward the rank of yellow cabs.

Gabriel took Maggie to a bar he knew well, in the basement of a brownstone building in the West Village. The walls were stone, the chairs and tables wooden. Small chandeliers above the bar sent a muted light throughout the room while candles in glasses flickered on the tables. There was soft jazz playing in the background and the murmur of conversation and laughter from the other people there. Gabriel went to the bar and ordered two whiskeys while Maggie found a spare table in the corner.

"It's the best they had," Gabriel said as he returned with two glasses of honey-colored liquid. "Actually, it's the only Irish whiskey they had."

"Then Dolly can't complain."

"I bet she could." He smiled. He lifted his glass. "To Dolly."

"To Dolly," she echoed. They clinked glasses, the noise musical.

"In light of the fact we don't have too many happy memories of her to share, shall we exchange bad memories?" Gabriel asked. "You start. Tell me what names she used to call you."

Maggie told him about being called a troll and a hobbit. "She also called me a whippersnapper once."

"Whippersnapper? Very nice. I got called a brat. An ignorant brat at that. A mama's boy. A good-for-nothing slacker draining our taxes and why didn't I spend a year or two in the military and see if that would knock some sense into me?"

Maggie smiled. "I got told to go back to my own country, to stop taking jobs from Americans."

"I was asked if I were gay, and when I told her I wasn't, she said it looked like I was, dying my hair this fancy-pants gray. And when I told her I didn't spend any time on it; in fact, it suddenly went gray all on its own a few years ago, she told me off and said I should take more care of my personal appearance or I would never get a wife."

They both took a sip from their drinks, then spoke at exactly the same time.

"So what brought you to New York?" Gabriel asked.

"So how long have you been working as a musician?" Maggie asked.

They laughed. "You first," they said in unison again.

"We'll toss for it." He pulled out a coin. "Head or tail?"

She called head. It landed on head. "I should be asking you a deep, philosophical question after that lead-in. So how long *have* you been a musician?"

"I'm not really a musician. I'm just moonlighting as one at the moment."

"What are you really?"

"A cameraman. News and current affairs, mostly. I trained in a studio, then went out on the road."

"But you're not doing it anymore?"

"Not at the moment, no. And what about you? Was there life before Rent-a-Grandchild?"

"I was a financial controller in a company in London. Or as Dolly saw it, a jumped-up accountant."

"Until one day you woke up and thought, No, I'd rather live in New York. So you fiddled the books, stole a million dollars, and here you are?"

"No, not exactly." To her own surprise, she told him what had happened, in even more detail than she had told Dolly. The whiskey had loosened her tongue. After weeks of trying to block it out of her mind, she was relating it for the second time in one day. She described the awful moment of seeing the gun emerge from the man's bag, the look in the man's eyes as he put it to his temple.

The smell of gunpowder afterward, combined with the sounds of screaming all around her. They were the two sensations that had been the hardest to forget. Some of his blood had landed on her jacket, which had been folded on the chair beside her. She hadn't noticed it until hours later, after the ambulance and police had gone. She hadn't taken it home. She'd put it straight in the bin.

"Do you regret resigning?"

She'd not been asked that before. She shook her head. "I couldn't have stayed there. I was told over and over that it wasn't anything directly to do with me, but I didn't feel that way. I still don't. I feel like it was my fault."

"I can see how you would think that."

At last, someone who understood. "Thank you."

"But you're wrong. It wasn't your fault."

"I think it is. I'd never been aware that my fun and games with numbers actually affected people's lives."

"Fun and games? That's how you thought of your work?"

She nodded. "I loved working with numbers. Any kind of math."

"You said you loved it. Past tense. So you don't anymore?"

She rubbed her nose. "I don't know yet. I've decided not to work in that area for a while. Not while I'm here, anyway."

"There's lots of other things you could do, isn't there? There must be a shortage of people who like numbers and math. Everyone I ever knew hated them."

"I was an oddity at my school, too. I haven't decided yet what I'll do next. I'm living off my savings. When they run out, I'll see."

He nodded. "You rub your nose a lot when you're talking. Did you know that?"

She stopped, embarrassed. "My mother used to say I'd wear the tip off if I wasn't careful. It's a habit I have when I'm thinking hard about something."

"So it's a good sign? It shows I'm a thought-provoking conversationalist? That's a relief."

They started talking about his music. He talked about the songs he played—Irish standards, Bob Dylan, Cat Stevens, all the old faithfuls. She asked how long he'd played guitar; since he was a twelve-year-old, he said, twenty-one years ago now. What was it like to sing in bars? Difficult, he told her, because people didn't really care if he was there, alive and kicking and singing, or if it was taped music playing. Could he make a living out of it? If he played seven evenings and seven lunchtimes a week, and in the middle of the night now and again, yes, he could. In his current situation, two nights a week in Irish bars? No, he couldn't. Which was why, in addition to helping his mother out in the office whenever she needed him to fill in, he was also her number-one window cleaner and dog walker. "I drew the line at the Avon selling at first, but I'm not ruling anything out now."

"And you still live at home?"

He winced. "Maggie, please. I'm thirty-three years old. No, I share an apartment off Lafayette Street with two friends. One's a doctor, so I never see him. The other's a writer who spends all his time watching TV instead of working on his book, so I see a little too much of him at the moment."

"Is that your dream? To be a full-time musician?"

"My dream? I don't think I've thought of anything as a dream, especially not the music."

"So why do you do it?"

He smiled. "Because I can."

She remembered something he had said earlier. Normally she wouldn't ask such a personal question, but this didn't feel like a normal conversation. It was as if they had leapfrogged from early awkwardness into a kind of intimacy.

"You said before that your hair turned gray suddenly. Why?"

He swallowed the last of his drink and sat quietly.

She'd made a mistake. It was obviously more sensitive than she realized. "Sorry, Gabriel. I shouldn't have asked."

"Of course you can ask. It's just the gray-hair story is what I'd call a long one. And here we are only finishing the getting-to-know-you stories. If we're both still standing later, I promise I'll start on the long stories. Speaking of which, can I get you another drink?"

He had evaded her very smoothly. Did she want another drink?

A combination of the day's events, a lack of food, and the whiskey was making her light-headed. Or perhaps it was the fun of talking to another human being that was having this effect on her. "If I have another, I'll be singing along with your Irish tunes."

"You're going to come and hear me?"

"Is that okay?"

"Of course. But in that case, I'm getting you a triple shot. A backing singer might make all the difference to my performance."

Somehow, without either of them noticing, three hours passed. They switched from whiskey to beer, alternating turns at the bar. She heard funny stories about his dog walking and told him stories in turn about Leo's inventions. They talked about their school days, which led to talk about their families, which led to talk about their fathers. Gabriel's parents had split up when he was four. He rarely saw his father. Maggie told him about David. "A friend of mine calls them celebration fathers. You only hear from them at Christmas and birthdays." They talked seriously about that, exchanged thoughts on whether it had affected their lives. Maggie was sure it hadn't in her case. Gabriel said the truth was, he did miss his father. Missed the idea of his father, that was. "The real one I'm not so keen on." It changed into a lighthearted conversation again when a person at the other end of the bar reminded Gabriel of a man he had worked with once, a sound technician in the TV station he trained at, sparking an anecdote about a newscaster swearing, not realizing she was on camera. Maggie was seconds from asking him about that work when he glanced down at his watch. He stood up, looking alarmed. "Oh, hell. I was supposed to be on stage twenty minutes ago."

They ran. It took them fifteen minutes to get there. Gabriel had trouble keeping the guitar case from crashing into people as they passed. He stopped and apologized every time. Maggie had trouble running and laughing at the same time.

"You go ahead," she called. "I'll meet you there."

He shouted back his thanks and was meters ahead when she realized something important. She called out again. "Gabriel, where are we going?"

"Rosie O'Grady's," he shouted back. "Corner of Ninth and West Seventeenth."

He was waiting out front by the time she arrived, only a few minutes after him. She could tell by the look on his face there was a problem. A glance into the bar confirmed it. There was someone else playing guitar on the stage.

"You were too late?" she asked.

He nodded. "I've been fired."

"But you're only half an hour late."

"He's been looking for an excuse. That's his nephew up there. I told you, the Irish bar scene in this city is a dog-eat-dog world."

"Gabriel, I'm so sorry. It's my fault."

"It's not your fault. It's Dolly's fault. I blame Dolly." He looked up and did a mock shake of his fist at the sky. "She told me she always hated Irish music. Music for maudlin, moaning old minnies, she called it. This is her revenge."

They were both still panting from the run. They stepped to one side as a group of people arrived, jostling into the bar. Maggie was momentarily pushed against Gabriel. She smelled his aftershave or deodorant—a subtle, woody smell—and just as briefly felt his body under the cotton T-shirt. A sudden image came to mind of Angus's slightly overweight pale body. Then, in another flash, an image of what Gabriel's body would be like. Tanned and lean. She stepped away quickly, glad of the flashing lights from the bar covering the blush she knew was on her face.

He hadn't noticed. "I know you're probably nearly in tears with disappointment at not getting to hear me sing, but can I take you for a meal instead? Unless you have other plans for tonight?"

She didn't have to think about it. "I'd like that very much."

They went to a small Italian restaurant Gabriel knew, back toward Greenwich Village. The streets were filling with people, out on a hot night.

They were shown to a table to the side of the room, against a window. There was opera playing in the background, murmured conversations all around them. It was like a date. Maggie felt self-conscious. She did what she always did when she was feeling nervous—tugged at her hair, pulling it over her ears.

"If you're trying to hide your ears because of me, don't," Gabriel said in a conversational tone. "I like them. They suit you."

Maggie went red again. "Sorry," she said, fighting the temptation to pull her hair over them again.

The food was delicious, the wine was good, the conversation lively. They talked over each other now and again, finishing each other's sentences, finding things in common, making each other laugh.

He apologized for telling a long story about a hitchhiking trip he'd once taken. "I should have saved that one up for another night. You've now heard every funny story I know. I'll have to go away and write some more before we meet up next."

She disguised her pleasure at his words. He wanted to meet up again? "No, there's still one story you haven't told me. Two, in fact."

"Two?"

"I wanted to ask why you stopped working as a cameraman. And you promised to tell me the one about your gray hair."

"That's right, so I did." He stirred the sugar into his coffee.

He wasn't smiling, she noticed. "Gabriel, I'm sorry. You don't have to tell me."

"You don't have to apologize. It's just I don't talk about it very much."

"You don't have to."

"I'd like to. It's probably time I did."

Gabriel began to talk. Yes, he had been a cameraman, up until two years before. He'd been working in TV since he was eighteen, fifteen years ago now. He'd started as a runner on one of the New York–based news programs, getting the job through a friend of his mother's. A year later he started training as a studio cameraman. That had led to a job as a trainee cameraman on local news programs, when he was twenty years old, then he moved to the network's Washington office. He'd gone freelance after that, taking jobs wherever they came up, constantly traveling. He did documentaries, music videos and the occasional advertisement even. He liked it that way, he said. He started getting work outside of the U.S. He went to Venezuela for a documentary. To Argentina to film elections. Then three years later he took a permanent job as a news cameraman with one of the cable TV networks.

Three months into the job he was sent to the Middle East, his first time in a war zone. Everyone told him it sounded more dangerous than it was. The footage on the bulletins was often dramatic, but there were days when nothing would happen. The producer would be the one out hunting stories, he was told. There'd be a lot of waiting around in his hotel.

That's how it was for the first two weeks, he told Maggie. Then, two days into week three, a big story broke. A leader of one of the opposition parties was assassinated, sparking tit-for-tat killings, riots, and demonstrations. An American soldier was killed. Gabriel was in the midst of it, working all hours, every day.

"It went from nothing to everything, all at once, eighteen-hour days, no breaks. We barely had time to edit pieces before we were out getting another story."

"Were you scared?" Maggie asked.

He shook his head. "It was like getting a shot of adrenaline after all the waiting around. It was exciting. One morning we got word there was something big going on in the center of the city. An attack on the American embassy, we were told. For once it was true. We heard the explosion on our way there, and then sirens and screaming. We got there and it was mayhem: people bleeding, bodies on the ground, a water pipe gushing, the smell of gas—" He stopped. He wasn't looking at her now, but fidgeting with the sugar packet on the table.

"We went right to work. I started filming general scenes while the reporter and our interpreter began talking to bystanders, trying to find out what had happened. I was walking away from the building to get a wider shot when a second explosion went off. Right in front of the embassy. Right where I had been. Where our reporter and interpreter still were."

Maggie didn't speak. Gabriel had now folded the sugar packet into tiny pieces.

"They were both killed instantly. They didn't have a chance. The people they were talking to were killed too. Another six died later from their injuries. I got hit by something; I don't know what. Something sharp. But it was nothing compared to the others. At least a dozen people were killed that day, maybe more, I never found out for sure."

She noticed then he was rubbing at a scar on his left arm. "Gabriel, I'm so sorry."

"It was chaos, Maggie. Complete chaos. The producer and I were lifted out of there. I had a week of medical treatment, some counseling. Then suddenly I was back in Washington, back to normal life. Except it wasn't normal. I'd turned into a different person." He looked at her then, as if coming out of a daze. "Maggie, I'm sorry. Why am I telling you this?"

"It's fine, please, go on."

"I stayed in Washington for another few months, but it just got stranger. Harder. I'd gotten scared. I'd lost the ability to be detached. Even with soft news stories or interviews with politicians, I was jumpy. If I heard a car backfire, I'd be a mess. We had a big memorial service for our reporter, and I had to leave halfway through. I kept thinking about the interpreter too. I'd only known him slightly, but he was my own age; we liked the same music; I'd promised to send him some CDs. But he was dead, and if I hadn't walked away when I did, I'd have been dead too. I should have felt like the lucky one, but I felt guilty. I got obsessed with news stories about similar events. All the fatalities and the near misses. One Monday morning I woke up and I knew I couldn't do it anymore. I was a liability in the studio and out in the field. This had started to happen." He gestured to his hair. "I turned gray in less than four months. The doctor said maybe it was coincidence. Mom said her grandfather went gray as a young man too. Maybe it wasn't connected, I still don't know. That same day I went into work and resigned. I moved back here, Mom took pity on me with some work,

I started singing in bars for extra money. And that's where I am now."

"Have you worked as a cameraman since?"

He shook his head. "About a year ago, I thought about it. I went in to see a friend here in New York, who works at NBC. I was in the newsroom, listening to the gossip, talking to the camera crew, and it happened again. I got scared. Not only of what I might film and what I might see, but fearful of what I might get wrong, what I might miss. You can't do a job like that if you're scared." He blinked, as if he could hardly believe all he had just said. "So there it is, Maggie. The whole messy story."

"Why is it messy?"

"It's not exactly a heroic tale, is it? I'm hardly the brave, fearless news gatherer."

"It must have been terrible. I can understand exactly why you had to leave."

He leaned across and almost absentmindedly took her hand, just for a moment. "Thank you for listening."

She touched his hand in return. "Thank you for telling me."

*   *   *

It was nearly midnight by the time they left the restaurant and started walking back toward Maggie's apartment. It was still warm, the streets still filled with people. They were two blocks away when Gabriel realized he'd forgotten his guitar, and they had to go back to the restaurant to get it.

"Hardly a dedicated musician, am I, leaving it behind as easily as that?"

"Perhaps you should switch to being a concert pianist. You wouldn't forget a Steinway so easily."

"I could buy a little cart and pull it along behind me," Gabriel suggested.

"That's the big disappointment of the evening," Maggie said. "You got fired, and I didn't get to hear you sing."

"Fired from only one job. I'm playing tomorrow night."

"You are? Where?"

"I'm not telling."

"I'll ring every Irish bar in the city."

"There are thousands of them, and I sing under a fake name."

"Really? What name?"

"Bono," he said.

They were walking through Washington Square Park when she stopped. "This is a perfect setting. Sing for me now, then. In Dolly's memory."

"Here? In public? Without the benefit of inebriated customers to cheer me on?"

"I dare you."

"You *dare* me?" He laughed. "As in, we're both eight years old, and, in that case, I dare you to, I don't know, eat a snail?"

"That's it." She laughed too. "If you sing, then I'll eat a snail. And I hate snails."

He held out his hand. She shook it. "Deal," they said in unison.

They stopped at a bench, and he took the guitar out of its case and took a seat. Maggie sat down next to him, watching as he placed it on his knee, strummed it, once, twice, then tweaked a tuning peg. He ran through several chords.

"You *can* play. That sounded great."

"No, it didn't, but yes, I can actually play. I take requests, too. What would you like to hear? Maudlin Irish, sexy Spanish, or a cross between the two?"

"What would that sound like?"

"This." He played softly, singing the words to "The Wild Rover" to a Spanish flamenco tune. Maggie started to laugh.

"Join in on the chorus," he said. " 'No nay never, no nay never no more, will I play the wild rover, no never, no more.' "

He had just started on the second verse when a string broke.

"That's Dolly at work, I think," Maggie said.

"It'll take more than that for her to silence me," Gabriel replied. "I've got spare strings in my case." He glanced around. "I just need a bit more light. I can't stop there, can I? Our poor hero's heart is breaking, and we need to get him into that boat and across the sea to Ireland before it's too late."

"In a Spanish galleon?"

"You've got it." Gabriel smiled.

"My apartment's just over there, and I've got plenty of lights. If I make you a cup of coffee while you fix the string, will you sing the rest to me?"

"That sounds like a fair deal. Is your apartment soundproof, though? I'd hate to upset your neighbors."

She assured him it would be fine. As they crossed the busy street, he put his arm across her back to guide her. He didn't take it away when they reached the other side.

CHAPTER 28

"Can I get you anything else, Leo?"

"I'm just fine, Ray, thanks very much."

Leo finished reading the copy of the *New York Post* the doorman had loaned him, leaned back in the armchair, settled the briefcase on his lap, and shut his eyes. He'd been waiting in the foyer of Maggie's building for nearly two hours now. He and Ray had become quite good friends. In retrospect, it would have made more sense to go to his hotel and ring Maggie every now and then from his room, but he was here now. Surely she wasn't that far away. Ray said that a young man had called for her earlier. She certainly hadn't mentioned anything about seeing anyone, not that she necessarily would have, Leo reasoned. She'd barely told her family what she was doing in New York in any case.

The sudden sound of a police siren on the street outside made him jump. He wondered what his daughters would say when they heard he'd made a trip to New York. Well, he'd find out soon enough. If his plan worked—if Maggie agreed to do what he was going to ask her—by the end of the week he'd be sitting around a dinner table with all five of them in Donegal, about to deliver some bombshell news.

How would he tell them? he wondered. Blurt it out as soon as they were all in the same room? Or wait a day or two for the usual meeting-up-again tensions to die down; for the clear, calm air of

Donegal to have its usual soothing effect on them? That was probably the best approach, he thought. They'd all waited twenty years
for this news, after all. What would a few more days matter?

He rehearsed several combinations before deciding he'd say it
as it was. "Girls, I've got some news." A pause. "I've found Sadie."

He pictured their reactions. Astonishment, amazement, disbelief. Where? How? What? When? All the questions he himself had
asked the private detective when he'd rung with the news.

"You're sure it's her? She's alive and well?"

"Alive and kicking," the man had said.

It was only the third time Leo had spoken to the detective. He'd
felt foolish the first time he rang him, as he explained the situation.
He'd kept it simple. He didn't tell the whole truth. He said that his
fourth daughter had made the decision to leave the family twenty
years ago. They'd always assumed, he didn't know why, that she had
stayed in Australia. She never seemed to have a lot of get-up-and-
go, you see, Leo explained. She was a homebody.

"You're sure she's still alive?"

Leo explained about the annual birthday cards to Maggie. The
most recent one had arrived just a few months before.

"And tell me again how you found this photo that you think is of
her?"

It had happened in a roundabout way, Leo explained. The thing
was, he was an inventor. Well, a retired inventor.

That sparked genuine interest. "Really? What have you invented?"

Leo had toyed with the idea of giving the man the details of his
two most successful inventions. The lawn mower fuel filter, which
had gone on to earn him hundreds of thousands of dollars, although that had been chicken feed compared to what its successor,
his petrol pump invention, had brought him. The royalties the
multinational oil company had paid him for the rights had made
him extremely comfortable, wealth-wise. His daughters, and Maggie, would be left that way after he'd gone, too. They'd be surprised, he knew that. They thought he was still living off the

earnings from the lawn mower invention. He was happy for them to think that way. He liked the idea of his real wealth being a surprise.

Just as coming across the photograph of Sadie had been a surprise. More than a surprise. A shock. It had happened five weeks earlier. He'd been at Heathrow Airport, almost his second home, waiting for his plane to Rome to board. He was going to visit the museum devoted to the drawings of Leonardo da Vinci; not just his namesake, but, in Leo's eyes, the original and best inventor in the world. As he sat, he'd watched a uniformed woman polish a nearby floor with an industrial cleaner. Back and forth, back and forth she had gone, missing sections each time. It was so inefficient, Leo thought. Not that it was the cleaner's fault. It was the equipment she was using. The machine was the wrong shape, with that round tip. It meant it couldn't get into the corners. It needed to be square. Possibly even diamond-shaped. Yes, diamond-shaped, but with a brush attachment that could swivel if necessary.

He jotted a few points down in the notebook he always carried with him, then forgot all about it. Until a week later, one idle afternoon in his Rome hotel room, he came across his notes and sketches. His imagination was sparked. He went down to the hotel's business center, intending to while away a few hours on the computer investigating it further, checking to see whether anyone had had the idea before him.

He checked the websites he knew that other inventors used to register early ideas. Nothing there. He checked the major cleaning equipment manufacturers' websites. No, they were all sticking with the traditional design. He keyed "industrial cleaning" into Google and watched as more than twenty million possible findings appeared. He laughed. Well, he didn't have much else to do that afternoon. He looked at sites based in the U.K. A subject heading caught his eye. A conference held eleven months earlier in Oslo. "Industrial Cleaning: The Future Is Green." He clicked on that.

He read the conference program. He looked at the list of speakers. He scrolled through the abstracts. Then, out of sheer curiosity, he clicked on the page marked "Delegates." There were dozens of shots of groups of people, smiling at the camera and dressed in their best, for the conference dinner, Leo guessed.

He spotted her immediately. She was in the third photo, in the front row, dressed in a red gown. She looked older than the last time he had seen her—of course she did, she was twenty years older—but it was her. Sadie. Sadie's face, Sadie's expression. Sadie's slightly uncertain smile. It was his missing daughter, his apparently hippie daughter, standing in a group of delegates concerned about the future of industrial cleaning products at a conference in Oslo.

He turned away from the computer. He went to the refreshments area of the business center, made himself a cup of tea, brought it back to the computer. He clicked the refresh button, and the same photograph came up. He tried to enlarge it, and was able to make it just slightly bigger.

He stared at her face again. He wasn't mistaken. It was Sadie smiling back at him.

There were no captions on the photograph, beyond a one-liner: "Delegates pictured prior to the conference dinner. A great night was had by all."

He didn't say or do anything about it for a week. Then he rang the number of the conference organizers. He thought he knew someone pictured on their website, he said. Could they give him the person's name and address? He was told that the person who had organized that particular conference had left the organization.

He contacted the Industrial Cleaners' Association itself and asked the same question. The woman who answered the phone was very unhelpful. They had more than two thousand members across Europe, the woman told him. It would take an age to find out who he was talking about.

"The woman in a red dress on the website," Leo said.

"I wore a red dress to that dinner," the woman said. "You'll have to do better than that."

On the phone to his lawyer three days later, he posed a hypothetical question: How would you track someone down if all you had was a photo from a website?

"The way smart people get anything done in this world. Pay someone else to do it."

It wasn't the first time the idea of a private detective had come up in regard to Sadie. In the early years, Leo had actively considered it. It was Juliet who had talked him out of it. "We write to her with Maggie's cards every year, Dad. She knows we want to see her. If she doesn't want to see us, we can't make her."

"But what if she needs our help? What if she's in trouble?"

"She doesn't want our help. I don't think she wants anything to do with us."

This felt different, though. Seeing Sadie's photo out of the blue like that seemed like a sign, from Tessa, or perhaps even from Sadie herself. Maybe things had changed by now. Maybe she was ready to see them?

His lawyer recommended the names of several firms. Leo chose one in London. If Sadie was a member of that association, she obviously was based in Europe somewhere. That narrowed it down to forty-seven or so countries.

Leo rang the agency, agreed to a fee, and briefed the investigator assigned to him. He sounded young. Confident. Smooth talking. More like a salesman than a detective, Leo thought. Perhaps that's what was needed in his job. Smooth-talking skills to prize information out of people who didn't want to give it.

Leo left him to it. He heard nothing for three weeks, rang to inquire, and was told investigations were underway and they'd be back to him with a full report as soon as possible.

A week after that, he'd gotten the call. The woman in the red dress had been found, alive and well and living very successfully in Dublin. Not only that—the woman Leo had thought was Sadie Faraday now called herself Sally O'Toole.

Leo had been shocked at both pieces of news. "A new name? And she's in Dublin? Dublin, *Ireland*? How did she get there? What is she doing? Is she all right?"

"I'm going there as soon as I can to find out. I'll be back to you with a full report."

Leo was expecting the report any day now. He'd had to stop

himself from ringing the detective too often to check on his progress. It seemed crucial to keep everything moving. He glanced at his watch. He would wait until twelve for Maggie, he decided. If she hadn't come home by then, he'd have to leave a message and come back in the morning.

He was longing to see her, he realized. They weren't just grandfather and granddaughter. They were friends. Allies. He thought back to the hours they had spent working together in Shed Land in Hobart. Everything revolved around numbers for them, even back then.

"I want you to find out five things about the moon landing for me, Maggie."

"Get me the names of six explorers."

"Tell me seven things about the early days of Australia."

"Who were King Henry VIII's six wives?"

She would go off to the library with Clementine or in later years on her own, returning with her little notebook—a copy of his own—filled with facts.

She'd always loved those games. Anything to do with numbers. They'd tricked her into doing household chores by the same method. Clementine would give her a list of tasks to be done. 1. Tidy bedroom. 2. Weed garden. 3. Sweep front veranda. It turned it into a game for Maggie. She always did it in the right order, too.

Perhaps that would be the best approach here. Explain that he had three things that he needed doing. Three very important things. And she was the only person in the whole world who could do them.

"That's bribery. Emotional blackmail." He could hear Miranda saying it to him. She had accused him of that sort of behavior in the past. He'd been hurt by that. It had made him sound manipulative, cunning. That wasn't how it was. He couldn't help it if his favorite thing in the whole world was to be surrounded by his daughters and his granddaughter. It wasn't a selfish thing, either. Not completely. He felt it was the best way of honoring Tessa's memory. The only way left to him.

He hadn't told his girls, but in his mind's eye, Tessa had been at every one of those family gatherings. Afterward, he had held imaginary conversations with her, the way they used to do when they'd been to work dinners together or parties. He had always enjoyed those chats, often more than the outings in question. He'd loved sitting up with Tessa in the kitchen, knowing the girls were all fast asleep in their bedrooms. They would talk about the evening, he would ask her who she had spoken to, who she had danced with, what she had thought of every moment. She always had such a turn of phrase. A bit wicked, sometimes. Miranda had inherited that, Leo knew. Tessa was always particularly scathing about some of his colleagues' wives, Leo remembered now, with a guilty pleasure. She'd make him laugh, even while he told her to be kinder.

See, you can still remember her, Leo said to himself, sitting up straighter in the chair, the relief giving him an extra burst of energy. He was panicking unnecessarily. All because of one silly incident a few months back, when for the first time ever, he hadn't been able to bring an image of Tessa to mind. It had set off a domino effect. He'd tried to recall her voice. Nothing. Her laugh. Nothing.

That's what had given him the idea of putting together a Tessa memorial. It was the perfect solution. Thoughts and memories and photographs of her all in one place. And what better way to do it than in scrapbook form, which she herself had loved? The more he'd thought about it, the more the idea appealed. He'd follow the same approach, he decided. Fill the Tessa scrapbook with memories of conversations, with impressions of her, photographs, recollections. If the worst thing happened, if he ever found himself struggling to recall her, all he would need to do is open the pages and there the memories would be.

And what better time and place to gather all those memories than during the July Christmas celebration in Donegal? He'd thought it all through. He would put Maggie in charge of it. It would be a perfect job for her. He'd ask her to interview him, Clementine, and her aunts; ask them for all their memories of Tessa, write them all down, bring them together into one place. It was important. Time was slipping away, and he wanted there to be a record of her, for after he had gone, after his daughters had gone. He wanted Maggie's children to know as much as they could about their great-grandmother. He also wanted to have a record himself, just in case his worst fear happened and he began to forget her.

That sudden blank moment had frightened him. He'd actually made an appointment with a doctor about it. He'd told him he was concerned he was losing his mind. When the doctor asked what the symptoms were, he hesitated only a moment. "I can't remember my wife as much as I used to."

"You're a widower?"

Leo nodded.

"How long since she passed away?"

"Thirty-five years," Leo said.

The doctor almost laughed. Leo noticed. It got his back up.

"Mr. Faraday, that's perfectly natural, I assure you. Time passes, memories fade, especially after such a long time."

"I know about other people. I don't want it to happen to me. I don't want to forget about her."

"But thirty-five years on? You haven't met anyone else since?"

"I haven't wanted to."

The doctor didn't understand. Leo left the doctor's office soon afterward.

He'd never wanted to get married again. Tessa's memory sustained him. As he knew the memory of her sustained his daughters. She was still a part of all their lives, remembered through all the beautiful traditions she had started: the birthday chair, the July Christmas. They had adapted them, as they should have done. Tessa would never have imagined their July Christmas celebrations taking place in Donegal, he was sure of that, but it kept her memory alive. Each of them had their own memories of her, special ones. He didn't want to change that. Any more than he didn't want to change his own memories of her. Precious, beautiful memories that had kept him going after her death. Kept all of them going.

Leo reached down and put his hand on the briefcase beside

him, checking once again it was there. It barely left his sight, not since he had carefully packed all nine of Tessa's diaries inside. He always traveled with them these days, cumbersome as they were sometimes. When he lived in Hobart, it had been enough to know they were in the shed beside him as he worked. Thirty-five years and he still hadn't read them. He hadn't needed to.

But things were different now. He needed to know what was in them, before he went to visit Sadie.

He had never told the girls all that Sadie had said to him that day in the caravan park, when he and Clementine had found her with Maggie. It had been a terrible time, and that had been a terrible day. He had never seen Clementine lose her temper, never seen her hit anyone, but that day he thought she would have killed Sadie if she could.

Sadie had stood, unmoved, as Clementine hit her. She had been as unmoved when Leo had taken her inside the trailer, begged her to tell him why she had done what she'd done, to explain herself. She had stared at him as if he was a stranger.

"We love you, Sadie. If you're unhappy, if something's wrong, tell me, please. Your mother would have hated to see you like this."

She had put her hands over her ears. "I can't listen to this anymore. No more lies."

"What are you talking about?"

"Don't pretend you didn't know. It's all there, in black and white."

His expression must have been blank.

"In Mum's diaries. The ones in your shed, remember?"

"Your mother's diaries? You found them? You read them? How dare you!" He was still ashamed of himself for losing his temper at her, for choosing that moment to do it, when he should have been calm, supportive, helping her. But he had seen red. She knew that the shed was out of bounds, the cupboard was out of bounds. All the tension of the past two weeks had spilled over as he accused her of snooping, of underhanded behavior, of poking her nose where she shouldn't . . .

Sadie didn't try to explain herself. She didn't tell him how she'd found them or when she'd read them or what she had read. She didn't say anything. She simply turned away from him while he kept shouting. He faltered, ordered her to pay attention, to look at him while he was talking to her. She didn't. She just sat there, as if he wasn't there, as if he wasn't talking to her.

He had no choice but to leave. He told her he'd be back the next day, that they'd all sleep on it, tomorrow was a new day. All the clichés poured out of him. None of them had mattered in the end. When he came back to the caravan park in the morning, she was gone.

When he, Clementine, and Maggie arrived back in Hobart the following day, one of the first things he did was go to the shed and unlock the cupboard. The red basket was pushed into the bottom shelf, roughly, on an angle. How had he not noticed that? He was always careful to put everything back neatly; keep his shed meticulously tidy. He took the basket out, lifted the magazines that were on top, saw the familiar nine notebooks underneath. He knew as soon he saw them that what Sadie had said was true. They were out of order. He had never left them like that.

He sat in the shed for a long time, the diaries on his lap. What had she read in there? What were the lies she mentioned? The fact is, he didn't know. He had never read the diaries. He still didn't want to read them now.

Two months after Tessa had died, when his whole world was in pieces, when it hurt even to get up, he had made the mistake of thinking it would help to read her words. He made a ritual of it. He made himself shower, shave, not be the haunted man who had looked back at him in the mirror for the past two months. He brought a cup of freshly brewed tea in her favorite blue cup down to the shed, prepared his desk, made it tidy. He unlocked the cupboard, took out the red basket, and picked out the first diary. He opened it at a random page, telling himself it was what Tessa would have wanted. That she would send him a message through her diaries. He knew it was fanciful thinking, but he was so desperate for her, so sure that she was watching over them all that he convinced himself this was the best way—the only way—to keep up contact with her.

He opened it at a page a third of the way in. He read the first three sentences: *"Bill took me to the heath today, for the most romantic picnic. It is love. I know it!"*

Leo almost physically recoiled. He shut the book, pushed it away as if he had been burned. He returned it to the basket, put the basket into the cupboard, locked it. His breathing was ragged. He realized he was crying. Sobbing. He couldn't read that. He couldn't read anything about her and Bill. Not now that it was too late to re-create memories. He couldn't bear to think of her and Bill together when she was alive. He could not allow any other memories to invade his memory of her now that she was dead.

Months passed before he looked at the diaries again. His grieving was still fierce, his sorrow deep. He didn't read them the second time. He held them, he put them back into the right order, he made himself think good thoughts—of Tessa laughing, of Tessa with the girls, of Tessa excited about one of their birthdays or about a trip home to the U.K. That thought was a jagged one. She had never gone into great detail about her trips home every two years. He had asked her lots about each one, all the questions except the one he didn't want to know the answer to. "Did you see Bill?"

He couldn't bear to know if she had.

He knew the answer would be in these diaries. She always took them with her to the U.K. If he wanted to know whether she had seen Bill, all he had to do was open the right diary, find the right page. He could read all about it. Know once and for all what had happened, whether his greatest fear had been true—that she had gone on loving Bill even after she had married him.

Is this what Sadie had read? Had she found out all about Tessa's history with Bill? Had she found out even more—that Tessa hadn't just had a history with Bill, she'd had an ongoing relationship, even after their marriage?

Was that what had caused her to run away and take Maggie with her? Once the thought wormed its way into his head, he found it almost impossible to remove. What could Sadie have read that would make her want to leave the family?

Deep down, he thought he knew. Had Sadie read that she wasn't Leo's daughter? That she was, in fact, Bill and Tessa's daughter?

The thought wouldn't go away. Yes, all five girls looked like him, but they could also just as easily be Bill's daughters. He found himself studying photos of all five of them, finding the resemblances, convincing himself that there were only his features replicated in them. But the voice inside continued to torment him. Did they all look like him, or did any of them look more like Bill? He and Bill had shared the same coloring, and they were alike in facial features and build, although Bill was the taller, nearly six foot. Tall, like Miranda and Juliet were tall. His hair was curlier, too, like Sadie and Eliza's hair was. He was prone to sunburn—as was Clementine. Leo was making a mental checklist, and he didn't like the findings.

He spent hours sitting and holding the diaries, knowing the truth was inside and fearing it. He imagined Sadie sitting in the same position, reading them, and discovering what? That she was the only one who wasn't his daughter? That none of them were his daughters? He couldn't bear to think about any of it.

So he'd had to lie to his other four daughters. He couldn't tell them the truth about his conversation with Sadie that day in the trailer park. If he said that she'd read the diaries, they would know he'd lied about burning them. They would insist on reading them, too. And if they did, everything might come tumbling down around him.

So he told them Sadie left for a different reason. That she had wanted to find herself. He had let them think that all these years, Sadie had been away. Then another equally unsettling thought had occurred to him. What if Sadie came back and shared what she had discovered with her sisters? He pictured the scene. She would arrive, different, confident and determined to tell the truth. She wouldn't let Miranda intimidate her, Juliet smother her, Eliza dismiss her or Clementine keep her away from Maggie again. She would stand there and tell them their whole family was based on lies, that Leo wasn't her father and wasn't their father either. And all he had worked for, all he loved, would collapse in front of him . . .

He had written to her each year, enclosing his letter with Maggie's cards, urging her to get in touch. Urging her to meet him somewhere, anywhere. He was careful with his wording. He didn't say, "Come home." He was too unsure, too scared to invite her back without knowing what it was she knew.

In the early years after Sadie left, Leo had thought about tracking down his brother and just asking him outright. It would be difficult. They had lost contact with each other in the years following Tessa's death. Leo hadn't even been sure where Bill was living; in the U.K. or South Africa or somewhere else. Then, while he was still deciding what to do, he'd got word from a lawyer in London that Bill had died. His daughters had been full of sympathy. Leo hadn't known how he felt. He and Bill hadn't been close for a very long time. Now all chance of a reunion, and of finding out the truth from him, were gone.

He'd put it out of his mind as best he could back then. But he couldn't live with the uncertainty anymore. Something had led him to find that photograph of Sadie—fate, Tessa, something. He had to put things right, while there was still time, while he was there to soothe any trouble between them all, to remind them of their closeness. But this time, he would meet her on equal ground. He would know what was in the diaries, too. Not because he had read them, though. He still wasn't able to face that.

He was going to ask Maggie to read them for him.

The idea had come to him two weeks previously. It was the perfect solution. Maggie had never known her grandmother. She had no personal memories that might be destroyed. She had grown up hearing wonderful things about Tessa—of course she had—but this went beyond changing any of those memories. He was going to ask her to read through them and tell him what it was Sadie must have discovered; why she had run away like that. That way, when Leo met her, he would be prepared. If it was true that Bill was Sadie's father—if Bill was the father of any of his daughters—then so be it. He felt differently now. Tessa was dead. Bill was dead. All that had happened had happened. What he had to do now was make peace with the living, with his daughters and with Sadie, most of all.

Once he had absorbed whatever it was that Maggie discovered, he was going to tell his four daughters that he thought he knew where Sadie was. Tell them the truth. All of it. That he hadn't burned their mother's diaries. That Sadie had read them. That the reason she had run away was, well, whatever that reason turned out to be.

Then his plans had gone awry. Maggie announcing she wasn't going to be in Donegal, and Clementine and Eliza following suit. All of them laughing at his insistence that it was important this time.

He'd had to concoct Plan B. It all relied on Maggie's agreeing with his plan. Not just agreeing to read the diaries. Agreeing to come to Donegal after all, which would hopefully also make Clementine and Eliza change their minds. He would have to tell Maggie everything, he'd realized. Express how important it was. Make it clear that time was of the essence.

He just wished she would hurry up and come home, so he could set everything in motion.

* * *

Nearly an hour passed before Maggie finally appeared. He spotted her before she saw him. From his seat he had a good view down the street. He smiled at the sight of her. His little Miss Maggie, living here in New York, all on her own. A second later he saw that she wasn't on her own. She was smiling up at a tall young man. A man who had his right arm around Maggie's shoulder and what looked like a large suitcase in his left hand. As they got closer, Leo saw it was a guitar case.

How long had Maggie had a boyfriend? he wondered. Surely he would have been told if one of his daughters knew. He hadn't heard a whisper about it. Perhaps they didn't know yet. He would be first with the news for once.

He stood up and straightened his light jacket. He was standing, beaming, as Maggie and Gabriel walked in through the door.

"Tadpole?" She was shocked. He could see it. "What on earth are you doing here?"

"Waiting for you," he said.

"What is it? Has something happened to Clementine?"

"Nothing's happened. Everyone's fine."

"But what are you doing here? You're supposed to be in Ireland."

"I'm on my way there."

"Via New York?"

"You know how much I like flying." Leo turned and put out his hand to the gray-haired man standing beside her. "Good evening. I'm Leo Faraday, Maggie's grandfather."

"Hello, Mr. Faraday. I'm Gabriel West, Maggie's . . . I'm a friend of Maggie's."

Maggie looked back and forth between them, as if thrown by the sudden display of introductory manners. "Tadpole, why didn't you ring me?"

"I did. I rang both your numbers and didn't get an answer from either."

"You rang tonight?"

He nodded. "From JFK airport, as soon as I got in. I'd have called you before I left Paris, but I was on my way before I realized it myself."

Gabriel spoke then. "Maggie, I think I should probably go."

She turned. "Gabriel, I'm sorry, I—"

"No, I'm the sorry one," Leo said. "You're right, Maggie, as always. It was bad of me to arrive like this. I apologize to you both."

"Oh, Tadpole. I'm sorry too." She hugged her grandfather. "I'm sorry not to sound more pleased. It's wonderful to see you. You just surprised me, that's all."

Leo hugged her back. "You'd think I'd have learned some manners by now, wouldn't you? At my age. Mind you, I think it's my age that is to blame." He turned toward Gabriel. "It's a theory I have, Gabriel. Keep on the move and that way the Grim Reaper doesn't know where to find you."

"It's an excellent theory. I'll keep it in mind."

Leo looked pleased at that. "Is that a guitar you have with you? How marvelous. I haven't got a musical bone in my body. What do you play?"

"Tadpole, please—" Maggie interrupted.

"Tadpole?" Gabriel said.

Leo beamed again. "It was her nickname for me when she was a little girl. She just couldn't seem to say grandpa."

Maggie interrupted. "I'm sure Gabriel doesn't want to hear all this—"

"He does, actually," Gabriel said.

Leo turned his attention back to Gabriel and his guitar. "So what kind of music do you play?"

"Background music, mostly, in Irish and Spanish bars."

"I take my hat off to you. Are you playing the next couple of nights? Perhaps I could pop along and listen to you? Maggie, what do you think about that?"

Maggie was looking a little red in the face.

Gabriel noticed. "I really should go." He put out his hand. "Mr. Faraday, it's been a pleasure to meet you."

"None of this Mr. Faraday nonsense, thank you. Call me Leo."

"Thanks, Leo. And thanks, Maggie, for a lovely evening. I really enjoyed it."

"I did too. Thanks again. For everything."

Leo watched them with keen interest. "You see him out, Maggie," he said. "I'm perfectly happy here for a few more minutes."

He watched as she accompanied Gabriel to the door and stood talking to him outside for a minute or two. He saw Gabriel lean down and kiss her cheek. Oh, how sweet. He seemed like a fine young man. Leo was still smiling when Maggie came back in. She, however, wasn't smiling. She looked very serious indeed.

She got straight to the point. "What's wrong, Leo? I appreciate you not telling me in front of Gabriel, but I need to know what it is. You wouldn't just turn up here out of the blue. I know you wouldn't."

He hated to see her so worried. He decided to change the subject. "He seems like a charming man. Is he your new boyfriend?"

"No, he's not. I just met him tonight."

"Tonight? You're getting on very well considering you just met him."

"I've known him for a while, but we only met tonight. I met him through his mother. She runs an agency—"

"A dating agency? I told your mother I was sure you'd be feeling lonely over here, in such a big city on your own."

"Tadpole, please listen to me. Gabriel's mother doesn't run a dating agency." She explained about the Rent-a-Grandchild scheme, about Dolly. She told him all that had happened that day. She felt the tears well again and wiped them away. "I shouldn't be this upset, I hardly knew her. It's your fault. You're here for less than ten minutes and you've made me cry."

"You cry as much as you need to. I have pockets full of tissues."

She took the tissue he was offering and wiped her eyes. "Sorry, Tadpole."

"It's me who should be apologizing. Your silly old grandfather turning up out of the blue like this, stepping on toes, butting in where he's not wanted."

"You're not silly. I'm glad you're here. Shocked, but glad."

"I've shocked myself, to tell you the truth. But I'm really glad I'm here too. For even more reasons now." He put his hand on her head, touched her cheek, then the end of her nose, the affectionate routine he'd done with her since she was a child. "What about you and I go and have a hot chocolate, or something soothing like that?"

"Aren't you too tired?"

"How can I be tired? I'm in the city that never sleeps, aren't I? Let's hit the town together until I collapse. If you can bear to be seen with your old grandpa, that is?"

She softened. She had never been able to stay mad at her grand-father. "We'll keep to badly lit places," she said as she linked her arm through his.

· · ·

An hour later, Maggie was back in her apartment on her own. She'd just waved Leo off in a cab, his suitcase and briefcase with him. He wouldn't dream of staying with her, he said. He already had a booking in an excellent hotel close to Central Park.

They had found a late-night café on Bleecker Street with several empty tables. It was too hot for hot chocolates. They'd settled on iced tea instead. He asked her all about her time in New York, but refused to answer any of her questions about why he was there. "It's too late. You've had a big day and I've had a long flight. Let's stay with desultory chat. I'm too tired now to have a serious conversa-tion tonight."

"I'm not surprised, considering you are nearly eighty years old and still flitting around the world like this."

"You're one to talk about flitting." He dropped the joking tone. "We've all been worried about you, you know."

"I'm fine, Tadpole. I needed to do it."

"I'm proud of you, Maggie." He reached across and squeezed her hand.

They arranged to meet the next morning at eleven, at his hotel. As he climbed into the cab, he had one final thing to say. "I need to ask you to do something else, Maggie. Just a small white lie. If your mother rings, or if any of your aunts ring, you haven't seen me, okay?"

"They don't know you're here?"

"Not exactly. Juliet possibly thinks I'm in London, on my way to Belfast, and after that on my way to Donegal."

"And the others?"

"I don't think they're too sure. They washed their hands of me years ago."

"You're incorrigible."

He had been delighted to hear it.

As she cleaned her teeth, pulled down the bed, and changed into her pajamas, she tried to guess what it was he wanted to talk to her about. He'd insisted he wasn't ill, so it wasn't that. He'd also assured her again that there was nothing wrong with Clementine or any of her aunts. What could it be?

She tossed and turned in the bed. After nearly three months of quiet time here in New York, today felt overwhelming. Dolly's death. Meeting Gabriel. Leo's arrival.

One of her grandfather's many sayings came to mind. Every cloud has a silver lining. If Dolly's death had been the cloud today, meeting Gabriel was the lining. She had liked him straightaway. Really liked him, she realized now.

What would have happened if Leo hadn't been waiting in the foyer when they got back from the restaurant? She tried to picture it. Gabriel would have come up to her apartment. She would have made him coffee. He would have taken out his guitar, sung her the song she'd dared him to sing. She imagined more conversation, more laughing. And then what?

It took her a long time that night to get to sleep.

Maggie met Leo in the foyer of his hotel the next morning. It was very grand, with plush carpets, glittering chandeliers, uniformed staff, and gleaming brassware. He assured her he had slept the sleep of the just and was in fine form. In the mood for a walk, he declared. He had his briefcase with him again. She offered to carry it, but he insisted he was well able to take care of it himself.

Together they strolled the four blocks up to Central Park, past the horse-drawn carriages, in through the Columbus Circle entrance. It was a warm, crisp day, the paths speckled with shadows, the sun sending flickers of light onto the ponds. The park was busy in patches, people already setting up rugs and towels on the grass, Rollerbladers slipping silently past them, trim mothers jogging past, pushing their babies in expensive space-age prams.

They walked for ten minutes until they came to a shady area with an empty bench.

"Let's sit down. Make ourselves comfortable. Are you hungry? Thirsty? Do you want a hot dog?" He nodded toward a cart in the distance.

Maggie shook her head.

Leo lowered himself to the bench with a mock groan. "Do you know, by the way, that there are more than twenty-five thousand trees in this park?"

"I did, as it happens." In her first few weeks she had seriously toyed with the idea of counting them all.

"Remarkable, isn't it? In the middle of a huge city like this. More than a hundred and fifty different species too."

"You've been reading up on it?"

"I couldn't just turn up without a bit of New York knowledge to offer you, could I?" He smiled at her.

"You're not here just to tell me about the trees, though, are you, Tadpole?"

"Of course I am. I've been wanting to see the Central Park trees for years. Once a tree man, always a tree man."

"You're just a kidder."

"Yes, but not all the time. Not today." He put his hand on hers. "I need your help, Maggie."

She waited, suddenly anxious.

Leo smiled at her. "Do you remember when you were little and I used to set those tasks for you, to find out lots of different things from the library? And the way your mum used to get you to help around the house?"

"The lists? Of course I remember them." She laughed. "I still live like that now. I can't do anything without a list."

He reached inside his pocket and withdrew a folded piece of paper. He handed it over without a word. She opened and read it. It was in exactly the same format the childhood tasks had been in.

Maggie's List for Today
1. Diaries
2. Donegal
3. Sadie
Signed,
Tadpole

She read it twice. "I'm sorry. I don't understand."

"Of course you don't. Not yet, anyway." He took a breath. "There's a lot I need to tell you, Maggie. I've thought long and hard about whether I'm the right one to tell you this, but if I don't, who will and when? It's gone on too long already. I'm not getting any younger."

"Tadpole, I'm sorry. I still don't know what you're talking about."

"How could you?" He turned so he was looking at her. "Maggie, I need to get a few things clear in my head before we go on. Why did you decide not to come to Donegal this year?"

"I know it would have disappointed you, and I'm sorry, but it just didn't seem right. I needed time away. I still do."

"It was important to me that you be there this year. There was something I wanted you to do for me. I'm an old man, Maggie. Getting older every day. And I realized there are things I want to organize before it's too late." He took out his wallet and opened it up to a photograph. "It's about Tessa, Maggie. My Tessa. Everything on that list comes back to her in some way."

Maggie took the photo. She had already seen it, many times before. It was a casual photograph of her grandmother as a young woman, laughing, the wind blowing her hair back, her red lips open to show perfect white teeth. She looked like a film star, Maggie had always thought. The love of Leo's life. Maggie had grown up hearing stories about her.

"I had this plan, you see, for this Christmas in Donegal. You know Tessa used to love to do scrapbooks?"

Maggie nodded. She'd grown up with those scrapbooks too, filled with recipes and colored pictures and tips about all sorts of things. She'd always liked them, thinking of them as a link to her grandmother. Not as much as she liked the special scrapbook Sadie had made for her fifth birthday, but close.

"A month or two ago I decided I was going to ask you all to help me put together a Tessa scrapbook. I thought it might make a good little job for you. Something to take your mind off things. I was going to hire you, pay you for your time." He smiled at her. "I also thought you might have had enough of numbers and it would do you good to spend time with some words instead. I had it all worked out. Once we were all together in Donegal, I was going to ask you to interview each of us, collect the memories of Tessa that we had, and write them up in the scrapbook, with photos of her. A collection of memories, so we'd never forget."

Maggie smiled. "I'd love to have done that. It's a beautiful idea. I think I would have gone to Donegal if I'd known about it."

"I should have told you. It's my own fault. As I said, I wanted to make a ceremony of it. I had it in my head that I would make an announcement about it on our first night together in Donegal. Have you ready—pen poised—as everyone started talking. But then something else happened. Something I didn't expect. And I realized that was all tied up with Tessa too. And I needed to think about it a bit more."

He was quiet for a few moments. Maggie waited, conscious then of the noise around them. Traffic noise, sirens, distant merry-go-round music. A crying child, a laughing child.

"It's about Sadie, Maggie. Your aunt Sadie. There's a lot about Sadie that I haven't told you. That none of us have told you. And I think it's time we did."

His serious tone unsettled her. "Is she dead? Is that what you mean?"

He shook his head. "No, she's not. I can tell you that for sure."

"Then what? It's you who has been sending me those cards all these years?"

"No, they've come from Sadie. As far as I can tell, anyway." He took his granddaughter's hand again and held it briefly. "Maggie, we've never told you the whole truth about Sadie. But I promise what I'm about to tell you about her *is* true. And I also promise that we have always felt uncomfortable lying to you about her."

"Lying?"

"Not so much lying as telling you a different story than the truth."

"Isn't that lying?"

"I don't know anymore. I don't know whether a lie told out of necessity is the same as a lie told for gain." He paused. "Maggie, the truth is your aunt Sadie didn't run away and join a hippie commune twenty years ago. She made a terrible mistake and did something very foolish, something that none of us have ever been able to fully understand. There was a fight, a very big fight, between your mother and her, and that was the last time any of us saw her."

"She's in prison?"

"No, she's not. But she did do something wrong and it involved you. I think it's time you knew about it."

He told her, in careful detail, everything about that time. He didn't look at her as he spoke, just stared ahead, as he told her the whole story. How Sadie had taken over full-time care of Maggie while Clementine went to university. How attached she had got. How upset she had been when Clementine wanted all her sisters to take turns caring for Maggie when she first started going away. He told her about the roster that had been drawn up, with Miranda coming first, the plan being that Maggie would go and stay with her for two weeks. How it had changed at the last minute.

Maggie thought she remembered her first flight with Sadie. She remembered—she thought she remembered—being in Melbourne with Sadie. But everything else? She couldn't recall any more details. She also couldn't take in the words Leo was using. Kidnap?

"How could she have kidnapped me? She was my aunt. That's not kidnapping. It's not like she took me off the street."

Leo tried to explain what those two weeks had been like. The terror that something bad had happened, or that something bad would happen. Clementine inconsolable, wracked with grief and guilt. They all had been. They had all blamed themselves, Leo knew that. All the conversations, as they waited by the phone for Sadie's calls. Leo had seen it in his daughters' faces. Miranda remembering a snap she had made at Sadie, her constant goading about her weight, her lack of boyfriends. Eliza barely taking any notice of her, except to complain about how messy she was. Clementine grateful but increasingly uncomfortable with Sadie's attachment to Maggie. Juliet guilty for not noticing it had all been happening. Leo too had been riddled with guilt. Hadn't he admitted to himself that he thought of Sadie as his runt, the girl in the wings while his other four daughters shone? He didn't tell Maggie that part of it. But the truth was they'd all felt partly to blame for Sadie's sudden disappearance. None of them had been kind to her. Only Maggie. And so she had taken Maggie with her.

Leo told Maggie why they had decided not to call the police; that Clementine particularly had been scared it might prompt something worse to happen. "We just didn't know what state of mind she was in, that was the worst of it. She rang every two nights and left messages on the machine saying you were all right, but she'd hang up if we answered. You were never in danger, though, Maggie, I'm sure of that. That was the one thing that kept us hopeful. Sadie would never have hurt you. She loved you too much."

He told her about finding that Sadie's passport and birth certificate were missing. The incredible moment when the school librarian had rung to inquire after Clementine's health, because she had run into Maggie herself on the beach near Byron Bay. The urgency of getting there as quickly as they could, both Clementine and Leo terrified they might have moved on before they found them.

Maggie was finding it all very difficult. Tiny scraps of images were flickering in and out of her mind. Were they lost memories? She didn't know. All she knew for sure was that she should have been told this long before now. She wasn't angry about it. Not yet. She was confused and upset. "I can't believe it's taken you, any of you, this long to tell me. Why not tell me the truth? Not when I was five, I can understand that, but when I was older. Why did you wait until now? Let me keep thinking she was a hippie—a stupid story like that?"

"It all just happened. We took the easy option, Maggie. I'm not proud to say it, but that's what we did."

"You should have told me before now. Clementine should have told me. It was part of my life."

"Yes, we should have."

"So what else isn't true?"

"What do you mean?"

"If you all lied to me about that, have you lied about other things?"

"Of course not."

"Is Sadie my mother? Is that what all of this is leading to?"

"No, Maggie. Clementine is your mother. I promise you."

"And David is my father?"

"David is your father."

"So why are you telling me about this now? Why did you come all this way to tell me this?"

"Because I've found out where Sadie is. I think I have, at least. I think she might be in Ireland. In Dublin."

"In *Dublin*? What is she doing there?"

"I don't know yet. I hired a private detective, after I happened across a photograph on the Internet of someone I was sure was Sadie. It seems I might be right."

"It seems? You haven't rung her? You haven't been to see her, now that you know where she is? But why not? She's your daughter. You must be desperate to find out how she is."

"I am. Of course I am." He hesitated. "But something made her leave all those years ago. Something she read in Tessa's diaries. And I need to know what that is before I go and talk to her. I need to be prepared."

"But she can't have read them. You burned them after Tessa died."

Leo shifted in his seat. "I didn't burn them, Maggie. I kept them. And Sadie found them and read something in them that badly upset her."

"You didn't burn the diaries? Another lie?" The look on Maggie's face saddened Leo. She ran her hand through her hair, unconsciously mimicking one of his own gestures. "I can't believe this. How can you have done that? She was their mother. They needed to read about her. They deserved it."

"Don't be angry with me, Maggie, please."

"How can I not be? And if you think I'm angry, how do you think Clementine and the others are going to feel? They'll be furious."

"I know why you might think that. Believe me, I do. I've had sleepless nights about this for years. But I had to do it. Not for their sake. For my sake." He stood up then. "Can we walk for a little while? I need to try and explain it to you."

As they walked down light-dappled paths, he talked. He didn't give her every detail, but he told her enough that she understood. He had adored Tessa. She had been the center of his life. "I wish you had known her, Maggie. She just glowed. She was pretty, funny, witty . . . If she walked into a room, people noticed her. And somehow, through some incredible stroke of luck, she and I met and we fell in love and we got married. She swept me off my feet."

She had heard him talk about Tessa like this many times before. She needed to hear it again. After the shock of his other announcements, she needed every piece of detail and explanation he could offer.

"She wasn't perfect, Maggie. I know love is blind, but I could see that sometimes she could be too impatient, with me and with the children. She was very quick-witted, and sometimes she was dismissive of people who couldn't keep up with her. But she energized me. I just loved being with her, watching her. Loving her."

"She was the love of your life?"

He nodded. "She truly was."

She heard the sadness in his voice and her heart went out to him. "I've always thought it was so romantic, the way you talked about her, all the ways you remember her. Don't be sad, Tadpole. You were the love of her life too. Even if it wasn't forever."

"I don't know if I was. That's what I'm frightened of." They walked on for a few moments in silence before he spoke again. "Your mother and your aunts don't know this, but I met Tessa because she was going out with my brother Bill. You never met him. Clementine would remember him a little, I think. He was hard to forget, you see. He had the same charm Tessa had. But he was so casual about her. He didn't appreciate her."

It was as if he'd forgotten his granddaughter was there now. As if he was airing thoughts he'd hidden away for years. Maggie listened as he spoke of days out with Bill and Tessa, being happy just to be the third person, until the day Tessa and Bill had broken up and she arrived at his house. "I thought at first I was just the rebound, but I was wrong. She loved me. We got married. Bill was best man. I was so confident of her love. And it helped that he'd got a job in

South Africa. Tessa became pregnant with Juliet, then Miranda and Eliza. We had a house filling with children. I'd always wanted that. Then Bill started visiting again. He was just the same—as funny and as witty as ever. He brought out the best in Tessa too. All I could do was watch them together. And worry. No matter how much I tried to ignore it, there was still an attraction between them. And then she told me she was pregnant again. I was delighted at first. It was wonderful news. Our fourth child on the way. But then I got worried. I got suspicious. I hated thinking that way, but it was like I couldn't help myself."

Maggie understood then. "You thought Sadie might have been Bill's—?" She left the sentence unfinished.

"I tried not to. When she arrived, I could see straightaway she looked like the others. I told myself it was just jealousy planting ideas in my head. Bill wasn't even around when she was born."

"Do you wish you had asked about it? Found out for sure one way or another?"

"I couldn't do it. I would have hated Tessa to think I didn't trust her." He breathed deeply. "If it was true, I didn't want to know." He stopped walking then and turned to her. She was struck by how sad he looked. By how old he looked. "But something Sadie read in Tessa's diaries made her want to run away from her family. What else could it be? She always felt like she didn't fit in. And the truth is, she didn't."

"But why take me with her?"

"I still don't know. Perhaps she was playing at her own family. She loved you. She already thought of you as her daughter."

Maggie wished she could remember those years. It was odd to be talked about like this, to hear herself being described and not be able to recall it vividly. Her own memories of her aunt were so slight; the scrapbook Sadie had made for her the strongest link between them. Not that she'd looked at it for a long time.

They reached another bench. Leo motioned toward it and they took a seat again. He put the briefcase on his lap. "Maggie, before I go to see Sadie, I want you to read Tessa's diaries and find out what it was that Sadie read. I don't want to know all the details. I just need the facts. I can handle facts."

"But they're private, Leo. If anyone should read them, it should be Clementine or one of the others, surely?"

He shook his head. "That would be impossible. If one read it before the other, there'd be an uproar."

"One already has. Sadie has."

"And look what happened. Look what she did as a result. I couldn't bear it if it happened with the others. It's been hard enough having one missing daughter. It would break my heart to upset the others. If I can find out what Sadie might have read, though, I can go to her as an equal. Because it will hurt me as much as it hurt her."

"But can't you read them yourself? Aren't you curious?"

He shook his head. He told her why not—the effect just one entry had on him, years before. "Perhaps if I knew exactly what Sadie read, if I knew which diary to go to, then I would chance it. But I'd have to read them all. Read through descriptions of her and Bill together."

She understood then. "When would I do it? Would you send them to me?"

"I don't need to. They're here." He opened the briefcase and she saw two bundles of blue notebooks. He handed one to her. She cautiously took off the rubber band holding them together and opened the cover of the one on top. *"Tessa Faraday"* was written flamboyantly on the inside page, with the date underneath. Maggie recognized the writing from the scrapbooks filled with recipes that Juliet still used. It gave her a little jolt to make the connection between her image of that Tessa—nurturing, homemaking, the loving mother—and the Tessa Leo had just described.

She closed it, put her hand on top of it. "I'm worried you're asking too much of me."

"It has to be you, Maggie. There's no one else I can ask."

Maggie stayed quiet, thinking. She remembered a conversation between Miranda and Clementine during one of the Donegal

Christmases. "He's a wily one, that father of ours," Miranda had said. "He might play the fool, but have you noticed we still do whatever he wants?"

"We don't do whatever he wants. I'm here because I want to be," Clementine answered.

"No, you're here because Leo wants you to be here. I tell myself every year, this is the last one, but I keep coming back. How does he get away with it? Because once I find out, I want some of it myself."

Clementine had laughed. "You haven't realized you've got it already? Miranda, we've been dancing to your tune all your life as well."

Had they been right? Had their lives always revolved around Leo? He was looking at her now with such eagerness, almost pleading, in his eyes. Three months ago she would have said yes, straightaway. But something had changed over the past weeks. The self-imposed separation from her family had forced her to be self-reliant, not to check everything, every decision and every piece of news with them. If she said yes to Leo, was she being a loving granddaughter, helping him as he had helped her so much all her life? Or did she need to say no, to somehow keep that distance?

"I need to think about it. It's a lot to take in. If I were to say yes, when would we go to Donegal?"

"As soon as possible. Juliet's there already. Miranda's due there at the end of the week. As soon as you say yes—" He stopped himself. "—if you say yes, I'll ring Clementine and Eliza and tell them you've changed your mind. They'd come then, I know they would."

He nearly had her, she realized. "I'll think about it. I'll tell you by tomorrow, I promise."

"Early tomorrow? It's just the sooner we tell Clementine and Eliza, the sooner they could get flights and—"

"Early tomorrow."

"Do you want to take the diaries now?"

She was tempted. He must have known that. Of course she would love to read her grandmother's diaries, to hear about her mother as a child, about her aunts. Who wouldn't want to do that? "Not yet," she said firmly. "You take care of them until I decide."

"Thank you, Maggie."

"You're welcome, Tadpole." As they stood up, she hooked her arm into his, the way she'd always done as a child. She was shaken by all she had heard, but she needed to show her grandfather she was fine; that everything was as normal as possible. She put on a bright face. "And that's enough family business for now. It's not every day my grandfather arrives out of the blue. I want to take you sightseeing. What about a bus tour? Or do you want to take the ferry to Staten Island?"

"I've already organized a little surprise for you tonight."

"You have? What?"

"It's a surprise. All you have to do is be ready in your finest evening wear by six o'clock tonight."

"You can't have organized anything yet. You just got here."

"No?" He gave her that big smile of his and her heart melted a little more. "Just you wait and see, Miss Maggie, just you wait and see."

CHAPTER 31

S he got home to her apartment just after four. She and Leo had enjoyed a long lunch, taken a carriage ride around Central Park and then she'd walked him back to his hotel. He wanted a nap before this evening, he told her. "You'd better have one too. We've got a lot to do," he said.

There was a message from Gabriel on the machine when she checked it. "Maggie, hi. I hope things are good with your grandfather. I just wanted to let you know I've told Mom about Dolly. She's been in touch with Dolly's nephew and passed on our sympathies. The funeral will be next week, family only, but we've sent a wreath, from you as well. And we'll understand if you don't want to work for us for a while. You've got the real McCoy now, with Leo, after all." A pause. "I enjoyed last night a lot, Maggie. Thanks again."

She checked the time. He'd rung at ten thirty that morning. Should she ring him back? She wanted to. But to say what? Thank him for his thanks?

It was all too much at once. Leo's revelations were spinning around her head. She decided to concentrate on getting ready. She had less than two hours. It had been so long since she'd been out for a gala night she would need every minute.

At exactly six p.m. Ray buzzed through her intercom to tell her Leo was waiting downstairs.

When she emerged from the lift, he and Ray wolf-whistled. She gave a small bow. She was wearing a black sleeveless dress, a gold pendant, beautiful vintage high-heeled shoes, and a vintage hair clip, its red flower vivid against her dark hair. She'd taken a long time over her makeup, carefully applying eyeliner and smoky eyeshadow, red lipstick and a touch of blush. She carried a light shawl in a vibrant red that matched her hair clip and lipstick.

"You remind me of Audrey Hepburn," Leo said.

"There's a touch of the young Elizabeth Taylor too, I think," Ray added.

"You both need your eyes tested," Maggie replied.

It was still hot, the evening air thick with humidity. A limousine was outside, the driver holding the door open for them. Maggie slid inside, grateful for its air-conditioning.

"Leo, you astonish me. How did you organize this?"

"Marvelous things, concierges. The fellow in my hotel is extraordinary. I do believe if I'd asked him to arrange a trip to the moon he would have given it his best shot."

It was like being in a film or playing at being a princess for a night, driving in a limousine through Manhattan in the hazy light. Their first stop was the Algonquin Hotel for cocktails in the Blue Bar and then dinner in the Round Table Room. Maggie had walked by the hotel several times over the past weeks, peeping inside at the opulent lobby, the rich fabrics and leather, but never feeling confident enough to go inside. It felt lovely to step inside now, with her grandfather beside her.

Leo was in sparkling form. He obviously hadn't napped that afternoon, but had spent the time memorizing facts about New York to share with her. He'd also announced in the limousine that he wasn't going to mention that day's conversation in the park and nor was she.

"This is a spoiling night, regardless of what you decide to do about Donegal and the diaries. And that's the last time I'll mention it tonight."

The atmosphere and elegance of their surroundings infected their mood. Leo regaled Maggie with snippets of poetry. It had become a new passion, he announced. Maggie told Leo tales from her early days in New York—getting lost in the subway, going to poetry readings. "All on your own?" he asked.

She nodded. She hadn't tried to make any friends. It had been hard to know where to find any, without a job to go to as a starting place. She'd grown used to her own company. She liked the thinking time.

"Don't do too much thinking," Leo said. "It's bad for the soul."

They had just finished their desserts and coffee when he reached inside his suit pocket and produced an envelope. At his urging, she opened it. Two tickets to see *The Producers* at the St. James Theatre, just two blocks away.

Her eyes widened. "This has been sold out for weeks. How did you get them?"

"Charm, mostly," Leo said.

They walked there, swept along in the throngs of people heading to other Broadway shows, the air rich with different languages, dressed-up couples beside groups in casual wear. Their seats were excellent and the show wonderful. It was exactly the diversion Maggie needed—an opportunity to put her own thoughts away and be swept up in pure spectacle, music, and wit instead. Beside her, Leo laughed so enthusiastically he nearly hit his head on the seat in front.

"You must be exhausted, Leo," she said as they walked through the crowds coming out of the theaters to where they'd arranged to meet their driver and car.

"Exhausted? Of course not. The night is still young."

"It's after eleven."

"That's young. You're young. I'm young at heart. We can't go home yet."

She expected the car to head downtown in the direction of Greenwich Village and was surprised when the driver took the opposite direction.

"Where are we going now?"

"Don't you feel like a nightcap?"

Ten minutes later the driver pulled into the curb just down from an Irish pub. She knew in that instant why they were there and who else was going to be there too.

"Gabriel is singing here tonight, isn't he?"

"I couldn't possibly say," Leo said. "I liked him, by the way. Much more than Angus, if you don't mind me saying."

"I don't mind at all," Maggie said. She felt the same way.

·   ·   ·

They could hear the conversation before they went in, underpinned by taped music. The Pogues, Maggie thought. "We could be in Donegal," Leo declared as they went inside, taking in the Guinness posters, shelves of battered books, and cabinets of old pottery. While Leo went to the bar, she found a seat between a leaning wooden post featuring road signs in Irish and English, nearly hitting her head on one. The main room was crowded, with three-quarters of the tables filled with people of different ages and accents. She heard Irish accents to her left, American accents in front of her. In the opposite corner was a small stage, a chair and microphone waiting in the center, under a red spotlight. There was no sign of Gabriel.

Until she turned around and there he was beside Leo, who was holding two glasses, one of Guinness, the other an amber fluid she guessed was whiskey.

Gabriel smiled at her. "Maggie, hello. What a nice surprise."

"Gabriel, has my grandfather been harassing you today? I don't want you to think we're stalking you."

"You mean you're not? No, he was very polite, weren't you, Leo? He phoned me at the office and I said I'd be delighted if you both came tonight. It's easier to sing in front of two people than an empty room."

"You've almost a full house."

"I can't take credit. There are two thirtieth-birthday parties in here tonight, a tour group from County Kerry, and a family reunion. I'll have my work cut out if they all start shouting requests."

"You don't mind us being here?"

The background music suddenly increased in volume. Gabriel leaned forward. "Sorry, what did you say?"

Maggie was very conscious of how close he was. She was equally conscious how good it was to be so close to him. She got that nice aftershave scent again. "I just wanted to make sure you don't mind us being here."

He touched her, fleetingly, on her bare arm. "It's great to see you here. I'll talk to you afterward." He turned to Leo and said a quick word in his ear too. Maggie couldn't hear what he said over the noise of the music, but whatever it was it made Leo laugh. Leo patted Gabriel on the shoulder and then took his seat next to Maggie.

Gabriel began his set without any fanfare. He simply walked up onto the stage, took a seat, and began to play. She already knew he was a talented guitarist; she'd seen that from the brief snippet he'd played for her in Washington Square. But it was his voice that was truly special. Warm, distinctive, confident. He began with "Raglan Road" and then U2's "A Sort of Homecoming." He sang "Trouble" by Ray Lamontagne and "Babylon" by David Gray. He did a rollicking version of Bob Dylan's "Like a Rolling Stone." The crowd gradually stopped talking and his background music became center stage. The applause was loud and genuine when he finished his set half an hour later with three more traditional Irish songs.

"Tessa would have loved that," Leo leaned over and said. "She adored Irish music. What did you think, Maggie?"

"I thought he was wonderful."

"Maggie thought you were wonderful, Gabriel, and so did I," Leo said in hearty greeting when he came over. "Sit down here and let me get you a drink."

Maggie couldn't send her elderly grandfather back to the bar a second time. She stood up. "I'll get this one. Whiskey, Leo? Gabriel?"

He smiled. "Thanks."

There was a crush at the bar. Nearly fifteen minutes passed before she returned. Leo and Gabriel were deep in conversation. The background music was too loud to be able to join in easily. She noticed Gabriel's respect for Leo, the way he listened so carefully to the older man. She noticed Gabriel's long fingers, the muscles on his tanned arms. She noticed the way lines appeared in his cheeks when he smiled, something he did often. She noticed how he threw his head back when he laughed. Leo was making him laugh a lot. She watched Leo grow serious as Gabriel answered a question. She wished she could lip-read. The background music finally lowered.

Leo leaned across. "Gabriel's never been to Ireland, Maggie. Did you know that? No Irish blood in him at all, yet he had those songs down perfectly."

"I have been to Spain, though," Gabriel said. "I apparently had a Spanish great-grandfather, so I'm much more authentic when I'm in a Spanish bar."

"I'd like to hear that too. Another time, I hope," Leo said, standing up. "Thank you again, Gabriel. It was an honor to hear you."

"We're going?" Maggie said. She was disappointed. She'd hardly exchanged a word with Gabriel all night.

"We've still got one more item on our agenda tonight, Maggie." He glanced at his watch. "Our patient driver will be expecting us any moment now."

"You've had a busy night already, I hear?" Gabriel said, as Maggie gathered her wrap and bag.

"He's rushed me off my feet. I think it's time he started acting his age," Maggie said. She took the opportunity to say some more. "Thanks for your message today about Dolly. I appreciated it very much."

"How are you? You're okay?"

"I am, I think. Are you?"

He nodded. "I'm glad for her that she had a visitor on her last day and that it was you. I think she would have liked that."

Leo was waiting. "Maggie, are you ready?"

She spoke impulsively. "Gabriel, would you like to come with us? I don't know where we're going, but you'd be more than welcome to come along too."

"I'd love to but I've got a second set in about ten minutes." He checked his watch. "In about three minutes, in fact."

"We'd better leave you to it, then. I don't want to get you fired from this place as well." She still didn't want to go. "It was good to see you again."

"Good to see you too, Maggie."

He shook hands with Leo, briefly touched Maggie's arm again, and then he was gone.

"What a charming young man," Leo said as he buckled himself into the backseat of the car. "He was a cameraman, you know. He's done everything—news, current affairs, documentaries. He's taking a career break at the moment, though. Like you. You've got a lot in common, now that I think about it."

"Do you think so?"

"He seemed very pleased to see you again tonight too."

"Is that right?"

Leo smiled. "I'd make a good matchmaker, wouldn't I?"

"Not a very subtle one."

"No?" Leo laughed. "Well, I'm too old for subtleties."

*   *   *

It was almost one a.m. before Maggie was back in her apartment. Leo's final surprise of the evening had been a beautiful nighttime tour of New York. The driver opened the partition between the front and back seats and joined in their conversation as he drove them across the Brooklyn Bridge, pointing out all the landmarks.

Maggie had the princess feeling again as she was dropped off in front of her apartment building. She leaned across and hugged her grandfather. "It was a wonderful night, Tadpole. Thank you."

"You're welcome, chicken. I'll see you in the morning." They arranged a time and place. Eleven at his hotel. "And I promised I wouldn't say anything about the other matter, so I won't. But I'll look forward to talking about it with you tomorrow."

She knew then what her decision would be. "You don't need to wait until tomorrow."

"I don't?"

"I'll do what you want. All three things. Read the diaries. Come to Donegal. And help you find Sadie."

He didn't gush or praise her. He just clasped her hands tightly in his. "Thank you, Maggie."

She could imagine Miranda's voice as she got ready for bed. "He's done it again, you realize that? Arranged it all, made you feel like you had no option but to do what he wanted. That's what tonight was all about, you know. He's a master at getting his own way."

Yes, he was, Maggie admitted. But he was also her grandfather.

*   *   *

He was bursting with news by the time she arrived at his hotel the next morning. He'd already rung Clementine in Hobart and Eliza in Melbourne.

"They both had to tell me off first, of course, for putting you under pressure by turning up in New York like this. And then they put up the usual arguments. But once I told them the whole story, they said of course they'd come. Clementine was particularly excited. I could hear it in her voice. She's got some wonderful news of her own. As I told her, now she'll be able to tell you face-to-face."

"Is she going to Antarctica again? That's fantastic. She'll be over the moon."

"She wants to tell you herself, so I'm not saying anything more."

"But what did you mean you told them both the whole story? About the Tessa scrapbook? I thought you weren't going to tell them any of that until we were there."

"No, I didn't mention that."

"You told them you'd found Sadie?"

"I promised you I wouldn't, Maggie, and I didn't. That has to be between you and me, for the time being at least."

"So what whole story did you tell them?"

He gave an airy gesture. "I just mentioned how important it was for them to be there for you."

"For me? What did you say about me?"

"I'll tell you in a minute. Now, just to discuss arrangements. I've rung the airlines this morning and we can get seats on a flight leaving New York this evening. We'll be in Donegal tomorrow, settled in beautifully by the time Miranda, Eliza, and Clementine arrive. I was lucky, I got the last three seats. I decided to splurge on business-class. There's nothing like it on these long flights. And we are going on business, aren't we?"

"Three? Why did you need to book three seats?"

Leo gave her an innocent smile. "Didn't I tell you? Gabriel's coming with us."

CHAPTER 32

Maggie was so angry by the time Leo finished telling her all he'd arranged that she was actually shaking.

"You can't do this. You have to stop it. You can't bring Gabriel into this as well."

"I haven't 'brought him' into it. I've hired him. It's a business arrangement. And it takes the pressure off you. I got the idea last night while he and I were talking. Please don't look so upset. Let me explain. I realized a scrapbook was too old-fashioned a way of collecting memories. I had to embrace the technology available to me. Videotape, for example. Not only that, but get an expert to help. Gabriel's an expert. We'll hire the equipment as soon as we get to Ireland and he'll film everyone talking about Tessa over two or three days. It's ingenious, if I say so myself. And so much easier on you, Maggie. You won't have to interview everyone, write everything down, worry about misquoting people or having to tape it and transcribe your notes. It leaves you free to read Tessa's diaries, too. I was worried when you were going to get time to do that, though you might want to make a start on the plane, of course. Don't you think it's the perfect solution?"

"Have you actually asked Gabriel yet? Or have you gone ahead and booked a plane seat for him without his permission?"

"Of course I've asked him. I spoke to him about it in a general way last night, when I heard that he used to be a cameraman and the idea first came to me. I asked him whether he was available for a freelance job. He said yes. And then I rang him this morning and we discussed it further. He said he'd think about it and let me know his final answer before lunchtime today. But he sounded keen. Very keen. He's never been to Ireland. He'll only need a few days with us to do the filming and then he can go off and visit all the music pubs he wants. It's all very businesslike, Maggie, I assure you. Return airfares, a living allowance, and a fee for his work. He's got the experience I want so I'm prepared to pay him for it."

"And what do you think Clementine and the others are going to make of this?"

"I thought it best not to worry them about it beforehand. It'll be much easier to tell them in person."

"What if they don't want to be filmed, though? You'll put Gabriel in a really awkward situation."

"But they want to meet him anyway, camera or no camera. Clementine and Eliza both said it, and so did Juliet when I told her we were on our way. I haven't spoken to Miranda yet, but I'm sure she'll feel the same way. You remember that document they drew up, 'The Commandments of Aunts' or whatever it was called. It's a legal arrangement between you."

Maggie was looking very confused now. "But that's got nothing in it about being in a film."

"I was thinking of another part of it. Not that I went into detail. All I said was he's a good friend of yours. A very good friend of yours."

The color rushed out of Maggie's face. "No. Please don't tell me they think Gabriel and I—"

"I didn't mean to, Maggie. I promise you it wasn't premeditated. I thought I heard them hesitate a little about making the trip, and before I quite knew what I was saying, I seemed to mention something about the fact this was a good opportunity for everyone to give you their approval, the way they'd promised . . ." His voice trailed off.

"But that document was just a joke, Tadpole. And it said nothing about a boyfriend, anyway. It said they had to approve the man I was going to marry."

"Yes, I know."

She stared at him. "You told them Gabriel was my *fiancé*?" Her voice was very low.

"Not in so many words."

"Tadpole, no! What a mess. Have you told Gabriel about this?"

"I mentioned it in passing. I just made light of it, kept it sketchy. There was no point in going into detail in case he decided not to come."

"And what did he say?"

"He laughed, I think. We both did. He seems to have a great sense of humor."

"It's not funny, Tadpole. It's not fair, either, on him or on me. How could you do this? I was here, going along nicely, living my own life, trying to get myself sorted out, and you arrive like some kind of tornado and turn everything upside down."

"Maggie, please, indulge your old grandfather. This is so important to me."

If it wasn't for the earnest expression on his face she would have completely lost her temper. "Miranda is right. You are the most manipulative person in the entire world."

"Miranda said that?"

"Yes, she did. You don't have to look so proud about it, either." She rubbed her nose. "I don't have much choice about any of this, do I? But Gabriel does. If you want to film everyone's memories, fine, but let's hire someone in Ireland. I'll ring Gabriel now and tell him he's off the hook and—"

"It's too late."

"Why is it too late?"

Leo was smiling at someone over her shoulder. "He's just come in the door behind you. And if my elderly eyes don't deceive me, he's carrying a suitcase."

• • •

Leo excused himself within a minute of Gabriel arriving. He managed in that time to give Gabriel a hearty greeting, a slap on his back, and a mention of how delighted he was to see the suitcase before saying he had to go and check something with the concierge.

If Maggie had had more time to think about the situation, she might have felt awkward. But her blood was still simmering. She wanted to get it all sorted out, then and there.

"My grandfather is impossible and I am so sorry you've been swept up in all of this," she said the moment Leo was out of earshot. Not that she would have minded if he heard it. "Gabriel, I'm embarrassed about this whole situation. You've been put in an incredibly awkward position. You don't know my aunts. They'll eat you alive. They'd eat you alive if you were there just as a cameraman, let alone as my fiancé."

"I think it sounds like fun."

"Are you serious? Are you seriously considering it?" She remembered something then and colored. "I'm sorry, I know Leo said it's a business arrangement and I can't tell you not to accept a job. It's just—"

"It's not about the money, Maggie. I just liked what Leo was suggesting. I haven't been to Ireland before. I haven't filmed for nearly two years. I thought about it all last night and this morning and I realized I was ready. That it was time I tried again. I liked the idea of this, too, something so different—no news angles, just people talking. And lots of scenery shots as well, Leo said. He described where the house is. It sounds beautiful."

"It is beautiful. It's incredible, so wild and—" She stopped there. "But it's the other little added extra that's made it impossible, Gabriel. For you and for me. It's not fair to either of us."

"Why not? Your grandfather made that part of it sound fun too. He painted a great picture. Come to Donegal, spend time with you and your family. Film you all talking about a much-loved mother and wife. Pretend to be your boyfriend—sorry, pretend to be your fiancé—to make sure they'll all come. I decided I was ready for the filming. But could I do that fiancé part? Could I pretend that Maggie Faraday—who already makes me laugh and gets me to tell her more than I've told anyone in two years, who rubs her nose and tries to hide her ears, and who is quite possibly the nicest person I've met in a very long time—could I spend five days pretending to be in love with her? And I decided that yes, I could. That I would find that fun as well."

"But it's crazy. You don't know me. I don't know you."

"How long does it take to fly to Ireland? Six hours or so? That's three hours talking time each. We'll be sick of each other by the time we get there."

She sank back into her chair. For the first time, she let herself picture the Donegal house. She saw all of them sitting around the table: herself, Leo, Juliet, Clementine, Miranda, and Eliza. She pictured Gabriel there, taking it all in, filming them, collecting their memories of Tessa. It wasn't just that that lay ahead, though. She thought of the diaries. Of Sadie. Of all that she had learned in the past two days.

Gabriel's voice broke into her thoughts. "Maggie, let's not take it too seriously. Let's just enjoy it. What do you think?"

She looked up at him. He was very relaxed. Amused, even.

"It's not as simple as you think. It never is with my grandfather."

"You'll have to fill me in on everything then. Prepare me. We're going to be married, after all. There shouldn't be any secrets between us."

If he only knew. She thought about it. What was the alternative? Staying in New York on her own? Passing up the opportunity to see her mother again? Her aunts? Perhaps it would be okay. And perhaps, in a way, it was also the best way to see all of her family again.

She gave in. "We'll have to have a big fight on your final day, then. Call off the engagement."

"No problem," he said. "I'll start it. I'm really good at dramatic fights."

"Are you sure you know what you're getting yourself into?"

He smiled then, that line appearing in his cheek. "No, but I'm looking forward to it anyway."

"I think you're mad."

"Mad? Maggie Faraday, how dare you talk to your fiancé like that?"

"I give up. You're as bad as my grandfather."

"Well?" It was Leo, back again. Behind him came the concierge, carrying a tray with a bottle of champagne and three glasses. "Was I gone long enough?"

"Your timing was perfect," Gabriel said. He reached across and took Maggie's hand in his. "Leo, we've got some wonderful news."

C H A P T E R *33*

Juliet's left ear was burning. She had spent all morning on the phone. First Leo, with his bombshell news. It was enough of a shock to hear he was in New York, let alone that he'd managed to convince Maggie, Clementine, and Eliza to come to Ireland after all, not to mention his final piece of news.

"So can you make up four more beds?" he'd asked her.

"Four?"

"One for Clementine, one for Eliza, one for Maggie and one for Gabriel."

"Gabrielle? Who's Gabrielle?"

"Maggie's friend."

"She's bringing a girlfriend?"

"Not a girlfriend. Gabriel." He spelled it. "As in the archangel. As in a man. As in her boyfriend."

"Maggie's bringing a *boyfriend*?"

"A little more than a boyfriend, I think. Not that I want to steal Maggie's thunder—"

"Maggie's *engaged*?"

Juliet had barely hung up, still reeling, when the phone rang again. Clementine from Hobart.

"Can you believe this?" Clementine said. "Maggie's engaged!"

Ten seconds after Juliet hung up from Clementine, Eliza rang from Melbourne. Ten minutes after that, Miranda from her villa on the Greek island of Santorini.

"I've just had the strangest text messages from Clementine and Eliza. Is it true? Maggie's coming? With a fiancé? What on earth is going on?"

Juliet filled her in. She kept it short. She was going to be busy enough now getting all the rooms ready. She wondered whether she should put Maggie and Gabriel in a room together. They were surely lovers, but she didn't think Leo would approve of that. He did still have the occasional old-fashioned idea about such things. Juliet did a quick count. There were just enough rooms for one each. If Maggie and Gabriel were to make their own arrangements in the middle of the night, then that was their business.

"Why hasn't Maggie told us about him?"

The million-dollar question. Juliet pondered the answer even after she'd said good-bye to Miranda. The truth was Maggie hadn't told them much about anything lately. They'd all realized that had been the whole idea behind her stay in New York—space and time to think things through on her own. But now the cat was out of the bag. She'd been enjoying a love affair the whole time. Good for her, Juliet thought.

And, best of all, it gave Juliet some more to do. Apart from getting more bedrooms ready she'd have to buy more food, more flowers, more wine. Good. More things to fill up her head, which was exactly what she needed.

She'd had an unhappy few days on her own. It should have been better. On her way to Donegal she'd told herself to use this time as rest and relaxation, as much as possible once all the preparations were done, of course. Perhaps she'd even get some reading time. Except she had done no relaxing and no reading. She had too much going on in her own head at the moment to be able to distract herself with fictional lives and dramas.

She checked the calendar again, even though she knew exactly what the date was. She was like a prisoner in a cell, ticking off the days, anxiously waiting for release. She knew when Myles expected to be back from his trip. She knew what flight he'd be arriving in on. She knew it would take him approximately one hour to get from Manchester Airport to their house. Three minutes to pay the cab driver. Less than two minutes to come inside, put down his case, walk around the house. Ten seconds after entering the kitchen he'd see the envelope propped up beside the fruit bowl. She'd left it against the vase first, then by the radio, then flat on the table, before deciding the fruit bowl was the most obvious place.

What would he think when he saw it? That it was a welcome-home note? He'd open it, take out the letter.

> *Dear Myles,* he would read:
> *It is cowardly to tell you like this, I know, and we will talk about it face-to-face, but I have to tell you in writing first, to give me a chance to put in words exactly how I feel, and you a chance to understand. I need to leave you and our marriage. I am too unhappy, every single day, and I am making you un-happy and I can't see any point in us staying together. I blame myself, I blame you, I blame the whole situation but I can't see any way around it. I haven't thought beyond that fact yet. I know it will be tricky, with the business and the cafés and every-thing, but I hope we can be civilized and keep the hurt as brief as possible for both of us.*
>
> *I'll be back from Donegal at the end of the month. See you then.*
>
> > *I'm sorry.*
> > *Juliet*

Was she sorry? Yes. She was sorry and sad and hurt, and sick of feeling all those things. She was sick of being surrounded by con-stant reminders that the life she and Myles had was not the life she wanted. She had set herself milestones for years. When I turn forty, I'll feel differently. When I turn forty-five, it will be okay. She was now fifty and she felt worse about it, not better.

She knew now she had been fooling herself that it would get better. It had changed, not improved. She wasn't just sad anymore. She was angry, angrier than she had thought it possible to feel. Not at herself, but at Myles.

The decision to leave him had still been a gradual one. At first, naively, she had thought the only way to get through it was together. It affected both of them, so they would have to mourn together. Then it had slowly dawned on her that he *had* gotten over it. He was fine. He thought it was okay. He actually thought they had a good life. He didn't see that he had played any role in this at all. All he did was fill their conversation with stupid platitudes.

"You can't have everything, Juliet. If we had been able to have children, who can say we wouldn't have had more heartache with them? Don't you think we've had a good life? We're better off than lots of people—we travel, have good holidays, do work we love. We've had good, full lives. You can't spend your life thinking 'what if.' You'll go mad that way."

She'd gone mad anyway. He didn't understand. No one did, not even her sisters. She'd only spoken to Miranda about it once, before losing her temper, furious at herself for even thinking she would understand, let alone care. Juliet hadn't bothered to discuss it with Eliza, already knowing what her reply would be. "Millions of women around the world don't have children, Juliet. I haven't and do I seem unhappy?"

"No, but you're some kind of ice woman," Juliet would have replied. "You don't need a man in your life, or children. You're perfectly happy with your business. Well, I'm not. I wanted more. I still want more."

Clementine would have been more sympathetic, to a point. But she would probably have explained that human beings were just like any other creature. She saw it all the time in her research projects. Some had chicks, others didn't. But no one lived happily every after, even in the bird world. Clementine would have cited case after case of chicks being abandoned, killed, or mistreated because they were different. Making her point as usual that the bird world and the human world weren't as far apart as people imagined.

Juliet knew all that. She knew having children wasn't the golden ticket to a life of happiness. She had always been realistic about it. After all, she'd seen Maggie from her first day. She knew the reality of caring for a small baby—the sleepless nights, the mess, the constant work. She'd been prepared for that, because she had also been there for the good side of it—the first smile, the first step, the sheer fun of having a baby, then a toddler and then a child in the house. For all the mess and chaos Maggie had somehow managed to create, there had also been great enjoyment. Juliet had never forgotten the sight of Maggie holding up her arms in the crib in greeting to the first person to come into her bedroom after a sleep. Or the sound of her laughter when she was being tickled. Or the funny things she would say, in that earnest way she'd had from the beginning. Juliet had seen it all with Maggie, loved it, and thought, blithely and innocently, that it would all be ahead for her and Myles when their own children started arriving.

Her experiences with Maggie had prepared her for the realities of adolescent life too. She'd been ready for a gaggle of her own teenagers, for the good times and bad: sleepless nights worrying when they weren't home yet; sullen days, moody days, drama-filled days. Temper tantrums from a teenage daughter. Monosyllabic answers from a teenage son. She had acted out scenarios in her head, over and over again, for years now. She had a parallel imaginary life, one filled with children, next to her real life's landscape. She'd done it as recently as this week, when she arrived here in Donegal. Her perfect life. It had kept her going through the darkest of times.

She shut her eyes and pictured a scene from it now. Some details didn't differ from the reality. She imagined herself as she was now, in her family's beautiful holiday house, preparing for the arrivals, food simmering on the stove, the fridge full, bottles of wine ready to be opened. It was the cast of characters that she changed. Sometimes she imagined her twin daughters arriving. Emily and Romy. One of them working as a teacher in London, the other a lab assistant in a hospital in Edinburgh. Bright, happy women. They fought a bit, of course, each of them coming to her and saying, "Mum, Emily said . . . ," and "Mum, Romy told me . . ."

Sometimes she thought of her boys arriving. Three of them. Rowdy, boisterous and fit. Adam, Lewis, and Henry. All of them with dark hair. Lewis was the quiet one, the more academic, still at university. She worried sometimes that he studied too hard, but he would assure her that he was getting plenty of fresh air and exercise. "Stop fussing, Mum." Adam was showing promising signs of being a professional cricketer. He'd hit three centuries the previous season. Harry had taken up soccer and was showing promise too. Juliet would stand with the other mothers and laugh. "I don't know where they get it from. I could barely throw a ball and the closest Myles got to a sports field was driving past it on the way to work."

Even one. A daughter, or a son. She wouldn't have minded. She would have felt the same, waiting for their arrival, making sure their bedroom was beautiful, that their favorite meals were in the oven, that she was ready to hear all their stories, offer any advice— or no advice. Whatever they wanted.

Myles never featured in any of these imaginings. It would confuse it too much; bring reality crashing in on her. Anger, disappointment. Why had she listened to him rather than her body? She'd wanted a baby since the first year they were married. "Let's establish ourselves first," he'd said. When the cafés took off in Australia, they'd been too busy. "There's no rush, Juliet."

She agreed, at first. Not for a moment had she thought they would have problems. The year she turned thirty-five she decided it was finally time. She'd stopped taking the pill for six months before she told Myles what she was doing. The mental picture of the end result stopped her feeling any guilt. She'd imagined herself setting the table for a romantic dinner, serving his favorite meal, pouring two glasses of wine and then after they had clinked glasses, putting hers down, going to his side of the table and saying, "I've got some news." Getting on the phone to Leo and the others, their congratulations ringing in her ears.

Except it didn't happen. Month after month came the disappointment. More than disappointment. It was a need, an ache, a space needing to be filled. She longed to feel a child in her arms, to feel a baby nestling against her neck. Not any baby—their baby. Her baby. It wasn't just physical. There seemed to be a whole area of her brain reserved for her child—for her children—as well. She was ready to worry about a child, be amused, be annoyed, angry and concerned about. To be consumed by. She had seen all that Maggie brought to Clementine; all that Maggie brought to all of them. The way a child in the house filled gaps and spaces with noise, laughter, warmth and love.

She was thirty-six by the time she and Myles started seeing doctors. Unexplained infertility, they told her. She had wanted to scream. How can it be unexplained? She needed them to explain it to her. She needed to know in the tiniest detail why what she wanted most in the world wasn't going to happen for her. She undertook test after test. So did Myles, even if she'd had to drag him in there. They met with counselors. They took relaxing holidays. They tried fertility treatment. Courses of drugs. Nothing worked.

Myles gave up first. "Perhaps it's just not meant to be."

She had gone into a fury with him, the temper fueled by the latest course of tablets she was on as much as her own feelings. "It is meant to be. I feel it. I don't just want a baby, Myles. I *need* a baby."

They had nearly broken up in those early days. Her distress was too much for him, his acceptance of the situation was too much for her. It was the business that kept them going. If they hadn't been working together, it would have been easy to stop talking to each other, to keep to their own parts of the house, to drift away. In the office together every morning, they had to speak to each other.

Maggie's visits had helped a little. As a child, then a teenager, and occasionally as an adult, she kept moving between all their houses, sure of their attention and love. In Sydney, and then when she and Myles moved to the U.K., in their house in Manchester, Juliet had always kept a room in her house ready for Maggie. There was a shelf in the bookcase full of her books, even some of her clothes in a cupboard. Juliet had treasured her company, all the while knowing that the bond and the love she'd feel for her own child would be even deeper than the feelings she had for Maggie.

When none of the treatments had worked, when they had spent

thousands of dollars in Australia and thousands of pounds in England, when she had cried more than she thought was possible, she decided to call a halt to it. Myles had begged her to stop months before. "You're destroying yourself," he said. Her own anguish and the hormones had made her fly at him. "I'm not destroying myself. This situation is destroying me." The words had been on the end of her tongue. She had pictured them, lined up, ready to go. "It's all your fault." She wanted to blame someone. She wanted to blame him. Because it *was* his fault. If he hadn't insisted they delay having children, for year after year, for the stupid, shallow reason of building their business, for the ridiculous, pointless goal of opening more cafés, then she may have had children now. The doctors had all said as much. She'd left it too late to start trying, too late to discover there were problems. The odds had been against her from the very beginning. And she had left it until too late because of Myles.

There had been distractions for a few years in their work. She couldn't deny it; she had found solace and pleasure in making a success of their cafés. She still loved cooking, thinking of recipes, preparing menus, working with all her staff.

What had changed in recent months was her home life. She couldn't pinpoint it, but one day at breakfast she had looked across at Myles and known it was over. He had been talking about a business trip he was planning to Glasgow. She looked at him and it was as if the volume had been turned down and she just saw his mouth opening and shutting. She wanted to get up from the table and walk away. So she did. He hadn't noticed. He kept on talking.

Their whole marriage was summed up in that moment, she realized. It had always been about him, not about the two of them, and definitely not about her. He had admitted to her once, in the middle of the IVF treatment that *she* had researched, that *she* had booked, that he had never wanted children as badly as she did. He was doing all of this for her. That had made her cry, as the smallest of things at that time had made her cry. "I need you to want it as much as I do, Myles. You have to."

"But I can't, Juliet. I can't lie about it."

The nurse had come in and not batted an eye at the tears or obvious argument. The IVF clinic was always a mass of emotions, Juliet discovered. Fights, anguish, elation; every couple who came in through the doors would soon be experiencing one or the other.

Juliet hadn't made the decision to stop the treatment completely on her own. Her doctor had told her bluntly that she was wasting her money, time, and hope. Myles did his best at that time, she conceded. He took her away for a two-week holiday in Spain. He spoiled her, brought her breakfast in bed every morning, didn't say anything when she insisted on staying in their room every day, sleeping or sometimes just lying there while the sun shone outside and the air filled with sounds of swimmers and windsurfers. All she could hear was children playing. She was being tormented by it. Everywhere she went she saw happy families.

It changed after a time. Everywhere she went she started to see unhappy families. People who didn't deserve children. Mothers in supermarkets slapping their toddlers. Teenagers roaming the streets late at night, uncared for. Every newspaper and TV news bulletin was filled with stories about neglected children, abandoned children.

She became obsessed with adoption and fostering, signing up with two agencies. Both of them told her she wasn't ready yet. "You're wrong," she insisted. "I'd be a perfect mother. I'm longing to be a mother."

They'd gently explained that was the reason they were asking her to wait. They felt she still had some way to go in the grieving process about not having her own children. They were concerned she had an idealistic view of motherhood. "We don't think you are quite ready for the reality of it," she was told. She disagreed. They stayed firm. She didn't go back to them.

That news affected her and Myles in different ways, too. Myles simply got on with his life. Juliet felt like her life was now at a standstill. Her marriage was at a standstill. On the outside it looked the same. The two of them working together, living together, sleeping together, though they hadn't had sex for months now. But all that time something had been changing. Her love for him. It had withered, as her hope for children of their own had withered and died.

She felt she had no other option than the one she had finally decided upon just the week before. She had to leave him. There was nothing left to keep them together. And soon he would be in their kitchen reading that note and he would realize that too.

She kept expecting to cry, but the truth was she had no tears left anymore. She'd shed them all already, years before. All there was left was a kind of emptiness. A resignation. A void that she had long been filling with work.

With a sudden, brisk movement, she stood up, turned on the radio, and gathered an armful of bed linen from the hot press under the stairs. Hadn't it always been Myles' own advice, whenever he found her in tears, month after month?

"Just keep busy, Juliet."

She would. She'd fill these next days with food, company, and her family, with the unexpected presence of Maggie and her surprise fiancé. And when they had all gone, and she and Myles had sorted out their separation and it was just her on her own, she'd still keep busy. What other choice did she have?

*   *   *

In Melbourne, Eliza was finishing her packing. She planned to be at Tullamarine Airport by seven, in time to meet Clementine's flight from Hobart. Their international flight left three hours later.

"I'll miss you," Mark said, lying on the bed and watching as Eliza put the final items into her suitcase. He'd called around to her apartment after finishing training work with one of his football team clients.

"I'll be back before you know it. I'm only going for a week."

"I'll still miss you."

"You're just a sentimental fool." Her smile took the sting out of her words.

"Why did you change your mind about going?"

"I realized I did have a few free days in my schedule. And the fact is my father isn't getting any younger." She left it at that. She had never gone into detail about her family with Mark and she didn't want to start now. That's what she loved so much about their relationship. It was just about them, the two of them, without other people complicating matters. She didn't want to take up the time they had complaining about Leo's latest antics, Juliet's dramas, Miranda's selfishness, or Clementine's success. She spoke about Maggie occasionally, but even that she kept as separate as she could. Maggie had never met Mark, in all the years she had stayed with Eliza. Eliza couldn't risk it. She didn't want to hear what her family would say if they knew about the situation.

"Have you finished packing yet?"

"Nearly. Why?"

"It seems a waste to be lying on the bed and not doing anything more interesting than watching you fold T-shirts."

"That's a very good point."

She moved her suitcase onto the floor and joined him on the bed, wrapping her body around his, placing her lips against his. Her desire for him was as strong now as it had always been. She kept waiting for it to fade, but it never did.

"What will I do if I need this while you're away?"

"You'll wait until I get back." She knew that he and his wife had long stopped being lovers. He'd told her and she believed him. Nearly believed him. If they did have sex occasionally, then there was nothing Eliza could do about it, in any case. It didn't change what they had. "You'll count down the days until I get home and you'll be here, waiting on my bed, just like this, when I do arrive back."

"Will I?"

"Yes."

"How do you know that?"

She smiled. "Because I know what you want and what you need, and I'm the only person in the world who can give it to you."

"I love it when you talk to me like that."

"That's why I do it," she said. Her next kiss silenced him.

•   •   •

Miranda woke up from her afternoon nap, reached up, and stretched, luxuriating in the feel of the warm air on her bare skin. Outside her window she heard a splash as one of the other guests jumped, or was pushed, into the pool. She preferred to stay indoors during the hottest part of the day. The bright Greek island light wasn't very forgiving to older skin, no matter how well looked after that skin was. Not that she ever gave that as her official reason for staying away from it.

Since she'd arrived here two days earlier, she'd made a habit of breakfasting early, swimming before ten, retiring to her room for a few hours in the middle of the day before stepping out onto the terrace around three, just in time for drinks and a late casual lunch. The villa had an enviable location, overlooking the Mediterranean Sea in one direction and the whitewashed houses of the nearest village in the other. The view wasn't the only wonderful thing about it. George was an extravagant host. The food was always sensational, yet simple: grilled fish, inventive salads, fresh fruit and local cheeses, all prepared by a very skilled chef that none of them ever saw. The wine cellar was extensive. The housekeeper was efficient: Miranda's clothes for the evening were already pressed and hanging in her wardrobe, her bed freshly made with the finest Egyptian cotton sheets and her marble bathroom gleaming clean and fully stocked with expensive toiletries. And all George expected of her in exchange was as much witty—and preferably bitchy—conversation as possible.

"It's a fair trade in my opinion, dearest Miranda," he'd said. "You provide the decoration and the entertainment, and I'll do all I can to make you happy."

Such a shame he was gay. Still, George always made sure there were plenty of other possible suitors in these gatherings of his. She'd been hugely flattered the previous evening when the twenty-something son of one of the other guests made a pass at her. A clumsy one, fueled by too much fine champagne, but a pass nevertheless. She'd let him down gently.

"Darling, you and that body of yours tempt me, I promise, but I'm old enough to be your big sister." She certainly hadn't said "old enough to be your mother" even if she was sure that was the case.

It was a shame to be leaving so soon. But at least the Donegal visit was looking brighter, now that Maggie and a sudden mystery boyfriend—fiancé, even!—were going to be there. Not to mention Eliza and Clementine as well. A full house, in fact. Thank heavens for that.

She glanced at her watch. Three p.m., on the dot. Perfect. She was longing for a glass of champagne. She draped her tanned and toned body in a flimsy silk caftan, pulled on a floppy sunhat and large dark glasses. A final check in the mirror, a reapplication of the pale-pink lipstick that went surprisingly well with her still-red hair and she was done.

"George?" she called as she strolled down the cool hallway toward the living area. "Where are you, my darling? I've got a sudden longing to hear something special."

"Of course, my sweet," his voice came back to her. "Classical? Jazz?"

"Neither," she said as she emerged onto the terrace. "What about the sound of one cork popping?"

.   .   .

Clementine was on the phone to Peter, the man she'd been dating for several months. She'd arranged to meet him for dinner on Saturday night. He wasn't happy.

"You can't come out with me because you're going to be in *Ireland*? You decided on the spur of the moment, did you?"

"I did, actually."

"Clementine, if you don't want to go out with me, you can just say. You don't have to come up with these outlandish excuses."

"It's not outlandish. It's the truth."

"Really? Well, as it happens, I wouldn't have been able to meet up with you on Saturday night either, because I'm taking a trip to the moon." He hung up.

Clementine stared at the phone for a moment. Had that really happened? He'd actually hung up in a sulk? What on earth was going on today? It had felt like an ordinary day when she got up. Then Leo had called from New York with his bombshell news. ("No,

Clementine, I'm not going to put Maggie on—you'll see both of them in less than two days so save all your questions until then.") Ten minutes later a call from Leo's travel agent to say it was all arranged; she and Eliza were booked on the same flight, business-class, direct to London, then on to Ireland. A call to Juliet to con-firm that it was actually all happening. And now this childish reaction from her would-be date. So much for an ordinary day.

No wonder she studied birds, she thought as she went into her room to start packing. They were far less complicated than hu-mans.

CHAPTER 34

In Dublin, in the northside suburb of Phibsboro, Sadie Faraday was gardening. She'd arrived home from the office after six as usual and changed straight out of her work clothes, wanting to take advantage of the warm summer evening. She'd started in the tiny front garden of her redbrick two-story terrace house. There was very little room for anything more than some ground cover and a hanging basket by the front door, but she was pleased with this year's display. She liked the colors and scents to greet her each morning and evening. Living with the long gray months of Irish autumns and winters, Sadie did everything possible to surround herself with color when she could.

She was now in her back garden, having decided it was time to pick off the dead roses from the three bushes that lined her fence. Three stems from finishing, she heard her neighbor's door open. She wondered if there was time to make a dash inside. She wasn't in the mood for one of Ivy's gossip sessions tonight.

"Lovely evening, Sally," Ivy called over their shared shoulder-high wall.

"Isn't it?" Sadie called back. Every now and then, it came as a surprise to hear herself called by a different name from the one she'd grown up with. But if she wasn't used to it by now, she never would be. "How are things with you?"

"Grand, thank God," Ivy said. "You're still living the single life, I see? I haven't seen that husband of yours for weeks now, it seems. Is everything all right?"

"Everything's great, Ivy. Thanks for asking." She snipped at another couple of roses and then took pity on the older woman. She was bursting with curiosity, Sadie knew that. "Were you starting to think I'd locked him in the cellar?"

"Oh, of course not. It's just that van of his hasn't been out in the front. A bit of a landmark that, you know. My Michael says that if it wasn't for the O'Toole Cleaners's van he wouldn't be able to find his way home from the pub some nights."

"Is it getting on your nerves again, Ivy?" Sadie asked. She'd long ago learned that Ivy had a roundabout way of making a complaint.

"Not at all, of course not. Well, only now and again."

"I'll tell Larry when he gets back. He's always happy to park it farther down the road. You only ever have to ask."

"I hate to be a bother. So everything's all right with Larry, is it?"

"He's in Galway at the moment for work."

"For work? Must be a big job. He's been gone nearly three weeks, hasn't he?"

Sadie had always suspected Ivy kept a running tally on the neighbors. Now she was convinced. For a moment she considered giving Ivy the complete answer. "Yes, Ivy, he's been gone exactly two weeks and four days. He's midway through a takeover of our biggest competitor in the pub- and restaurant-cleaning business. There was a last minute hitch with the lawyers and the contracts, so he's had to extend his trip." He hadn't been happy about it. "I can't leave you on your own, Sally," he said. "Some fancy man will come and whisk you away from me."

Sadie had laughed. He'd always talked to her like that—praising her, flattering her, building up her confidence in tiny ways ever since she had met him nearly twenty years ago. It was one of the many reasons she loved him.

Ivy was still waiting in position over the fence, keen for news. Sadie felt sorry for her. The poor woman, stuck inside all day caring for her elderly mother and selfish husband, she was always longing for some distraction.

"He'll be back on the weekend, we hope," Sadie said, deciding on an edited version. "Just as well. You'll all start to think we've split up if he's gone any longer."

"Split up? Not you two," Ivy replied. "I've never heard a couple get on as well as you two do. Talking and laughing all the time. You're like two newlyweds."

"A long way from newlyweds."

"I saw Maudie the other night. Did she tell you? She's back living with you, is she?"

"Just while Lorcan's working down the country for a few weeks."

"You'll be planning that wedding soon, I suppose? Before people do too much more talking."

Sadie kept the smile on her face with some difficulty. She knew that it was Ivy who had been doing all the talking on that particular subject. "Oh, I don't know. It's their decision, not ours."

"Well, I suppose if you look at it like that. It's just, you know, in the circumstances—"

Sadie kept snipping at the roses. "Marriage is out of fashion these days, anyway, isn't it? I'm sure I read something in the *Irish Times* about that."

"I don't know," Ivy said, her tone slightly deflated. "I only read the *Independent*."

Sadie gave a final satisfying snip and then gathered up the dead blooms. "Excuse me, Ivy. I want to go in and make a start on dinner. Say hello to your mother for me, won't you? I'll try and drop in later in the week."

"She'd like that. Bye now, Sally."

Sadie was barely inside before she dialed the number. Her husband answered on the third ring.

"Thank God it's you," he said. "If I speak to one more lawyer today I'm going to self-combust. The sooner I'm back in Dublin the better."

"You're telling me." She sat down on a kitchen chair and put her feet up on the nearby stool. "I've just been Ivy-ed again. Wait till you hear this one."

Ten minutes later, still on the phone, she heard a key turning in the front door. Moments later a young woman walked through the hallway into the kitchen, a rucksack slung over her left shoulder. Her pretty, lightly freckled face had a slight sheen of sweat. Her shoulder-length brown hair was caught back in a clasp, showing off two impressive displays of earrings. She was wearing a red cardigan over a blue cotton dress, its close-fitting design highlighting rather than disguising the fact she was in the late stages of pregnancy.

Sadie smiled in welcome, interrupting her story with a "Hello, sweetheart," before moving off the chair and motioning to her daughter to take her place. "Yes, that's Maudie I'm talking to," she said into the phone. "Yes, she looks better than well. And of course she wants to talk to you."

Maudie took the phone from Sadie and lowered herself onto the chair. "Da, are you there?" She laughed into the phone, resting her head back against the wall and placing her free hand protectively on her bump. "I'm healthy as a trout. Mum's right. Not a bother on me. What about you? Are you ever coming home again?"

Sadie fetched a glass of ice water and passed it to her daughter, getting a grateful smile and a whispered thanks before Maudie turned her attention back to the story her father was telling. Sadie knew once the two of them got going they could be on the phone for an hour or more. She decided the evening was too nice to stay inside. She collected her gloves and pruning shears, gestured to Maudie that she'd be outside, and stepped out into the warm air again.

.   .   .

It wasn't until much later that night, Maudie already asleep in her bedroom upstairs, that Sadie remembered the story she'd been about to tell Larry when Maudie arrived.

It had happened that afternoon. Sadie had been in her office reading through the advertising agency submissions for the final time. They had put her into a reflective mood. She'd found it hard to believe what she was hearing in the middle of their presentations, stranger still to read it all in black-and-white like this. But the facts were the facts. O'Toole Cleaners was the most successful company of its kind in the country. A dozen full-time employees in the Dublin office, a Cork office of eight, and if the Galway takeover went through, they'd have an office of six employees in the west of Ireland. They had more than two hundred part-time employees as well. All that business built on the back of dirt.

Her work had been interrupted by a call from her secretary. A journalist from a magazine was on hold on line one, wanting to talk to her. "He asked for you specifically."

The journalist was English, youthful-sounding, well-educated, and very businesslike. He got straight to the point. He was the business editor of a magazine called *Entrepreneurial Europe* and was working on a major article about successful businesses, particularly those employing immigrants from the EU states. He'd attended a recent industry conference in Oslo, he told her, and had heard good things about O'Toole Cleaners. He was in Dublin for the day, and was sorry for the short notice, but could she spare thirty minutes to talk to him that afternoon?

Normally Larry dealt with any media or publicity inquiries, but Sadie's interest was sparked. He had obviously done his research. O'Toole Cleaners was one of the country's largest employers of newly arrived workers from Poland, Latvia, and other EU countries. She could meet him at three, she said.

He was ten minutes early. She liked that. He apologized for not having a copy of the magazine with him. He'd hoped to bring the most recent issue but there had been difficulties with stock deliveries. He would send her a selection of back issues as soon as he returned to London.

"Thanks very much for sparing the time, Mrs. O'Toole. I'm sure you're very busy." He smiled. "I have to admit, your accent surprised me. I expected an Irish accent with a name like O'Toole."

"It surprises everyone," Sadie said, as she led the way back to her office. "I grew up in Australia."

He took a seat and got straight down to it. "What we like to do with our magazine, Mrs. O'Toole, is give the background to business success stories. It's helpful for our readers—up-and-coming entrepreneurs—to realize it can be a long and winding road to the top."

"I'm afraid I can't help you, then. My husband and I actually had an easy run of it."

"You did? Perhaps you could fill me in?"

She gave him the potted history. O'Toole Cleaners was owned and run by her husband Larry and herself. They'd moved to Ireland from Australia fifteen years previously, having worked in the cleaning industry in Queensland for some years. They'd immediately recognized a gap in the market in Ireland. They'd started in Dublin, offering full cleaning services to pubs in the city center, then to pubs outside the city center. They did the work themselves in the beginning, as they had done in Queensland, starting at three o'clock some mornings, moving from client to client, their day's work done before ten a.m.

The journalist was taking notes. "Our readers will love hearing that. It's a great image, the two of you, on your hands and knees, scrubbing pub floors."

"It wasn't the Dark Ages," she said. "We did have machines. Those machines you heard us talking about at the conference, in fact."

"The conference?"

"In Oslo. Where you first heard about us."

"Of course."

They expanded to restaurants, Sadie told him. The work flooded in. They had to start hiring extra staff, more each week. Irish people to begin with, and then as new immigrants came into the country, Polish, Nigerian and Chinese workers too.

"I've seen your brochures and I have to say you have a very straightforward image. What you see is what you get."

"My husband's idea," Sadie said with a smile. Straightforward was Larry's middle name. The company brochures featured photographs of O'Toole Cleaners' staff wearing their distinctive green overalls and driving the green vans, all with the O'Toole Cleaners logo and slogan. Nothing fancy, Larry had insisted. Let's say it as it is: "The Cleanest Cleaners are O'Toole Cleaners."

He asked her several more questions about the sort of market-
ing they did. "And what about your own background, Mrs.
O'Toole? If you don't mind telling me, how did you and Mr.
O'Toole meet?"

"In Australia. We were both backpackers in Brisbane. We started
working together, and it grew from there."

"You've been married for how long?"

"Nineteen years."

"And your age? Larry's age?"

She shifted slightly in her chair. "Do you really need this kind of
personal detail for a business story?"

"Only as much as you're happy to give. I'm sorry if I seem intru-
sive. I like to include what we call a break-out section in the article,
a box to the side with quick facts, a photo, that kind of thing. Nothing too personal, I promise."

Sadie relaxed. "I'm forty-five. Larry is a year older."

"And do you live in Dublin? Don't tell me, you're in one of the
seaview mansions in Killiney, next to Bono and Enya and the rest of
them?"

She laughed. "No, we haven't quite hit those heights. My husband grew up on the northside of Dublin and he still prefers it
there. We're in a suburb called Phibsboro." She spelled it for him.

He reached into his briefcase and took out a color print. "Now,
I found this photo on the website of the Oslo conference and I'm
happy to use it to accompany the article, unless you've another one
you'd prefer to supply?"

He passed over the photo. Sadie recognized it from the night of
the conference dinner. Herself in the red dress she'd immediately
regretted buying, Larry beside her looking uncomfortable in a suit.
She pulled a face. "I'll give you another one, if you don't mind."

"Whatever you're most happy with," the journalist said. He
pointed up to the bulletin board by her desk. "Are those family
photos? Because casual ones are just fine. In fact they're often better than posed ones. Would you mind if I had a look?"

She was happy to let him. He asked a few questions, "You have a
daughter? What age? Eighteen? She's very like you, isn't she?" be-

fore choosing a photo of the three of them, taken two years before on holiday in Spain.

"It would be nice to include a photo of your daughter as well, if you're happy for me to do that, especially as it's a story about a family business. She works for you too, I presume?"

Sadie explained that no, Maudie was working as a secretary. "Her boyfriend's setting up a plumbing business. Eventually she'll go into partnership with him."

"I'll have to come back in a few years and do another article then; two generations of an entrepreneurial family. Now, I could get this photo scanned here in Dublin and drop it back to you this afternoon. I've a few others I need to do, so it's no problem."

"That sounds grand, thank you."

He smiled. "You've picked up the Irish vocabulary, I see. Hard not to, I suppose." He started to pack away his notebook, his conversation becoming more informal. "Do you manage to get back to Australia very often?"

"No, not since we left."

"I was in Tasmania myself a year or two back. Beautiful place. The cleanest air in the world, apparently."

"Yes." Sadie stood up. Larry had taught her that was the best way to bring a meeting to a close. He was right. It worked every time. "I hope that's been helpful—"

"Very, and once again, I really appreciate your time. Just before I leave, would you be able to give me a few extra copies of your brochures? In case our art department needs them?"

"Of course." She rang through to her assistant but her phone was engaged. "Let me get them for you myself."

When she returned he was back behind her desk, looking at the photographs again.

"Excuse my curiosity," he said, not embarrassed at all. "Perfect character trait for a journalist, I suppose."

"I suppose. Let me show you out," she said. Larry had also taught her that line. It worked just as well.

He shook her hand, promising to send her the article as soon as it appeared.

She hadn't had a chance to think about it any more after he'd gone, distracted straightaway by a meeting with their personnel manager, and then two appointments with prospective restaurant clients. Now, in the peace of the evening, alone in the living room, something was niggling at her. What was it? Something he did? Something he said? It wasn't the photo. He'd done as he promised—dropped it back at reception within the hour.

She decided to do what she had done for the last twenty years whenever she felt uncertain about something. Talk to Larry about it. She checked the time. It was late, but not too late.

He was in his Galway hotel room, still working at his computer, happy to be disturbed. She launched straight into the story. Midway through, he stopped her. "I think I know where this is leading to. Tell me, did you check out his magazine? Make sure it actually existed?"

"Well, no. He sounded so businesslike when he rang and he looked the part. Tape recorder, notebook, all the right questions."

"Hold on," he said. "I'm online at the moment. Let me check. What did you say it was called?"

She spelled it out, heard the click of his computer keys down the phone, and waited. More clicking, then Larry came back on the line.

"Oh, my Sally. My innocent little Sally." He was laughing, not mad at all at her. "There's no magazine with that name. I'd bet you a thousand euros he was a snoop, sent by one of our competitors. It's an excellent cover, I'll give them that. Was he asking about clients? Staff numbers? Marketing approaches?"

He'd asked about all those things. Sadie shut her eyes. "How could I have been so stupid?"

"You're not in the least bit stupid. It's just that you're so honest yourself, you don't expect other people to be dishonest. Don't worry about it. You didn't tell him anything that wasn't common knowledge. So what if they know we're successful, that we've got clients all over the country? The dogs in the street know that. Besides, we've got a fifteen-year head start on the business. They'll never be able to catch up, ill-gotten research or not."

"Are you ever pessimistic, Larry O'Toole?"

"Never. What's the point? Now, go to sleep and stop worrying. It's my fault, not yours, anyway. I leave you alone for a few weeks and look what happens."

"I fall to pieces and get taken in by a wily competitor."

"You didn't get taken in, so stop your worrying. Good night, love. Sleep well. Talk to you tomorrow."

As she went upstairs to bed, her mind eased by the conversation, she thanked her stars for the hundredth time that Larry O'Toole had come into her life all those years ago. Where would she be, what would she be doing, what sort of person would she have turned out to be if he hadn't? She hated to think.

CHAPTER 35

"So let me see if I've got this straight," Gabriel said to Maggie as they sat side by side in the plane's business-class section. Leo was just across the aisle. "You've got three brothers, two sisters, your mother is a ballerina, and you grew up in Africa?"

"That's it. Well done. You'll pass with flying colors."

"Thank you, Millie. Your name is Millie, isn't it?"

"You really do have a mind like a steel trap, don't you?"

"Steelier than that, even."

"Would you mind if I pulled my blanket over my head and screamed?"

"Why? Is that another Faraday family tradition? You certainly are an active family in that regard."

For the past few hours she had been giving Gabriel a crash course in her family history. At first he'd taken her very seriously, asking questions, taking it all in. Over the past few minutes it had fallen in a heap.

"It's not too late, Gabriel, seriously. You can change your mind about going through with this."

"And do what? Jump out over—" He looked past her, out the tiny window. "—what look like shark-infested waters? No, a challenge is a challenge. I'm here till the end." He smiled. "Please don't look so worried, Maggie. If we manage to pull it off, fantastic. If we don't, we'll tell your family it was a delayed April Fool's Day trick."

"They won't be happy either way."

"Leave it with me then. I'll come up with something spectacular to finish it and you'll be blame-free, I promise. In the meantime, just correct me in front of them if I get anything too wrong. Isn't that what is so wonderful about our relationship? Discovering new things about each other every day?" He spoke the final two sentences in a saccharine voice.

She relaxed. "If you talk to me like that, I'm going to tell my family that you earn your living as an Avon lady."

"Oh really? Well, I'm going to tell your family that I met you when you were go-go dancing in a seedy nightclub in SoHo."

"Go-go dancing?" She started to laugh.

Across the aisle, Leo called for Gabriel's attention.

"Excuse me, darling," Gabriel said to Maggie.

"Of course, darling," Maggie answered.

She shut her eyes and leaned her head back, still smiling. She would never have thought it possible, not when Leo first broke all of this to her, but she was starting to enjoy herself. She had never laughed with Angus the way she laughed with Gabriel. He kept her on her toes too. Quick witticisms, lots of storytelling. They'd spent most of the day in each other's company, between waiting at the airport when their flight was delayed and now the flight itself, and not once had Maggie felt bored or uncomfortable. They kept finding things to talk about. She'd asked him a lot about his childhood, and been thoroughly entertained by his stories—a New York City upbringing a long way from her own relaxed Hobart days. The more he told her, the more she wanted to know. She needed to know as much about him as he knew about her, after all. She could already imagine the third degree she'd get from her aunts, not to mention Clementine. She had another shimmer of guilt about lying to them, but quickly pushed it down. It was Leo's idea, not hers. He was the one who was behind all of this.

That thought reminded her that this visit wasn't going to be all fun and games. There were the diaries to read. Just as important, the question of Sadie. Leo had tried calling the private detective before they left New York, but had got only his voice mail. "No news is good news," he said to Maggie. "I just have to be patient."

Maggie had debated whether to tell Gabriel the whole Sadie story. If all Leo hoped was true, that Sadie had been found alive and well and living in Dublin, then Gabriel would probably meet her one day and—she stopped herself. Why would he meet Sadie? For one silly moment, she seemed to have convinced herself that Gabriel really was her fiancé.

Wishful thinking, said a voice in her mind.

It was true. The more time she spent with him, the more she liked him. Not just because he was easy to talk to, though he was. Not just because he was good-looking, though he was definitely that as well. It was the whole combination, she realized. The intelligence, the humor and the looks. How on earth he hadn't been snapped up by any other woman she didn't know, but the fact was—

Oh God. She actually had a crush on Gabriel.

"Maggie?"

She turned, convinced her thoughts were somehow visible.

"Would you like a drink?"

She hadn't noticed the flight attendant with the drinks trolley. "No, I'm fine, thanks."

Leo and Gabriel returned to their conversation. Maggie took a breath. She had to get back to the business at hand. The diaries were the most urgent thing. She'd done a calculation—nine of them, each with one hundred pages. Nine hundred pages. It would take her several minutes to read each page. A few days' solid reading at least. She really had to get started.

The briefcase and the diaries were in her overhead locker. She stood up, moving past Gabriel and opening the hatch.

He stood up too. "Let me do that for you," he said. He took down the briefcase and handed it to Maggie.

"I thought I'd make a start," she said to Leo.

"Thank you, love." He smiled at her, that glimpse of vulnerability evident again. "It's all part of this project we have you working on, Gabriel. Collecting memories of my wife and Maggie's grandmother. This needs to stay between the three of us, but I've appointed Maggie chief reader and editor of some diaries Tessa kept. Now, stop me if I'm repeating myself, but did I tell you about my very first invention?"

That would keep Gabriel occupied until they landed in Ireland, Maggie knew.

She opened the briefcase and took out the first of the blue notebooks. Settling herself in her seat, she opened the front cover, traced her fingers over the flamboyant script on the inside page: *Tessa Faraday—Private and Confidential,* and began to read.

CHAPTER 36

Tasmania. He'd mentioned Tasmania.

Sadie sat upright in bed. She didn't know what time it was or what had woken her, but she suddenly knew why she had been so bothered by the journalist that afternoon. He had mentioned Tasmania.

How had he known of her links there? She hadn't told him. There was nothing about it in any of the company's promotional material. She'd never spoken about Tasmania to Larry or Maudie, either. Both of them believed she had been brought up in Adelaide.

She traced back over the conversation again. Perhaps she'd been mistaken. Imagined it. Her family had been on her mind all week, as they always were this time of the year, especially the past few years, knowing they were gathering less than five hours from Dublin.

She could still remember the shock she'd got receiving Maggie's letter that year. It had finished with the casual announcement that Leo had surprised them all again, buying a "holiday house in Donegal, of all places. We've decided to spend our July Christmas celebrations there each year. You know you'd be welcome, if you ever felt like making a trip to Ireland."

For once, she had read the letter Leo enclosed with that one straightaway. She didn't always read his the day they arrived. It depended on how she was feeling. His letter also mentioned the Donegal house. "If you ever want to go there, to feel close to Tessa, you know I would pay your airfare in a shot."

She had shredded his letter immediately, then Maggie's. She had shredded all their letters and cards over the years. She'd had to. She couldn't risk Larry or Maudie finding them. She knew only too well the dangers of leaving personal material lying around. But while the letters were shredded, the news of the house in Donegal had stayed with her.

It had been very simple to discover which house it was. A phone call to an auctioneer in Letterkenny, the main town in Donegal, a casual inquiry about recently sold properties in the southwest of the county, near the village of Glencolmcille. She was directed to several different websites, each featuring dozens of properties in the area. She found it within the hour: a beautiful extended white-washed house, with views of the sea and mountains.

She'd driven past it once. She and Larry had been in Letterkenny on business. Driving back to Dublin she'd suggested they take a scenic drive. She drove into the village, took the road that wound up the hill, following all the directions from memory. It was easy to spot the house, the largest one in the area. There was a discreet signpost in the front garden: *Available for rent*. A local caretaker's number was listed below.

She stopped the car, leaving the engine running. "What do you think? Will we rent this place one summer?"

Larry shuddered. "No, thanks. Too much scenery around here for me." He was a city man through and through.

She had been tempted. She couldn't pretend she hadn't been. To stay there on her own, in their house, without them knowing. To stay nearby when they were all there. Shop in the same shops, drink in the same pubs. Would they know her? Would she know them? She hadn't changed that much in twenty years. A few gray hairs these days and she was still battling with her weight, but she was certainly not plump anymore. They'd recognize her, as she knew she would recognize them.

They'd be there now, she realized. If she wanted to, she could get up, drive for five hours, and walk right into the house. "Hi, everyone. I'm back."

Hell would freeze over before she would do that.

She got up, too unsettled to sleep. She tried to be rational about it. That man's reference to Tasmania was just a fluke.

She went into the kitchen and made herself a hot milk drink, despite it being a warm night. She wished again that Larry was home. If he was there, all she would have to do is wrap herself around him to feel safe and secure. She'd told him that once. That being with him made her feel so protected, peaceful. Complete.

"That's because we're soulmates," he'd said, very matter-of-factly. "We were destined to be together. Look at the odds. The gods were looking down on us when we met. Blessed with luck, the pair of us."

Sadie had felt cursed, not blessed, at that time. Those five months before she met Larry in Brisbane had been the loneliest and scariest of her life. It still shocked her sometimes to think back. It was like someone else's life. Someone so unhappy, so desperate.

She knew exactly why she had run away. But if someone were to ask her now why she had taken Maggie with her, she still wasn't sure what she would say. Anger? Desperation? Shock? To hurt her family, to make them feel as bad as she was feeling? Or for another, quite simple, reason?

So many things had been going wrong for her at that time. She had felt so lost, so out of place. Unappreciated. A stranger in her own family. If it had been possible to do so without Eliza hearing, she would have cried herself to sleep most nights. The only good thing in her life had been Maggie. She was the only person in her family with whom she felt a connection. Maggie didn't pick on her, judge her, put her down, or compete with her. She just enjoyed being with her. Sometimes when they were out together she would catch someone smiling at the two of them. "How old is your daughter?" "Hasn't your daughter got a lovely smile?" It didn't mean anything, Sadie knew that. But she liked hearing it. It made her feel like she and Maggie were a family. It made her feel good at a time when not much else did. She knew she drove her sisters crazy. She could feel Leo's disappointment in her. She couldn't keep up with any of them, achieve even half of what they achieved. Why was she like that? Where had it all gone wrong for her?

Reading the diaries, she had finally known why. It all made sense. She could never forget how it felt to read her mother's words. The further she read the more distressed she'd become. How had Leo been able to keep talking about Tessa with such love? He must have read all of this, yet he had chosen to keep up her traditions, paint a picture of the perfect mother, the happy family.

It was an entry written two days after Sadie's own tenth birthday, just a few months before Tessa died, that had hurt the most. She could remember herself so clearly at that age. So ungainly, so clumsy; desperate to be as pretty and witty and clever as her sisters. She'd asked for a birthday party and been told by Tessa and Leo that she could invite three friends over. She'd taken ages making the list, trying to choose between the girls in her class. Eventually she had whittled it down to three. She'd drawn the invitations herself, ignoring Miranda's teasing that her pictures of cats looked like deformed mice. She'd gone to school the next day with the invitations in her bag and at recess had proudly walked over to the three girls. She handed them out and waited, grinning, imagining their responses: "A party? Great! Thanks, Sadie." One by one they opened them. The tallest, Kym, had the grace to look embarrassed. "We can't come that day, Sadie. Sorry."

"Why not?"

They had shuffled their feet, looked at each other, not at her, until one of them spoke. "Because we're all going to another party."

Kym's birthday party, the same day, to which everyone had been invited except for her and three other girls who Sadie herself thought of as the dregs of the class.

She'd run home after school, desperate for her mother. Her uncle Bill had been on holiday from England, sitting out on the veranda smoking a cigarette. She ignored him. She had run inside the house in tears, wanting a hug, wanting to be consoled. Her mother was in bed. All of them knew never to wake her up from her afternoon naps, but this was different. Sadie needed her. She remembered running into the room, crying, starting to tell her mother all about it, and the shock she had got when her mother had sat up, told her to be quiet and leave her alone.

Reading the diaries, reading her mother's account of that day had felt like a blade going through her. She had obviously picked up the diary straight after Sadie had gone away and put down all her feelings on the page.

Sadie remembered sitting in the shed in the middle of the night, reading it, recalling the same event from her own perspective, feeling the tears fall down her face. She had decided to leave her family that night. If Leo wanted to live a life of lies, paint Tessa as the perfect wife and perfect mother, then that was his choice, but Sadie knew she couldn't be a part of it anymore. She had to leave, get as far away from the family as she could.

She had planned to use the two weeks in Melbourne with Maggie only as thinking time. Her intention was to wait until Miranda returned and let her take Maggie back to Hobart. She was going to move on then, to Perth, or perhaps even Darwin. Somewhere as far from her family as possible.

It was just circumstances that led to her taking Maggie with her. Talking to her about having an adventure, seeing how excited she was. Having so much fun together. Maggie telling her that night, in that beautiful way she had, "I have to tell you a secret. You're my favorite auntie." It had gone straight to Sadie's heart. She'd decided then that she couldn't say good-bye to Maggie. Not yet, anyway.

She still remembered every detail of the night Leo and Clementine turned up. The shock of it—Clementine hitting her, Leo snatching Maggie away from her as though she had been in some danger, then coming back and saying over and over again, "Why, Sadie? Why did you do this? Has something happened to you? We love you. We're your family. Tell me."

He couldn't have chosen worse words if he'd tried. She hadn't intended to tell him, but the words blurted out of her. "Don't lie to me, Leo. I read her diaries. I know the truth."

She'd never forgotten the look on his face. Like one mask falling away and another being revealed behind it. He knew exactly what she was talking about. Any hope she might have had of Leo saying, "No, you have it wrong," died in that moment. She'd turned away, unable to bear listening to him anymore.

She ran. She left the caravan park before seven a.m., startling the owner who was barely awake, settling her bill, handing over Maggie's belongings in a plastic bag. She waited at a bus stop outside the town for half an hour, stepping in and out of the shadow of the trees, terrified Leo and Clementine would drive past. Leo had said he would come back that morning. She wanted to be miles away before he appeared.

She hitchhiked in the end. An elderly woman on her way to visit her sister up the coast stopped for her. She disapproved of anyone hitching, she told Sadie, and proceeded to lecture her for the duration of the journey. Sadie was happy to listen, hanging her head, looking chastened, inwardly urging the woman to drive faster, to get her as far away as she could.

Two hours later she was in Brisbane. It was her first time there. She was terrified, short of money, and alone. She wouldn't let herself think about anything that had happened or what might happen next. She told herself this was a holiday, an adventure. She talked to herself as she had talked to Maggie over the past two weeks. Tried to make it exciting and fun. She had to fight to keep thoughts of her family out of her mind. They kept breaking through. Miranda, sneering at her: "What the hell did you think you were doing? Have you gone even madder than usual?" Juliet, motherly, concerned and lecturing: "Have you any idea how worried everyone's been? How could you be so thoughtless?" Eliza, as judgmental as ever. She didn't have to imagine what Clementine and Leo would have said. They had made it clear. Leo veering from anger to shock when he realized that she had read the diaries, that she knew his charade of the perfect marriage, the perfect mother, had been just that.

She spent her first night in a hostel, the cheapest she could find, surrounded by cheerful, loud girls from Germany, Ireland, Switzerland, and the U.S. on the latest stop of their year-long adventures.

She lay in bed listening to them exchange traveling tips, funny stories from the road and checklists of the must-sees of Australia. At breakfast the next day she joined two of them in the communal kitchen. She had some fruit leftover in her bag. She offered it around and received some cheese and crackers in return.

They'd fired questions at her: "You're Australian, aren't you?" "What's your name?"

"Sally," she said, without even a second's hesitation. "Sally Donovan," she added, even more firmly.

It was so easy to make up a story. She told the two girls that she'd just finished her university degree and was taking a year out.

They told her about towns they'd stayed in in far north Queensland, where they received food and board in exchange for fruit picking, cleaning, and packing jobs. They told her which hostel in Darwin to avoid because of its sleazy owner. They told her about a café in Cairns that acted as an informal employment exchange for backpackers. If you're not fussy, there's work everywhere, they said. Especially in Brisbane.

Sadie wasn't fussy. She didn't care what she did. All she knew for sure was she didn't want to go back to Hobart. Ever.

Over the next few weeks she washed dishes and cleaned bathrooms, and kitchens in pubs and restaurants in the city center. She worked hard during the day so she would be exhausted at bedtime. She shared a dormitory with a changing cast of backpackers. She added more details to her own story. It was so easy, when there wasn't someone like Miranda waiting with a smart put-down to contradict her.

She dyed her hair black, using a cheap mix from the pharmacy and getting the hostel bathroom into such a mess it took her two hours and a whole bottle of bleach to clean. She waited for the other girls to tell her off, the way Juliet or Eliza would have done. An Italian girl called Maria just laughed. Another girl offered to give her a hand when she found Sadie on her hands and knees scrubbing at the black splatters of dye.

In the daytime she managed to keep thoughts of her family at bay. All of them except for Maggie. It shocked her how much she was missing her niece. She hadn't even had a chance to say good-bye to her. What if Maggie thought Sadie had forgotten all about her? What had they all told Maggie? The thought gnawed at her. What could she do about it? She couldn't ring home and ask to speak to her; try to explain to a five-year-old what the situation was. She was also unsure what Clementine might have decided to do. Press charges against her?

It was when she was walking back to the hostel from one of her casual jobs that she had the idea about contacting Maggie via Father Cavalli in Hobart. She'd passed a priest in the street, chatting to a young woman. The image stayed in her mind. Three days later she went to a phone booth and made the call. Father Cavalli himself answered. If he hadn't, Sadie knew she would have hung up. She didn't say much. She wondered if he knew anything about the whole business yet. She suspected not. The Faradays had stopped going to mass in recent years. She told him that there had been a fight, without going into details. She wanted to be on her own for a while, but she didn't want Maggie to think it was her fault. If she was to send a card to Maggie care of the priest's house, would he pass it on to her?

He mouthed some platitudes to her, which she did her best to block out. It was his job, she supposed, so she made some pretense at listening. He urged her to find forgiveness in her heart, to understand that all families went through rocky periods, but stressed how important it was to let love cancel out conflict.

"And what if there is no love there, Father?"

He went quiet.

"Family love is the strongest of all, Sadie."

She said good-bye soon after that. But she was grateful to him. He'd said he would act as a go-between. She gave him a general delivery address at the Brisbane GPO. If it changed, she would let him know.

"Keep praying, Sadie," he urged her.

She hadn't prayed for years and wasn't about to start. She didn't tell him that.

She sent a birthday card to Maggie the next day, a cheerful one with dancing mice on the front that she knew Maggie would love. Two weeks later her daily visit to the GPO was rewarded. There was a card waiting for her, in an envelope with unfamiliar writing. Father Cavalli's, she presumed. Inside, a card from Maggie, thanking her and telling her that she had got two gold stars at school that week. *I miss you and I love you, Maggie xxxxx*. There was a note tucked inside it from Leo. Sadie didn't read it.

Over the next few months she lived the life of any happy-go-lucky backpacker. She went north for the mango picking, sleeping in hostels open to the weather and unfortunately also open to large spiders, snakes, and flying fruit bats. She woke up one day with a spider crawling across her pillow. She was back in Brisbane and her old hostel by nightfall. The next day she found work behind the bar of a city center pub. It was that easy.

Why hadn't she ever done this before? She'd never known there was this way to live, the sheer freedom of it. The incredible pleasure of being taken for herself, not as one of those Faraday girls, not as Miranda's less glamorous sister, Clementine's less clever sister, Juliet's less hardworking sister, or Eliza's less athletic sister. She was just herself.

She added more layers to her story as necessary, depending on the questions she was asked. She told people she came from Adelaide. That both her parents were teachers. That they were putting on pressure for her to go into teaching too but she wanted to explore the world a bit first. She got sympathy and understanding from her fellow hostelers. Everyone took her as she was.

It surprised her to discover that the hostel held its own July Christmas celebration. She'd thought that was only a Faraday family tradition. All of the backpackers from the U.K., Ireland and other parts of Europe threw themselves into the celebrations. Sadie chose not to get involved, spending the day at the cinema instead, seeing three films in a row and coming back late after it was all over.

There was equal enthusiasm when the first December came around—lots of talk about how funny it was to have a hot Christmas, phone calls back to families on the other side of the world, all of them lining up to use the phone. One of the girls, a soft-hearted Scottish girl called Ruth, noticed that Sadie didn't make any calls.

"Can't you afford it?" she whispered. "I'm happy to give you the money if you want."

"No, but thanks."

"Is everything all right?"

"We had a big fight," she said. It was the closest she'd ever come to telling the truth.

"That's what families are for, aren't they? You'll make it up, won't you?" Ruth had been so eager and optimistic.

"I don't think so," she said.

"Don't you want to? Don't you miss them?"

Sadie didn't miss them. Not yet. Every day she felt better than she had ever felt when she was with them. The only person she missed was Maggie.

Sadie went out for a walk. By the time she came back Ruth had told the others that Sadie was feeling sad because she'd had a fight with her family. A group of the other girls came over to her, all sympathy and hugs. "We're here if you want to talk about it," a young Canadian woman said.

So Sadie talked. She told them the whole story. Not the real one. Another story just came tumbling out of her. That her father was violent. That he had beaten up her mother for years and that Sadie had come in one day and tried to stop it, and he had thrown a chair at her. She showed them the scar on her forehead. She'd got it falling off a swing at primary school when she was six.

The other girls sat around the table, staring at her, mouths open. She'd never felt that kind of attention before. She had the faintest spike of guilt, thinking of Leo who had never raised a hand to any of them. Then she looked back at her audience and noticed how they were hanging on her every word.

Overnight in the hostel, she became the poster girl for survival. She felt guilty about it. There were people who had truly gone through what she was pretending to have experienced. But it was too late by then to take back her story.

She moved out of the hostel into a four-bedroom share-house a month later. One of the other girls from the hostel moved in too. The house was a timber Queenslander, up on stilts to let the cool air circulate, and with as much furniture out on the veranda as inside. Sadie didn't have much furniture but she had her own room, a foam mattress on the floor, a clothes rack, and a mirror. All she needed.

One of her new flatmates told her about a job going at a big hotel in the city. A cleaning job. Terrible hours, he said. She'd have to be there by six a.m., but she'd be finished by eleven and have the rest of the day to herself.

She liked the idea of it. She'd started doing a lot of swimming, enjoying the feel of her body in the water, getting stronger and fitter. If she got her work over in the morning, she could head to one of the beaches and spend all day swimming and reading.

She went for the interview, told the truth about all the cleaning jobs she'd had, told the usual lies about her name and background, so good at it now there was no way the interviewer would have picked it up. She got the call the next day. They wanted her to start on Monday. She'd be working in a pair, with an Irish guy called Peter O'Toole.

"Call me Larry," he said when they met.

She liked him straightaway. He had such a happy smile. Happy as Larry, she thought. When they told the story to friends in later years she couldn't ever say it was love at first sight. "It was like at first sight," she'd explain.

"It was love at first sight for me," Larry always said.

Her first impression was good and, as she soon learned, accurate. He looked happy because he was happy. He'd been nicknamed Larry after Lawrence of Arabia, the Irish actor Peter O'Toole's most famous role. He was short for a man, only five foot seven. He had a round face, freckled skin, a stocky body, blue eyes, and the widest, cheeriest smile Sadie had ever seen.

He was also the most enthusiastic person she had ever met. He thought Australia was amazing. He thought the cleaning job was "the biz," as he put it. "Five hours' work in the morning and that's us free for the day. Call this work?"

They made a great team. They discovered that in the first week. They were assigned the nightclub areas of the hotel on the weekends, the conference rooms and lobby bar during the week. Larry did the heavy work: the furniture shifting, the industrial mopping, the lugging of trays of empty bottles out to the bottle bank. Sadie worked behind him, polishing, sweeping and restocking shelves. They took it in turns with the toilets, though if they were particularly bad, they did them together. They got such a routine going that one of the managers actually came down one morning to compliment them on the good job they were doing.

It was Larry's idea to start even earlier than six, so they'd be finished and out even earlier too. "We could start at five and be free by ten. What do you think?"

"What would we do then?"

"Whatever we wanted. That extra hour would make all the difference. I want to learn how to surf, et cetera." He often said "et cetera" instead of "for example," in the wrong context. She found it very endearing. "Come and learn to surf with me, Sally."

They learned how to surf, then decided to also try windsurfing. Larry didn't tease her when she turned out to be very bad at both activities. "Don't worry about it. Get up and try again," he said each time. So she did.

They talked while they were working in the hotel together, talked while they were going to the beach, talked over cheap pizzas and games of pool. He called over to her share-house several nights a week. When a room became spare, he moved out of his hostel into her place. They talked even more. He told her about growing up in Dublin. She kept to her Adelaide story. She slowly learned that things hadn't been easy for him as a child. His mother had left his father when he was only five. They'd moved around a bit. She worked in local hotels as a barmaid. It kept her too close to the drink, unfortunately.

"That's why you don't drink?" She only realized then that she'd never seen him have so much as a beer.

He wasn't maudlin about it. "It never looked like much fun to me."

So she didn't drink when she was with him either. It didn't make sense when they both had to be up at four a.m. anyway.

She heard bad stories about nights with his mother, having to help her upstairs to bed, finding her slumped outside the house, a series of men coming in and out of her bed and their life. He asked her about her family. She knew that he'd heard a hint of the story she'd first told in the hostel. She felt guilty and hedged around the subject. Hers was make-believe. His had been real. He was hurt when she closed up, hurt that she wouldn't trust him enough to tell him, so she did. To compensate, she added more detail, describing a difficult childhood, a violent father and how scared she had been. She didn't know where all the stories were coming from, but she couldn't stop them, adding details of bullying at school and night after night of her parents fighting. The more she told, the more real it seemed to become.

One evening they were sitting out on the veranda together, enjoying the warm air and listening to the sound of cicadas. He had asked her a question about her school days. She had responded with a tragic tale about being in a school play and neither of her parents turning up, coming home to find her father beating her mother, and him then turning on her. It had just come out of her mouth. He'd been silent for a while afterward and she'd felt terrible. Guilt and shame. She'd gone too far this time.

Then Larry took her hand and held it against his heart as he spoke. "We're peas in a pod, you and I." He told her how much he admired her. How amazing he thought she was to be so strong and cheerful and happy, with all that she had been through. And then he kissed her.

Sadie had never had a long-term boyfriend. She'd never really had any boyfriend. She'd had kissing sessions as a teenager and lost her virginity as a nineteen-year-old at an awful party she and a friend had gate-crashed. She'd known the boy from university, had sex with him in one of the spare bedrooms, given him her number, and never heard from him again.

She tentatively kissed Larry back. He stopped midway and pulled away from her.

"I'm not very good at this," he said.

"Me either."

"You? You must have had loads of fellas chasing you."

Sadie told him the truth. He didn't believe her. "You've never had a proper boyfriend? It's true. Aussie men are thick as planks."

They kissed again. When they drew away from each other the next time she noticed he was smiling. Beaming at her.

"What's so funny?"

"Nothing's funny," he said.

"So why are you smiling?"

"Because I've been waiting for this for weeks." He loved her, he said. It was as simple as that. He thought she was just great. He loved the way she looked, the things she said, the way she worked, the way she laughed.

She felt the same way about him, she replied, in a kind of wonder. She had never realized until that moment. All she'd known was she loved being with him. That working with Larry didn't seem like work. That it didn't matter if they were scraping muck off dance floors, washing hundreds of glasses, or scrubbing filthy bathrooms; he somehow made it fun.

They kissed again, until one of their flatmates came out and applauded. "At bloody last."

Larry moved into her room that night and they became lovers from then on. They worked together, played together and socialized together.

Sadie had never felt this way in her life. Not just loved, but protected. He was always on her side. He built her up in little ways, every day, with compliments and encouragement. It wasn't all roses. They fought occasionally, but he was quick to apologize if it was his fault, and she sought his forgiveness if it was hers.

Getting married just seemed the obvious thing to do. They decided on a registry office. He had been a resident of Australia for two years. She had her birth certificate and passport. There were no difficulties. Until Sadie realized something. Once they got to the registry office he would see her name wasn't Sally Donovan.

She worried about it for days. One night, in bed beside him, she heard his voice in the darkness.

"Have you changed your mind, Sally?"

"About what?"

"Marrying me."

"No. Of course I haven't."

"What's wrong, then? You've been tossing and turning every night since we decided to get married."

She made her decision. "Larry, there's something I haven't told you."

"You're already married?"

"It's not that." She hesitated. "I'm not Sally Donovan. It's not my real name. I changed it when I ran away. I needed to."

"What's your real name?"

"Sadie. Sadie Faraday."

"I'd have changed it too. Sally Donovan's a much nicer name."

"You don't mind?"

"Of course I don't. I can hardly talk. Larry's not my real name either." He pulled her close then, and became serious. "Sally, we both did what we had to do to try and make our lives better. You changed your name, ran to Queensland. I changed my name and ran to Australia. And then we met and now we'll have the same name. If you want to change it to O'Toole, that is? I think Sally O'Toole's an even better name."

She found herself in tears. "So do I. I'd love to change it to O'Toole."

"Stop that crying, then. We can't live happily ever after if you keep crying, can we?"

He was right. They were starting afresh together now. She decided in that moment there was no need to tell him anything else about her background. "What did I do to deserve you?" she asked. She wasn't fishing for compliments. She genuinely wondered.

He kissed her. "I ask myself the same thing about you."

They got married and had a small party. They kept working, agreeing that they'd have a honeymoon down the track, when they had more money saved. They moved into their own cheap flat. They didn't bother with contraception. Six weeks after the wedding they realized they wouldn't need to for a while, either. Sadie was already pregnant. Ten months after the wedding, Maudie was born.

Larry chose her name. It wasn't from his family. "It's sentimental, but there was a poem I loved when I was a kid. It was the only one I ever managed to memorize at school. But if you think it's too old-fashioned . . . ?"

He recited the poem for her. It was "Come into the Garden, Maud," by Tennyson.

> *Come into the garden, Maud,*
> *For the black bat, night, has flown.*
> *Come into the garden, Maud,*
> *I am here at the gate alone;*
> *And the woodbine spices are wafted abroad,*
> *And the musk of the rose is blown.*

Sadie loved it too. Larry had unknowingly continued a Faraday tradition, choosing a name from a poem or a song. It made her sad for a few days, until she reminded herself that it was Larry who had chosen the name, not her. And soon she was too busy caring for Maudie to give her family and their traditions much thought.

She would never have believed her life would turn out this way. She had a husband who loved her; a husband she loved. A daughter who had arrived in an easy, uncomplicated fashion, and had brought them nothing but joy since. Sadie had literally fallen in love with her at first sight, the moment the midwife passed her daughter to her. She hadn't been out of love with her since.

Larry was equally smitten. He marveled at Sadie's mothering skills. "You're a natural at this, Sally," he often said, watching her change their daughter's nappy, or, later teaching her to count. "You didn't train as a kindergarten teacher before you met me, did you?"

She laughed it off. It was just instinct, she told him. Instinct and love. And it was. If she had enjoyed and loved Maggie, and she truly had, nothing had prepared her for how she would feel about her own daughter. She reveled in every moment. The look of her. The smell of her. The feel of her. The changing expressions, the little starfish movements of her hands, the intense concentration on her face when she stretched. Sadie's fascination increased the older Maudie grew. She recorded every highlight. Not in a scrapbook. Something stopped her from doing that. She kept photo albums instead. Lots of them, with detailed captions underneath each photo.

The more involved she got in her own little family in Brisbane, the more her family in Hobart receded in her mind. She continued to write a birthday card to Maggie each year, sent care of the priests, her message brief: "I am very well and happy and hope you are too." She always received a letter back from Maggie, filled with news. There was always a letter from Leo enclosed, and occasionally letters or notes from her sisters too. Sometimes she read them, sometimes she didn't. That annual contact was all she needed. It eased her conscience. She knew they were all right. They knew she was all right. That was enough for her. She was too busy, anyway, to worry about them. She and Larry had set up their own cleaning agency, working nearly sixteen hours a day. It was easy to juggle it around caring for Maudie. They just brought her with them whenever possible, or took turns looking after her at home.

Maudie was four when Larry received a letter from a solicitor in Ireland. His mother had died. He was the sole beneficiary of her will. To his great surprise, she had saved a lot of money over the years.

They moved to Dublin three months later. They had enough money to be able to buy a house almost immediately, the same house in Phibsboro they still lived in. Larry set to work researching cleaning companies in Dublin. There was definitely a gap in the market, he declared. If they were prepared to work long hours again, share the workload and get as much as possible done while Maudie was at school, they could set up their own business there as they had done in Australia.

Slowly, it happened. They came in at the right time, with the right approach, and gained a reputation for hard work and reliability. They also kept trying for another baby. Month after month Sadie was disappointed.

Larry wouldn't let her get too sad about it. "We got it so right the first time with Maudie, why try again?"

"Don't you want a big family too? How can you always be so optimistic?"

He hadn't risen to her bait. "You get a choice in life, Sally. You can see the bright side or the dark side in everything. I always choose the bright side."

Would he always, though? She sometimes imagined telling him the truth about her own life. She imagined two reactions. The bright side: "You've been lying all this time? You didn't have an abusive family? Maudie has a cousin and a grandfather and four aunts? That's fantastic! Do you want to go to Tasmania? Will we organize a reunion?"

Or the dark side: "You lied to me from the start? You invented a terrible childhood, knowing that I had been through it for real? All these years have been built on a lie? And you expect me to ever be able to trust you again?"

Truth was too important to Larry. She had seen him with Maudie, expressing disappointment when she told even the smallest of white lies. She couldn't risk it.

The truth would come as too much of a shock to Maudie too. Sadie couldn't do it to her daughter. Maudie knew only that her mother had had a difficult childhood in South Australia and that she had chosen to be separate from her family. Maudie had just accepted it, never questioned it. She had no reason to, after all. Why would her mother lie to her about something as important as that?

Sadie rarely missed her family. Once she had made her decision, it was easy to stick with it. Larry and Maudie were her family now. And it wasn't a complete estrangement. Sadie knew about Leo's success with his inventions, Myles and Juliet's move to Manchester and their expanding business empire, Miranda's life in Singapore, Eliza's accident and her reincarnation as a life coach, Clementine's research projects in Antarctica, Maggie's work success and life in

London. At any time over the twenty years she could have picked up the phone and slipped right into their lives. And destroyed the new life she'd built for herself in an instant.

Sitting alone in the living room, staring out at the garden, Sadie decided she had to stop worrying so much. That journalist's mention of Tasmania had been pure coincidence. She had to focus on all the great things in her life—Larry, Maudie and her first grandchild on its way. They were the real things. She wasn't going to tell Larry the truth. There was no point. She had made the decision twenty years ago to leave her family. It had been the right one then and it was the right one now.

Time for bed. She walked around the living room, closing curtains, moving newspapers off the table and smoothing down the cushions on the sofa. As she plumped the red one on the armchair, she noticed an odd bulge. She reached inside the cover. It was a bottle made from purple glass. A bottle of perfume. The Moonstruck.

She smiled. She'd been waiting for this. It had been several weeks since she had managed to slip it into Maudie's bag one afternoon, disguised inside a parenting magazine.

They'd been passing the Moonstruck back and forth between them like this for more than two years, ever since Maudie had found it in Sadie's wardrobe. Sadie had kept it all those years, carrying it around Australia, from hostel to hostel, bringing it to Ireland with her. It was her one link with her sisters. One that brought good memories.

Sadie didn't tell Maudie that it had once belonged to her mother. She made up a story on the spot, telling her daughter that she and a school friend used to play a game, passing it back and forth between them, the rule being that it was never to be spoken about. Maudie had opened the stopper and pulled a face. "No wonder you didn't want to keep it. It's disgusting."

Sadie pretended not to notice when Maudie slipped the bottle into her own handbag. She had also said nothing to Maudie when exactly a week later she was having breakfast and it fell out of the cornflakes packet and into her bowl with a clatter.

"Good God," Larry said across the table. "Those free plastic toys are getting huge these days."

Once, during a visit to Maudie and Lorca's flat, Sadie hid it in their fruit bowl. A fortnight later, she found it in her own house again, tucked in one of the window boxes. One Christmas she noticed it hanging from a branch of their Christmas tree. Back and forth it had gone, with never a word said about it between them.

She was smiling as she went upstairs to bed.

CHAPTER 37

They heard Miranda's car arriving long before she herself appeared. A beeping of the horn all the way up the laneway. Moments later, her voice from the yard outside.

"Where is he? Where is this mystery man? Let me take a look."

Inside the kitchen, Leo, Maggie, Gabriel, Juliet, Clementine, and Eliza sprang up from the table. They had all been there together since early that day. Arriving from different countries into different airports, they'd somehow managed to get to the Donegal house within ten minutes of each other.

Miranda had phoned to say her flight had been delayed. "You're not even allowed to speak to each other until I get there, though. Do you hear me?" she said. "Go to your rooms and wait. I'll be there as soon as I can."

Juliet had been the first to meet Gabriel. She was instantly welcoming. "You've shocked us. I hope you don't mind me telling you that. But it's a pleasure to meet you. If you can survive the next few days, you'll survive anything."

Maggie anxiously kept an eye on Gabriel, but he was more relaxed than she was, laughing with Juliet, enjoying Leo's tour around the house and yard. Juliet had the house looking beautiful. It was festooned in Christmas decorations, with a small pine tree in the hallway. Maggie's presents—the ones she had sent to Donegal, at least—were in a colorful pile underneath. Gabriel was taking in everything. He'd been like that since they arrived at Belfast Airport—asking questions and making observations. They'd taken a detour into the city to collect the hired camera equipment that Leo—or his wonder concierge, at least—had managed to organize from New York.

Maggie had continued reading the diaries as Leo drove, anxious to get through them all as soon as possible. She'd been conscious of her grandfather watching her throughout the flight too, obviously trying to gauge her reaction. She'd told him she wanted to read through all nine notebooks before she spoke to him about them. It had almost been a relief to arrive in Glencolmcille and tuck them away out of sight in her bag. His anxiety was making her anxious.

Clementine and Eliza had arrived next. Maggie hugged her mother close for a long time, before introducing Gabriel, feeling as shy as if he were her real fiancé. The excitement in the house increased with Miranda's arrival. There were more rapid exchanges of news; details from Clementine about Antarctica; comments about how well everyone was looking, that New York was obviously good for Maggie. And most especially, remark after remark about the surprise engagement.

Between Leo, Gabriel, and Maggie, they somehow pulled it off. There was one awkward moment when Maggie realized she and Gabriel hadn't actually discussed the question of public shows of affection. As they all sat talking in the living room, the two of them should have been side by side, even arm in arm. Maggie was too self-conscious to be able to make the first move. Gabriel somehow picked up her concern. He quite naturally came over to where she was sitting in one of the big armchairs, sat on the side, and draped his arm across the back. He gave her the quickest of winks. She gave him the quickest of winks in return.

She knew Clementine was noticing everything. As soon as it was possible, her mother came across and spoke to Maggie on her own.

She gently touched her daughter's cheek. "Are you all right, Maggie? Really?"

Maggie nodded. "I am, really. I'm glad to be here."

"Not as glad as I am." Clementine lowered her voice. "He seems lovely."

"He is. I really like him." It was nice not to have to lie all the time.

Clementine laughed out loud. "Well, I'd hope so."

In the center of the room, Miranda was looking like a film star and behaving like a queen. Maggie shot Gabriel a glance. He was smiling. He'd enjoyed her stories about Miranda. It seemed he was planning on enjoying the real thing too.

Miranda gave him an exaggerated inspection. "Yes, our surveillance reports have been accurate. You are handsome." Then she shook her finger at him. "So far so good, young man. But let me warn you, you had better look after that Maggie of ours or there will be trouble. The reason we look like a coven of witches is because we are a coven of witches."

"She's in safe hands, I promise," Gabriel said.

"It's all very well living love's young and spontaneous dream, but I really think we need to get to the nitty-gritty. When did you meet? Where are you planning on living? Have you set a date?"

"Miranda, would you leave them alone?" Juliet said. "Maggie, Gabriel, ignore her, would you?"

"I know we've been trying to for years," Eliza added.

"I'm only asking what you're all thinking," Miranda said.

Leo leaned across to Gabriel, smiling. He hadn't stopped smiling since they arrived. "Gabriel, imagine. I've had nearly fifty years of this."

"You deserve a medal," Gabriel said.

"Good ploy, Gabriel," Miranda said, disgusted. "Sucking up to the grandfather-in-law."

"I wasn't sucking up," Gabriel began, before Maggie, Clementine, Eliza, and Juliet all laughed, telling him, in unison, to just ignore her.

Maggie didn't get any time alone with Gabriel until after dinner. They had all gathered around the dining table in the large room that had the best view over the sea and the fields. Leo sat at the head, telling stories, so happy to be at the center of them. Juliet moved back and forth from the kitchen, delivering several different casseroles, fluffy mashed potatoes and crisp green salads. This wasn't their July Christmas dinner—that would take place the following evening.

Conversation flowed easily. Clementine talked about her research. Miranda talked about a recent passenger, a famous film star who had locked herself in the first-class toilet with her boyfriend and unfortunately been unable to get out again. Eliza spoke about a new client management plan she was devising, until Miranda too obviously yawned, and changed the subject.

Leo waited until coffee was served before making his other announcement. "I know I told you I wanted you all here for a special reason, and I think this is the perfect time to tell you. Of course, the main one was to hear Maggie and Gabriel's news—"

"To Maggie and Gabriel," Miranda declared, holding up her glass. It was the third toast to them that evening. The champagne and wine were flowing very freely. "Thank heavens you went to New York, Leo, or we would never have discovered Maggie's little secret life."

"Yes, Maggie," Clementine said, in a pretend stern voice. "When were you going to tell us?"

Maggie shifted in her seat. She knew she looked as uncomfortable as she felt. "I would have got around to it, I promise. It's—"

"She's lying, actually."

It was Gabriel speaking. They all turned to him. Maggie's heart started thumping.

"Maggie and I were going to live there secretly together forever. She'd told me so much about all of you that I thought our best chance of survival was to stay as far away as possible."

"Gabriel!" Maggie said.

"I'm joking, I promise. Leo beat us to it with the news, but only by a few days. We were planning on ringing you all when we first decided, but Maggie wanted to take it slowly. I think after all that happened with Andrew—"

"Angus," Maggie said quickly.

"Angus," he corrected smoothly, "she was worried that you

might think it was just a rebound relationship. But it's not. Well, I hope it's not." He turned to Maggie, his face serious, his eyes twinkling. "Please tell me it's not, Maggie."

"It's not, Gabriel." He didn't have to lay it on quite so thick, did he?

Leo smiled approvingly and then clinked his glass to get their attention again. "The other reason I wanted you all here was something to do with Tessa. Gabriel and Maggie already know this, so I hope they won't mind me repeating myself."

They fell quiet. Maggie tensed, wondering whether he was going to surprise her too, announce that he hadn't burned the diaries all those years before. As he started to speak, she relaxed.

He put it beautifully, talking about his longing to have a collection of all the best memories of his life to look back on. He explained that his original plan had been to ask Maggie to compile a scrapbook, but after meeting Gabriel, he'd decided to be modern and film them instead.

They liked the idea very much. All of them except Miranda. She'd drunk a lot of wine and wasn't letting anyone get away with anything.

"Gabriel, this isn't some clever ruse, is it? You're not here in disguise, putting together one of those real-life freak-show independent film festival documentaries, are you?"

"I wasn't, no, but it's looking more promising by the hour."

That earned him a laugh from Miranda.

Leo gazed around the table again. "Don't you think it would be something special? A record of all of us, for all of us."

"All of us except Sadie, you mean," Miranda said. "Gabriel, I don't know if you know, but there is another sister—"

Juliet interrupted. "Miranda, please, you don't need to—"

"It's fine, Juliet," Gabriel said. "Maggie's already told me the whole story."

She hadn't, actually. She didn't look at Gabriel or Leo. She was worried she might give something away.

"Will we get started in the morning?" Leo said eagerly. "Get it under way as quickly as we can? I don't want Gabriel to spend his entire first visit to Ireland working. He and Maggie want to get away and soak up the music and pub atmosphere too."

"Get away and talk about us, more like it," Miranda said.

"They probably want to go and talk about us right now," Juliet said, standing up and beginning to collect the dishes. "Off you go, you two. Maggie, go and show Gabriel the nice view from the top of the lane. You're let off the dishes tonight."

Maggie did as she was told, getting up from the table, kissing Leo and each of her aunts and giving her mother a special hug. She and Gabriel left through the kitchen door, across the yard and up to the back field. From there it was just a quick climb over the little stone stile to the top lane, which wound its way to the top of the hill. The view from there was a glorious one, especially at this time of evening. The sky was still bright in patches. The sea in the distance had a silvery sheen. There was the sound of the wind rustling through the gorse bushes, sheep bleating and the distant noise of a tractor across the valley.

As they walked side by side, Maggie looked up at him. "I can give you the car keys if you want to make a dash for it."

"A dash for it? Leave all this?" Gabriel gave her a smile. "No way. Miranda's right. I can already see myself accepting first prize at Sundance for this film. There are more secrets and dynamics flying around down there than I ever saw in the White House."

"They're not that bad."

"They're not bad at all. They're great. Fascinating."

"Fascinating? Why?"

He was thoughtful for a moment. "It's like a solar system. Leo is the sun and you all orbit around him."

About to protest, Maggie pictured it. Gabriel was right.

They walked on a little while in silence. She spoke first. "Thanks for smoothing over that moment about Sadie, by the way."

"You're welcome. Have you told me the whole story?"

"Not exactly, no." She couldn't give the old standard answer about Sadie being a hippie anymore, she realized. Not if she was to be truthful about it. "It's a long one. A complicated one too. You don't have to hear it if you don't want to."

"I want to."

They walked as Maggie talked. It struck her that she and Leo had been walking in Central Park just two days ago when she had heard this story herself for the first time. Now here she was in Ireland, retelling it, to a man she barely knew.

It took her fifteen minutes. Gabriel asked her questions along the way. They were at the very top of the hillside by the time she finished. It was the strange in-between light of an Irish summer, the sea now a white mass, the mountains across the valley a brown-black, shadows and sounds around them. All the warmth had gone. She shivered. "We should start going back. They'll get worried."

"No, they won't. They'd be more worried if we came back too soon." He turned nevertheless, putting out a hand and steadying her when she stumbled on a rock in the dim light. He returned to the subject of Sadie.

"What if the private detective finds her? If she is in Dublin? What then?"

Maggie hadn't thought about that yet. She didn't know if Leo had either. There had been other things on their minds. "I guess he'll go and see her. As soon as I've read Tessa's diaries and can tell him what I think it was Sadie read."

"There are a lot of ghosts flying around your family, aren't there?"

"What do you mean?"

"Sadie. Tessa. Maybe I had it wrong that it's Leo who's the sun. Maybe you've all been orbiting around them instead. Around their memories, at least."

"But they're not here."

"Leo seems to think they are."

"I think you're wrong."

"I can't see you clearly in this Celtic mist, Maggie, but I'd swear I just heard your hackles unfurling."

He was right. She didn't like hearing any criticism of her family. "It's jet lag. I'm oversensitive. They're my family and I love them. And I want you to like them too." She did, she realized. It felt important that he liked them.

"And I do. But I'm an only child, remember. I'm not used to crowds like this. It's like, I don't know, Tom Thumb suddenly finding himself staying with the Old Woman Who Lived in the Shoe. People everywhere. A serious danger of being squashed."

She smiled, glad of the change in mood. "I meant it about the car keys. You make a run for it whenever you want."

"You don't get rid of me that easily."

The smile was back in his voice again too. It reminded her of the first time she'd heard it on her answering machine in Greenwich Village.

"I hope Sadie does come back," he said. "For extra dramatic tension, I'd like it to happen just in the middle of filming. Can you imagine the scene, Maggie? One of your aunts recalling her, we hear a noise outside, I pan to the front door, which opens, and there—"

"Dressed in a batik dress, with her hair in dreadlocks, is Sadie? I'm sorry, Gabriel, but I really don't think it's going to happen like that."

"She'll drive up in a Rover, dressed in a pinstripe suit?"

"Maybe." He was trying to cheer her up, she knew. "We're just sport to you, aren't we? And there I was feeling guilty that my scheming grandfather has dragged you across to Ireland to pretend to be in love with me." She was fishing for compliments, she knew. He disappointed her.

"Maggie, don't worry about it, please. It's just a week out of my life, playing make-believe. I promise you I'm enjoying myself. Even if your aunt Miranda is watching me like a hawk. I don't think she completely trusts me."

"She's just protective. She was there in London with me when it all finished with Angus."

"Ah, yes, Angus. Angus of the tweed pants and running nose."

Angus had had a perpetual cold. "Did I tell you that?"

"No, Miranda did. In between Clementine telling me about the way you used to count all the time as a child, Eliza telling me about your dress-ups and Juliet telling me about your university results."

"It's just as well this is all make-believe or you would be completely overwhelmed."

"Just as well," he said.

They reached the stile, the lights of the house warm and inviting over the rise of the hill. He helped her across, taking her hand as she climbed up the stone steps, holding it until she was safely on the other side. His skin felt warm, his hold strong. She was glad it was almost dark. She wouldn't have liked him to see the color that she had felt come into her cheeks.

*   *   *

Maggie woke late the next morning. She could hear noises from downstairs, music playing in the kitchen, a chatter of conversation, then something more than that. Furniture being moved and someone hushing, saying, "Maggie's still asleep," followed by Miranda, or perhaps it was Eliza, replying, "Then it's time she was up."

They'd all gone to bed early the night before, the five new arrivals suffering various degrees of jet lag. Juliet showed them to their rooms, giving Maggie a little smile as she pointed out that Gabriel was just down the corridor. Maggie had calmed down by then, talking herself out of her crush on him as best she could. She'd obviously imagined any attraction between them. If Gabriel had wanted to kiss her, then he'd just had the perfect opportunity, out walking in the twilight together. Yet he'd passed on it. She had to realize that as much as she liked him, this was just a job in his eyes. A slightly unusual job, granted, but that was all.

She checked her watch. Nearly ten. She'd slept for more than twelve hours. She reached up and pulled back the curtains. Half the sky was blue, the other half was cloudy. She came downstairs in her dressing gown and stopped at the doorway to the living room. It was transformed. All the furniture had been shifted. Mini sets had been arranged in three corners: a backdrop of the nicest painting, a watercolor of a local beach scene, with one of the elegant armchairs in front; in another corner, a side table, a vase of flowers and a straight-backed chair; in the third, the sofa, roomy enough to hold three or four people.

Gabriel was in the middle of the room, the camera equipment on a tripod beside him and cables snaking on the floor at his feet.

He was dressed in black jeans and a white T-shirt. His hair was still damp from the shower, the gray almost black in the morning light.

He turned and smiled. "Good morning."

"Good morning. You've been busy."

"We want to get started. Leo wants to get started, at least. Miranda says she won't possibly be camera-ready before noon and insists I have to hire a makeup artist, but we'll try and work around that."

"Vaseline on the lens at the very least, darling, all right?" Miranda came in behind Maggie and kissed her on the cheek. "How nice of you to drop in, sleepyhead. Coffee? A shot of something stronger to get your memories flowing?"

"I don't have any memories of Tessa."

"I'm not talking about Tessa. I want you to sit in front of the camera for half an hour and wax lyrical about me."

The others came in then too, all fully dressed and made-up, carrying cups of coffee. The mood was bright. Clementine handed Maggie a cup and the two of them sat down on the sofa together.

Gabriel looked up from the camera. "I'm sure you've heard this a thousand times already, but you two could be sisters."

"That's because Clementine was a teenager of loose morals and had Maggie when she was only thirteen years old. Or was it twelve, Clementine?"

Clementine refused to take Miranda's bait. "I was seventeen, Gabriel. My sisters were at a loose end so I decided to give them a niece to play with."

"And Maggie's the only one of the next generation?"

"She's all we ever needed," Miranda said. "If you get it perfect the first time, why try for another?"

They all laughed. All except Juliet, Maggie noticed.

"Very unfair to Maggie," Gabriel said. "That's a lot of pressure to be under."

"Pressure? The little pet has been showered with love, attention, and unwanted gifts all her life, not pressure. Isn't that right, Maggie?" Miranda said. "We like to think of Maggie as our own little creation, Gabriel. A sort of Frankenstein's monster, all of us having a hand in her makeup."

"Well, everyone? What do you think? The perfect look for a director?" It was Leo, standing in the doorway, dressed in a long gray coat, a white scarf, and a baseball cap turned backward, all obviously gathered from the cloakroom under the stairs. Some of it belonged to the Faradays. Other items had been left by holiday tenants over the years.

"I think you've got more of a raggy old farmer look going on, Leo," Miranda said. She went over and adjusted his cap. "You're not the director, anyway. Gabriel's in charge. Our hotshot American filmmaker, direct from New York."

"Absolutely." Gabriel checked his watch. "So, who's first? I want to do some test shots."

Maggie realized they were quite serious about this. She was tempted to stay and watch, but this was her best opportunity to read the diaries. She waited until the others were occupied with Gabriel and went across to Leo.

"Any word?" She knew he would know she was talking about Sadie.

"Nothing yet." He took out his mobile. "I keep checking the signal is okay, but it's so unreliable here. I didn't want to give him the landline number in case one of the others answered."

"I'll go upstairs and get on with the diaries then."

He clasped her hand. "Thank you, Miss Maggie. Some lovely reading there, I'm sure." He lowered his voice. "Nothing yet?"

She shook her head. No, Tadpole, nothing yet to prove that your wife was having an affair with your brother.

"What are you two whispering about?" It was Miranda, from across the room.

"I've just told Maggie that I've decided to change my will and leave everything to her," Leo replied.

Eliza looked up. "I hope you're joking. The only reason I've turned up here year after year is to stay in your good books."

"Of course he's joking," Juliet said. "He decided years ago to leave it all to me. I'm the one who's kept this show on the road all these years, after all."

"You're wrong there," Miranda said. "It's easy to hire a caterer and party planner. It's much harder to hire someone with my wit and humor to keep things lively. Isn't that right, Leo?"

Juliet's face hardened. Clementine didn't say anything, but Maggie saw her gently touch Juliet on the arm and whisper something to her. She saw that Gabriel had noticed too.

Maggie wasn't imagining it. There were tensions in the room that she had never picked up on before. Why now? What was so different? She remembered Gabriel's comment the night before, talking about the ghosts of Tessa and Sadie filling the air. She'd denied it last night. Today she wasn't so sure. Something was different. Or perhaps the difference was she was noticing it.

It was definitely time to leave. Maggie went into the kitchen, made herself a pot of coffee and a plate of raisin toast, and slipped back upstairs to the diaries.

CHAPTER 38

I t was nearly five by the time Maggie finished reading through another two diaries. She'd had to battle interruptions all day, quickly hiding the notebooks anytime she heard one of the others come up the stairs. She'd set herself up in a corner of her bedroom, curled up in the comfortable armchair by the window, the diaries tucked in beside her, decoy books on the table in front of her. They'd all visited. Clementine to make sure she was all right and have a proper catch-up chat. Juliet to ask her did she want lunch. Eliza to say how impressed she was with Gabriel's work ethic.

Miranda called in to ask advice on which outfit she should wear for her solo interview. One was a bright-red silk kimono-style dress, the other a suit made from a soft cream material with leopard-skin collar and cuffs. Maggie thought both of them looked glamorous, expensive, and completely out of place in a Donegal farmhouse. When she'd gently pointed that out, Miranda just raised an eyebrow. "Of course they do. *I* am completely out of place in a Donegal farmhouse."

Maggie called down to the living room twice. Eliza was right. Gabriel was extremely professional. He was still relaxed, joking with everyone, but he was getting it done, keeping them moving and asking enough questions to get the memories flowing. Maggie heard him explain to Leo that he would edit it afterward so it was only their voices on the soundtrack, not his. "That's what will give it the intimate feel," he explained. "It will seem as though they are just remembering details without being prompted."

Leo thought that sounded perfect.

Beside Maggie, Clementine whispered, "He even knows how to control Leo, Maggie. You definitely need to hang on to him. He's just what we need in the family."

She was glad to go back to her room. The pretend romance had seemed a playful joke in New York. Here in Donegal it just felt like lies. One on top of the other.

They all asked her what she was doing upstairs. "Catching up on some reading," she said.

"She's being kind," Gabriel said. "She knows I get all clumsy when she's around."

During a break for lunch, Maggie managed a moment alone with him. They walked outside to the courtyard and leaned against the wall, looking over the valley toward the sea.

"I think you may have got yourself the job as official filmmaker to the Faraday family," she said. "Leo's so excited about all of this. He wants a documentary crew to follow him for the rest of his days."

"If he can find one to keep up with him. Has he always been this energetic?"

"Always," Maggie said.

"And the others? Have they always been this tense with each other?"

"Tense?"

"I asked them to do a scene, all four of them sitting on the couch together. Talking to each other, ignoring the camera. They could have been four strangers."

"It's a while since they've seen each other."

"But they're sisters. I thought sisters get on well."

Until now, Maggie would have argued that her mother and aunts did get on well. But perhaps she had been wrong. "It takes a few days for everyone to get used to each other again. It's probably always like this. It's just I've never noticed it before."

"You've been having these reunions every year?"

"Twice a year."

"Twice a year? For how many years?"

"All my life," Maggie said.

He gave a low whistle. "And you're surprised about tensions? Hasn't anyone ever said they didn't want to join in? That they couldn't make it?"

Only her, Maggie realized. But look what had happened when she did that anyway. "There's been some discussion now and again," she said, choosing her words carefully. "But we're here now. All because of you, I hope you realize."

"Oh, I do, believe me. Not everyone's happy about it, though."

"They're not?"

"I heard Eliza telling Clementine that they needn't have come because—actually, I've just realized I can't tell you what I heard. It's far too flattering about me."

"You have to tell me now."

"All right, but I'm just reporting what I heard. Eliza told Clementine that in her opinion Leo had brought them all here under false pretenses, because it was obvious you and I were made for each other and that I was, let me think how she put it, that's right, 'a real catch.' "

"No!"

Gabriel nodded. "It gets better. Then she said, 'Maggie's nuts about him, that's obvious. Far more than she ever was about Angus.' "

Maggie went bright red. "She didn't."

"She did. And Clementine agreed. And then they both went on to say mean things about Angus, which I also found interesting, though not quite as interesting as it was when they were talking about me."

"You're making this up." She was extremely embarrassed.

"I'm not, I promise you. Congratulations, Maggie. I thought I was doing a great acting job as your loving fiancé, but you're obviously miles ahead of me."

"My acting job?" She recovered quickly. "Oh, yes. Thanks. You're doing brilliantly too. Except for that line about you getting clumsy when I'm around."

"But it's true. My hands start to shake and my heart beats faster when I see you."

"That's jet lag."

They both heard the crunch of gravel behind them and smelled cigarette smoke. Miranda, coming toward them. Gabriel spoke louder. "Please, Maggie, take pity on a workingman and leave me in peace this afternoon."

Miranda reached them, leaned against the wall and raised an eyebrow. "My word, Maggie, he is a silver-tongued devil, isn't he?"

"Silver hair, silver tongue," Gabriel said.

"It's natural, that hair of yours, is it?"

"One hundred percent," Gabriel said.

"I hope so. I'd hate to think it was fake." She waited just a beat before smiling at them both. "Ready when you are, Mr. Scorsese."

. . .

Maggie was back up in her room, about to start reading again, when Leo came in to say he'd just had a call from the detective. He'd completed his report.

"And?"

Leo lowered his voice. "I couldn't ask him for details. The girls were all around me. I asked him to courier it to me. By the fastest method possible."

"But is it her?"

"He's ninety percent sure. He's got a recent photo, extra details, her home address. But he said the final decision will be mine. Ours, at least."

That gave Maggie the extra impetus to keep reading Tessa's diaries. She was halfway through. Maggie had read about Tessa's years in London as a young woman, before she met Leo. In the one she was reading now, Tessa and Leo were married, Juliet was a three-year-old and Miranda a toddler.

Maggie read ten more pages, then put the blue notebook down.

She felt strange. Downstairs, Gabriel was filming memories and anecdotes about a much-loved wife and mother. Here, upstairs, Maggie was reading her actual words. Two perspectives on the same person. But which was the true one?

Maggie couldn't fully make up her mind yet, with four diaries still to be read, but there was no getting away from the impression she'd formed of her grandmother so far.

Tessa was horrible.

Mean-spirited. Spoiled. Bitchy. Catty. Cruel. Manipulative. Conceited. Vain. Impatient.

As she'd read Tessa's words, Maggie had tried hard to stay balanced about it. She hadn't trusted her own reaction at first. Of course Tessa would seem self-centered. They were her diaries, after all. They had to be all about her. But the more she read, the harder it was to form any other opinion. Tessa was cruel about her friends, calling them dowdy and boring. She was much more interested in her own good looks. There were pages devoted to descriptions of the clothes she'd worn and the compliments she'd received.

Maggie was glad Leo had already told her that Tessa had first gone out with his brother Bill. She would have been shocked to read about it, otherwise. Even so, it had hurt Maggie to read Tessa's thoughts about Leo, to hear him being dismissed and to be compared unfavorably to Bill: *"The puppy dog followed us around all day again today."*

It had got worse. Reading on, she'd learned that Tessa had only started going out with Leo as a way of making Bill jealous. That for a time she had been seeing both of them. Even when she had decided to stay with Leo, she had been dismissive of him. She was more interested in being spoiled by Leo than returning his love for her.

Maggie had hoped her grandmother would change when she became a mother. Perhaps that would have softened her, turned her into the woman Leo idolized. In the beginning, it did. There was a lovely account of her feelings during her first pregnancy. Detailed descriptions of Juliet and, less than two years later, Miranda, as babies.

It didn't last, though. Two hours' reading and three years of entries later, Tessa's tone was now constantly petulant, her complaints loud. She was feeling housebound with her young daughters. She was bored with housework too, though as far as Maggie could make out, it was Leo who did it all. He came home from his job at the forestry nursery at lunchtime, made dinner, and did the washing. Not that Tessa put it like that.

> Leo had the hide to ask me if I would be able to make dinner this week. It's easy for him, he can come and go as he pleases—he's not home all day with the babies.
> Miranda won't stop crying. My neighbor told me to try some whiskey in her milk. It worked a treat, for me as well as her!
> I'm pregnant again! With Eliza, Maggie realized. The other girls on my street are so jealous.

As the family grew, one thing didn't change. Leo's brother Bill was a constant visitor to the house.

> Bill made a move on me today.

Maggie held her breath.

> I told him to keep his hands to himself. If he thinks he can march in here and have whatever he wants from me he can think again. Even if he was much better in bed than Leo. The funny thing is I think Bill is actually jealous of Leo and me, so I get to have the last laugh after all! Wish I could make one Faraday man out of the two of them, though. That would be the perfect man.

Maggie tried to imagine Leo reading this. It would kill him.

Tessa must have had some redeeming feature. Maggie was trying hard to find it. Her sense of humor, perhaps. Despite herself, Maggie had laughed out loud several times. Tessa's turn of phrase reminded her of someone. Miranda, she realized. That same wickedness and cutting humor. But deep down, Miranda was kind.

Maggie knew that. She had been at the receiving end of Miranda's kindness many times over the years. She couldn't see any evidence of kindness in Tessa.

"Maggie? Are you still alive up here?" Miranda appeared in the doorway. "You've been too quiet. It makes me nervous. What's that you're reading? We haven't seen you for hours."

"*Anna Karenina,*" Maggie lied. She'd just had time to push the diaries under her mattress. She'd taken the Tolstoy off the shelves downstairs, deliberately choosing the thickest book she could find.

"Can I get you a little afternoon pick-me-up? My fingers are itching to open a bottle of wine and no one else will join me."

"Not yet, thanks."

Her next visitor was Gabriel. He appeared at the doorway, on his way back from his bedroom, holding a Windbreaker. The bright morning had turned cold and the house chilly, despite the sunshine filtering through the windows. Maggie had wrapped the colored quilt from her bed around her feet and pulled her chair into a ray of sunlight, like a dozing cat.

"Are you receiving visitors?" he asked. "Tucked up here on your own."

"Like mad Mrs. Rochester in the attic?"

"I didn't like to say."

"How's the filming going?"

"Miranda's right. I may enter it in the Sundance festival yet. I'm playing with different titles at the moment."

"*Inside the Asylum?*"

"Catchy. I was thinking more along the lines of *Leo and His Daughters.* Or *Truths, Tensions, and Lies.*"

"Who's telling lies?"

"Well, you, me, and Leo for starters. But we're not the only ones."

"My mother and my aunts are too?"

"To different degrees."

"About what?"

"It depends on the questions they're being asked."

"But what makes you think they're lying?"

"Their body language, for starters. And it's all too positive." He went over to the window and stood beside it, just a meter or so from her. "I'm sorry to sound so cynical, Maggie, but the way they're talking, their early life was like a cross between *The Sound of Music* and *The King and I*. All laughs, never a cross word spoken, nothing but fun and games with their mother before she died. Was it actually like that?"

Just a day before, Maggie would have said yes. She would have defended Clementine and her aunts, said that of course their stories were true. Tessa had been the most wonderful, warm, fun, loving mother possible. But did she believe that now? How could she, when she had spent hours reading how impatient Tessa could be, how bored she was sometimes, how dismissive she was, not just of her life as a mother, but of her husband too. They must all have felt that from her, surely? Had they all blocked out those bad times somehow? Or not noticed what was going on around them when they were children? Maggie was very confused.

"Perhaps it was that good," she said, still needing to stand up for her family. "Just because they're talking about happy memories doesn't mean they're lying. It's not as if you have a lie detector attached to the camera, is it?"

"I don't need one. People lie all the time. I learned how to watch for it when I was in Washington. Being a cameraman's like being a waiter. People forget you're there. I'd hear the politicians chat in between takes, the whispers to their advisers, and then watch them change when the camera was rolling. I'd see it all through the lens."

"I can imagine politicians lying. But why would my mother and aunts do it now?"

"Perhaps for the same reason they all came across the world at a moment's notice. To please your grandfather."

Maggie hesitated. Was that it? Was that why they were all being so positive about Tessa? For Leo's sake? Even if it was true, she wasn't comfortable hearing it from Gabriel. "He's an old man. They love him. I thought you liked him too."

"I do like him. I like him a lot. He's great company. But I'm glad he doesn't have a hold over me."

"I think you're being very rude."

Gabriel stayed calm. "Maggie, you must see it."

"See what?"

"All the tensions there are about Leo and his traditions. The tensions between your mother and your aunts. I asked each of them to tell me about themselves. I thought it would be a good way of relaxing them, but none of them told the truth. It was all 'I couldn't be happier. I have the perfect life and Leo has been the perfect father and Tessa was a wonderful mother,' and yet their body language said something else."

"Perhaps they're nervous in front of a camera."

"They're nervous in front of each other, if you ask me."

"Did you ask the others to leave the room?"

"I suggested it, but they wouldn't. Everyone wanted to see what everyone else was saying."

"And you thought that's when they were lying?"

He nodded. "To Leo and to each other. All morning."

Not just all morning. And not just to Leo and each other. They'd been lying to her about Sadie all these years, hadn't they? They'd all known that Sadie hadn't run away to become a hippie. They had all known the circumstances of her disappearing. Yet none of them had ever told her the truth. If they could lie about that, what else could they lie about? Not just to each other, but to her?

Gabriel was now looking out the window, out across the bay. It gave her an opportunity to study him. As upset as she was, she couldn't be angry with him for making these comments about her family. He'd been invited to Donegal to observe them, after all. She'd willingly told him all about her upbringing, about her mother and each of her aunts. But his comments, on top of all she had read in the diaries, had left her unsettled. He had got close to the heart of her family in a very short space of time. She imagined how Angus would have reacted to any of the events of the past few days. Badly, on every count. He'd never had any time for her family. Gabriel was different. He was curious. More than that. It was as if he actually cared.

He turned back and caught her staring at him. "Penny for your thoughts?"

"I was thinking about you, actually. About what a good family therapist you'd make if you ever decided to give up the windows and the dogs."

"Are you being sarcastic?"

"No, I'm serious. You're doing a very thorough job with my family."

He smiled down at her. "It's easy with someone else's. Wait until you meet my extended family. You'll get your revenge on me, I promise."

They were interrupted before Maggie had time to respond to his casual suggestion that she would meet the rest of his family.

"Okay, you two lovebirds." It was Juliet. "Cocktail hour. Miranda's insisting."

"Thanks, Juliet, " Maggie said. "We'll be right down." She waited until she heard her aunt reach the creaking floorboard at the end of the hall. "You might be right about some things, but not all of them. I know for a fact that Juliet is truly happy. She and her husband have a great life. They're really successful, they travel all the time—"

"I think you're wrong about that."

"You do?"

He nodded. "If you ask me, Juliet is the unhappiest of all."

• • •

Maggie tried to see her family through Gabriel's eyes that night. At first glance, it seemed like their usual Faraday July Christmas. Juliet had obviously been preparing for it since she arrived. The dining room looked beautiful, lit only by candles. There was carol music playing, the open fire gently glowed. The blinds were pulled down for added atmosphere.

The table was decorated with red flowers, silver tinsel, and garlands of fake ivy. They had an abbreviated present ceremony around the small Christmas tree, with half of Maggie's presents unfortunately en route to other destinations. Maggie gave Gabriel a bottle of fine Irish whiskey, bought hurriedly at the airport. Leo gave him the same thing. He accepted both with a smile, before giving one straight back to Leo.

Leo made a production, as usual, of unwrapping each of his presents, immediately putting on anything wearable—a tie from Eliza, a scarf from Juliet, a leather belt from Clementine. He splashed on the aftershave Miranda gave him. He exclaimed over the selection of chocolates Maggie had sent from New York.

As they took their seats at the table, he opened a bottle of expensive French Champagne, another July Christmas tradition. They pulled crackers, wore the paper hats, told each other the predictable jokes. Miranda related one of her funny work stories, but she didn't have the captive audience she might have liked. Leo was laughing, but he was the only one. Juliet was occupied with her dinner preparations, carrying dishes in from the kitchen, declining all offers of help. Clementine appeared to be listening to Miranda, but Maggie knew from her expression that she was miles away, in Antarctica probably. Eliza wasn't even smiling, just looking at Miranda in a blank-faced way. Gabriel was filming again. Leo had asked him to take just a few minutes of footage of all of them at dinner.

Apart from the gift-giving and joke-telling, there were plenty of other rituals throughout the evening to keep everyone busy. Leo had insisted on them over the years. The toast to Tessa. The toast to Sadie. Maggie caught Leo's eye as they made it. She knew what he was thinking. Perhaps the next time they made that toast, Sadie herself would be there.

Juliet's food was wonderful, as always. The long table was covered in an array of colorful, perfectly cooked Thai dishes: light curry puffs, tangy beef salads and spicy curries, the rich scents of fresh coriander, garlic, lime, and chili filling the room. As they passed the food around, Leo entertained them all with quirky facts about Thailand. Another tradition of their multicultural feasts.

The final ritual before the dessert of mango and coconut sticky rice was served was the roundtable wishes, each member of the family expressing a wish for something to happen in the forthcoming year. Maggie had the sudden feeling that they were all like actors, playing roles, reciting lines that had long lost any meaning.

Who was playing what role, though? Maggie watched and listened. Miranda, still the wisecracking, sharp-tongued, sarcastic one. On the surface she was the most independent. Juliet—always on the move, cooking, serving or clearing away. Perhaps she hated doing it, but she never let anyone help her. Maggie had long ago given up trying. Eliza was as reserved as usual, keeping herself to herself. She was no different here—speaking when spoken to, talking in general terms about her work, but never in any detail. And Clementine? Maggie looked across the table at her mother. She was talking to Leo, animated as she explained what her new study would be in Antarctica, basking in Leo's interest and pride. Maggie had always felt confident that there were two great loves in Clementine's life: Maggie herself and Clementine's work. But had Clementine ever wanted more? A different life? One that she hadn't been able to have because Maggie had arrived?

And Sadie? The invisible but ever-present Sadie. If she had been here, what sort of night would it have been?

"Maggie?"

They were all looking at her.

"Your turn."

"For what?"

"To make your wish for the year ahead."

"Sorry. I was miles away. You go next, Gabriel. Come back to me."

He was back behind the camera. "I'm working. I'm also not family. So I'd rather watch, if you don't mind."

"You're almost family," Juliet said.

"Come on, Gabriel," Miranda said. "It's just a wish."

He was silent for a moment and then held up his glass. "I wish for truth and happiness for everyone here."

"Truth and happiness," the Faradays echoed, holding up their glasses.

"Maggie?" Leo asked.

"I second that."

"Oh, come now, Maggie," Miranda said. "Just because you're engaged doesn't mean you can't think for yourself."

"I'm not copying Gabriel. I want the same thing. Truth and happiness."

They made the toast a second time.

CHAPTER 39

Maggie was awake when the courier called to the house early the next morning. She had been awake most of the night.

She'd had a visitor to her room just as she was about to fall asleep the night before. And then another. Then another. The different conversations had filled her head with so many thoughts it had been hard to relax again.

The first to arrive was Miranda. She'd knocked three times on Maggie's door, come in, sat on the edge of her bed, and cut straight to the chase. "Maggie, I'm worried about Gabriel. Something's not right about him. About this whole situation."

Maggie sat up, switching on her bedside lamp. She wished again she could tell her the truth, but she couldn't. Not yet. She laughed instead, deciding to make light of the question. "Miranda, stop it, would you? Just because I made a mistake with Angus doesn't mean I'm going to do it again."

"I'm concerned you're in a vulnerable state of mind at the moment and I'm worried he's taken advantage of you."

She heard a faint slur in Miranda's voice. Her aunt had drunk a lot of wine at dinner. Maggie imagined the fallout if she was to tell Miranda the truth right now. She would be outraged to think she'd been conned. She'd tear strips off Leo first, then off Maggie, and Gabriel too, for being part of it. She would probably storm off in a temper. Eliza would more than likely follow. Leo would be so upset. Any chance of bringing Sadie—if the woman in Dublin was Sadie—back to Donegal while they were all gathered together would be ruined. Maggie had to keep up the pretense.

Miranda was still talking. "I just want you to be careful. It's all been so quick with Gabriel. You don't even mention him—in fact, you refuse to tell us any details about your life in New York—and then here he is. He's able to give up his work at a moment's notice. He won't answer any direct questions—"

"That's why you're suspicious. You've met your match for once."

"I'm suspicious because I love you very much and I don't want to see you hurt again. Don't rush into anything. Get to know him better. Listen to your own instincts."

"I don't need to have any instincts. I have a mother and four aunts thinking for me."

"Four?"

"Four. You. Juliet. Eliza. Sadie."

"Three working aunts. As for your mother protecting you—" Miranda scoffed. "She wouldn't notice if you came home engaged to a meerkat."

"She would so. Clementine is a wonderful mother."

"When it suits her, yes. When she can fit it in between research projects."

"That's not fair." Maggie realized then that her aunt was quite drunk.

"We all have a share in you, Maggie. We all helped raise you. Which is why I know I have every right to talk to you like this."

"You don't have a right. I'm not a child anymore."

"You don't stop being my niece just because you're old enough to vote."

"I've been making my own decisions for years. I've managed on my own the past three months, haven't I?"

Another scoff. "In a rent-free apartment in one of the best areas of Manhattan that a friend of mine loaned to you, because you are my niece. That's not managing on your own, Maggie. That's being looked after."

Maggie wasn't amused anymore. She was angry. "Were you like this with Sadie?"

"Like what with Sadie?"

"Bossy? Controlling? Insulting?" She didn't know what had made her ask the questions, but they suddenly seemed important.

"Well, well, the little mouse that roared." Miranda smiled to take the sting out of her words. She wasn't completely successful. "What makes you say that? Don't tell me you and Sadie have been secretly meeting all these years, have you? Having little bitching sessions about how mean all of us were to her?"

"Is that why she left?"

Miranda stood up then. "I have no idea why she left. But I can tell you why she didn't come back. Because she was the smartest one of all of us in the end. She chose freedom over family. I sometimes wish I'd done the same thing."

Maggie barely had time to take in all that Miranda had said. Five minutes after she left, there was another knock at her door. It was Eliza.

"Maggie, are you awake? Can I come in?"

Eliza had never needed alcohol to fuel her strong opinions. Maggie knew within a second she was about to hear a few of them now. She would never have admitted it to anyone, but Eliza had always been her least favorite aunt. It seemed so childish to think of them in terms of favorites, but she'd always had a faint stomachache when she was sent to Eliza's. It wasn't that she was cruel or mean. She'd just never been much fun. Eliza saw the world and life as something to be endured and worked through. She had been bad enough when she was a personal trainer. Since she had become a life coach the advice and pronouncements had multiplied.

She sat on the chair beside Maggie's bed, her face solemn. "Maggie, I hope you don't mind, but I've been worried about you since I got here, and there just doesn't ever seem a chance to talk to you during the day."

"What are you worried about?"

Eliza leaned forward. "You don't seem to have much direction in your life at the moment. No goals, no ambitions. You have a true gift with numbers, Maggie, and I would hate to see you waste it. I just wanted you to know that I'm here for you if you want to sit down and talk through your options. Reassess your career to date. Explore new avenues. Make serious plans."

Maggie suddenly wondered what Eliza would say if she were to tell her to mind her own business. Instead, she surprised herself, and her aunt, with another question. "Have you ever done anything spontaneous, Eliza?"

"Pardon?"

"Have you ever made a mistake, or done something you've regretted? Been swept off your feet, fallen head over heels in love?

"Why do you ask that?"

Maggie realized that she truly wanted to know. If Eliza was going to come and lecture her, then Maggie wanted to voice a few opinions of her own. "It's just you are the most controlled person I have ever met in my life. The most organized. The most together. And I was trying to imagine how you would cope if you were to do something out of character—like fall in love at first sight, or make a rash decision about something. Throw caution to the wind."

Eliza didn't answer.

"Sorry," Maggie said, abashed. "It's none of my business."

"I forget sometimes that you're an adult now, you know that. Yes, Maggie. I have made rash decisions. I have thrown caution to the wind. And I have been in love. I still am in love."

"You are? Really? Why haven't we met him?"

Eliza didn't answer.

Something occurred to Maggie. "Is it a her?"

"No, it's a him. The same him I've been in love with for twenty-six years. We've been together for thirteen of those years."

"Together? Are you married? And none of us knew?"

"You can have love without marriage, Maggie."

"But why don't you bring him home? Why haven't we met him?"

"Because I don't want you to. Because that would change everything. I don't want to hear anyone's opinions about him. I don't want to see him putting up with Leo's waffle, Miranda's insults, Juliet's mothering—" She stopped there. "I'm not risking it."

"Could I meet him?"

Eliza shook her head. "You don't need to. He doesn't need to meet you either."

"But we're your family."

"Yes." Eliza seemed to come to her senses then. "Maggie, I don't want you to tell the others what I've just told you. Not Clementine. Not Gabriel. I don't even know why I told you myself."

"I won't. I promise." Maggie was genuinely shocked. Eliza, of all people, having a secret love affair. There were a dozen questions she longed to ask.

It was too late. Eliza had returned to her businesslike self. She stood up, smoothed down her silk dressing gown. "But think about what I said. If you need to talk about your work goals or your career path, I'm always here for you, okay?"

"Thanks, Eliza."

"You're welcome. Good night."

Maggie wasn't surprised when Juliet arrived, ten minutes later. She knocked gently on the door. "Maggie, are you awake? Up for a little chat?"

"I'd love one."

Juliet came over and sat beside Maggie's bed, straightening the covers, tucking the sheet around her the way she had often done many years ago. "I just wanted to make sure you're okay. There's been a lot for you to handle the past few days. But I'm so glad you're here. And I'm so glad to meet Gabriel."

"I'm glad to be here too."

Juliet started stroking the bedcover again. "Maggie, there's just a couple of things I wanted to say to you, in private." She paused. "It's about marriage. About relationships. I've watched you and Gabriel and you obviously get on so well, and that's great, but do you feel like you can stand your ground with him? That your opinion matters? That you're sure about him?"

"Well, I think so, but it is early days."

"But you're engaged, so you must love him. Well, you clearly do and he clearly loves you—"

"He does?"

Juliet laughed softly. "Don't sound so surprised. He wouldn't have proposed if he didn't. He did propose, didn't he? Or did you propose to him?"

"It was kind of a mutual agreement," she said. She imagined telling Juliet the truth. *"Actually, it was Leo who proposed for us both."*

"Have you talked about children yet, Maggie?"

She was taken aback. "It's a bit soon, don't you think?"

"It's not. It's not too soon. You're already twenty-six, and you know that a woman's fertility decreases every year after she turns twenty-five. You need to find out as soon as you can if there will be any difficulties." Another pause. "You know that Myles and I aren't childless by choice, don't you?"

Maggie nodded. She'd never asked Juliet directly but she had heard talk about IVF treatments over the years.

"We left it too late, Maggie. I left it too late. If we had started trying earlier, then there might have been time to sort out any problems we had. You'd have cousins, maybe lots of cousins."

"You wanted lots of children?"

To Maggie's shock, Juliet's eyes filled with tears. "As many as I could. And I couldn't even have one."

She put her arms around her aunt, held her close, shocked and sad at once. She had never thought that Juliet would still be so upset about it. She must have known for years. Surely she was used to the idea. And she and Myles had a great life; their business so successful, traveling all the time . . . She tried to say all that, to console Juliet, and was shocked when her aunt pulled away from her.

"None of that ever mattered to me, Maggie. It mattered to Myles, not to me, and I went along with it. I stupidly, foolishly let him make the decisions and now I'm left with what? Nothing. A perfect kitchen and an empty life. I don't want that to happen to you. I couldn't bear it if you went through what I did."

"But, Juliet, Miranda doesn't have kids, Eliza doesn't. It doesn't have to be everything—"

"Not to them, perhaps, but it was to me. It still is to me." She sat up straight then. "I just wanted to give you my advice. If you want children, Maggie, don't put it off. Men don't understand what it means to a woman. They'll talk about it from an intellectual or financial point of view, and it's not that kind of decision, it's pure emotion and feeling. Men don't think like that."

"But Myles—"

"Maggie, I may as well tell you. You'll all know in a few days, anyway. I'm leaving Myles. We're separating."

"You're what?"

Juliet explained about the note that would be waiting for him at their house in Manchester.

"But why didn't you say anything to anyone?"

"There's enough talk in this family as it is."

Maggie didn't know what to say to that. "I'm sorry, Juliet. I always really liked Myles." She truly had.

"I've no choice, Maggie. I can't forgive him and I can't forget so I've no choice. Please don't make the same mistake I did." Juliet abruptly stood up and left the room.

Maggie sat up in her bed for some time afterward. She wasn't imagining it. Things were different this July. Her aunts had never spoken to her like this, told her these kinds of things. But she had never spoken to them as she had tonight either. She'd never stood her ground with Miranda, challenged Eliza or spoken so honestly to Juliet. Had she also just missed a perfect, important opportunity? Should she have asked each of them about Sadie? Told them she knew the truth? Watched them react?

Maggie didn't wait for Clementine to come to her. She went to her mother herself. She stepped quietly down the corridor, avoiding the creaking floorboard, and slipped into her mother's room at the front of the house. It was bright with the moonlight through the open window. Clementine always slept with her curtains open.

Maggie spoke in a whisper. "Clementine?"

"Maggie?" Clementine sat up immediately. "Is everything all right?"

"Can I hop in with you for a minute?" It was the same sentence she used to say when she was little.

Clementine smiled, obviously remembering it too. "Of course you can." She lifted the bedcover and Maggie slipped in beside her. She hadn't been in the same bed with her mother since she was a child. She wished she hadn't left it so long. It was as comforting now as it had been then.

Clementine didn't switch on the light. She just turned on her side and smoothed the hair back from her daughter's face. "What is it, Maggie? What's wrong?"

Maggie wanted to tell her everything, about Leo's plotting, about the fake engagement. It didn't feel right to hide things from her mother. She wanted to tell her she knew all about Sadie. She wanted to ask her what that had been like, how Clementine had felt when she was missing, whether she had forgiven her sister. She wanted to ask her why she hadn't been told the truth all these years.

But she thought of the fallout again and it stopped her. Clementine wouldn't be as dramatic about it as the others, but she would be upset. It would cause a row with Leo. And they needed everything to stay as it was for a few more days, just in case Sadie did want to come and join them . . .

"What's up, Maggie?" Clementine asked again.

"I've had a few visitors tonight."

"A few aunts, do you mean?"

Maggie nodded. "All three of them."

"Like Three Wise Men bearing gifts?"

"Not exactly gifts."

"Oh dear." Clementine tucked her pillow behind her and smiled. "I might be wrong, but did Miranda have a few things to say to you about Gabriel?"

"How did you know?"

"She's been talking about nothing else since she got here. Don't listen to her, Maggie. You know your own heart and mind. I've hardly had a chance to talk to him, but Gabriel seems lovely. He's thoughtful, he's clever, and he obviously cares about you."

"You like him?"

"From what I've seen, yes, I do. What did Eliza have to say about him?"

"It wasn't Gabriel she was concerned about." Maggie hesitated. "Do you think I should have another job by now?"

"No, not yet. You don't know what you want to do yet, do you?"

"No."

"Why rush into it, then? You take all the time you need."

"And do you think I should have children as soon as I can?"

"Before you get married?"

"While I'm young."

"Is it something you and Gabriel are talking about already?"

"Not yet, no."

"Well, wait and see. If you want to and if you can, wonderful."

There was another question she needed to ask. "You don't regret having me, do you?"

"I have never regretted you for one minute. Not even one second."

"You don't think you could have done more with your career? Had a different sort of life, if you weren't tied down with a baby?"

"I've done everything with my career I could have wanted to do. I'm still doing that. Because of you, Maggie. I couldn't have done it without your understanding."

Her understanding? Had she always understood? Maggie wasn't sure of anything anymore. She was too unsettled by the revelations and events of the past few days. Because the truth was there had been times in her childhood when she wished Clementine hadn't gone away so often. Times she would rather not have stayed with her aunts. Events in Maggie's life that Clementine missed because she was away on an island somewhere, or on top of a mountain. Maggie was very proud of her, but if she was honest with herself, had she resented Clementine's work sometimes? Miranda's words came to mind. That Clementine had been Maggie's mother when it suited her. Was that true? That she wasn't always there for her?

There was something she needed to know. "When that thing happened in London, with that man at work and with Angus—"

Clementine nodded.

"Would you have come if Miranda wasn't able to?"

"Of course. We wouldn't have let you go through something like that on your own."

"We?"

"Any of us. Me. Leo. Your aunts. I'd have brought you back to Hobart with me, but before any of us knew what was happening, you'd gone to New York."

"You'd have brought me back home?"

"If you'd wanted to come, yes, I would have."

It hadn't even occurred to Maggie to go home to Tasmania. She thought now about being back in Hobart, living in the old family home, surrounded by all that beauty every day—the water, the mountains, the clean air, the vivid sunsets. Every day. Having her mother there, every day. Except she wouldn't be there. She'd be in Antarctica.

It was as if her mother had read her mind. Clementine stroked Maggie's hair away from her forehead again. "I don't leave for four months, Maggie. There's plenty of time for you to decide if that's what you'd like to do next. If you want me to stay home, I will."

"You actually mean that, don't you?"

"Of course I mean that."

To both their surprise, Maggie started to cry.

Clementine sat up and pulled her into her arms. "Maggie, what is it? Why are you crying?"

"I thought you'd say no."

"Why would I say no? You're my daughter. You mean more to me than anything."

"Do I?"

Clementine laughed. "Maggie! Of course you do. Where has all this come from? What did those sisters of mine say to you?"

"It wasn't just them. I couldn't sleep. I started thinking about things—" So many things. Sadie. The diaries. The lies. She wished she could talk to Clementine about all of them.

Clementine stroked her hair again. "Maggie, you're tired, I can see it. You've had a lot going on the past while. You've just brought your fiancé home to meet the family. That's enough stress to knock anyone out, even you. Will you do something for me?"

Maggie nodded.

"Stop thinking so much. Relax a little. And try to get some sleep. Do you want to stay here with me? I can get you another pillow."

"No, I'll go back to my own bed." She began to climb out from under the covers, then stopped. "Do you mind me calling you Clementine? Would you rather I called you Mum?"

"You can call me whatever you like."

"I think I might stick with Mum for a while."

"Mum it is, then."

Maggie hugged her closely. "I love you, you know."

"And I love you, you know."

"How many times?"

Clementine smiled. "You know exactly how many times. Twenty-six. Now go to bed."

Maggie had managed just an hour or two of sleep before she woke before eight to the noise of an engine straining up the steep hill toward their house. She got up, looked out her window, and saw an orange courier van making its way up the road.

When she got downstairs Leo was already at the front door in his dressing gown. "They rang to say they were on their way," Leo explained, talking quietly. "My mobile worked for once, a miracle. Incredibly efficient company to get it to me so quickly. I asked them to use the fastest service money could buy. They must have sent it via rocket."

The delivery man got out of his van, came up the path, and handed over a satchel. Leo signed for it. Maggie wanted to snatch it out of his hands and tear it open. Leo was just turning it over when Miranda appeared behind them.

"What on earth are you two up to?"

"It's a document from my lawyer in London," Leo said, after just a moment's hesitation. "A new patent going through on the lawn mower device." Leo tucked the satchel under his arm. "Maggie, why don't we get dressed and head up the laneway for a morning walk? We need some time together, don't you think?"

They were just leaving when Gabriel appeared, dressed in black jeans and a blue shirt, the sleeves rolled up.

Leo greeted him. "We're going for a walk. Will you join us?"

"Sure, thanks," Gabriel said.

"But the report?" Maggie whispered. "I thought you wanted to—"

"We can trust Gabriel," Leo said.

Leo filled Gabriel in within minutes of leaving the house. Gabriel asked Leo several questions, curious about the private detective's methods.

Leo opened the envelope as soon as they were out of sight of the house. Maggie realized she was holding her breath as Leo carefully withdrew a folder. He leaned it on the wall nearby, so they could all see. It was a businesslike report. Name, age, description. Brochures for the company the woman ran. The address and a photo of her house in the Dublin suburb of Phibsboro. Another photo. The woman with her husband and daughter.

Leo picked it up. Maggie noticed his hands were shaking. He stared at it for a long time. "She's married. She's got a daughter." His voice was a whisper. He checked the report again. "A daughter of eighteen. My second granddaughter. Your cousin, Maggie."

Maggie took the photo from her grandfather. As she looked at it, she realized she was holding her breath. It was an informal shot. A woman with a smiling face, relaxed in the sunshine. A round-faced man, also smiling. A brown-haired young woman. A happy family.

"Is it her, Tadpole?" she asked. "Is it Sadie?"

He took the photo back again and studied it intently. "It's her. It has to be her." He was quite agitated. "She's practically down the road, Maggie. It must be fate that she's ended up in Ireland too. Have you finished the diaries? Do you know enough yet? I think we need to move quickly, if we're to get Sadie back here to meet everyone. It's the best chance. Eliza's already talking about seeing if she can change her flights and go home early."

"I'm reading as fast as I can, I promise." She was. She wanted to get it over and done with. "I've got about four more to go."

"And nothing yet? You haven't found what might have upset Sadie so badly?"

Maggie hesitated, then shook her head. She needed to read all nine, let them sink in, before she would be able to talk to Leo about them.

Leo gazed at the photograph again. "I'm worried, Maggie. I haven't thought this through enough. What if it is Sadie, but she doesn't want to see me? Slams the door in my face? And she might. All these years I've written to her and she's never written back."

"She's always written back to me," Maggie said. She hoped he hadn't set her up, that this was what he had been intending the whole time. Even if it was, she knew what she had to do next. She made the offer. "I could go."

His shock seemed genuine. "What? Drive down to Dublin yourself?"

"I could go too," Gabriel said. "If you don't want the others to know, perhaps that's the best way. We could leave this afternoon, tell them that Maggie and I are going to do some exploring and will be back tomorrow."

"That's too soon," Maggie said. "I still need to read the diaries."

"I could drive while you read."

"What if all three of us went down?" Leo asked.

"You can't leave," Maggie said. "Not when everyone's come all this way."

"They came to see you, not me."

"They've seen me. I think Gabriel's right. The two of us could be there and back within a day. We'll do some more filming this morning, then head off this afternoon."

"But what if it isn't Sadie? What if the detective has made a mistake?" Leo asked anxiously.

Maggie had never seen her grandfather this upset. She put her hand on his arm. "We'll find out, Tadpole. And if we can bring her back, we will."

CHAPTER 40

Maggie and Gabriel were on the road to Dublin before eleven. They'd been met by a delegation of Faraday women when they came back in from their walk with Leo. It was going to be a beautiful day, the warmest yet that summer. Too good to spend inside filming, Miranda had decided on behalf of everyone. They were going to take a picnic lunch down to the beach and spend the day there.

"In that case, Maggie and I can take off earlier than we'd planned," Gabriel said easily.

It took them less than half an hour to get organized. Everyone gathered in front of the house to wave good-bye. They promised they'd be back within twenty-four hours.

"Good luck," Leo said quietly, hugging Maggie.

"Thanks, Gabriel," Maggie said, as they drove down through the village, turning at the old church before taking the road that led up through the heather-covered hills. "This is really going above and beyond the call of duty."

"No, it's not. I checked the Charter of Fake Fiancés this morning and it was there, number seven in a list of twenty: 'Thou must drive to Dublin if necessary.' "

"I'm serious, Gabriel. If you'd known what you were getting yourself into—"

"Maggie, I told you, it's no problem. All of this is much harder for you than me."

"Me?"

"Maybe I'm wrong, but I'd find it difficult if I were you. They all seem to want a piece of you. The only one who doesn't is Clementine, who has the most claim to you. She's the calmest of them all."

"She always has been."

"I think you chose the right mother out of all of them. Well done."

"Thank you."

They made their way across the hills, bare except for the turf bogs here and there, the drying sods of turf heaped into piles to dry in the sun. Maggie took the opportunity to read over the detective's report about Sadie again. It was strange to see someone's life laid out in a stark, factual way like this. Stranger still to think that Sadie might have been living this false life for nearly twenty years, calling herself a different name, living with her husband and daughter in Dublin. It was that photo of the three of them that had shocked Leo the most, Maggie knew that. If it was her, there was the proof that she truly did have another life somewhere that they all knew nothing about. Not just a new life, but a new family. All these years Maggie had imagined her living as a hippie, part of a commune somewhere in tropical Australia. She still couldn't bring herself to let go of that image.

She looked at the photo again now, focusing on the woman. In some ways it was like looking at a stranger; in other ways there were echoes of her mother and her aunts. She had the same dark eyes and a similar-shaped face. Her hair looked dyed, though it was hard to tell, windswept as it was. The husband looked nice. Smiley-faced. Freckled. Very blue-eyed. And their daughter. Maggie's cousin. It was harder to tell from her photo what she was like. Her face was turned upward to her parents, laughing too. All three of them looked happy.

Gabriel interrupted her thoughts. "Is Leo going to tell the others that he's found Sadie? At least, that he thinks he's found Sadie?"

"Not yet. He wants to wait until he's sure."

"Will they be pleased?"

"Of course they will. She's their sister."

"Didn't anyone ever go looking for her before now?"

"I don't know," she said. "They might have. But if they did, I was never told about it."

The same question had been gnawing at Maggie too. Perhaps they had gone looking. Perhaps each of them in turn had tried to find Sadie and failed. Layer by layer, the truth of the situation, all that had been hidden from her over the years not just by Leo, but by Clementine and her aunts, was filtering into her mind.

"Can I ask you something personal, Maggie?"

"That sounds serious."

"I'm curious about it, rather than serious. Why do your aunts have such a hold over you?"

"A hold?" She laughed. "Gabriel, they're aunts, not alien controllers."

"I know that. I understand the concept of aunts; I have a few of them myself. But mine draw the line at socks at birthdays. Yours seem to have a stake in your entire life."

"They all brought me up. I suppose they do have a stake in me. And it's not like it's some awful torture. They're my family, I love being with them."

"Do you?"

"I do. I do." She was silent for a moment. "I like walking into a room and it being filled with my mother and my aunts and my grandfather. I loved it when I was a child and I still love it now. It was obviously different for you, just you and your mother."

"Maybe that's why I'm so fascinated."

"I'm glad we're keeping you entertained."

"Completely. I'm intrigued too. About these reunions, especially. It's like you have all gotten into a habit none of you can break."

His observations were making her feel uncomfortable and annoyed in equal measure. "Gabriel, we're here because we want to be here." She corrected herself. "Because we feel we should be here. For Leo, more than for ourselves, but what's wrong with that?

When Tessa died, he had to be everything to five young daughters, mother and father. I think that's something to admire."

"He talks about her so much still, doesn't he? You'll see it on the film tomorrow night. She was quite something, by the sound of things."

Maggie wished she could agree. Wished she could say, Yes, Tessa had been a wonderful woman and her diaries were the proof of it.

Gabriel noticed her hesitation. "You don't agree?"

She chose her words carefully. "I don't know anymore. Her diaries don't quite match up to that public image." She needed to talk about it. "Have you ever kept a diary, Gabriel?"

He shook his head. "I already know what's in my head. I don't need to see it on paper to make it real."

"But if you did write things down, they would be your real thoughts? The real you? Show the sort of person you really are?"

"They would have to. There'd be some self-delusion, some hedging of the facts, but the truth would come through eventually."

"I thought the same thing. But if that's the case, then the real Tessa is nothing like the person Leo has described all my life. The Tessa he's told my mother and aunts about, every day for years. The Tessa we celebrate with these July Christmases, this holiday house, all of it." Maggie thought back to all she'd read and tried to put it into words. "I thought it would be an honor to read her diaries, Gabriel. To get to know my grandmother in an intimate way like that."

"And it hasn't been?"

She shook her head. "I wish I hadn't read them. I wish I'd never found out what she was really like. She's selfish and self-centered and dismissive. There's page after page of it. She's mean about Leo; about everyone around her."

"But Leo said that they were the loves of each other's lives."

"That's what he believes. But I don't think he was, not for her." She didn't say it out loud but from what Maggie had read, the only love of Tessa's life had been Tessa herself.

"Then why did Leo want you to read them?"

Gabriel knew everything else about her family. There was no reason not to tell him this as well. As briefly as possible, she explained about Tessa and Bill, and of Leo's theory that Sadie had read some-thing shocking about them in the diaries, something that had caused her to run away.

"That Bill is her father, not Leo?"

Maggie nodded. "I don't think Leo actually wants me to find it. I'm sure he hopes I won't. But I think it's coming up in the diary I'm reading now. The timing is right."

"You haven't jumped ahead? Skipped a few years? I wouldn't be able to resist it."

"I needed to get the whole picture of her first. I wish I hadn't now. I actually wish Leo had done as he said and burned them all, years ago."

A beep of an arriving text message sounded in the car. Gabriel signaled and pulled over to the side of the road, taking out his mo-bile phone. "Sorry, Maggie. I've been expecting this. I might need to call them back."

He read the text. It was from his writer flatmate, letting him know he'd had a story accepted by a small literary magazine. "Good for him. He says he was going to keep some champagne for me but unfortunately he and his girlfriend have just drunk it all."

He put the phone away and pulled back onto the road.

"What did they think about you coming on this trip to Ireland?" Maggie asked.

"They were sick with jealousy. They wanted to know why they never got a job offer like this."

A job offer. There it was. The fact of the matter. She was making the mistake again of thinking this meant as much to him as it did to her. They came up to the motorway then, the surface instantly be-coming smoother after the bumps of the country road they'd been traveling on. Better for reading too, Maggie realized. The quicker she got it done, the better. And that's what this trip was about, after all: Sadie and the diaries, not her and Gabriel. She reached into the backseat for her leather bag. She'd pushed all nine notebooks into the bottom of it that morning, covering them with a scarf.

"I'd better get back to work," she said.

"Of course. Happy reading."

"Thanks." She wished it was going to be.

.   .   .

She read for the entire journey, having a brief break when Gabriel stopped to refuel and buy a map of Dublin. She was soon oblivious again to her surroundings, to the passing towns, fields, and housing estates. She was back in the 1960s, inside her grandmother's mind, hearing her thoughts. Tessa was now pregnant with Sadie.

> I've been sick this entire pregnancy. A friend of mine told me there's an old wives' tale that if you don't want to be pregnant, your body tries to get rid of the baby. Well, mine isn't trying hard enough. Bloody Leo, it's all his fault. I told him three children were enough for me.

There was a gap between entries.

> My first diary entry in three months. Still recovering from the most painful birth yet. Sadie Mary. Not an easy baby. A crier. I leave her to Leo at nighttime. I have enough to do in the day-times as it is with the other girls. I've told Leo we have to get help in the house or I will surely collapse.

Another gap of six months.

> Feel like I am losing my mind. Sadie is like a cat, mewing mewing mewing all day and all night long, the noise constant in my head. Growing pains, the doctor said. She'll get over it. I just want to leave her to it. I confessed as much to the nurse and got all the usual guff about giving myself time to bond. How much more time do I need??? I'm not imagining it, this baby feels different.

Five months later, the news that Maggie had been waiting to read.

> Pregnant again! Told Leo this is the last time. Five babies are enough for any woman. Barely a year between this one and

Sadie. If she's as difficult as Sadie I truly don't know how I will cope.

She held her breath as she started to read about the arrival of her own mother.

Another girl. I was disappointed for a second when I heard it wasn't a boy but this one has the face of an angel. The other girls very excited. Juliet wanting to take it home straightaway, told me she will look after it until I get home! Miranda disgusted that it's another girl, wanted to know if we could swap it for one of the newborn boys in the ward. She does make me laugh. Eliza slightly interested. Leo besotted, yet again. Picked her up yesterday and called her his little darling, strangely just as I had heard "Oh My Darling, Clementine" playing on the ward radio. Clementine it is! She is the most wonderful baby, so peaceful, calm, a pleasure to look after. Feeds when she should, sleeps when she should. So pretty.

Maggie felt her eyes fill with tears. For a moment she had nothing but warm thoughts toward Tessa. The feeling didn't last long.

Sadie is driving me crazy! So jealous of her little sister, whining all the time, wanting to take her bottle from her. Caught her trying to climb into Clementine's cot today. Told the nurse about it. She said to be careful not to leave them alone together, that there have been reports of older siblings suffocating new arrivals. Wish it was the other way around. Feel guilty for saying that!!!

The entries for the next two years were few and far between. Snippets about Juliet's love of cooking. Funny things Miranda had said. Complaints about Leo, how exhausted she was, how much work there always was to do, how suffocated she was feeling. Talk about her scrapbooks, how they at least gave her something to do that didn't involve washing or cleaning. There were enthusiastic reports about Bill's visits, but nothing that Maggie could tell hinted at a physical relationship between them.

The year Clementine turned four there was an important entry.

> Bombshell news today. We are off to Tasmania. Didn't even
> know where it was until Leo got the map but like the sound of
> adventure. Older girls very excited. Miranda very funny,
> parading around with an apple when Leo told her it was called
> the Apple Isle. Sadie upset. Scared to go on the boat. Whine,
> whine. That child would find something to complain about
> even at Christmas, I'm sure of it.

There was a four-month break before the next entry. Maggie
read each word even more carefully. They were now in Hobart—in
the house she had grown up in, the city she called home, and
among the scenery she loved. It quickly became clear that Tessa
wasn't as impressed.

There was little about Hobart itself, or about Leo and his job,
apart from her being glad there was more money coming in. The
new house was too drafty. Hobart was beautiful, so clean after London, but where were all the people? She was also getting even
crosser with Leo.

> He's back in his bloody inventing phase again. Jokes all the
> time that it's in his blood. Out in the shed for hours each
> night, fine by me.
>
> No kindred spirit at the girls' school, all the women a bit
> behind the times if you ask me. Girls have settled in, except
> for Sadie. Tears all the time again, doesn't want to go to
> school, says she is scared of the teacher. She has to be the most
> annoying child to walk this planet. So whining. So hesitant all
> the time. I watch her hanging around the edges of groups of
> kids and want to push her forward.

There were more funny little stories about the other four, but
none about Sadie. Maggie read back, just to double-check. There
wasn't a single one.

Sadie having nightmares again. Sent Leo in to her the last few nights, she seems to settle better for him than me. At least he agrees with me. As he put it, there's a runt in every litter, and Sadie's our runt. Don't expect too much of her, he tells me. I just wish she didn't annoy me so much. It's almost a physical thing. She is so needy, wanting to be hugged and petted all the time. It's like she's the cuckoo in the nest.

Twice Maggie found herself wiping away a tear. Gabriel noticed. "Are you all right? Do you need to stop?"

"No, thank you." She didn't know who she was crying for. Sadie? Leo? Her whole family?

She finished reading the final diary as they reached the outskirts of Dublin. She closed the cover. She didn't speak. She didn't know what to say.

"That's it?" Gabriel asked, glancing over.

She nodded.

"Did it get any better?"

She shook her head.

She now knew all it was possible to know. She'd read every page; knew what Tessa had thought and felt about her life, her husband and her daughters, right up until a few days before she died. She also knew exactly what Sadie had read.

Maggie was angry. She was confused. Mostly, though, she was sad. Sad for Sadie, and how she must have felt reading this. For Leo, who must have suspected how Tessa really felt about him, who had spent so many years jealous of his own brother, who had tried, endlessly, optimistically, constantly, to make Tessa love him as much as he had loved her.

Maggie even felt sad for Tessa, in a strange way. So full of conceit, writing so carelessly and cruelly, unaware that in two weeks' time she would be dead. There was a passing reference to her forthcoming operation—a hysterectomy, Maggie realized. She had winced at her words: *Can't keep Leo away from me, so at least this will mean I can't get pregnant AGAIN.* Her final entry was about how bad the hospital food was, how bored she was, and how pleased she was that the woman in the opposite bed had gone home. There were four lines about the idea of the July Christmas: *I'm hoping it will help convince Leo that it's time we went back to the U.K. I've had enough of being here. If he doesn't agree, I'm tempted to just stay there myself next time I go back on holiday. That'd bring him over quick-smart!*

All these years the family had been celebrating the July Christmas, thinking it was a wonderful tribute to Tessa and her imagination. Yet the only reason she had proposed it was as part of a plan to get Leo to agree to returning to the U.K. A purely selfish reason.

All Maggie had read the past two days filled her head. It was hard to make sense of it. Even harder to imagine talking to Sadie about it. "Gabriel, can we stop somewhere? I think I need some fresh air."

"Of course." They were on a motorway, coming into Dublin. He saw it first, a signpost for the Phoenix Park, two kilometers away.

They drove in through wrought-iron gates, the park opening up in front of them, all meadows and green fields. The trees were lush with summer growth. Gabriel drove for a short while before pulling into a side road. They were the only people there.

They got out of the car and began to walk. Maggie brought her leather bag with her, hitching it over one shoulder, the diaries a heavy weight inside. They had gone only a short way, across a small wooded area toward a path, when she started to talk.

"Leo will be pleased about one thing. Bill isn't Sadie's father. It wasn't that."

"That was all he wanted to know, wasn't it? The most important thing for him?"

Maggie nodded. "Leo is definitely the father of them all."

"But if it wasn't that that made Sadie go, it must have been something else. Do you think you found it?"

"I think so." She didn't think it. She knew it. She glanced up at him. "Gabriel, does your mother love you?"

"What?"

"Does your mother love you?"

"Of course she does."

"Would it matter if she didn't love you? Didn't like you?"

"Would it matter?" He thought about it. "It would be very hard. I'd think there was something wrong with me. That it was my fault."

"Why?"

"Because all mothers love their children."

"Do they? Can I read you something?" She reached into her bag, opened the diary at random, and began to read some of Tessa's words about Sadie.

Gabriel could hardly believe it.

"The diaries are filled with it," Maggie said. "It goes on and on like this, from when Sadie was born, until just before Tessa died." She flicked forward to the end of the final diary and read it aloud to Gabriel:

> Have just canceled Sadie's birthday party. More tears, of course. She's been carrying on so much, all upset because the girls she invited can't come or some such nonsense. As I said to her, it's a hard world out there and the sooner she realizes that the better. She started to go on and on about it, as usual. What's wrong with me, Mum? Why haven't I got any friends at school? Do you love me? What was I supposed to say, the truth? No, Sadie, I don't think I do love you. You actually drive me crazy. I told her to just put it behind her, she could have a party another year, and of course I got hit by another flood of tears. It's a terrible thing not to like one of your own children, but I can't help it.

Maggie shut the diary and pushed it back into her bag as if she wanted to hide it. "What would you do if you read that, Gabriel? If you read that your mother didn't like you; in fact, was sure she didn't even love you; that your father thought of you as the runt and that both parents thought your four sisters were better in every way than you?"

"I'd want to get as far away from that family as I could."

"I would too."

"You think that's what happened?"

"I'm sure of it."

"But why take you with her?"

"Because I was there? Because I didn't hate her? I don't know."

They started walking again. "Why would Leo keep up the charade, Maggie? It's like he's remembering a different woman."

"Maybe it was easier for him that way. Maybe that was the only way he could keep the family together after she died."

"She can't have been all bad, can she?"

"I honestly don't know."

"Was she beautiful?"

"Very."

"Perhaps that was it. Sometimes that's enough. People get bewitched by beautiful women."

"But would that feeling last for years?"

"There must have been more. From what Leo was saying, she entertained him. Amused him. She gave him a family. All those things would count for something."

Maggie didn't know what she should do next. "It would have been simpler if Bill was Sadie's father. At least Leo is expecting that. I can't tell Leo all of this. And I can't go to Sadie and ask her to come to Donegal and rejoin the family. Why would she want to? She read everything I did. She knows what Leo said about her. She knows that the July Christmas wasn't some lovely family tradition. It was just Tessa hatching a plan." That had hurt Maggie more than she expected. "What do I do now, Gabriel?" It wasn't fair to ask him, but she was lost.

He was quiet for a moment. "I think you've got three options. Maybe even four. You can go to her work, or to her house. You can phone her. Or you can do nothing and we can go straight back to Donegal. Tell Leo exactly what you read, what you think, and leave it to him to figure out."

She couldn't do that. Not yet. Not after coming all this way. Not just from Donegal, from New York too. "If I ring, she might say no. It's easier to hang up on someone than to say no face-to-face."

"Do you want to go to her office?"

"She might not even be in Dublin. We should have rung before we got here. She could be away somewhere."

"Yes, she might. Or she could be sitting at home right now."

"Why did I let Leo talk me into this?"

"He didn't. You offered."

He was right. She had.

"I checked the map, Maggie. We're not far from Phibsboro. Two kilometers at the most."

"That close?" Maggie tried to picture a scene. A suburban house, one of the terraced houses they'd passed on their way. Sadie in her kitchen, making tea. Or in her garden, or watching TV. Unaware that her niece was so close. That her entire family was in the same country. The choice was Maggie's. She could come crashing into that life and upset who knew what, or she could decide to do nothing; leave everything as it had been for the past twenty years. "That woman might not even be her," she said again.

"Don't you want to find out for sure?"

She thought about it for a few minutes. She couldn't stop the search here. "Let's go to her house."

.   .   .

In her Dame Street office, Sadie checked her watch. Larry had phoned that morning to say he hoped to be home by five. She decided she wanted to be there to meet him. They hadn't seen each other for nearly three weeks now. Too long. The longest they'd ever been apart, in fact. She picked up her bag, tied her silk scarf around her neck, and walked through to her assistant's office. "I'm going to finish up early, Anne. Larry's due home and I want to get the house ready for him."

"You old romantic, Sally O'Toole." Anne smiled. "Say hi from me. See you both tomorrow."

Sadie usually caught the bus home. Stepping out onto the street, she decided it was such a beautiful day she'd walk instead. It would take her half an hour. She'd easily be home before Larry.

.   .   .

In Donegal, Leo was in the living room on his own. He'd decided not to join the others on the trip to the beach. He wasn't a fan of

swimming in an icy-cold sea. Besides, he'd had an idea during the
night that he wanted to explore. The seed had been planted while
he was watching Gabriel operate the camera, noticing that he
needed to move the equipment each time he wanted a different
angle. Surely there was another, more efficient method? What if
the camera was to swivel on the tripod in some way, not just around
but up and down, on a sort of extendable arm? That way the oper-
ator wouldn't have to physically move the tripod, just the camera itself. It would be a simple enough mechanism, Leo thought. The
trick would be how the camera attached to it. The wires would
need to be inside a swiveling case, so they could rotate in different
directions.

All the camera equipment was still set up from the previous day,
all the wires neatly coiled, like a proper TV studio. Leo circled the
camera, cautiously touching this lever and that button. Extraordinary to think such a small apparatus could hold hours of footage.
Gabriel had given him a brief lesson on how it worked, pointing
out the viewfinder, the different focus buttons. The technology had
changed in a big way even during the time Gabriel had been working with cameras, apparently. It really was marvelous.

Leo put on his spectacles and started carefully undoing the
screws holding the camera to the tripod. The lever was tightly fastened and fiddly to get at. He steadied himself as the tripod started
to tilt, grabbing at the camera to steady it, smiling sheepishly to
himself. That wouldn't do, he thought. All those hours of filming
the previous day going to waste because he had dropped the camera.

"Ah, there we are," he said, as the camera came loose from the
tripod. "Now we can get to work."

·   ·   ·

In Manchester, Myles Stottington stepped back as the cabdriver
pulled away from the curb. He juggled his suitcase, briefcase, and
jacket, finding his front door key and letting himself into the
house. He didn't call out to Juliet as he normally would. He knew
she wasn't due back from Donegal for a few days yet.

He left his case in the hallway, hung his jacket on the hook, walked into the living room and opened the window to let in some fresh air. He was hungry, thirsty, and tired. It had been a long trip, but a successful one. If all the negotiations came to pass, they'd have another five cafés to add to their portfolio. He'd ring Juliet that night to tell her the good news.

He came into the kitchen. The first thing he saw was an envelope leaning against the fruit bowl. An envelope with his name on it. Puzzled, he went across. It was Juliet's handwriting. He picked it up, slit open the envelope, and took out the letter inside.

CHAPTER 41

I t was four thirty. Maggie and Gabriel were parked down the road from what they hoped was Sadie's house.

It had taken them less than five minutes to get there. They had driven along the tree-lined main road of the park, past the zoo, through another set of ornate white gates and onto the North Circular Road. Maggie had called out the directions from there. On the way they had passed a guesthouse taking up two of the terrace houses, with a sign saying VACANCIES hanging out the front. Maggie took note of the name. If—*if*—this was Sadie's house, they might need to stay the night nearby.

Sadie lived on an attractive street. The terraced houses were of redbrick, each with small, well-kept gardens in the front, surrounded by iron railings. There were hanging baskets by each front door: masses of tumbling color, blue, white, and red flowers.

They sat in the parked car, waiting and watching. There was no sign of life in the house.

"Perhaps I should have gone to where she worked." According to the detective's report, O'Toole Cleaners' office was in Dame Street, in the center of the city. "But if it is her"—everything they said was prefaced with that—"perhaps it's better to talk to her at home, do you think? What do I say, though? What if her daughter answers when I knock? Or her husband? Do I say who I am? Would she have told them about me? About any of us?"

Gabriel smiled at her. "Do you want me to try and answer all twenty of those questions or can I pick just one or two?"

"Sorry." She was growing more anxious by the minute. It had been much easier to think about this when it was hypothetical, when she wasn't sitting just meters from Sadie's house.

Gabriel was reading the report again. "You're quite like her daughter, you know. She looks like you, I mean. Not identical, but there are similarities."

Maggie had noticed that too. They had similar coloring: dark hair and pale skin. She wasn't going to point this out to Gabriel, but Sadie's daughter had slightly sticky-out ears too. She wore a lot more earrings than Maggie ever had, though. In the photo it looked like she had about ten silver hoops in each ear.

They sat for five minutes, not speaking. Maggie had a lot to think about. She couldn't get Tessa's words out of her head. She kept picturing Sadie reading them. She tried to imagine how it would feel to read something like that about yourself. It would be devastating. Not just hurtful, but crushing. Something else occurred to her too. What if Leo decided he wanted to read the diaries now as well? She knew that once she told him that Bill definitely wasn't Sadie's father, he would want to. Now that his great fear had been dismissed, he would surely be curious to read everything Tessa had written; her thoughts on their life together. She pictured how hurt he would be. Not only that. He would be reminded of all he'd said about Sadie being the runt of the family. He would realize that Sadie had also read that; that he had somehow contributed to her deciding to leave the family. Around and around her thoughts went. Maggie wished again that Leo had destroyed the diaries all those years ago. None of this would have happened if he had.

She was roused from her thoughts by a sudden touch on her arm. "Maggie, is that her?"

They watched a woman coming down the road. She had a purposeful step. She looked to be in her midforties. Dark-brown hair. She was dressed in dark-blue trousers and a light-colored shirt, with a colorful scarf around her neck.

They were too far away to tell for sure, but Maggie recognized something familiar about the woman. She realized what it was. She walked like her aunts. That same brisk, easy stride they all had. She walked like that too.

She froze. "I can't talk to her."

"Maggie, of course you can. She's right there."

"But what do I say? 'Are you Sadie? Hello, I'm Maggie, the niece you haven't seen for twenty years'? It doesn't seem fair. Not just on the street like that."

The woman was getting closer.

"Do you want me to do it?" Gabriel asked. "Break the ice, if you like? I can ask her outright."

"Would you?"

"Of course I would. But is it the right thing?"

"Please, Gabriel. Quickly. Before she goes inside."

Maggie could feel her heart thumping as Gabriel got out of the car and crossed the road. She heard his voice calling out, his American accent distinct. "Excuse me."

The woman turned, a polite smile, clearly thinking she was about to help a lost tourist. Maggie sat still, watching as Gabriel said something. She saw the woman's hand go up to her neck. She wasn't shaking her head or nodding. She was just listening, staring at Gabriel. The two of them turned and looked at the car Maggie was sitting in. She didn't know what to do, whether to wave or acknowledge them. She didn't do anything. Should she go over there? Had he asked her?

The woman ran her hands through her hair. Her hand went back to the scarf around her neck. She looked at her watch. Gesture after gesture, but still no nod. Gabriel touched her arm, then turned away. She opened the gate to her house and went inside, not looking back. He came back toward Maggie, his face not giving anything away. He opened the door, got in and shut the door.

"It's her, Maggie. It's Sadie."

Her heart started thumping. "What did you say to her?"

"I asked her outright. I said I was a friend of the Faraday family from Tasmania. I didn't want to shock her, but I needed to know, was she Sadie Faraday?"

"And she said she was? Just like that?"

"Not at first. She said no, I must have confused her with someone else, that her name was Sally O'Toole. And I said yes, I knew that, but that her family thought she may once have been called Sadie Faraday and that her niece was here and she would very much like to talk to her. And she said, 'Maggie? Maggie's here?' I hadn't said your name before then."

"Will she talk to me? Does she want to? Now?"

He nodded. "She said she just needs some time on her own first."

"Is her daughter there? Her husband?"

"She didn't say. She was pretty shocked, Maggie."

"What does she sound like?"

"Australian but with a bit of an Irish accent. She sounds like Juliet actually. That same tone to her voice."

"Does she look just like the others?"

His voice was gentle. "Maggie, you'll see for yourself in a few minutes."

Maggie realized her hands were shaking. She pulled down the mirror, checked her appearance and smoothed down her hair. "Do I look all right?"

"You look great. You always look great."

"Wish me luck."

"You don't need luck, Maggie. She's your aunt, remember."

She opened the car door and started walking toward the house. She was at the gate when the front door opened. The woman was standing there, a mobile phone in her hand. She looked agitated.

Maggie stopped. "Sadie?"

"Maggie, I'm so sorry. I can't talk to you now."

As they spoke, a green van came around the corner. It had "O'Toole Cleaners" written in white letters on the side.

"That's my husband. He's just phoned. He's back earlier than expected. He doesn't know about you. Maggie, please, don't say anything. Just go, now, as quickly as you can."

"But, Sadie—"

"Please don't call me that. It's Sally now."

"I need to talk to you. Leo has—"

"Leo's dead?"

Maggie shook her head. "No, that's not it. It's just—"

The van was pulling into a gap five houses down.

"Sadie—Sally, please. I need to talk to you."

Sadie hesitated, glancing anxiously down the road at the van. "Where are you staying?"

Maggie named the guesthouse on the main road, hoping she remembered it right.

Sadie nodded. "I'll call you there, in the morning. First thing in the morning. I promise. But I need you to go now."

The van door opened and a man got out. As Maggie walked as quickly as she could back to their car, she glanced across. Sadie had left her front door open as she ran up to the van. The man put down his suitcases and hugged her. Maggie heard snatches of their conversation. "Welcome home!" As they walked arm in arm back toward their house, Maggie saw the man glance across in her direction, ask a question, and nod at Sadie's answer. What had she said? Maggie wondered. That she was a lost tourist? A door-to-door saleswoman? Anything but her long-lost niece.

They went inside just as Maggie reached the car, opened the door, and got in.

"Maggie? Are you okay?"

She couldn't stop herself. She burst into tears.

CHAPTER 42

Sadie finished tidying up after dinner. It was the hardest night she'd ever spent in Larry's company. On the surface, she hoped she'd been her usual self. The conversation flowed as easily as it always had between them. She asked questions about the Galway merger, even though they'd spoken several times a day and there wasn't much she didn't know. She talked about her work, about a possible new client. They discussed a political scandal in the news. They talked about Maudie.

They talked and they laughed and for a few minutes Sadie managed to forget that her old life had just come crashing into her new life.

She felt Larry come into the kitchen behind her, slip his arms around her waist, and press a kiss on her hair. "I missed you, Sally."

She turned around in the circle of his arms and kissed him back. "I missed you too."

"I don't ever want to be away from you for that long again."

"I didn't like it either."

He kissed her again. She gave herself up to it, to the pleasure, the comfort and safety of his familiar touch. This was what was real in her life now. Larry, Maudie, this house, this country. Not her old life, not Tasmania, not her old family. Not even Maggie. She had all she needed, more than she ever thought she would have. She couldn't bear to lose it. She couldn't risk doing anything that might change things.

As Larry whispered in her ear, as he gently started to undo the buttons on her shirt, ignoring her protests that the neighbors could be watching through the window, one part of her was thinking of something else. As she laughed at him pulling the blind down, she came to a decision.

She wouldn't ring Maggie in the morning. There was no point.

.   .   .

It was past midnight. Three hundred meters up the road from Sadie's house, Maggie was wide awake. She and Gabriel had spent a subdued evening in each other's company.

He had been very understanding about her tears in the car. She'd been embarrassed, wiping her eyes, as he drove away from Sadie's house.

They checked into the guesthouse that Maggie had noticed earlier. The first thing she did was confirm there was a phone in the room.

She wasn't sure when Gabriel suggested they go and find somewhere to eat.

"What if she rings?"

"She said she'll ring tomorrow."

"I'll take a message if anyone does ring," the receptionist said, overhearing every word.

They walked down the main road, closer to the city center. The receptionist had recommended an Indian restaurant four streets away. Over dinner, Maggie tried to talk about general things, but she kept returning to the subject of Sadie. Perhaps she should have done things differently.

Gabriel stayed patient with her. "Maggie, you can't change it. You've made the first move and now you can't do anything until the morning, until she rings."

"What if she doesn't?"

"Wait and see."

As they came out of the restaurant, Maggie tried to convince herself Gabriel was right. There was no point going over and over what had happened or what might happen. There was nothing more she could do. It was up to Sadie now.

"You're doing that nose-rubbing again," Gabriel said. "Should I be scared? Is it a sign that the weather is about to change?"

"No, it's a sign that you have probably heard more than enough about the Faraday family for one day. It's also a sign that it's time someone took you to an Irish pub to hear some Irish music."

"We're in Ireland? I keep forgetting that. New York one day, Donegal the next, Dublin the day after. I like knowing you, Maggie Faraday. You're one of the jet set."

They crossed the busy street, dodging between green double-decker buses and taxis heading in the direction of the city center. The area was a mixture of rundown and prosperous: modern shops and cafés next to abandoned buildings; dilapidated terraced houses beside smart new apartments. Maggie counted five pubs in less than a hundred feet, painted in bright colors and decorated with window boxes, with small groups of smokers in every doorway. Maggie and Gabriel walked into one, lured by a large sign announcing MUSIC TONIGHT on a blackboard on the footpath.

"You should have brought your guitar," Maggie said as they walked inside.

"I stole two spoons from the restaurant. I'll play those if the mood takes me." He smiled at her expression. "Maggie, I'm joking. I took forks, not spoons."

The band was just starting as they walked in. Not Irish ballads. It was a techno duo, with synthesizers and a drum machine. Maggie and Gabriel turned around and walked out again. The next pub had three large video screens, each showing a different football match, all at high volume. The pub after that smelled of industrial disinfectant. The next was playing loud pop music via a badly tuned radio.

They finally settled on a pub at the end of the street: music-free, disinfectant-free and sports screen–free. It was like a country pub in the center of the city, with red-painted exterior walls, the interior like someone's lounge room with an unusual selection of photos arranged higgledy-piggledy on the walls: hurling teams, a poster of the *Titanic*'s maiden voyage and a black-and-white photograph of a young boy standing in the middle of an expanse of cobblestones. It was quiet; just a group of young women laughing and talking in one corner, the other tables and stools empty. The barman greeted them warmly and took their orders for two pints of Guinness. "Take a seat. I'll bring them over." He delivered them with a smile several minutes later.

Gabriel picked up the glass. *"Sláinte."*

Maggie repeated the Irish toast. *"Sláinte."*

They both took a sip.

"Here we are," he said.

"Here we are," she said in return.

"How are you, Maggie?"

She thought about it. "Stunned. Shocked. Sad."

"All those *s* words. Dolly would be proud of you."

"I'm also scared."

"Scared?"

"I'm scared of her not ringing me tomorrow. What do I do then?"

He smiled at her. "Maggie Faraday, have you always been like this? Wanting to control things, wanting to know everything that's going to happen? You can't do that all the time. You need to let things unfold for themselves sometimes."

"You're right. I know that. It was one of the reasons I was glad to be in New York. To be outside my normal life; let things happen of their own accord. To take a step back from myself."

"It was a good thing to do. And don't you see how your brave step was rewarded? The wonderful thing that happened next?" he prompted. "Maggie, please. You met me." Another smile. "See? Good things come to those who go to New York on a whim."

She felt herself relax a little. "Thank you, Gabriel."

"Thank you? For what? And yes, I am fishing for compliments."

"Ten things." She counted them off on her fingers. "For coming to Donegal. For being so nice to Leo. For filming my aunts and mother. For standing up to Miranda. For listening to all of this. For driving to Dublin today. For talking to Sadie in the street when I couldn't. For being so understanding."

He was counting too. "That's only eight. Come on. You can think of two more."

Number nine. For being so lovely that I want to kiss you. Number ten. The same thing again. She wanted to kiss him more than once.

"I'll save those two up for another time," she said.

"I'll look forward to hearing them," he said.

His next words surprised her.

"I've had an idea how to end things between us," he replied.

She stared at him.

"Our engagement. Don't you remember? When we were in New York, you were worried about your family, what they'd think. I promised you I'd come up with a way of ending it."

"You did?" That seemed like a hundred years ago.

"You've got so much else to think about at the moment, I didn't want you to worry about that as well. I've asked a friend of mine at home to call the house in Donegal in the next couple of days, to come up with an excuse for me to go back urgently. We'll have finished the filming by then. And then once I'm gone you can tell your family you've been having doubts and you're thinking of calling it off. It'll be much easier to say all that if I'm not there."

She hoped her reaction wasn't obvious on her face. She didn't want to end it. She liked pretending to be engaged to him. She wished they weren't pretending. It was a sudden reminder, again, that this was just a job to him.

She managed a smile. "That sounds great, thanks very much. That'll make it much easier."

They walked back to the guesthouse after their drink. They said good night to each other at reception. Another time, it might have been different. In Dublin for just one night, they might have gone on to another pub, kept talking, found some live music, even gone to a club. They might have come back to the guesthouse, whispering and hushing each other, going to his room or hers to keep talking. To keep laughing. Perhaps to do even more.

But tonight wasn't that sort of night. They were almost businesslike in their good nights. He wished her luck with the call in the morning. She promised to let him know as soon as she heard anything.

She'd been in bed for more than an hour and not come anywhere close to sleep. She lay listening to the traffic passing outside, watching the moonlight flickering on the wallpaper, listening to the faint sound of conversations of people walking home from pubs and parties.

Part of her wanted to go to Gabriel's room. To knock on his door and just tell him what she was feeling. That she was finding it too hard to pretend to be his girlfriend—his fiancée—when her real feelings were so strong. She'd thought it every day since they had started this charade, the feeling growing by the day. Sitting in the pub with him tonight, listening to him talk, watching his face, noticing tiny details—the color of his eyes, the creases in his cheeks when he smiled, the way he used his hands to express himself. She wanted to touch his hands, kiss his face, be close to him . . .

She turned over in bed. It was impossible. She wasn't in a normal situation. Her family was crowding in on her, in her mind and in reality.

She had needed that New York break from them, from the part she played when she was with them. The role of bright, clever, loyal Maggie—daughter, niece, and granddaughter. She wanted to be something different than that. She wanted to be just Maggie. Her own person. Was that possible, though? If you were part of a family, was that family always with you, following you, surrounding you, enclosing you?

Certainly her grandfather thought so. Leo was so convinced everything could be made right, that all it needed was a bit of tweaking here, a bit of engineering there and, like one of his inventions, everything would fall into place. He would create the perfect happy family, memories of Tessa intact and Sadie back in the fold.

He was wrong. Maggie knew that. There was no such thing as a perfect, happy family. She knew that for sure because she had once believed there was. That she had been at the heart of one. Now she knew the truth. Her family was made up of layers and layers of lies and untruths and secrets, twisting and binding one member to the next. Maggie had thought it was just love that kept them close and connected. It was more than that. It was like a mathematical sum. Love plus lies plus secrets, truths, history, hopes, fear, and happiness. What did it equal, though? She wished she knew.

 * * *

Sadie couldn't get back to sleep. She and Larry had come upstairs to bed, made love, and then fallen asleep in each other's arms. Sadie's last thought before sleep had been contentment and certainty that she had made the right decision not to ring Maggie.

Now, as the digital clock beside her switched to three o'clock, she wasn't so sure. She'd woken with a start, perhaps by her own thoughts. She lay there, picturing Maggie. She'd barely had a chance to look at her yesterday. It had been a quick impression, a sudden knowledge that this was the grown-up version of that beautiful five-year-old. Then Larry arrived and she'd sent her away.

She'd sent Maggie away. It felt like a terrible thing to have done. She pictured her niece now, in the guesthouse just up the road. Sadie knew it well. She could even picture the rooms, the beds, the decoration.

It seemed extraordinary that Maggie was so close. How had she found her? After all these years, why had she tracked her down now? She knew now that the English journalist must have had something to do with it. But there were still so many questions. Was the whole family in Donegal? Did they all know Maggie was here, turning up on Sadie's doorstep? Were they in fact all staying at the guesthouse at this minute? And who was the American man? What part had he played in all of this?

Sadie thought of all the letters she had received from Maggie over the past twenty years. She'd watched her niece's handwriting change, her vocabulary increase and her life expand. She'd read stories of Maggie's trips to Melbourne and Sydney to stay with her other aunts. She'd heard about math competitions, university results, high-flying job offers, job placements in Canada and her move to London. She'd heard details of Leo's inventions, Clementine's study, Miranda's exploits, Eliza's accident and recovery and Juliet's business success. It was because of Maggie's letters that Sadie had been able to stay away. They had kept her in touch and allowed her to keep away at the same time.

She thought back to the days she and Maggie had spent together in Hobart all those years ago. The fun they'd had. The conversations. What good company Maggie had been. She could recall her expressions, her earnestness, her sense of fun. Another memory came to her, one she often liked to recall; one that had cheered her up so much when it happened in Melbourne and still cheered her up now. A five-year-old girl putting her arms around her neck and saying she had a secret. "You're my favorite auntie."

A favorite auntie wouldn't send her niece away after twenty years without talking to her first, no matter what the circumstances.

Sadie turned over in the bed and whispered. "Larry?"

"Mmm."

"Are you awake?"

"Mmm."

"I've just remembered, I have to go and see one of the suppliers tomorrow morning and we've got the weekly staff meeting. Do you mind going into the office early instead of me?"

"Of course not." His voice was thick with sleep. "They've all been pining for me anyway, have they?"

"Badly. Worse than me."

"I'll go in extra early, then."

"Thanks, Larry."

He put his arm around her and pulled her close in against his body. "You're welcome, love."

CHAPTER 43

M aggie rang down to the front desk three times before eight o'clock. The morning receptionist, a young Polish woman, was polite each time.

"I'll put the call through to your room as soon as it comes."

"It's just I don't know if she'll ask for me by my full name or what. She might just say Maggie. Or it might be Maggie Faraday."

"Whatever she calls you, I'll put her through."

The phone beside the bed rang at exactly eight thirty. Maggie snatched it up. "Hello, Maggie speaking."

"Maggie, it's Sadie." It sounded like she was calling from a mobile phone.

"Sadie. Hello." So much to say and no way to say it over the phone. "How are you?"

"I'm fine. I'm good. How are you?"

"Good."

"And the others?"

"Everyone's good."

"Are you all up in Donegal?"

"How did you know that?"

"From your letters, Maggie. You're a very good letter writer."

"So are you." She paused. "Well, actually, no you're not. But you're a good card writer." They both laughed awkwardly.

"I'm sorry about last night. I must have seemed rude."

"It's fine."

"My husband doesn't know about you, Maggie. About any of my family."

"He doesn't? But—"

Sadie interrupted. "Maggie, how did you find me?"

"Leo hired a detective."

"After all these years?"

"He found a photograph . . ." She told Sadie the whole story. She was babbling, she knew that. She could tell that Sadie was listening intently to every word, though. She looked down and saw that her free hand was clenched. She made herself breathe deeply. This was her aunt. It was Sadie. "Will you meet me, Sadie? Can I come to your house again? Talk to you?"

"You can't, Maggie. I can't see you here. It's too difficult."

"Somewhere else then? Wherever you want."

Sadie suggested a meeting place in the nearby Phoenix Park. The polo grounds, just next to the zoo. There was a car park beside the pavilion. It was usually quiet, she said, especially this time of day. They could take a walk from there.

"I won't have much time, Maggie, I'm sorry."

"I can be there as quickly as you like."

They agreed to meet in fifteen minutes. Maggie immediately rang through to Gabriel's room and told him the news. He sounded happy for her. "I'll meet you in reception to give you the car keys."

"You're not coming?"

"Don't you want to be on your own?"

"I'd like it if you were there too."

"Then of course I'll come."

.   .   .

Maggie and Gabriel arrived first. It was a beautiful summer morning. There was the glow of soft sunlight through the trees, highlighting the clipped green neatness of the polo playing field and the fresh white paint of the pavilion, with its border decoration of colorful window boxes, each one tumbling with flowers. They heard the faint hum of traffic, the noise of a mower far off in the distance and bursts of birdsong. Maggie could see deer grazing under a nearby copse of trees. Gabriel pointed out a squirrel darting across the grass, its tail an upright flash of white.

They heard Sadie's car arriving before they saw it.

"Wish me luck," Maggie said to Gabriel again.

"You still don't need it," he said.

It felt different from the start. This time they hugged. Maggie moved toward her and Sadie opened her arms straightaway.

"Maggie," she said. "Let me look at you." She took a step back, still holding onto Maggie's shoulders, staring at her intently. "You were gorgeous as a child and you're even lovelier now. You're beautiful."

"I'm not, but thank you. But you are. You look wonderful." Close up, Maggie saw the bloom in Sadie's cheeks, the laughter lines around her eyes. She had a contented face. A happy face.

"Not wonderful or beautiful. I never was. But you are." She reached across and tucked Maggie's hair behind her ears. "And so are these. I'm glad they never changed."

"Your daughter got off more lightly than me."

Sadie tensed. "You've seen Maudie?"

"Just a photograph. The detective . . ." She briefly explained.

Sadie smiled then at the mention of her daughter. "I noticed her ears the moment she was born. But they were never as lovely as yours."

Her name was Maudie. It felt funny to hear her name, the cousin she had never met.

Their conversation was just skimming the surface, both of them as nervous as the other, Maggie was sure of it.

"Who is that with you?" Sadie asked, nodding toward the car. "The man from yesterday?"

"Gabriel. He's a friend of mine. From New York."

"New York?"

"I've been living there for the past three months."

"You have? You didn't tell me that."

"I've told you all about it in my Christmas letter. You haven't got it yet?"

"Not yet. Those priests aren't always the most reliable of post-men, I have to admit."

"I've sent you writing paper again. You're probably sick of it by now."

"No, never, Maggie. I promise you."

There was another pause, a sudden awkward moment. Maggie hurried to fill it. "I don't know where to start, what to say. I don't even know what to call you. I can't think of you as Sally."

"Then call me Sadie. I don't mind, not here. We're on our own."

They started walking. They moved away from Sadie's car, taking a path that wound its way alongside iron fencing. It was the bound-ary of the President of Ireland's house and grounds, Sadie ex-plained. They'd see the house itself in a few minutes. Casual facts, filling the spaces and easing them past the first strange moments.

Sadie raised the subject first. "Why are you here, Maggie? Why now, after all these years?"

"Leo wants to see you."

Sadie nodded, but didn't answer.

"He wants you back."

Still nothing.

"He's an old man," Maggie said. "He's nearly eighty. I think he's trying to make everything as right as he can."

"I understand that. I promise you I do." They walked a short dis-tance before she spoke again. "I can't see him, Maggie. I left a long time ago. I'm too different now. I'm a different person. I can't go back."

There was no time to hedge around. She needed to ask the main questions. "Sadie, why did you go?"

"For lots of reasons. And I can't come back for even more rea-sons."

"It was the diaries that made you leave, wasn't it? Tessa's diaries?"

Sadie stopped walking. "You know about them? Leo told you?" Her hand moved toward her neck.

Maggie recognized the gesture from the previous day. A sign of anxiety. She explained everything. She owed it to her aunt. She told her about Leo arriving in New York, asking Maggie to read the diaries, needing to know if Sadie had left because she'd learned that Bill was her father.

"That's what he thought?" She was upset. "It wasn't anything like that. Leo must have read the diaries himself. He must have known exactly why I left."

"He's never read them, Sadie. He was always worried there was something in them about Bill and Tessa. He said he couldn't face it if there was."

Sadie's face was suddenly hard. "Leo has lived his whole life like that."

A week ago, Maggie would have defended her grandfather. Now she couldn't. Sadie was right. "I've read the diaries, Sadie. I finished them yesterday."

They were now facing each other on the path. "And what did you think?"

"What did I think?" Maggie didn't hesitate. "I thought Tessa was a horrible, mean old witch, actually."

Sadie started to laugh. Really laugh. A release of tension rather than the moment being funny. "I suppose that's one way to put it."

"I'm sorry, Sadie. I know she was your mother but I didn't like her. I thought she was selfish and cruel and conceited." She had to say it. She had to acknowledge the worst part of Tessa's diaries. "And she was awful to you. From the very beginning."

"Yes, she was."

"You must have felt terrible. You must have wanted to get as far away as you could when you read those things."

Sadie didn't answer that. She didn't need to.

There was more walking and more silence before Sadie spoke again. "It was my own fault. I shouldn't have been snooping in Leo's shed. I should have put the diaries back, forgotten all about them. Or told the others." Her first mention of her sisters. "But I couldn't do it. I was desperate to read them. Desperate to know something my sisters didn't. And once I started reading I couldn't stop, Maggie. Even after the first pages, when I realized that the Tessa I thought I remembered, the Tessa Leo had always spoken about, was a sham. A fake. That the Tessa in the diaries was the real one. Not a loving mother, not a caring wife, but a—" She tried to find the words. "What did you call her, Maggie?"

"A horrible, mean old witch."

"I tried not to think that. She was my mother. I tried to like her. I tried to see beyond her words, tried to excuse her—that she was young, she was just letting off steam. Sometimes I almost did like her. She was very funny sometimes. So witty. Mean about people but in a very clever way. She actually reminded me of Miranda. Or at least Miranda reminded me of her."

Maggie nodded. "Me too," she said quietly.

"I was so excited to read them. I used to go down to the shed as often as I could and read just a few pages—save them up, like a treat. Someone else might have skipped ahead to their own birth, but it was like reading a secret novel about our family. I wanted to go with the story, watch it unfold, even though I knew the ending. At least, I thought I knew the ending. I hadn't known about Bill and Tessa being lovers, so that was the first shock. And then Leo coming onto the scene, falling head-over-heels in love with her. It was like eavesdropping on the past, seeing them get married, Juliet arrive, Miranda arrive, Eliza arrive, all so quickly." She went quiet again for a little while. Maggie wanted to touch her, console her, but Sadie was keeping her distance now. "Then I arrived, Maggie, and spoiled everything."

"You didn't. You can't see it that way."

"I couldn't find any other way to see it. I still can't. It was the truth. Tessa didn't like me from the start and she certainly didn't love me. I annoyed her, I bored her, I drove her crazy. She found good things to write about all of the others, but there was never anything like that about me. Not one funny story, not one nice observation. I know, Maggie, because I read back over them, twice, to check."

Twenty years on and Maggie could see how hurt Sadie still was, how fresh all the memories of the diaries still were.

"I was the runt of the family, you see. Perhaps you don't remember reading that, Maggie, but they were Leo's words for me. I was the one to feel sorry for. The one to pity. Perhaps he loved me—I think he did, more than Tessa did in any case—but he wasn't proud of me. He wasn't amused by me. He didn't have great hopes for me. That's what hurt so badly. I'd always had a feeling he treated me differently than he treated the others, but I'd never realized what it was. It only became clear when I read the diaries."

Maggie did remember Leo's words. Sadie's memory was perfect.

"I couldn't stay there. Not knowing what I knew—that not only was I a disappointment to Leo in my adult life, but I'd been an annoyance to my mother as a child too. Not just an annoyance—a bore. I couldn't bear to hear Leo talk about Tessa as that angel, to go through the rituals year after year in her memory. I found it hard enough to be part of the family as it was, never being able to keep up with Miranda's wit, fighting with Juliet all the time, annoying Eliza, even Clementine—" She hesitated there. "Especially Clementine, in the last few years."

"After I was born?"

Sadie nodded.

"What happened, Sadie? Why did you take me with you that time? You must have known how upset everyone would be."

Sadie turned and looked at her then. "Because when I got to Melbourne and I decided I wasn't going back, I couldn't say good-bye to you. I loved you too much, Maggie. I knew you loved me too. And back then I needed all the love I could get."

Maggie didn't ask, she just acted on impulse. She closed the gap between them and hugged her aunt close.

When Sadie drew back, her eyes were filled with tears. "I was running for my life, Maggie, and I just took you with me. I didn't even think about them, about how they would feel. I look back and it's truly as if I had gone mad. I have Maudie now. I can't begin to imagine how Clementine must have felt. If someone took Maudie—" She shook her head. "I'm lucky that Clementine didn't kill me."

"Leo said she came close."

"I must have caused her so much pain. I still can't forgive myself for doing that, even though I know why I did."

"But what about Leo, Sadie? He's your father. He's been so sad to lose you. Don't you want to see him? To write to him at least?"

"It's not that simple. I've thought about it so much over the years and I've never been able to decide the best thing to do. Part of me wants to see him, but I know that every time I looked at him, I would remember he thought of me as the failure of his family. And I would become that person. I would become all those things Tessa said about me in her diaries. I know it would happen. And I can't do it, Maggie. Because I know whatever each of us is like outside our family, in our own lives, as soon as we came together, it would be like those days again. Can I guess what they're like? Miranda as sharp-tongued as ever, but getting away with it because she's funny? Juliet trying to mother everyone? Eliza still on her high horse?"

Maggie didn't need to answer. Sadie was right.

"And Clementine?" Sadie continued. "Would she ever be able to forgive me, trust me with you? I don't think so, and I can't blame her. It's as if each of us was somehow assigned a role to play in our family and I got the short straw. It wouldn't matter what I've done with my life since then, all I've achieved, no matter that I have Larry and a successful business and Maudie and a grandchild on the way—"

"A *grandchild*? You're going to be a grandmother?"

Sadie nodded, a beautiful smile appearing on her face. "Maudie's seven months pregnant. She's only young, not nineteen yet, but she's in a great relationship. Larry and I are very happy about it."

There were so many questions Maggie wanted to ask. "How did you meet Larry? How did you get to be here?" She managed a laugh. "What have you been doing for the past twenty years?"

Sadie told Maggie the bare facts of her story. She described the months after she left Hobart. Meeting Larry. Starting their business together; getting married; having Maudie. Coming to Ireland. She told her about the fake stories; her pretend background. The reason why Maggie couldn't ever meet Larry or Maudie.

Maggie listened intently to every word. She imagined herself in Sadie's position. Sadie kept calling it "being on the run." It didn't sound like that to Maggie. It sounded brave. She told her as much.

"I didn't feel brave. I felt desperate and scared. I felt like I'd made a mess of my life. And I know that if I was to see Leo—to see all of them—again, I'd go straight back to being that old Sadie. And I didn't like being her. I don't ever want to be her again."

Maggie understood. More than Sadie could have known. Hadn't she spent most of her adult life trying to be each of the different nieces her aunts wanted her to be?

"I would never have hurt you," Sadie said again. "They thought you were in danger, but you never were."

"I wish I could remember."

"You can't remember anything from that time?"

"I don't think so. If I think back to my childhood it's just women everywhere, and Leo in the middle of it." She smiled again. "I still have your scrapbook, you know."

"You do?"

"Of course."

"I thought Clementine would have thrown it out."

"She might have wanted to, but she didn't. I still love it. Did you do that for Maudie?"

"No, I did something different for her."

"Can I meet her, Sadie? Can I meet Larry?"

Sadie didn't hesitate. "I'm sorry, Maggie, but you can't. You are from one part of my life and they are from another part. I can't mix the two. I don't dare, in case I lose my own family. And I couldn't bear that."

"You don't want to see the others? Not even Leo?"

"I can't, Maggie. I just can't."

"He loves you. He misses you. I know he does. He's been like a driven man since he tracked you down. He's gone to so much trouble. If he could just see you—talk to you. Know that you're all right."

"He knows I'm all right. That's why I send you that card every year."

"If he even saw you just for a minute, Sadie. So he could see that you're okay. Even if he spoke to you on the phone."

Sadie shook her head.

Maggie had to try again, for Leo's sake. "Sadie, why not? It would mean so much to him—"

"Why not?" All the hurt, the pain and the vulnerability was suddenly visible on Sadie's face. "Because I'm too scared, Maggie. Because I know how fragile a good life is. How flimsy good luck is. I could have gone another way, but I met Larry, we had Maudie and piece by piece I have rebuilt and remade my life. And if I let Leo in, then there will be a crack, a tiny chink in that life, and I risk it all. Because what if that one conversation isn't enough for him, or for me? What if I want to see him again? If I want him to meet Larry and Maudie? If I tell him he's about to become a great-grandfather? When would it stop? Where would it end? In ruin. It would all come tumbling down around me again and I don't know if I could rebuild my life again. I don't know if I can be this lucky twice."

Maggie didn't say anything. She felt her eyes well with tears, but if they were for Sadie, or Leo, or for all of her family, she didn't know.

"I'm sorry, Maggie." Sadie's voice was soft.

"You don't have to apologize to me."

"But I do. Because I'm about to ask you to do something difficult. I need you to promise me that you won't tell Leo, or your mother or your aunts, that you've seen me."

"Sadie, I—"

"You have to promise me, Maggie. Please. I didn't ask anyone to come looking for me. I need you to respect my privacy. My whole family's privacy."

Sadie's whole family. A different, new family.

"What do I say to Leo?"

"I don't know. I don't mind what you say to him. Tell him it wasn't me. That the detective made a mistake. Whatever you think is best."

"What if he comes looking for you himself?"

"He won't if you tell him that it was all a mistake. That it wasn't me."

"I can't even tell him you're okay? Give him a message from you? A hello? Anything?"

Sadie didn't answer her that time. She just shook her head.

Maggie didn't push her again. It was clear that Sadie had made up her mind. "Can I keep writing to you?"

"Of course you can. I'd hate it if you didn't."

"Will you write back to me, properly? Not just a card? Tell me about your granddaughter? I can give you my address."

"I need to keep things the way they are, Maggie."

"But can I see you? If I come back to Ireland again?" She didn't say next July. She didn't know yet whether there would be another July Christmas here.

"I don't know. I need to think about that."

They walked back toward the two cars. Gabriel was still sitting inside their car.

"What happened to your boyfriend in London?" Sadie asked.

"We ended it."

"And this man? Is he more than a friend? Is he—?"

"No. But he's a very good friend. Would you like to meet him? He knows, not all of it, but a lot of it—"

Sadie stopped again. "I'm sorry, Maggie, but no. I don't think it's a good idea. I shouldn't even have asked you about him. I need to keep a distance from anyone connected with the family. If I met him, I know I would want to know more, talk to you both. I already have so many things I want to ask you and I can't. It wouldn't be fair to you or to me. It would get even more complicated. I'm sorry. I hope you understand."

"I do. And so will he."

Sadie glanced at her watch. "I have to go, Maggie. I'm late already."

"Thank you for coming, Sadie."

Sadie smiled. A sad smile. "Thank *you* for coming, Maggie."

"I miss you. I wish you hadn't gone away."

"I miss you too."

Maggie felt the tears welling again. She didn't try to stop them.

They hugged each other, close and tight. Sadie pulled back first. "Let me look at you again, one more time."

"You're just double-checking my ears stick out more than Maudie's."

Sadie smiled. "Yours win, Maggie. I promise. They were always the best in the world." She hugged her again. "Thank you, for understanding and for listening and for finding me. I can't stop you from saying anything. It's up to you. But I won't go back, Maggie. If I ever had doubts, I haven't now. I can't. All I ask is that you please don't spoil what I have. What my life is now. I couldn't bear it if I lost Larry and Maudie, and I'm scared I would if they found out. Perhaps I'm wrong, but I can't risk it."

"I won't do anything to hurt you, I promise."

"Thank you, Maggie."

They hugged once more before Sadie got into her car, waved and drove away. Maggie stood and waved until her aunt had driven out of sight.

•   •   •

Gabriel didn't get out of the car until Sadie was gone. She walked toward him. It felt natural and right for him to open his arms, to be enfolded in a hug. It felt good to be close to him, to feel his arms around her back. To feel his chest against her cheek, to breathe in the scent of his body. She wanted to stay there.

"Are you okay?"

She pulled back from him, reluctantly, then nodded. "I'm so glad to have seen her."

"And does she want to come to Donegal? See everyone?"

"No. She won't even consider it."

Gabriel didn't ask why not. She was grateful for his understanding. She needed time to think it through before she could talk more about it.

"What will you tell Leo?"

"I can't tell him anything. Sadie doesn't want me to. She asked me to promise."

"Not even a message?"

"Nothing."

"But he's seen the photograph."

"I have to say it wasn't her. She's asked me to do it."

"But Leo—"

"I know. What can I do?" She was in an impossible position. Caught between a promise and a lie. If she honored what Sadie had asked, she had to lie to Leo. If she honored Leo, she would break her promise to Sadie. She also knew that Leo wouldn't leave it at knowing that Sadie was all right. He would come to Dublin to see her. Complication upon complication.

Maggie was sure of only one thing at that moment. "I wish we hadn't found her, Gabriel. That Leo hadn't seen that photo and tracked her down. I wish it hadn't been her. Because what choice do I have but to lie to him? To tell him that we made a mistake? Even if I told him the truth it would break his heart. That it was her, that I spoke to her, but she doesn't ever want to see him again or have anything to do with us as a family. The only good thing I can tell him is that Bill isn't her father. That I finished the diaries and I know that for sure."

"That's something, isn't it? That will give him some solace?"

"But it won't, don't you see? Because once he hears that, he'll want to read the diaries. He'll decide that he can, because the thing that he feared most isn't in it. And then what happens? He reads all the terrible things Tessa said about him. The way she thought about her life, how bored she was with him, how she felt about Hobart. The terrible things she said about Sadie. He feels bad enough about Sadie being gone. The truth about Tessa would destroy him."

Gabriel was silent for a little while. "It all comes back to the diaries, doesn't it?"

Maggie thought about it. He was right. None of this would be happening if Tessa hadn't written them. If Leo had destroyed them as he said he had. If Sadie hadn't found them. And now she, Maggie, had read them and the knowledge of them felt like a bruise, something bad inside her, something she wished she didn't know. "I can't do it, Gabriel. I can't take them back to him and hand them over and say, 'Sorry, it wasn't Sadie and here, read these.' "

"What else can you do, though? Tell him that you met her? You can't. You promised Sadie."

"I can't break that promise. But I don't have to give him back the diaries."

"But you do. He's kept them for so many years. What are you going to do with them?"

Maggie looked around, anxious, upset. "I wish I could destroy them. Here and now. Get rid of them. Get them out of my family, out of our lives."

"They're not yours to do that with, Maggie."

"Whose are they, then? They were Tessa's. She apparently told Leo to burn them and he didn't. So they're not lawfully his property any more than they are my property, are they? They shouldn't belong to anyone."

"You have to let Leo decide that."

"But I can't, Gabriel, can't you see? Perhaps he decides not to read them, then what? He hides them away somewhere else. And then he dies one day, and who finds them? Miranda? Juliet? My mother? Eliza? And then they'd be angry with him for lying to them all these years. And they would; I know they would. They dearly wanted to read them all those years ago and he said they were gone. And once the anger with Leo passed, what next? They would read them and they would feel as sick as I did. Even worse, because it was their mother. And believe me, Gabriel, she's not the mother any of them would want to remember."

"I still think you have to give them back."

"I don't."

"Maggie—"

"She was *my* grandmother. I have a say in this too. And I want to destroy her diaries before they hurt my family even more." She took a breath. "You know what I wish, Gabriel? I wish the park rangers had decided today was the perfect day to have a big bonfire. And I wish I could take those diaries, throw them onto the flames and watch them turn to ashes. It's what Leo should have done thirty-five years ago."

"But what would you tell him?"

"That I'd tripped and accidentally thrown them into the fire. All nine of them."

"You could, I guess." Gabriel changed position, and leaned back against the car. He was quiet for a moment. "I meant to tell you, I read a very interesting article in the paper at breakfast this morning."

"Did you?" she said, puzzled, even a bit annoyed, at the change of subject.

He nodded. "Apparently Dublin has one of the highest levels of petty crime in Europe. Car theft and vandalism, especially. Particularly directed at tourists' cars. It's terrible, I believe. Tourists come back to their cars and discover they've been broken into and bags taken, contents and all. It's happening all the time, apparently."

"It is?"

He nodded. "The thieves take whatever happens to be lying on the backseat."

Maggie looked into their backseat, at her bag containing the diaries.

"They don't even have to smash the windows sometimes," Gabriel said. "Apparently the tourists often forget to lock the car properly. They leave a back window open."

"And the thieves just reach in and take things?"

Gabriel nodded.

"And what do the tourists say to their families when they get home? To their grandfather, for example?" Maggie stopped all pretense that they were talking hypothetically. "Would Leo believe it?"

Before Gabriel had a chance to reply, she answered her own question. "He would have to, wouldn't he? Because the diaries would be gone."

She thought about it. She imagined knowing the diaries were no more and that no one else, not Leo, not Clementine, not any of her aunts, could read them, deliberately or accidentally. She felt immediate relief—a lifting of stress and worry. Tessa's words would be silenced, as they should have been silenced many years before.

There was only one obstacle. It would mean lying to Leo. Not only about Sadie, which was going to be hard enough, but about the theft of the diaries. She would have to lie to the man she had loved all her life, who had looked after her and encouraged her and spoiled her for as long as she could remember. She didn't know if she could do it.

Then she thought of the alternative. Everyone reading Tessa's words. The distress that would cause. She thought of the story she had been told all her life, about Sadie running away to become a hippie. She thought of Leo's stories about Tessa, the myth he had created around her. She thought of Clementine and her aunts being told the diaries had been burned, when all that time Leo had kept them.

Maggie knew then that she could lie if she had to. It was a Faraday family tradition, after all.

CHAPTER 44

As they drove up the laneway to the house five hours later, Maggie felt calm. She and Gabriel had gone over all the possible scenarios. Gabriel had posed different questions that Leo might ask. She hoped she could answer them all.

They had decided not to stay in Dublin any longer. They returned to the guesthouse, gathered their bags and checked out. They were on the road to Donegal by ten. Maggie didn't phone or text Leo to let him know they were on their way. She knew he would want to know how she had got on. She needed to wait until she saw him face-to-face.

They made a stop on the way out of Dublin. Gabriel had asked at the guesthouse. There was a recycling station on the main road from Dublin to Donegal. They did it together, standing in front of the metal bin, tearing each diary up one by one. Gabriel had asked her before they started if she was sure. There was a moment when she could have changed her mind. She could have put the diaries back in the bag, gone back to the car, returned to Donegal and handed them all back to Leo.

No. Getting rid of them was hard. The alternative would be worse.

"Do you want to do it yourself?" he asked.

She shook her head. "It'll be quicker if we both do it."

It took less than five minutes. She left her brown leather bag beside the bin. It was a small price to pay.

He gently touched her arm as they walked side by side back to the car. "Are you all right?"

Was she? She didn't know yet. She had no regrets about getting rid of the diaries. She was glad to leave them behind, glad to have seen Tessa's words being ripped up and thrown away. What she felt uncertain about was telling Leo. How to lie to him.

Three hours into the journey they stopped for lunch. It was Gabriel's idea. He called into a small store in a village just over the border into Northern Ireland, came back with two bags and wouldn't tell her what was in them. Half an hour later, as they passed into County Fermanagh, the expanse of Lough Erne appeared. Maggie hadn't even noticed it on the journey down, her attention too taken with the diaries. She gazed out at it now. It stretched for as far as she could see, a silver-blue expanse of rippling color, dotted with tiny tree-covered islands, a shadow fringe of dark-purple mountains visible on its farthest reaches.

Gabriel indicated right, taking a small lane off the main road, through a thicket of trees. They emerged into a small picnic area right on the shore of the lake. The sunlight glittered off the surface. It was a beautiful spot.

"Water, sunlight and a picnic area. You think of everything," Maggie said.

"No, I don't. I checked the Charter of Fake Fiancés again this morning. It's very strict on the issue of picnics. A necessity, apparently. Especially when one of the fake fiancées has had a difficult couple of days."

They didn't have a blanket but he spread out his jacket for her to sit on. He unpacked the bag. There was brown bread, olives, smoked salmon and cheese.

Maggie was very touched. "Gabriel West, you are the kindest man I've ever met."

"Really?" He looked up from unwrapping the bread, his face serious. "I'm not, you know. I entered a poll to find the Kindest Man in New York last year and I came in last. I let myself down on the helping old ladies across the road question. I said, let them be independent. Let them run free. Let them find their own way across the road. Apparently that was the wrong answer."

She smiled. "You're also the funniest."

"No, that's not true either. There were five hundred and three funnier men than me."

"The best looking?"

"No. I came equal two hundredth with a troll."

"Most talented singer?"

Another shake of his head. "Came in last, behind a howling dog and a fire siren."

He sat down beside her, stretched out his legs and leaned back on his arms. He had rolled up his shirtsleeves and his forearms were bare. Maggie noticed the muscles on his arms. His tanned skin. Sitting this close, she also noticed the color of his eyes. She'd thought they were a dark hazel. She saw now that they were a very dark blue. She saw the laughter lines again, the ready smile. She meant what she'd said. He was the best-looking man she'd ever seen.

"You just can't take a compliment, can you?" she said.

"Where do you want me to take it? See, I'm not funny. That's why I did so badly in the poll." He smiled and dipped his head. "How ungracious of me. Thank you, Maggie. While we're on the subject, I think you are very kind too. And very funny. And very good-looking. You're beautiful, in fact. And talented too. Scarily talented, from what your aunts have told me. I can't even add up. Four plus four is nine. See?"

"I might be able to add up but I can't play the guitar or sing."

"You can't? What a relief. We're equals then."

"It looks that way."

"Neck and neck."

She nodded.

He was just inches away from her. Just the two of them, alone, in the sunlight, looking out over a beautiful lake.

"We couldn't get any closer," he said.

"No, we couldn't."

Kiss him. The voice was strong in her head. Kiss him, Maggie.

He beat her to it. Leaning across, he gently kissed her on the lips. She kissed him back. His arms came around her. Another kiss, gentle, exploratory, slowly building, slowly becoming more passionate . . .

Two cars drove down the laneway, halting inches from theirs. Eight doors opened to produce four adults, five noisy children and a barking dog.

Maggie moved away. Gabriel sat up. She knew her cheeks were flushed. She could see that Gabriel's eyes had darkened. They just looked at each other for a moment, before Gabriel spoke very matter-of-factly.

"So, I was thinking of doing something along those lines every time Miranda comes into the room, if that's all right with you? Just to pull the wool over her eyes."

"That's fine. That's great," Maggie said.

The moment was lost. They finished their lunch quickly, surrounded on all sides by the two families, a ball bouncing across their picnic at one point, followed by an apologetic smile from one of the women. They packed everything back into the car. Maggie was about to get into the passenger seat again when Gabriel spoke.

"Maggie, could you hold on for a minute there?"

He came around to her side, leaned down and kissed her again. Just like that. He skipped the gentle stage and went straight to the deep, stirring stage. Maggie kissed him back. It lasted only a minute but her head was spinning as she stepped away.

A child watching down by the water's edge made a bad attempt at a wolf whistle. "That man kissed that lady, Mammy."

Gabriel smiled. "I hate not finishing something I started, don't you?"

Maggie could only nod.

As they drove into the yard of the house now, she asked Gabriel to beep the horn five times.

"Let me guess, a family tradition?"

She expected her mother or her aunts, even Leo, to appear.

None of them did. That was odd. She noticed the front door was open. They were all still home, then. They decided to leave their bags in the car and walked across the gravel into the house.

Maggie knew as soon as they came into the living room that something had happened. They were all seated: Leo, Miranda, Clementine, Eliza, and Juliet. They were serious-faced. There were no greetings, nothing.

"What is it?" Maggie said, alarmed. "What's happened?"

There was an exchange of glances. They all looked toward Miranda.

Her expression didn't give anything away. "We had a phone call this morning, Maggie," she said. "From America. From New York, to be precise."

Maggie glanced at Gabriel, standing beside her. It was the call he'd told her he'd arranged. "Is everything all right?"

"Not particularly, no," Miranda said. Her voice was very cold. She was now looking at Gabriel, not Maggie. "It was Gabriel's girlfriend. She was wondering when he was coming home."

Maggie spun around and looked up at Gabriel. She was shocked. More than shocked. She felt Miranda's eyes on hers. She sensed her pleasure. She could almost hear her thoughts. *Told you so, Maggie.*

Gabriel ran his hand through his hair. He didn't look at her. He didn't say anything.

"Gabriel?" Maggie said.

"Lost for words, Gabriel?" Miranda said, unfurling herself from her seat. She strolled across the room and leaned against the table next to them. "She sounded lovely. So polite. She's missing you, she said. We had such a nice chat. I have to say, she was a bit surprised to hear you'd been here for the past few days with your fiancée and your fiancée's family, though."

Maggie stared back and forth between the two of them.

Gabriel was still silent.

Miranda was triumphant. "I told her everything I could. She was so interested. I told her you've been seeing Maggie for the past three months. That you were engaged to Maggie, in fact. That you seemed to be head over heels about her. Or should I say head over heels about what you thought you could get out of her."

Gabriel finally spoke. "You're wrong, Miranda. It wasn't like that." He looked at Maggie. "I'm sorry you found out like this, Maggie. I should have told you."

"You have a girlfriend?" Maggie said.

Gabriel nodded. "We've been together for—"

Miranda interrupted. "Eighteen months, she told me. Susanna, her name is, Gabriel, in case you've forgotten that as well. You know, she didn't sound that surprised to hear about Maggie. Is this something you've done before? Perhaps you were in on this together? Is it a little game you like to play?"

"It wasn't like that, Miranda. Maggie, I hope you believe that."

Maggie felt Clementine come up behind her, felt her mother's arms wrap around her. Across the room, Eliza looked angry. Juliet shocked. Leo just looked stunned.

Maggie didn't know what to say or do. Should she tell them the truth, that Gabriel wasn't her fiancé? That he was entitled to have a dozen girlfriends in New York waiting for him to come home? She realized she couldn't do it. She felt as though it was true. That she had just discovered her beloved fiancé had been deceiving her.

He touched her arm. She stepped back, pure reflex. "Maggie, I'm so sorry. All I can say is that I never meant to hurt you. I just couldn't decide between the two of you."

"But I can't understand. Were you going to break up with her or with me?" She asked as if it were true. It felt true.

He gave an embarrassed smile. "I was actually hoping to keep you both going."

She couldn't stop herself. She slapped him, across the face. The face she had been kissing less than an hour before.

"Maggie, no!" Clementine pulled her back. She was led out of the living room into the kitchen. A cup of tea was placed in her hands. She felt dazed. In the background, she heard Miranda's voice.

"I'm sure I'm speaking on behalf of the whole Faraday family,

Gabriel, when I say that we'd like you to leave. Right now. Go and pack your things."

"But what about the filming?"

Miranda laughed. "You actually think we'd let you continue filming us? That we'd want you around any longer?"

"I promised Leo."

"It's all right, Gabriel." Leo spoke at last. "Miranda's right. I think you should leave. If you get your bags, I'll drive you to the airport."

"You will not, Leo." Miranda again. "There's a bus from Glencolmcille. Let him take that."

Maggie could hear every word. "He can't take the bus," she said to her mother. "That's a terrible way to treat him."

Clementine put her hand on her shoulder. "Let Miranda deal with this, Maggie. She's good in these sorts of situations."

Through the doorway, Maggie could see Gabriel talking to Leo. Her grandfather was pointing at the camera equipment. Miranda stood beside them, her arms crossed. Juliet and Eliza were still sitting on the sofa, looking stunned. When Gabriel finished explaining whatever it was to Leo, he left the room. To pack, Maggie guessed.

It was all too unreal. She didn't want it to end like this. She turned into her mother's arms and let herself be hugged. She was still there, a minute later, when she heard the sound of a car. No beeping horn, just the engine. She waited for it to go past, to the houses farther up the road. It didn't. It drove in through the gate, pulled into the yard, stopped just meters from the front door. It was a silver car with Irish registration plates.

"Who on earth is that?" Clementine said, letting go of Maggie. "They nearly drove into the house."

She didn't have to wait long to find out. The front door flew open.

"Is Juliet here?"

It was Myles.

He stood in the hallway, looked left into the kitchen, right into the living room.

Juliet stood up. "Myles? What are you doing here?"

"What am I doing here?" He didn't look at any of the others in the room. He stood in the doorway, reached inside his jacket and took out a letter. "Why do you think, Juliet?"

"Please, Myles. Not in front of everyone."

He acknowledged them then. He nodded to Leo, to the others. His attention returned to Juliet. "We have to talk some time, Juliet. Why not now? Let them hear. It feels like they've been part of our entire marriage anyway."

"Myles, please."

Myles was very upset. "It's true, isn't it? Princess Diana had nothing on us. What was it she said? 'There were three of us in this marriage.' What did we have? Six? Seven? Eight? All of your sisters, your niece, your father, your mother, through every tradition and ritual possible. Even now, Juliet? You leave me a note, telling me you're leaving me, and run and hide behind your family again? You don't even want to talk to me about it, to hear my side of it first?"

"It was the only way I could do it."

"The only way?"

Eliza silently got up and moved out of the room. Leo followed her. Miranda stayed where she was.

"I couldn't think of any other way to tell you."

Myles stepped forward. "You thought I would find your letter, shrug, and go, 'Oh well, those twenty years were good while they lasted. I wonder what's on TV tonight?' "

"I can't talk about this now. Not here."

"Yes, you can," Miranda said. "Don't mind me."

Juliet spun around. "Shut up, Miranda, would you?"

"I agree," Myles said. "If we want a smart remark, we'll ask for it, all right?"

Miranda glared at him. "Don't you talk to me like that. Don't you talk to my sister like this either. Who do you think you are, barging in here like this?"

"Who do I think I am? I'm her husband, Miranda. That's why I can come barging in here like this. I'm her husband and I am try-

ing to save our marriage. And I'll tell you why. Because I love your
sister one hundred times more than you do. I care about her one
hundred times more. I know her one hundred times better than
you. So don't you tell me about your sister and how I can or cannot
talk to her."

"Miranda, can you please leave?" Juliet said.

"Leave or stay, Miranda, I don't mind anymore," Myles said. "I
want all of this out in the open. It's been avoided for too long."

"I'm leaving," Miranda said. "But it's my choice to go."

Myles waited until she had left the room, then turned back to
Juliet.

"Did you mean it? You want to leave me?"

Her hands were shaking. She held them tightly together. "I have
to, Myles."

"But why?"

"Everything."

"I know it's about the children. I know you're hurting and it has
killed me to see it. I've tried to make it better. I've tried to keep us
busy. But I can't change the world, Juliet. I can't make life fair. I
can't fix it for you. All I can do is tell you over and over again that I
love you, that I will do all I can to make you happy. But I can't live
with the blame every second of every day for something that isn't
my fault."

"You made me wait to have children. You told me over and over
again to wait, to put it off. And so I did."

"I didn't know we'd have trouble. If I had known, do you truly
think I would have said that? Why would I want to hurt you like
that? You think that's why I wanted to marry you, to give you a really terrible life?"

"You were never as sad about it as I was."

"Of course I was sad. But I can't stay sad forever. I can't spend
every day being sad when I keep finding things not to be sad about.
The rest of our lives, our business, us. They don't cancel out the
other sadness but they give me something else to think about. We
aren't parents, no, but we are bloody good businesspeople. We care

about our staff. We care about our cafés, the food we serve. I'm trying to see all the positive things around us and all you ever see are
the bad things."

"I can't help it. It's how I feel."

"I know that. And it breaks my heart to see it." Myles's voice softened. "You've gone behind a glass wall, Juliet. Ten feet high, two
feet thick. It didn't matter what I said, you wouldn't listen to me. I
thought I just needed to stay patient, to keep waiting and hoping
you'd see things the way I did. And then this." He looked down at
the letter. "I'm sorry, Juliet, but I don't accept it. I don't believe our
marriage is over yet. I know I still love you and I think, I hope—"
He stumbled over his words. "I hope that you still love me, somewhere deep down, underneath all of this sadness you've wrapped
yourself in. Because we do have a good life together, Juliet. We
don't have everything. We don't have the perfect happy ending,
but we still have a great deal. Don't forget the good things, Juliet,
please."

He moved toward her. She didn't turn away. She didn't stop him
when he gathered her close to him. "We can't end like this. Not
with a note. Not us. We've too much going for us. We've been
through too much already. We can get through this. I know we
can."

"I'm too sad, Myles. I'm too sad, every single day."

"Be sad. But tell me when you're sad and I'll tell you when I'm
sad. And maybe together we can try and be something else. Something other than sad all the time."

"But it's not what I wanted. I wanted us to have a family. I wanted
to be a mother. I wanted you to be a father."

"I wanted those things too. But it didn't happen for us. So we
have to do something else. We can't change it. We can't have what's
impossible for us."

"I know that. But I can't stop wanting it."

"You don't have to stop wanting it or feeling sad about it. You
just have to find a way to work around it. With me. For both of us."

Juliet began to cry, wrenching sobs from deep inside her. Myles
held her even closer.

CHAPTER 45

I n the kitchen, the others were all gathered around the table. Gabriel hadn't reappeared yet. The mood was quiet. Myles and Juliet's voices were just audible through the closed door. They'd heard the different rhythms, the raised voices. They could hear Juliet crying now.

Miranda opened her mouth as if to speak.

Eliza snapped. "No, Miranda. I'm sure you've thought of something funny and witty to say, but I don't want to hear it right now. I bet Clementine and Leo don't want to hear it, and I triple-bet Maggie doesn't want to hear it. She's had enough of a shock today as it is."

Miranda shut her mouth.

They stayed silent. They heard the murmur of voices from the living room again. Five more minutes passed before the door opened.

It was Juliet. They could see Myles standing in the room behind her. Her eyes were puffy, but she was calm. She managed a brief smile. "I'm sorry, everyone. You didn't need to hear all that."

They all spoke over one another, telling her it was fine, they were sorry.

She cut into their talk. "I've decided to leave today. I'm going home with Myles. We're going to go right away."

"Oh, Juliet," Leo said. "But what about—"

"Of course, Juliet." Clementine shot Leo a warning glance. "You do whatever's best for you both."

Juliet still looked teary. Myles came up behind her. She leaned back against him, taking the hand he put on her shoulder. "I'm sorry, Leo. I know I said I'd stay until the weekend. And I know it means I'm leaving you all with the cleaning and—"

"Juliet, it's fine," Eliza said. "We're fine. We'll manage."

"Speak for yourself, Eliza," Miranda said. "You couldn't rustle up a quick dinner for us before you leave, Juliet?"

There was a sharp intake of breath from Eliza. Clementine glared at Miranda. Even Leo was shocked. "Miranda, please—"

"It's just a joke," Miranda snapped. "Remember jokes? Those lines of words with something funny at the end of them?"

Juliet didn't seem bothered. "You're right, Miranda, I'm sorry. It is selfish of me." She let go of Myles's hand and moved past them all to the refrigerator. They watched as she opened it, leaned inside and took out a round glass dish. Without a word, she carried it across and emptied it over Miranda's lap. "There's your dinner, Miranda. One hour in a moderate oven. *Bon appetit.*"

She walked out, Myles following. They left behind a room of shocked people. Miranda looked down at her white linen pants, her silk top, now covered in tomatoes, herbs, pieces of chicken, and red wine.

"Has she gone absolutely mad?" She glared at the others. "Don't just stand there. Do something."

Clementine did. She started to laugh. Two seconds later, so did everyone else.

•   •   •

Over the next half hour, the house was all movement. Doors opening and closing, bags being fetched from the cloakroom under the stairs. Maggie helped Miranda clear up most of the tomato mess. They had just mopped the floor when Eliza appeared again. She was carrying her suitcase.

"I've decided to go today too. I'm going to get a lift to the airport with Myles and Juliet and try to change my flights when I get there."

Leo appeared behind her. He looked sad and old. Eliza had obviously just told him. "It's an exodus," he said. "Maggie, Gabriel's going to go with them. It makes sense, I suppose."

Maggie just nodded. She felt Clementine's presence behind her, felt a touch on her arm.

"Clementine, do you want to go today as well?" Leo asked, his expression forlorn. "Miranda, do you? Maggie?"

They all shook their heads.

Even if Maggie had wanted to leave, she couldn't. There'd been no chance to talk to Leo about Sadie yet. He would be desperate for news, she knew that. There had been no chance to talk to Gabriel either. Either by chance or design, he'd stayed out of the way during Juliet and Myles's confrontation. He was now back in the living room, packing the lighting equipment away. She couldn't read his expression from where she sat. There'd be no chance for privacy even if she did go in and talk to him. The others kept walking back and forth through the room.

She was too confused to know what to say to him, in any case. She knew she had no right to be upset with him. It had been a fake engagement. And of course he had a girlfriend. It would have been more surprising if he was single. She just wished he hadn't kissed her that afternoon. That she hadn't felt so attracted to him. That she hadn't begun to imagine that he was attracted to her too.

They were all soon ready to leave. Myles was anxious to get going, to try to make the early-evening flight to Manchester. The farewells were hurried. Maggie managed just a few minutes alone with Juliet, and even less with Eliza.

Juliet hugged her close. "I'm sorry about Gabriel, Maggie. I can't give you any advice, either. I obviously don't have a clue about relationships myself."

"Don't worry about me. Are you all right? Will you and Myles be all right?"

"I don't know yet. I didn't know he felt half of the things he said. I want to hear everything and I can't do that here."

Maggie hugged her again. "I'll ring you when I get back to New York."

"I'll probably ring you first."

Eliza hugged her too. "Don't forget my offer, will you? I want to help you as much as I can." She didn't mention Gabriel. It was as if she had wiped him out of her mind already.

In the kitchen, Miranda was still in her tomato-covered clothes, dabbing at them with a sponge, cursing under her breath. "No, I'm not changing yet. Let Juliet see the consequences of her actions. I've a good mind to send her the drycleaning bill."

Maggie glanced out the kitchen window. Gabriel was outside, leaning against the wall, looking out across the sea. She couldn't let him go without talking to him. She'd have to be quick. Myles was already at the car, loading in the bags. Juliet was in the living room saying good-bye to Leo. Eliza was looking for her jacket on the crowded coat-stand. This was her best chance, while everyone was occupied.

She was just opening the door to go out to him when she heard a voice.

"Don't, Maggie." It was Miranda.

"I need to talk to him," Maggie said.

"What on earth is there to say? Be dignified about this. He's the one who should be seeking you out. Let him crawl to you."

"I just want to say good-bye."

"I didn't trust him and I was right. He's a liar and a cheat."

"He's not. He's an honorable, kind, lovely man."

Maggie moved to go outside. Gabriel was standing in the doorway. If he'd heard what Miranda or Maggie had said, he didn't show it.

"I've come to say good-bye," he said, looking only at Maggie.

"Make it snappy, then," Miranda said. "Maggie wants to get on with her life."

He ignored her. "Maggie, I'm sorry it ended like this. Especially after today."

"Why?" Miranda said. "What happened today?"

Maggie spun around. "Miranda, could you please give me some privacy?"

"No," Miranda said. She crossed her arms. "I want to hear whatever he's got to say."

Maggie turned back to Gabriel. "I'm sorry too. Especially after today."

He hugged her. She hugged him back. He felt so good. She heard a whisper in her ear. "Bravo, fantastic performance."

She pulled back, startled. "What?"

Miranda was watching everything. "Don't listen to him, Maggie."

He kept his voice low. "When are you back in New York?"

"Sunday," she whispered, confused. What did it matter to him now?

"Don't fall for it, Maggie." Miranda's tone was stern.

Outside, Myles started the car. "I'd better go," Gabriel said, picking up his bag. "Good-bye, Maggie."

She wanted to hug him again. "Good-bye, Gabriel."

"Good-bye, Miranda."

"Good-bye, Gabriel." She said it in a mock-sincere voice. "Let me give you a tip before you go. Next time you think it might be fun to cheat on someone, don't."

"Thank you, Miranda." He turned to go, then turned back. "Can I offer you a tip too?"

Maggie tensed.

Miranda glared at him. "Go ahead."

"Salt and soda water on those stains. My mother swears by it."

Maggie smiled. Miranda didn't.

*   *   *

The house felt instantly different after they drove away. From eight people to four in less than half an hour. Leo was overly cheery. Maggie knew he was also desperate to talk to her. She didn't want to put it off any longer either. She also didn't want to hear her mother and aunt discussing Gabriel.

"Miranda and Clementine, Maggie and I are going for a walk. She needs some grandfatherly advice. If we're not back in three hours, come looking for us."

She walked alongside him, their pace slow. She realized for the first time that he was getting frail. Not in manner, not in energy, but physically. She hadn't noticed it in New York.

He took her hand, gave it a squeeze and then released it. "Let's wait until we're out of earshot."

They walked up the laneway, the late-afternoon sun warm on their faces. The hedges on either side were heavy with bright-red fuchsia flowers and blackberries.

They reached Leo's favorite spot, the stone wall that was not just a sun trap but a perfect leaning point, with views over the sea and valley. They stood there silently for a moment, side by side. Maggie felt an unexpected rush of sadness. How many more times would she get to spend moments like this with Leo? It felt even harder, knowing she was about to lie to him.

He turned to her. "We have a lot to talk about, you and I, but before we do, let me say thank you. I thought you and Gabriel managed beautifully the past few days and I'm very grateful to you both. It worked a treat. I got to have everyone around me even if it was just for a few days. I'm only sorry he had to leave so quickly. I'm going to ring him in New York and thank him myself."

"You are?"

"It was good timing in a way, I suppose, that his girlfriend rang. It makes it easier for you, doesn't it? You don't have to come up with any explanation about the two of you breaking up. I'm glad Myles arrived when he did as well. I'd be heartbroken if he and Juliet separated. Tessa would have been too."

Tessa again. Her ghost, and the subject of Sadie, was hanging heavy between them. Maggie tried to find the words to tell him. Leo beat her to it.

He put his hand on hers. "Tell me, Maggie. Tell me everything that happened in Dublin. It wasn't good, I know that. I can see it in your face." He paused. "That woman in Dublin wasn't Sadie, was she?"

Maggie turned. "How did you know that?"

"Because you would have rung me if she was. I knew you would. I kept my mobile with me, I stayed near the other phone, and when you didn't call, I knew."

She nodded. Lie number one. "I'm sorry, Tadpole. She did look like Sadie might have. I could see it straightaway. And she was Australian, from Adelaide originally. She's been living in Ireland for years, with her husband and daughter. She's about to become a grandmother, in fact. But it wasn't Sadie."

"You met her? To make sure? Asked her all the right questions?"

Maggie nodded.

Leo gave a deep sigh. "It was too much to hope that Sadie would be here in Ireland. I should have known better. I was thinking that Tessa was sending me messages, thinking how perfect it would have been if we'd found Sadie while we were all here. I'm a foolish old man, Maggie."

"You're not, Tadpole. You're not."

"You finished reading the diaries too, did you?" The anxiety was obvious in his face.

She was thankful for one thing. She could tell him that Bill wasn't Sadie's father. That much was true. Yes, she had finished, she told him. And he had nothing to worry about. He was most definitely the father of all five of his daughters.

He smiled, a radiant smile that broke her heart. Then his expression changed as he realized something. "But what could Sadie have read, then? There must have been something there. She mentioned the diaries the last night I saw her. She said I must have known."

"I don't know what she meant, Tadpole. There was nothing in there that I could imagine upsetting her. Tessa mostly wrote about people she'd met, things she'd done, the funny things her daughters did and said. The funny things you said." Lie after lie after lie.

Leo smiled again. "I bet it was a good read, Maggie, was it? She could be so funny. She had a real gift with words, I thought."

Maggie had to tell him now. She couldn't wait any longer. "Tadpole, I've got some terrible news about the diaries. Something bad happened when we were in Dublin." She told him quickly, speaking in a hurry, hoping the lie wouldn't feel as terrible that way.

He was shocked, she could see it. She wasn't sure if he believed her, either. "You're sure you didn't just leave your bag somewhere?

In the guesthouse? In the car? Oh, Maggie, after I've kept them for all these years, for this to happen. Are you sure you looked everywhere?"

She felt sick inside. For one moment, she wished she hadn't done it. But in the next second, she pictured the scene. If she did still have them, what would be happening now? Would she be handing the diaries back to Leo? Would he start reading them that same night? Reading all she had read? That thought was worse. She could live with the guilt more easily than she could live with the thought of Leo being so hurt. "We looked everywhere, Tadpole, I promise. We reported it to the police; they said it's happening all the time at the moment. It was my fault. I left my bag on the seat. I'm to blame."

He asked more questions. Was the car damaged? Did anyone see anything? What else was stolen?

She answered each one, just as she and Gabriel had rehearsed, speaking quickly, desperate to convince him. "I'm so sorry, Tadpole." Another lie. She was sorry about many things that had happened the past two days, but not about getting rid of the diaries. "I know how much they meant to you. I know you would have read them now yourself."

"They meant a lot, Maggie, yes. But I wouldn't have read them."

She stared at him. "But I thought you wanted to. I thought it was only because of Bill and Tessa that you hadn't."

"It was originally, but I decided in the past few days that I wouldn't read them, no matter what you told me was in them. I always liked having them. I liked thinking about them. I liked knowing Tessa had poured her heart and soul into them. But while we were doing that filming and I was hearing the girls talking about her, I realized I didn't need to know any more about her. I already knew the sort of person she was—so kind and funny and full of life. I didn't need to read her diaries to remind myself of that. Besides, Tessa always said to me, 'You're not to read these. You have to burn them if anything ever happens to me. Promise me.' I'd decided I would finally honor that promise."

"You were going to burn the diaries?" She couldn't believe what she was hearing, after all the turmoil she'd felt making the decision to get rid of the diaries herself.

He nodded.

"But what about Mum and the others? Didn't you want them to read them?"

"I couldn't. If I produced them out of the blue, they would know I'd lied to them all those years ago. It would have been too upsetting for everyone." He reached for her hand again. "Perhaps those thieves have done us all a favor. They made the final decision. Who knows, they might even be sitting somewhere in Dublin right now having a good read."

"I'm so sorry, Tadpole," Maggie said again. "I've been feeling sick about telling you." The truth, at last.

He squeezed her hand. "I'm your grandfather, Maggie. Your grandfather who loves you dearly. Never feel sick about telling me anything." He stood up straight then. "Now, how about you help me back down that laneway? We can't stay up here all day. We've got a film to watch."

They started walking back. "You don't mind that you didn't get to finish the project?"

"We have plenty to be getting on with. I can't wait for you to see it."

*   *   *

The four of them gathered in front of the TV that night after dinner. Miranda had done the cooking. Baked beans on toast. She served it with a bottle of very expensive Italian red wine.

Leo knelt in front of the TV, checking that the cables were connected correctly to the camera, that the tape was inside, that all was as it should be. He referred to Gabriel's notes several times, before pressing the "play" button with a flourish.

Nothing happened.

He checked again, pressed "play" again, then looked up, perplexed. "I don't understand it. He made it sound so simple."

It was Maggie who noticed the TV wasn't switched on.

Leo smiled sheepishly. "Sorry. We'll try that again."

The screen flickered into life. An image appeared on the screen: Juliet, Miranda, Eliza, and Clementine on the sofa. The composition was perfect, the lighting excellent.

Leo beamed. "Look at you. My beautiful girls, all in a row."

Maggie wondered if she was the only one thinking of Sadie.

They could hear Gabriel's voice off camera, asking them to talk about themselves. There was a minute of looking at one another, each one saying to another that they should go first. Some nervous laughter. Gabriel's voice again, suggesting that they start with the oldest: *"Miranda, that's you, isn't it?"*

Maggie tried to ignore the dart of pleasure she got just hearing his voice. She had to try to forget about him, starting right now.

"How insulting, Gabriel," Miranda said. *"With this perfect skin? How could I possibly be the oldest?"*

"You carry on like you're the oldest," Eliza muttered.

"She carries on, at least," Clementine smiled.

"I am the actual oldest so I'll go first," Juliet said firmly. She looked into the camera. *"My name is Juliet and I'd like to start by sharing some memories of—"*

The screen went blank. There were a few seconds of nothing, then the picture flickered. The four women were nowhere to be seen. There was a shot of the floorboards instead. A shaking shot.

Clementine looked at Leo. "What's happened? Is it a loose cable?"

Leo checked. "No, they're all fine. It's not the equipment. It's what's on the tape. Hold on, there must have been a little hitch. It'll come back, I'm sure."

They kept watching. The floorboards stayed on the screen. They heard creaking sounds in the background. Then a voice. Leo's voice.

"Turn it up, Tadpole," Maggie said.

He did. They could clearly hear him. Only him. He was talking to himself. *"It should just be a matter of this attachment here. If there was a swiveling mechanism, though, of course I would need to—"*

As they realized what was happening, Clementine and Miranda started to laugh.

"This is what you were doing when we went down to the beach, wasn't it?" Clementine said.

"You were in here, messing with the camera, weren't you?" Miranda added.

"I had an idea for a new kind of tripod. I just couldn't figure out how it would attach to the camera."

"I *knew* you'd been up to something," Clementine said.

"Don't worry, Tadpole. It'll come back to the other pictures, won't it?" Maggie said. "How long were you working on the camera?"

He looked very embarrassed now. "Quite a while."

"Ten minutes?"

"Two hours," he said.

Maggie reached across and took the remote control. She pressed fast-forward. The shot of the floorboards didn't change for a long time. A high-speed version of Leo's voice created a funny soundtrack. Now and again another image appeared; a shot of the window or a quick flash of the door as Leo moved the camera. There was nearly a minute of Leo's face close to the lens, muttering away to himself, moving the camera up and down as he inspected it from all angles.

Clementine and Miranda were now laughing so hard they had tears in their eyes. They asked Maggie to get it to play normally. It was even funnier in normal time.

It ended with a final shot of the floorboards before the screen flickered to show a four-second image of Miranda getting up from the table where she had just finished her reminiscences. Gabriel's voice was heard again. *"That was great. Thanks, everyone."* The screen went black.

Leo had his head in his hands, rocking back and forth. Maggie and his two daughters went over and sat next to him, still laughing, putting their arms around him.

"My beautiful idea, ruined," he said. He was truly upset. "When will I ever get to do that again? Are we too late to get to the airport with the camera? Maybe they're all still there?"

"No!" the three of them answered in unison.

"Don't worry, Leo, really," Clementine said. "That was much more fun than watching ourselves."

"No, it wasn't. I had it all planned. It was going to be a special gift for you and for Maggie in years to come. Now what do I have to give you? A film of a mad old man alone in a room talking to himself."

"That's why it's so good, Tadpole." Maggie spoke for them all, laughing again. "It's the perfect record of you."

CHAPTER 46

There was no chance of sleep for Maggie that night. An outsider would have watched them all eating dinner, laughing at the tape, thinking, What a happy family. Perhaps they *were* happier than some families's she thought. Perhaps every family had a sadness at its heart—disappointments, bereavements and estrangements. Perhaps it was moments of laughter like tonight that was the glue, holding everyone steady against all the difficult times.

Maggie now knew more about her family than she had ever known. She had met up with Sadie again. She knew the truth about why she had left. She had read the diaries and knew more than she wanted to know about her grandmother. She knew that her mother, her aunts, and her grandfather had been lying to her about Sadie for twenty years. It was this fact that was haunting her now. She wanted to know more. She needed to know more. And there was only one person she could talk to about it.

Her mother.

She realized as she sat up in bed, looking out the open window, that she couldn't leave Donegal without having that conversation with Clementine. There might never be another opportunity like this. She didn't want to wait any longer, either. She was already caught in a new web of lies, about the diaries being stolen, about the woman in Dublin not being Sadie. She was caught between promises made to Sadie not to destroy her new life, and a need, deep inside, to tell her mother that she knew what had happened twenty years ago.

For the second time in three days she made her way down the corridor for a middle-of-the-night visit to Clementine's bedroom. She gave a gentle knock at the door, then let herself in. Once again, the room was bright with moonlight, the curtains open. Clementine stirred.

"Mum?" Maggie whispered.

Clementine sat up, instantly awake. "Maggie? Is everything okay?"

"No, it's not."

"What is it, are you sick? Is it Leo?"

"It's me. I need to talk to you."

"What is it? About Gabriel? Oh, Maggie, of course you can, let me—"

"It's not about Gabriel. It's about Sadie." She saw her mother go still and rushed ahead, before she lost courage. "I'm sorry to bring it up like this, without warning. And to wake you up. Can I get you a cup of tea or—"

Clementine was now fully awake. She reached across and turned on the bedside lamp. "No. No, I'm fine. Sit down. Talk to me."

Maggie shut the door first, then came across and sat beside her mother on the bed. She hesitated for one moment only. "I know about Sadie. I know what happened when I was five. That she took me. I know she's not a hippie."

Clementine's hand went to her throat. The exact gesture Sadie had made. "Who told you?"

"Leo." Leo, not Tadpole. It was time to leave some more of her childhood behind. "Why didn't you tell me? Not just you, why didn't anyone ever tell me?"

Clementine sat up straighter. Maggie had another moment of guilt, that she had caught her mother too unawares, waking her like this. But when would have been the right time? It had to be now. In the moment while her mother gathered her thoughts, her expression serious as she seemed to be weighing up what to say, Maggie had the odd sensation that Clementine looked different.

Not physically. The short hair, the dark eyes, the pale skin was familiar and the same. It felt as though she was seeing Clementine as a woman, not just her mother, for the first time in her life.

Clementine smoothed the covers on her bed. "Can you tell me what Leo has already told you?"

Maggie was surprised by a flash of anger. "So you can lie about it again if you have to?"

Clementine remained calm. "No, so I don't have to tell you what you've already heard."

Maggie immediately felt guilty. "I'm sorry, I shouldn't have said that." She began to recount all that Leo had told her in New York about that time. Midway through she stopped, realizing she had stepped out into a minefield. Yes, she could tell Clementine all Leo had told her, as long as she didn't mention anything about the diaries or meeting Sadie. She recognized the irony of it. Even as she was fighting back anger at the lies *she'd* been told, she was lying by omission, to her own mother. For a moment she was tempted to tell her everything. But with what consequences? It would mean breaking her promise to Sadie. And putting Clementine in a difficult position, knowing something that neither her father nor her sisters knew.

"Go on, Maggie." Clementine's voice was soft.

Maggie continued, picking and tiptoeing her way around all the things she couldn't say.

Clementine was silent at first afterward. She reached across and took Maggie's hand, holding it between both of hers. "All he told you is true. I'm sorry, Maggie."

"That it happened or that you never told me the truth?"

"Both."

"Why? Was it too hard to tell your daughter about something that split up her whole family?"

"It was too hard at first, and then it got too easy to let the lie continue."

"You all let me write to her year after year—"

"For what we thought were the right reasons, yes. To protect you, and to protect Sadie from gossip if she ever came back to us."

Maggie's temper was flickering and dying. Clementine had always talked about things in this calm, rational way. If it was Miranda she was talking to now, there would be fireworks and high drama. Juliet would be overly emotional and apologetic. Eliza would coldly lay out the facts. Gabriel's words came to mind. She had indeed chosen the right sister to be her mother.

Clementine's next words surprised her, though.

"I wish Leo had checked with me first. He shouldn't have told you out of the blue like that."

"Why not?"

"I'm your mother. He should have asked me first."

"I'm no one's property. Even though everyone in this family seems to have a stake in me."

"Is that what you think?"

"It's true, isn't it?"

"Don't we all have a stake in each other?"

"I don't know." Maggie stood up, out of reach of her mother; why, she wasn't sure. She crossed her arms in front of her. "This has been a strange July Christmas."

"Hasn't it? On again, off again. Over before we knew what had happened."

"Like my engagement." It was a bad attempt to lighten the mood.

Clementine's expression changed. "Oh, Maggie. Tell me really, how are you feeling about it?"

Maggie was grateful for a change of subject, even if briefly. She also realized something. She could at least tell Clementine the truth about that. "Gabriel wasn't really my fiancé. I only met him a few days ago." She explained how. "It was Leo's idea, to bring you all over. To lure everyone here."

Clementine was shocked. "And you went along with it?"

Maggie nodded.

"Even though it was a lie? Why?"

"Because Leo wanted it. Because it was important to him that we keep the family traditions going—" She stopped, suddenly unsure of all the reasons why herself. "I wanted to make Leo happy."

"And was it all fake between you and Gabriel?"

"Why?"

"Because it didn't seem to me like either of you were pretending."

Maggie hesitated. "I liked him. Very much. Did you speak to his girlfriend?"

"No, only Miranda did. You didn't know about her? You seemed genuinely shocked."

"I knew there was going to be a phone call from New York. I just didn't know it was his girlfriend who would be ringing."

"I'm sorry," Clementine said again.

There wasn't any more to say about it, Maggie realized. She was still several feet away from her mother. For a moment she was uncertain about the next step.

Clementine made the decision for her. "Maggie, please come and sit down again. I want to talk to you some more about Sadie. I need to talk to you."

Maggie sat down beside her. She felt like they were in uncharted waters. She had never had a conversation like this with her mother. There had never been a reason to. There was now. There were so many questions. "I can't understand why you all kept it secret for so long. Especially you. Didn't you ever want to tell me?"

Clementine was quiet. "I couldn't, Maggie. I felt too guilty about it."

"Why were you guilty? Sadie was the one who took me. You had nothing to be guilty about, except for reacting like any mother would. Leo told me you hit her. Is that what you mean?"

Clementine shook her head. "It was much more than that. I had everything to be guilty about, Maggie. I still do. It was all my fault. It's my fault that the family has been apart all these years."

"No, it's not. Sadie chose to stay away. That's not your fault."

"It was my fault she went in the first place. None of this would have happened if it hadn't been for me."

"What do you mean?"

"It happened because she was a better mother than me, Maggie. She was a much better mother to you than I ever was."

"That's not true."

"It is true. She had more confidence; she had more patience. She managed everything so easily—all the cooking for you, washing your clothes. She played wonderful games with you. She took you on trips to the beach. She did that beautiful scrapbook for you. And I—"

Maggie waited.

"I wasn't good at it, Maggie. Not as good as her."

"You were only seventeen when you had me. Just a—"

"It wasn't my age. It was everything else. The constancy. The worry. The isolation, even though I was in a house full of people. I felt like I didn't have any room in my head. I felt so guilty that I wanted to keep studying, but I couldn't bear not to. I let Sadie take you over, Maggie. The harder parts of you. I let her come in and do all the work and look after you, while I got the cream at the end of the day—the hugs and the love and the beautiful sound of you calling me Mummy. I let it happen. And then I had the gall to be angry when she took you, when she wanted more of that for herself."

"That's not why she took me."

Clementine didn't seem to have heard her. "Her leaving felt like my punishment, Maggie. I was being punished for taking you for granted. For taking Sadie for granted."

"You never took me for granted. I never felt that."

"I loved you so much, I promise. I've always loved you, but—" Clementine stopped there.

"You can tell me. I need to hear this."

"Maggie, it was so hard at times. Harder than I expected. I'd thought it would be a matter of doing my study and looking after you. But what happened was you filled my whole brain, every day. And that was a wonderful thing, but I needed room for other things, too. I wanted to prove to myself—to Leo, to everyone—that I could manage. And I did. But the only reason I managed was because of Sadie. That's why it's all my fault. I accepted her help, let her look after you, but I still wasn't happy about it. I was the one who drove her away."

"You didn't drive her away."

"I did. I know I had something to do with it. Perhaps we all did. Miranda always picked on her. Juliet got exasperated by her. Eliza barely noticed her, or if she did, it was to get annoyed with her. We all felt so guilty when she left, Maggie. We never admitted it openly to each other, but I know that's how we felt. I'm sure we all still do."

"Did you go looking for her?"

"I thought about it. Not at first, I was too upset, too angry. Too confused. As time passed, though, we all wrote to her, enclosed letters with your cards, asking her to come back. But she never answered us. She only ever wrote cards to you, saying nothing about us. It couldn't have been clearer. She didn't want anything to do with us or with Leo. Only with you. And that's never changed. It makes me so sad. I think about her so often; she's there in the back of my mind the whole time. I worry that wherever she is she's unhappy or lonely, and that we should have done more to try to bring her back. Then I tell myself she's doing what she wants. That she doesn't want to be with us. And that ridiculous hippie story Miranda made up . . . it began to feel real, not just to me, but to all of us. That's how we imagined her. Living in a commune with lots of friends—with a partner maybe. But none of us knew—know—the truth. That's the hardest thing of all. All we can do is hope she's happy, wherever she is."

Maggie realized she could tell her. She could sit here now, in the moonlight, and tell her mother that Sadie was indeed happy. She was married to a man she loved. She had a beautiful daughter. A great business. Not only that, she was about to become a grandmother. There was so much she could tell, and yet she could tell her nothing.

It was happening again. Just free of one set of lies, she was bound up in new ones. As guilty of lying as the rest of her family. But she had promised Leo, and she had promised Sadie. Was a promise more important than telling the truth?

She chose her next words carefully. "Perhaps she is happy," she said. "Perhaps that's why she hasn't needed to come back to us. She's made a whole other life. Maybe she's got kids of her own, a husband—"

"Do you think? I don't know, Maggie. Sadie was always different. She was—"

"What was she?"

"An unsure person. A lost person."

"The runt of the family?"

"That's a horrible term. Please never think of her like that. She was just different."

"Perhaps that's why she stayed away. She had to have a different life than the rest of you."

"Do you remember anything from that time? When the two of you . . ."

Maggie shook her head. She nearly said, "Sadie asked me the same thing." "It's all jumbled together. When I think about my childhood, all I remember is being happy. People everywhere. Going on planes to stay with Miranda and Juliet and Eliza. Going on trips with you. Being happy."

"Really?"

"Of course." Maggie realized then that her mother was crying. "Why does that make you sad?"

"I'm not sad. I'm happy. I'm relieved. I was always so worried I hadn't been good enough. After Sadie left. Even before then."

"Good enough at what?"

"At being your mother."

"But you were a wonderful mother."

"Not always, Maggie. I should have been there more."

"More?" Maggie reached for her mother's hand, trying to console her, to lighten the mood. "I would have got sick of you if you'd been there the whole time."

"You didn't ever resent me going away?"

Maggie hesitated. Perhaps it was time for more truth. "Sometimes, I did, of course. But then Tadpole would take me to the museum, or Miranda would take me to the theater or something else great would happen to distract me. And you always came back. I always knew you would. I always felt like I had everything I needed. I still have everything."

"Not a father. Not Sadie."

"I have everything I need," Maggie repeated.

"I'm sorry, Maggie. I'm sorry I wasn't the one to tell you the truth about Sadie."

"It's all right. I know now. I can talk about it with you now, can't I?"

"Any time you want to."

"And I'll tell the others I know too. Not yet, but I will."

"I think they'll be glad you know. I'm sure they'll be glad."

"And you're not a bad mother. You're not. You've been the best mother and I'm going to say it as many times as you need to hear it."

"A hundred times?" Clementine smiled.

"A thousand times, if you like," Maggie said. She closed the gap between them. Her mother's arms came around her too.

"I love you so much, Maggie," Clementine said. "I can't even put an amount on it or make a joke of it. And I'm so proud of you."

"Then we're even. Because I'm proud of you and I love you too."

They hugged for a long moment. Clementine was the one who eventually drew back, stroking her daughter's hair. "And I'm sorry again about Gabriel."

"About me lying to you? I'm sorry too. I shouldn't have said yes to Leo."

"Not that. You just seemed such a good match. Are you sure it's not something you can work out?"

Maggie managed a laugh. "Explain to his girlfriend that he and I make a much better pair? I don't think so. Besides, Miranda would kill me if I saw him again."

"Oh, don't listen to her. Miranda's just a drama queen." Clementine laughed at Maggie's expression. "You think I don't know my own sister? Of course she's a drama queen. She always has been. She's wonderful, but she needs constant melodrama to keep herself amused. And while we're on the subject of my sisters, all of whom I promise you I do love dearly, I also know that Juliet mothers all of us too much. And yes, Eliza can be a dry old stick-in-the-mud and she terrifies the wits out of me sometimes as well."

Maggie was laughing. "Why didn't you ever tell me those things before?"

"I didn't need to. You could see it for yourself, couldn't you?"

Maggie nodded.

"See, I don't need to tell you everything."

"Just the big things. Like the truth about Sadie."

"Like Sadie." Clementine became serious. "I'm sorry. I'm sorry she's not with us, and I'm sorry for not telling you."

"I am too."

Clementine smoothed Maggie's hair over her ears. "I'm sorry most of all that I wasn't the perfect mother to you. I'm not making excuses; I won't say that I should be let off lightly because I don't remember my own mother very well, even if I wish I could. But if you ever felt that you came second to my work, I need you to know that you didn't."

"You've been the perfect mother for me. The best mother I could have had. And I should know, because I had five of you to choose from."

This time it was Maggie who wiped away Clementine's tears.

CHAPTER 47

Throughout the six-hour flight from Ireland to New York, Maggie didn't watch a film, read a newspaper, or look at a magazine. She had her thoughts to keep her occupied.

She thought about her final day in the Donegal house. They had woken to find the weather had changed, the blue skies gray and rain thundering down. They lit the fire, pulled the curtains, and played board games all day. They didn't worry about cooking dinner. Miranda announced she'd got the hang of "this catering lark" as she called it. She heated four frozen pizzas and opened two even more expensive bottles of Italian wine. For dessert, they ate nearly all of chocolate that Maggie had sent Leo for his July Christmas present. They tried to cheat one another at the games, laughed a lot, and drank too much, as the rain pelted against the windows and the wind howled outside.

The weather was still stormy the next day as they cleaned, washed and dried the linen and prepared the house for the next lot of holiday tenants. They stood outside afterward, their cars packed, looking back at the house.

"I wonder how long until we're all here together again," Clementine said.

"Next July, of course." Leo sounded surprised at her question.

"But I won't be able to come, Leo," she said. "I'll be in Antarctica next July."

"Well, if she's not coming, I'm not coming," Miranda said. "She's the only one that keeps me sane."

"And if they're not coming, I'm not coming," Maggie added.

Leo looked back and forth between them. "Well, if you're all not coming, I'm not coming either."

"I'll believe that when I see it." Miranda laughed, moving toward her car. "You know full well you'll conjure up some trick to get us all here. A polar ice melt, for example, so Clementine has no choice but to leave the Antarctic and fly to Donegal."

"And if she comes, I'll come," Maggie said.

Miranda grinned. "And if they both come, I'll come."

"We don't have to decide now," Leo said. "Besides, you all know I'd never make you do anything you didn't want to do." He looked at them. "Why are you laughing? What's so funny?"

The car journey from Donegal was followed by four sets of farewells at the airport in Belfast. Leo was going to London. He was hatching an idea for a new invention, he told them. He wanted to investigate a few museums for designs. Talk to a few people in the field. He wouldn't tell them what it was.

"Not the camera idea, I hope?" Miranda asked.

He put his hands over his ears. "Don't remind me. Haven't I suffered enough humiliation already?"

Miranda was flying back to Greece. Another group of her friends had arrived at the villa. There was possibly a yacht involved. A week cruising in the Mediterranean was just what she needed to recover from the trauma of a family holiday, she told them.

Clementine was flying back to Tasmania. Before she left, she made Maggie promise her something. "If you want to come home to Hobart, and if you want your mother to be there to wait on you hand and foot, you only have to ask. My penguins have been there for hundreds of years and they'll be there for hundreds of years yet."

"I thought they might not be. Isn't that the whole point of your research, to find out if they're becoming extinct?"

Clementine had just smiled. "I mean it, Maggie. In fact, you don't even have to ask. I can tell you now my answer would be yes."

Maggie was giving it serious thought. It would be such a contrast, to go from the crowds, smog, humidity, and intensity of New York to the clean air, mountains, water and space of Hobart. She could go bushwalking. She could read all the books she hadn't had time to read for years. She could see her school friends. Or she could do nothing but laze around with Clementine. The last thing sounded the most attractive of all.

She did her best to distract herself with thoughts of family and Hobart, but it didn't work for long. She kept coming back to one subject. One person. Gabriel. She couldn't stop herself from thinking about him.

Why hadn't he ever mentioned his girlfriend? Why had he asked her when she was coming back to New York? And why had he kissed her that day by the lake? She kept remembering something he'd said during the confrontation with Miranda: "I was actually hoping to keep you both going." Could he have meant that? Did he seriously think that she—or this Susanna—would consider such an arrangement? Or did he just want to see her out of politeness? To apologize some more? It had to be that. He would think it only good manners to ring her and arrange to have a coffee together after all that had happened between them. A coffee would be nice, she thought.

No, it wouldn't be nice. It would be terrible. Too hard. She didn't want to see him for a quick cup of coffee knowing that he would probably be going on to meet Susanna. She didn't want to meet him knowing he had probably just come back from seeing Susanna. She didn't want to meet Susanna. She didn't want to see Susanna and Gabriel together. She also decided that Susanna was a silly name.

She could always ring him first. Set the tone. Call him a day or two after she got back. She'd have to call him at the Rent-a-Grandchild agency, she realized. She didn't have his home number. Even better. Less personal. She'd ring and leave a message at the agency to say she was back, that she hoped he was well and that perhaps they'd catch up for a coffee some time. Perfect. Nice and casual.

She didn't fool herself for a moment. She couldn't ring him. She couldn't go back to being just an acquaintance, just a friend, not feeling the way she felt about him. She would have to stay away from him. Stay away from him and Susanna. Leave the two of them to live happily ever after. While she did what? Stayed in New York for a few more months? Returned to London? Moved back to Hobart? See? she told herself firmly. She had plenty of options. Gabriel didn't need to feature in any of them.

*   *   *

The sun was just setting as she stepped out of JFK Airport and joined the cab rank. She felt the humidity immediately, smelled the pollution, and saw the haze of smog hanging over the city. As her cab drew closer to Manhattan, she found herself looking at the buildings in a different way. The last time she'd taken this cab ride she'd come from London, distressed, uncertain, and scared. This time was different. She knew she had changed. She knew more about her family than she had ever imagined knowing. She also knew New York better too. Only tiny pockets of it: her area of Greenwich Village, Dolly's area and Central Park. But she'd had experiences there that no one else in this city of eight million people had had. Maybe she had noticed things that no one else had noticed. She could leave right now—go straight back to the airport—and the city wouldn't even feel her absence. But she knew the memories would stay with her.

Ray the doorman greeted her as if she'd been gone for years, not less than a week. He asked after Leo. He was delighted with the can of shamrock-shaped chocolates she'd brought back for him.

Nothing had changed on the sixth floor. There was still the faint smell of cooking oil in the corridor. She heard the sound of the TV from the neighbor that she never saw. Everything inside her apartment was exactly as she had left it.

She unpacked. She showered. She wasn't tired enough to go to bed. She sat out on the balcony, breathed in the humid air and listened to the sounds of late summer. She looked down at the garden below, noticing the faint tinge of autumnal yellow and orange beginning to appear on the trees. She decided to count them. It might make her feel better. It took her less than a minute. Forty-five. She counted them again.

She was counting them for the third time when the sound of the buzzer made her jump. It was Ray.

"Hi, Maggie. That boy named Sue is here again." She heard Ray talk to someone, then a quick burst of laughter. "My little joke. I mean Gabriel."

"*Gabriel?* Gabriel's downstairs?"

"I told him you've only just arrived back. Want me to tell him to come by again later?"

"No. No, I'll be right down."

She told herself it was the jet lag that was making her hands shake as she quickly changed into her favorite dress. She told herself it was only the humidity that had brought the sudden color to her cheeks as she checked her appearance in the bathroom mirror. The lift seemed to take an hour to go down the six floors. She said the numbers aloud as each one was illuminated. Six. Five. Four. Three. Two. One. It calmed her down, just a little. She nearly made it go up again so she could do some more counting.

He was waiting in the same spot he'd been waiting the first night she met him. He was watching the lift this time too. He was smiling. She wanted to smile back at him. She wanted to go over and hug him. She made herself be serious. She thought of Miranda's advice. Be dignified.

"Gabriel." She was almost funereal.

"Welcome home, Maggie."

She joined him at the window seat. So far, so good. She was cool, calm, and collected. All those *c*s. Dolly would be proud of her.

"How did you know I'd be here? I'm just in from the airport."

"I was up cleaning the windows of the Rockefeller Center and I saw your plane come in." He smiled. "I rang Leo and got your flight details. I'm sorry I couldn't be there at the airport to meet you. I got called in at the last minute to do some dog-walking. I'm not too early, am I? I gave you a few hours to clear immigration, wait in the cab line, get stuck in traffic, try and find your key, get inside, put down your bags, and then I gave you an extra five minutes, just in case. Do you want me to go and walk around the block a few times?"

She was confused. Why was he talking in this normal kind of way? She thought of Miranda again. She knew her aunt would urge her to cut to the chase. "Gabriel, why are you here?"

"To see you."

"But why?"

He seemed puzzled by her question. "Why do you think?"

"I thought you'd be with Susanna."

"Susanna? Oh yes, Susanna." He smiled. "You should have heard the fight we had when I got back from Ireland, Maggie. She was furious with me. Threw everything of mine that was in her apartment out onto the street. Broke all my CDs. Smashed my guitar in two."

"She did?" He seemed to think it was funny. "But you made up afterward? After the fight?"

"Oh, of course. She's great like that. Hot-tempered, but it passes in an instant. I think it's the Latin blood in her. Or is it Spanish blood? One of the two, anyway."

Latin or Spanish, Maggie thought. She'd be beautiful as well as fiery, then.

"I just wish she'd rung a day later, as we'd arranged," Gabriel said. "She told me she messed up the time zones. She thought Ireland was behind New York, not ahead of it. But I suppose it worked out well enough, didn't it? I was able to go to the airport with Juliet, Myles, and Eliza. Not that they spoke to me. You will tell them the truth, Maggie, won't you? I was going to, but I didn't know how much longer we needed to keep it up."

Maggie stared at him. If this was jet lag, it was the strongest dose of it she'd ever had. "Gabriel, I'm sorry, but I have absolutely no idea what you are talking about."

"I'm so sorry. I forgot you're just off a long flight. Why don't we go outside and I'll fill you in on the whole story?"

They walked through to the communal garden, taking a seat at a bench just inside the doorway. The air was warm and the sky hazy. They sat side by side.

Gabriel began. "Let me start at the beginning. We'd been in Dublin, and then we drove back to Donegal—"

She knew that much. "And then we got back to the house and everyone was sitting—"

He interrupted. "You left out something."

"I did?"

"When I finally got to kiss you. After wanting to kiss you since the first night I met you."

She wished he hadn't reminded her about that. She ignored it and continued. "And then we got back to the house and Miranda told us that your girlfriend had just rung."

"And you reacted perfectly. Especially the slap across the face. Well done."

Well done? Was he being sarcastic? "I'm sorry. I shouldn't have hit you."

"Don't be sorry. It was the perfect touch. Even if we'd rehearsed it, I wouldn't have thought to ask you to do it."

"The perfect touch?" How could he be so lighthearted about this?

"Even Leo looked shocked and he knew it was all make-believe. Maggie, I'm so sorry. I should have asked you before now. Did you get to talk to Leo about Sadie? About the diaries?"

She explained what had happened and answered his questions. She couldn't understand why he was so interested. The job was over, after all.

"And he was okay? He wasn't upset?"

"No, he was actually more upset by what happened later." She told him about Leo's idea for a new camera and how he had somehow erased the film and replaced it with footage of floorboards.

Gabriel's attention was instantly captured by the camera idea. "A swiveling tripod? That's ingenious. What was he going to do with the connecting wires, though? That would be the tricky part—"

She needed to bring this strange meeting to an end. "Gabriel, why are you really here?"

"I thought you might like to go out to dinner. I didn't like to think of you in your apartment on your own, not after the week you've had. There's a great Vietnamese restaurant a few streets from here. We could sit outside. I think you'd like it."

"Susanna doesn't mind?"

He smiled. "Oh, she's furious, but I told her she'll just have to get used to you being around as well."

"I don't think that's very funny."

Gabriel stopped smiling then. He stared at her as if he'd just realized something. "Maggie, do you think there really is a Susanna?"

"Isn't there?"

"No, of course not."

"You don't have a girlfriend called Susanna?"

"Of course I don't. Do you think I'd be kissing you if I had another girlfriend?"

"Some men would."

"I'm not some men, Maggie."

"But what about that phone call? All the things you said in the house about her?"

"My roommate's sister Gina made the phone call. I asked her. Don't you remember? I told you in Dublin I'd organized a way to end it, to make it easier for you in front of your family."

"You didn't say anything about a girlfriend."

"I didn't know that's what it was going to be. I asked Gina to ring and say there was a crisis back here. She got carried away with the girlfriend story herself. So I made it up as I went along too. I can't even remember what I said."

"You said you were hoping to keep us both going. Susanna and I."

"I did?" He fought a smile. "No wonder you slapped me. But that probably worked in our favor too, because you looked genuinely shocked, as if I really was two-timing—" He stopped there. His expression changed, as if he had just realized something else. "Is that why you slapped me? Because you actually believed that I had a girlfriend here in New York?"

She nodded.

"Can I therefore assume that you weren't happy about that?"

She nodded again. She could have pretended. She could have

told him she'd been feeling shocked after all that had happened with Sadie. That the slap had been a reaction to all of that. She didn't want to lie. She wanted him to know the truth. "I didn't want you to have another girlfriend."

"Why not?"

"I wanted to be your only girlfriend. Your only real girlfriend."

"You wanted? Past tense?"

"Want. Present tense."

He nodded. His face was solemn. "I see. So if that was the case— if you were my girlfriend—that would mean I would have to be your boyfriend. Is that right?"

"Yes, it is."

"Would that also mean I'd have to spend time with you every day? Or call you on the days we didn't see each other? That I would have to take you out to dinner or to see a movie or some comedy or some music as often as possible? Basically take you wherever you wanted to go?"

She nodded.

"Would I also have to kiss you quite often?"

"I think that would be part of it, yes."

"Here and now, for example?"

She nodded.

He kissed her. She kissed him back. It was even better than it had been by the lake in Ireland. The feel of his skin under his T-shirt. The touch of his lips on hers, on her skin. His hands holding her tight against his body, his fingers caressing her skin, as their bodies moved closer and closer and . . .

Ray knocked on the window. "Public place, folks," they heard him call.

They broke away from each other. Maggie could tell Gabriel was as affected by the kiss as she was.

He gently touched her cheek. A touch rich with promise. "Do you know, I really think this sounds like a good arrangement."

"I think so too," Maggie said.

"I'm sure there are terms and conditions we need to sort out, though, don't you? Points to discuss. It's probably just as well I've got a table booked for dinner in—" He checked his watch. "Ten minutes ago."

He stood up and held out his hand. "May I escort you through the streets of New York, Ms. Faraday? Very quickly, so we don't lose our reservation?"

"I'd like that very much." She more than liked it. She couldn't stop smiling about it. All the sadness she'd felt, the confusion, seemed to have disappeared into the air. She was exactly where she wanted to be, with the person she most wanted to be with.

He kissed her again, quickly, beautifully, as if he had read her mind. "I wouldn't ever two-time you, Maggie. I thought you'd guessed what was happening. I'm sorry I upset you."

"I should have asked you about it in Donegal, but it all happened so quickly."

"Next time I'll make sure you know exactly what's going on."

"Next time?"

He smiled. "Next time we pretend to be engaged to each other. I enjoyed it so much I thought we could make a career out of it."

They had just said good night to Ray and were outside the building when Gabriel stopped. "There's actually something else I've wanted to ask you. Ever since I met your family in Donegal. But perhaps it's not fair. You've just had a long flight—"

"I'm fine, really."

"I don't want to put you in an awkward position."

"You won't. I'm sure you won't."

"It's just the question's been on my mind and you're the only one who can answer it."

She was worried now. "Please, ask me."

His face was very serious. "Maggie, what's nine hundred and forty-seven multiplied by forty-two?"

She didn't hesitate. "Thirty-nine thousand seven hundred and seventy-four."

He smiled at her. A beautiful smile. "That's amazing. That's exactly what I thought too." He took her hand as they started walking down the street. "Do you know what I think, Maggie Faraday? I think the two of us are going to get along very well indeed."

One Year Later

The house in Glencolmcille looked magnificent, if Miranda did say so herself. She'd been busy all day, hanging fairy lights in the trees outside, arranging fresh flowers and unpacking all the supplies into the freezer and refrigerator.

It was a cool day, so she lit the fire. She arranged candles all around the house. She didn't light them. She would wait until she heard the first sound of the cars arriving. They expected to be there around seven, they'd told her. Three carloads of them.

That reminded her. She still hadn't finished making the beds. She ran up and down the stairs with armfuls of linen. How on earth had Juliet managed this every year? Miranda was only one day into it and she was exhausted.

An hour later, everything was finally ready. The dining table was set. The dinner—a rich, spicy *boeuf bourguignon*—was ready in the oven. She'd cheated, of course. She'd bought everything premade in Donegal town and driven across the county with it carefully packed into an ice chest. She'd picked up fresh seafood in Killybegs. She'd bought local cheese for dessert. There was also enough champagne and wine to last a week. They would very possibly get through it in a night or two.

She'd warned them all what to expect. "You might not see any sunshine at all, even though it's summer. It might be lashing rain every single day."

They all told her they weren't coming for the weather. No one came to Ireland for the weather, did they? They were coming for the scenery, the atmosphere, and to see this wonderful house she'd been going on about for years.

There would be six in total. Her friend George from Greece. Two friends from London. One from Barcelona. One from Sydney. And another new friend from Hong Kong. He was a manager of one of the hotels there. It was early days in their relationship, but things looked promising.

Her family had been astonished when she rang around to see if they minded her taking over the house for the last week in July. They'd all agreed six months previously that they weren't going to be able to keep up their July Christmas tradition this year. It was getting too hard for everyone, with their different commitments. For Clementine, particularly. Miranda was the last person they'd expected to continue it.

"I'm not doing it for me. I'm doing it for my friends," she said. "They always thought it sounded so quaint."

She heard the sound of a car. Her first arrival. Behind it, a second car. Fantastic, an instant crowd. She hurriedly lit the candles, then ran to the refrigerator and opened one of the bottles of French champagne. As they pulled into the laneway, she was standing in front of the house with a tray of brimming glasses and a big smile.

This was what life was about, Miranda decided, as they started beeping their horns and waving at her. Friends, food, fizz, and fun.

And family, of course. Just not all the time.

.   .   .

In Melbourne, Eliza was trying not to look too obviously at the clock on her desk. The woman sitting opposite her was one of her least favorite clients. Katherine had been coming to her for over a year now, but it didn't seem to matter how many times Eliza made suggestions or helped her reset her goals. She came back each month having done absolutely nothing different.

"—and so I tell my son, over and over again, that if he doesn't lift his game, I'm going to—"

Eliza thought about dinner the previous evening. She'd met Mark in a wine bar on the beach at St. Kilda. He had good news to tell her. The separation was happening. Not just happening, but happening amicably. His wife was ready to leave the marriage too. She hadn't been happy for years, apparently. Eliza had almost laughed at the look on Mark's face.

"You don't seem pleased about that."

"I thought I'd done all I could to make her happy."

"Including having an affair with me for years?"

He looked abashed at that.

They would take the next stage slowly. She hadn't invited him to come and live with her. He hadn't suggested it. He talked about finding a place of his own. She said she'd look forward to seeing it.

"This will be different for us, Eliza, won't it?" he'd said. He sounded as nervous about it as she was. It would be different. She hoped it wouldn't become ordinary. She was going to do all she could to stop that from happening.

The woman was still talking. "And then my husband said I was putting on weight, not losing any, and I said to him—"

"Blah, blah, blah, blah," Eliza said.

"I'm sorry?" The woman looked at her. "Did you just say, 'blah, blah, blah, blah'?"

Eliza looked alarmed for a brief moment. "I don't know. Did I?"

"Yes, you did."

"How rude of me."

"Yes, it was."

"Why would I have said that, do you think?"

The woman shifted in her seat. "I don't know."

"I must have had a reason. Can you think of one?"

"Because you thought I was going on and on too much . . . ?"

"That could have been it, yes. Can you think of another reason?"

"That you are probably thinking that I come back here every appointment saying the same old boring things."

"Yes, that would be another reason."

The woman sat up straighter in her chair. "Is that what you think? That I don't do anything that you suggest? That I just come back and go 'blah, blah, blah, blah' every time?"

"Don't you?"

There was a long, uncomfortable silence; the woman glaring, Eliza unblinking.

The woman sat up even straighter. "Yes. Yes, I do. But not anymore. You're right, Eliza. I've been self-indulgent. This time I am going to change. I was thinking about not coming to see you anymore, you know. You didn't seem to be helping me at all. But not now. I'm going to start coming every fortnight. And I'm going to tell my friends to come to you too. I needed a good talking to and you gave it to me. You're incredible."

Damn, Eliza thought.

*   *   *

Juliet stood nervously at the side of the stage. Across the other side, Myles winked at her. He mouthed something.

What? she mouthed back.

He mouthed it again.

She still couldn't figure it out.

He reached for a piece of paper beside him, scribbled something in black marker and held it up. She could just read it: *You'll be GREAT!*

Thanks, she mouthed. She just had time to smooth down her skirt before the MC introduced her. She just hoped no one could see that her legs were shaking.

It was the gala awards presentation of their Young Chef competition, ten months in preparation. It had started as a tentative idea, just a seed of a thought, in the weeks after she and Myles had returned home from Donegal. They had talked more in those weeks than they had in years. They had both cried a lot as well. He told her how isolated he'd felt from her. She explained to him about the gap there had been in her life, how nothing had ever seemed to fill it. It was the part of her that wanted to look after something, nurture something. See it grow. She'd always assumed it had to be a child. Maggie had come some way in filling it, but she was an adult now. Independent. She didn't need aunts fussing over her. Juliet thought that might have triggered her attempt to separate from him. That and turning fifty.

"What you need is some more Maggies, perhaps," Myles said. "Boy Maggies and girl Maggies that need looking after."

They talked about it. Ideas sparked between them. At first they discussed developing mentor schemes with the dozens of young waiters and waitresses who worked in their cafés. It was Myles who suggested they do more than that. "You have a gift for cooking, Juliet. You're brilliant at it. Why don't we do something to help young chefs?"

They launched it properly. They advertised it in all of their cafés. Juliet did interviews with local newspapers and radio. One of the national papers did an article about her. They described her as a passionate advocate for good food and nutrition. A strong believer in what young people had to offer.

More than a hundred young people applied for the twelve scholarships. She met with them all. They were all sizes, nationalities, and personalities, ranging from fifteen-year-olds just out of school up to twenty-four-year-olds, the age limit they had set. There were cheery ones, moody ones, grumpy ones, ones with natural talent and others who had to be encouraged. Juliet chose twelve contenders and tried to coax the best out of them all. Three fell to the wayside in the early days. She learned not to blame herself for that. She took on another three instead. She traveled around the U.K., running workshops in their cafés. The students' work was assessed over six months. The winner tonight would be offered a position as her assistant, eventually being put in charge of his or her own café. The other eleven would be offered further training, and then full-time positions in their other cafés, either in the U.K. or Australia.

She stayed realistic about it. She didn't see them as her own children. She wasn't their mother and Myles wasn't their father. But she was proud of them, she believed in them, and she wanted them all to do well and be happy. And if that was the closest she could come to being a mother herself, then that was fine.

She looked out into the crowd, and then briefly at Myles standing in the wings. She could feel his love and encouragement. As she opened the envelope, her hands trembled only slightly.

She smiled. "And the winner of the inaugural Young Chef Award is . . ."

* * *

Clementine had to laugh. She'd come all the way to the bottom of the world, joined one of the most isolated communities on earth, and what had she discovered? That they celebrated a July Christmas.

Maggie had been extremely amused about it. Clementine had e-mailed her with the news.

> They're worse than us, Clementine wrote. Everyone dresses up. They take turns being Santa. At least we never did that.
> Everyone dresses up? Maggie wrote back. Even you?? What as??
> Clementine's reply was brief. I'll send photos. I can't begin to describe it.

She'd been down south for nine months now, with another five to go. Her research into the breeding habits of the Adélie penguins was progressing slowly, but well.

She checked the time and did a calculation. If she had it right, Maggie would be just about to land. Clementine knew her daughter would love it if there was a welcome-home e-mail waiting for her. She quickly wrote the message, ending with lots of love and good wishes for the days ahead. She'd just sent it when she heard a knock on her door. "Clementine? Are you ready? We're all going across."

"Coming," she called. She pulled on her antlers, double-checked her reindeer suit was on the right way around, and made her way out of her room.

* * *

In London, Leo was getting very excited. He thought he'd done well with his lawn mower invention. His petrol pump device was used all over the world. But this one had the potential to be even bigger. The best of them all. He decided he was going to give this one a name. Not any name. His name. It would be called "The Faraday Cleaner." Catchy and to the point.

The idea had never gone away, not since he'd seen the cleaner in the airport that day, more than a year ago now. He'd been in a lot of airports since then, and seen the same situation time and time again. It was so obvious. The machines were the wrong shape.

He had done his research. He went to the manufacturers to investigate every industrial cleaner already on the market. He pretended he had his own cleaning business and was looking to upgrade his stock. He got a lot of information that way. He made sketches of alternative designs. He visited factories specializing in molded plastic shells, in cleaning bristle production and in swiveling wheel design. He made a prototype. The first one was a disaster. He'd misjudged the length of the brush. It left more dirt behind than it collected. The motor also wasn't anywhere near powerful enough.

He started again. He decided to start small and build his way up this time. The first prototype had cost him a lot of money to produce. He decided to make a mini version. If it worked on a small scale, it would work on a big scale.

It did. It performed better than he might have hoped. He laughed now, setting it to work again to clean the top of his desk. He had rented this serviced office in east London several months earlier. It made sense to be based in the U.K. while he was developing a product like this. Bigger population and the right manufacturing capabilities as well.

He set up some obstacles on his desk. A pile of books, the phone and a fax machine. The mini Faraday Cleaner worked around them with ease, the angled body adjusting to suit the different spaces, the little brush underneath lifting and changing shape as required.

"Leo Faraday, you are a genius, if I do say so myself," he said aloud.

That was the first step. Now he had to get serious about it. He needed to find out if it would do more than clean one desk in London. It needed testing. It needed to be put to work in heavy-duty situations. He'd thought about approaching hospitals and hotels himself, before realizing how he might appear. An old man with a miniature cleaner under his arm? They'd laugh at him.

The previous night he'd had a brain wave. When in doubt, go to the experts. Talk to the people who would be the end user of his product, as the phraseology went. It had taken him some time to locate the file, but eventually he had. The slight drawback was they were based in Dublin, but he could fly across easily enough.

Best of all, he could drive up to Miranda afterward. What a surprise that would be for her. It made him happy to think of the Donegal house being used. Even though the rest of them had decided not to go there this year—and he hoped it would only be this year that they missed their July Christmas—he liked to know it was being celebrated in some way, that Tessa's beautiful idea was still being perpetuated. Ireland was very fashionable at present, Miranda had told him. Much more so than Greece or Spain. She'd had to turn some friends down. They'd all wanted to come and stay in her rustic Celtic hideaway, she had told him.

He moved his phone back into the middle of his spotlessly clean desk and dialed the number. Zero zero to get out of the U.K., 353 for Ireland and 1 for Dublin. He heard the ringtone.

A woman answered. "Good afternoon, O'Toole Cleaners. Can I help you?"

"Oh, good afternoon. Yes, I hope you can. My name is Leo Faraday and I am an inventor. Now, this might sound odd . . ." He spoke quickly, putting his case succinctly. "I'm now at the stage where I need to do a test run with someone in the business. Last year I had some dealings"—he allowed himself the small white lie—"with Mrs. Sally O'Toole. I wonder if she is there now? Could I have a quick word?"

"I'm sorry, Mr. Farrelly—"

"Faraday."

"I'm sorry, Mr. Faraday, but both Mrs. and Mr. O'Toole are away

on holiday at the moment. If you like, I can take a message and
they could get in touch with you when they return."

"When will that be?"

Not for another fortnight, she told him. Leo thought about it.
No, he couldn't wait that long. He'd approach another cleaning
company instead. One in the U.K. Perhaps that would make more
sense, anyway.

"Would you like to leave a message, sir?"

He hesitated. He looked at the folder; at the information about
the company; at the photo of the woman on the front who looked
uncannily like Sadie. The brochures did say they were the most successful company of their kind. But he was too impatient. He wanted
to talk to someone about it now, not in two weeks' time.

"No, thank you all the same. Have a lovely day."

He hung up, put the folder to one side and reached for the yellow pages instead.

*   *   *

Sadie laughed at the expression on Larry's face. They'd been there
for four days now and he didn't look any more impressed with the
scenery or the view than he had when they first arrived.

"Where's the asphalt? Where are all the cars? What's that green
stuff over there?"

"It's called grass."

"And that watery stuff? Next to that sandy stuff?"

Sadie laughed. "It's called the sea. And that sandy stuff is a
beach. Children love it. That's why we're here, remember?"

"Constance wouldn't know if she was in a sandpit or a bag of
kitty litter yet. Don't blame her for this disaster of a holiday."

From her seat under the umbrella a few meters away, Maudie
laughed too. "You stop that moaning. I know you're having a great
time. You're just pretending. I think he wants to move down here,
don't you, Mum?"

It was a beautiful house, newly renovated, looking out over the
sea and the valley, on the southwest coast of County Kerry, the bottom tip of the country. It had made sense to stay in Ireland for their

summer holidays rather than try to carry everything to Spain or France. They needed so much luggage these days. Sadie had forgotten how much equipment a baby needed. At ten months of age, Constance was a beautifully behaved baby, sunny-natured like her mother and grandfather, but she still made a big mess too. Another good reason to have this kind of self-catering holiday. The washing machine had been going constantly since they arrived.

It had been Sadie's decision to come to this particular spot. She'd spent an afternoon on her computer looking up holiday websites before finding this one. It was perfect, just four hours from Dublin. Lorcan, Maudie's partner, would be joining them for a week of it, but they were so close he'd been able to come down for the weekend as well, in between jobs. It was also at the opposite end of the country from Donegal.

The key to this holiday for all of them was relaxation. Larry had been forced to slow down. He'd had a minor heart attack six months earlier. It had been one of the most frightening nights of Sadie's life. From now on, it was less work and more fun.

Larry had been easy to convince. He'd frightened himself, too. "I don't want my granddaughter growing up without her grandfather to look out for her."

Sadie ignored the pang his words gave her. She'd learned to ignore it. Especially during the past year, when she had thought many times about how easy it would be to reconnect with her own family. Had she made the right decision that day with Maggie? She had to believe it. Not just for her sake, for her own peace of mind, but for Larry, Maudie, Lorcan, and Constance. That was part of being a family. Realizing that any decision she made, any action she took, wouldn't affect only her but all of them as well. A ripple effect or a tidal wave—either way, she knew she wasn't going to allow it to happen. She would still write to Maggie and she would still love receiving her letters. But she could never have more than that. She had done just one thing differently since she met Maggie. She had sent her a birthday card as usual, but she had added a new sentence: "Please give Leo and the others my love." She meant it too. She had thought of Leo going to all that trouble, hiring a private detective. She remembered all the letters she had received from her sisters in the early years. She knew she couldn't see them again. But she could send a message, at least.

She looked at her husband stretched on the sun lounge beside her, wearing a ridiculous hat, bouncing Constance on his knee and singing her a nonsense song that made her laugh. She could hear Maudie in the kitchen now, beginning to prepare their lunch, humming to herself.

It was true what people said, Sadie realized. You couldn't have everything. But sometimes you could come close.

·   ·   ·

Maggie moved her passport from one hand to the other. She'd been in the immigration line for nearly an hour now. She'd kept herself busy looking at everyone around her. She counted the people in the different lines. She counted the number of desks, the number of immigration officers. She divided one into the other. She counted the posters carrying warnings. She counted the number of people with red hair, black hair and blond hair.

She counted the minutes until she would see Gabriel again.

"Come forward, ma'am."

She stepped toward the desk, handed over her passport, her heart thumping, even though she knew all her permits were in order. Dora, Gabriel's mother, had helped her with those. Not just with the permits either. She'd found the job for her in the first place.

They'd received the message from her while they were sitting in a seaside café in Italy. She and Gabriel were midway through their six months of traveling. They'd started in London, spending time with Leo, before going up to Manchester to see Juliet and Myles. From there they had flown to Paris. After that, they had gone wherever the urge took them. They had one rucksack each. They stood at railway-station platforms, looked up at the boards and chose destinations at random. They crisscrossed Europe. If they liked a town, they stayed for a week. If they didn't like it, they still stayed for a minimum of two days, to give the place another chance. Those were the only rules they'd set themselves. The rest they took as it came.

The text from Dora had been brief but to the point: *Juicy job for Maggie. Ring asap.*

A friend of hers, a very rich woman, had set up a philanthropic fund, financing projects all around New York. She was generous and she had the ideas, but she had no business experience. She'd told Dora she needed someone with a brain, a conscience, and a flair for numbers. Someone like that doesn't exist, though, do they? she'd lamented.

Oh, yes they do, Dora had said.

Maggie had talked about it with Gabriel. She'd rung Dora's friend from a phone booth on the esplanade of the Italian village. They'd spoken for an hour. Maggie had made her decision before she hung up. She'd do it.

It had changed their plans. They had intended to fly to Tasmania and spend time with Clementine before she went to Antarctica. She hadn't delayed her trip in the end. Maggie hadn't asked her to. She wanted Clementine to go ahead with her research. She knew what it meant to her. And as Clementine had said, there was e-mail these days. It wasn't as if she was completely cut off. They'd e-mailed each other more since Clementine had been down there than they ever had before, in fact.

Maggie would soon see it all for herself. Instead of visiting Clementine in Hobart, they'd decided to fly to Antarctica instead. They'd already booked the tickets. One of the few tourist flights. They'd get to spend a night with her. It made perfect sense, Miranda had said. Clementine in her natural habitat.

"That's fine, ma'am, thank you." Maggie was finally cleared to go through by the immigration official.

Gabriel was waiting just outside the doors for her. He'd gone through the fast channel with his U.S. passport.

"Welcome to New York," he said, kissing her, as though it had been months, not minutes, since they'd seen each other. "I was starting to think they weren't going to let you in."

"I was getting worried myself."

"Here, let me take that." As she passed her bag over, a frayed piece of the strap caught on her ring. On one of her rings, at least. They stopped, heads bent over, trying to untangle it.

"My own fault for being so showy," she said.

"My own fault for being such a generous fiancé," he replied, smiling back.

She had worn both engagement rings for the past six months. They were simple designs, each with thin silver bands—one a tiny diamond, the other a delicate emerald. He had given them to her just a few weeks before they left on their trip. She had moved out of Miranda's friend's apartment the month before. She had been staying with Gabriel since then. His doctor roommate had gone to live with his girlfriend, and his writer friend had decided to move to New Orleans. They had the apartment to themselves.

They'd become lovers the first night they were there together. It had been all Maggie had hoped, and it had got even better every time since. They made love to each other as well as they made each other laugh. They enjoyed long lazy days in bed as much as they enjoyed long conversations in bars and over restaurant tables. They were hungry for each other. They felt right together. Maggie still felt a small jolt of happiness each time she looked at him. She felt something else too. Love, certainty, and contentment. She knew he felt the same way about her. He told her often.

On the way back home from seeing a film one night, they'd crossed Washington Square. He remembered another promise they had made in that same place, more than a year before, the first night they met. She had dared him to sing in public, and in return she had promised to eat snails.

She reminded him she hated snails. He said he was sorry to hear that, but a dare was a dare. The following night, he took her to the finest French restaurant he could find. They both dressed up, Gabriel in a suit, Maggie in a black dress with a jet necklace. The waiters were polite, with just the right amount of superciliousness.

They delivered the snails, six of them, on a specially shaped silver plate.

Maggie looked down at them in disgust. "Do I really have to?"

"I think so. Our whole relationship depends on it. It's all about give and take, Maggie. You know that."

She picked one up with the tiny silver fork. She could smell the garlic. The butter dripped onto her finger.

"I don't think I can."

"Of course you can. We can't tell our children in years to come that their parents' marriage proposal fell in a heap because their mother refused to do the first part of it."

Maggie dropped the snail.

"What marriage proposal?"

"The one I'm about to propose. You can propose a proposal, can't you? Or is that bad English?"

"It's good English. I like the sound of it anyway." She looked down at the snails again and back up at him. "The marriage proposal depends on me eating these?"

"I'm afraid so."

"Why?"

"Because I've hidden the rings inside two of the snail shells and you have to find them."

"The rings? Plural?"

"It's our second engagement, I realized. Then I realized I didn't give you a ring for our first engagement. So I'm making up for it now."

"You've put the rings inside the snails?"

"I didn't. The chef did."

"Oh, Gabriel." She swallowed. "I'm just not sure—"

"About getting married?"

"No, I'm completely sure about that. Sorry, didn't I say yes?"

"Well, no. But I didn't put it to you as a question either."

"Could you do that now? Make it romantic? And we could worry about the rings later?"

"It's not very romantic to do it without the rings."

"It's more romantic than doing it with the snails, I promise."

He reached across, moved the snails, took her hand, and asked, very solemnly, "Maggie Faraday, would you please do me the honor of getting engaged to me again? Only this time for real. And we have to get married at the end of this one."

"I would love to. I would love that very much. But you do know what you're getting yourself into? I come with a complete, ready-made family. Too many aunts. A mad grandfather—"

"That's why I'm marrying you. For them, not you." He smiled. "That's not why I'm marrying you. I'm marrying you because you are the best person I have ever met in my life. And not only that, the most beautiful. And the kindest—"

As it turned out, he had a long list of reasons why he wanted to marry her. She gave him a long list of the reasons why she wanted to marry him too.

By the time they'd finished, the snails had gone cold.

"What a shame. I can't eat them now, can I? The chef would be very angry." She picked one up and started shaking it. Butter flew across the table.

Gabriel ducked. "Why are you doing that?"

"I'm trying to find the rings."

"Look behind you."

The waiter was carrying a tray. On it were two small boxes. He passed them across to Gabriel with dignity. No fanfare, no corny music, no balloons.

"These are for you, Maggie," Gabriel said. "With all my love."

She accepted them, with as much love. She had worn them every day since.

The crowds were growing bigger all around them in the airport as more people came through immigration. Gabriel finally untangled the thread from her rings. He helped her put her rucksack back on. She helped him with his.

"Ready?" he said now.

She smiled. "Ready," she replied.

It was time to go home.

ACKNOWLEDGMENTS

My love and thanks to my families and friends in Australia and Ireland for their constant support and encouragement, with special thanks to my three sisters, Maura, Marie and Lea and my mum, Mary. My extra-special thanks to Maura for getting insomnia just when I needed her beautiful e-mails and expert help twenty-four hours a day.

Thank you for the loan of family stories, help with research and much more to: Max and Jean Fatchen, Noelle Harrison, Madonna Noonan, Fiona Gillies, Merran Gillies, Imojen Pearce, Bill Page, Sarah Conroy, Brona Looby, Maria Dickenson, Stephanie Dickenson, Carol George, Lyn Vernon, Kristin Gill, Jenny Newman, Margie Arnold, Sinead Moriarty, Helen Peakin, Melanie Scaife, Fiona McIntosh, Karen O'Connor, Maeve O'Meara, Noelene Turner, James Williams, Marea Fox, Andrew Storey, Margaret, Tony and Julie Fox, Jane Melross, Rod, Lizzie and Joe Arnold, Marie Harrington, Jean Weir, Janet Grecian, Christopher Pearce, Amanda Wojtowicz, and Bruce and Vicki Montgomery.

Thank you to my niece Ruby Clements for being the perfect five-year-old.

Thanks to all my publishers, especially Laura Ford, Lisa Barnes and all at Random House in the U.S.; Ali Watts, Saskia Adams, Anne Rogan, Dan Ruffino, Sally Bateman, Cathy Larsen, Robert Sessions, Gabrielle Coyne and everyone at Penguin Australia; Imogen Taylor, Trisha Jackson and David Adamson at Pan Macmillan in the U.K. and Cormac Kinsella of Repforce in Ireland. My thanks also to the Books Alive team in Australia, especially Brett Osmond, Margaret Burke, Andy Palmer, Tim Fitzgerald and to Sue Hill of the Big Book Club.

Thank you to my agents: Fiona Inglis and all at Curtis Brown Australia; Jonathan Lloyd, Camilla Goslett, Kate Cooper and Alice Lutyens at Curtis Brown UK; Christy Fletcher at Fletcher Parry in New York; Anoukh Foerg in Munich; and Roberto Santachiara in Italy.

And, as always, all my love and thanks to my husband, John.

THE FARADAY GIRLS

Monica McInerney

A READER'S GUIDE

RC: With its themes of family estrangement and betrayal, *The Faraday Girls* is more emotionally intense than your previous novels. Did you set out to write a more serious book, or did it naturally evolve this way?

Monica McInerney: I let the subject matter lead me, in many ways. My starting point for *The Faraday Girls* was simple—I wanted to explore the relationship between nieces and aunts and the impact that particular bond can have on our lives. As I began to write the story of Maggie and her four aunts, though, I found myself stepping out into deeper water, thinking and writing about not just the idea of aunts but the whole theme of motherhood and children—the idea of good mothers, bad mothers, those who want to be a mother but discover it's not possible, those who choose not to be mothers. The more I wrote, the more questions I found myself facing. What would it be like to feel like a stranger in your own family? Is it possible to re-invent yourself? Can you ever leave your family behind? When—if ever—is it right to lie to your family?

I'm also intrigued by the impact of past events on present-day life in families, how decisions made years ago can resurface and cause great ripples or damage, or sometimes lead to greater understanding and closer relationships. Those ideas are at the heart of *The Faraday Girls,* and I also explored them in *Family Baggage* and *The Alphabet Sisters.* I find family life such rich material for fiction—every family, real or fictional, is an emotional ecosystem, each member reliant on one another in some way.

RC: The Faraday sisters' relationships are so realistically and vividly drawn. Did growing up with a number of siblings help you create these characters and shape their interactions? Is any part of this novel autobiographical?

MM: Growing up in a big family (I'm one of seven children) has definitely made its mark on me as a person and as a writer. I'm the middle child, which I think helped me become an observer—I had people above and below me to watch and interact with, and I could easily go unnoticed, too. I do try hard not to use any elements from my own family life in any recognizable way in my novels, though, to keep it as fiction not memoir. That said, I know firsthand what it's like to be in a room with many siblings and feel the snip-snap of conversation, the teasing, the quick remarks which can also turn from light into shade in an instant. All of those experiences fed into the scenes between the five Faraday sisters.

The actual events in the book aren't autobiographical, but the emotions behind them are. I know how it feels within—and outside—a family to share times of great fun, happiness, camaraderie, but equally, I've experienced loss, pain, jealousy, anger, grief and sadness. I wanted to portray all the different ways we interact with the people in our families, from the older members to the youngest, and how one event years before can impact on family members many years later.

RC: The novel shifts between many different points of view. Which character do you personally identify with most? Which was the easiest to create, and which the most difficult?

MM: I actually identified with all of them. I enjoyed Miranda very much, though I did wince sometimes at her wit and casual cruelty. I related to Juliet's tendency to mother, Eliza's need to keep herself separate and private, Clementine's self-sufficiency, and even Sadie's hurt and feeling of isolation. I really liked Maggie, too—her earnestness, her courage, and her loyalty. In a big family—in all families—the landscape shifts and changes and so do the relationships and personalities within that group. I wrote many scenes involving the Faradays which didn't end up in the final book but which helped me understand each of their characters. Once I'd done that, each of the sisters, as well as Leo and Maggie, felt so real to me that I knew exactly how each of them would react or behave in any situation I placed them. There were times in the writing where I felt like I was watching it all unfold, rather than being the person making it happen.

RC: *The Faraday Girls* takes place in many far-flung areas of the world, including Australia, Ireland, Singapore, and the United States, and travel is an important part of all of your novels. Can you explain why this is?

MM: A quick version of my biography is probably the best answer here! Since I left my hometown in the Clare Valley of South Australia as a seventeen-year-old, I've moved nearly twenty times, living and working all around Australia, in London, and in Ireland. For the past sixteen years my Irish husband and I have moved back and forth between Australia and Ireland and we've also traveled extensively through Asia, Europe, and the United States. I know so well the feeling of arriving in another country, either to start a new job or life, or just on holiday: There's excitement, fear, anticipation, and so many other feelings at the same time. It's rich emotional ground for fictional characters, too—taking a person out of their usual surroundings and dropping them into a new city or country and seeing what unfolds and how they react.

As a child growing up in a small town in South Australia, my first experience of other countries was through the pages of books. I read about English villages, American cities, imagined myself in snow (even while I was experiencing scorching Australian summers); I loved being taken into other landscapes through the pages of a book and I love to do that with my own writing now.

RC: You spent last summer touring Australia as the keynote speaker for the Books Alive campaign. Can you tell us a little about this program and your experience? What was the most rewarding element for you?

MM: The Books Alive campaign is an annual Australian government initiative to encourage all Australians to read more. As the "ambassador" for the 2006 promotion, I wrote a short novel called *Odd One Out* which was used as a giveaway book in conjunction with a selection of 50 Great Reads—a terrific selection of Australian and international books: thrillers, fiction, crime, history, science, memoirs, fantasy and children's stories. During the five-week campaign I traveled to every state and territory of Australia, visiting more than twenty-five cities and towns to give talks in bookshops, libraries, and schools about the importance and especially the joy of reading. It was a wonderful experience—I met and did talks with many other authors and had the opportunity to talk about books and share reading tips with people of all ages all over the country. That was the most rewarding element for me—to be in a position to share my love of books and all they offer, and to be part of a campaign designed to encourage a love of reading.

RC: What authors or books have influenced your work? Are there any authors you admire and emulate?

MM: I'm sure that every book I read influences me in some way. I read a great deal and have done since I was a child. I average three books a week, from all genres. I've many favorite authors and books, including Laurie Graham, John le Carré, Patricia Highsmith, David Sedaris, Tim Winton, Joanna Trollope, Garrison Keillor, Adriana Trigiani, Rosamunde Pilcher, and classic books like *Jane Eyre, Anna Karenina,* and *Little Women.* I don't think I can say that one particular author has influenced me, or that I try to emulate any one writer, either. With each book I write I feel more confident that I am finding my own voice. As a reader, I love it when I feel like I am part of the book, in the rooms with the characters, hearing their dialogue, feeling and seeing what they are going through. I want to care about the characters. As a writer, I want to create that same mood, by writing fast-moving, entertaining but also emotionally charged stories with recognizable characters. The loveliest feedback is when I hear from someone who has read my books and felt that they were part of the family in the story, and that they missed them after they'd finished the book.

RC: What are you working on next?

MM: I have three or four ideas for my next book bubbling away and I'm waiting to see which one wins. I've also had an idea for a TV series that I'd like to explore, and an idea for a children's book that I'd like to write. My husband and I want to do lots more traveling too—one of the ideas I have for the next book involves several different countries so our next trip is going to be more research than holiday, I suspect. . . .

1. The five Faraday sisters have very distinct personalities. Which did you get to know best through the course of the novel? Whom did you identify most with?

2. Why do you think Sadie has so much trouble fitting in with her family? Is she simply a lost soul, or does her family situation exacerbate her problems? Do you think her drastic action at the end of Part One was at all justified?

3. Early in the narrative, when discussing Leo with her sisters, Miranda states "Sometimes I think he enjoys it, you know. It's like he's been cast in a lead role, as the eccentric brave father of five little motherless girls" (page 19). Do you think her assessment of Leo is correct and fair? Does Leo, as Gabriel later states, exert an unhealthy control over his daughters, even with the best intentions?

4. Why do you think Leo idolizes Tessa so greatly? Do you agree with Gabriel that her beauty may have played a large part in his attraction? Have you ever found yourself in love with a person who may not be the best match?

5. Do you believe each of the five Faraday sisters would have turned out differently if their mother had been alive to raise them through adulthood?

6. The traumatizing events Maggie experiences send her into a huge tailspin. Anyone would be traumatized, but why do you think she is so extremely affected by what happened? Do you think her reaction has anything to do with how she was brought up?

7. Family rituals, such as the Faraday Christmases in July, play an important role in this novel. In which ways do these traditions strengthen the Faraday family relations, and in which ways do they strain them?

8. Maggie makes the important decision to keep the family secret she's discovered to herself. What would you have done under the same circumstances? Do you believe the truth is sometimes better left unknown?

9. Nearly every character in *The Faraday Girls* romanticizes their past. In each case, how has this process hampered a sense of reality? Does sentimentality ever help any members of the Faraday family?

10. Aside from the way she was raised, how is Maggie's relationship with her mother unconventional? How is Maggie similar to Clementine, and how is she different? Explore the breakthrough they have in their emotional conversation toward the end of the novel.

11. As an outsider, Gabriel is the only person who can point out and clarify the Faraday family dynamics to Maggie. Have you ever been in the situation of gaining new perspective on your family? How have your own family dynamics changed over the course of your life?

12. How has the Faraday family as a whole changed by the end of the novel? Do you think Leo, the sisters, and Maggie are closer? How do they understand one another better?